NAUSICAÄ

OF THE VALLEY OF THE WIND

Picture Book

Original Story and Screenplay
Written and Directed by

HAYAO MIYAZAKI

VIZ Media
San Francisco

Meet the Characters

The Valley of the Wind

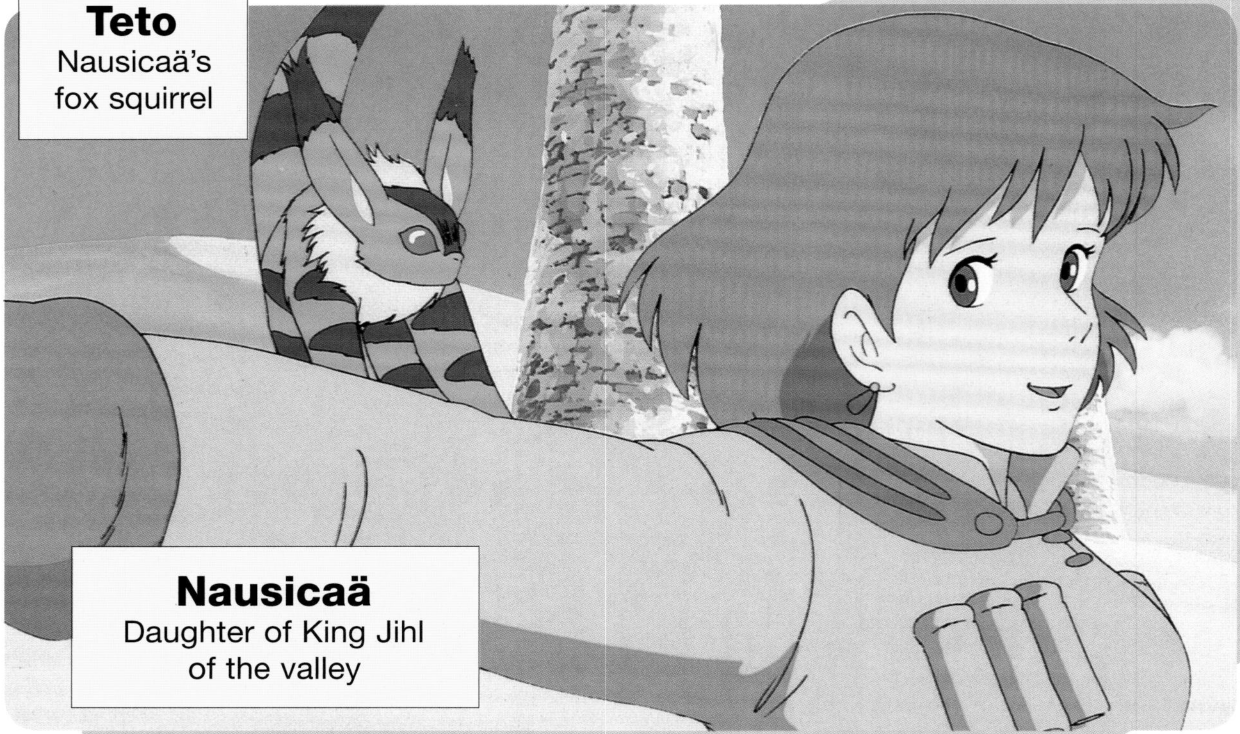

Teto
Nausicaä's
fox squirrel

Nausicaä
Daughter of King Jihl
of the valley

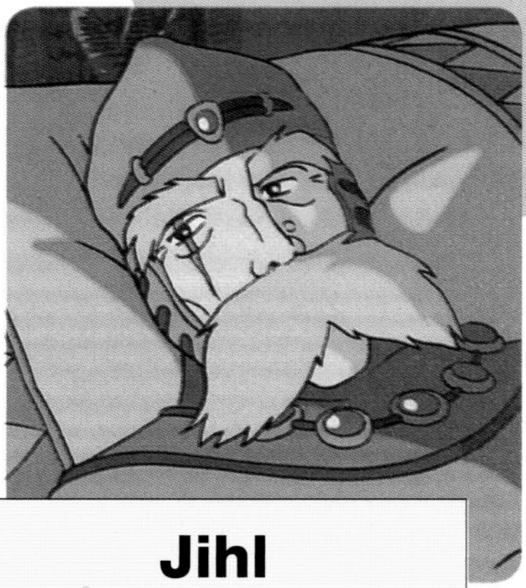

Jihl
Nausicaä's father and
king of the valley

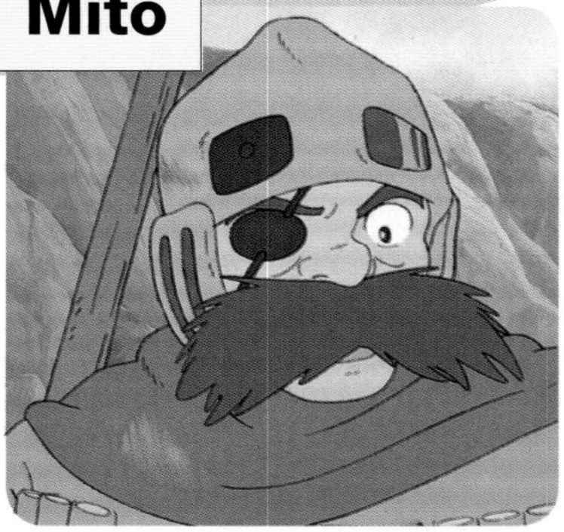

Mito

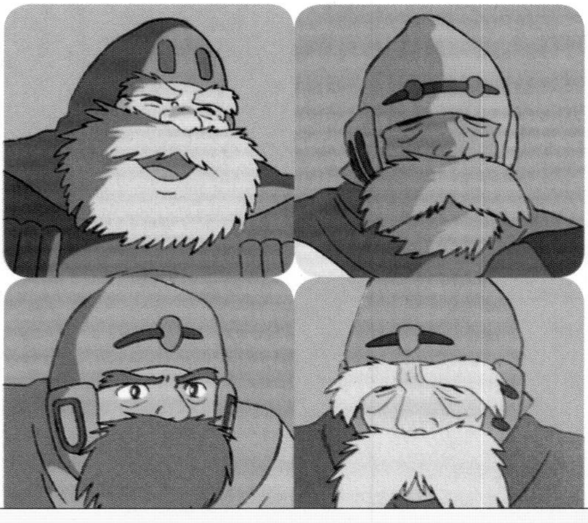

Old Men of the Castle

Lord Yupa
A skilled swordsman
on a secret quest

Obaba
The sage of the valley

Pejite

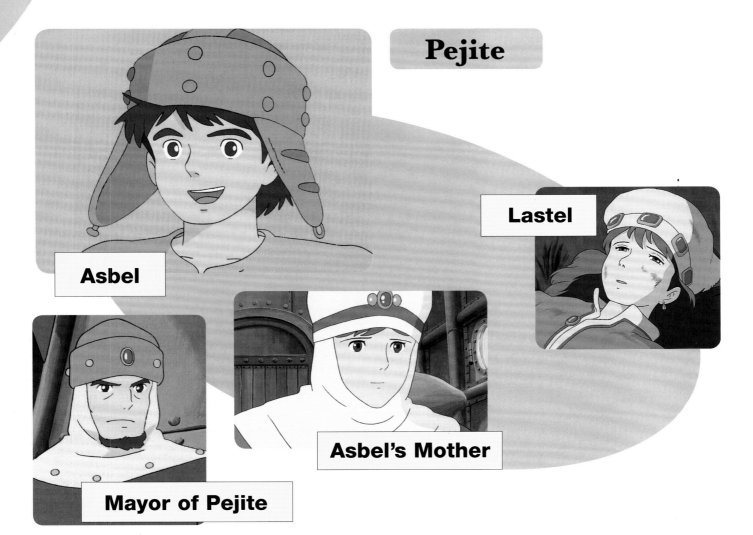

Asbel

Lastel

Asbel's Mother

Mayor of Pejite

Tolmekia

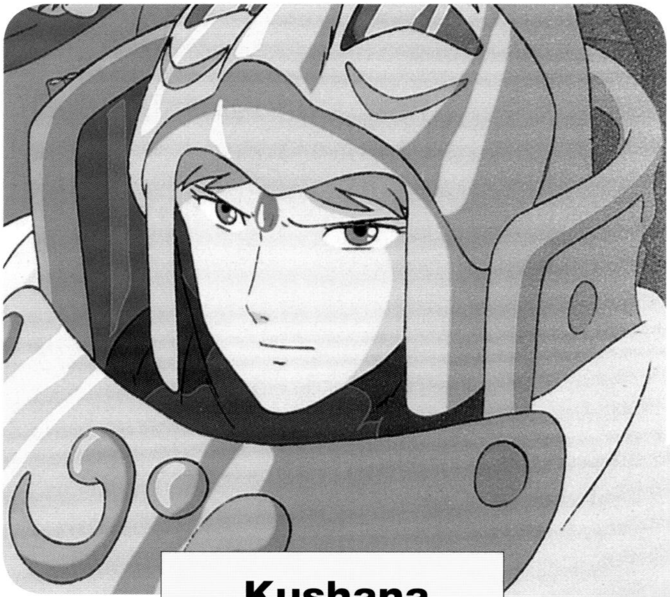

Kushana
Queen of Tolmekia

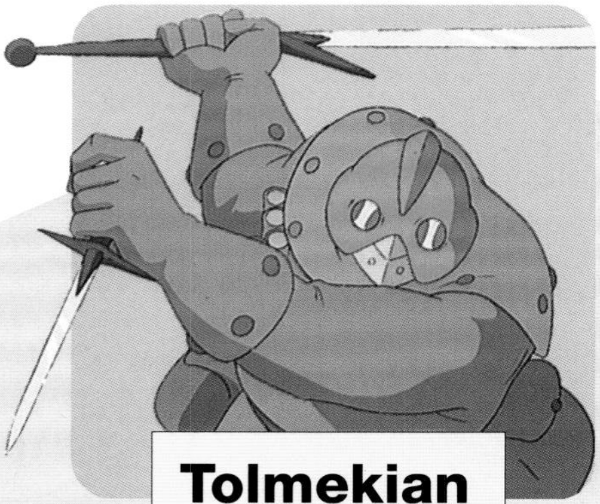

Tolmekian soldiers

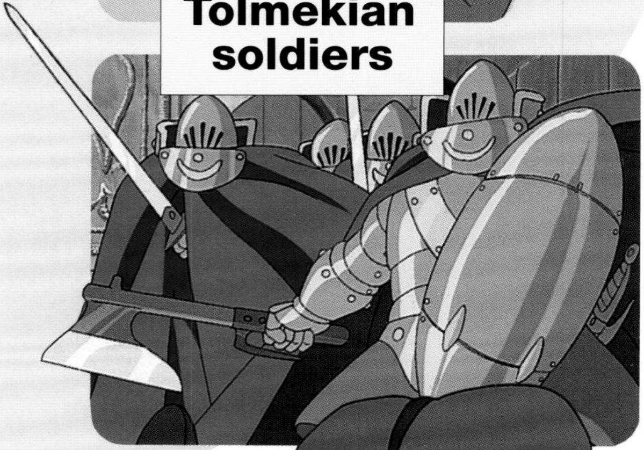

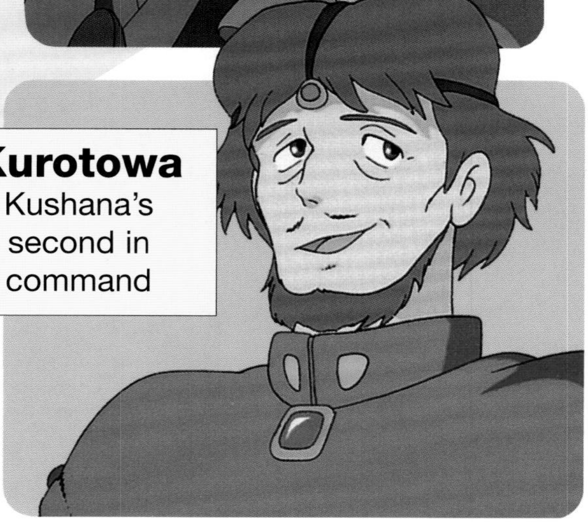

Kurotowa
Kushana's second in command

Flying Machines

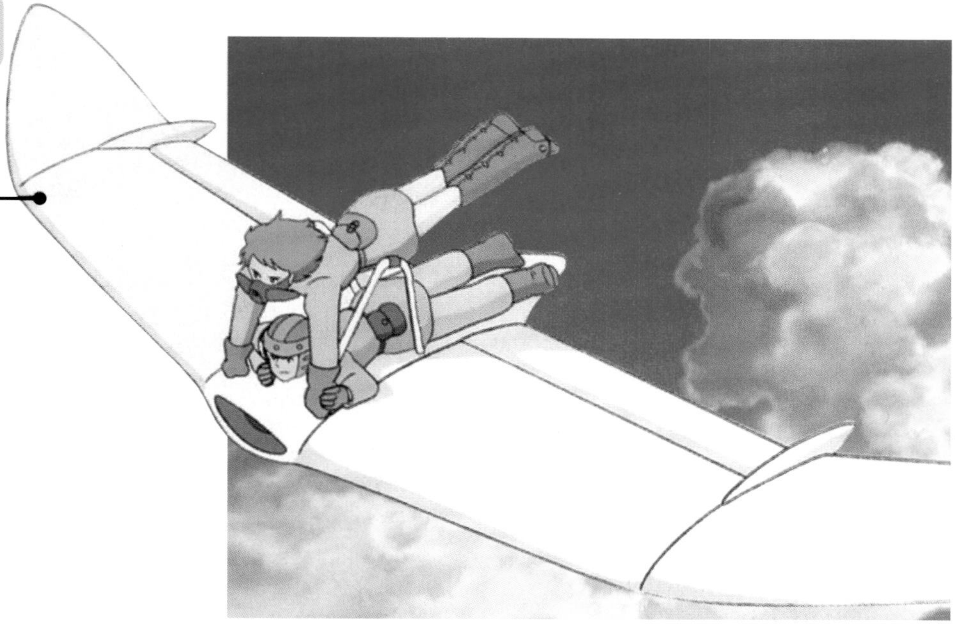

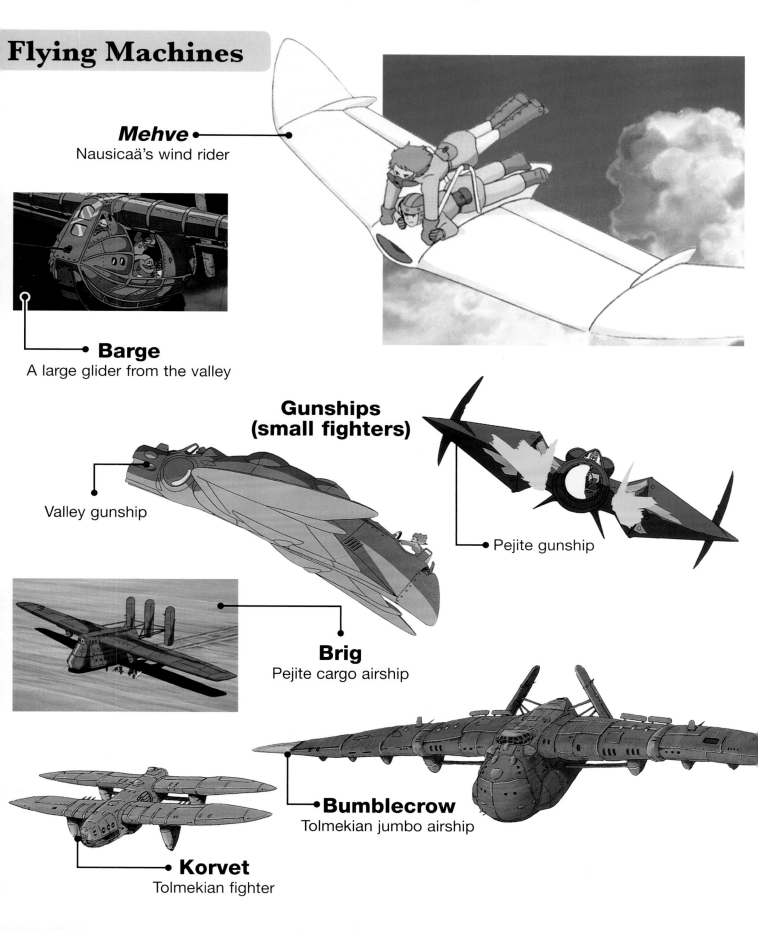

Mehve
Nausicaä's wind rider

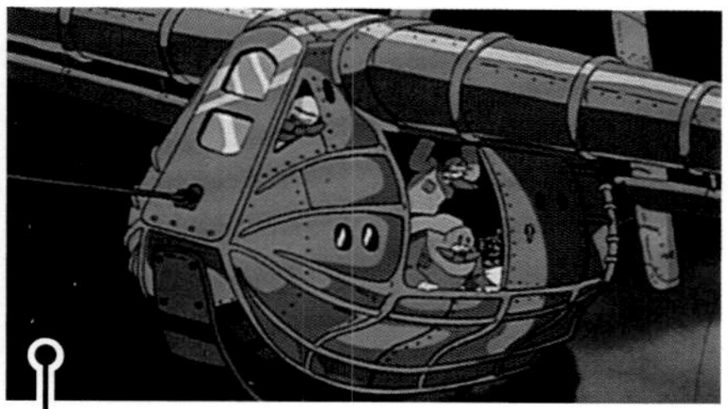

Barge
A large glider from the valley

Gunships (small fighters)

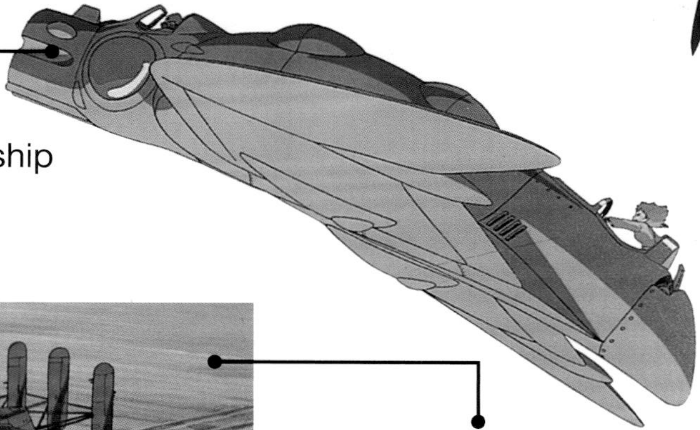

Valley gunship

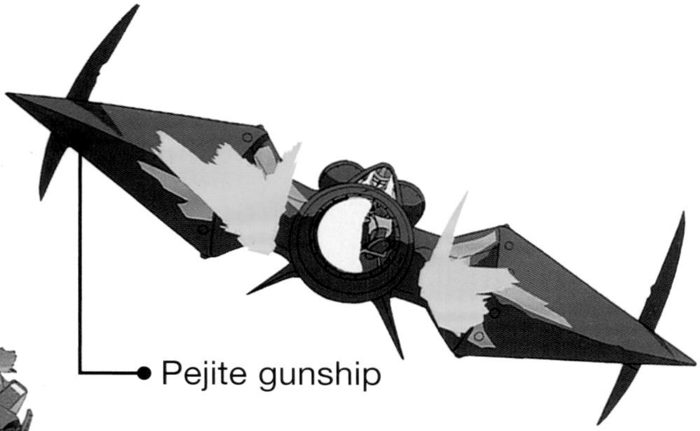

Pejite gunship

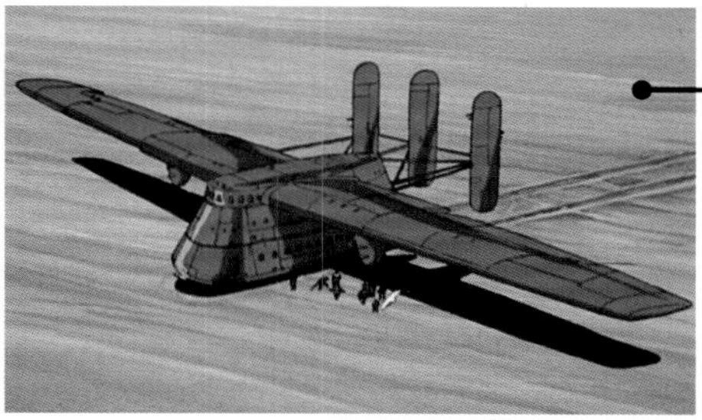

Brig
Pejite cargo airship

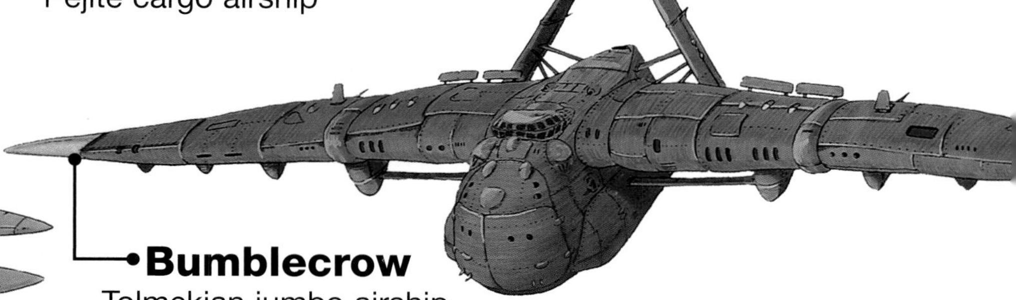

Bumblecrow
Tolmekian jumbo airship

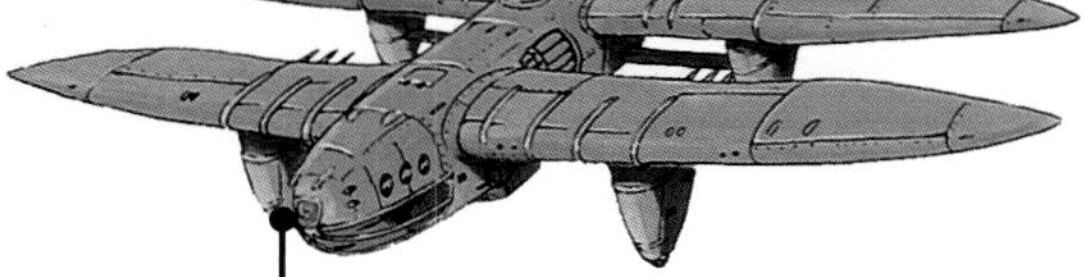

Korvet
Tolmekian fighter

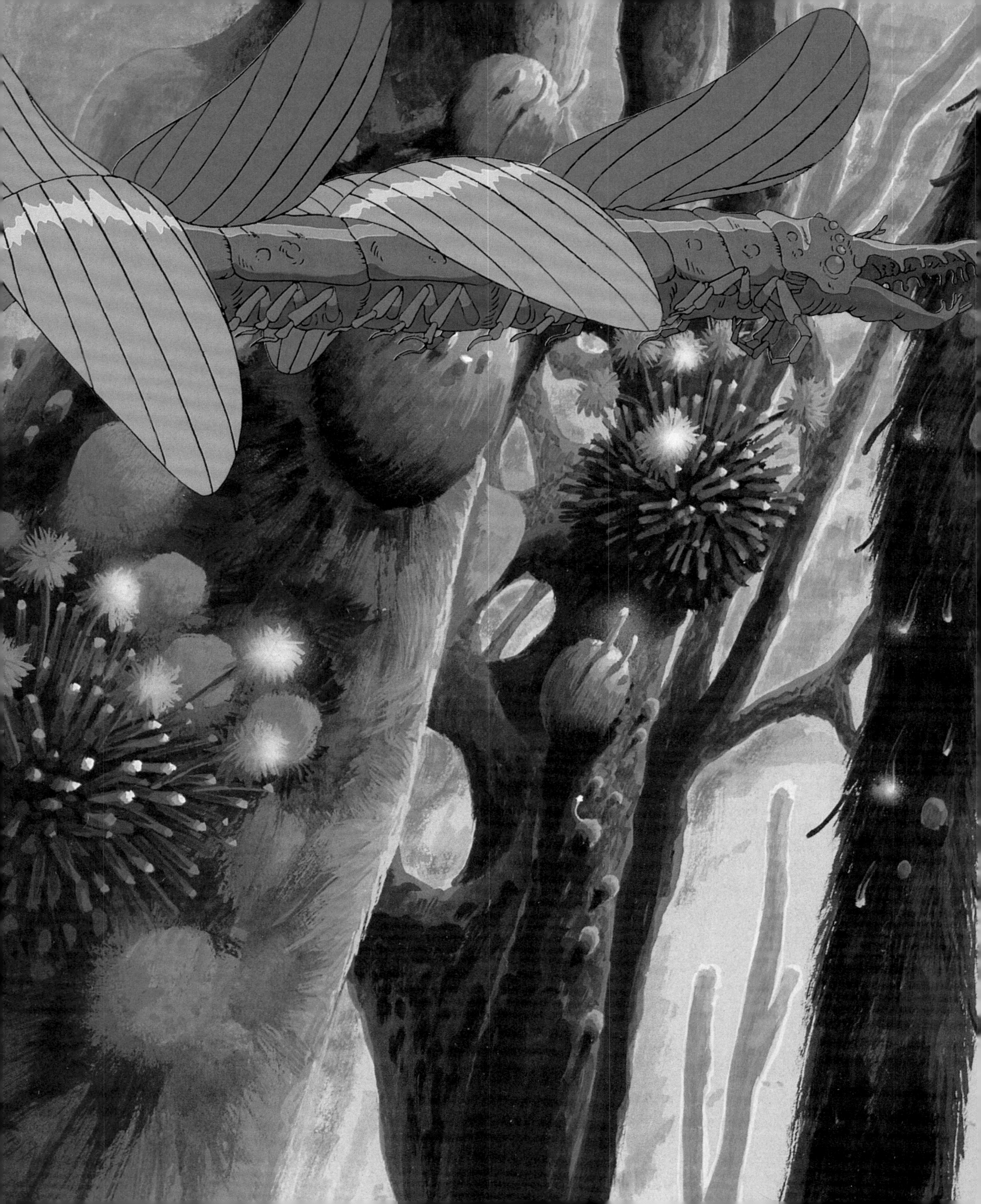

The Seven Days of Fire…

The story, handed down for generations, told how a terrible war destroyed civilization.

A thousand years later, most of the earth was covered with a toxic jungle called the Sea of Decay. The jungle was full of strange plants dispersing deadly spores. Swarms of giant insects waited to attack any intruder.

A few scattered kingdoms survived on the outskirts of the jungle. People lived in fear of the relentlessly spreading jungle and the giant insects.

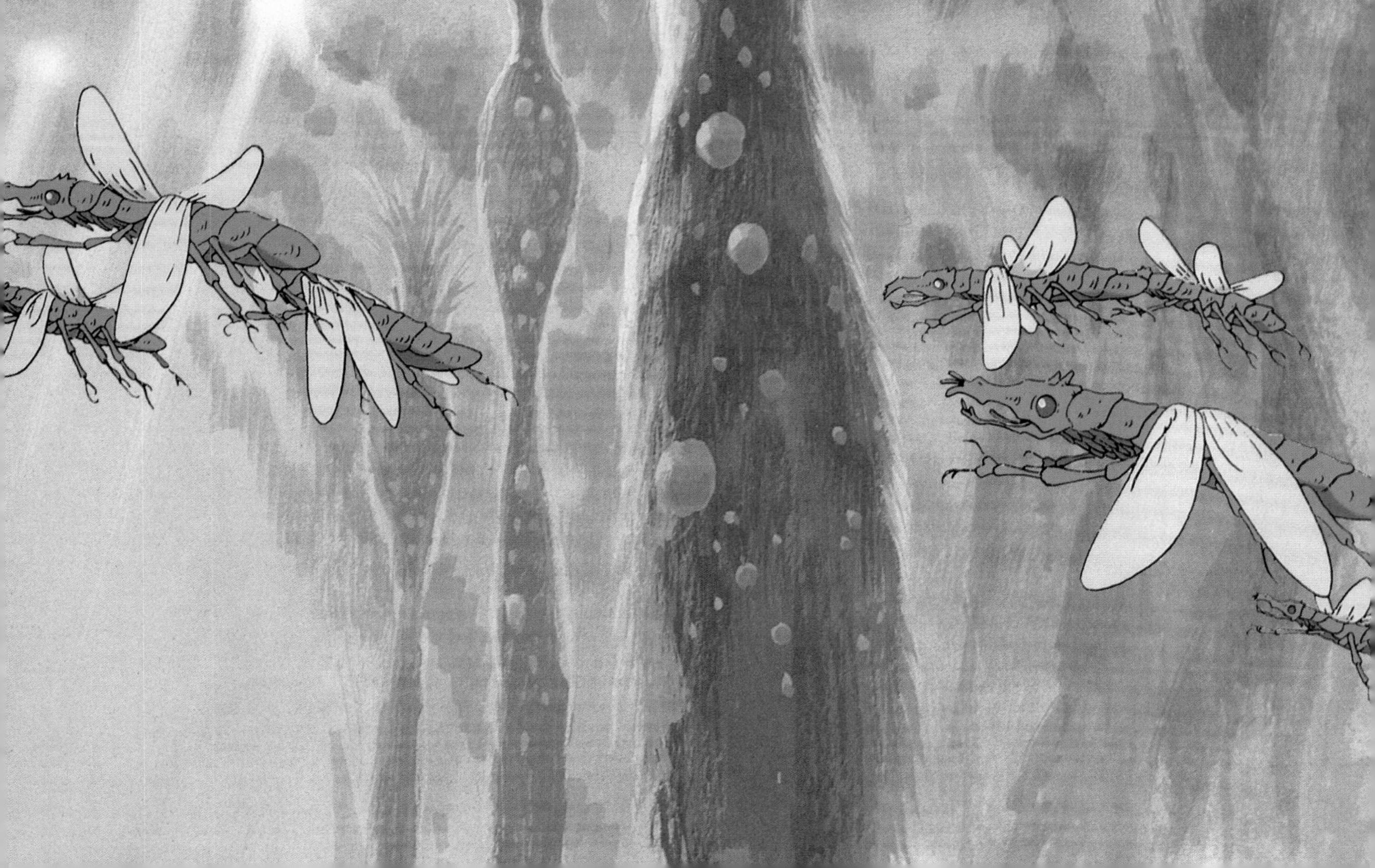

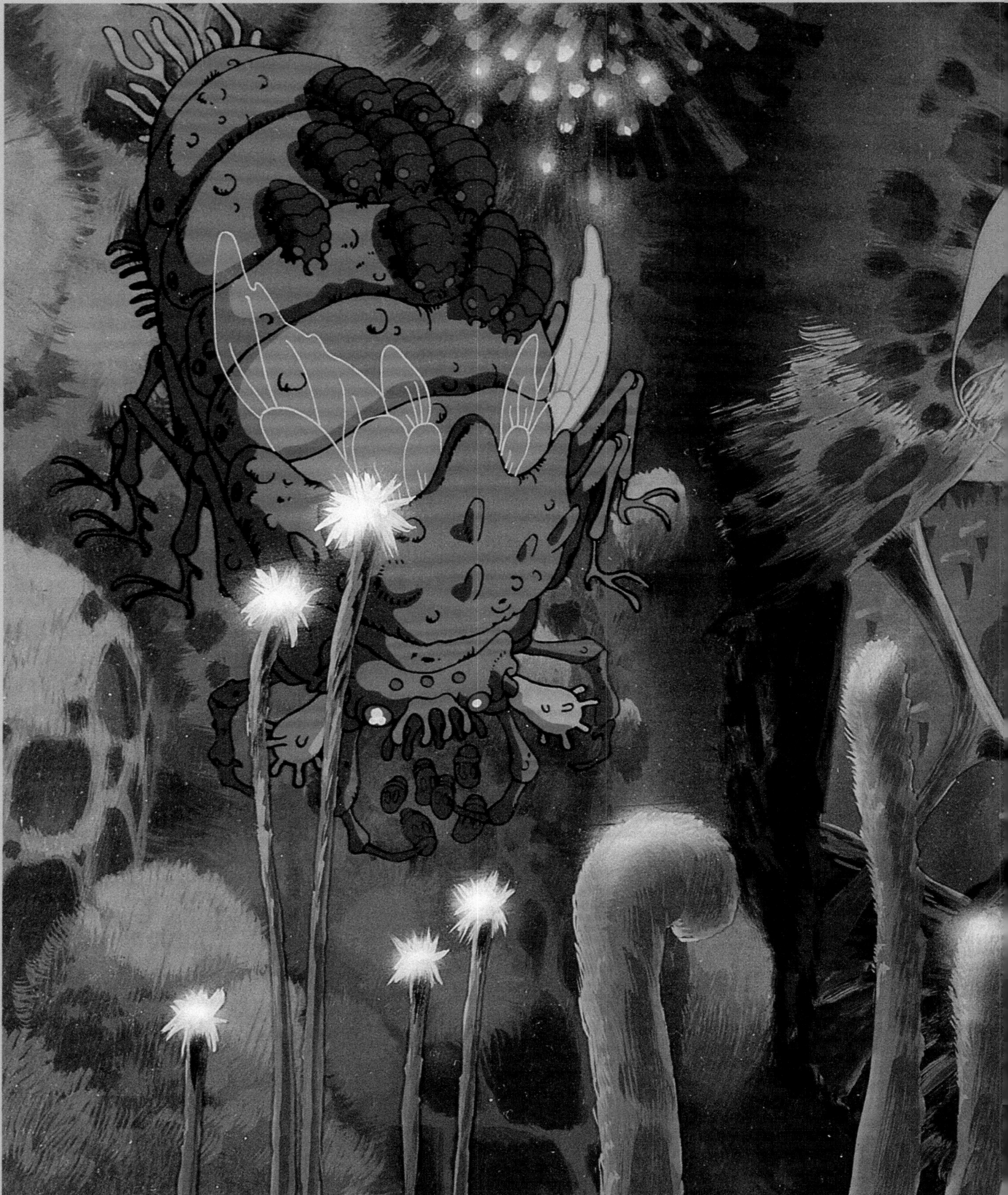

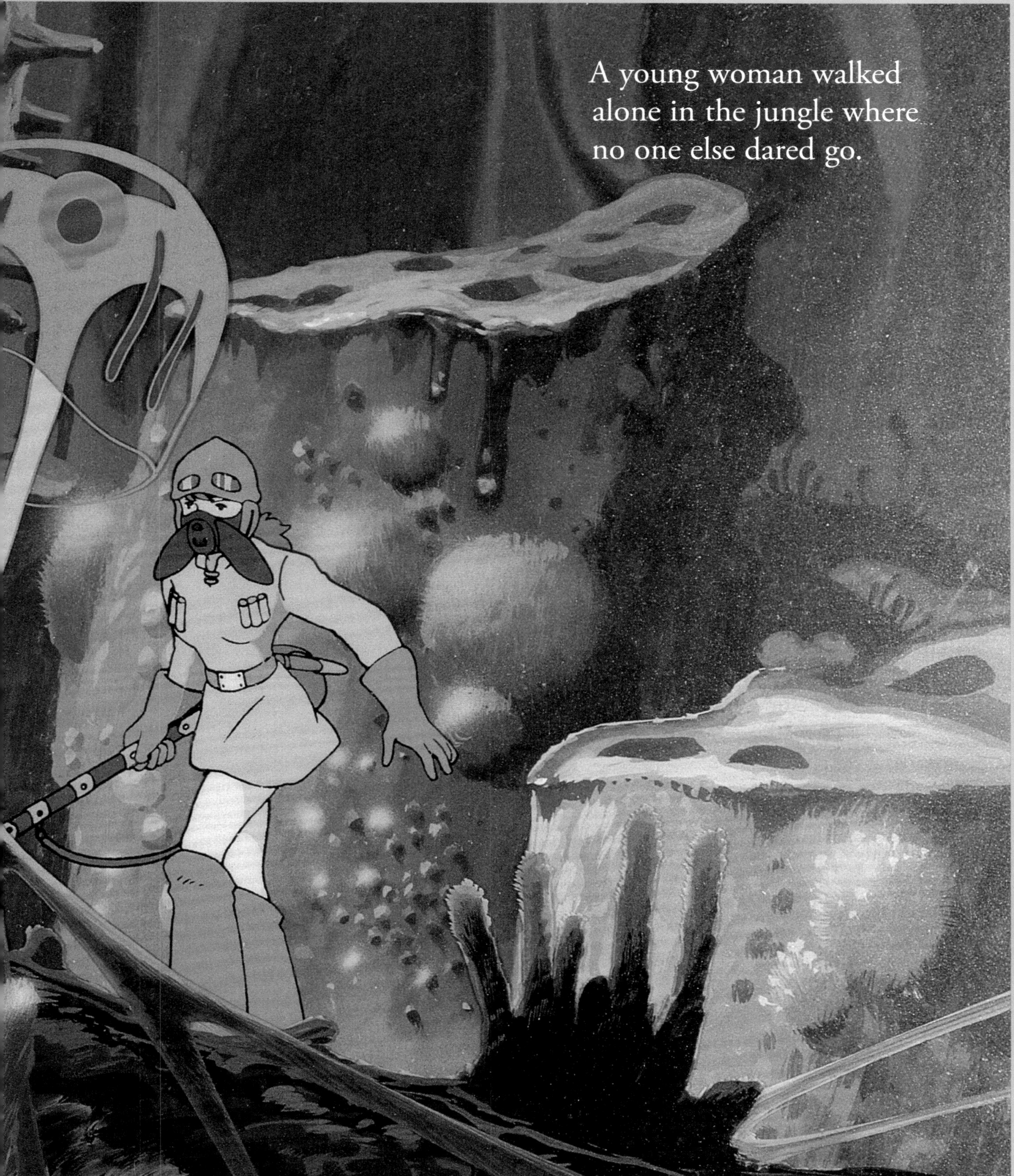
A young woman walked alone in the jungle where no one else dared go.

NAUSICAÄ THE WIND RIDER

The girl was Nausicaä, the daughter of a king. She came from the Valley of the Wind, a small kingdom nestled between the sea and the toxic jungle.

Nausicaä was a gentle princess. She loved nature and all living things.

Deep in the jungle, she found a plant that glowed with a soft blue light.

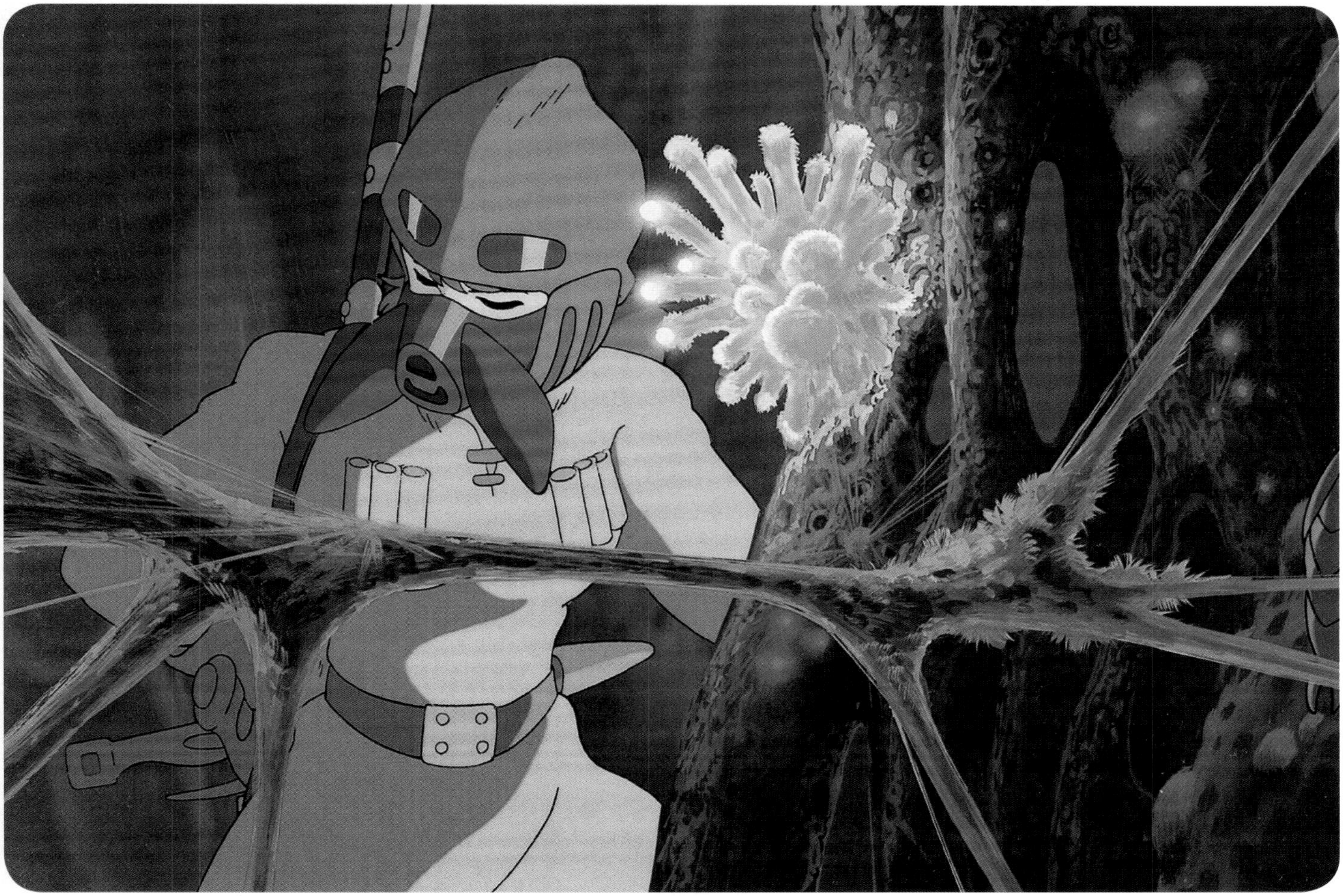

Nausicaä held a glass tube under the plant and tapped it with a fingertip. A tiny blue spore dropped into the tube, and she sealed it carefully.

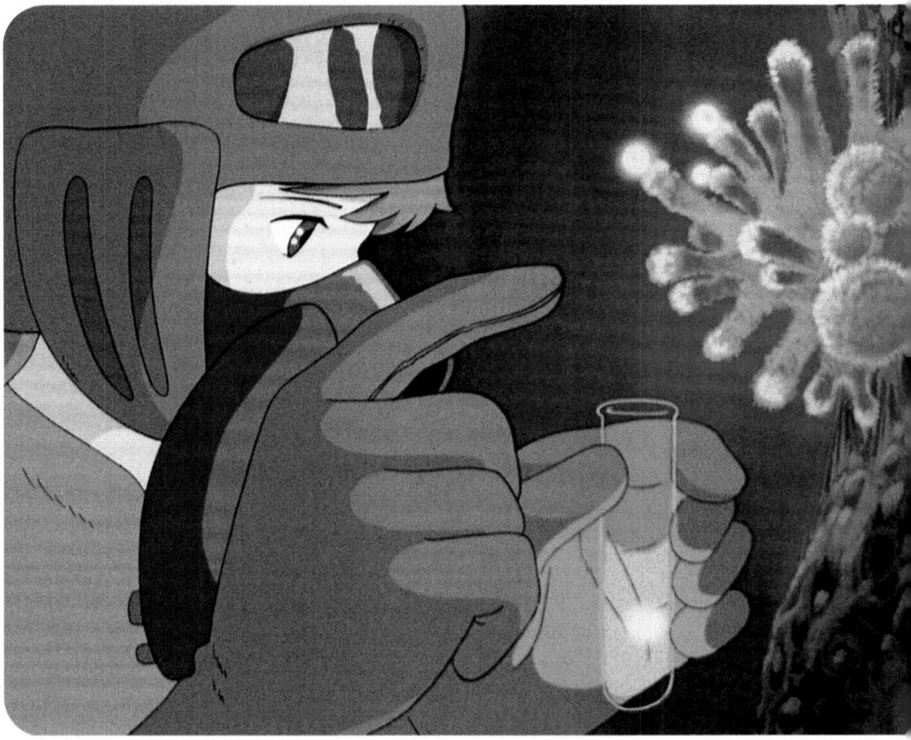

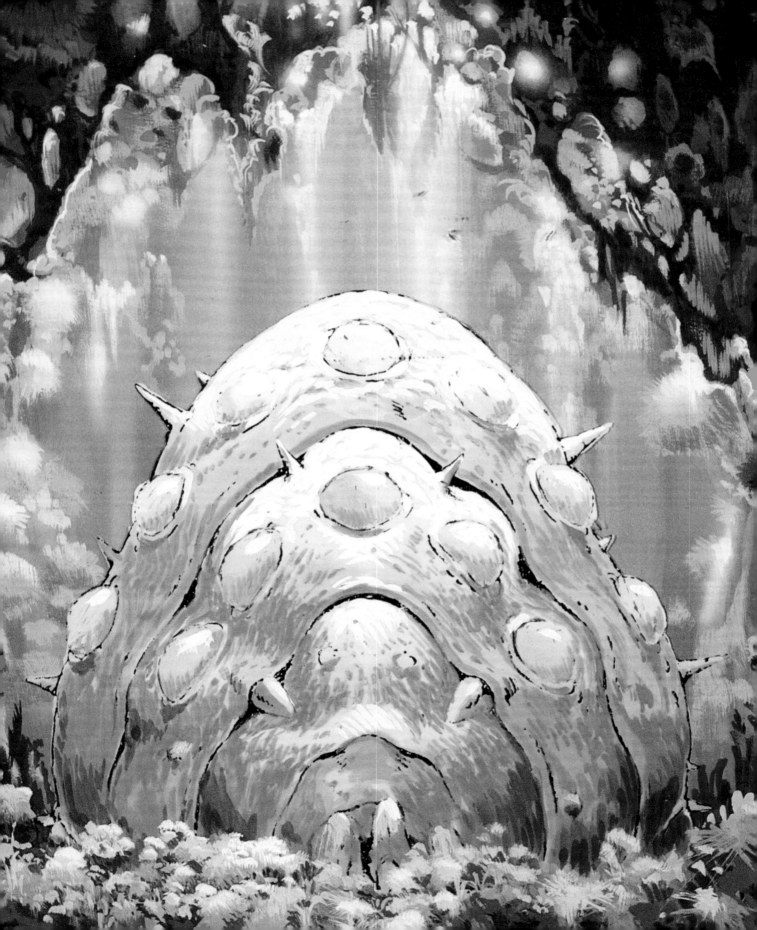

She walked deeper into the jungle. Suddenly she stopped. "A perfect Ohm shell!" she exclaimed with amazement.

The Ohm was a giant insect with fourteen eyes, the king of the toxic jungle. It shed its thick carapace many times as it grew to immense size.

A cast-off Ohm carapace was harder than steel and prized by the people of the valley. It was the perfect material for making all sorts of useful things.

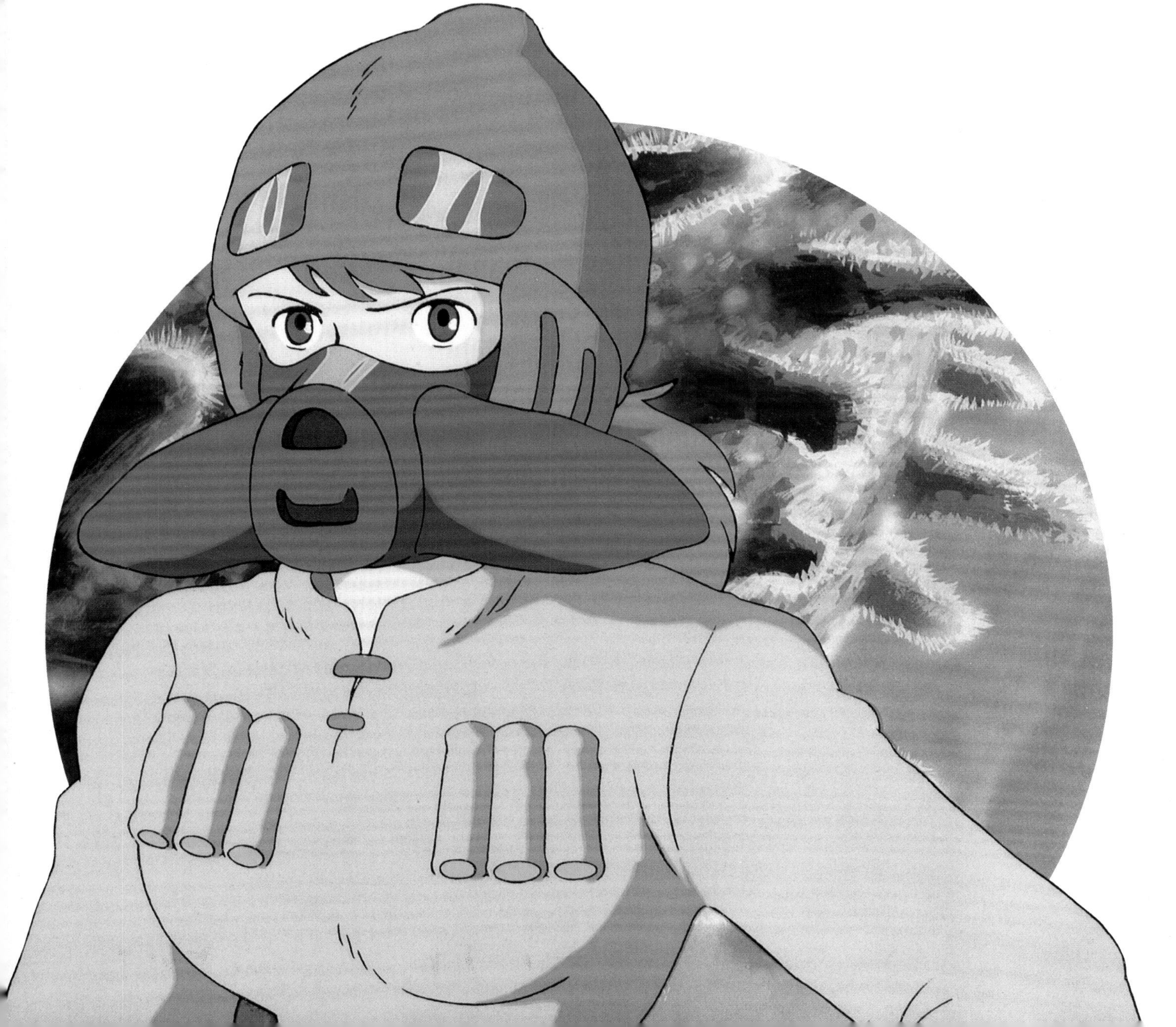

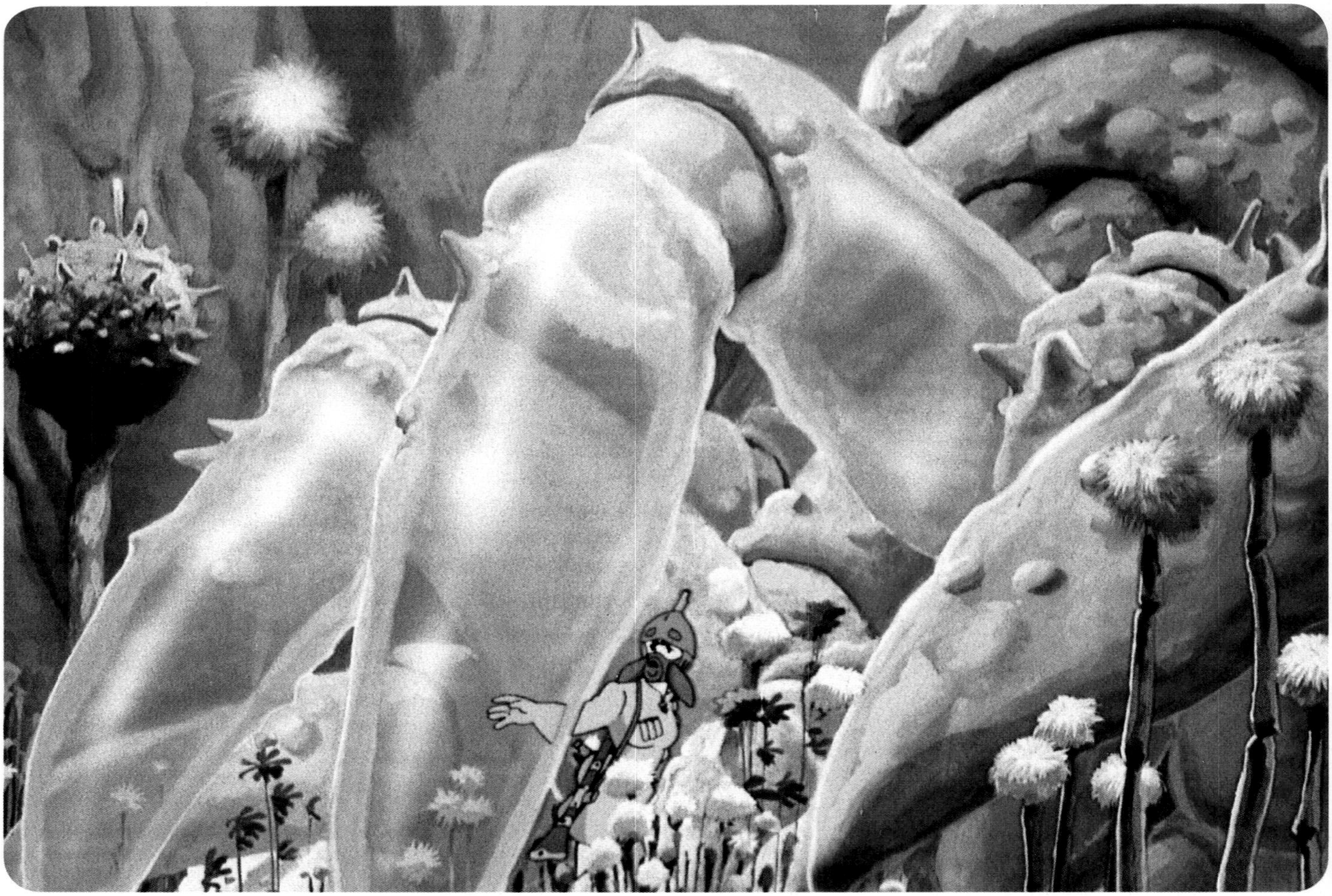

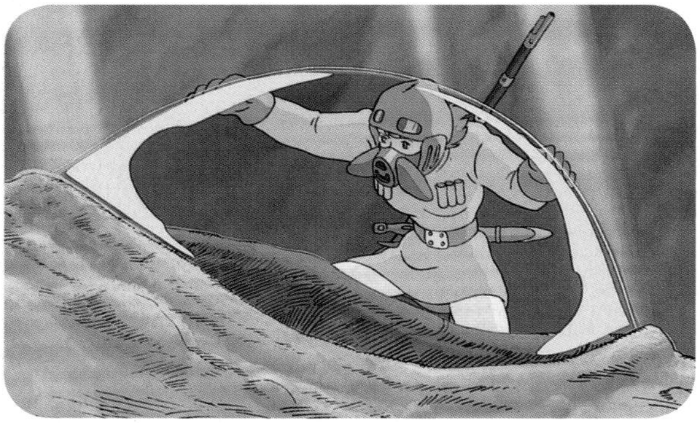

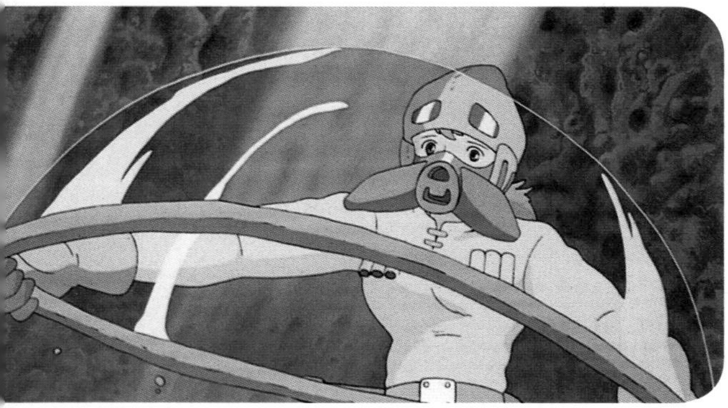

"This should make the people of the valley happy. They won't have to worry about finding materials for making tools for a long time."

Nausicaä climbed up onto the enormous carapace and pried off one of its crystal-clear lenses. She held it over her head. "It's so light!"

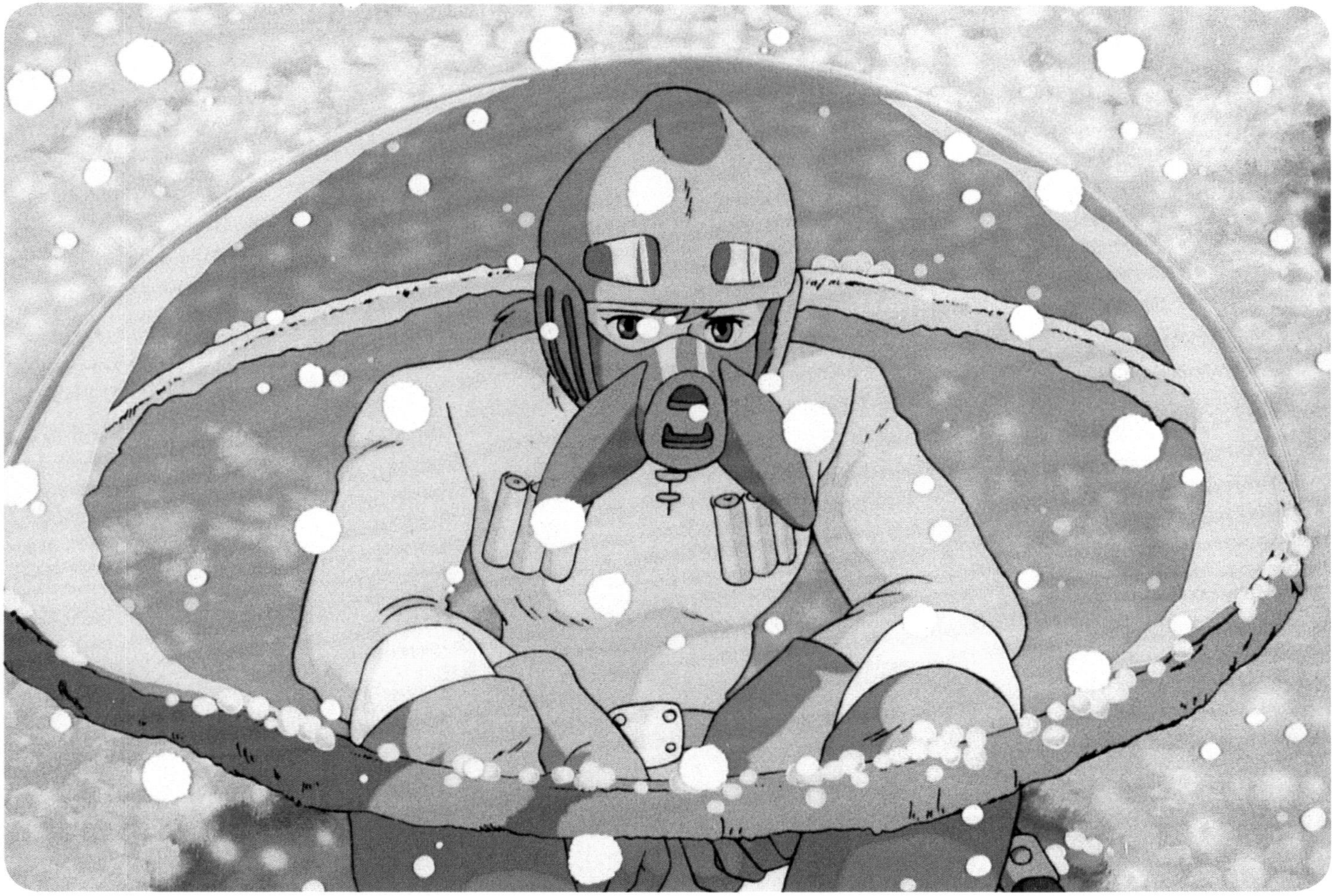

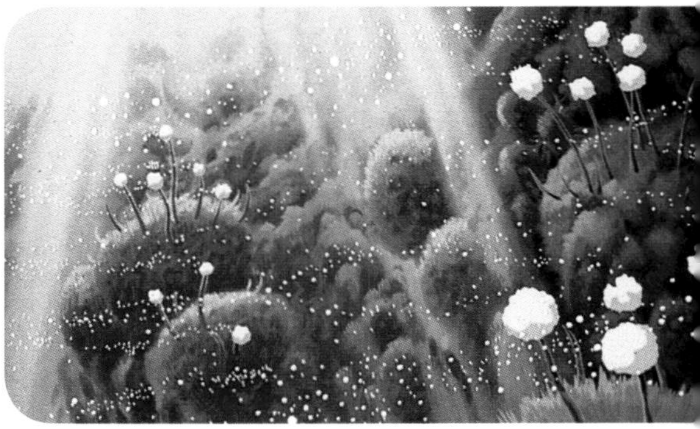

Small, white objects like puffballs started floating down. The plants of the jungle were spreading their deadly spores.

The calls of the insects faded away. Now there was deep silence, like the depths of a vast ocean.

"It's so beautiful," Nausicaä murmured. "It's hard to believe these spores could kill me. Five minutes without a mask and I'd be dead."

But then…

The sound of gunfire! Someone was shooting wildly.

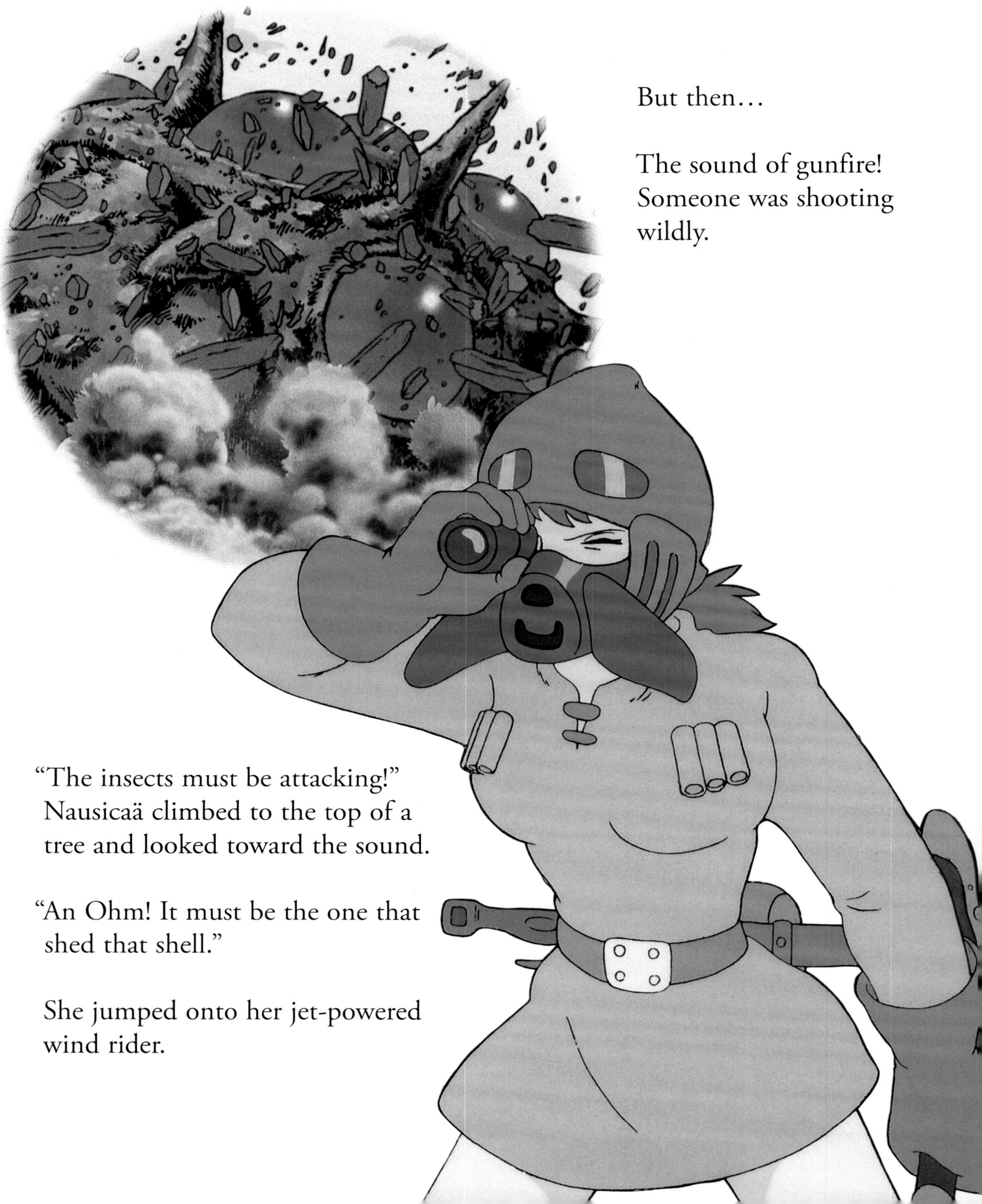

"The insects must be attacking!" Nausicaä climbed to the top of a tree and looked toward the sound.

"An Ohm! It must be the one that shed that shell."

She jumped onto her jet-powered wind rider.

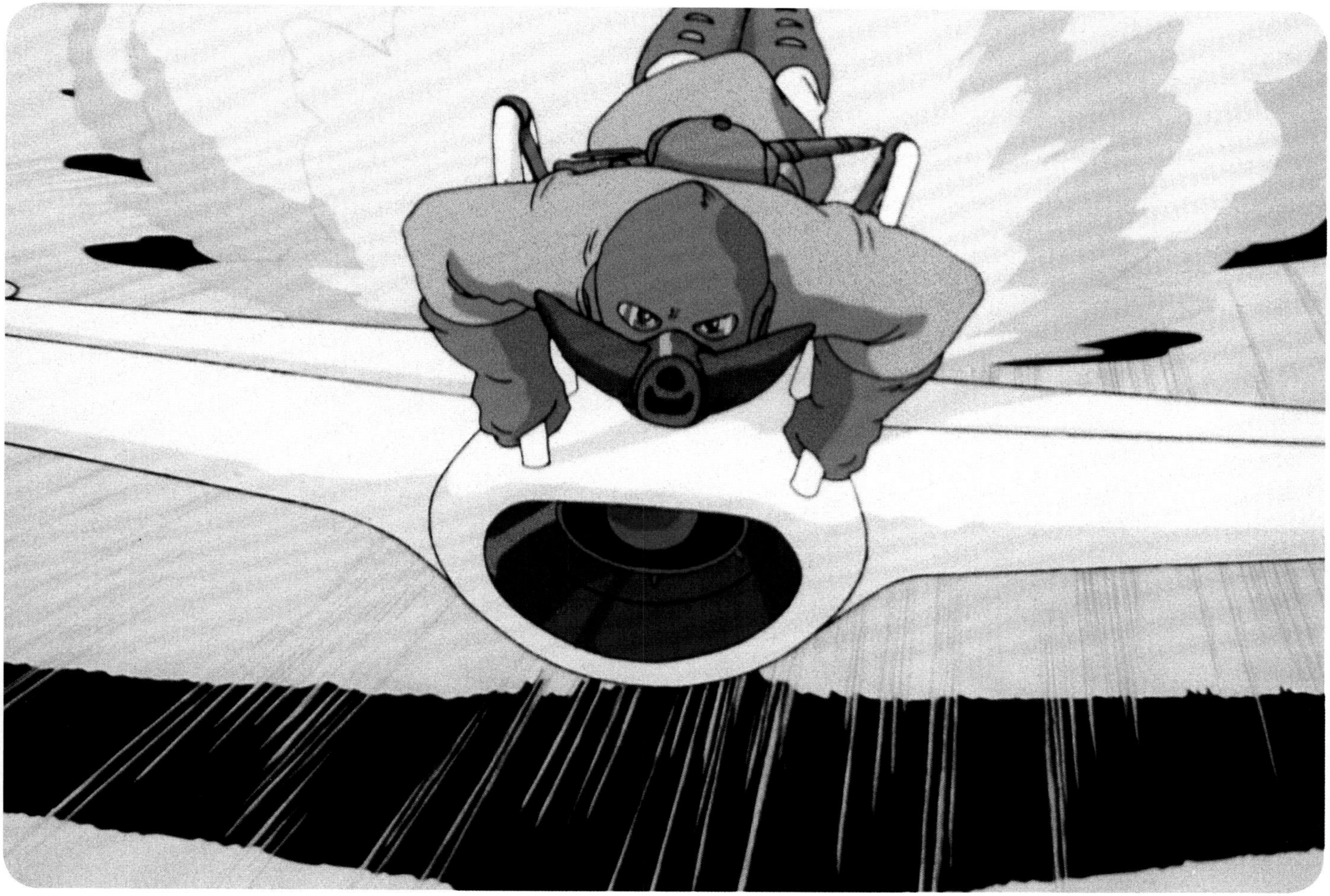

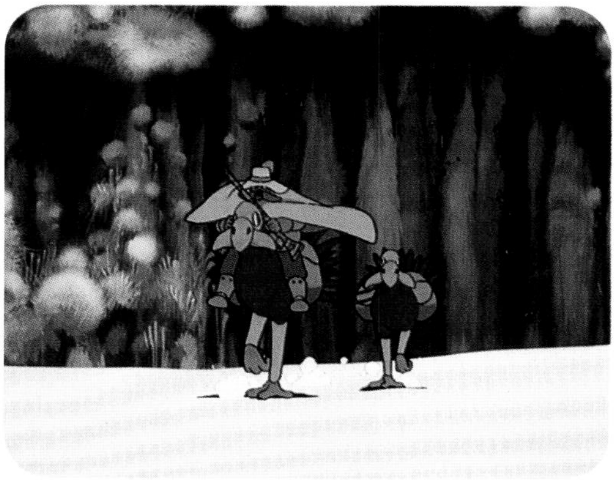

Nausicaä was a master of the wind. She could use it to take her anywhere she wanted to go.

She opened the throttle and flew as fast as she could. Soon she saw a man galloping out of the jungle on a strange, two-legged beast.

"There he is!"

As she watched, a huge Ohm charged out of the jungle and came bearing straight toward the man.

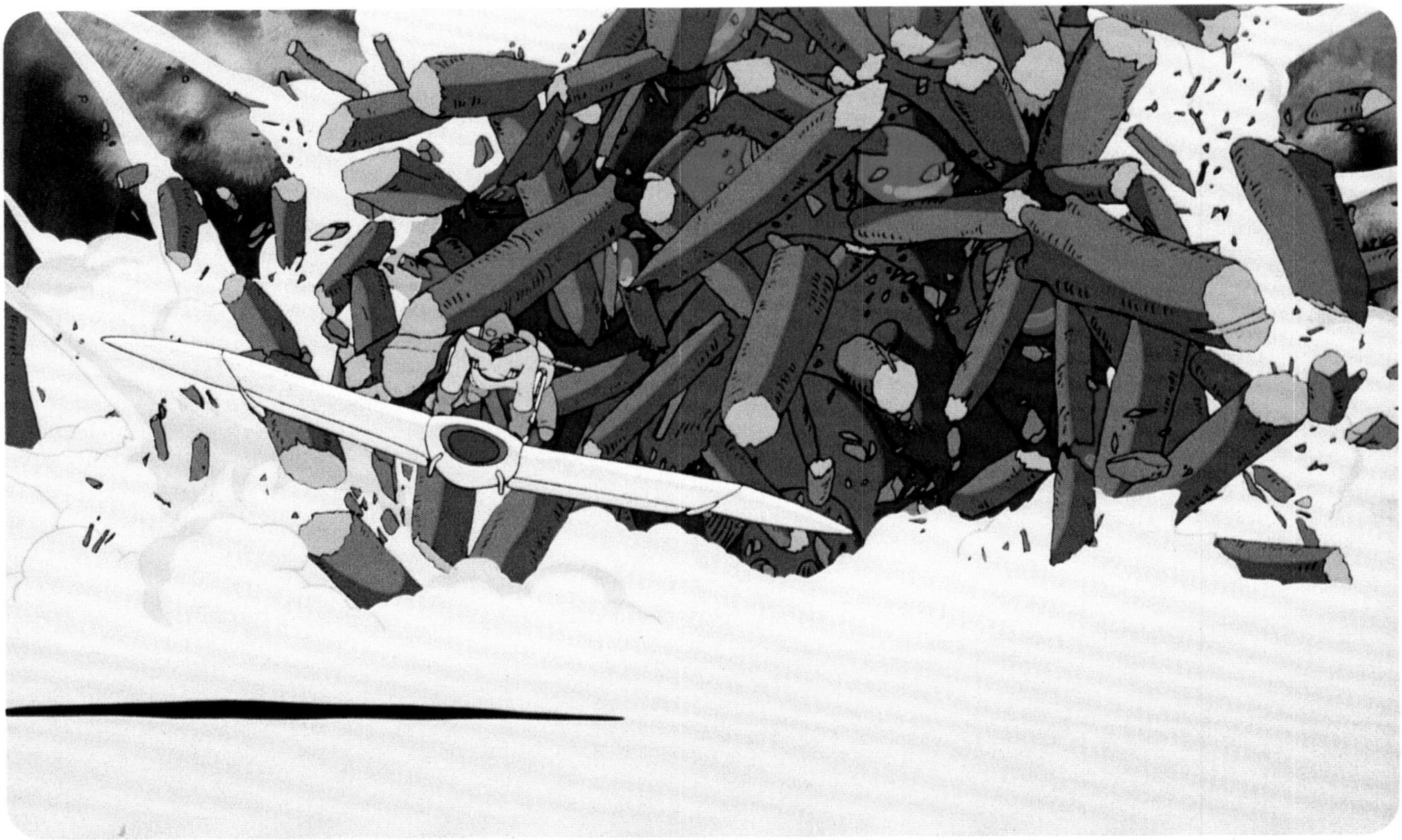

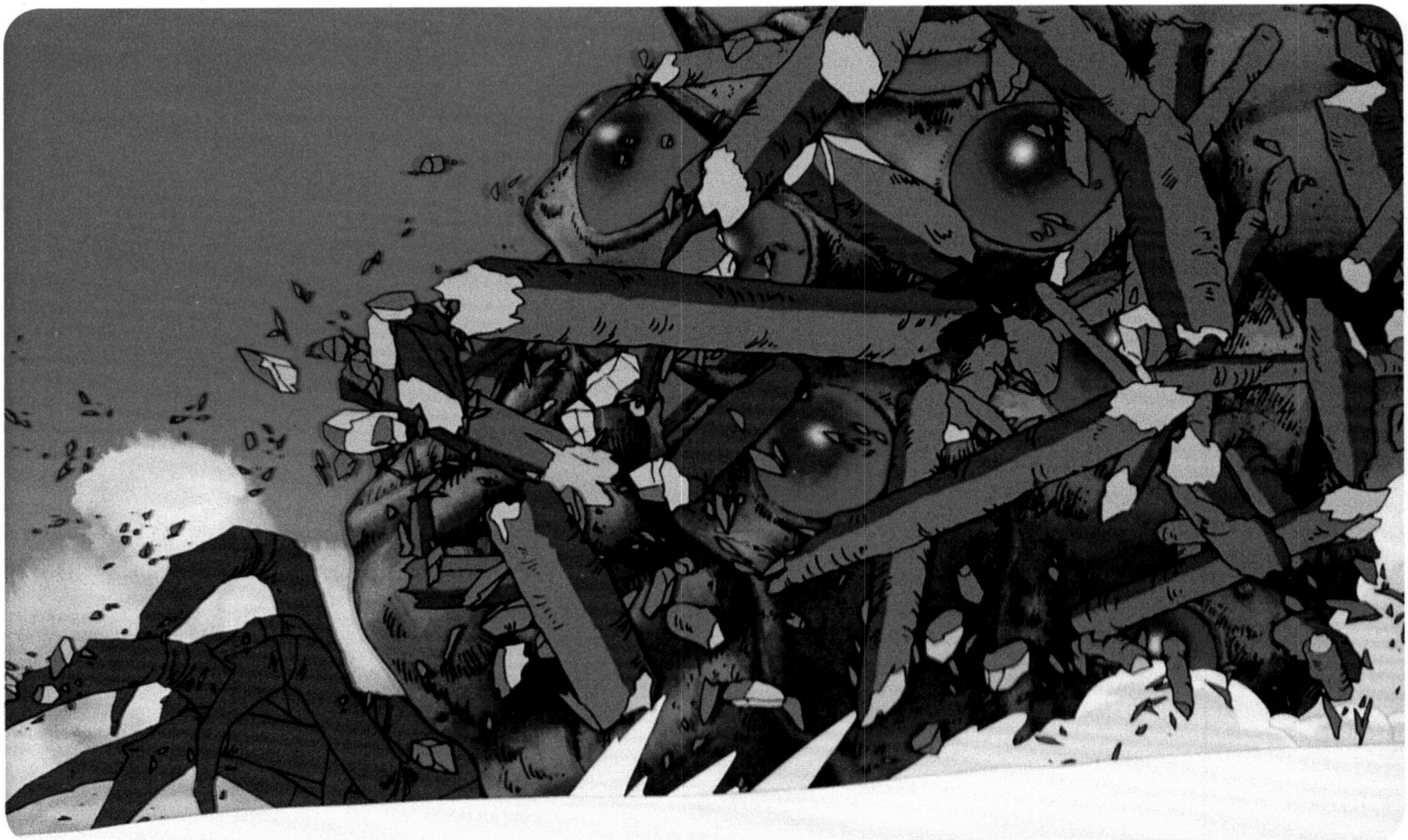

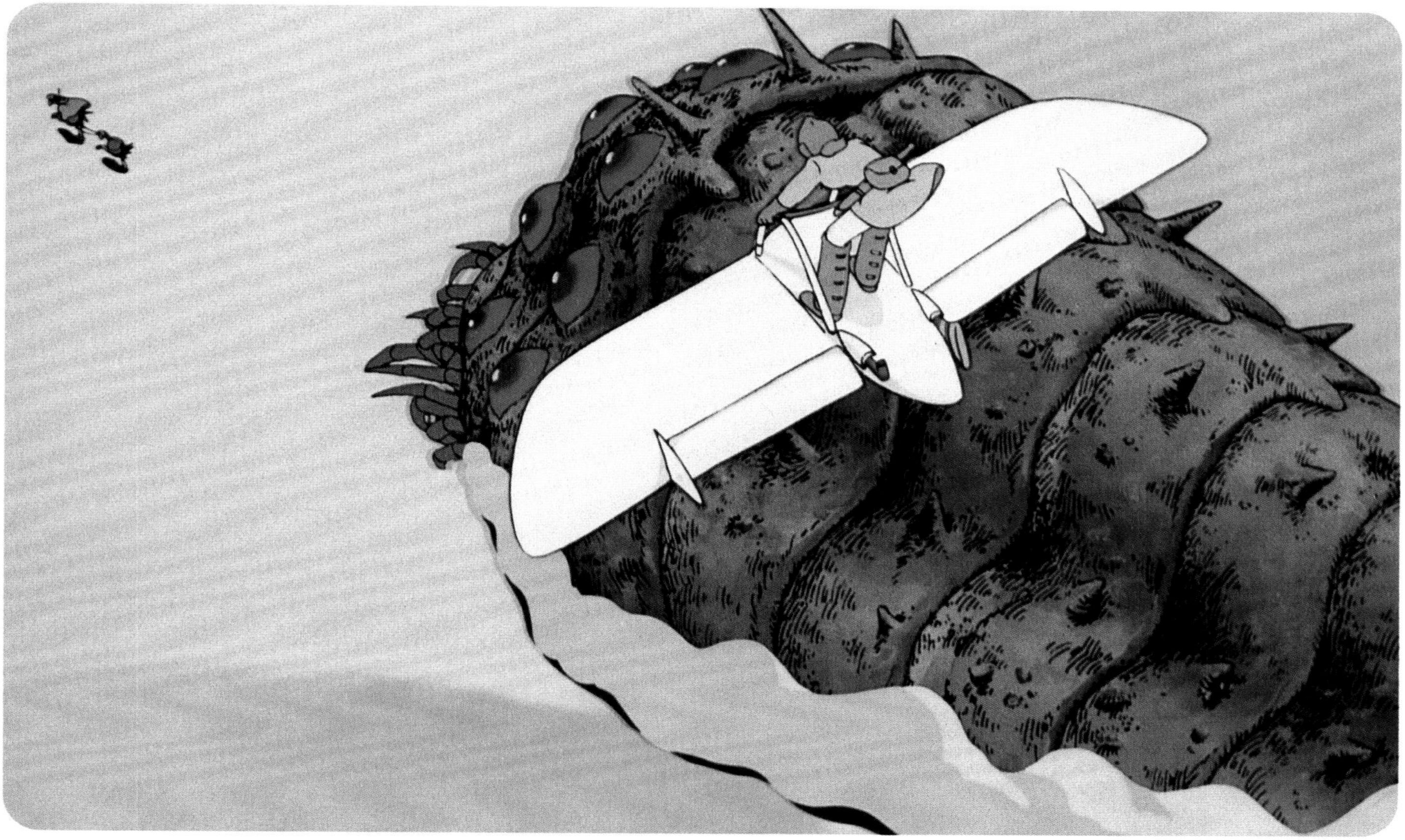
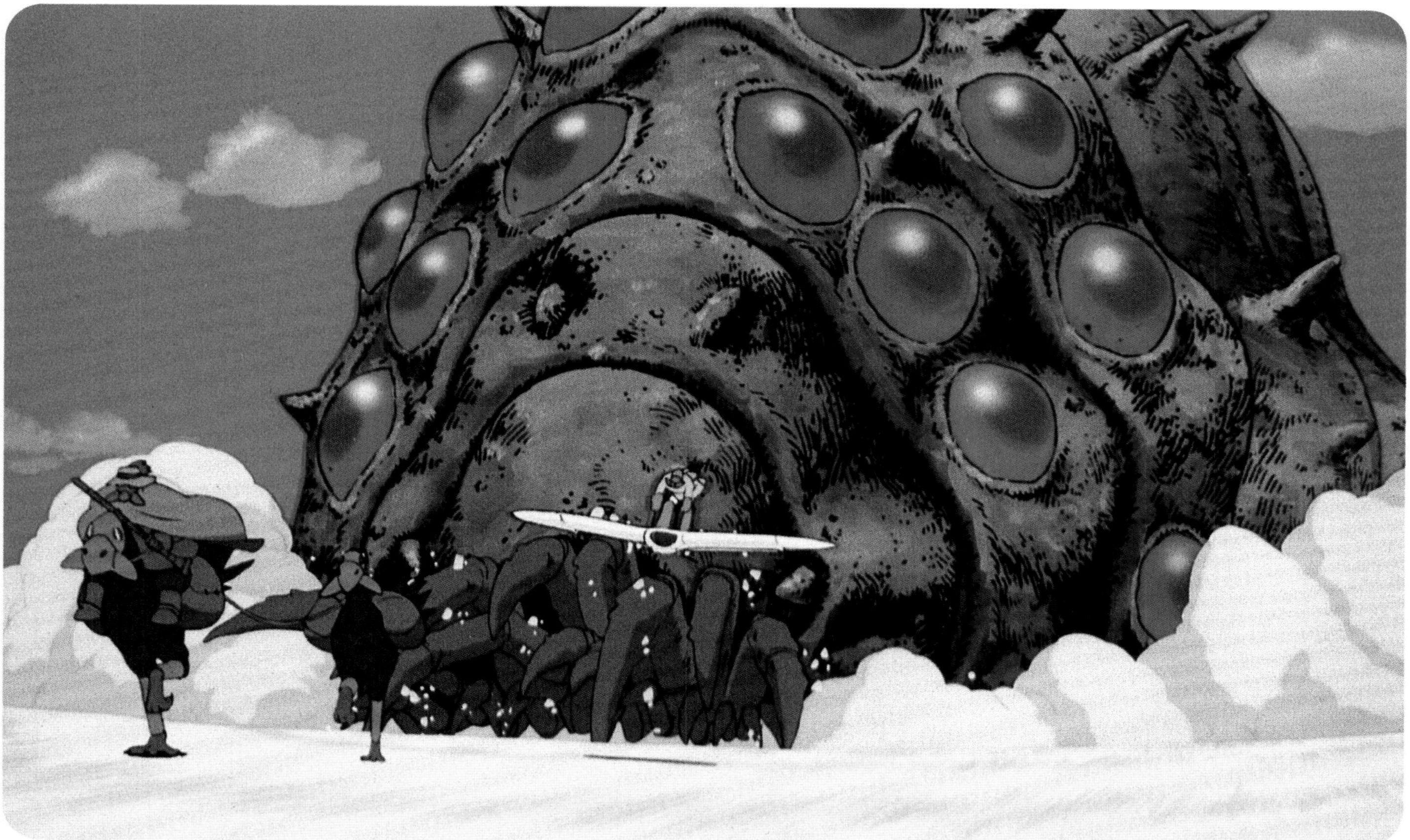

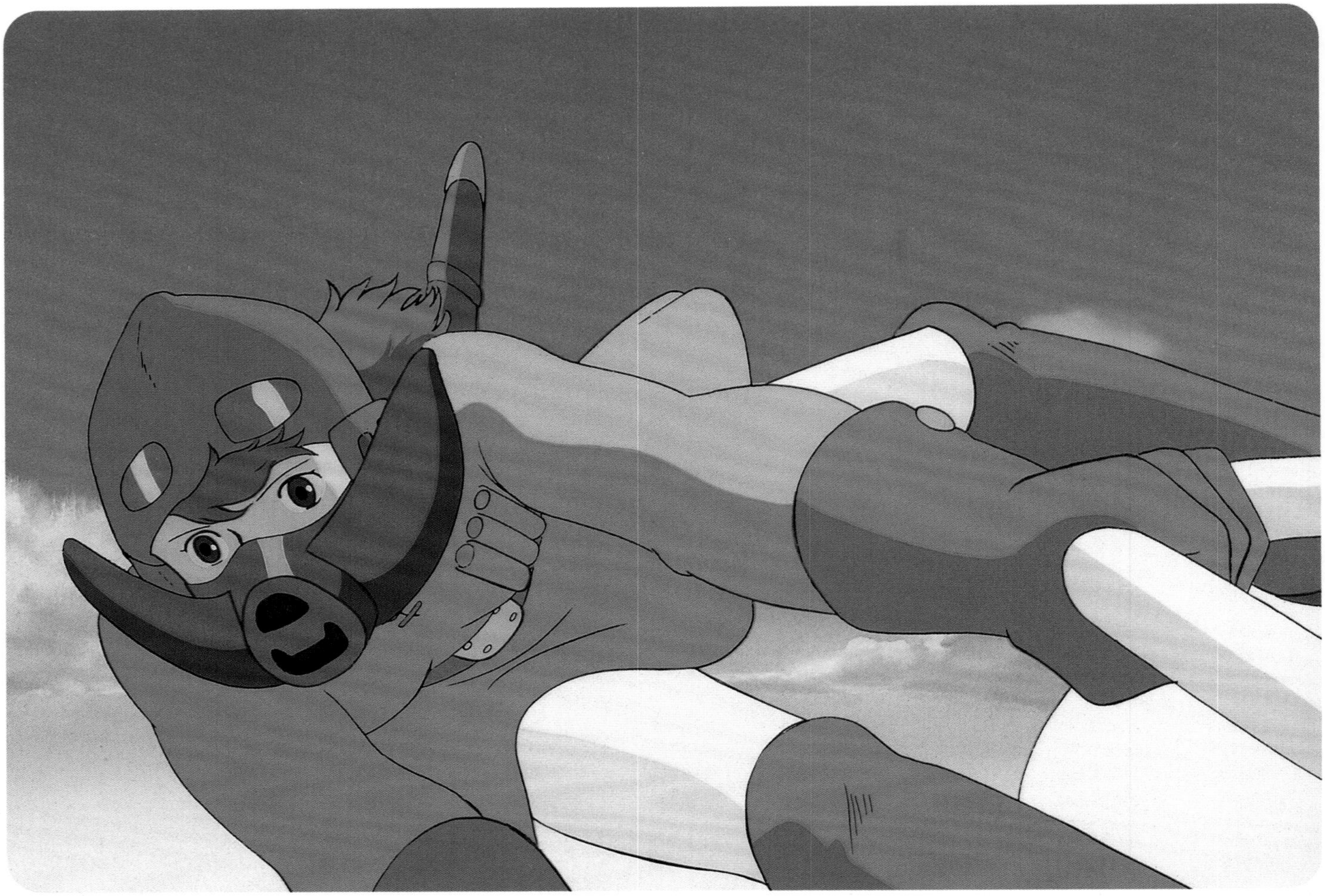

The great insect's eyes were crimson with rage.

"Ohm! Go back to the jungle," Nausicaä called. "This is not your world."

But no matter how many times she called, the Ohm wouldn't listen. It kept stampeding toward the man.

"It's blind with rage. I've got to calm it."

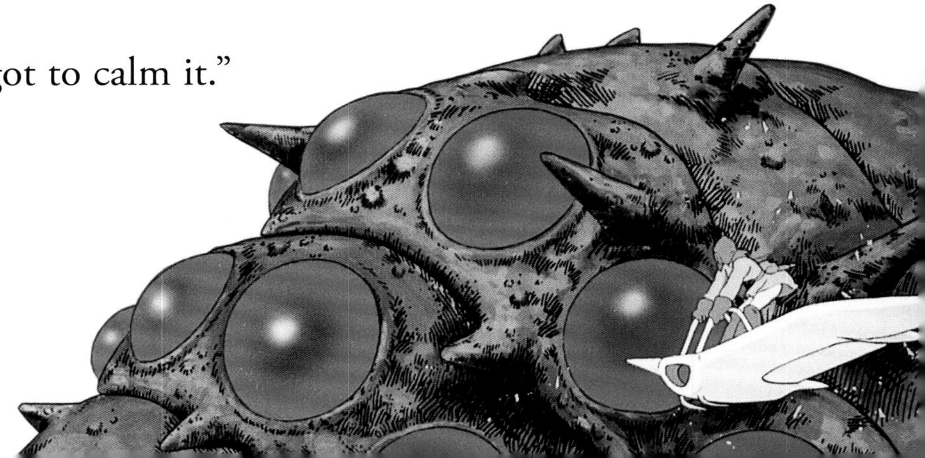

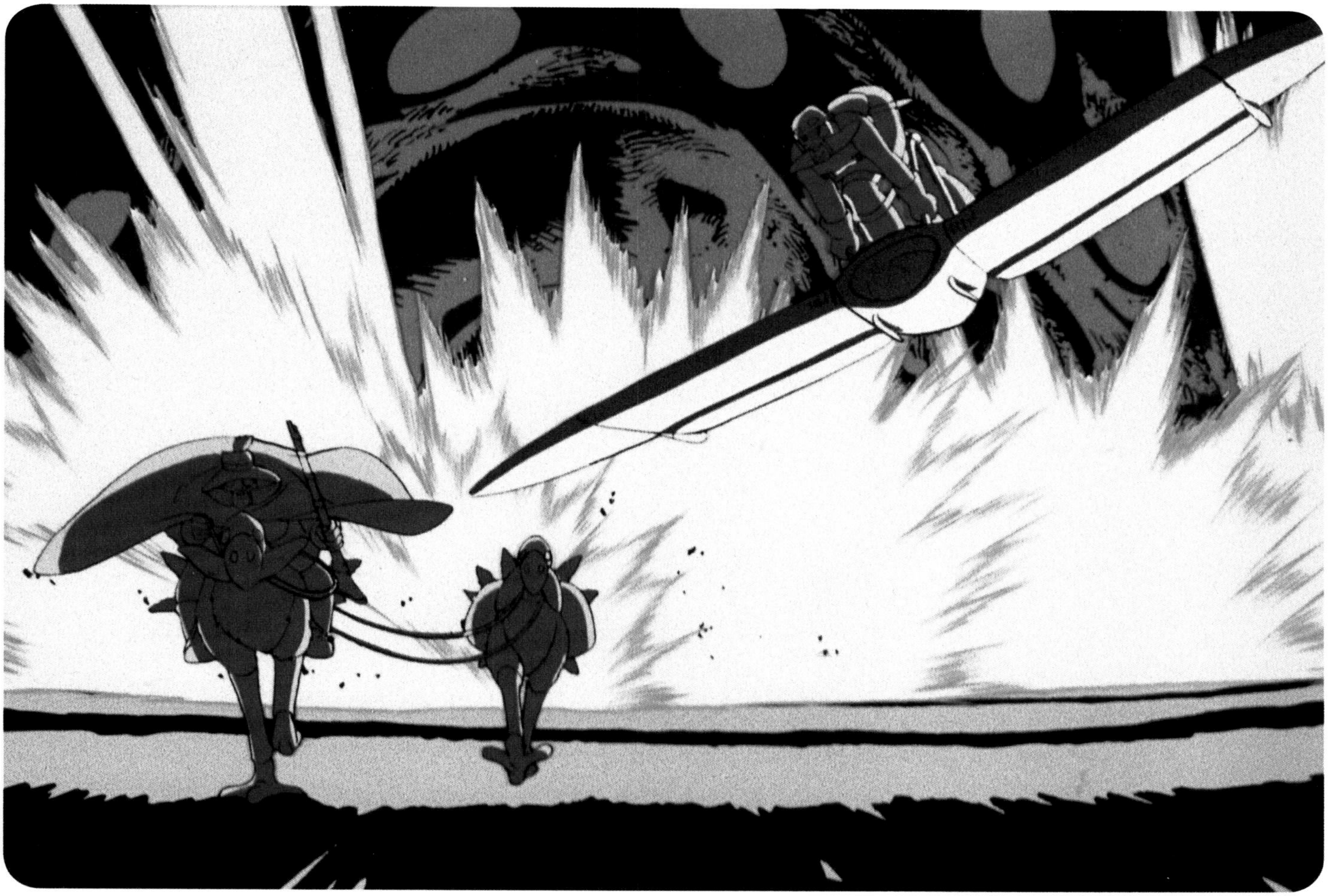

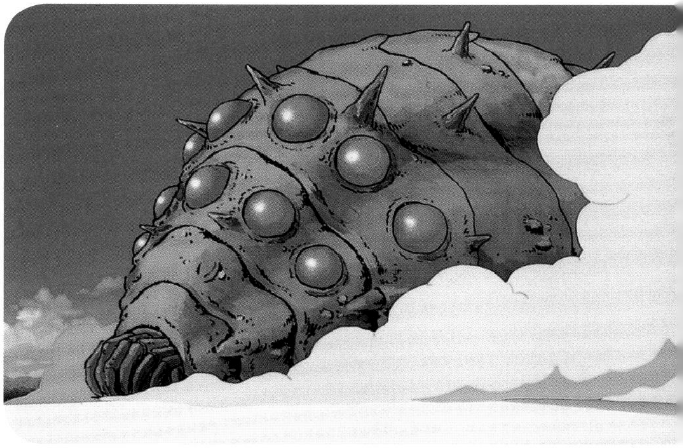

She dropped a handful of flash bombs in the Ohm's path. They went off with a loud bang, showering the Ohm with blinding light.

The huge creature skidded to a stop in a cloud of dust. The blazing fire in its eyes was gone. It was very still now.

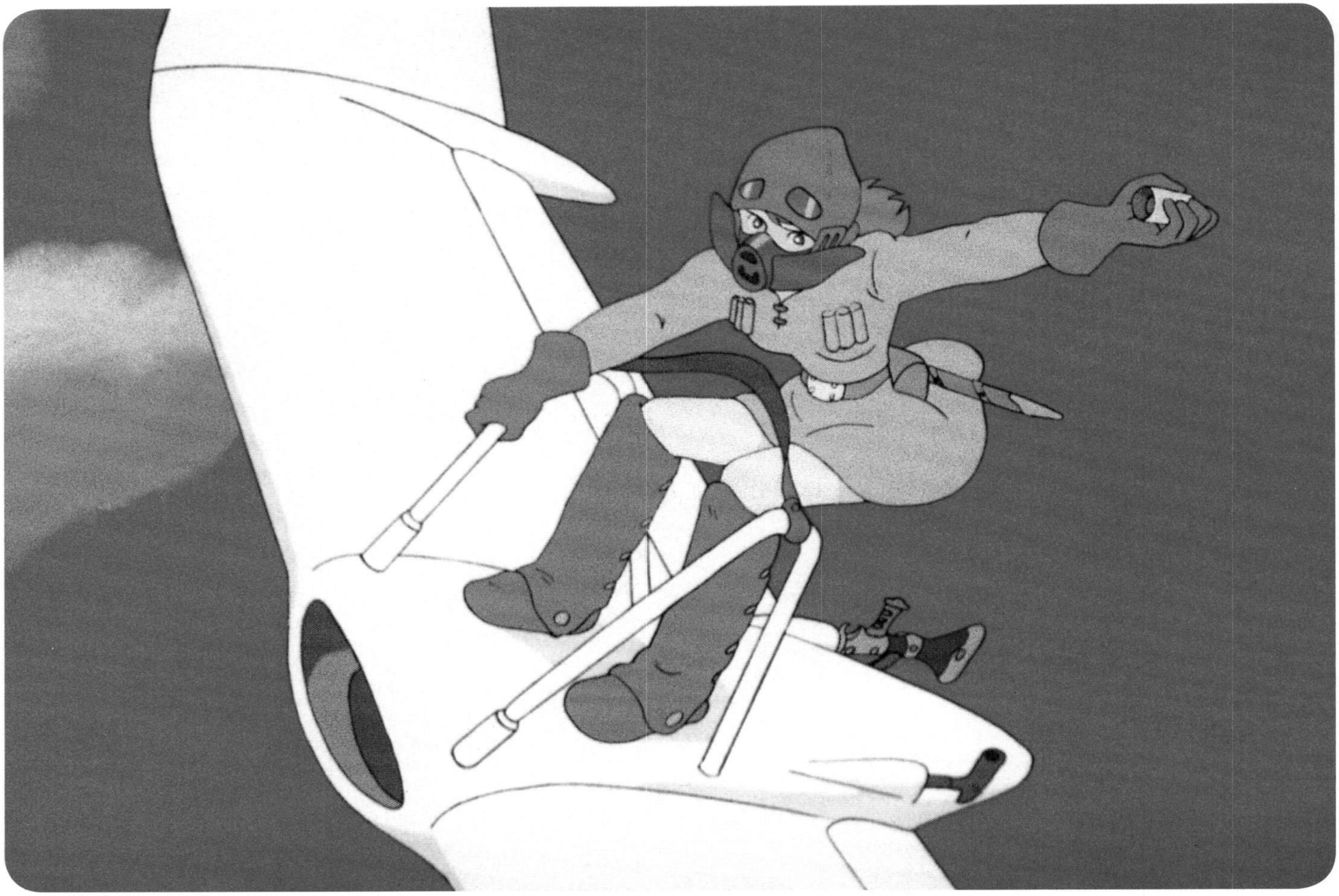

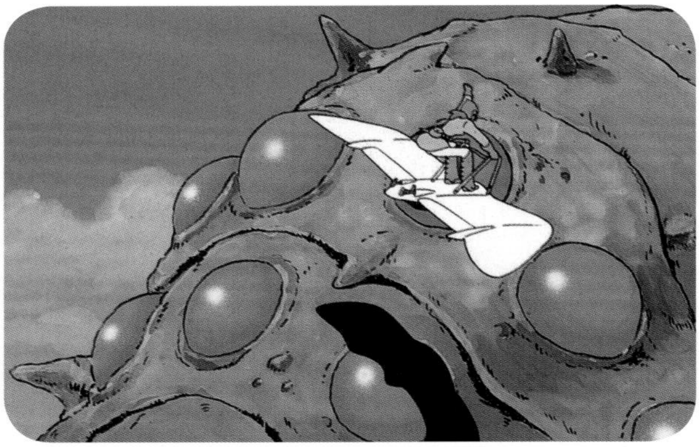

"Ohm, wake up! You need to go back to your jungle," Nausicaä called as she held her insect charm in the wind. It gave off an eerie, pulsing hum.

The Ohm seemed to hear the charm. A blue light rose in its eyes. Slowly, it began to turn away.

As he watched the Ohm returning to the jungle, the man murmured in wonder.

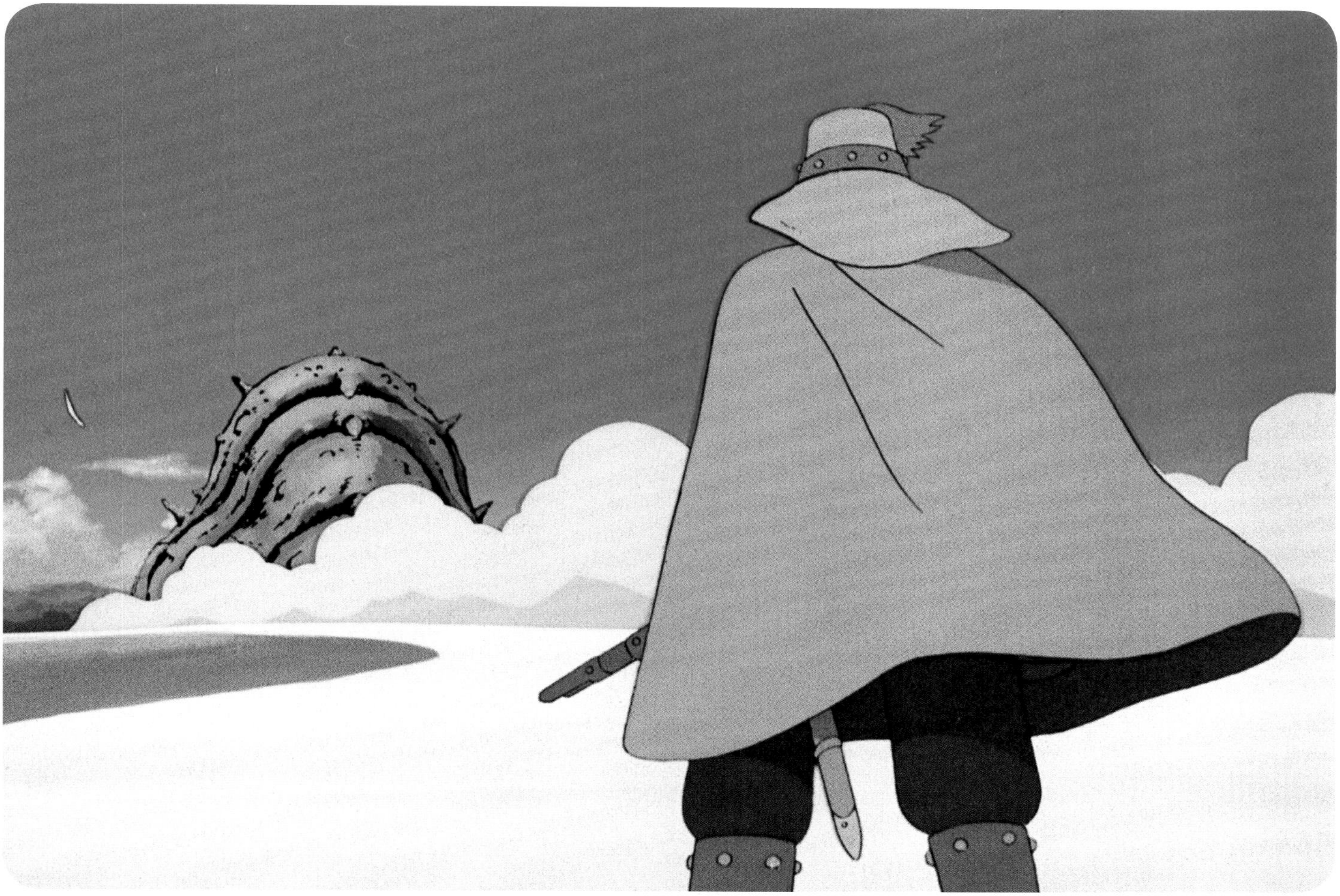

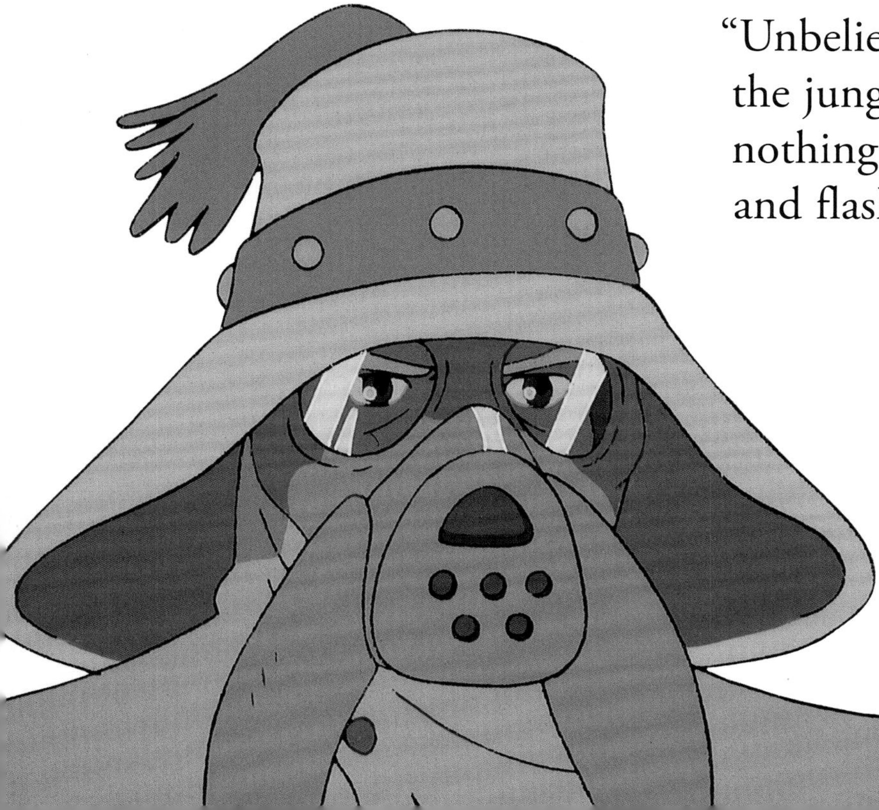

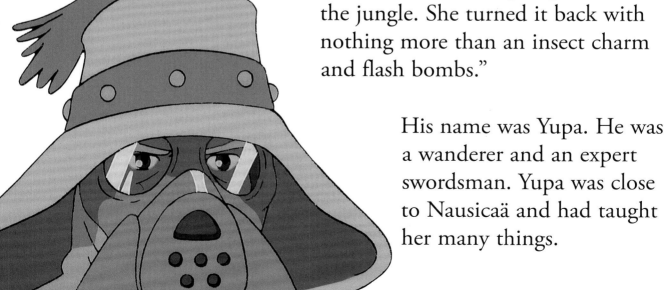

"Unbelievable... It's going back to the jungle. She turned it back with nothing more than an insect charm and flash bombs."

His name was Yupa. He was a wanderer and an expert swordsman. Yupa was close to Nausicaä and had taught her many things.

"Lord Yupa!"

Nausicaä leaped into his arms. It had been a long time since they'd last met.

"It's been over a year now. It's great to see you."

"Thank you for helping me with that Ohm. You've certainly mastered that wind rider of yours."

Nausicaä was gazing at Yupa with affection when a rustling sound came from the pouch on his belt.

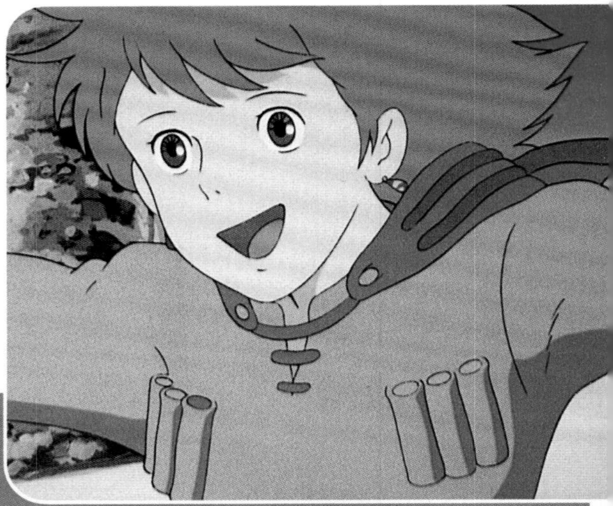

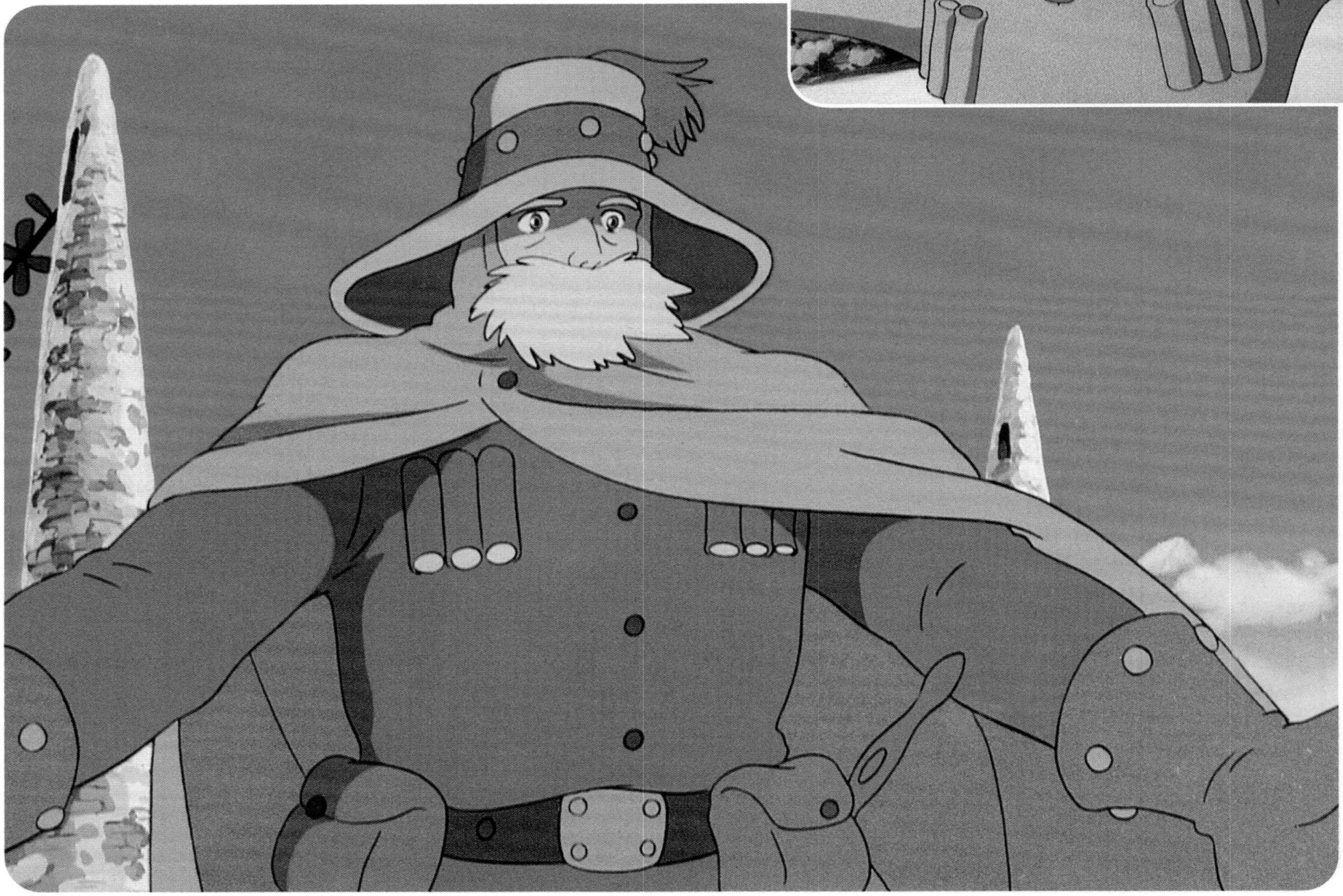

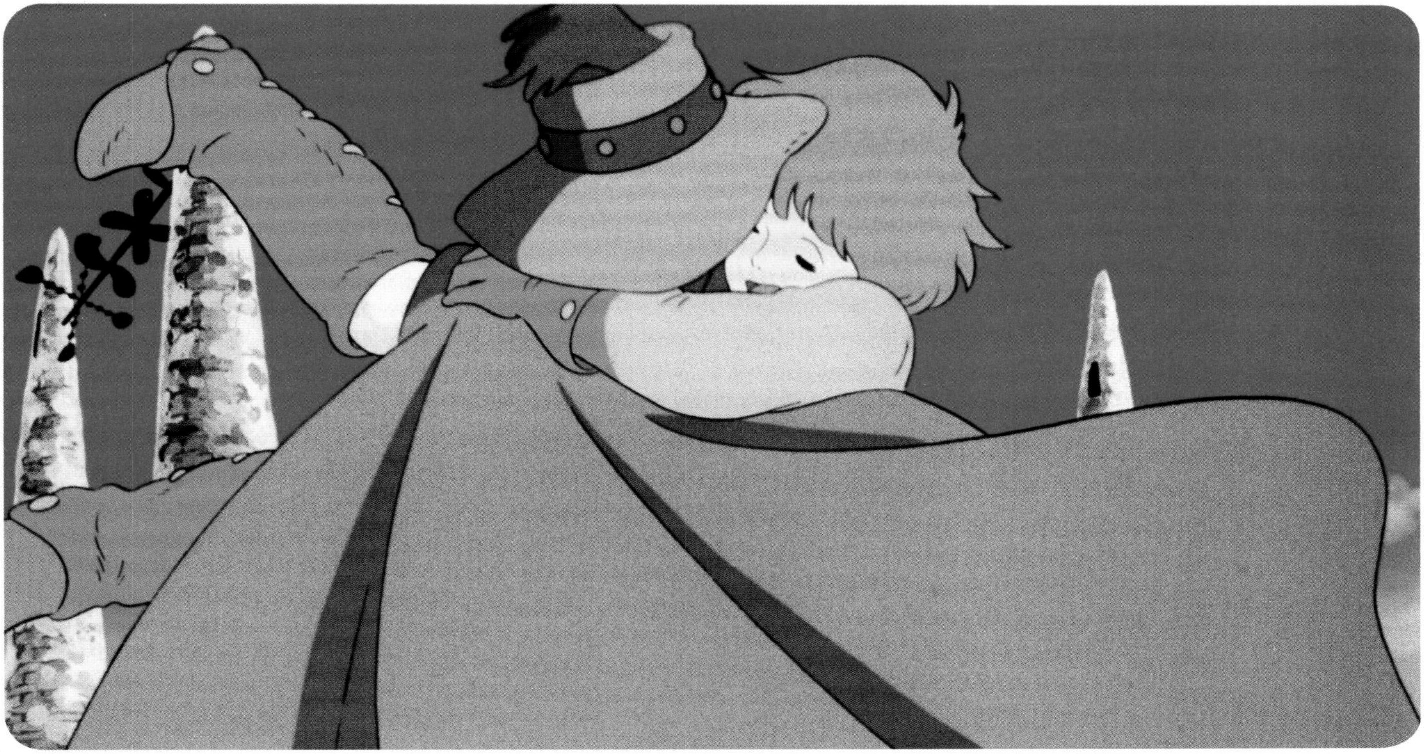
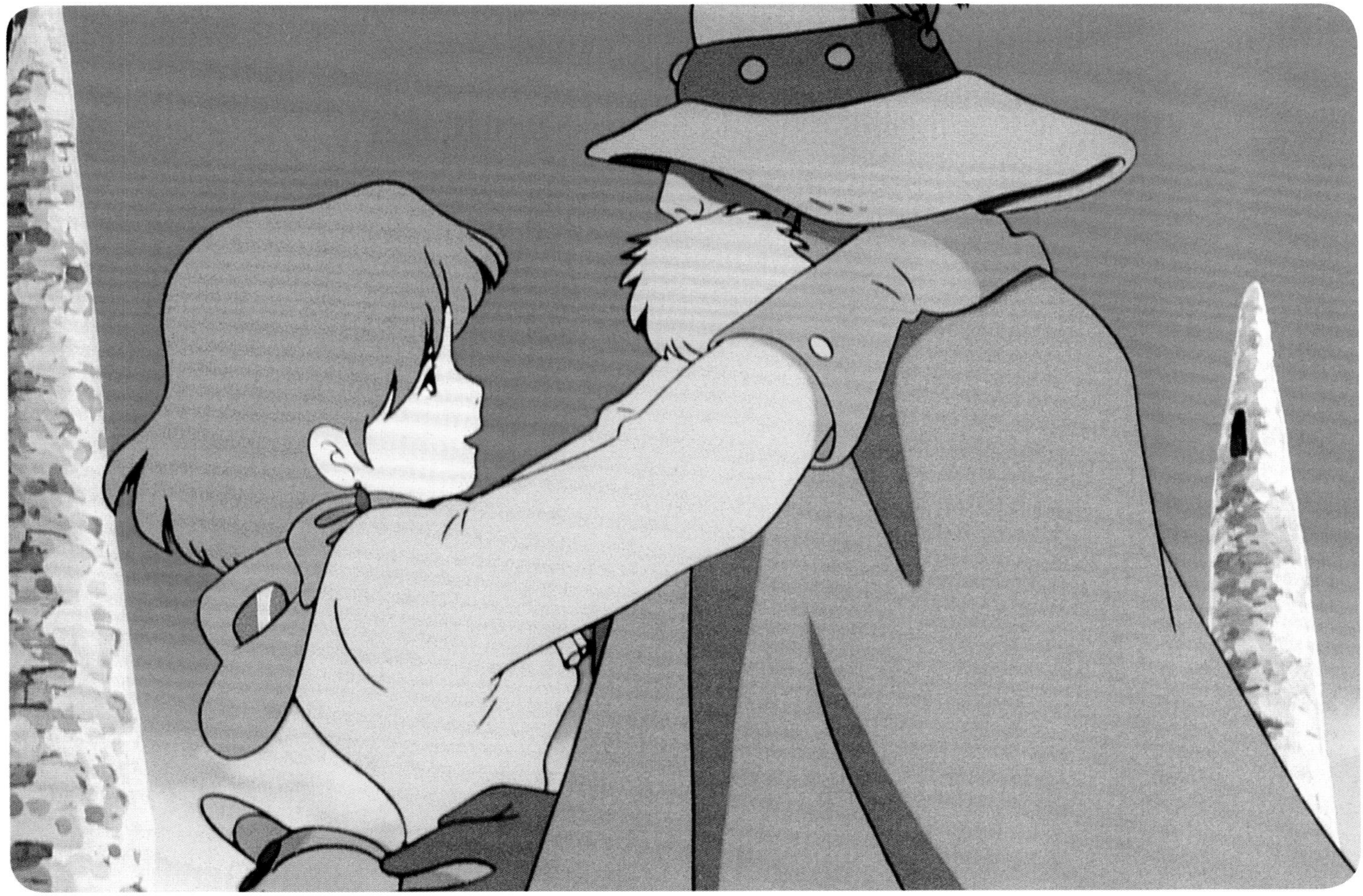

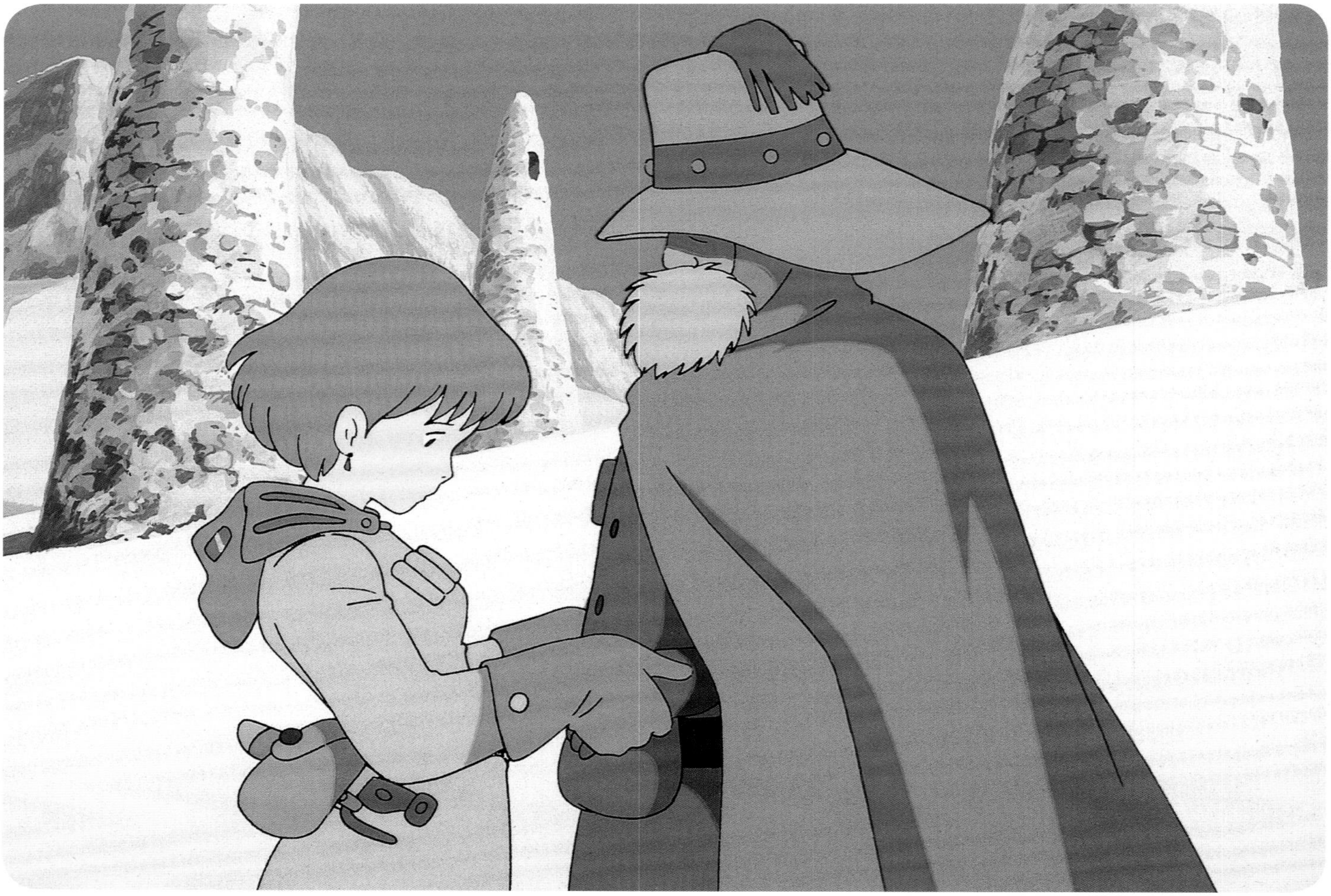

Yupa unbuttoned the pouch and a baby fox squirrel peeked out.

"Oh yes, I forgot all about this little fellow. Rescuing him is what got me in trouble with the Ohm. I saw an insect carrying him off. I had no choice but to use my gun."

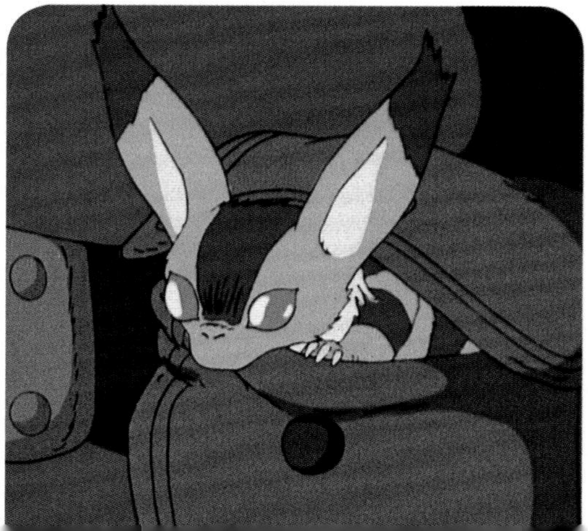

"So that's why the Ohm was so angry with you," Nausicaä said.

"Better not touch him. Even the babies are vicious."

"Come on, it's okay."

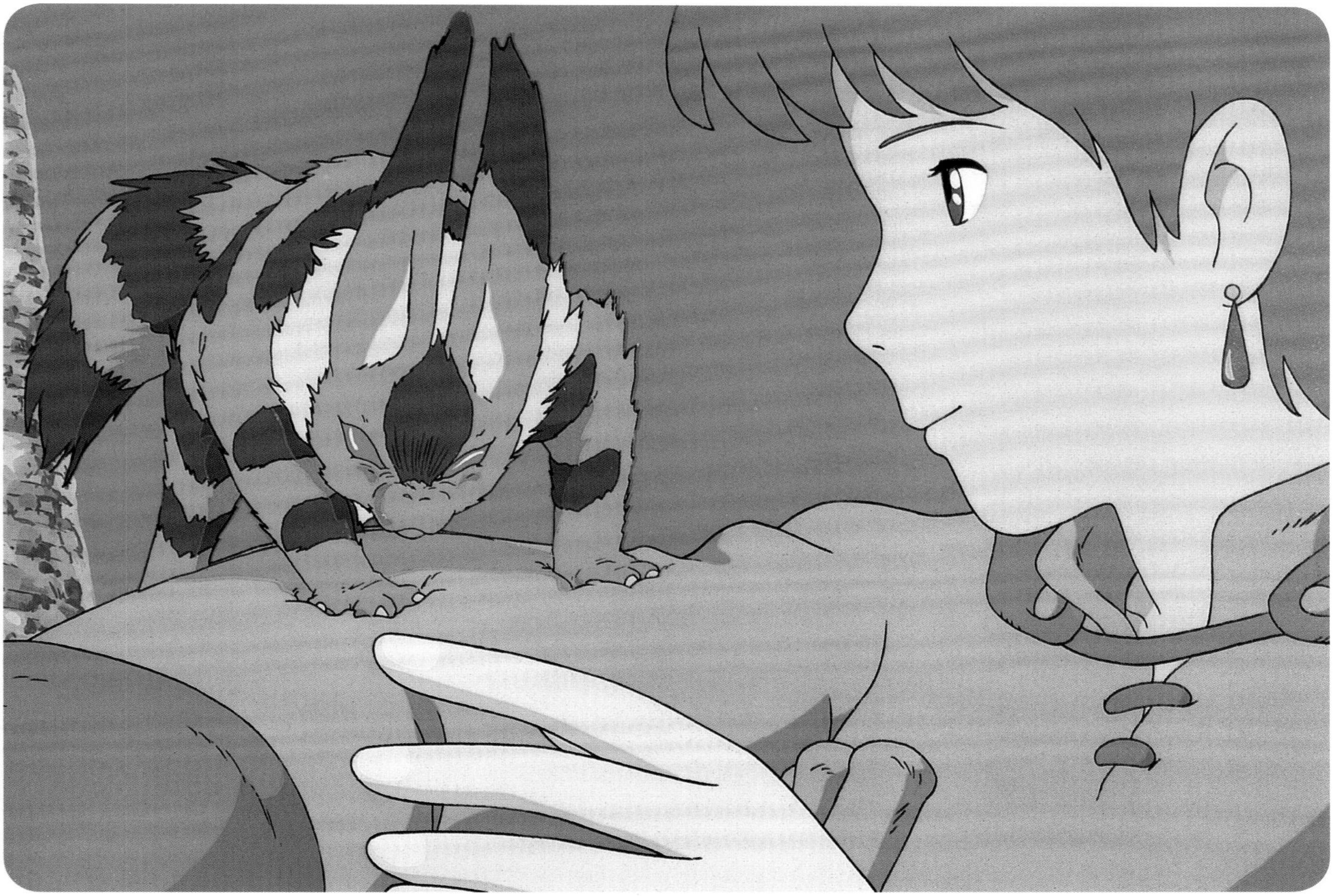

She held out her hand, and the little animal leaped out of the pouch and ran up her arm.

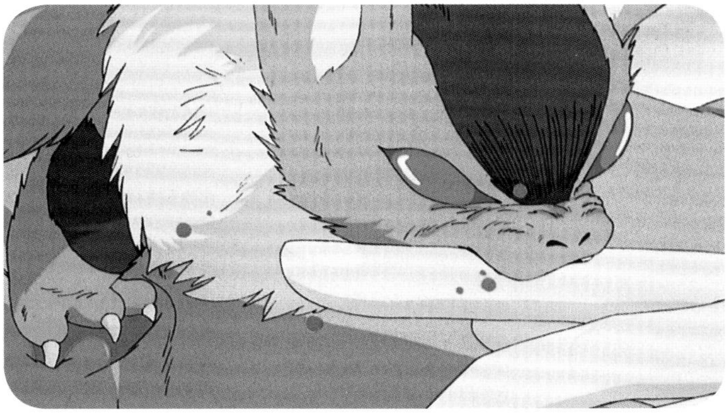

The fox squirrel's fur stood on end with fear as it bared its fangs.

"There's nothing to fear." Gently, Nausicaä extended a finger. With a high-pitched snarl, the animal sank its teeth into her finger.

Nausicaä didn't pull away. She just kept talking quietly.

"There's nothing to fear. See?"

Slowly, the animal relaxed its jaws and gently licked her finger.

"You were just a little scared, weren't you? I'm going to name you Teto."

Nausicaä smiled, and the fox squirrel began to run happily back and forth across her outstretched arms. She had a new, loyal friend.

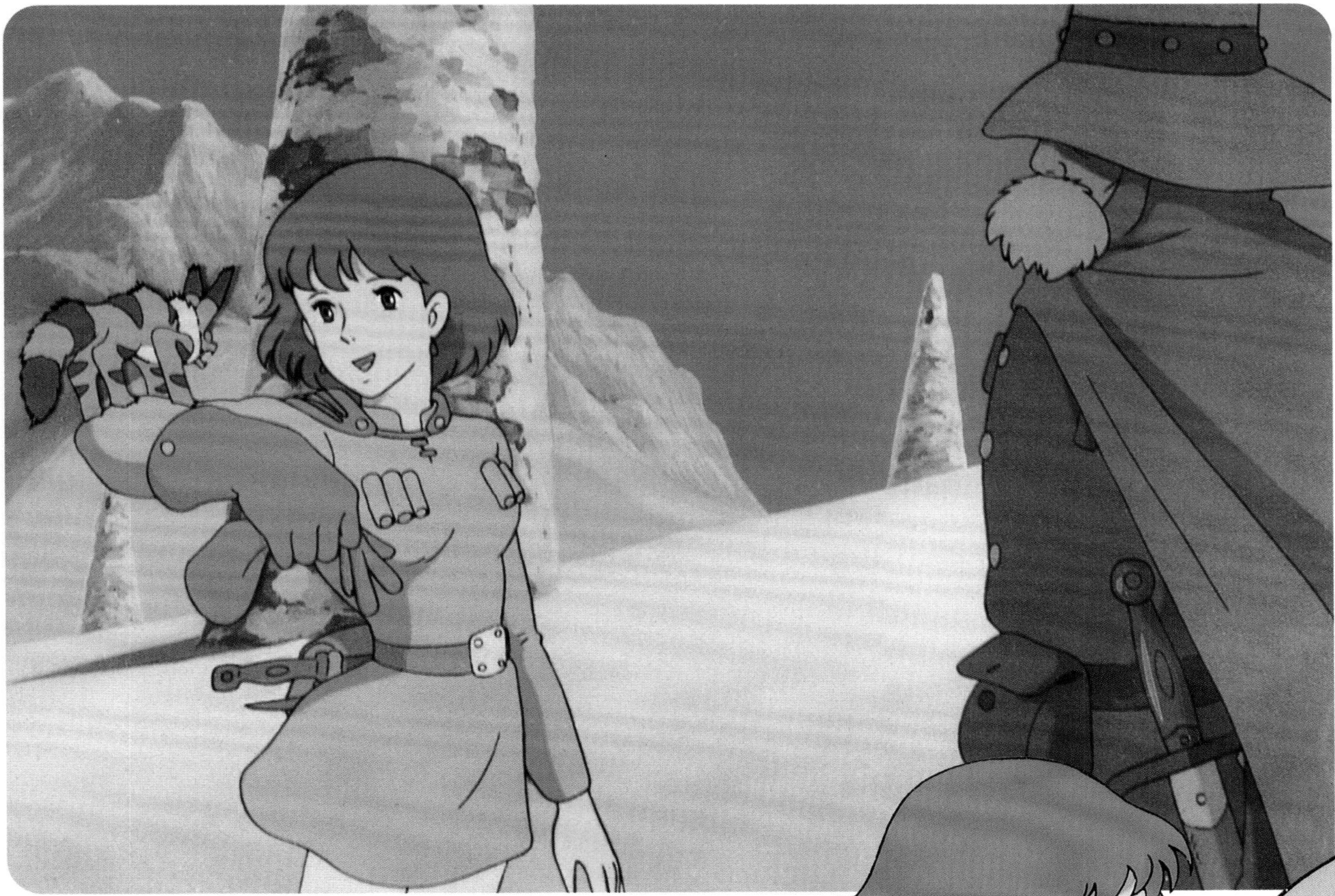

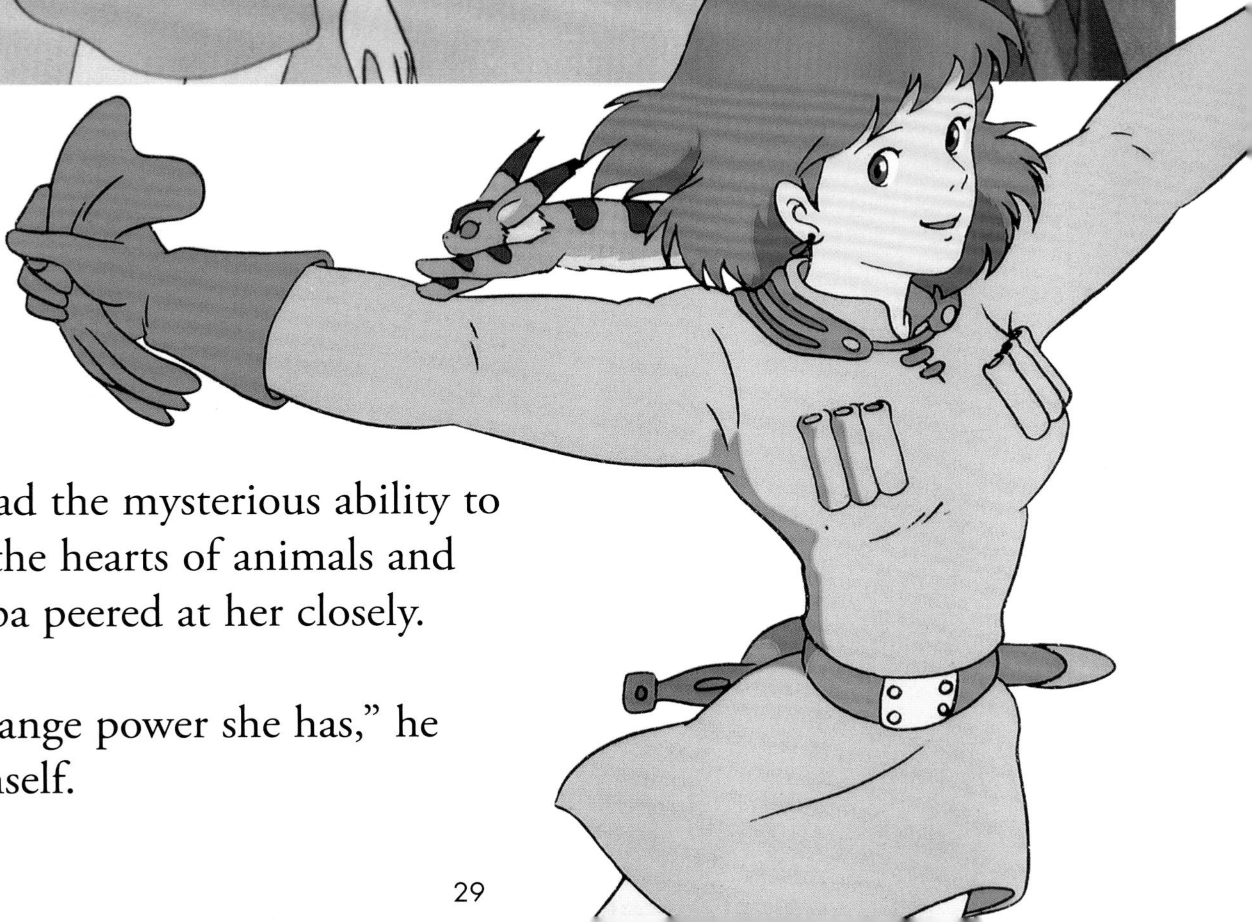

Nausicaä had the mysterious ability to enter into the hearts of animals and insects. Yupa peered at her closely.

"What a strange power she has," he said to himself.

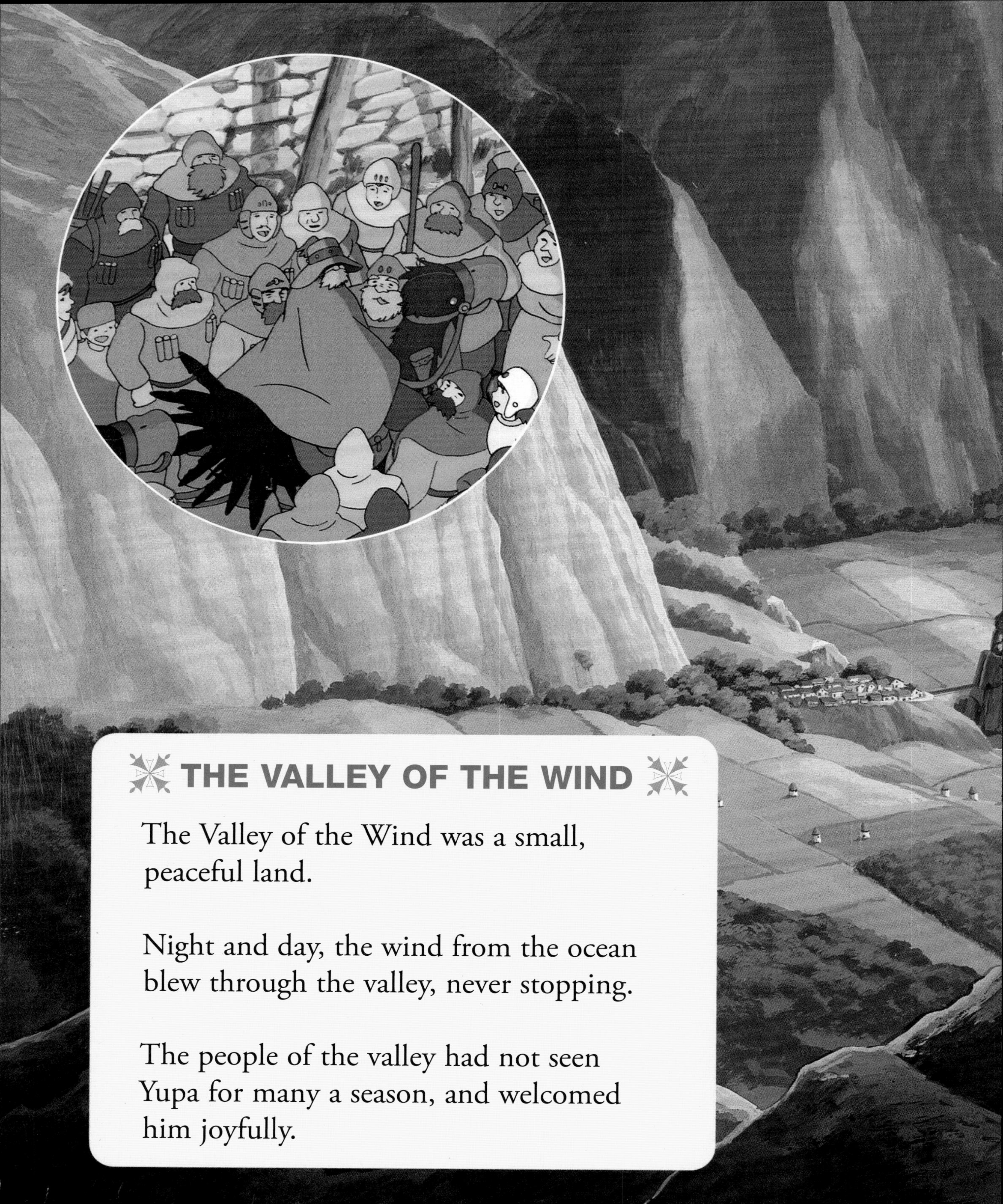

THE VALLEY OF THE WIND

The Valley of the Wind was a small, peaceful land.

Night and day, the wind from the ocean blew through the valley, never stopping.

The people of the valley had not seen Yupa for many a season, and welcomed him joyfully.

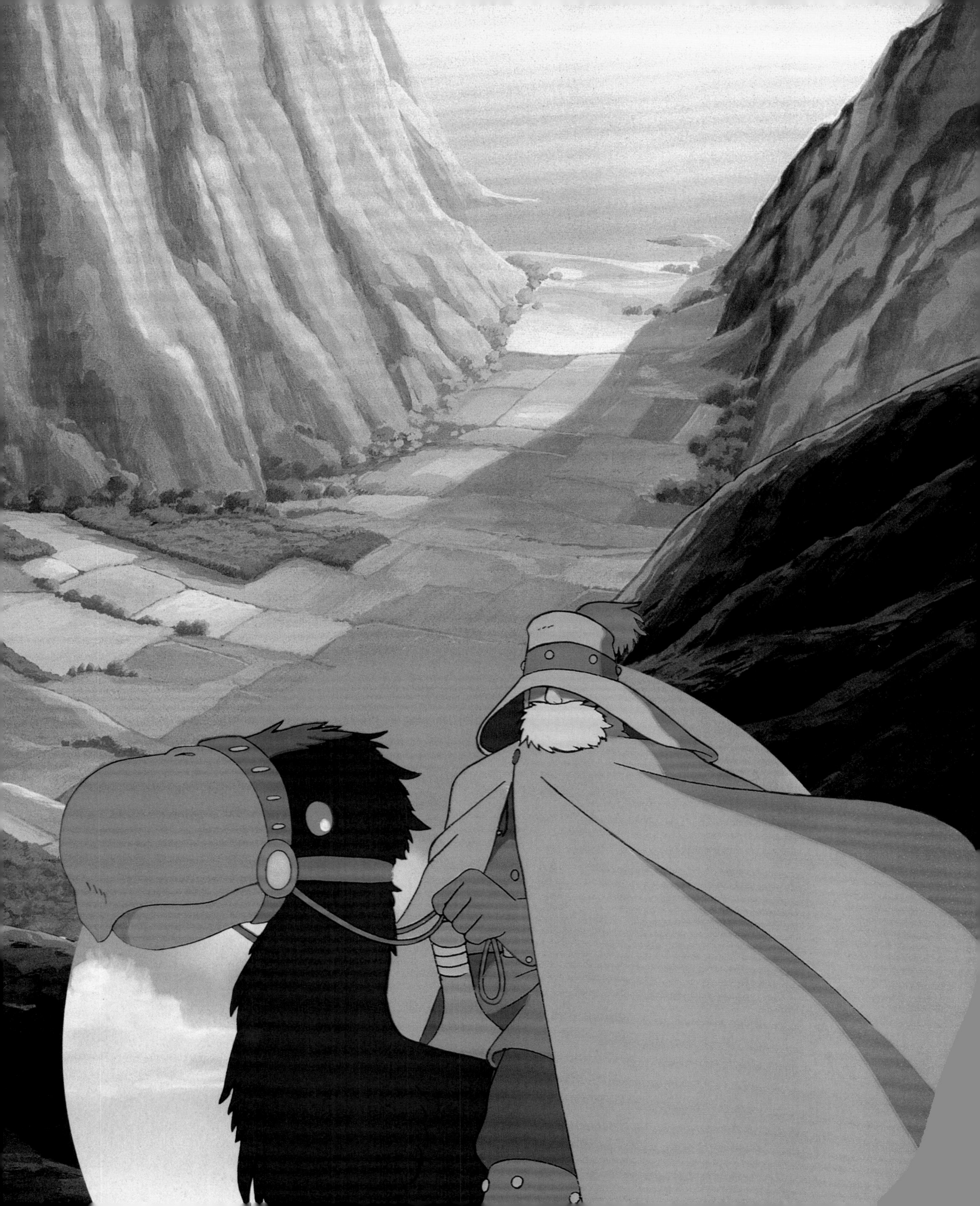

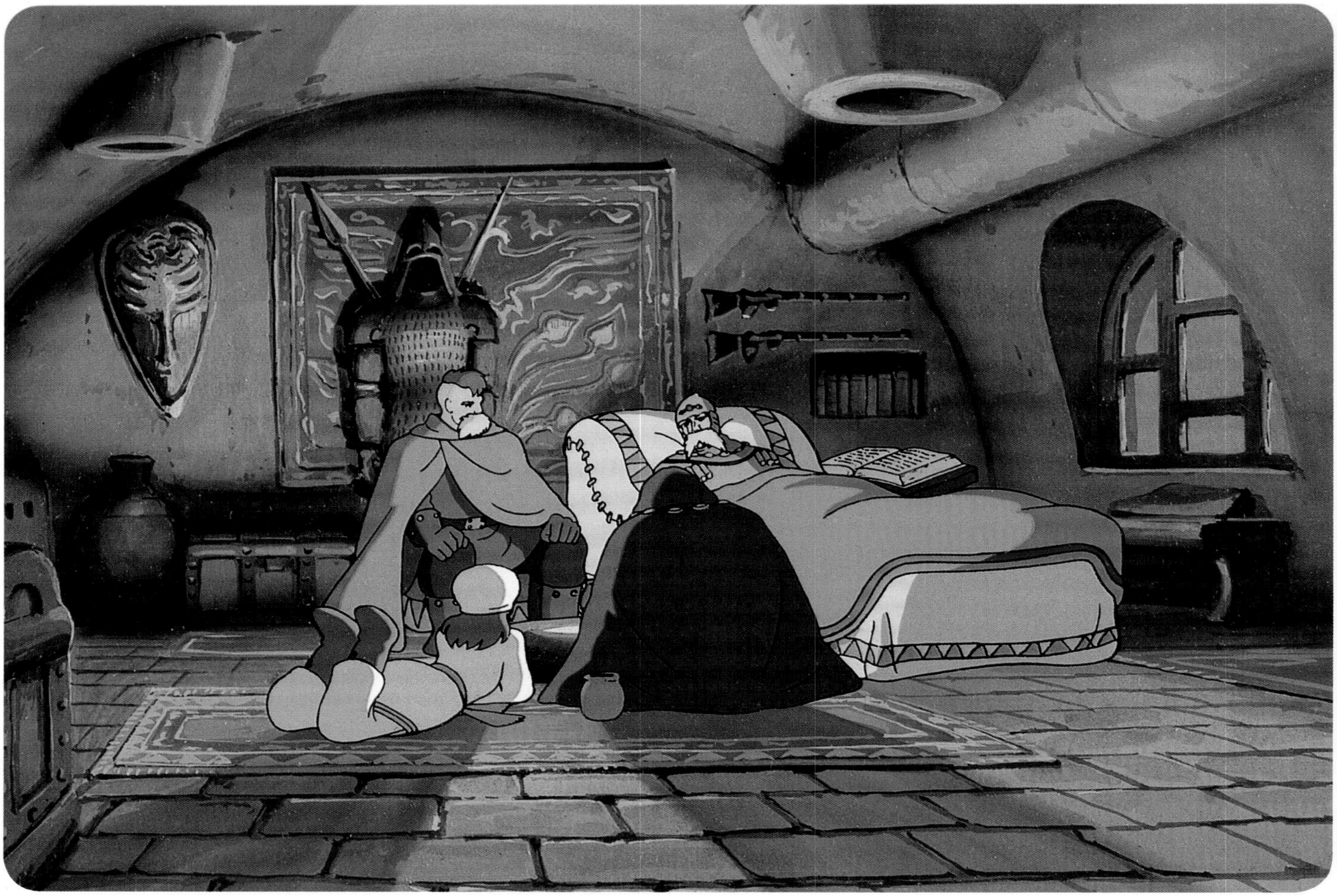

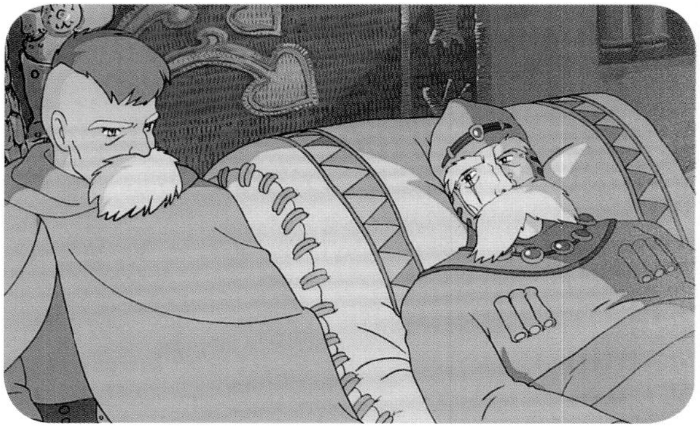

Nausicaä's father, King Jihl, lay propped up in bed. Years of living not far from the toxic jungle had left him unable to walk.

Yupa sat by his bed and told Jihl, Nausicaä, and Obaba what he had seen during his wanderings.

"Things are grim. I found two more kingdoms to the south that have been consumed by the jungle. It seems to spread faster every day."

"And the kingdoms that survive are torn by war and starvation."

"Lord Yupa, isn't it about time you settled down here?" Jihl said. "It would bring peace of mind to us all."

Obaba laughed. "That's impossible. Lord Yupa must continue his search. It's his destiny."

Nausicaä looked up at her. "Obaba, what is Lord Yupa searching for?"

"How could you not know, child? The answer stands before you." Obaba nodded toward a tapestry hanging on the wall.

"I can no longer see it, but I remember it well. There is a figure in the upper-left corner."

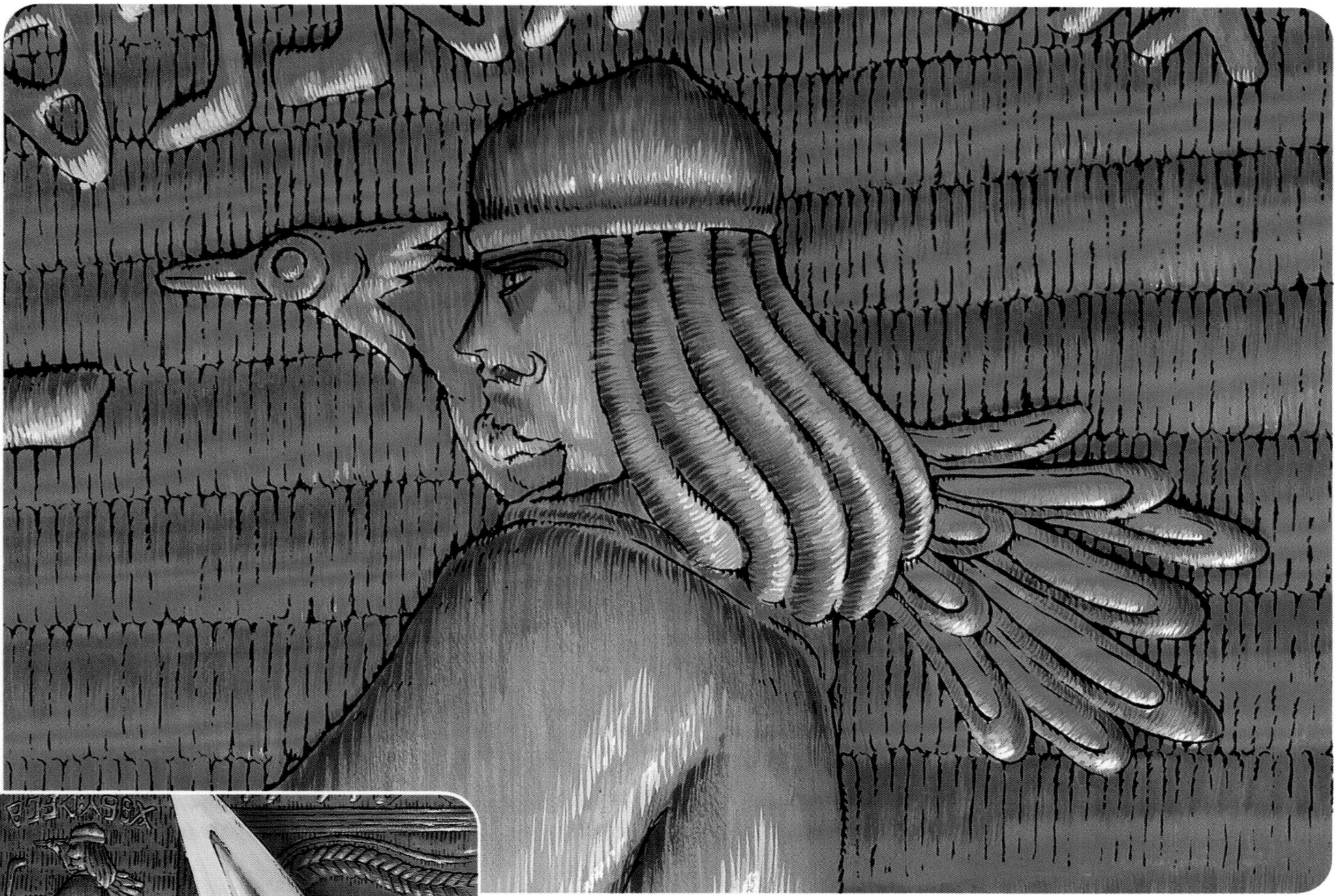

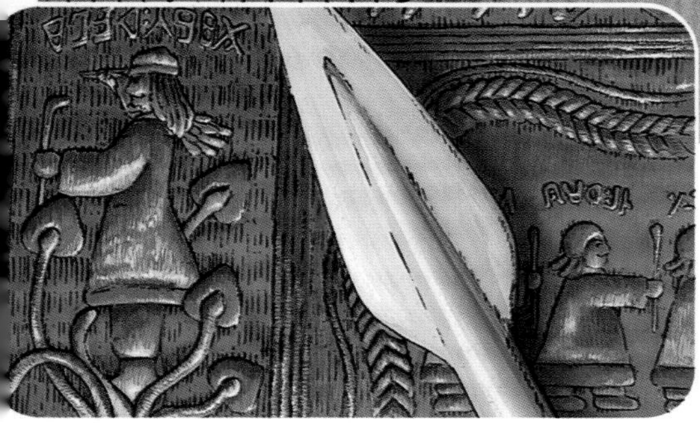

“The legend says that after a thousand years of darkness he will come, clad in blue on a plain of gold, to restore our connection with the earth.”

Nausicaä listened intently, then turned to Yupa.

“Lord Yupa, are you searching for the man in blue?”

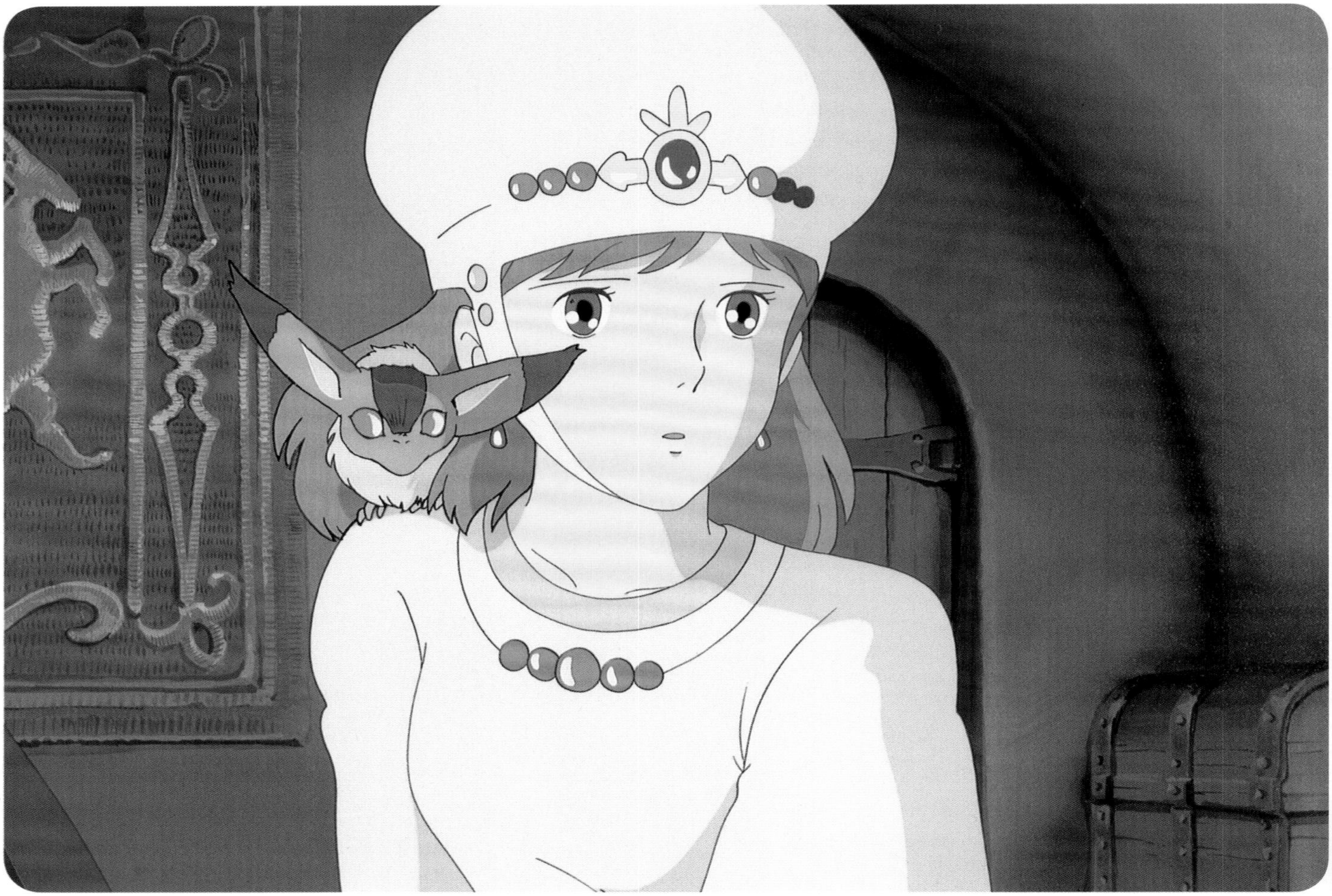

“The only goal I seek is to understand the mysteries of the toxic jungle,” Yupa replied. “I want to know if there is hope that we may survive.”

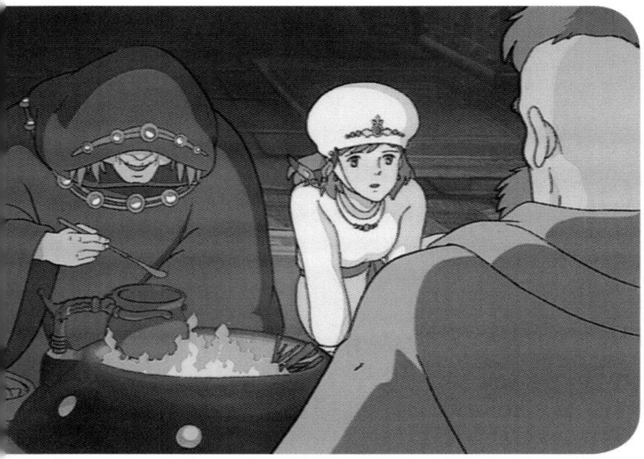

For the first time, Nausicaä heard the reason for his travels from Yupa himself. She wished there was something she could do to help.

That night, as she was about to drift off to sleep…

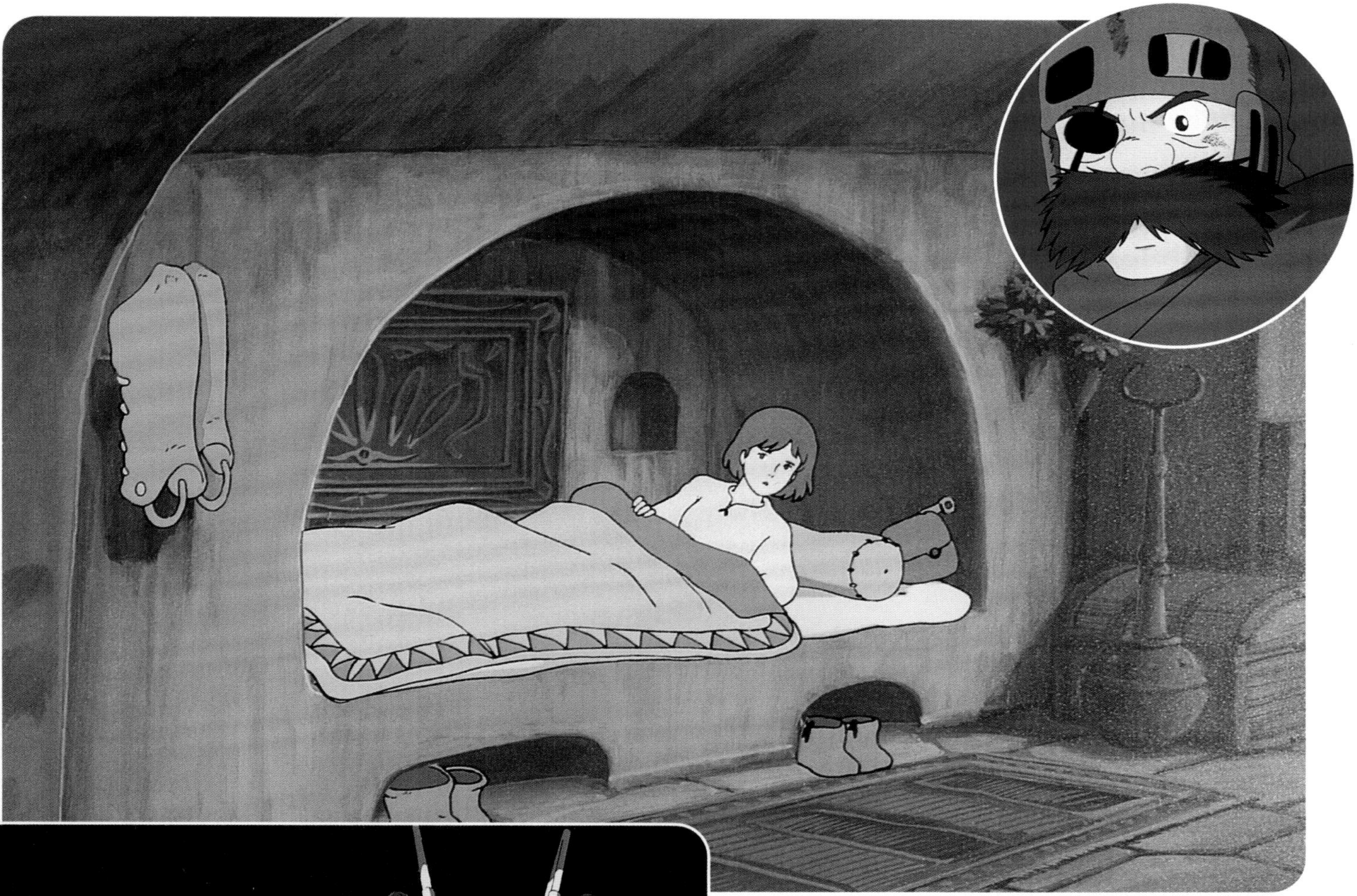

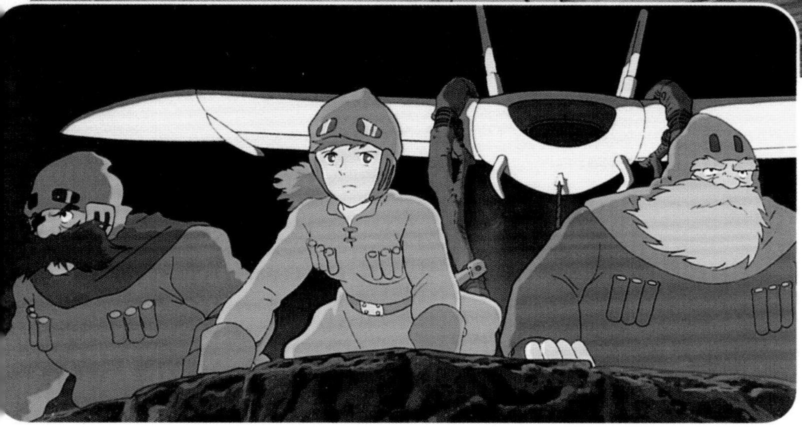

"Princess? Princess!" Someone was pounding on the door. It was Mito, one of the old men of the castle. Nausicaä sat up with a start.

"There's something in the wind!" Mito sounded scared.

She followed him to the top of the tower. The wind was booming, scattering the leaves from the trees as she gazed up into the moonless sky.

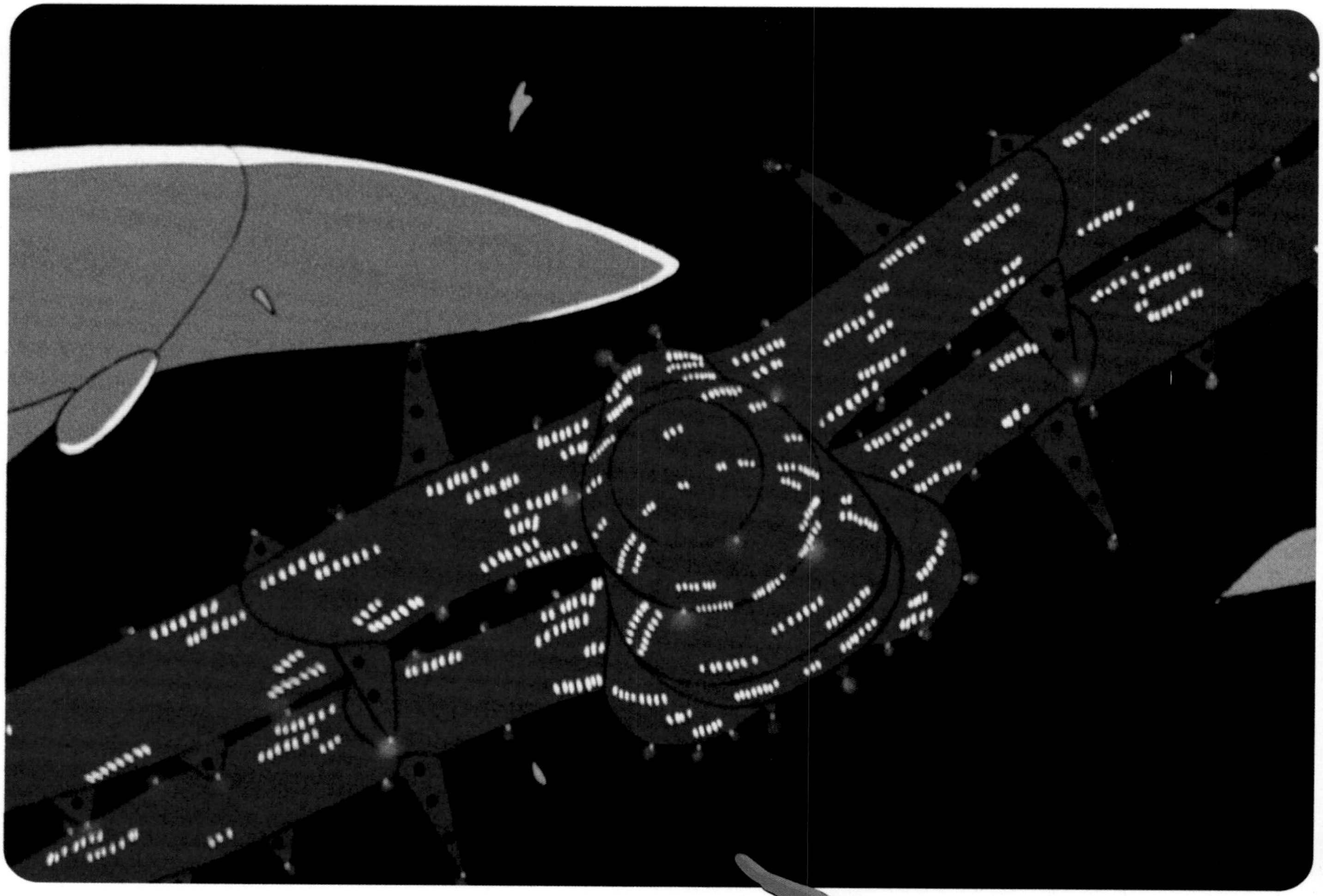

Far above, partly hidden by clouds darker than the night, Nausicaä saw a dim light rushing through the sky. It was coming closer and closer.

“It’s a Tolmekian airship. It’s in trouble!”

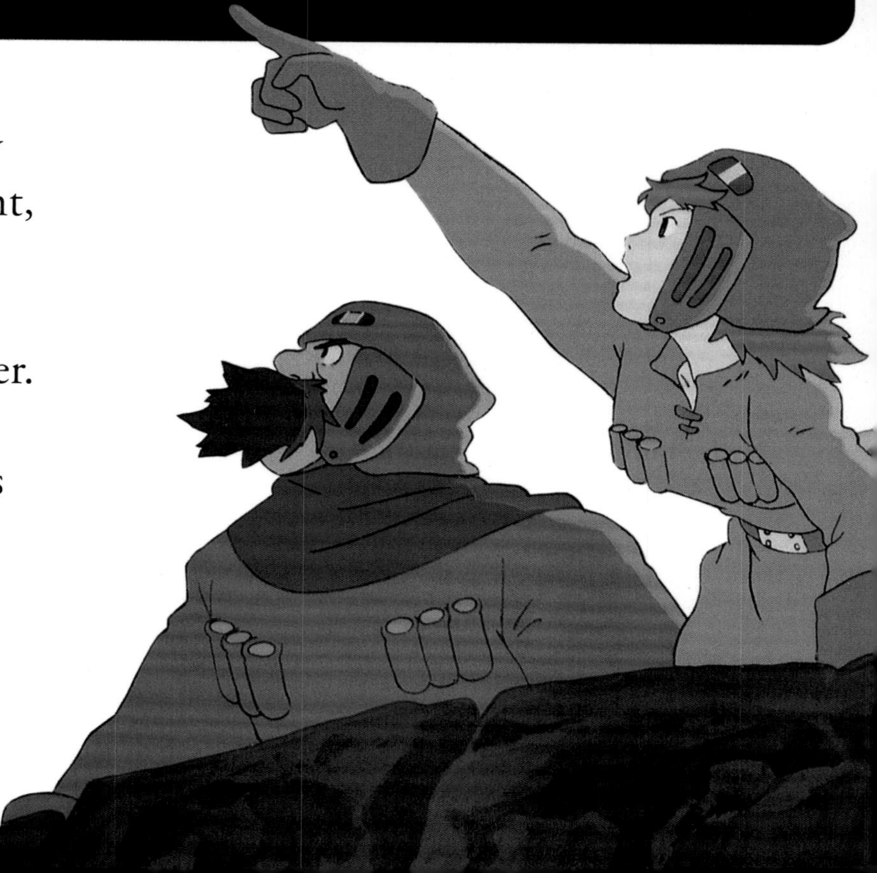

"They're trying to land! I've got to guide them."

Nausicaä leaped aboard her wind rider and flew off in pursuit.

But when she drew closer, she saw that the bridge of the airship was swarming with landgrubs from the jungle.

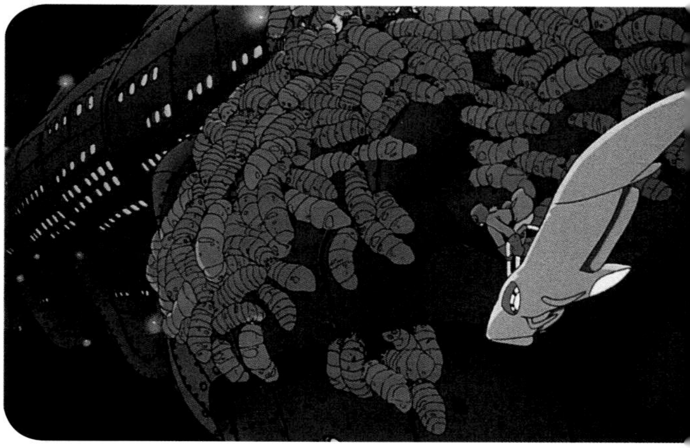

"Oh no! They must've landed in the jungle and angered the insects!"

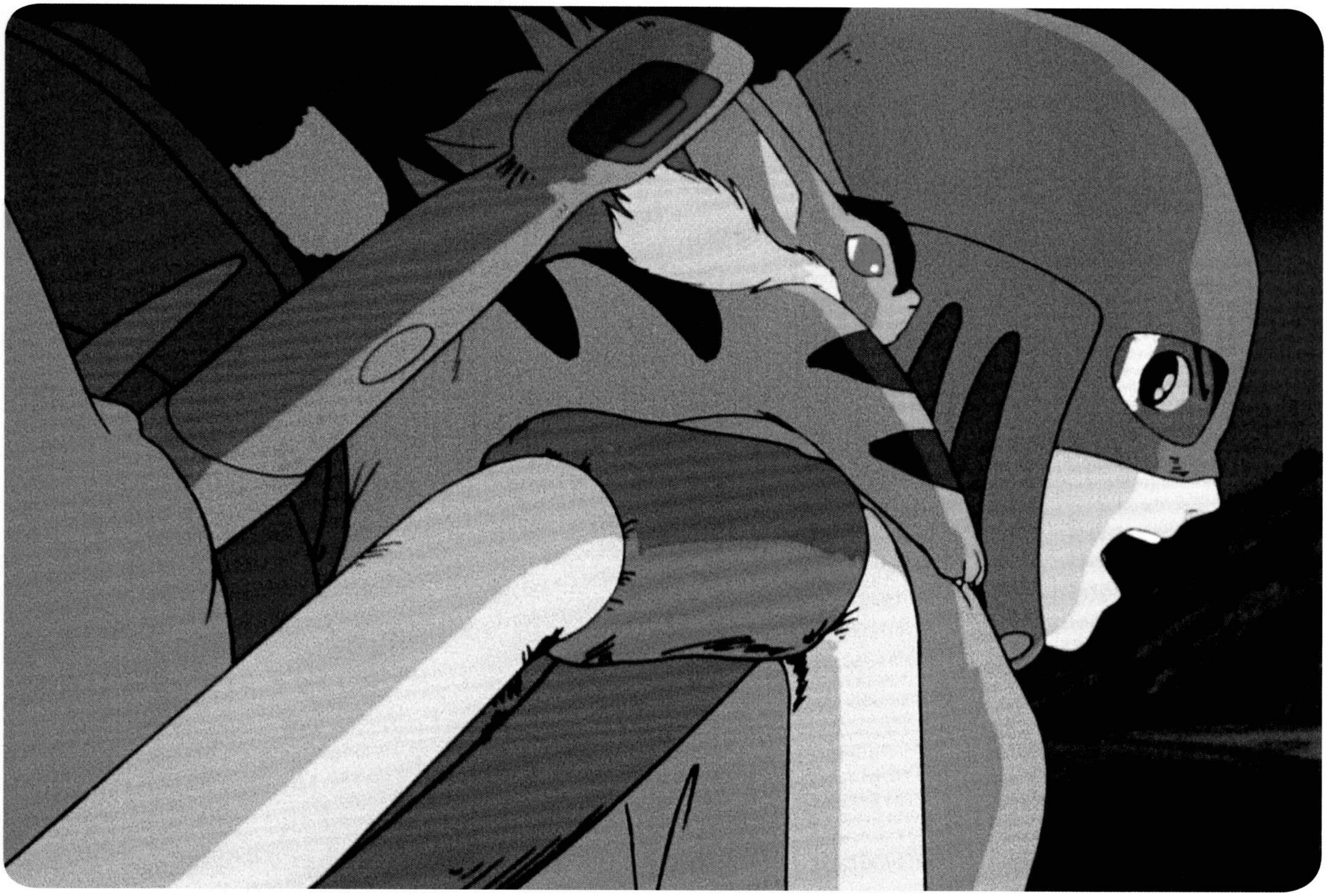

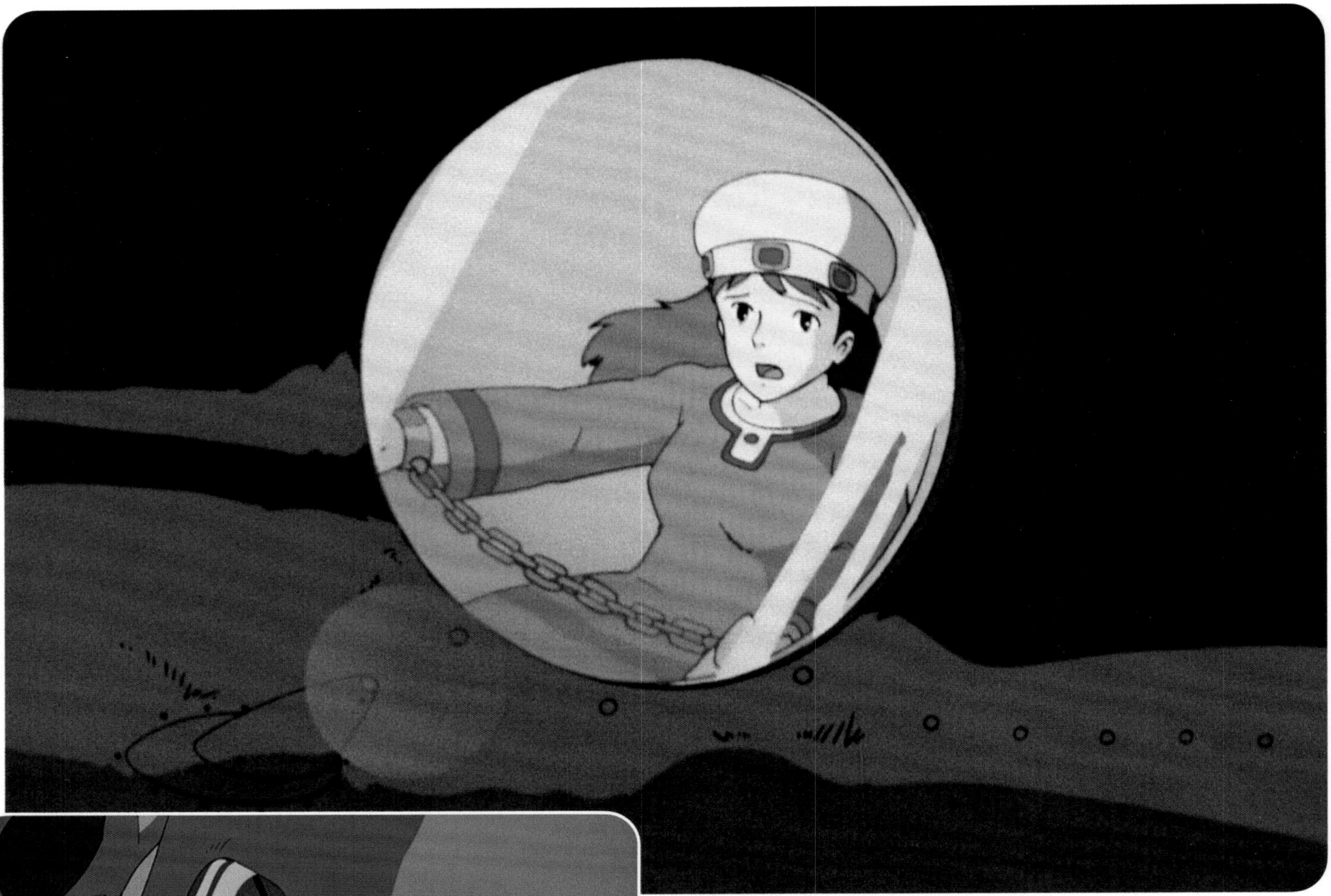

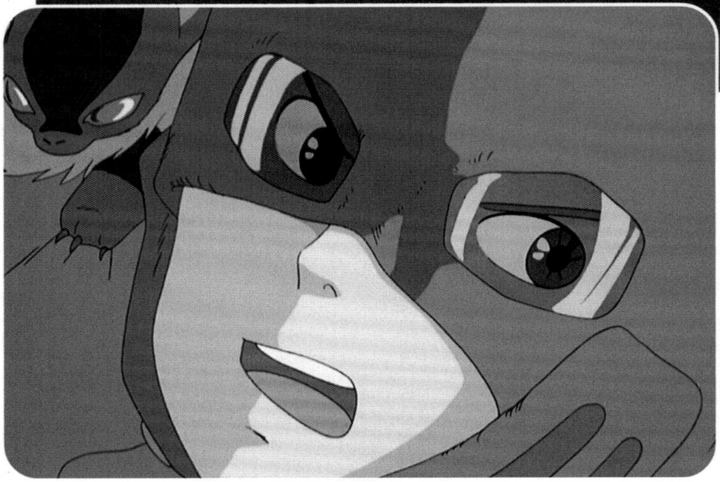

With the windows of the bridge blocked by the landgrubs, the Tolmekian airship was flying blind. It hurtled toward the cliffs overlooking the sea.

Nausicaä cried out desperately. "Turn your ship! You're going to crash!"

For one moment, as the ship flew past her, Nausicaä saw the frightened face of a little girl through one of the portholes.

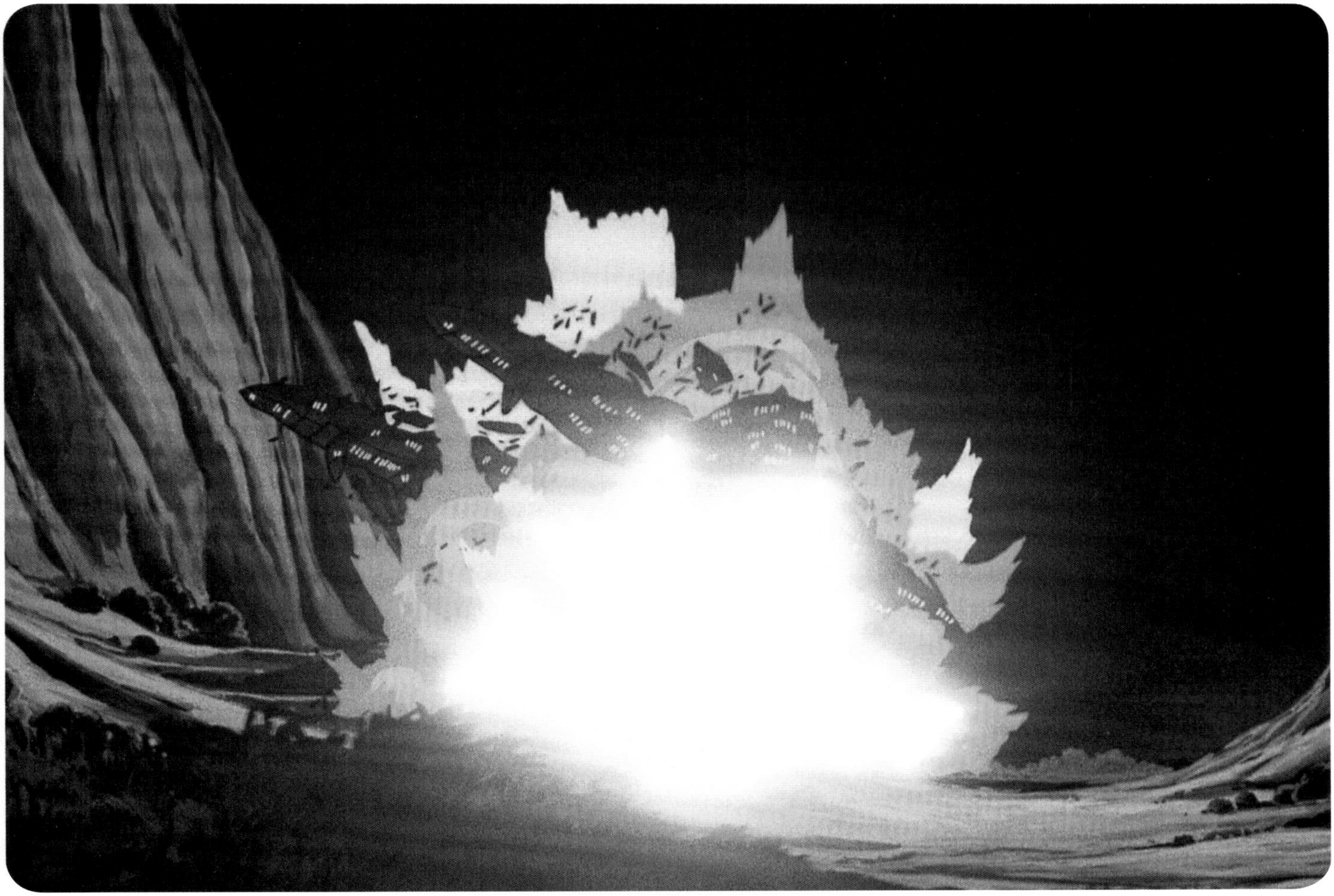

With a great explosion, the ship slammed into the cliffs and burst into flames.

The valley beneath the cliffs became a sea of fire. Nausicaä landed her wind rider, jumped off and ran straight into the roaring inferno.

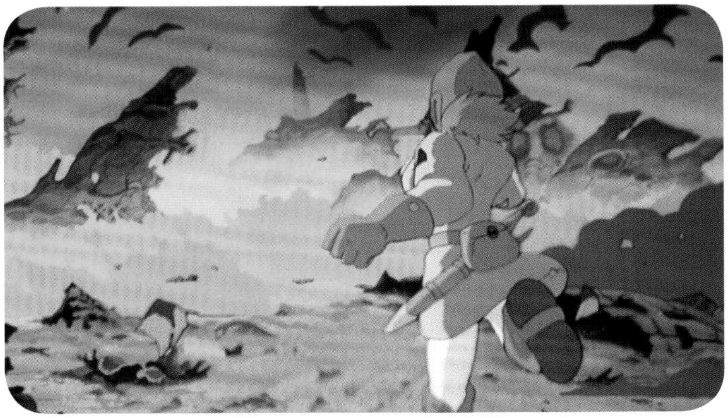

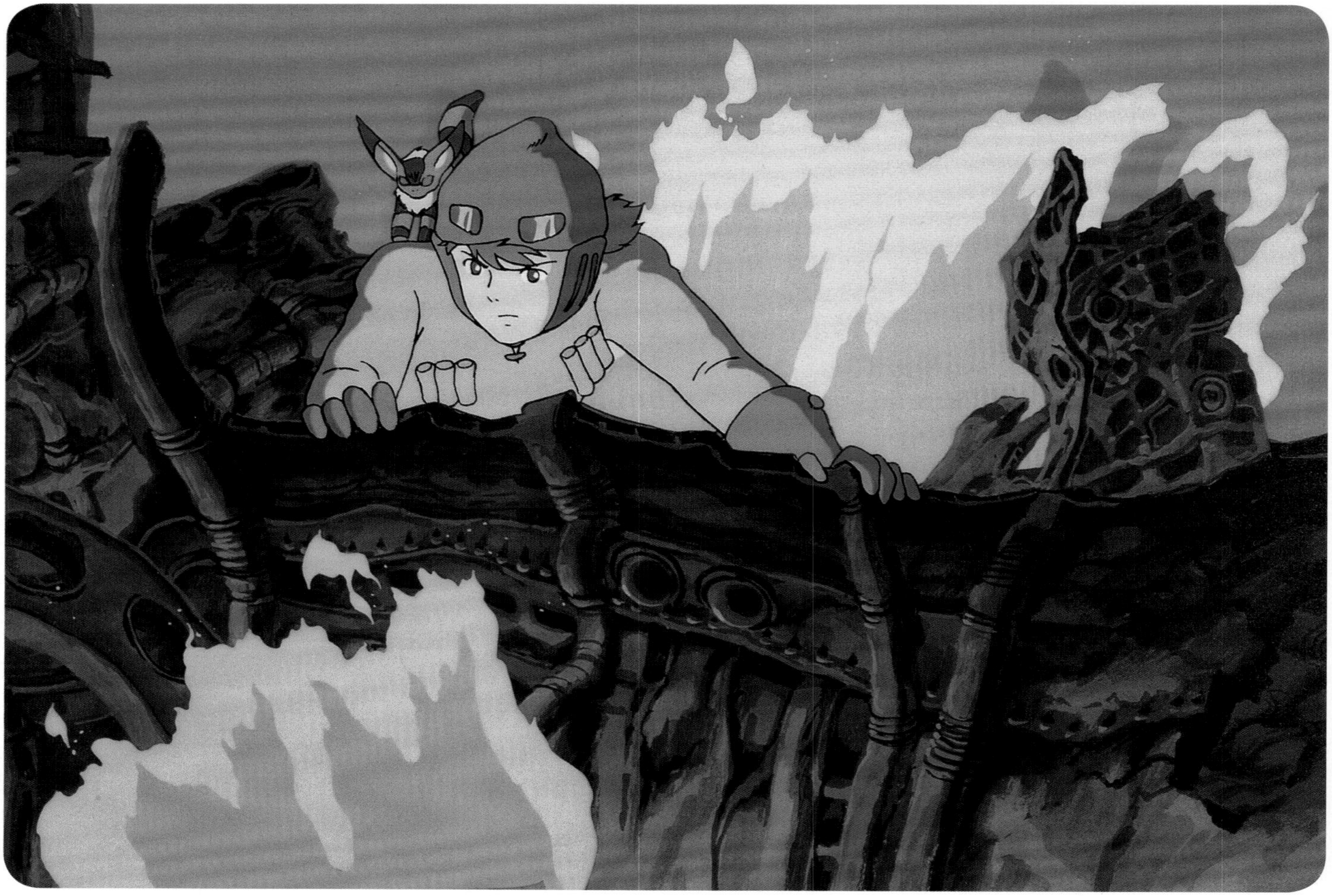

“There she is. She’s alive!”

Nausicaä found the little girl lying unconscious amid the flaming wreckage. Her wrists were chained. She was a prisoner!

Nausicaä gathered the girl into her arms and carried her away from the flames to a safe spot, where she laid her gently on the grass.

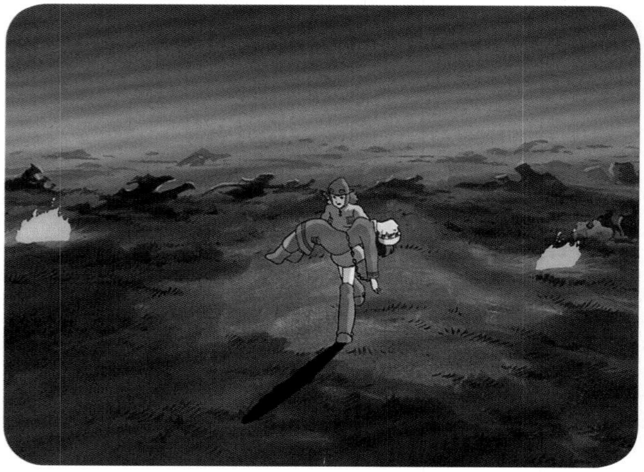

The girl opened her eyes and whispered weakly.

"I am Princess Lastel of Pejite. I beg you—burn the cargo. Something terrible is on board..."

Nausicaä looked at her intently. "I understand. Everything is burning."

"Thank God," the girl said. She smiled peacefully, and breathed her last.

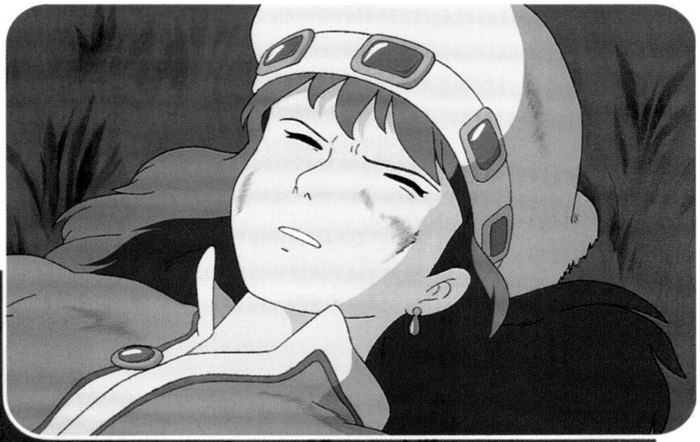

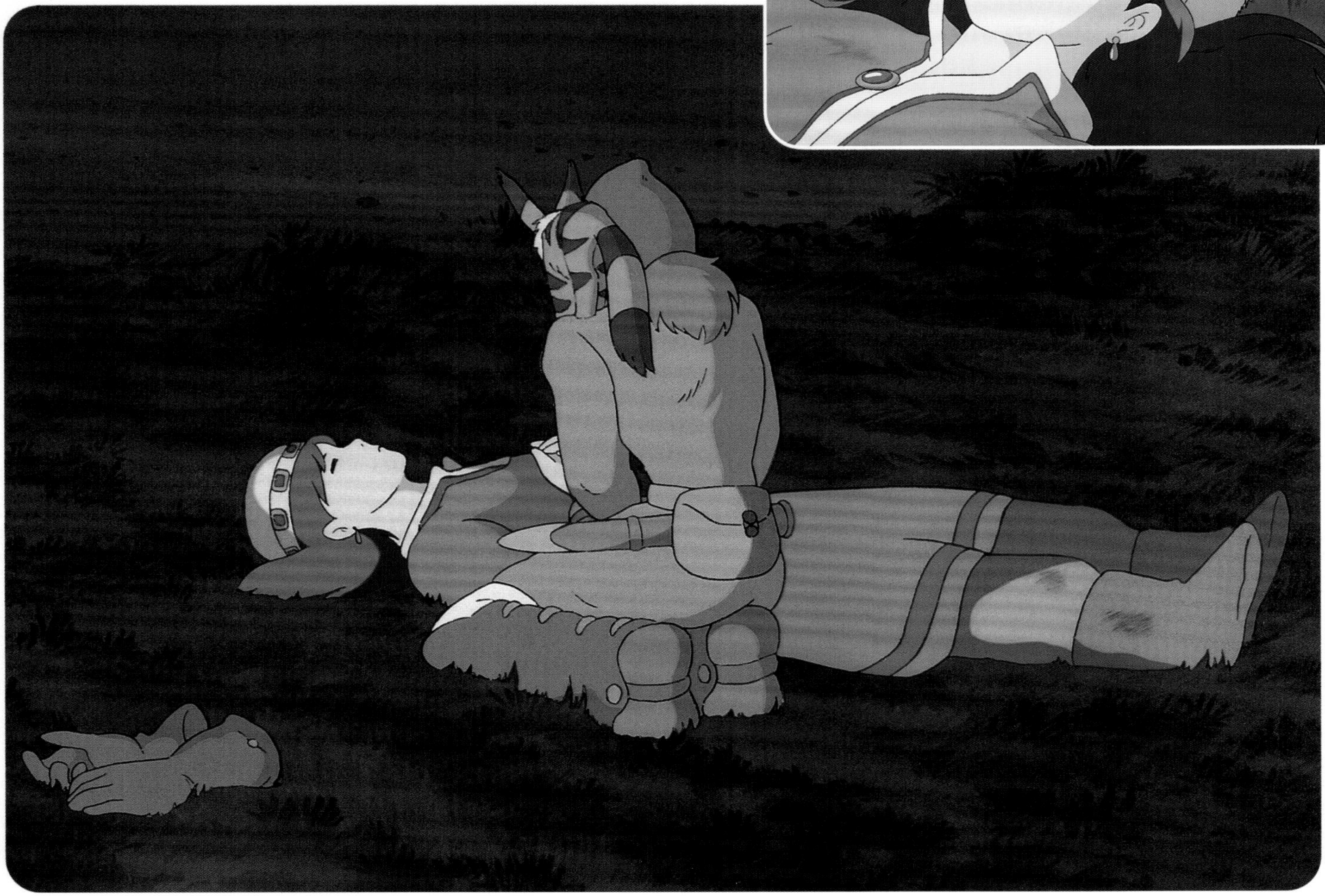

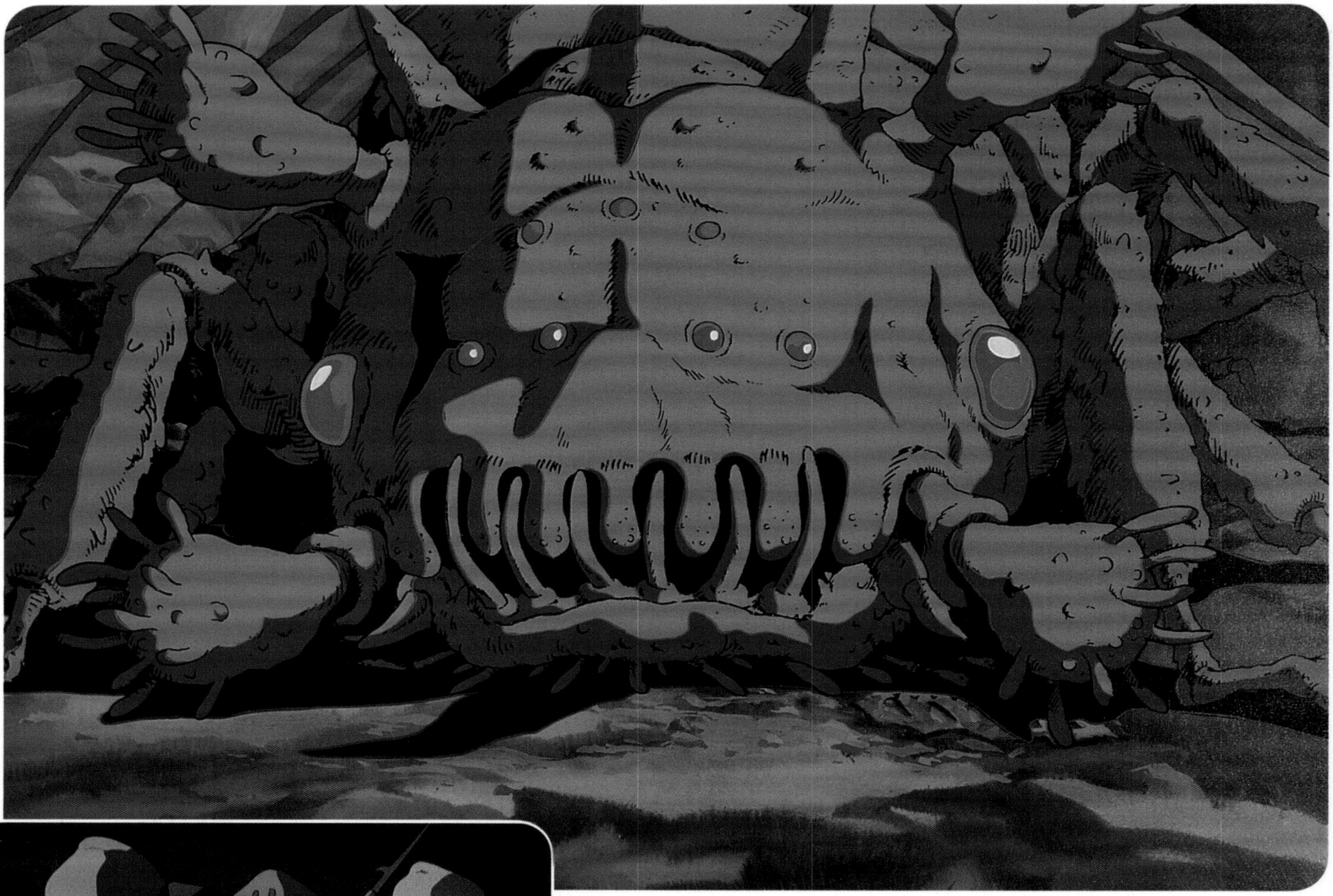

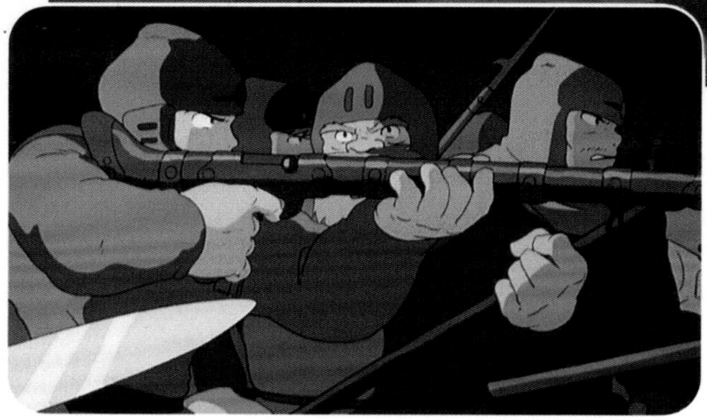

"Everybody, look out! One of the insects is still alive!"

A giant Ushiabu struggled to its feet and faced the young men of the valley. The insect sent out a strange call.

"Oh no! It's calling for help!" shouted one of the men.

"Maybe it's wounded and can't fly. Don't shoot, you'll enrage every insect in the jungle!" called another.

But some of the men raised their weapons.

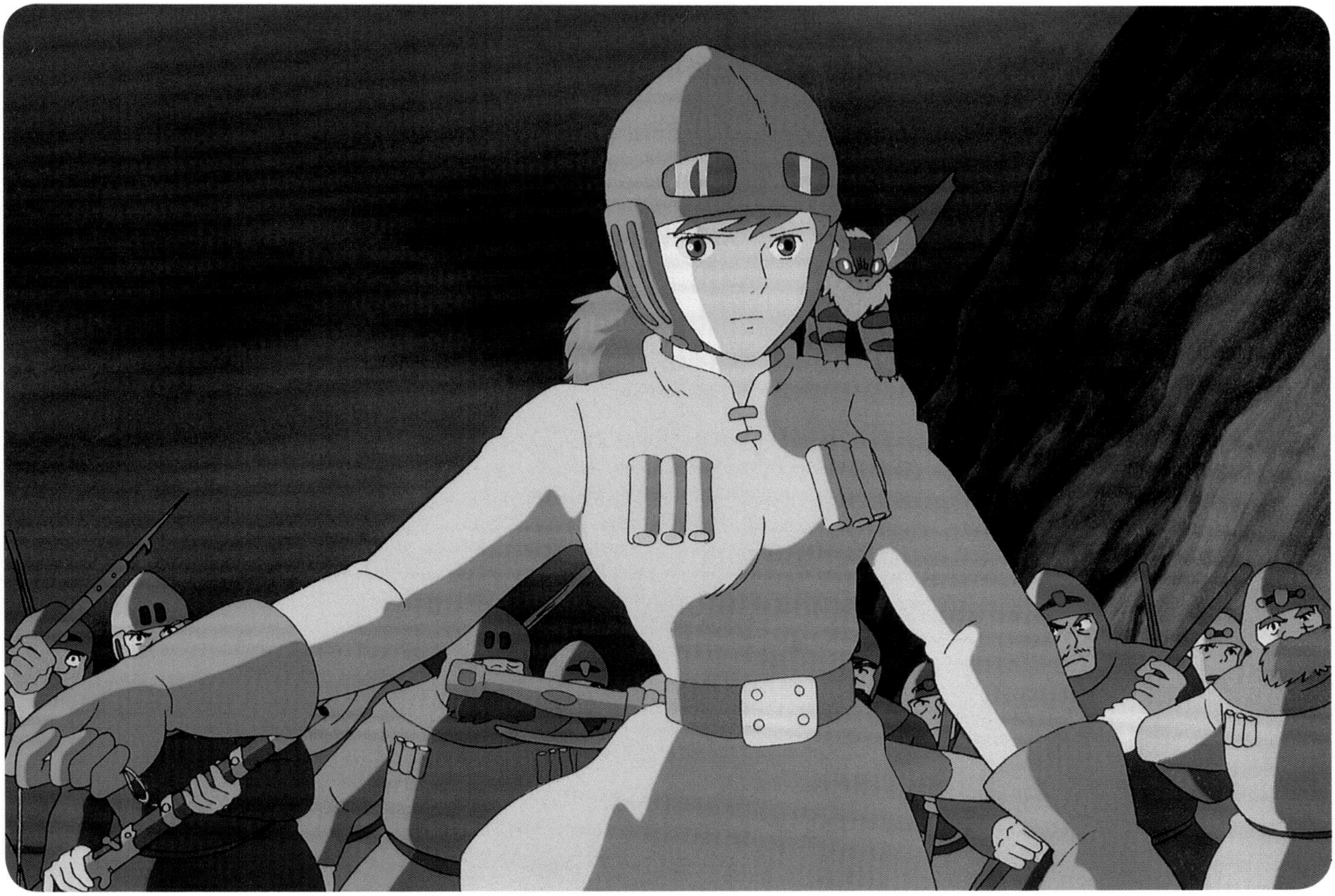

"Wait!"

Nausicaä stood before the giant Ushiabu. She began to whirl her insect charm.

"Go back to the jungle." She spoke gently to the creature. "You're strong. You can fly."

At the sound of the charm, the Ushiabu slowly raised its tattered wings.

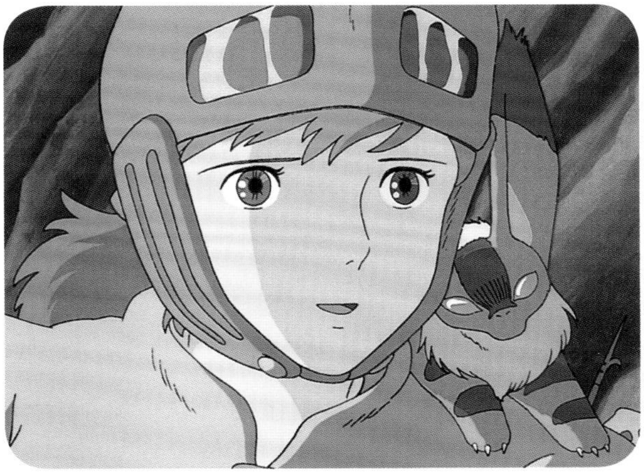

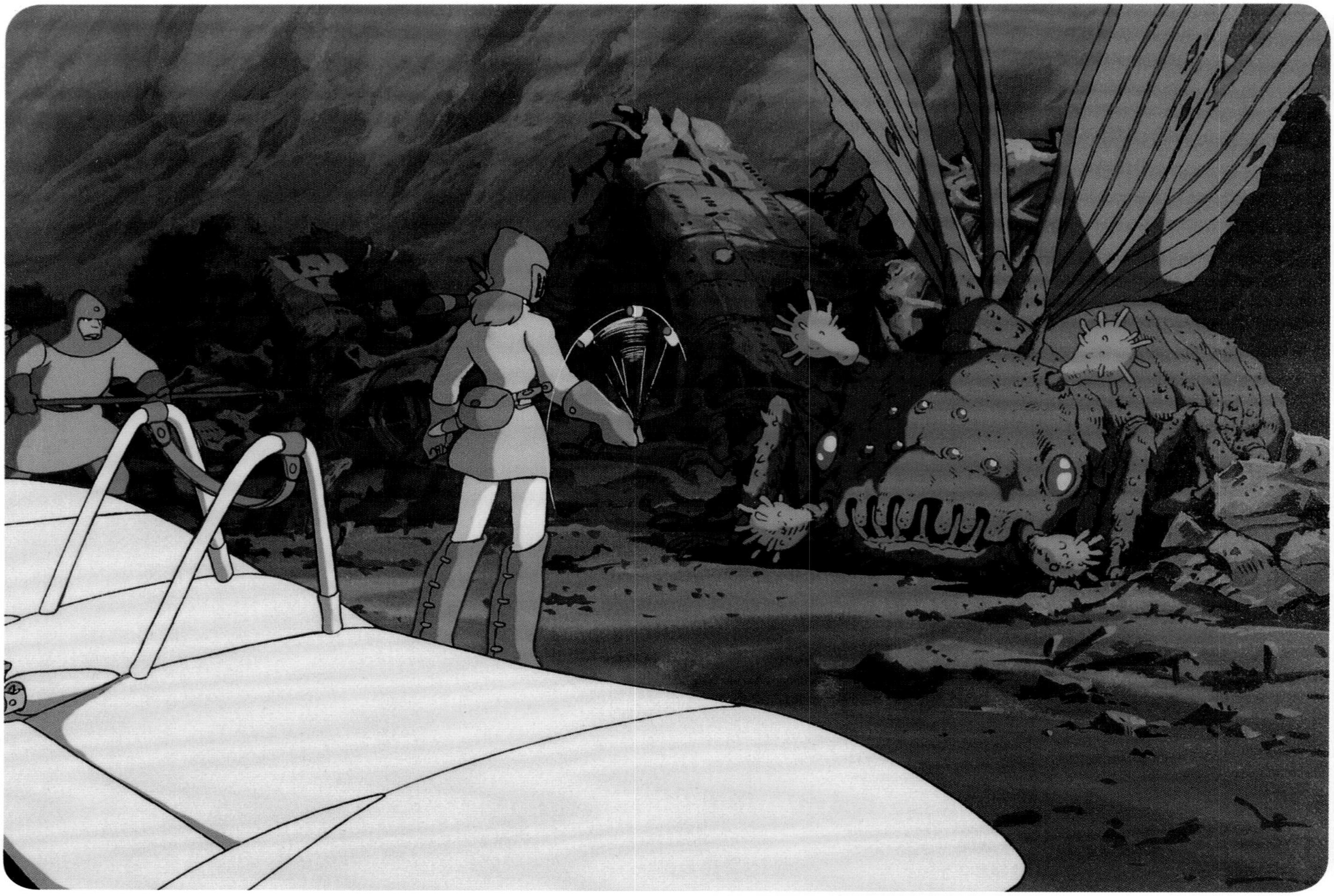

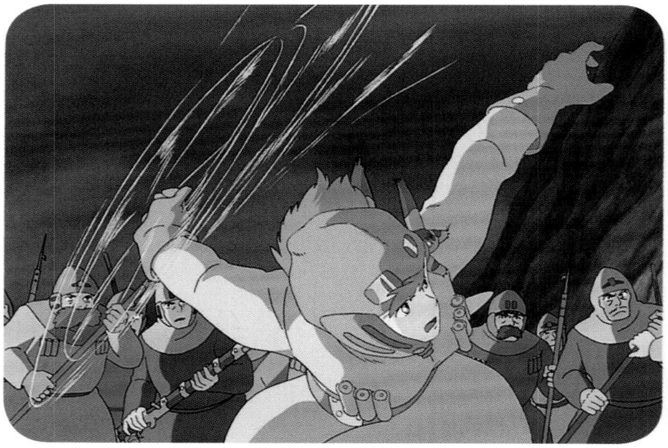

With a rustling sound, the Ushiabu beat its wings. Nausicaä drew back her arm and sent the insect charm sailing into the sky. As if drawn by its humming call, the Ushiabu took off after it.

Nausicaä jumped onto her wind rider, caught her falling charm, and raced after the insect.

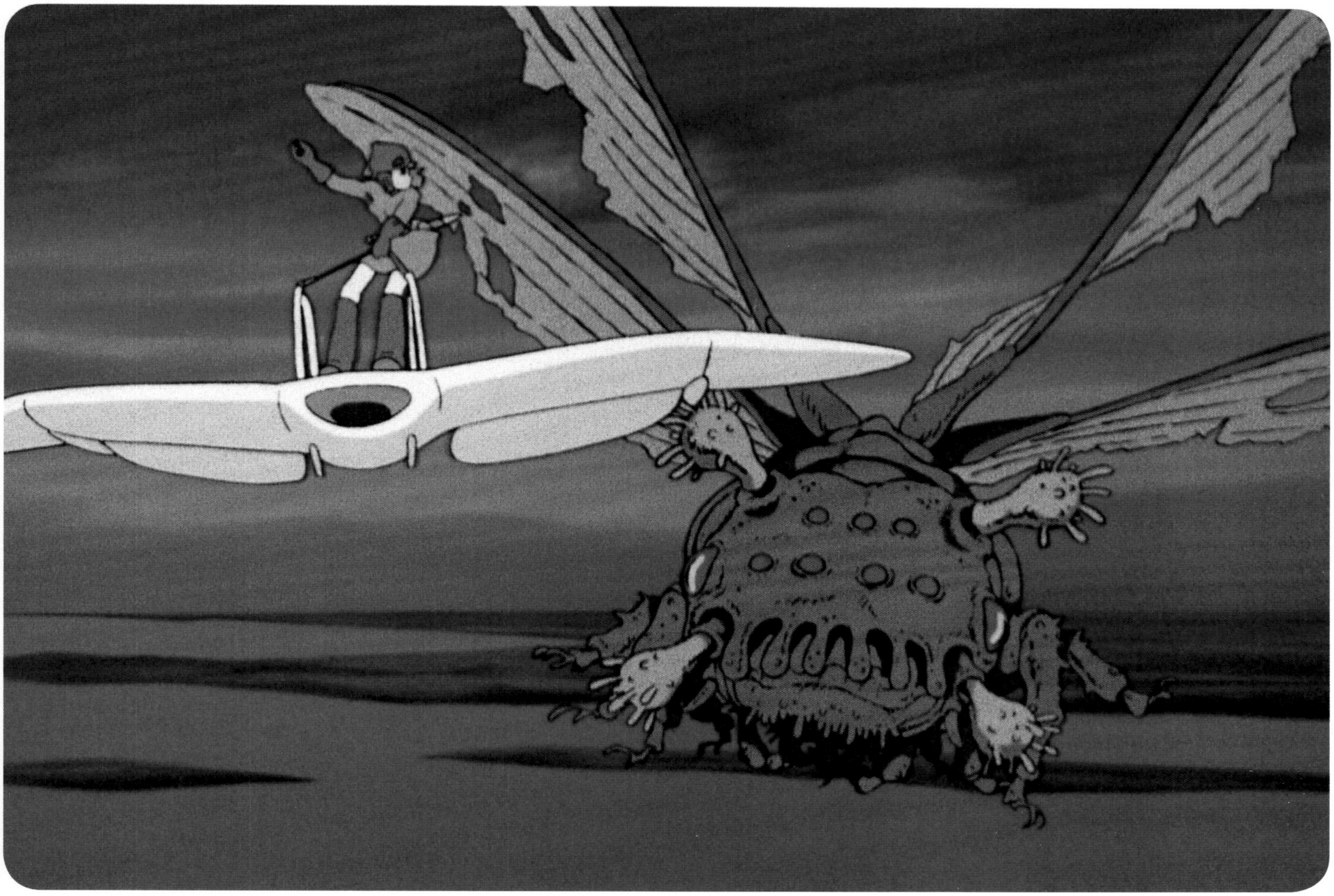

It was almost dawn now. As the sky turned from black to blue, Nausicaä flew ahead of the Ushiabu, guiding it home with the sound of her charm.

She landed at the top of a dune by the edge of the toxic jungle and watched the Ushiabu growing smaller in the distance.

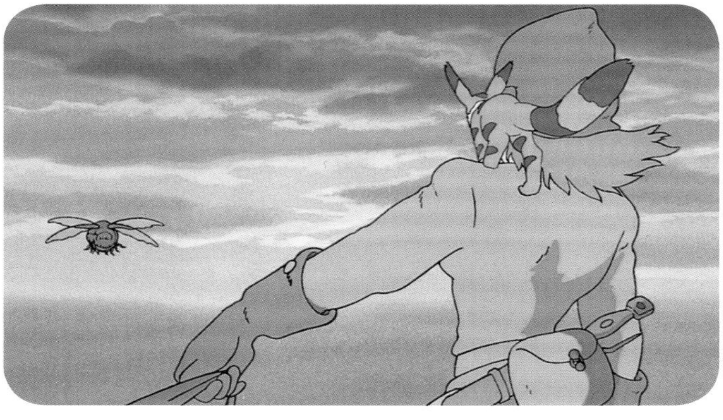

It was then that she saw an Ohm approaching from the jungle.

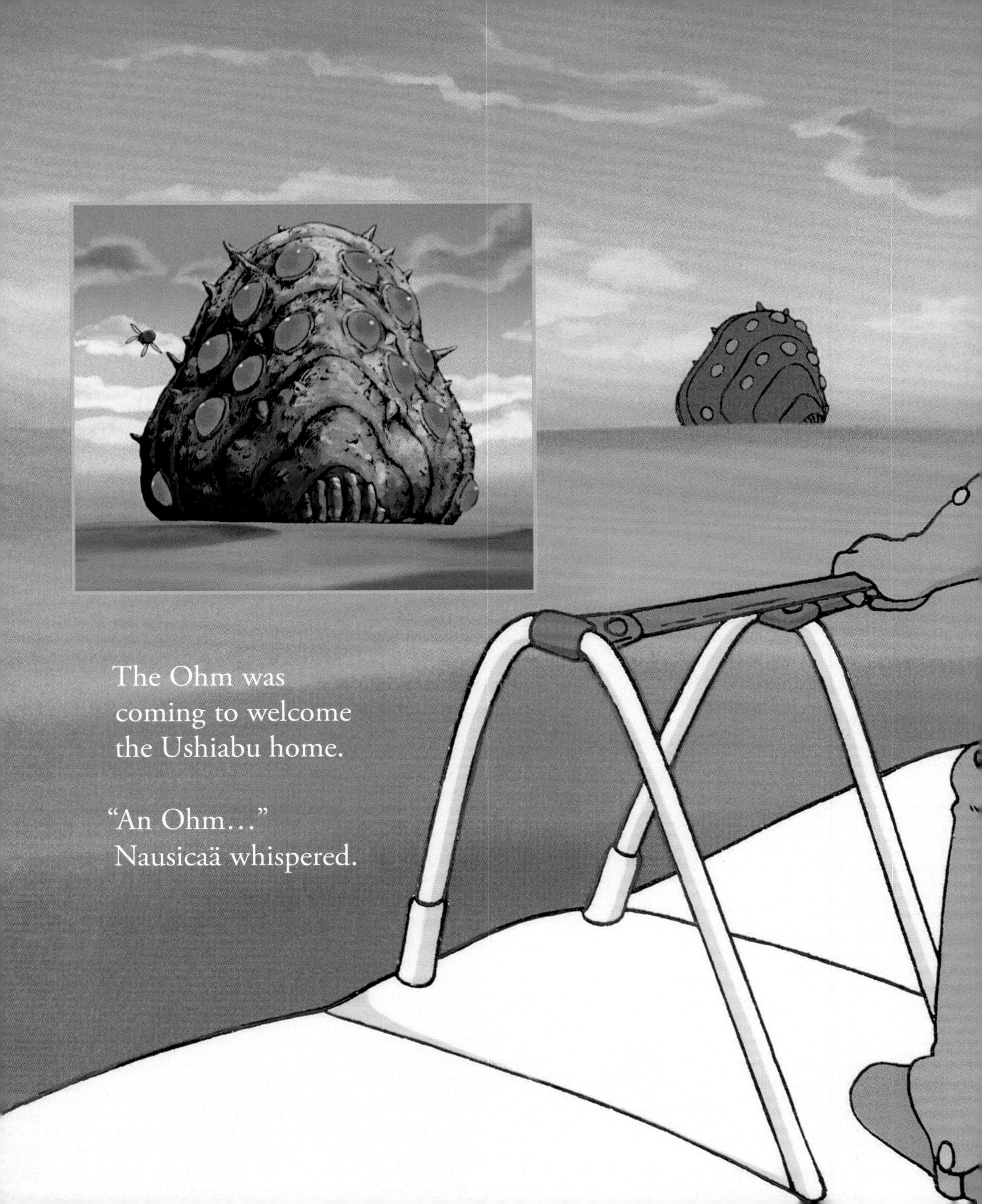

The Ohm was
coming to welcome
the Ushiabu home.

"An Ohm…"
Nausicaä whispered.

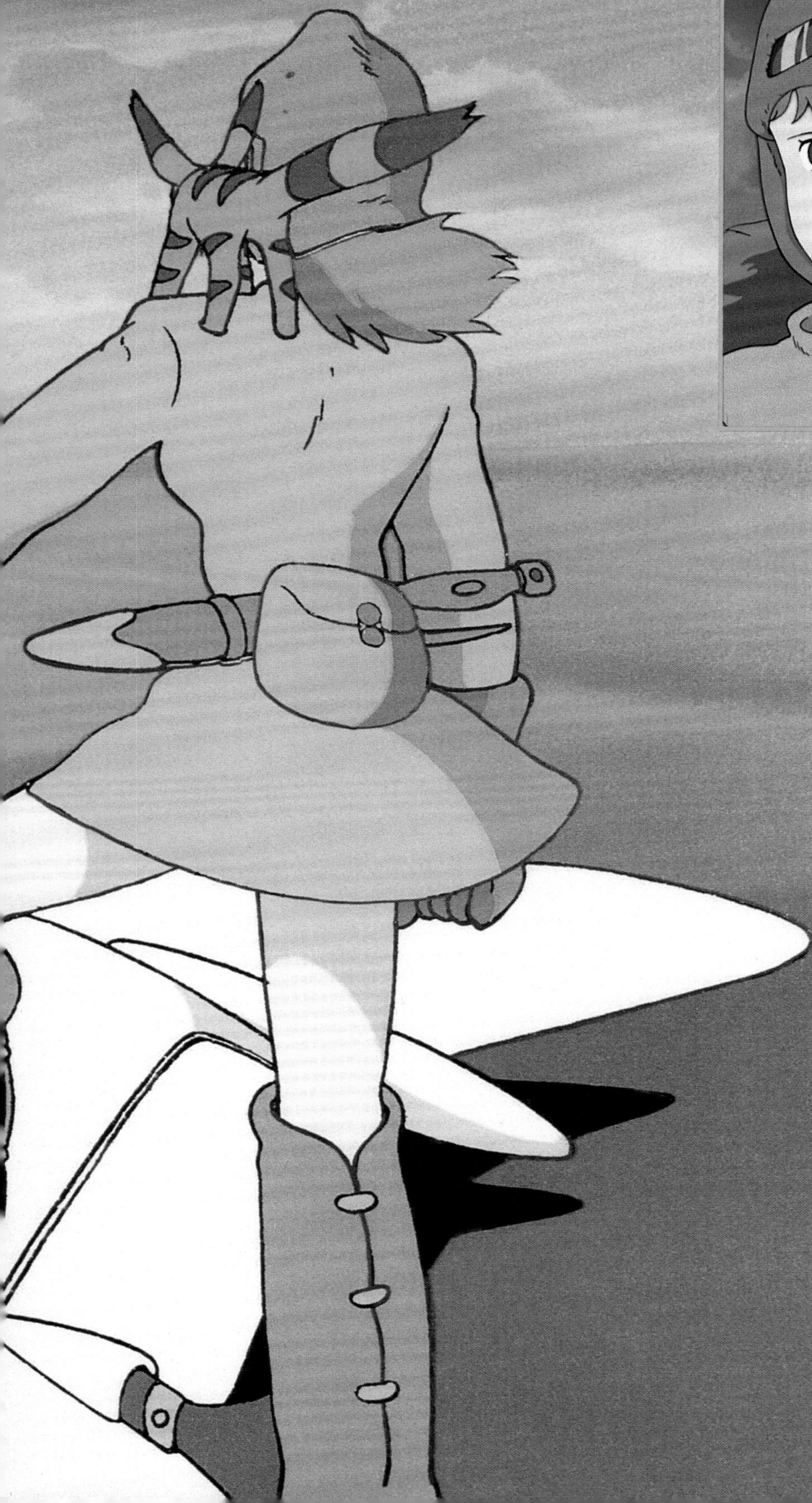

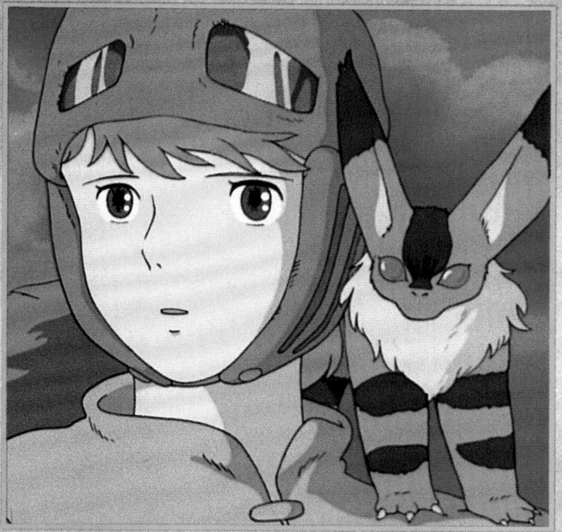

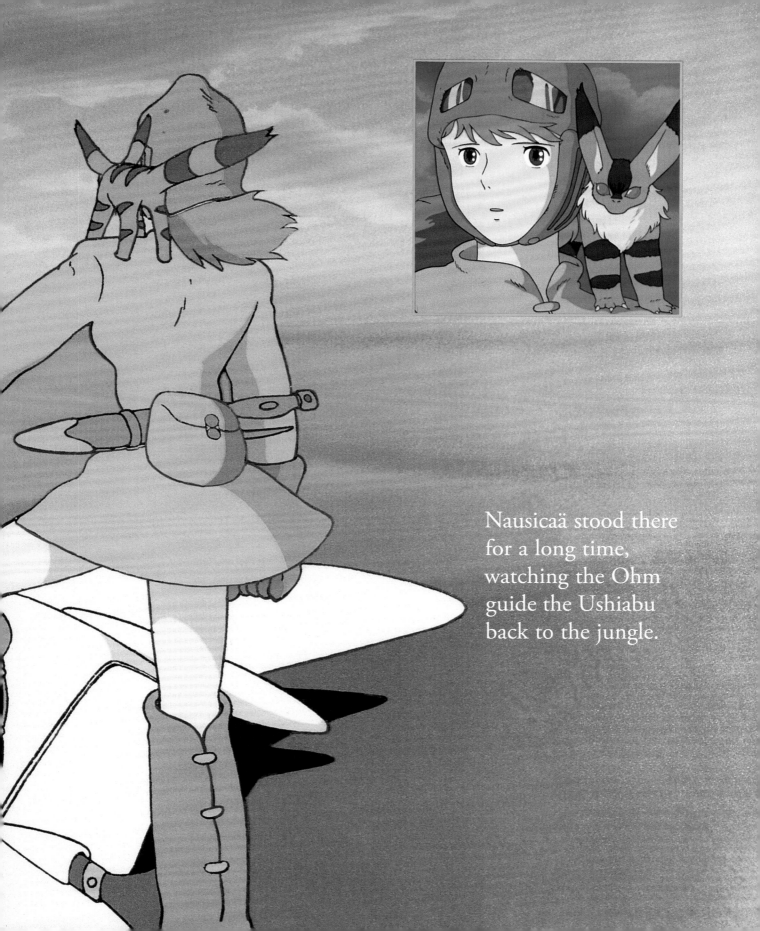

Nausicaä stood there for a long time, watching the Ohm guide the Ushiabu back to the jungle.

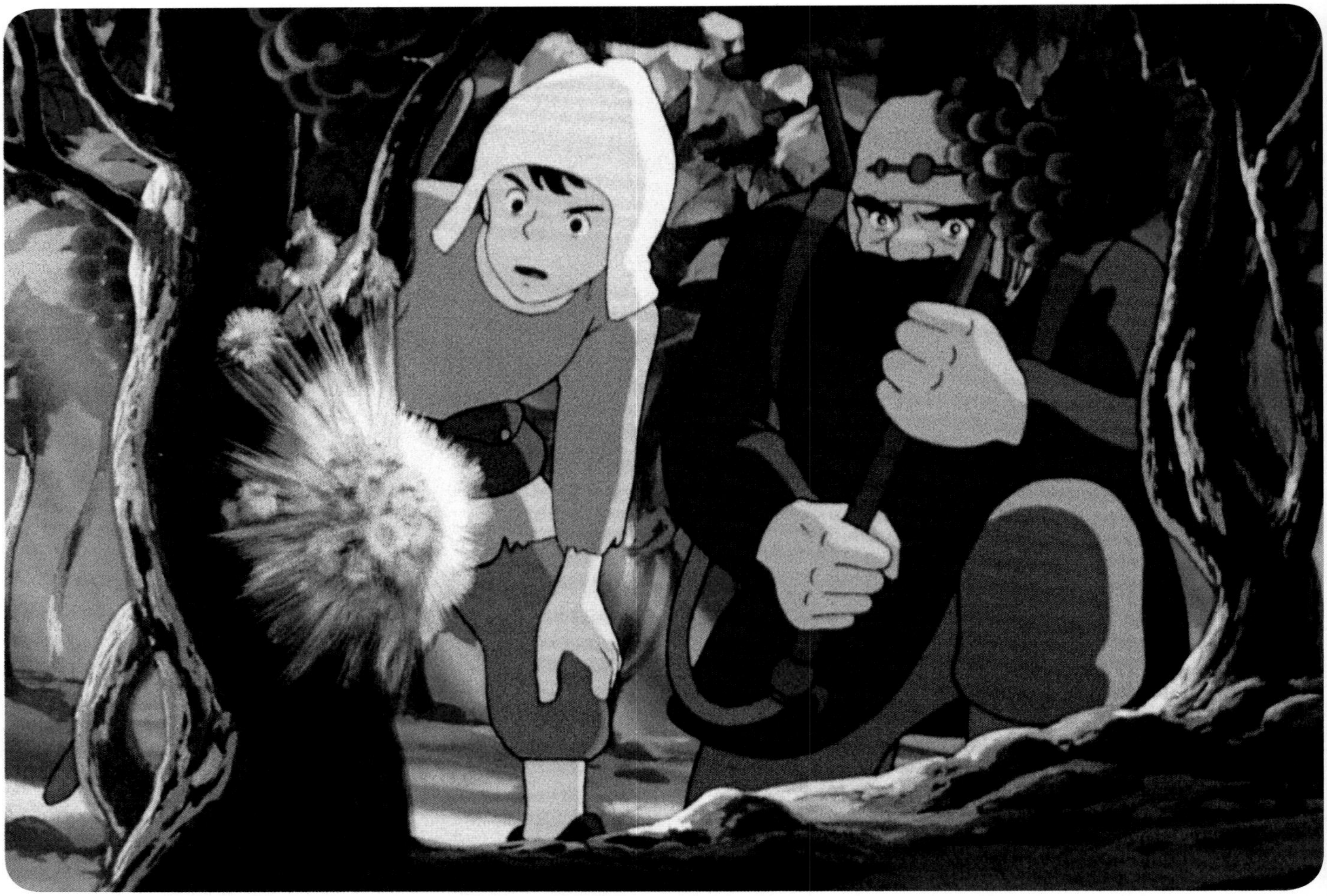

THE TOLMEKIANS ATTACK

The next day, the people of the valley were up before dawn. They had work to do.

The Tolmekian freighter that had crashed the night before was covered with deadly spores from the toxic jungle.

As soon as they infested a healthy tree or plant, the spores started releasing poison. A boy from the castle found one in the vineyard.

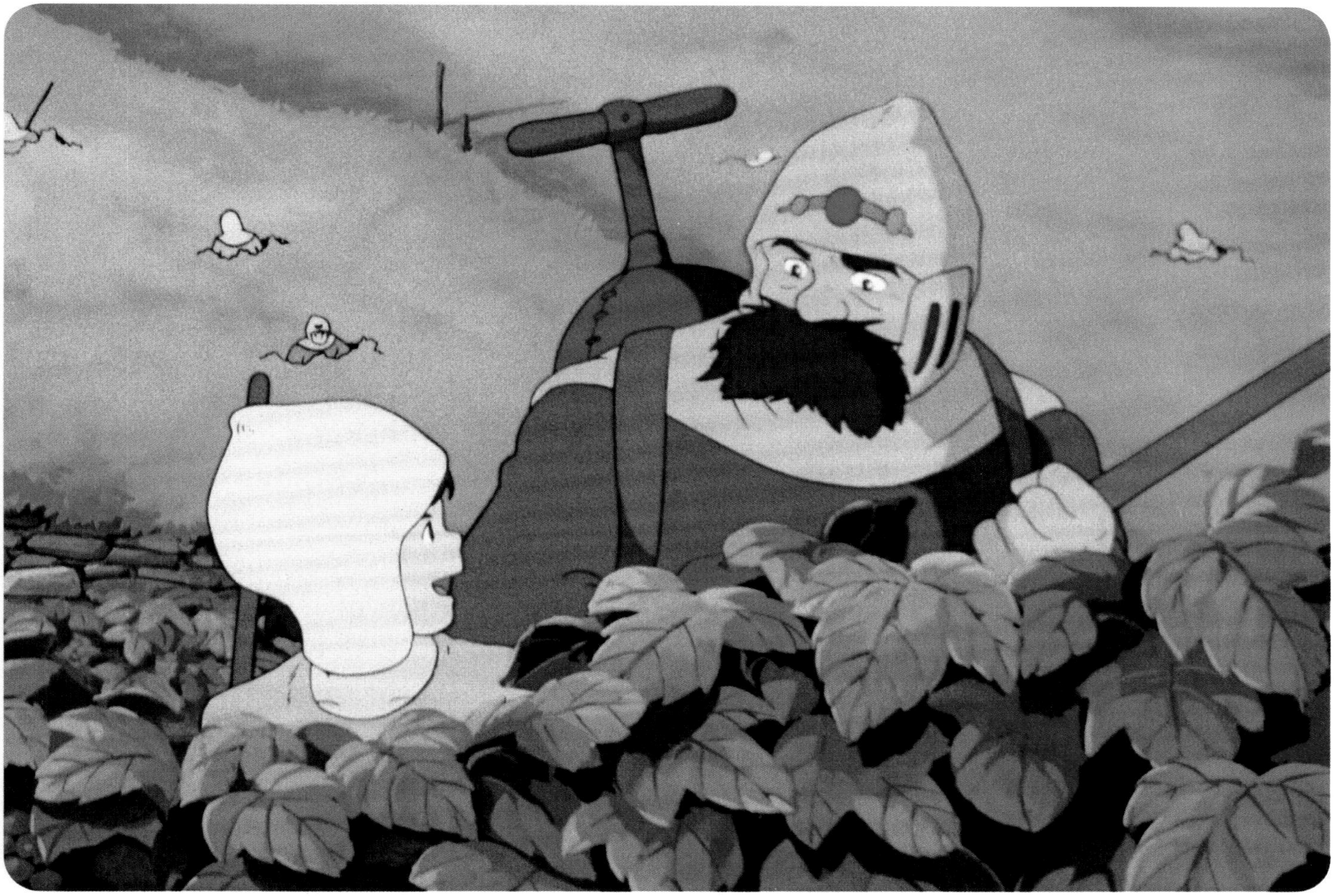

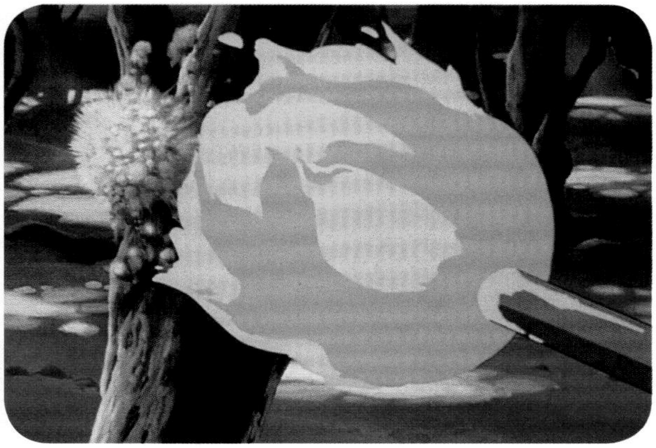

Carried by the wind, the spores spread from tree to tree. If they were not stopped, the Valley of the Wind would soon become part of the toxic jungle, a place unfit for people to live.

“Let’s keep searching till we find every last one,” the boy said.

The people of the valley worked together to find every spore.

But the crashed freighter was carrying something much more dangerous than spores. It was a gigantic, red-black object, like an alien egg.

"What is this thing? The fire didn't seem to harm it at all," Mito murmured with wonder.

Yupa gestured toward the egg.

"Mito, take a look at this."

The object was slowly pulsating.

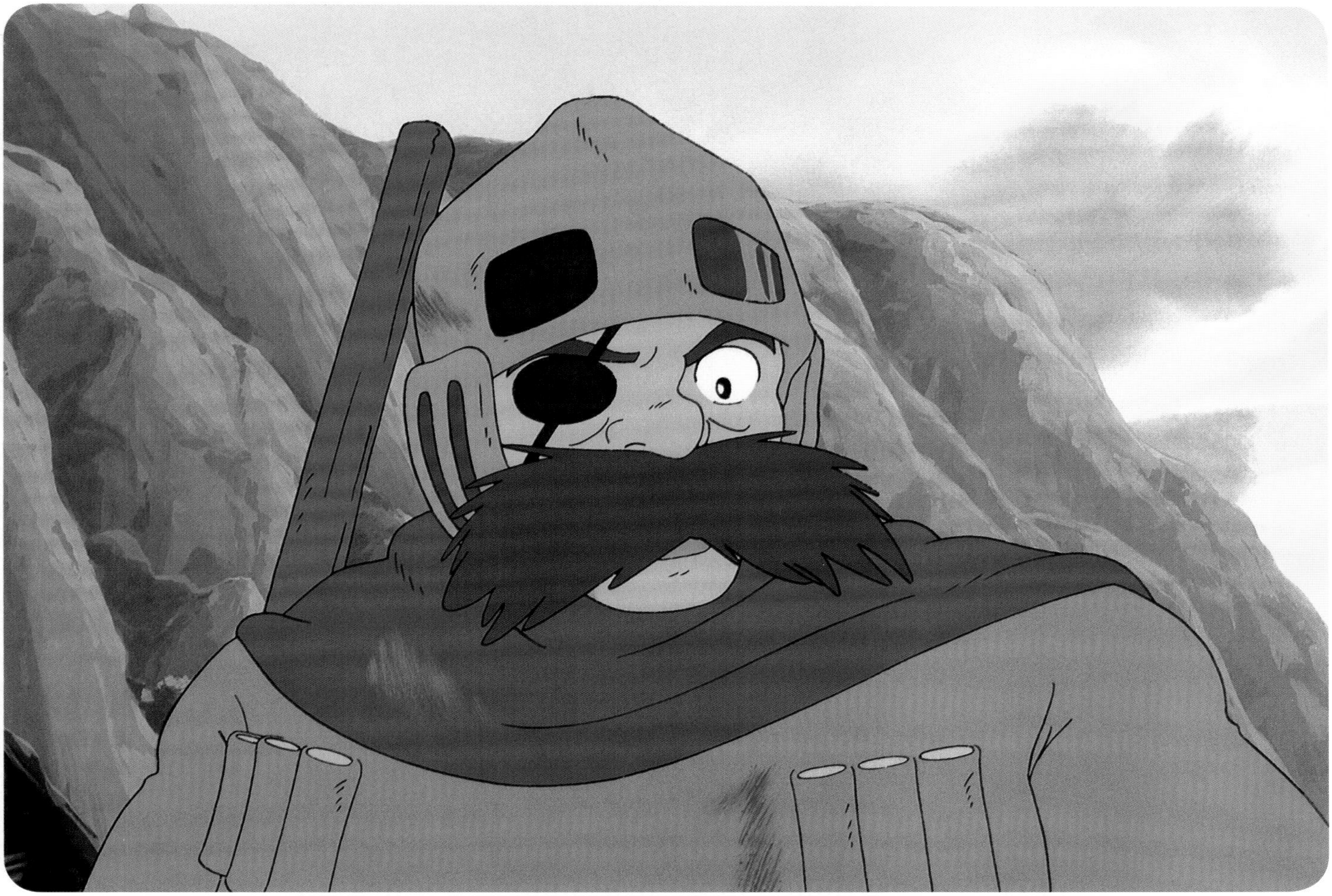

Mito stared in surprise.

"It's beating like a heart. Looks like this thing is alive. Lord Yupa, what is this?"

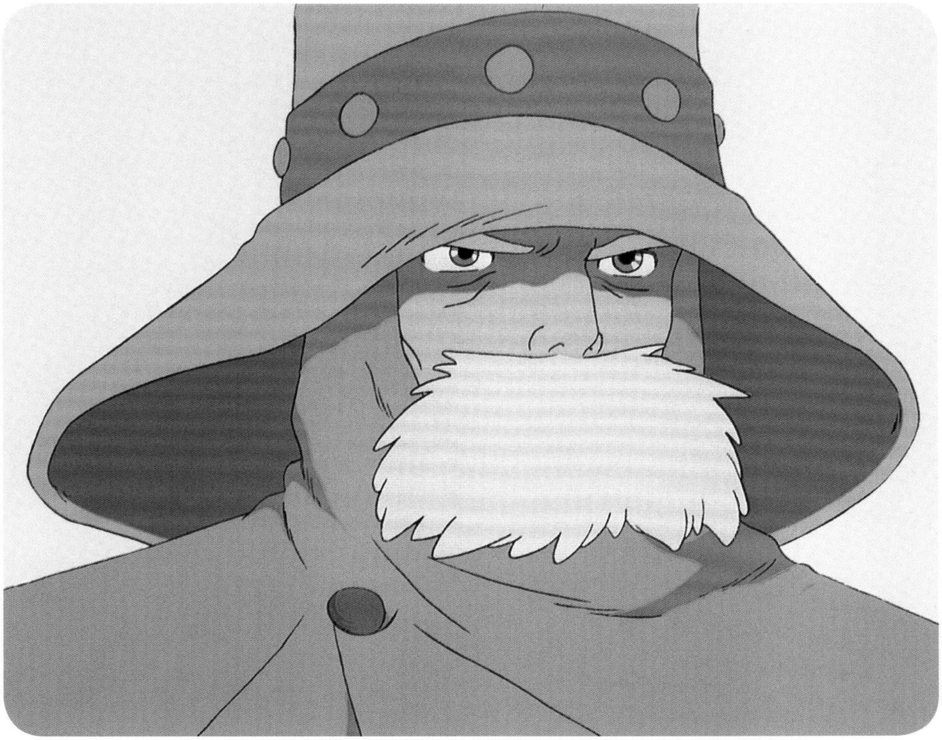

Yupa gazed up at the gigantic egg.

"While I was traveling, I heard a frightening rumor. It was said that a monster from the old world was found buried deep beneath the city of Pejite."

Mito shrank back in surprise. "One of the monsters who destroyed civilization in the Seven Days of Fire? But that was a thousand years ago. It can't be!"

Yupa looked at him gravely.

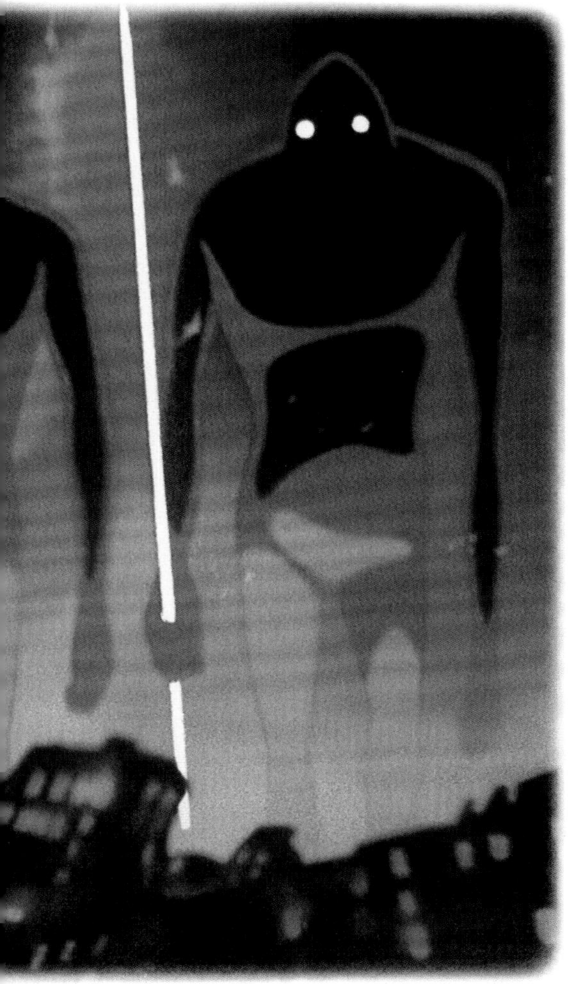

“After they incinerated the earth, all the Giant Warriors were said to have turned to stone. But one of them must have remained, deep underground.”

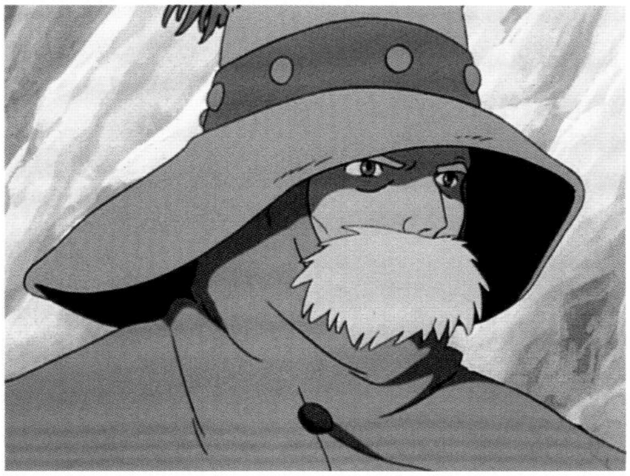

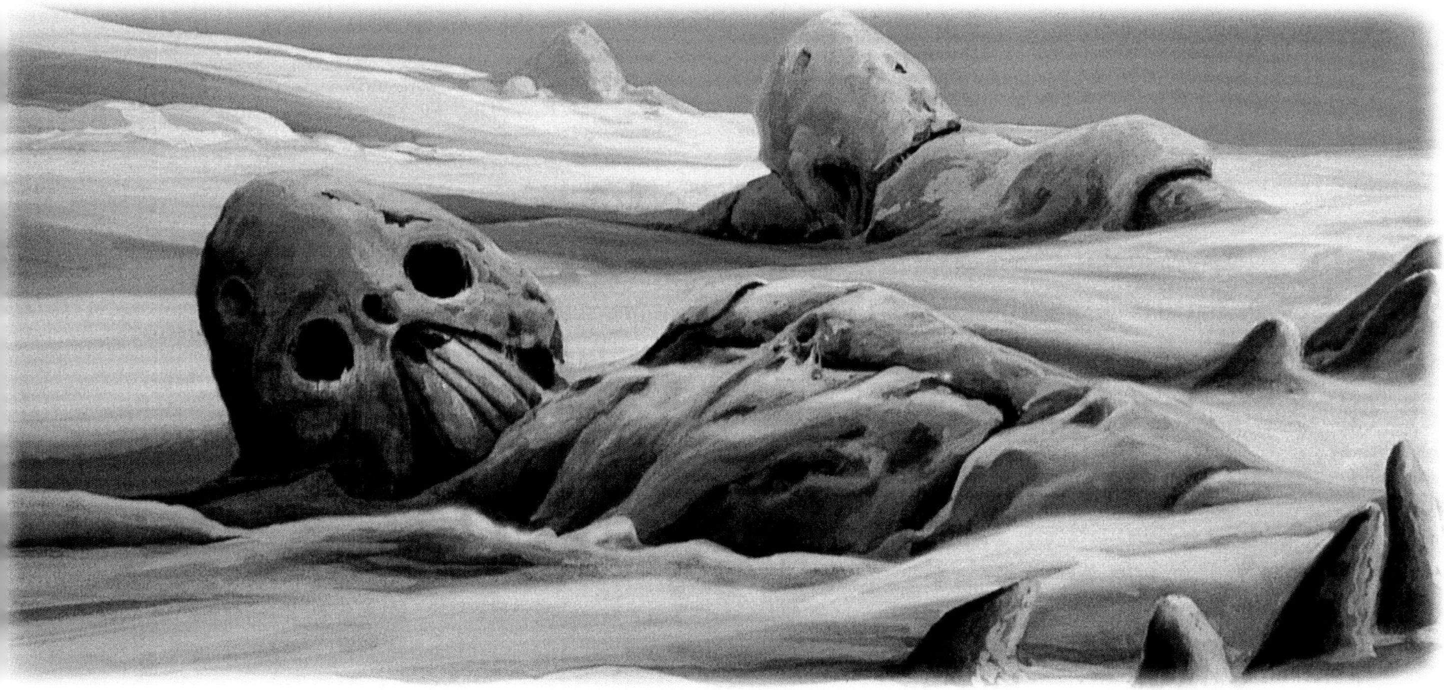

Just then, Nausicaä heard the far-off roar of approaching aircraft.

It was a fleet of giant airships from Tolmekia, carrying an invading army.

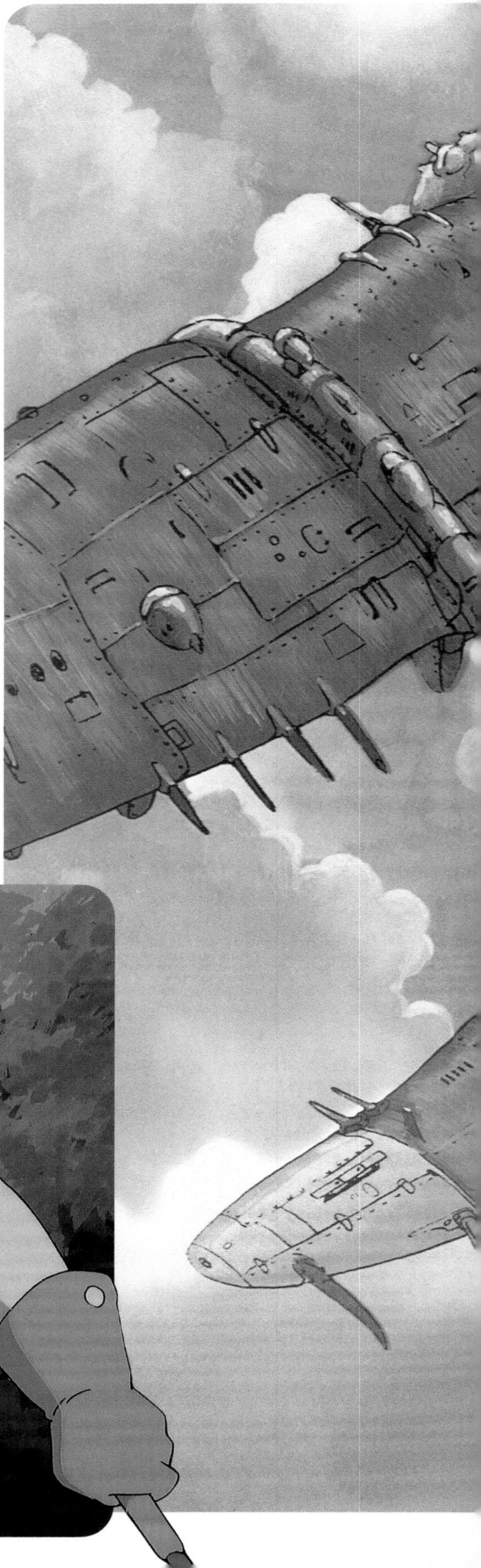

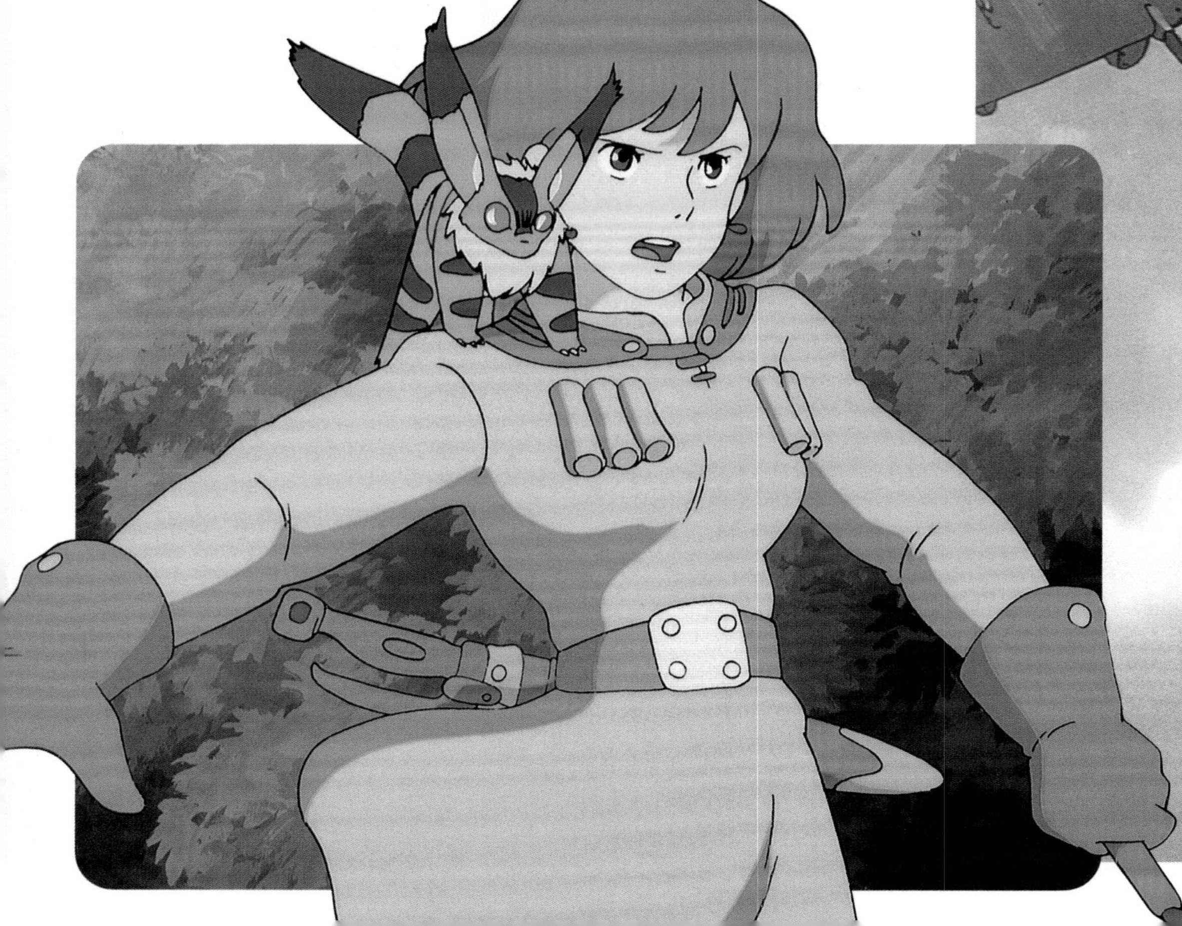

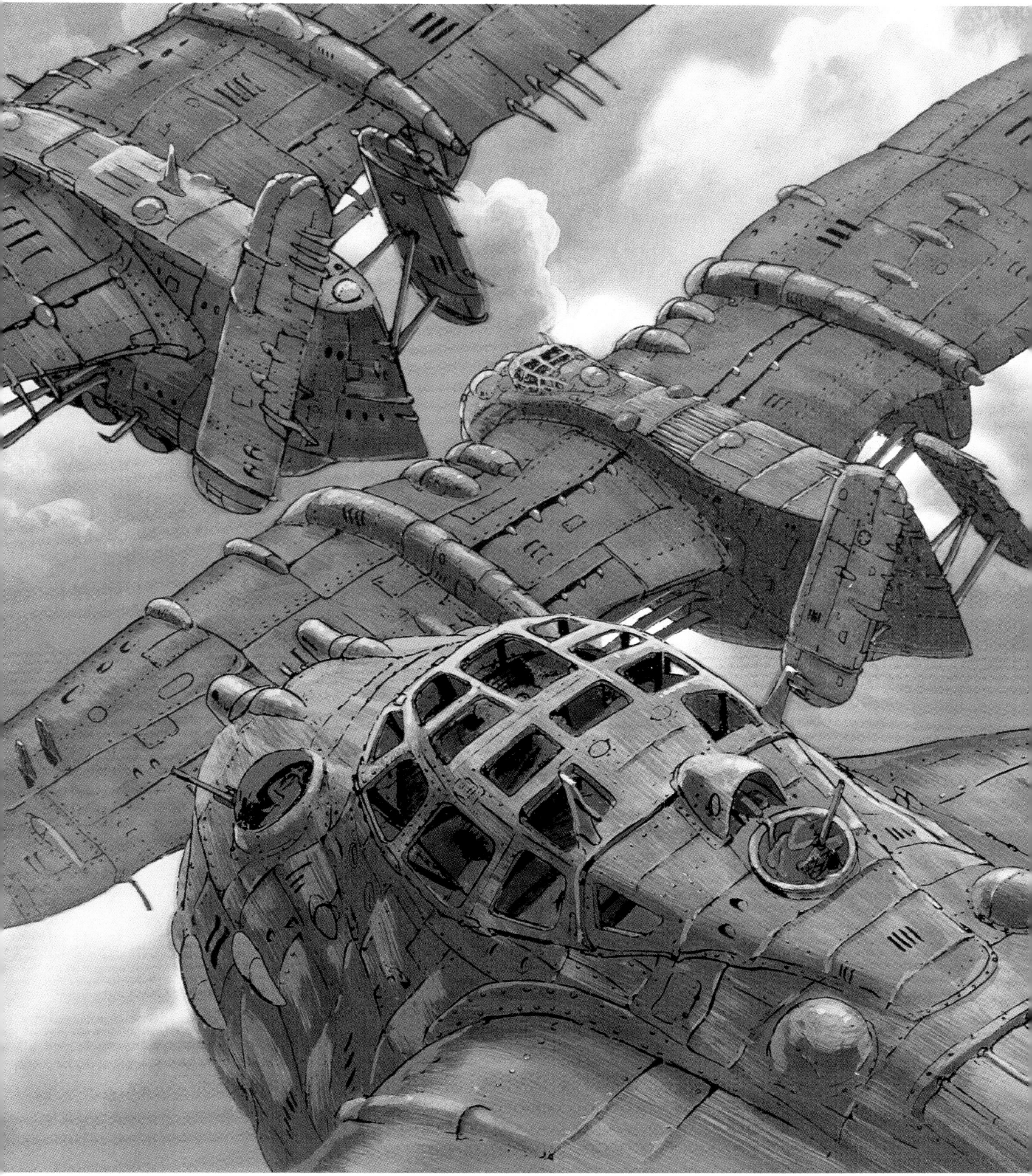

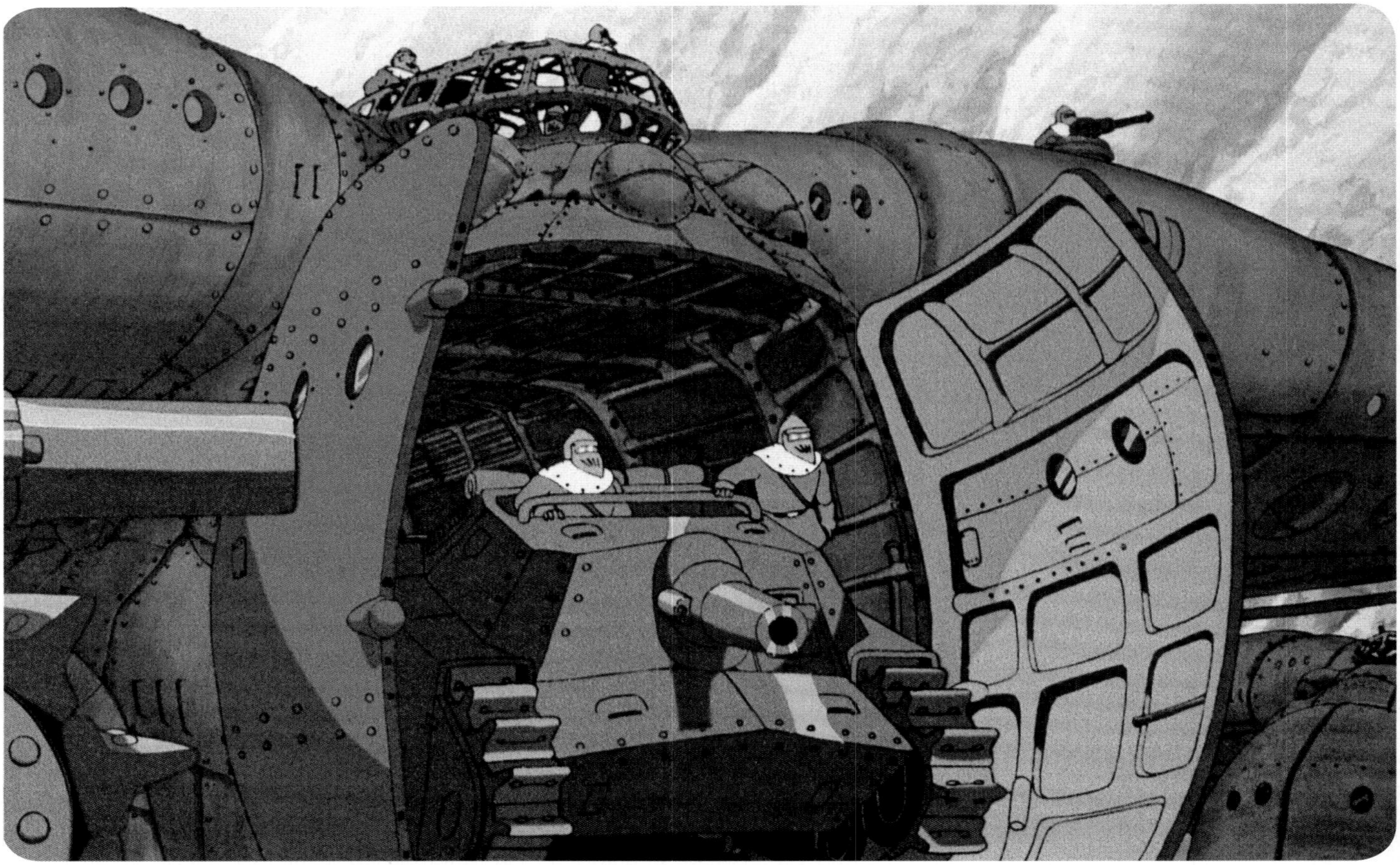

The airships landed and tanks and soldiers came swarming out. The people of the valley were terrified by the sudden attack.

Nausicaä heard sounds of gunfire coming from the castle. “Father!” she cried.

She ran to Jihl’s room as fast as her legs would take her. But when she got there…

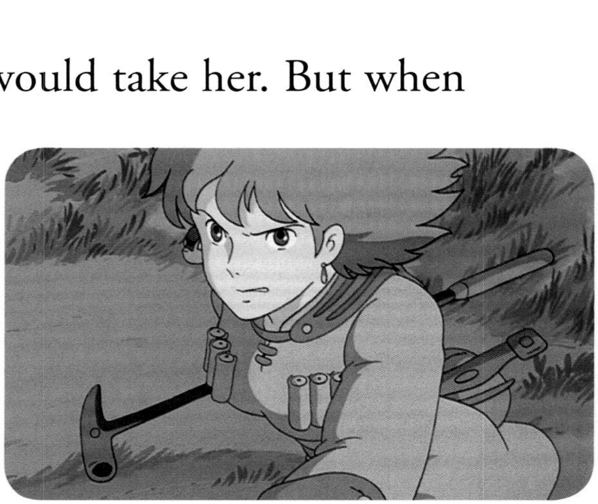

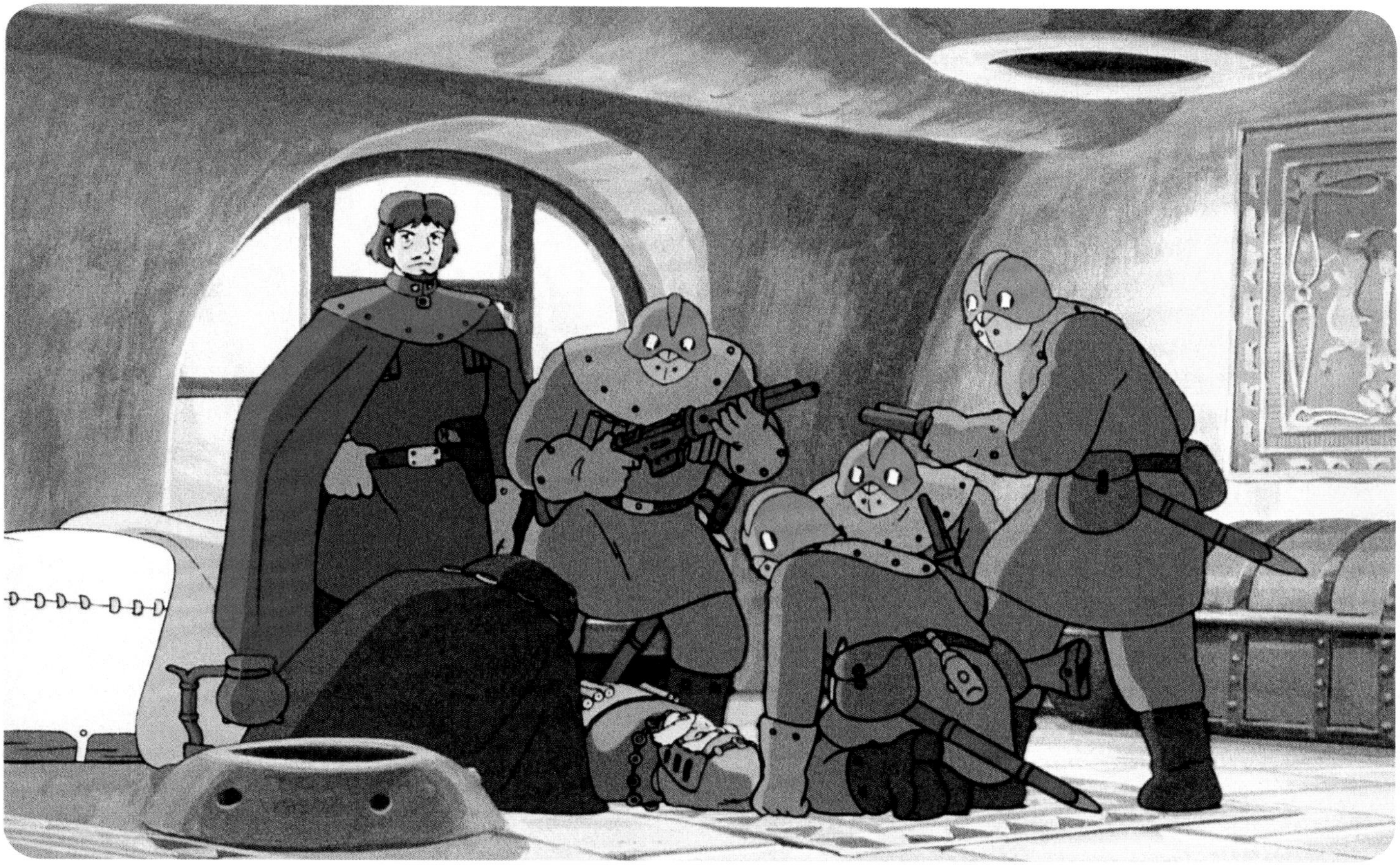

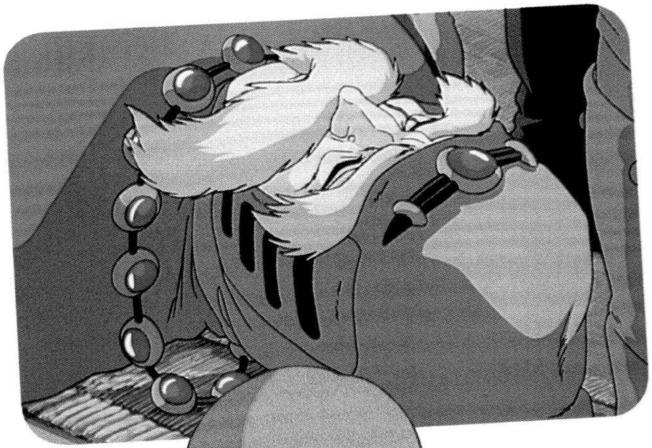

She saw her father lying on the cold stone floor. Rage and hate rose up in her.

Without a moment's hesitation, she charged fearlessly at the soldiers gathered around Jihl.

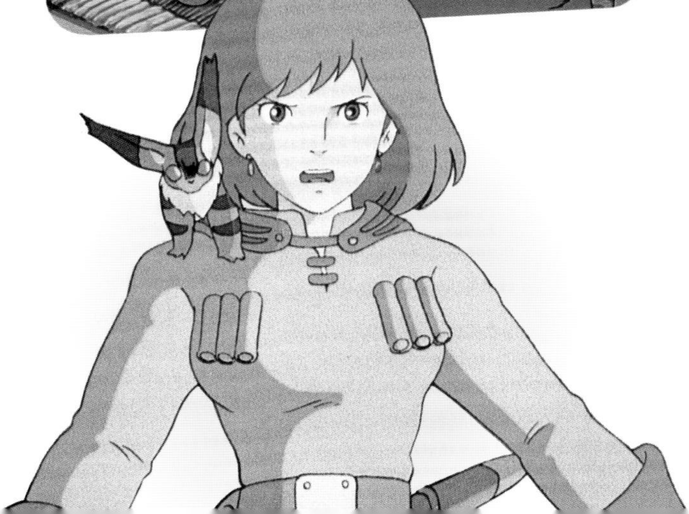

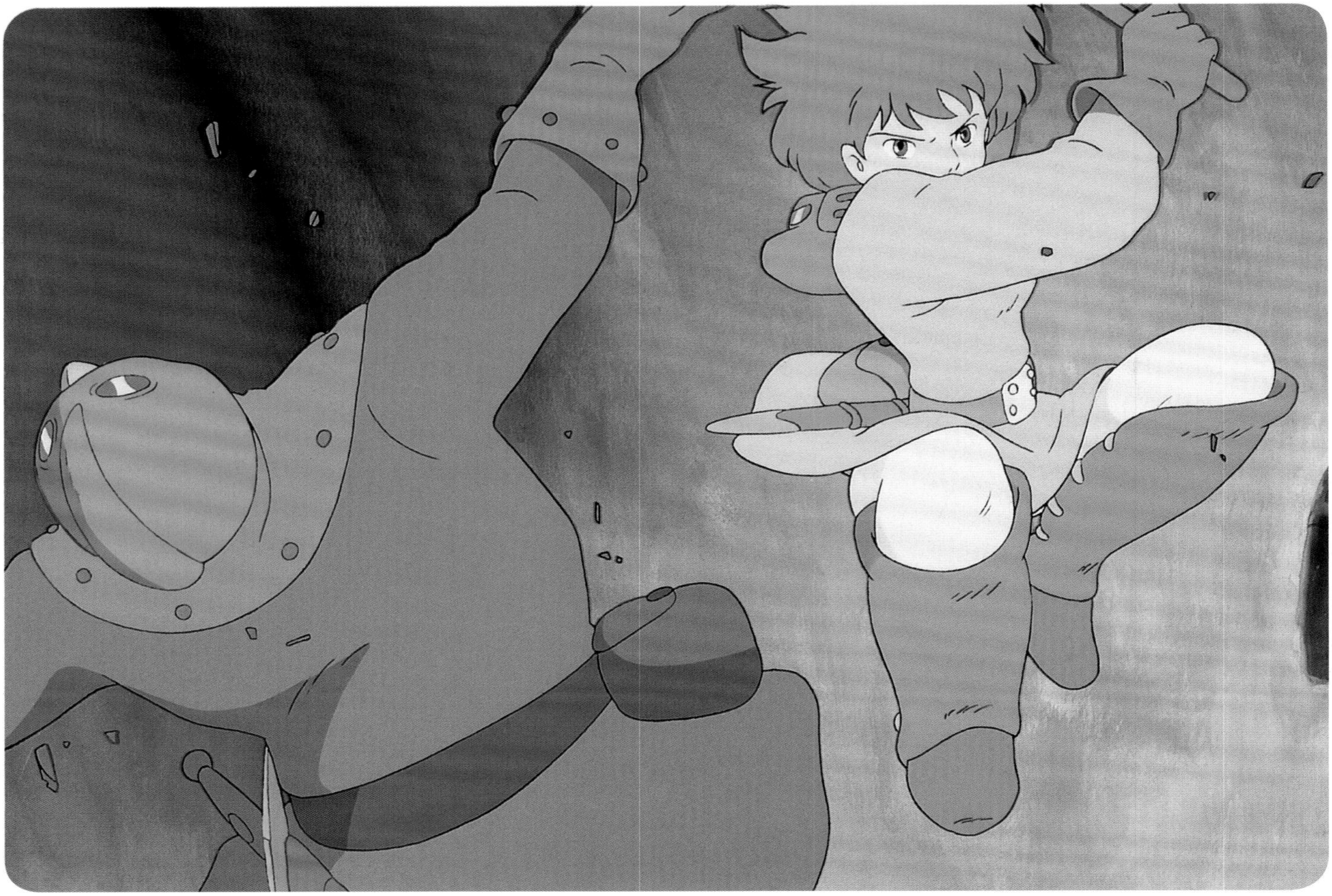

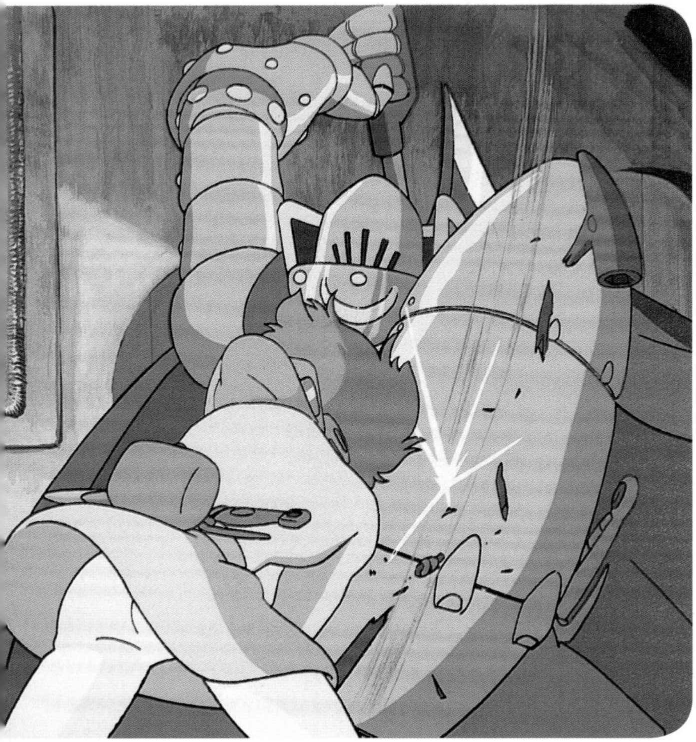

Nausicaä was filled with fury as she attacked her father's killers.

She struck down one soldier after another. Suddenly another man burst into the room.

It was Yupa!

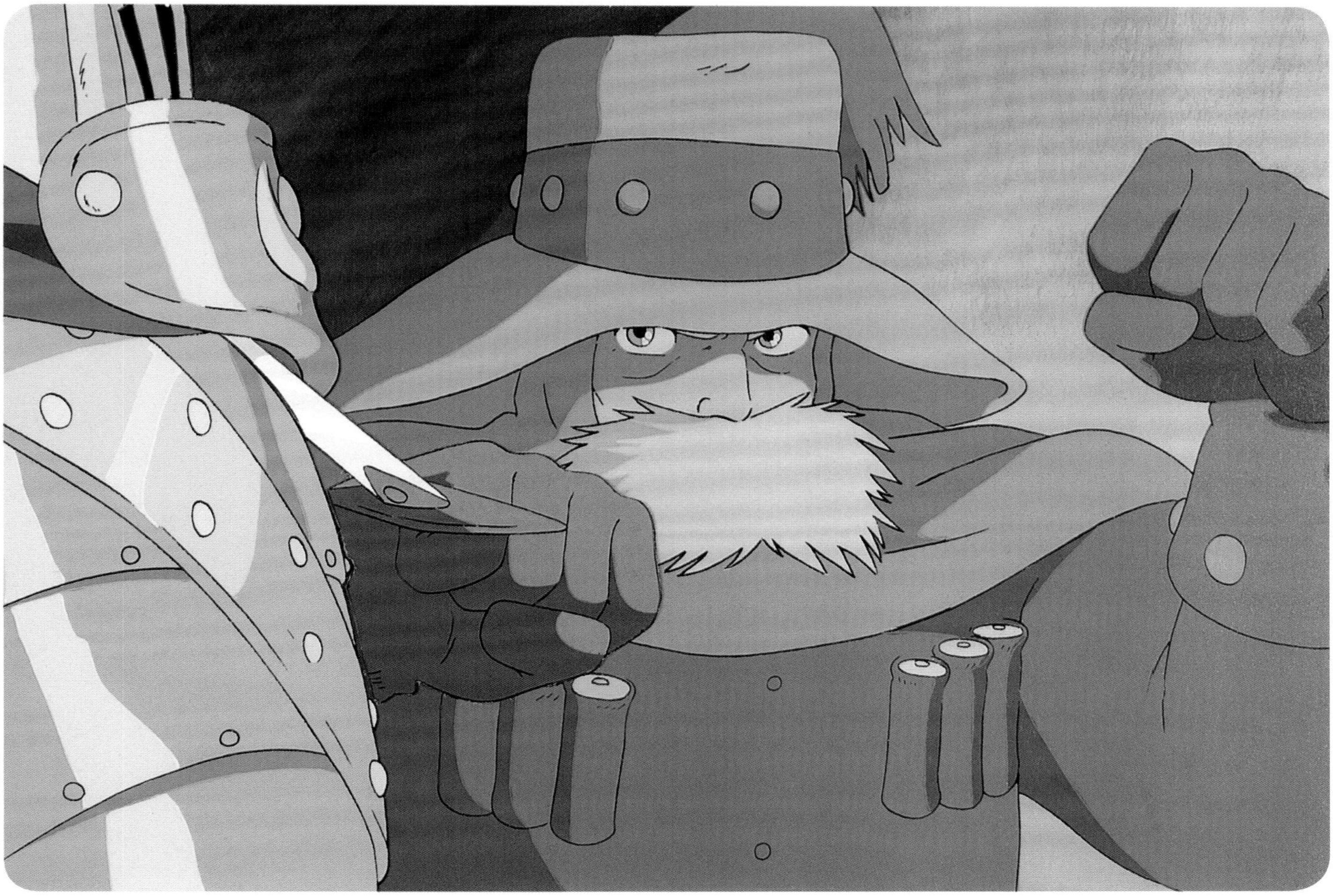

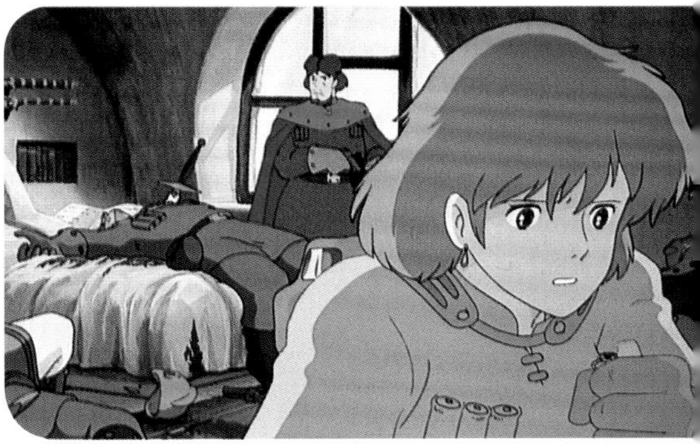

Yupa held his dagger to a soldier's throat as he blocked Nausicaä's sword.

"Nausicaä, be calm," he said quietly. "If you fight now, the people of the valley will be massacred. We must survive and wait for the right opportunity."

Hearing his words, Nausicaä came to her senses. She knew then that in her rage, she had taken the lives of other human beings.

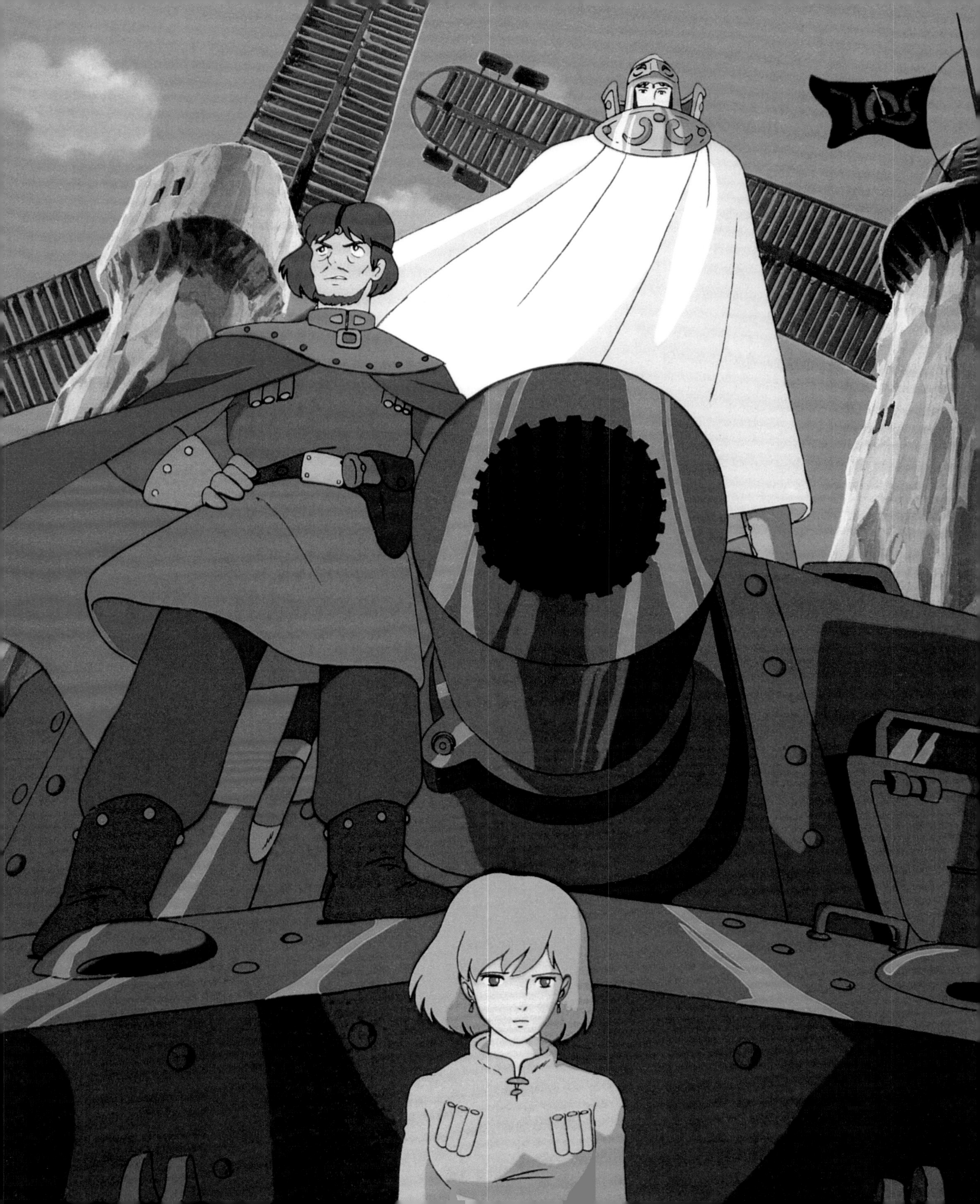

Kushana, the queen of Tolmekia, stood atop a tank with her
lieutenant, Kurotowa. She spoke to the people of the valley as her
soldiers stood guard.

"We shall put the toxic jungle to the torch. I have obtained the
world's greatest weapon, the awesome force that once allowed
humanity to rule the earth."

Kushana was determined to take over the world with the Giant
Warrior she had stolen from Pejite.

"Stop! Stop, I say!"

Obaba stepped forward. "You must not touch the toxic jungle. Yes, people have tried time and again to burn it. But their attempts did nothing but enrage the Ohm. They came out of the jungle and stampeded across the land. They toppled cities, destroyed kingdoms, and killed thousands. And the jungle only spread further. You must not touch it!"

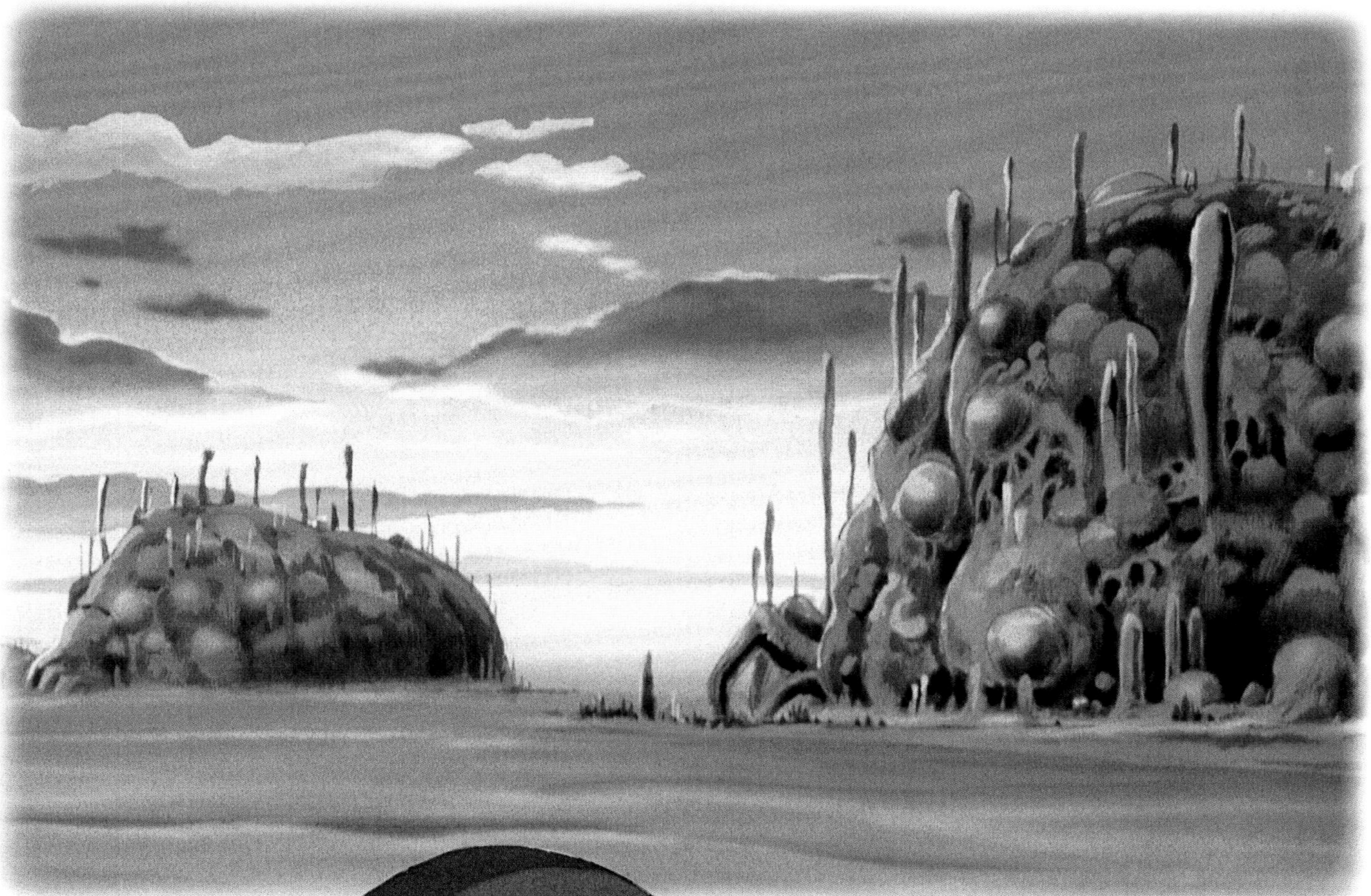
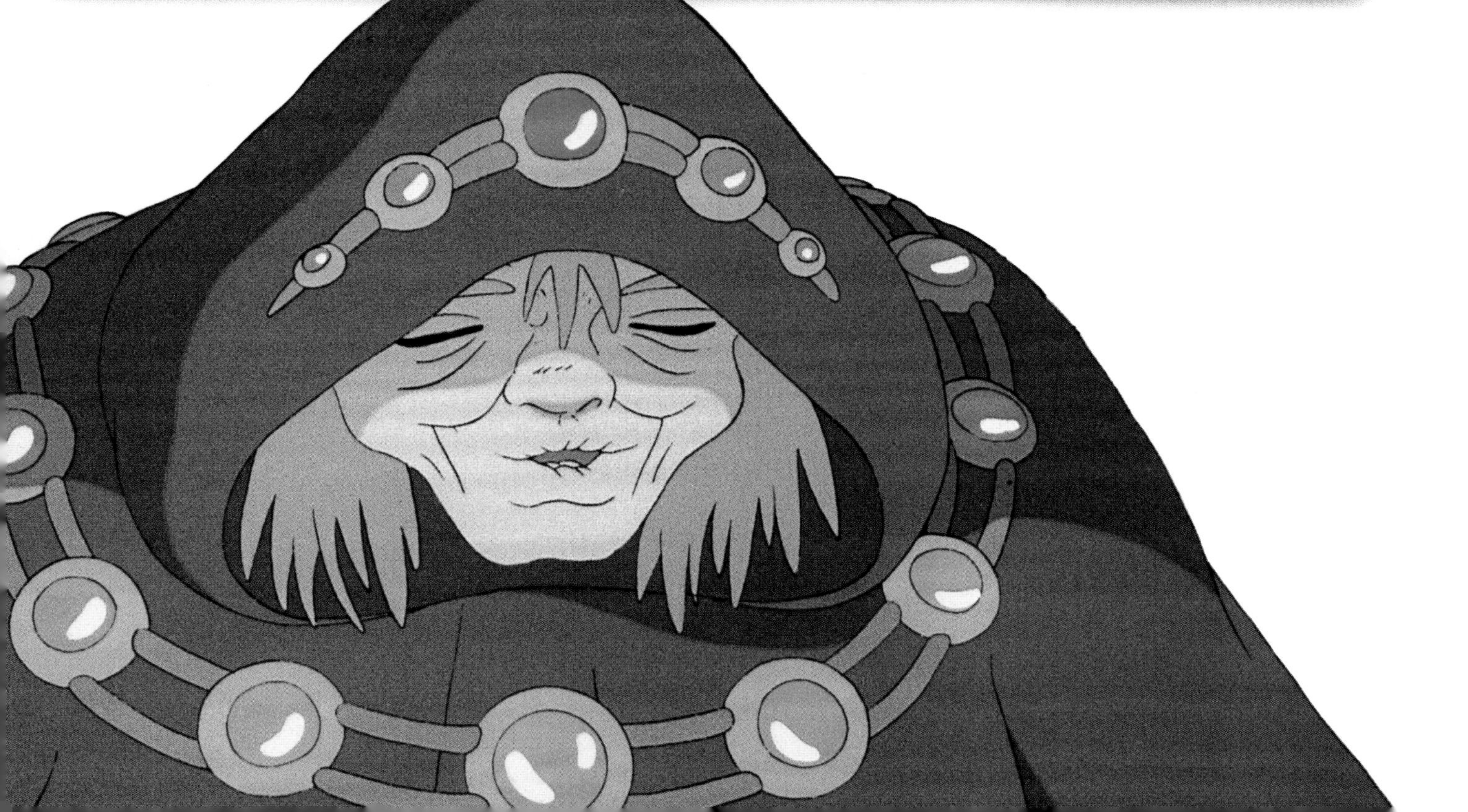

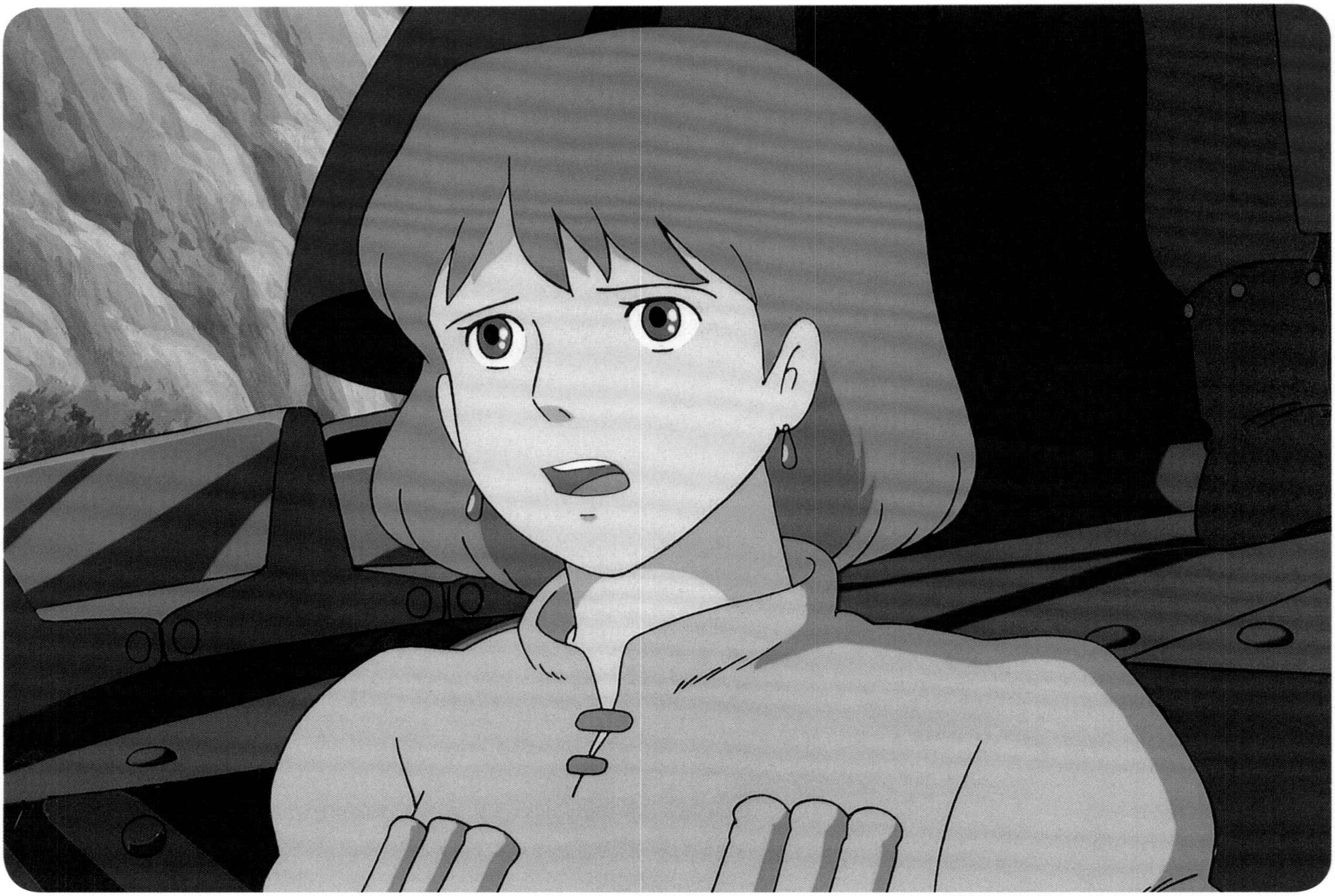

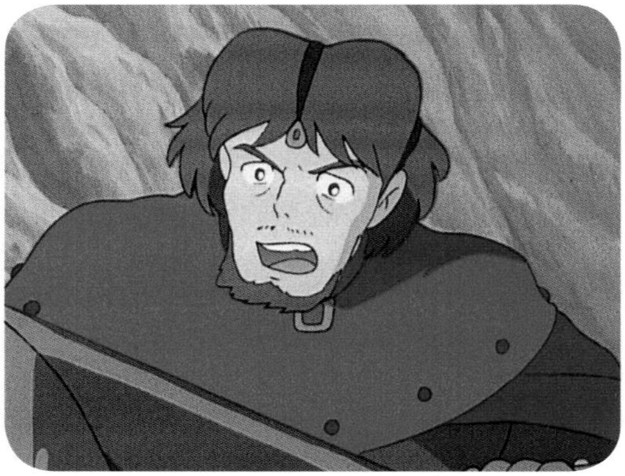

"Silence! Or you will meet the same end as your king," Kurotowa shouted.

On hearing this, the people bristled with rage. The soldiers drew their swords.

"Everyone, please!" Nausicaä called to her people. "I can't bear for anyone else to die. Obaba, please understand. We must do as they say."

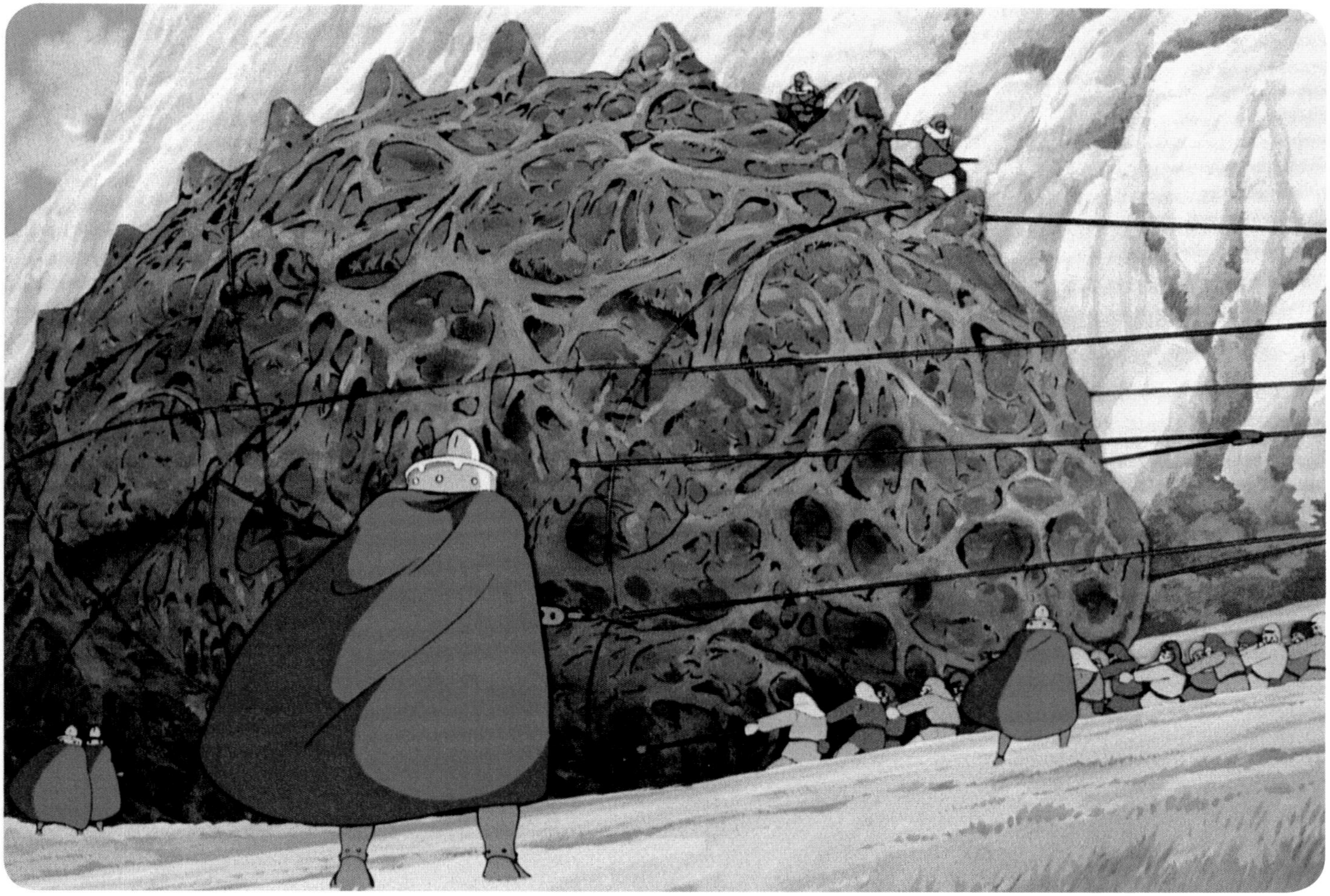

Kushana forced the men of the valley to haul the giant egg.

"The Giant Warrior is so heavy, even our largest ship couldn't handle it," she said to Kurotowa. "We can't take it back to Tolmekia. I'm going back to Pejite to report. While I'm gone, awaken the warrior."

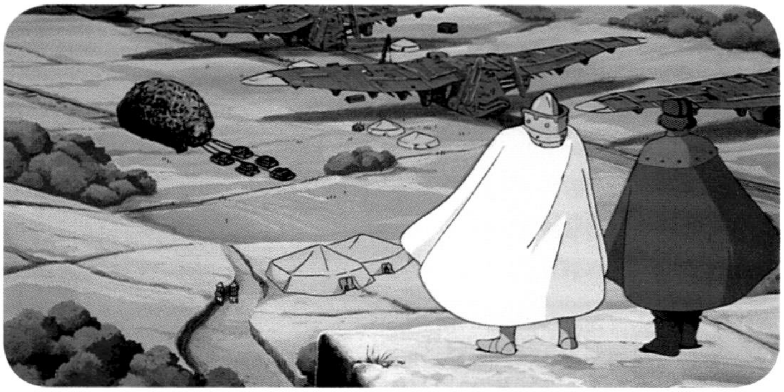

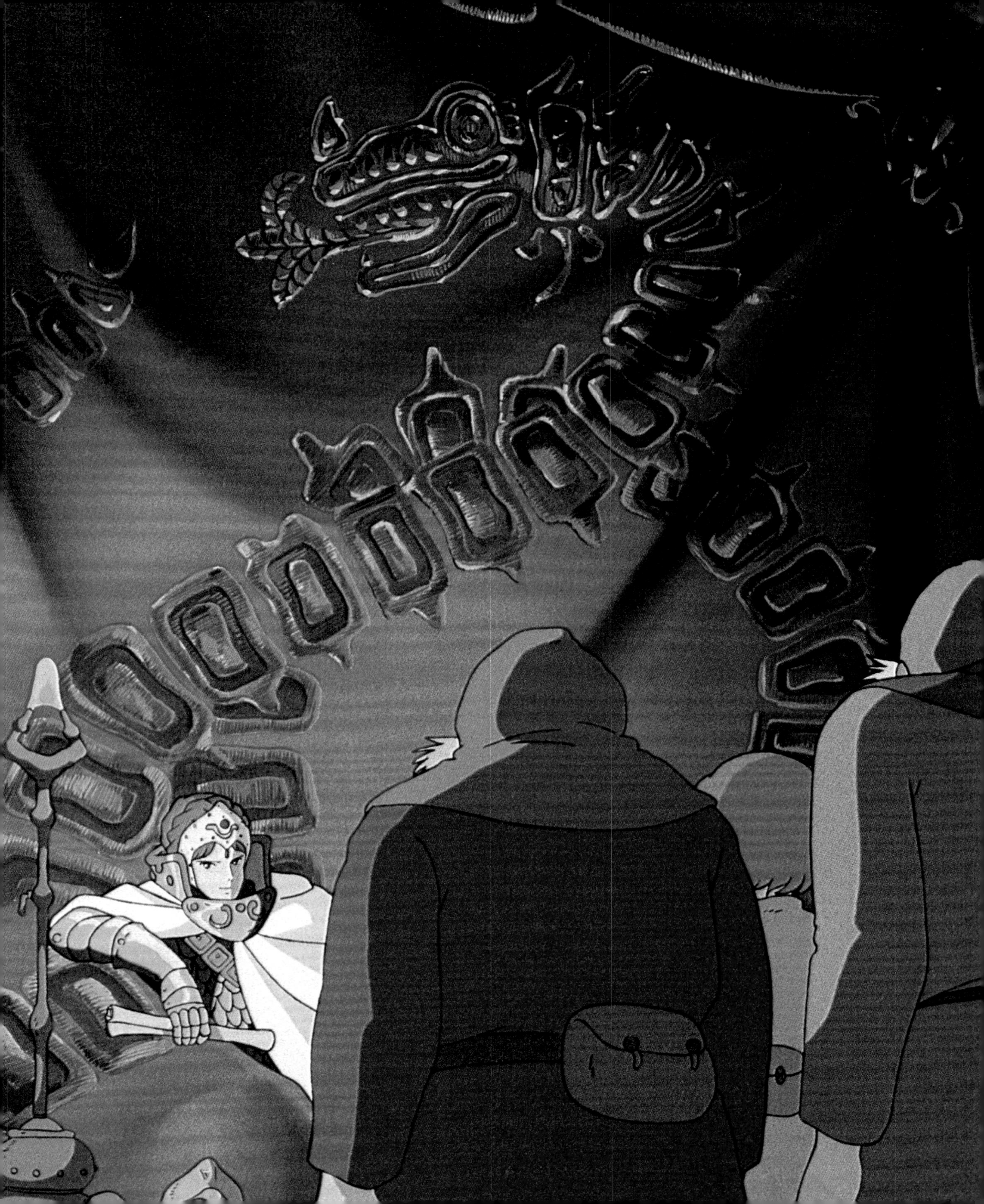

Kushana decided to take Nausicaä and the old men of the castle with her to Pejite.

"You will be my hostages, to guarantee your people's cooperation," Kushana said. "We leave in the morning."

The valley only had one gunship for defense. The Tolmekian soldiers seized it and loaded it onto the cargo barge. Their plan was to steal everything of value from the people of the valley.

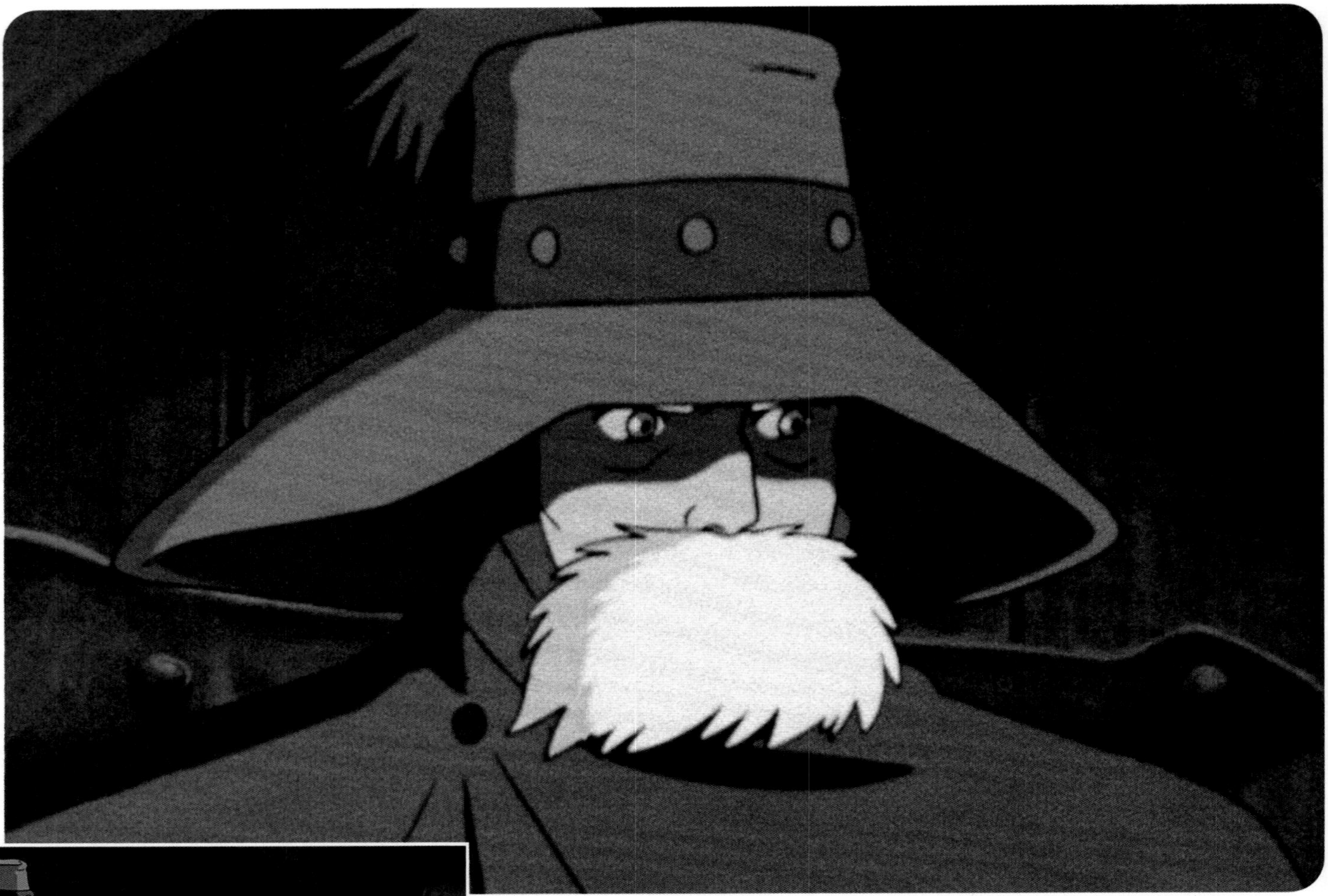

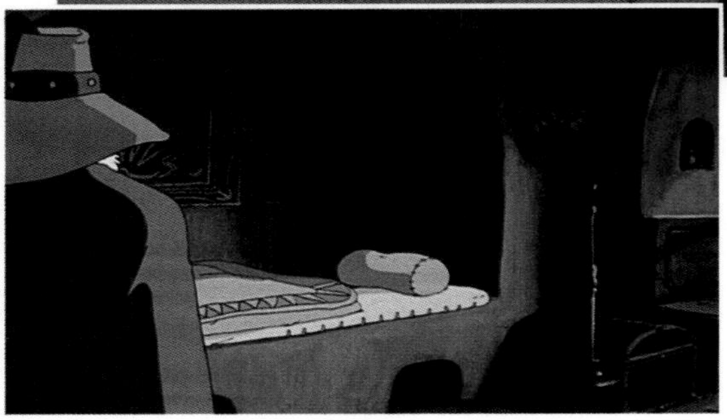

Late that night, Yupa visited Nausicaä's room. But she was nowhere to be seen.

Teto the fox squirrel was scratching with his claws at the stone wall.

"Teto, where has Nausicaä gone?"

Yupa was curious. He came closer to the wall and touched it gently. A hidden door swung open.

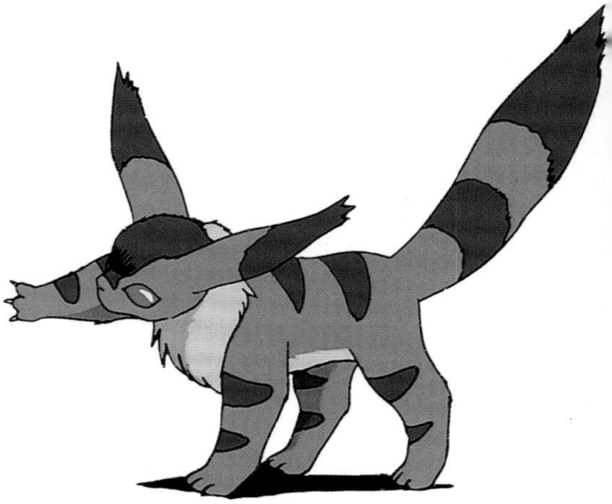

A stone stairway led down into darkness.

Yupa went down the stairs into a lighted room. Nausicaä was sitting at a table with her head cradled on her arms.

Yupa looked around the room and cried out in amazement.

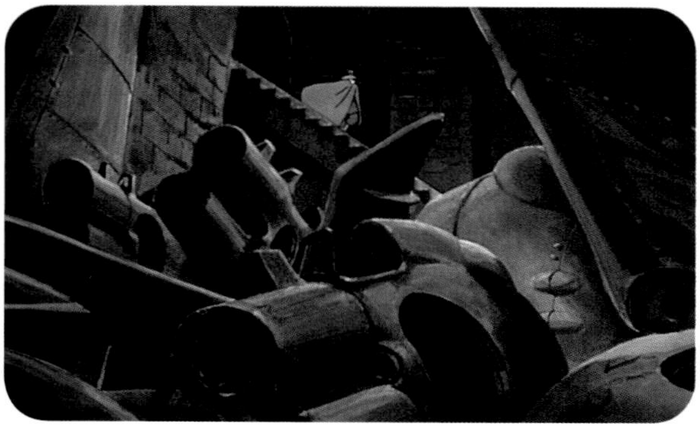

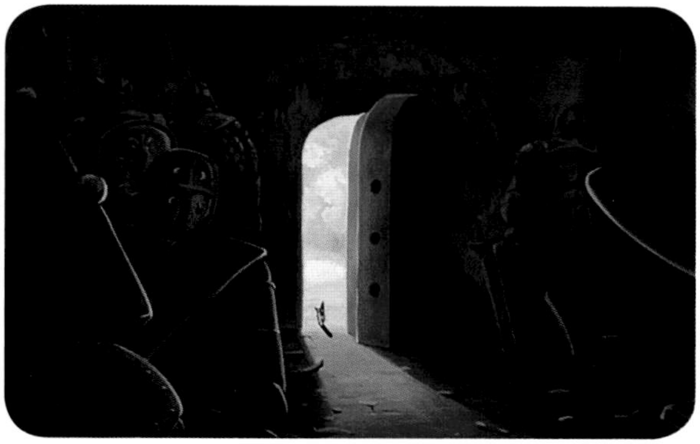

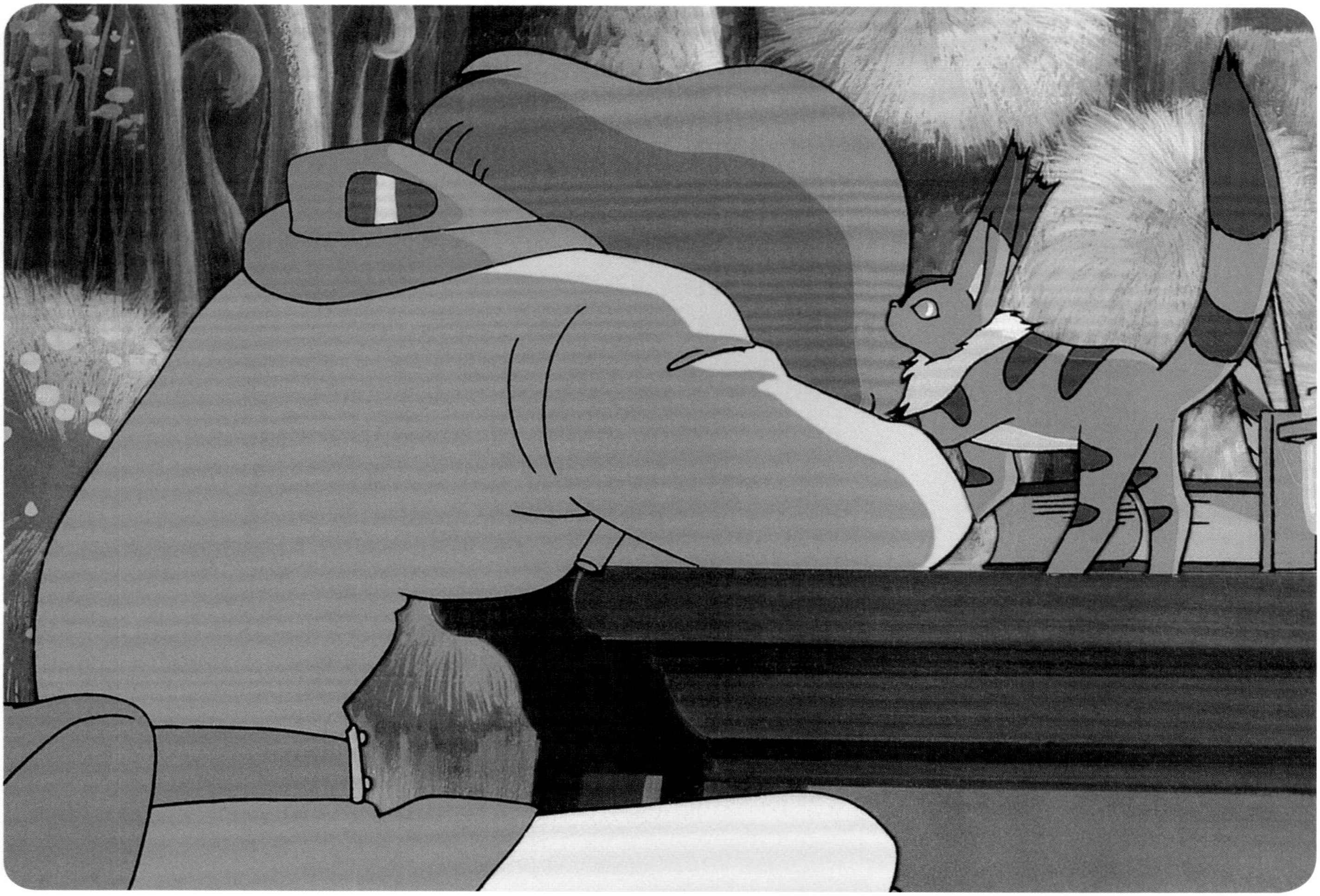

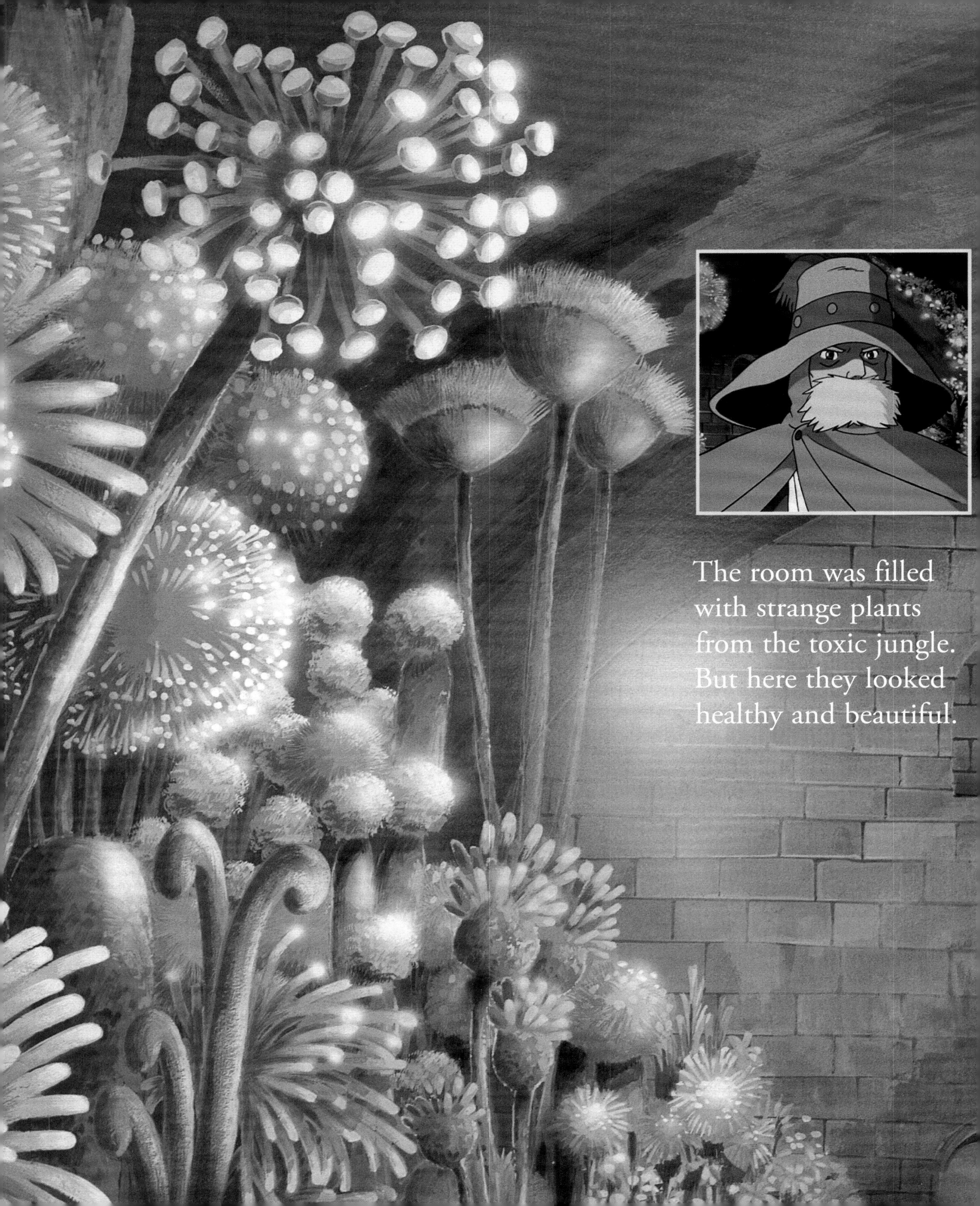

The room was filled with strange plants from the toxic jungle. But here they looked healthy and beautiful.

"I collected the spores and grew them myself," Nausicaä said to the startled Yupa.

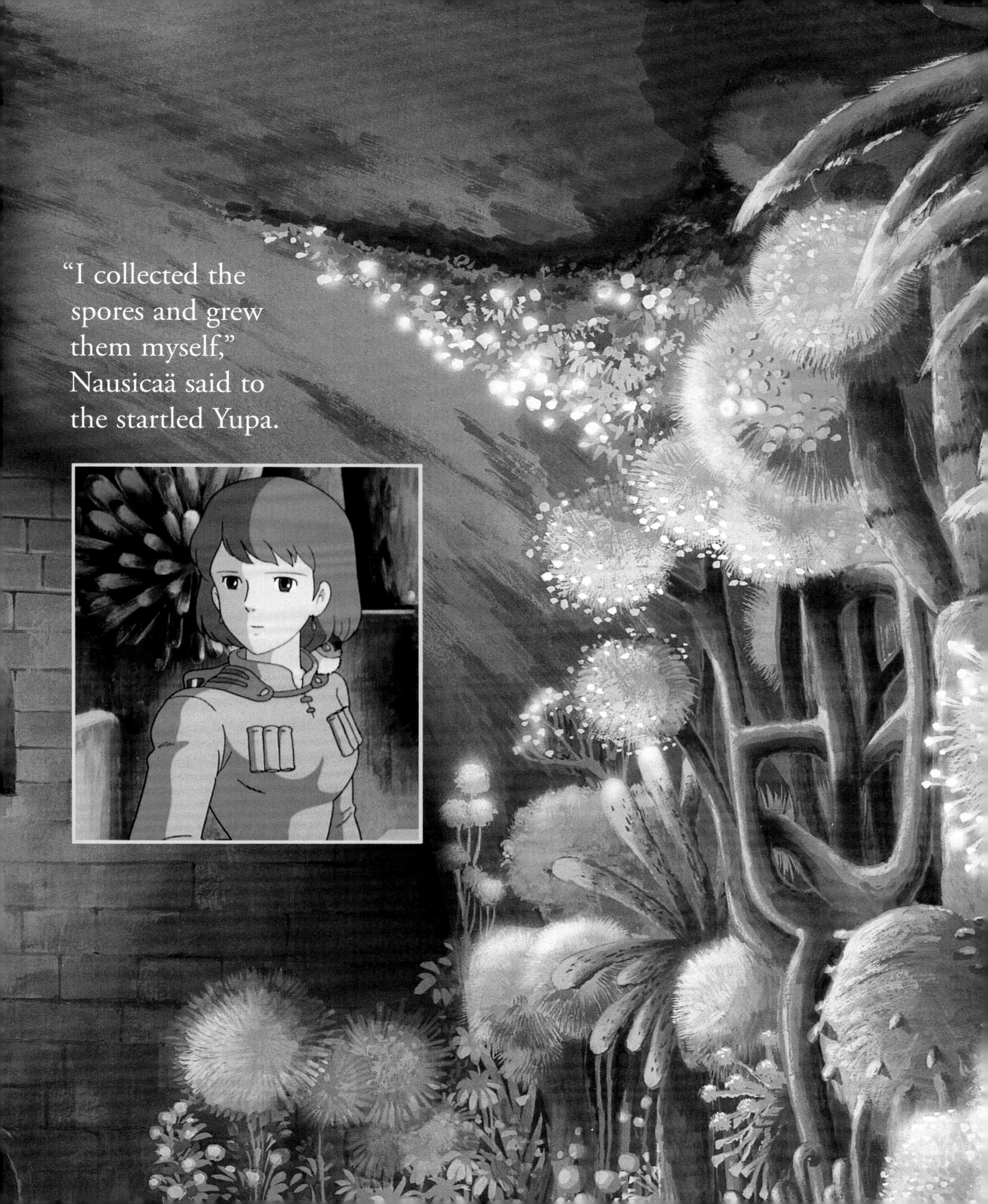

"Don't worry, they're not poisonous. I'm using water drawn from deep underground by the castle windmill. I used soil from the bottom of the well too. With clean water and soil, the plants from the toxic jungle aren't poisonous. All the poison is in the soil."

Yupa couldn't contain his surprise. "You discovered this all on your own?"

"Yes. I was hoping to find a cure for father's illness. But it's too late now."

Suddenly, Nausicaä threw herself into Yupa's arms. "I'm afraid of myself, Lord Yupa," she sobbed. "I had no idea that my rage could drive me to kill."

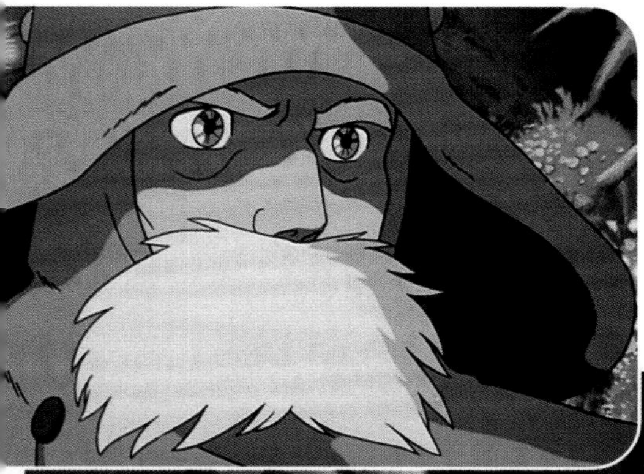

Yupa held her gently as she wept.

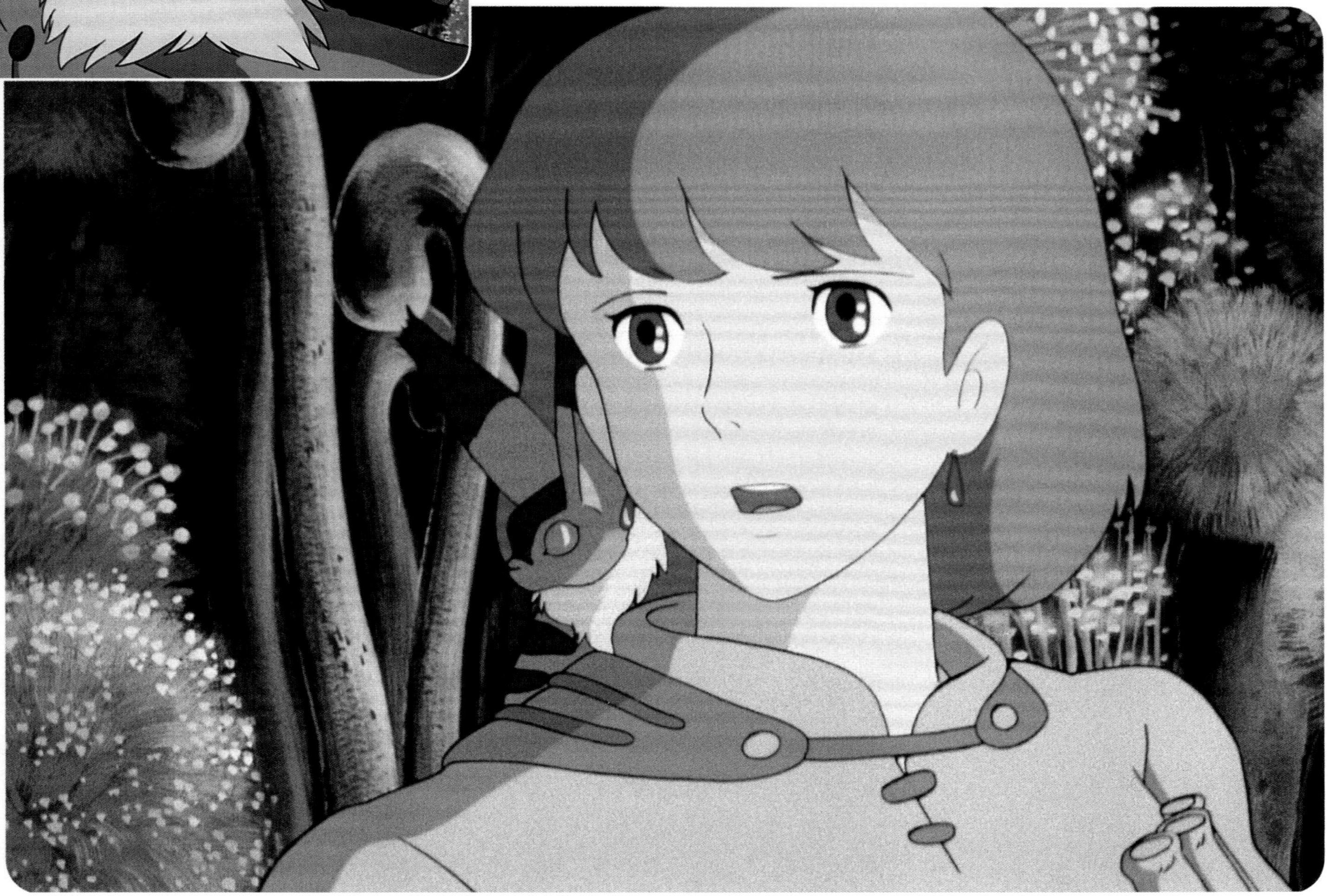

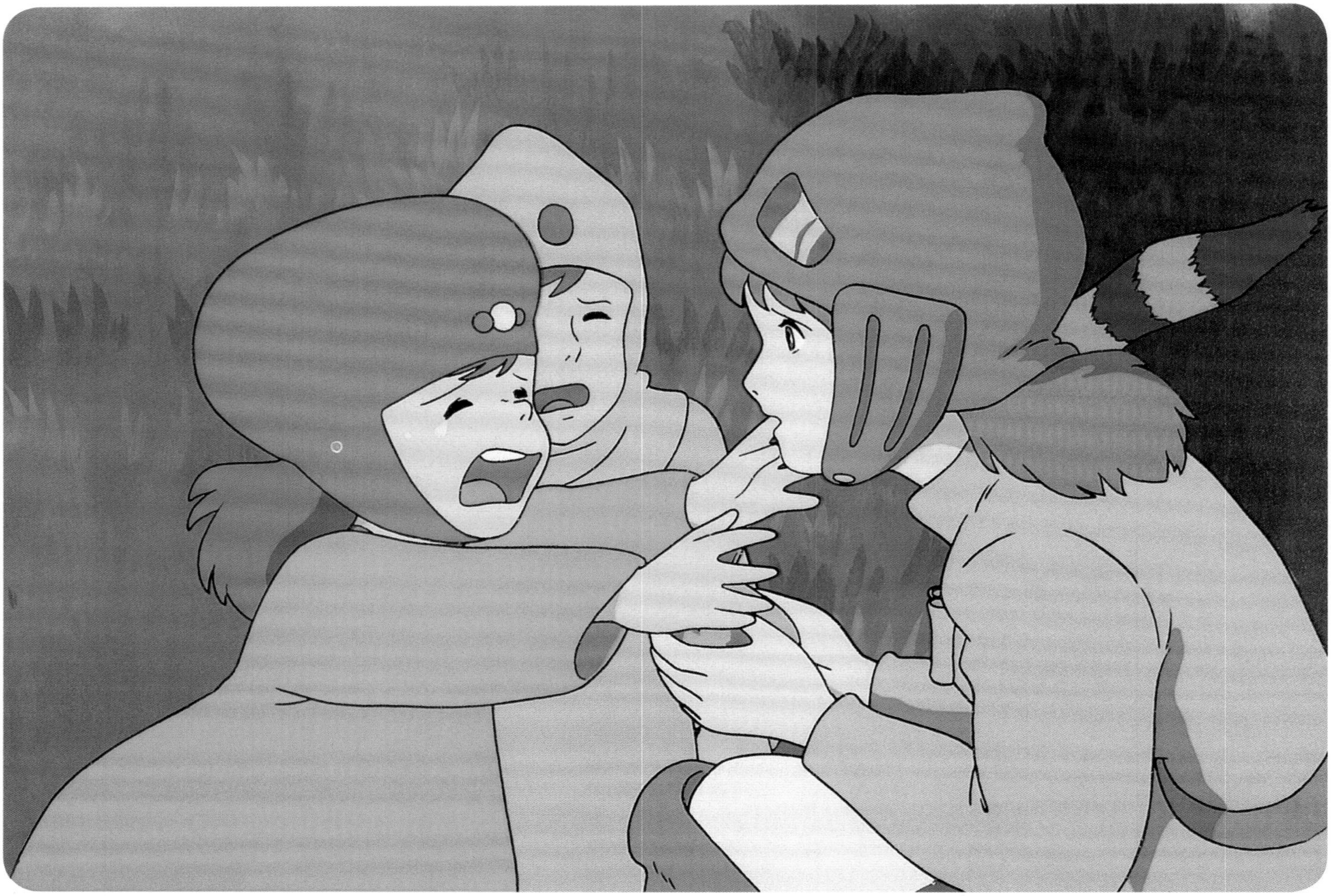

The next morning, as Nausicaä was about to board the airship that would take her to Pejite, the children of the valley surrounded her sorrowfully.

"Princess Nausicaä!"

"We don't want you to go."

Nausicaä knelt and comforted them. "Don't cry. I'll be back very soon."

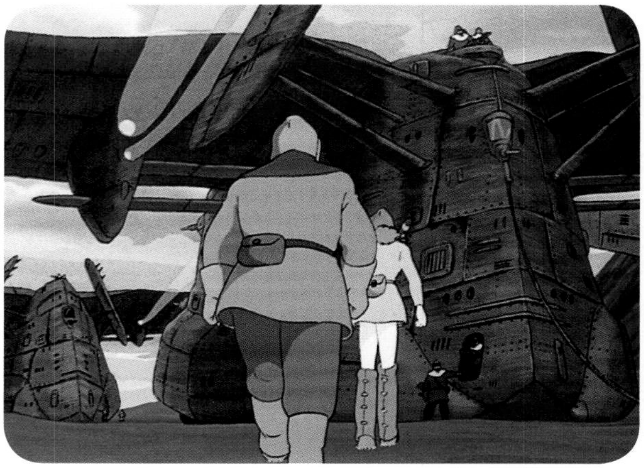

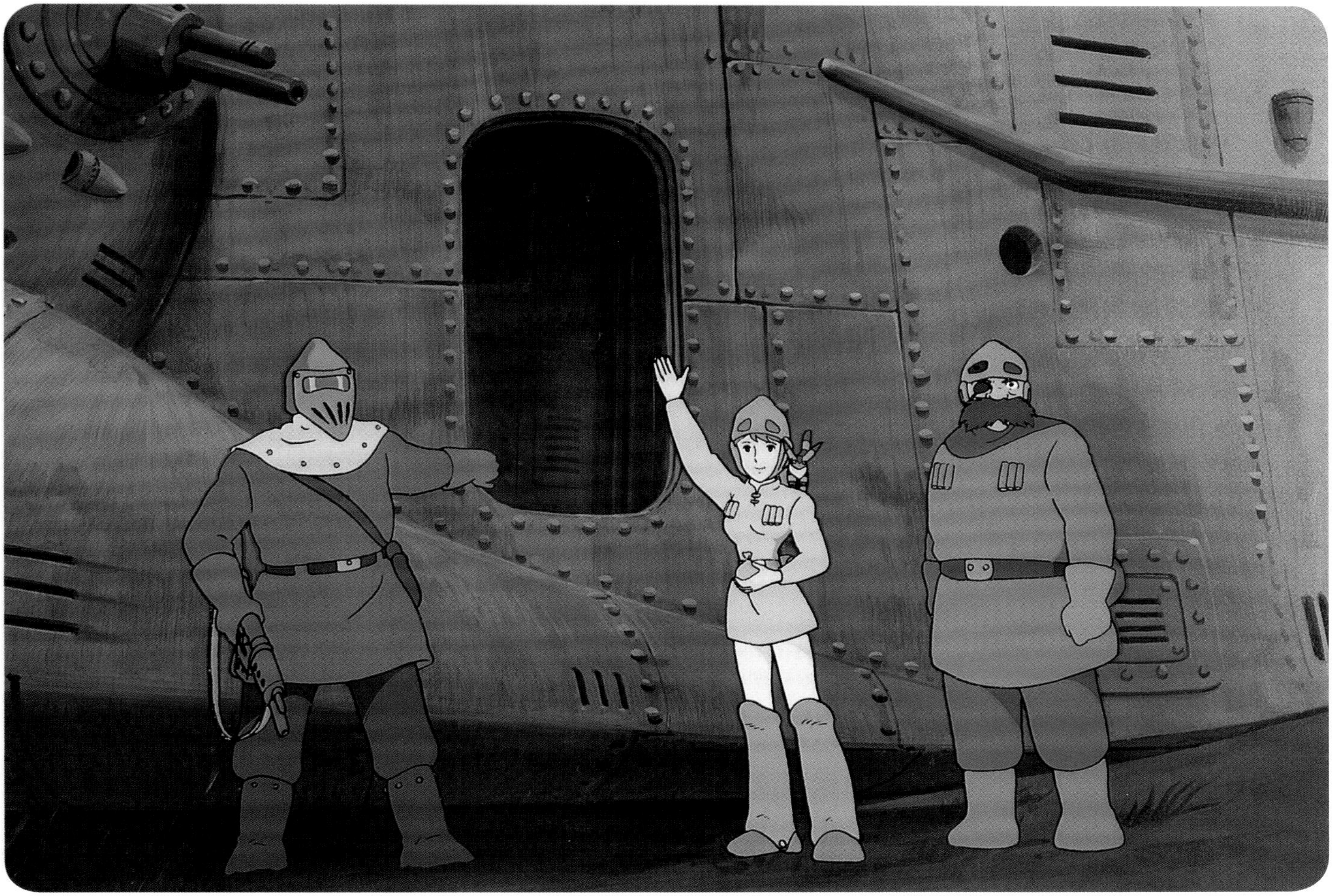

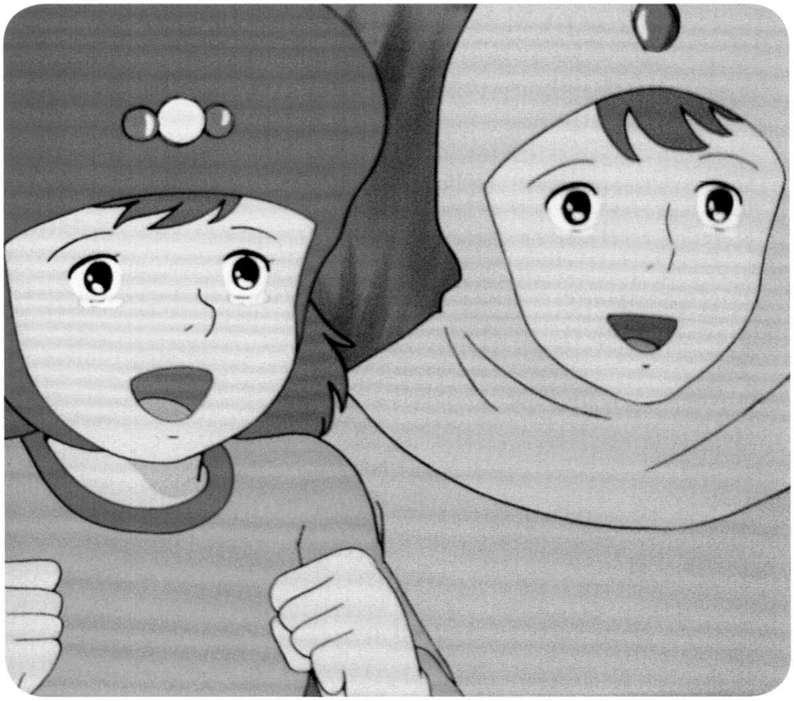

“Do you mean it?” the children said.

Nausicaä gave a big nod. “Of course. Have I ever broken a promise to you?”

As she smiled and waved farewell, the children smiled too.

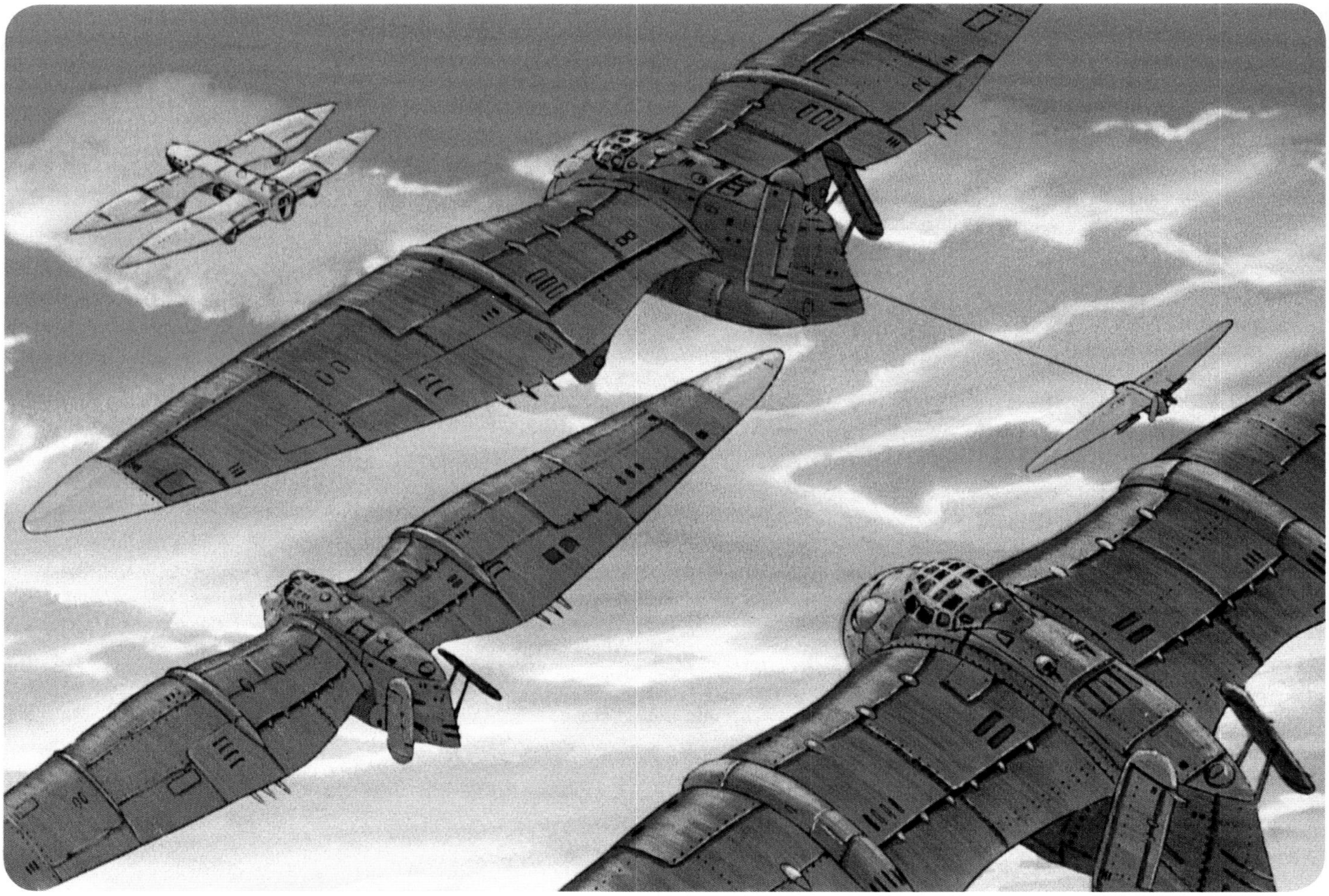

Mito followed Nausicaä into the airship. The other hostages went aboard the cargo barge, which was attached to one of the airships with a tow line. The people of the valley watched as the great Tolmekian ships took off one after another.

Pejite was far from the valley. The airships flew over the Sea of Decay for what seemed like hours.

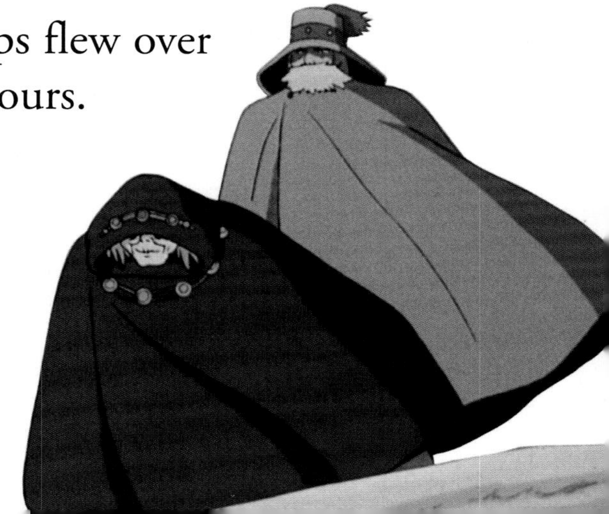

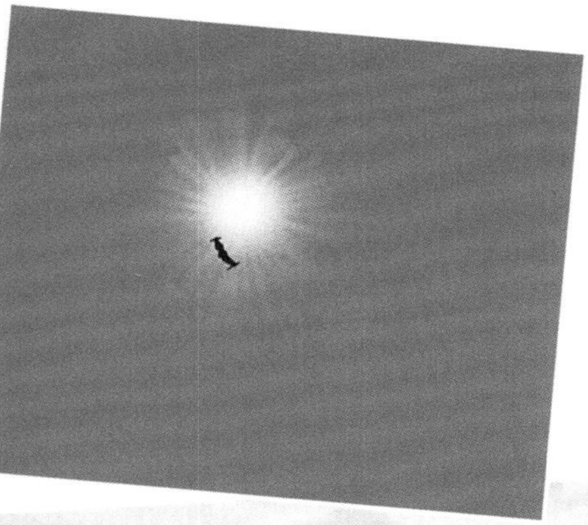

Far off in the sky ahead, Nausicaä saw sudden flashes of light.

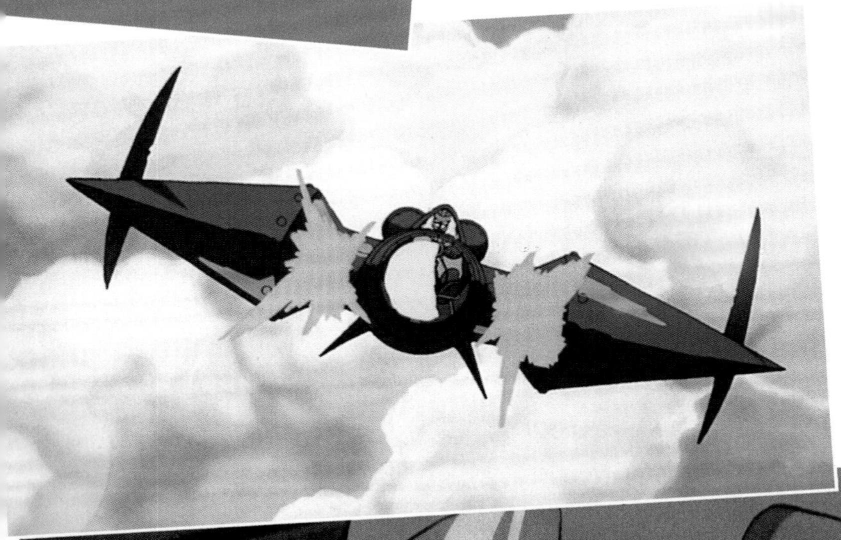

It was a gunship from Pejite, and it was firing in her direction! The little fighter hurtled out of the blue, guns blazing.

The pilot was making straight for the Tolmekian airships.

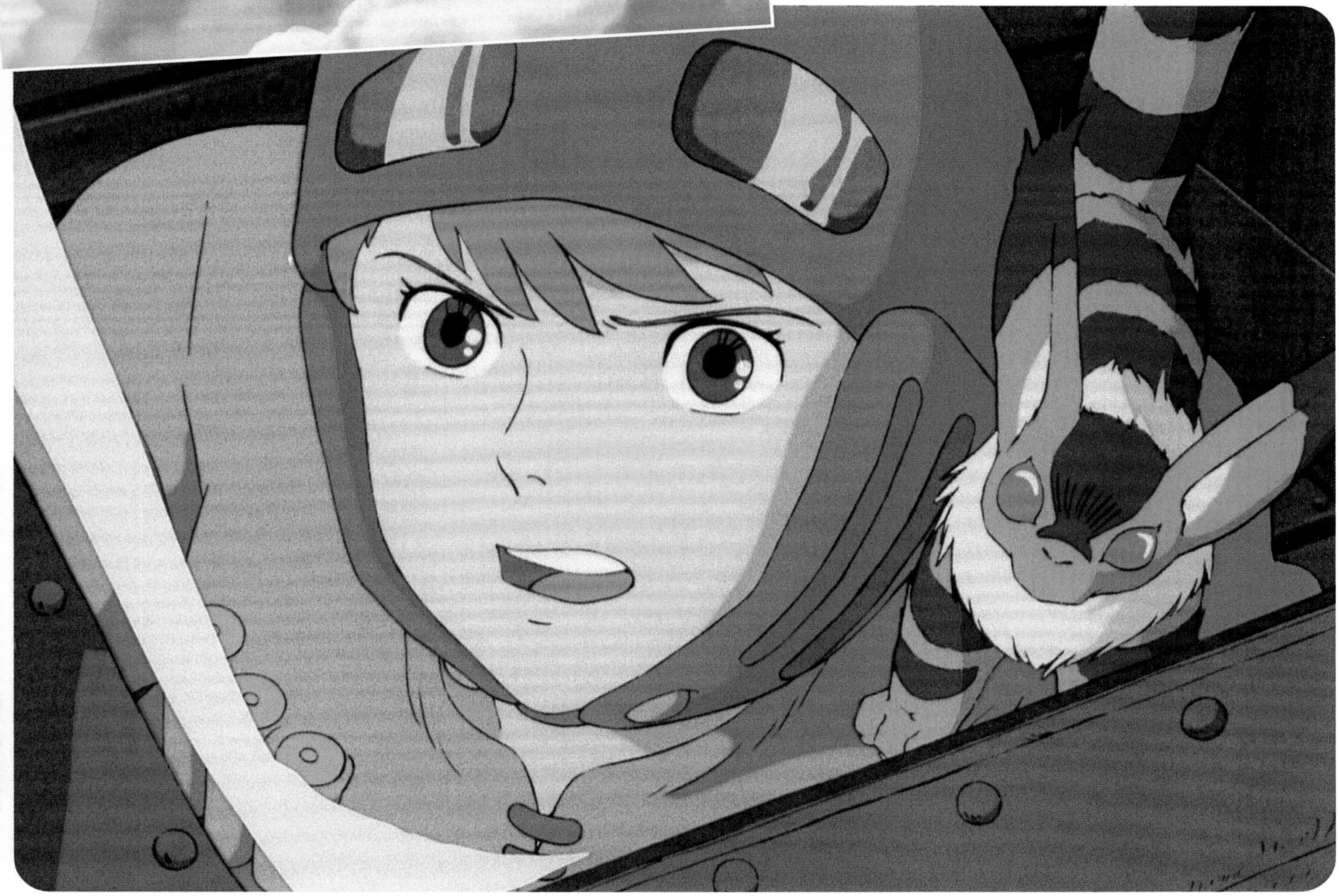

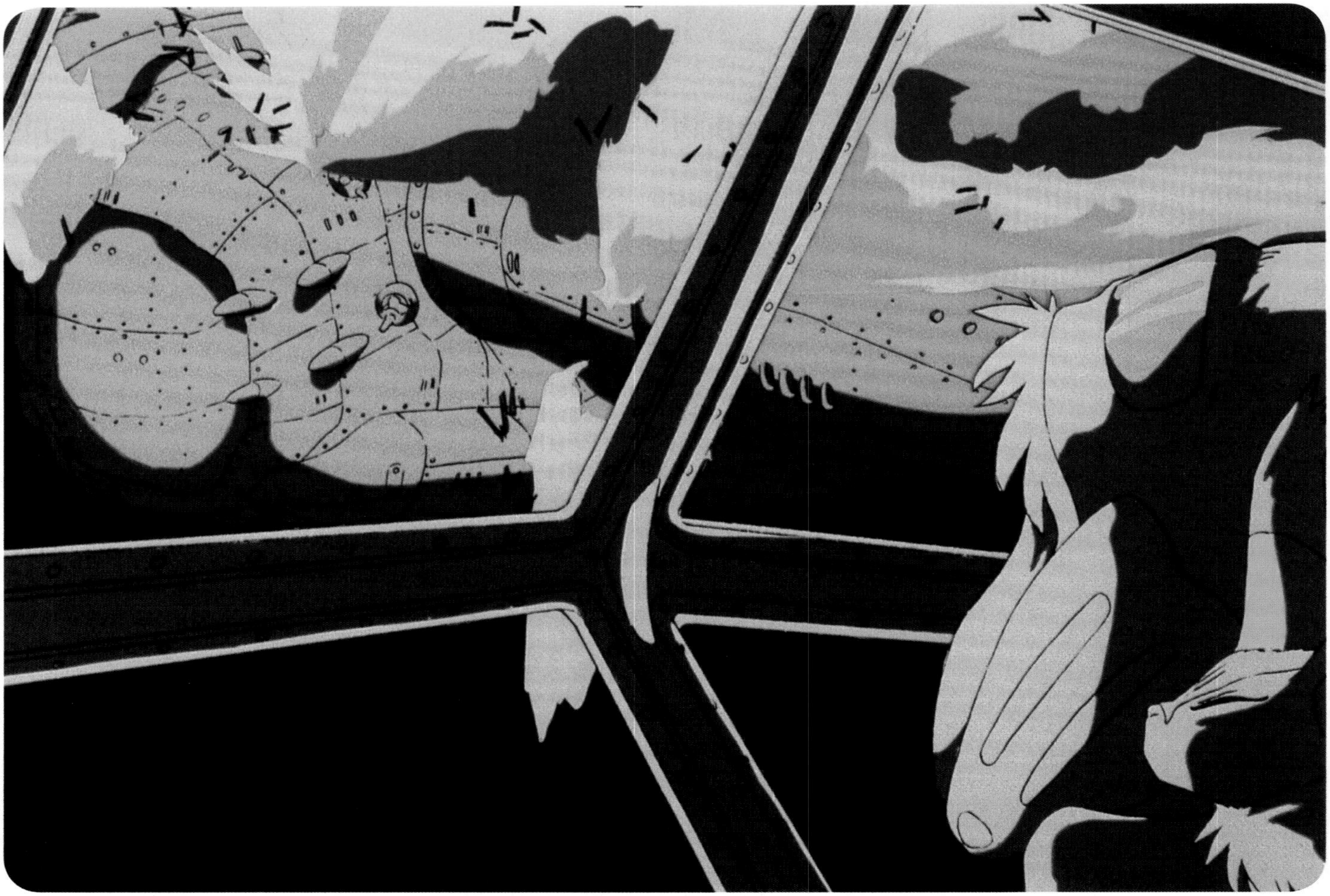

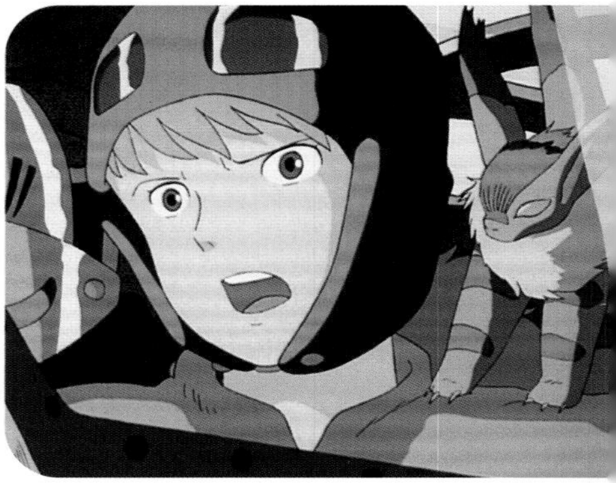

One by one, the giant ships were hit. They burst into flames and went crashing to earth. The Tolmekians were taken completely by surprise.

Nausicaä looked out the window and gasped. The barge, carrying the old men from the castle, was diving down into the poison clouds.

The gunship kept attacking. Nausicaä's airship was soon hit and engulfed in flames.

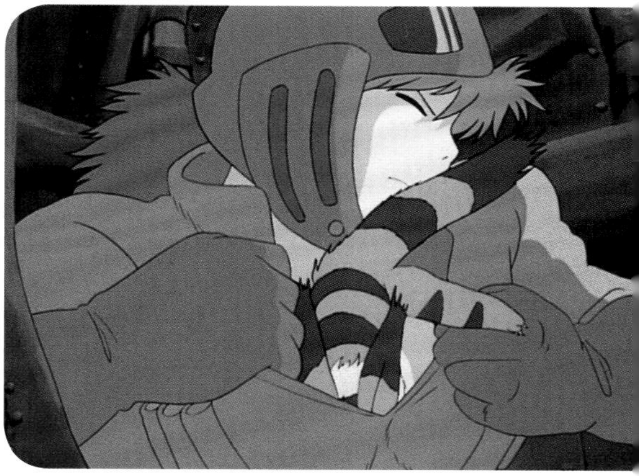

She tucked Teto inside her suit for protection and climbed outside the cockpit.

"Stop it!" she cried. "All this killing must stop!"

But the gunship came straight toward her.

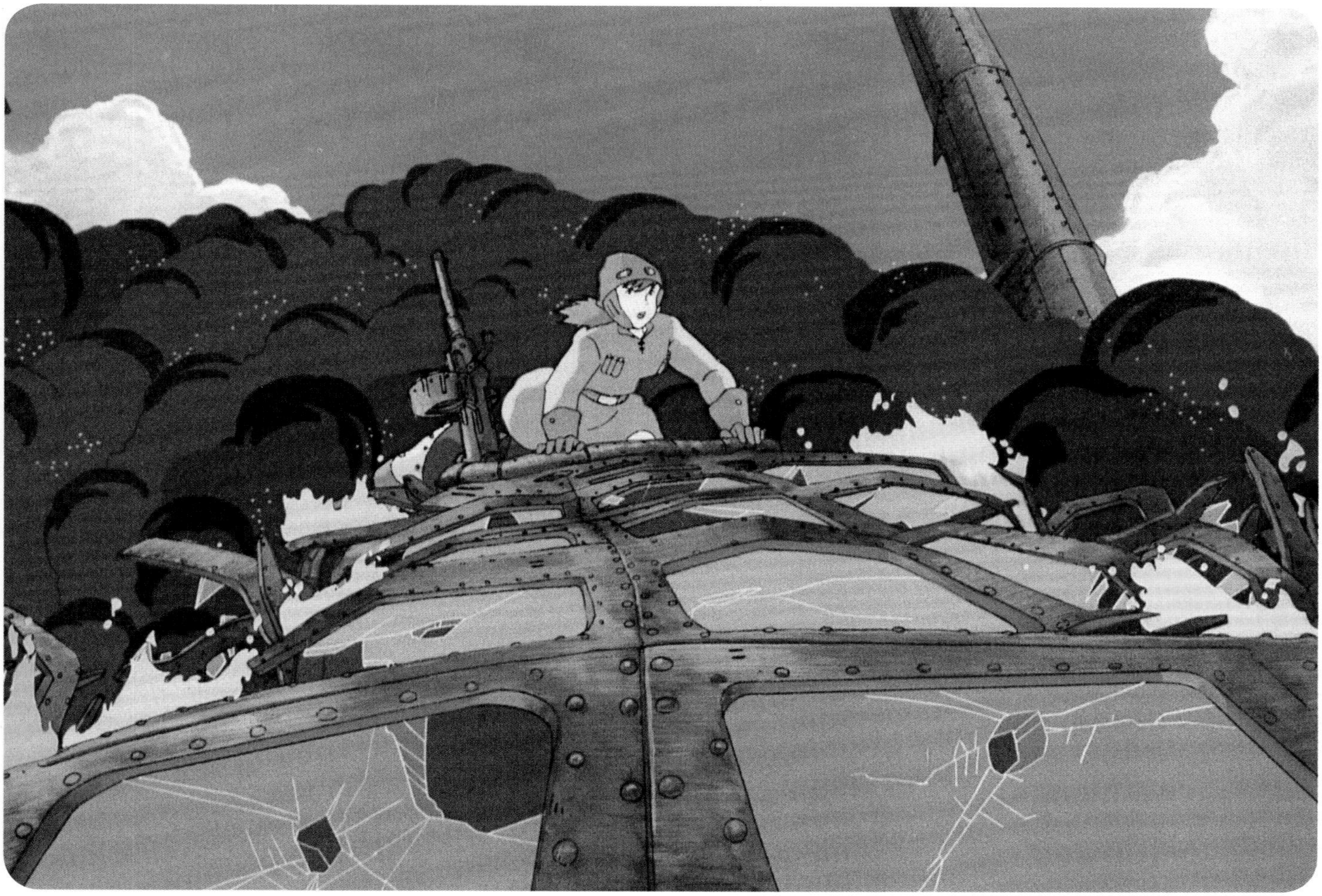

There was a young pilot in the cockpit of the gunship.

He could see Nausicaä standing on the airship surrounded by the flames.

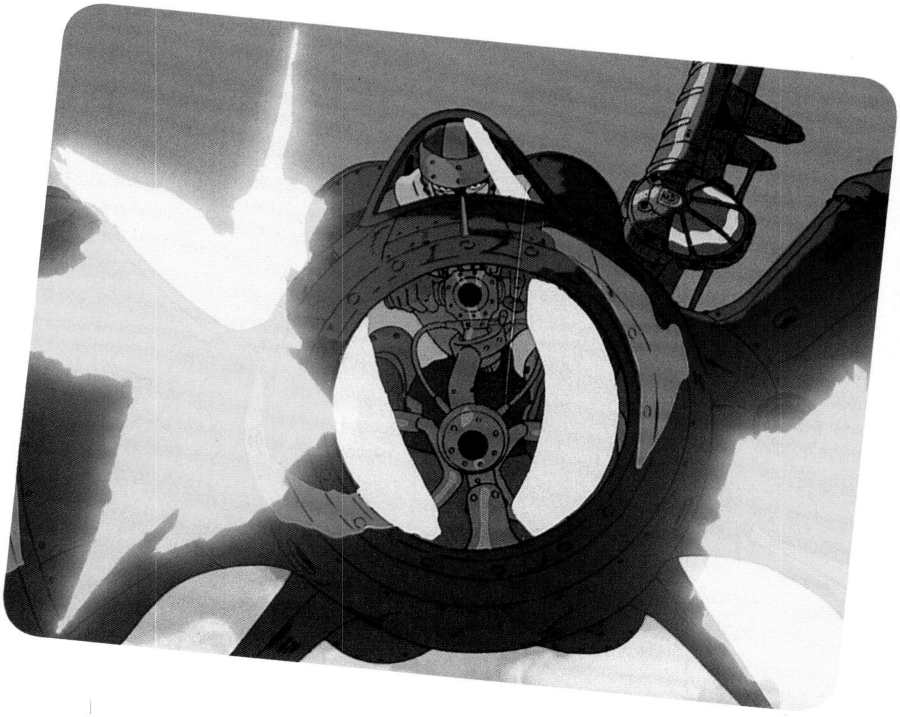

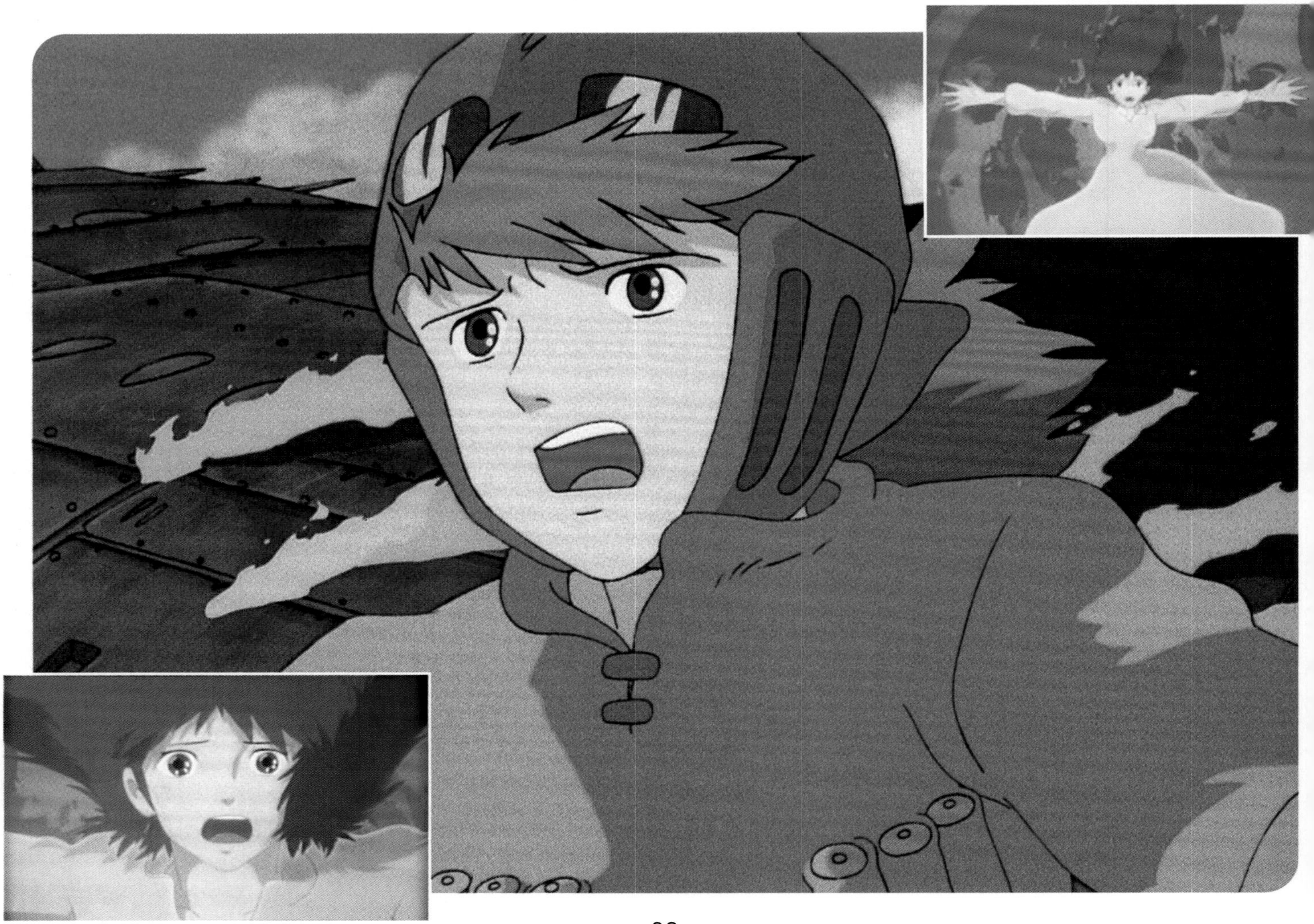

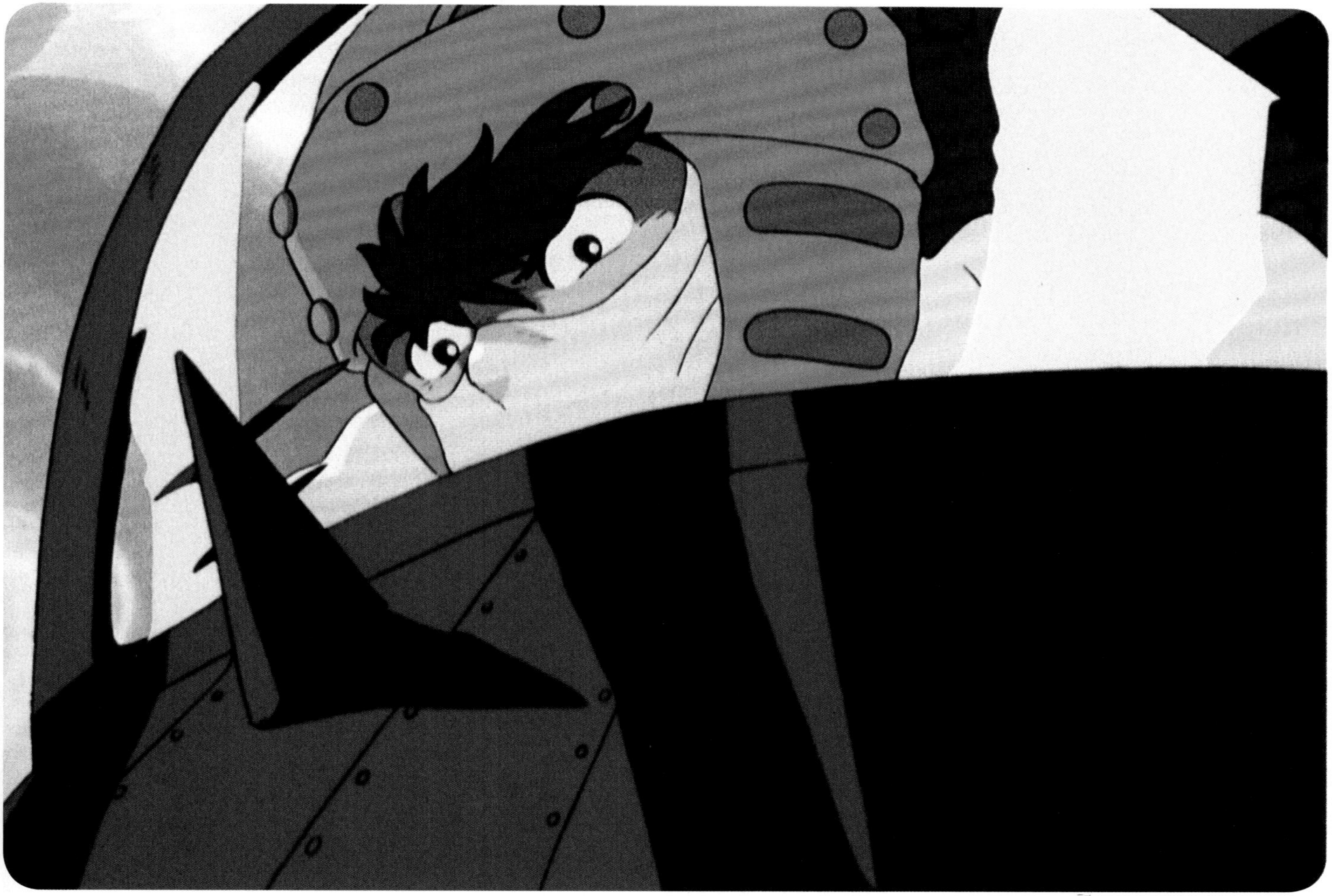

The figure of Nausicaä with arms held wide seemed to waver in the heat of the fire.

The pilot stared with astonishment at this mysterious girl. Somehow he couldn't bring himself to shoot. But when he broke off his attack and banked away, he was hit by Tolmekian gunfire. His ship burst into flames and plunged toward the toxic jungle below.

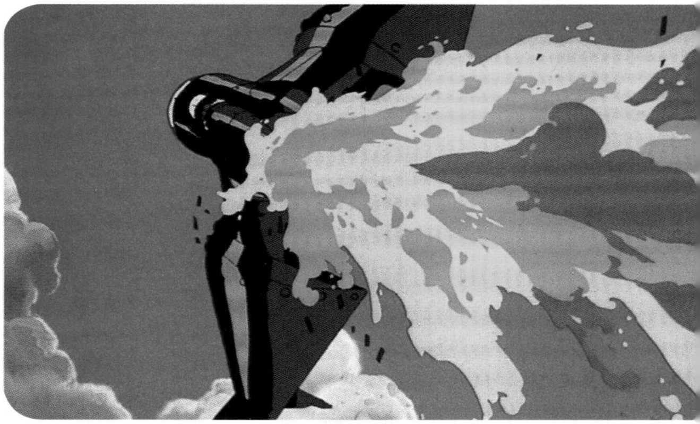

Mito called urgently to Nausicaä. "Princess, we're going down!"

They made their way through the flames to the cargo hold, where the Tolmekians had stored the gunship from the valley. Nausicaä leaped into the cockpit and started the engine. Suddenly she looked up. Someone was standing in the door of the cargo bay.

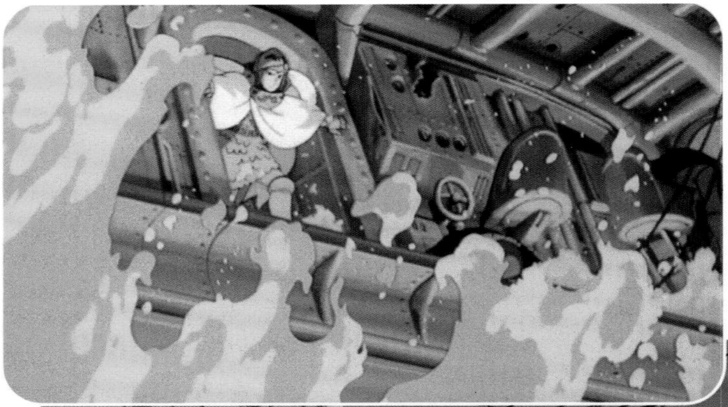

It was Kushana. As the flames rose around her, she stared intently at Nausicaä.

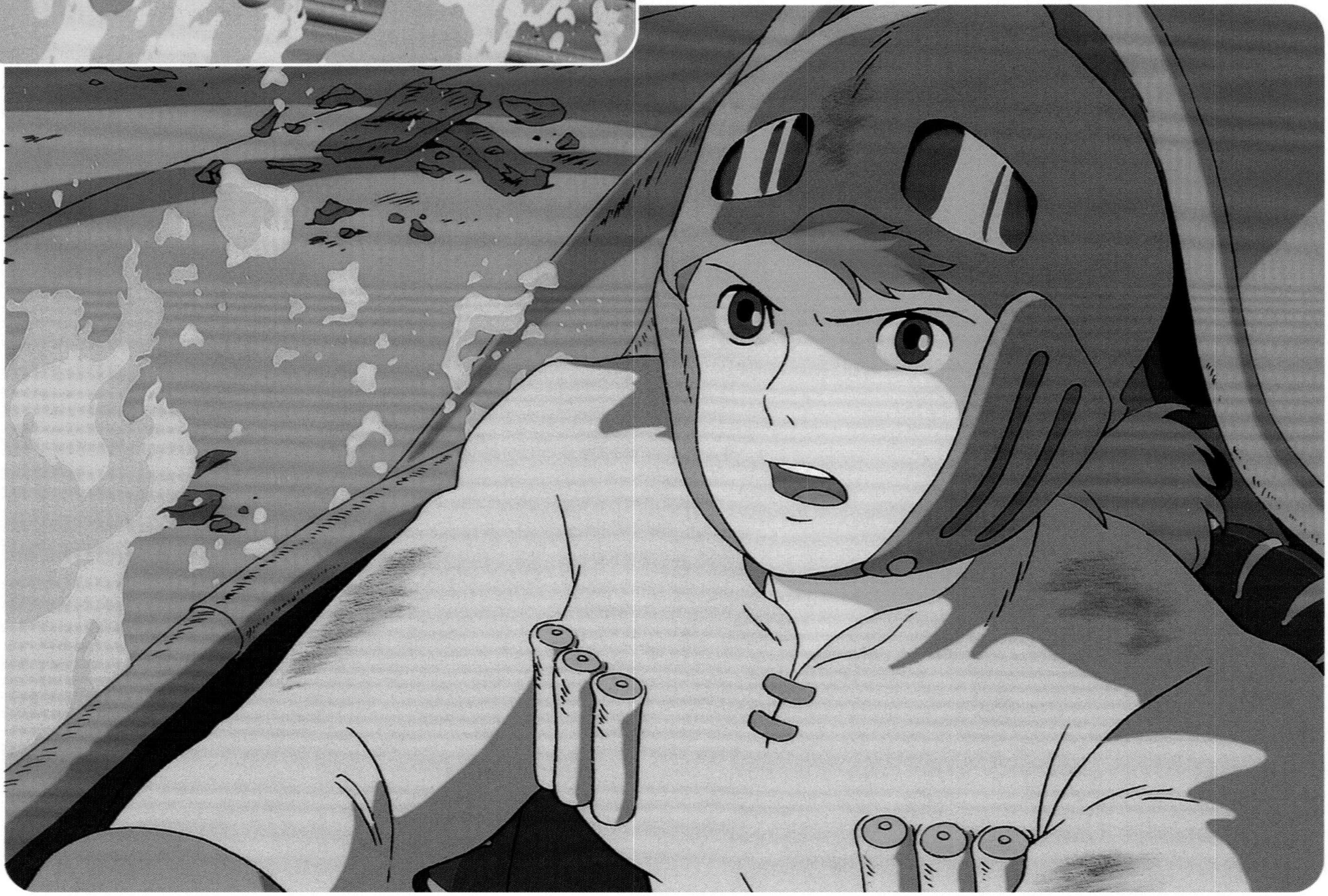

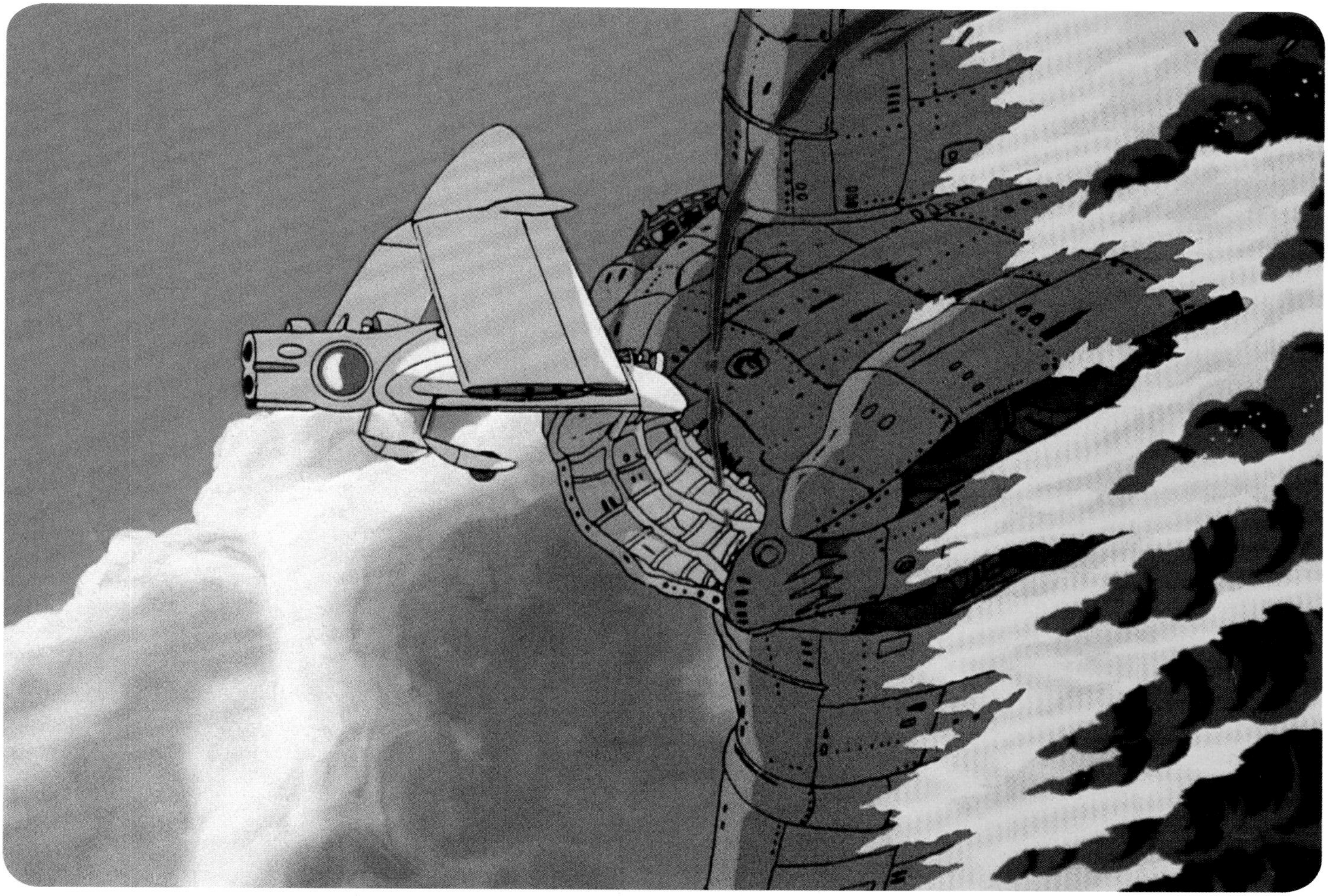

Nausicaä didn't hesitate. "Come on! Hurry!"

Kushana leaped into the gunship. Mito fired up the engine, and the gunship burst from the cargo bay into the sky.

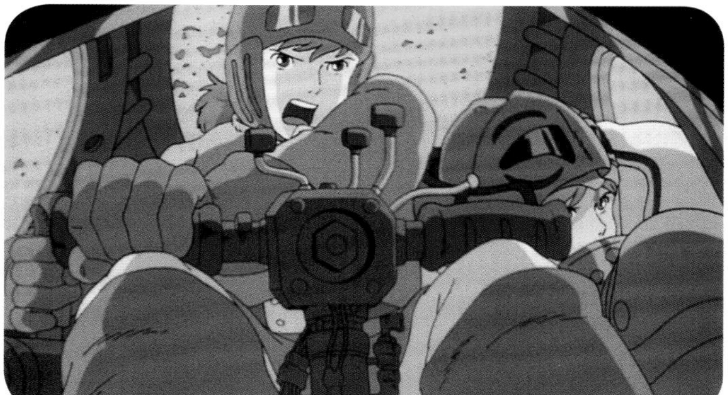

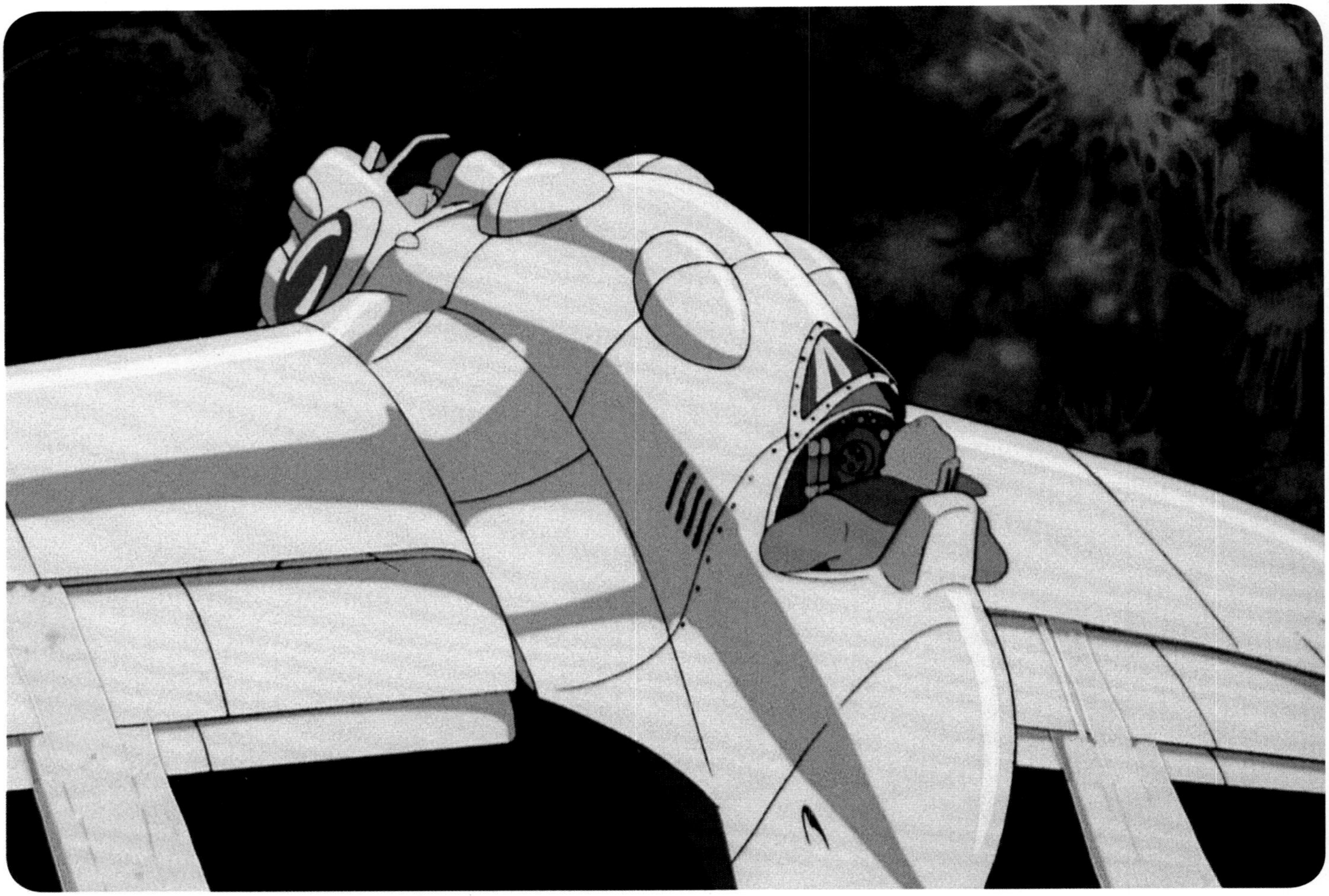

BENEATH THE TOXIC JUNGLE

"Put on your masks! I'm going below the clouds to rescue the cargo barge."

Kushana and Mito followed Nausicaä's order as the gunship descended toward the jungle.

Below the clouds, the landscape was dark and forbidding. Even with their masks on, the three survivors could almost feel the thick waves of poison rising from the plants.

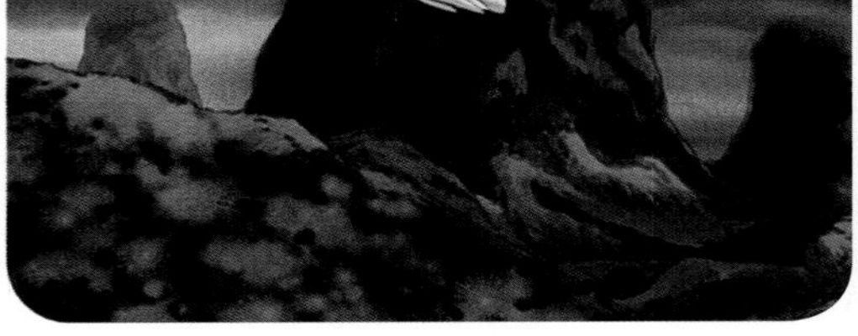

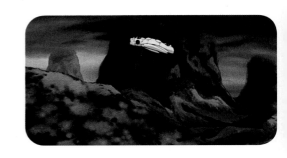

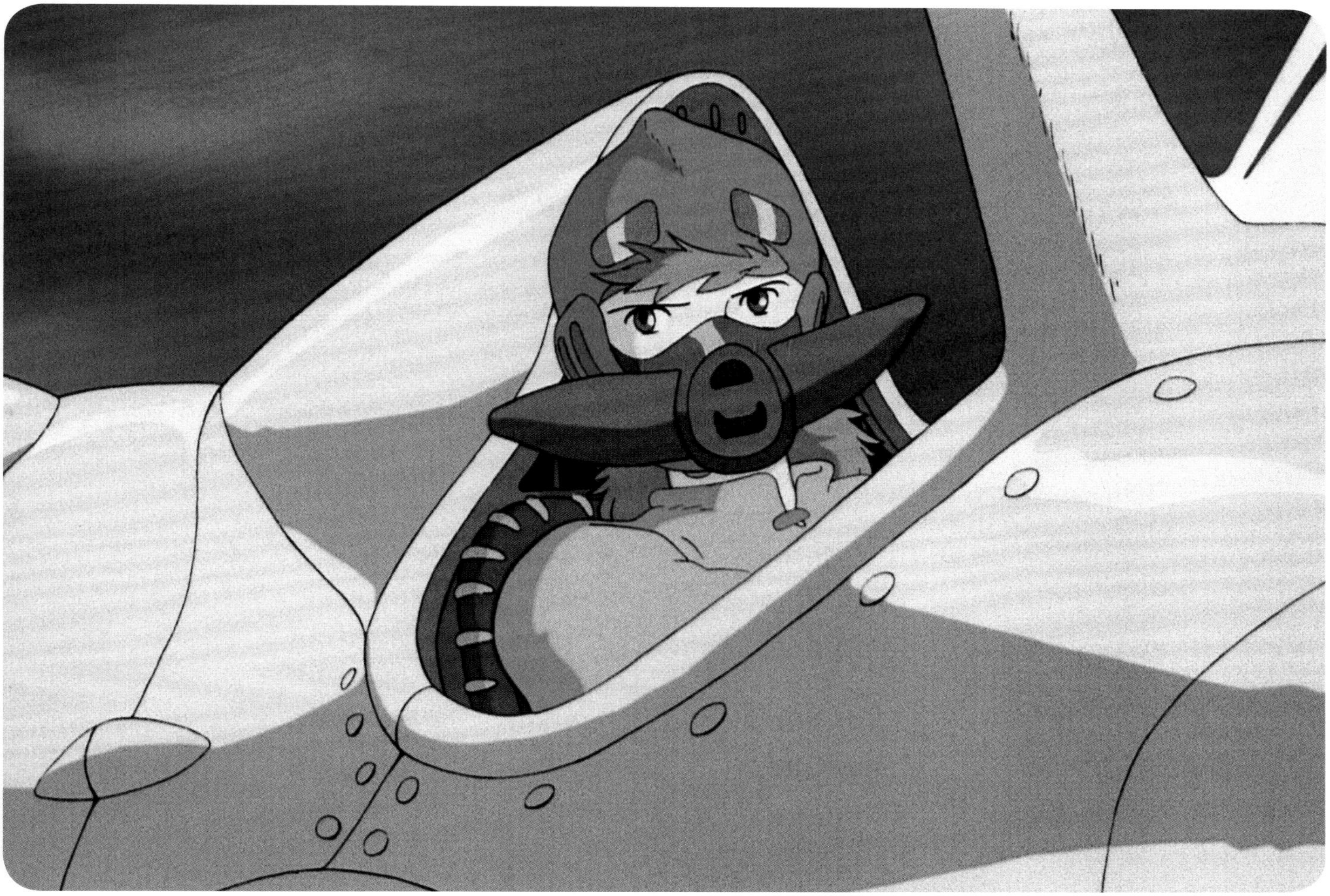

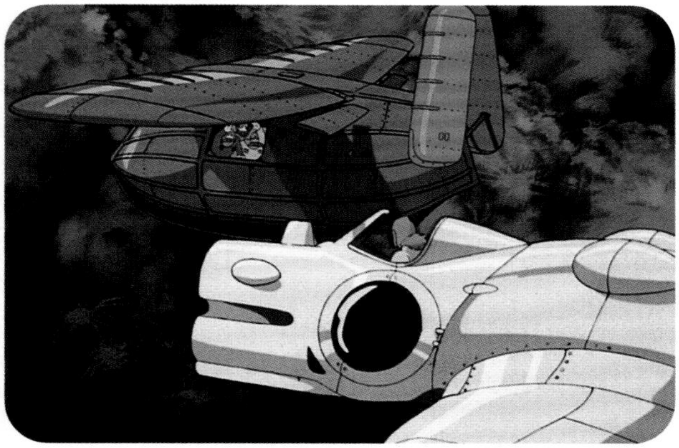

"Hold on," she called to the men in the barge. "I'll throw you a tow rope!"

But the old men had already given up.

"The towing hook broke. If we land, the insects will eat us alive!"

"We'd rather jump to our deaths!"

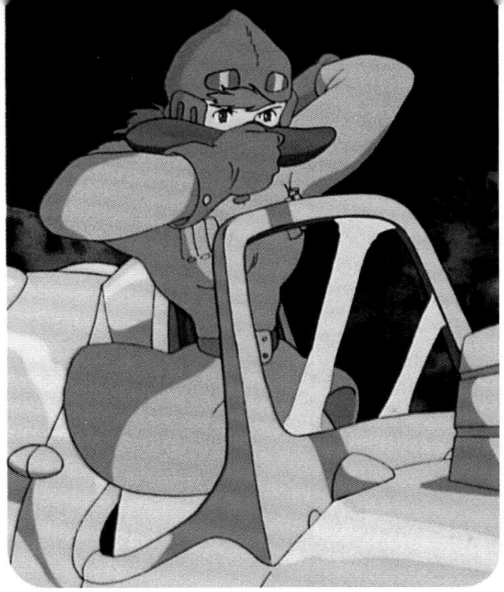

Nausicaä stood up in the cockpit—and took off her mask!

“Princess, what are you doing?” the men shouted. “Put your mask on! You’ll die!” They stared at her with astonishment.

“Dump your cargo and follow us down! You’ll be just fine,” Nausicaä called back.

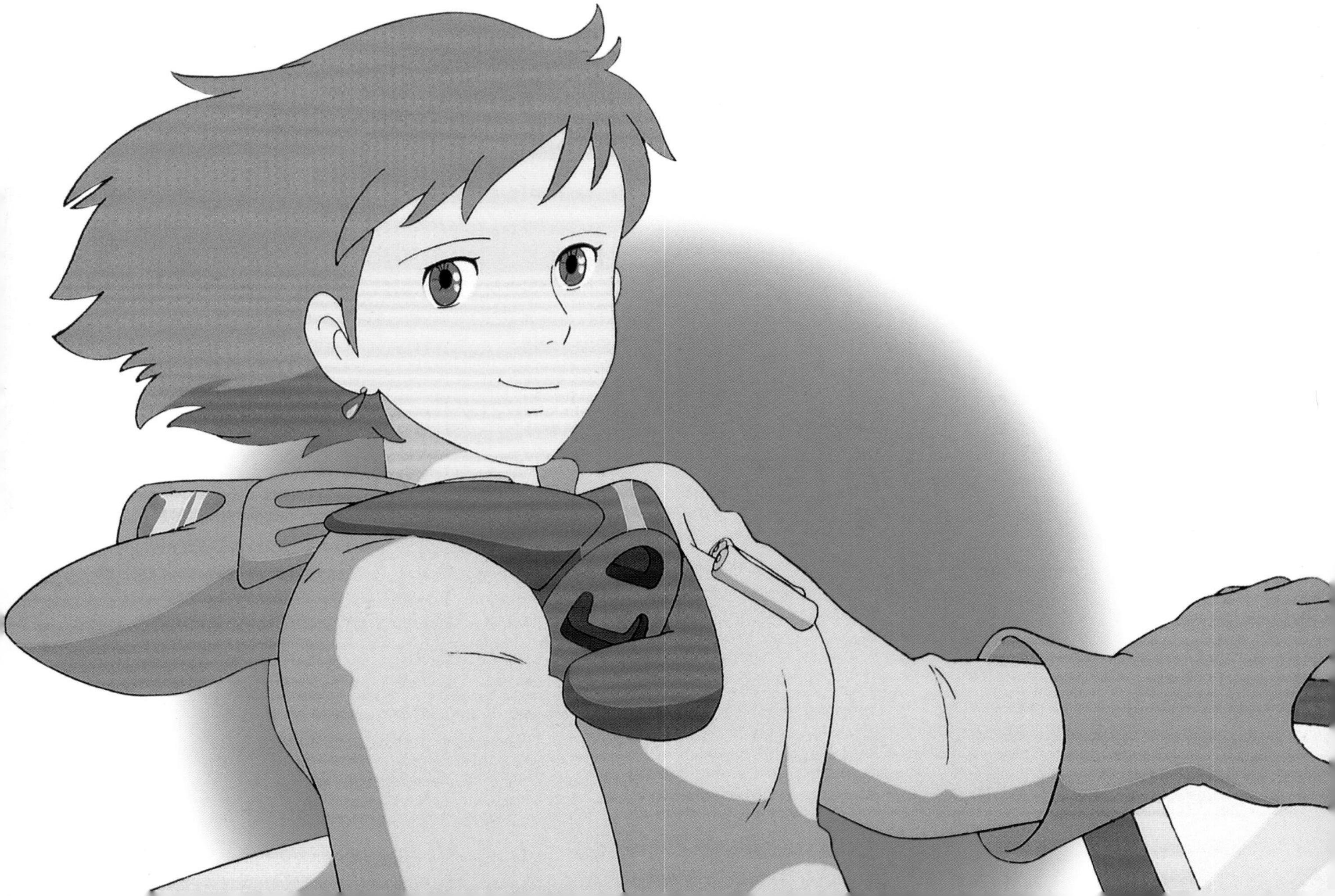

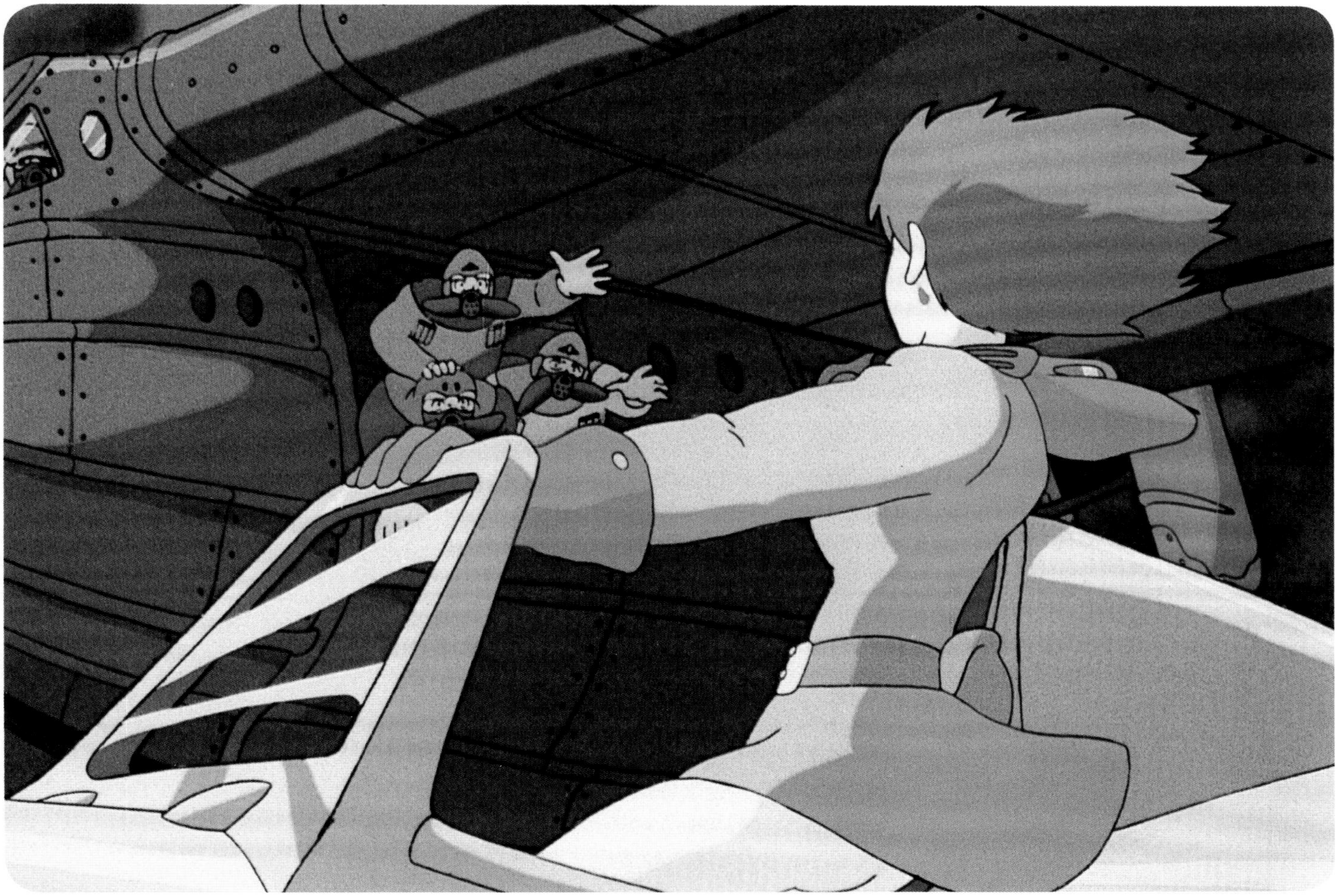

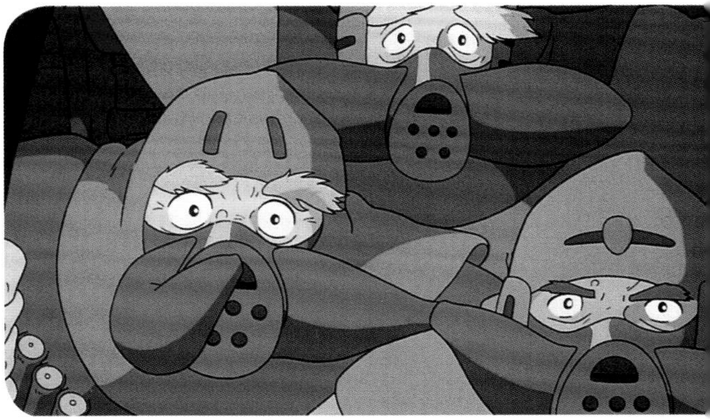

“All right, we’ll do as you say. Now put your mask on!” they shouted.

But Nausicaä just smiled encouragingly as she flew off ahead of them.

“She actually thinks we’re going to be okay…”

“Hurry, dump the cargo!”

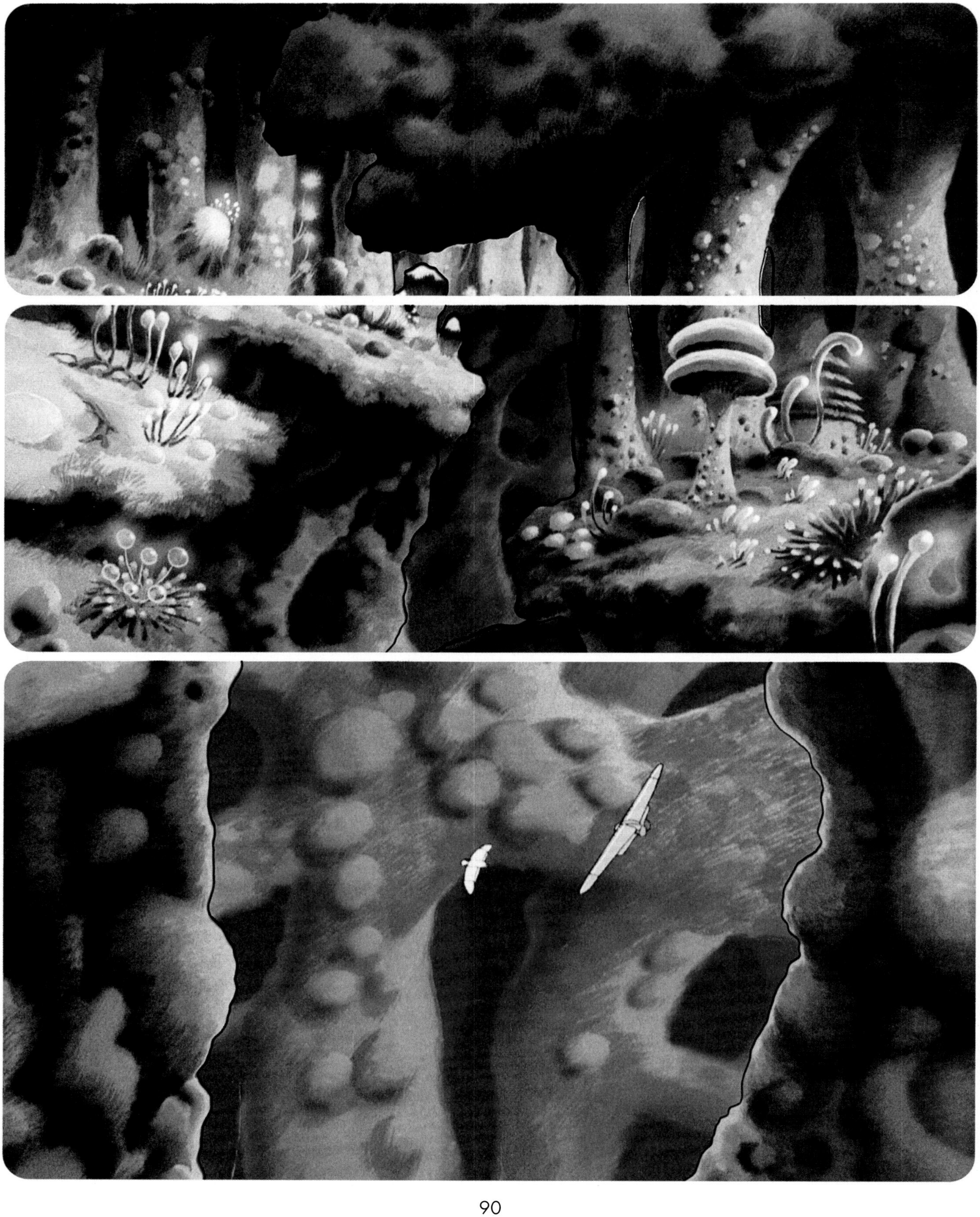

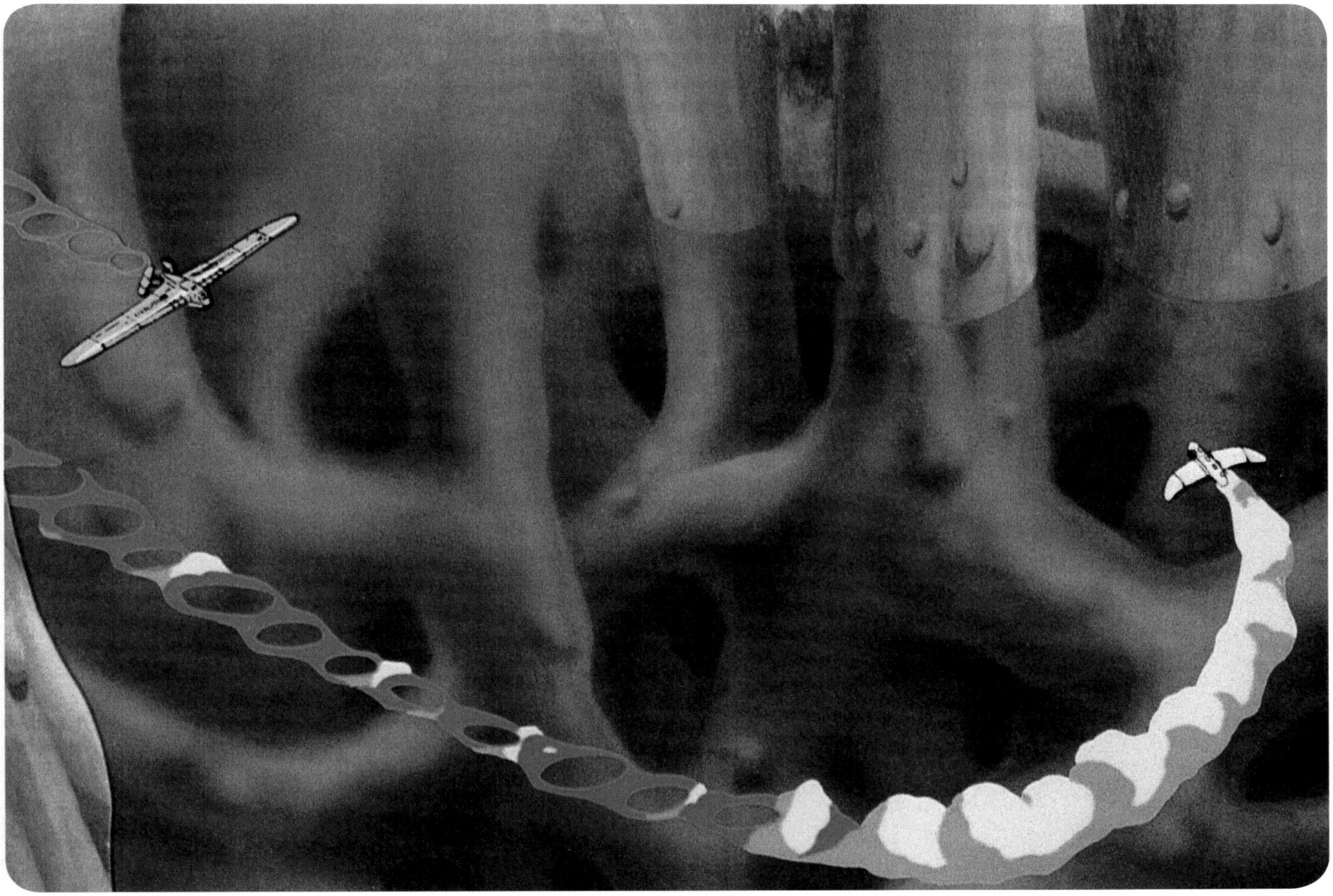

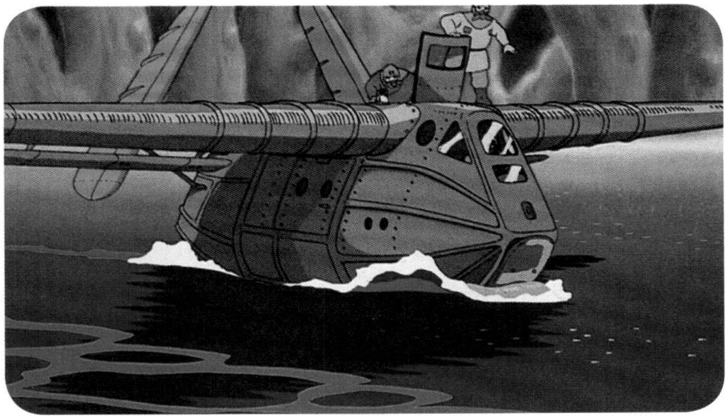

Nausicaä hurried to put her mask on as she guided the barge toward a landing place in the jungle. She finally found a lake surrounded by huge trees where they could touch down safely.

The water in the lake was crystal clear. The two aircraft glided onto the surface and drifted to a halt.

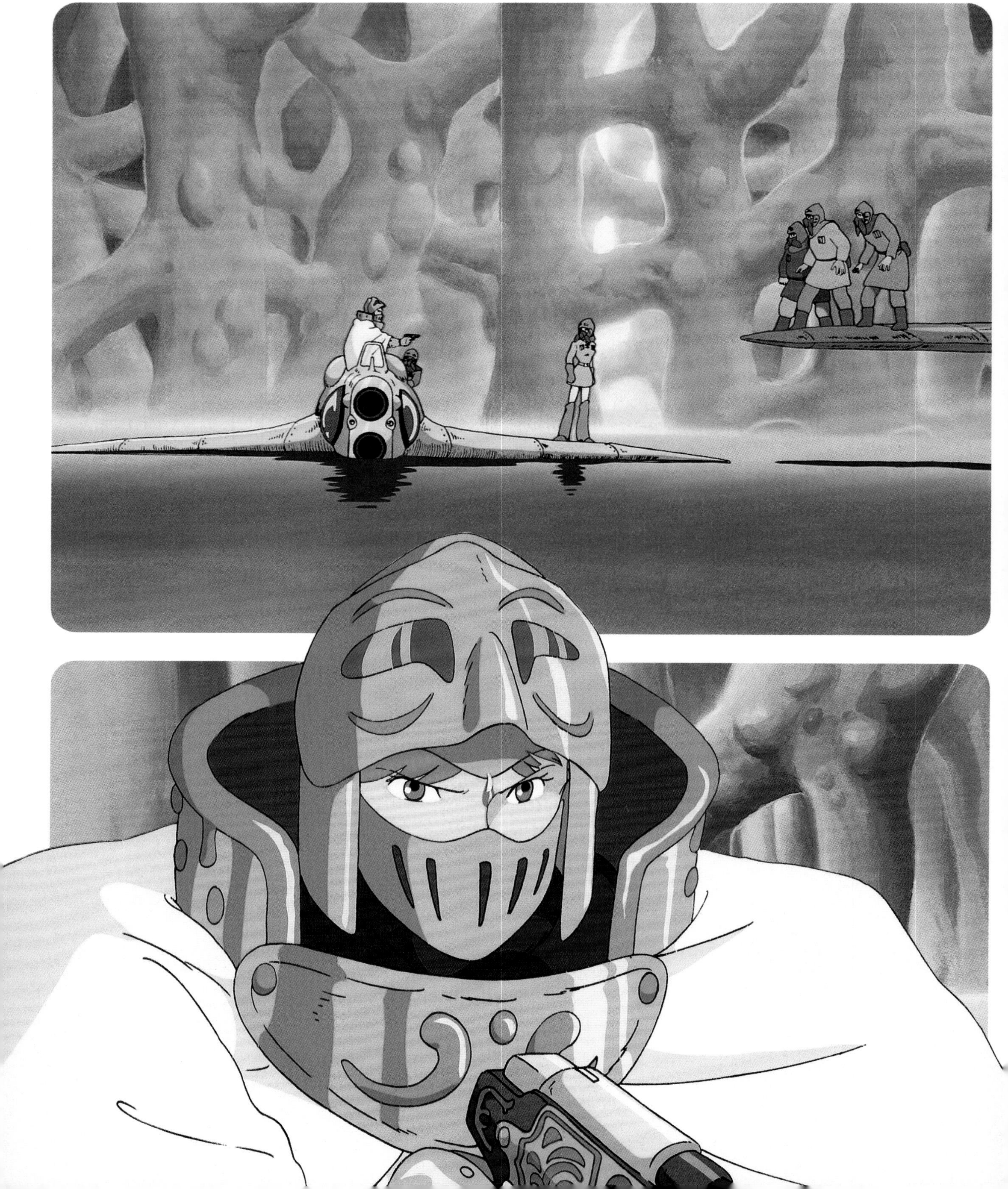

Nausicaä had just climbed out onto the wing to greet the old men when she heard a voice behind her.

"Don't move!"

"This is no place for guns," Nausicaä said. "The insects are already swarming because of your airships crashing into their jungle. We have to get out of here, now!"

Kushana shouted and fired a warning shot. The silence of the jungle was shattered.

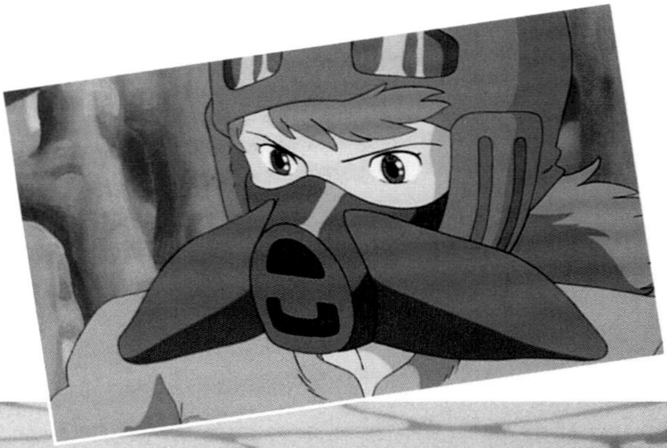

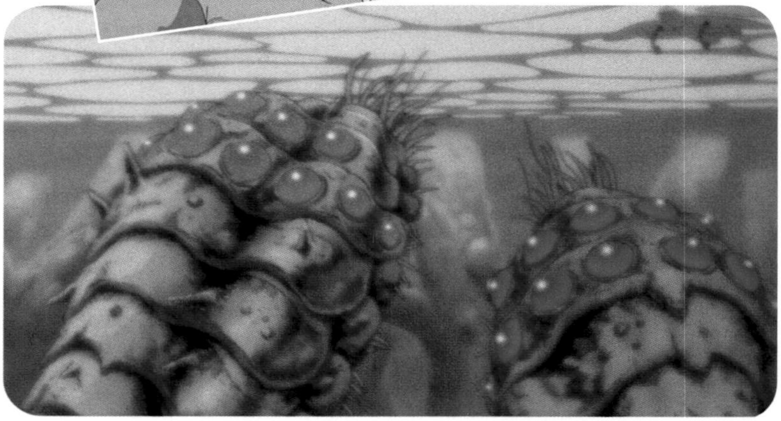

Suddenly the surface of the lake began to churn violently.

"They're here!"

As Nausicaä and the others watched, a group of huge Ohms rose out of the water.

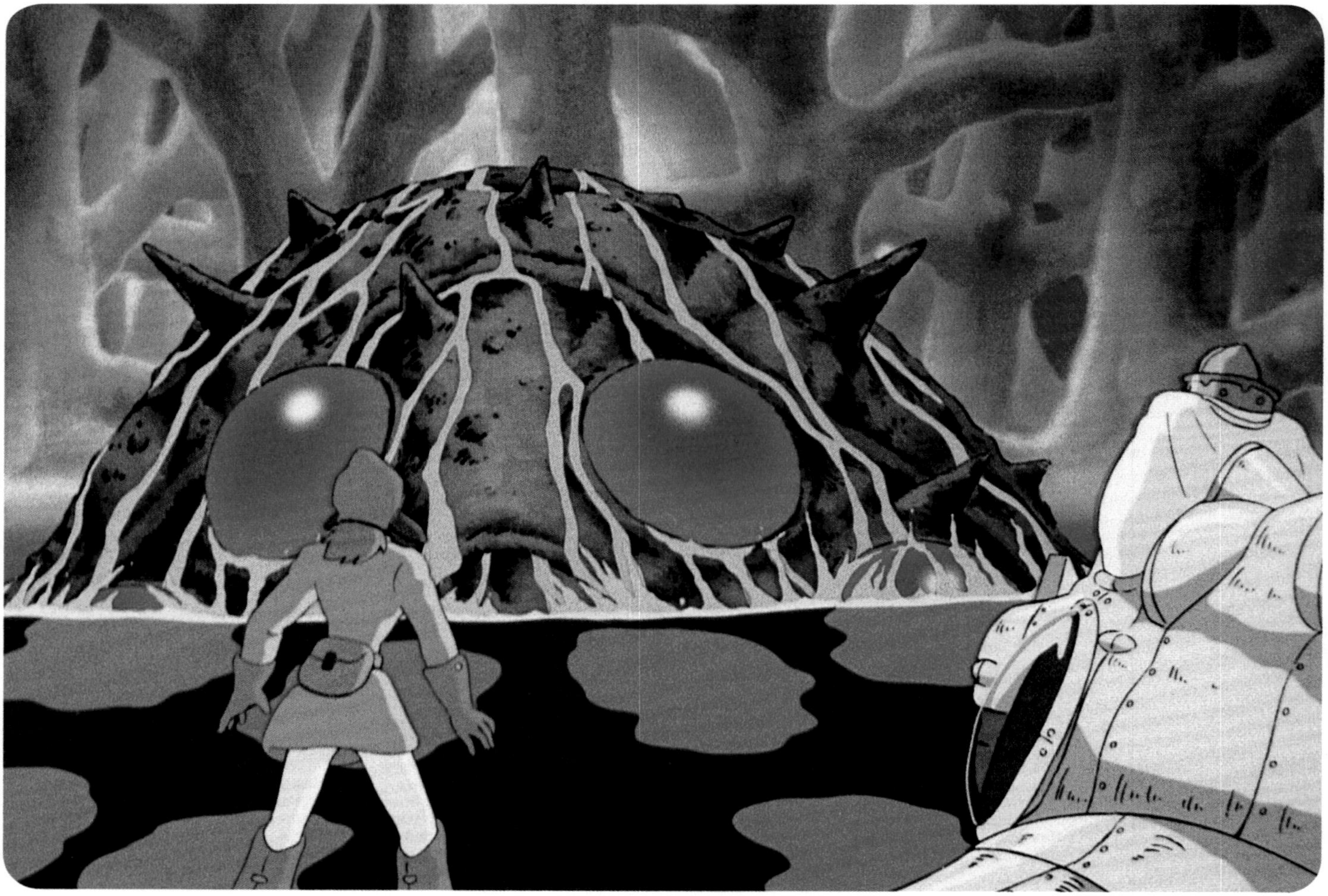

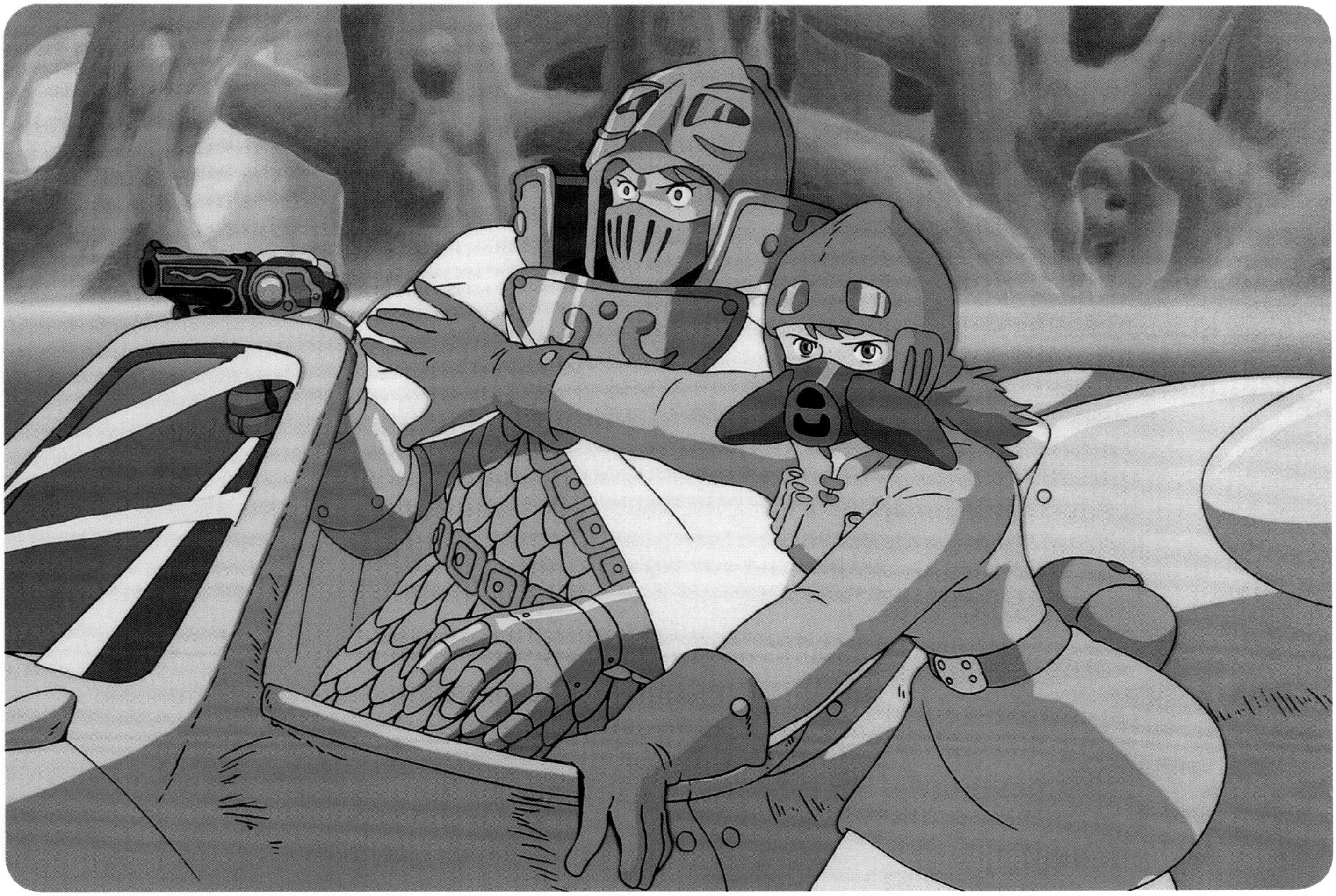

"Stay calm," Nausicaä said. "Whatever you do, don't startle them."

"We're in the middle of an Ohm nest!" cried one of the old men. The Ohms surrounded the two aircraft. The humans had landed on the very lake where the giant insects made their home.

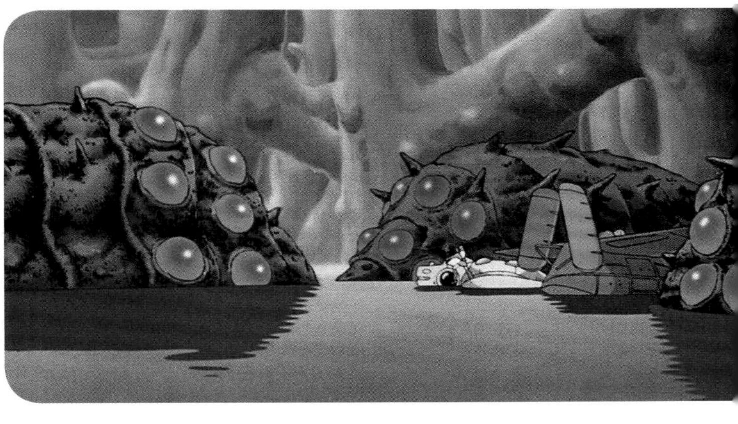

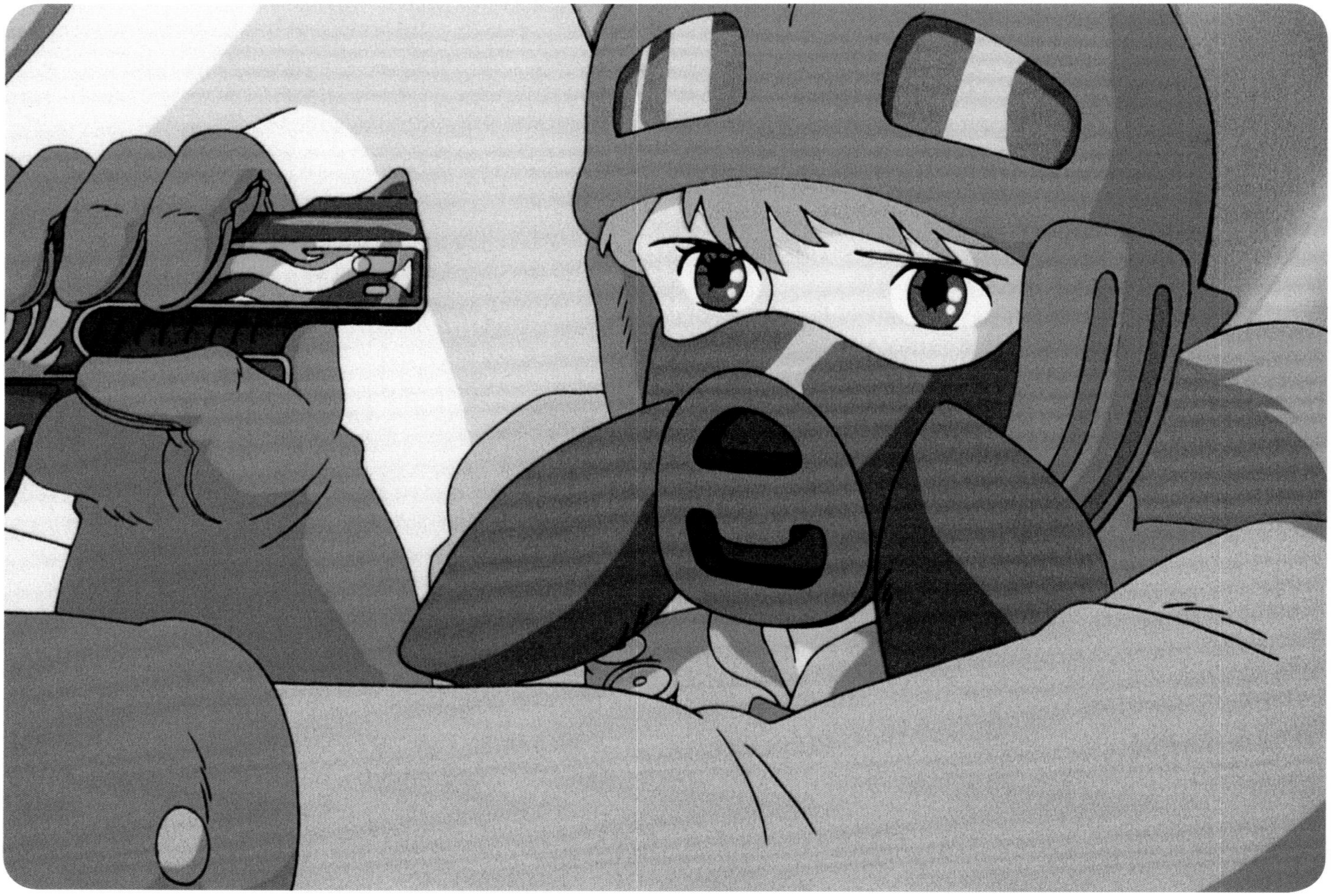

The Ohms gazed at Nausicaä and the others with their huge blue eyes.

"They're examining us," she said and took a step toward them. "Please forgive us for disturbing your nest! We're not your enemies. We mean you no harm."

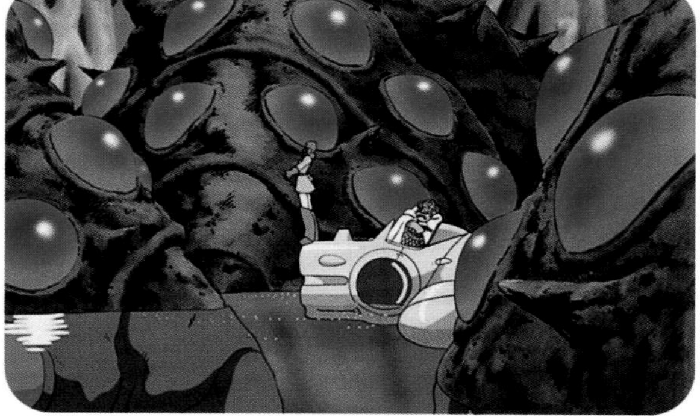

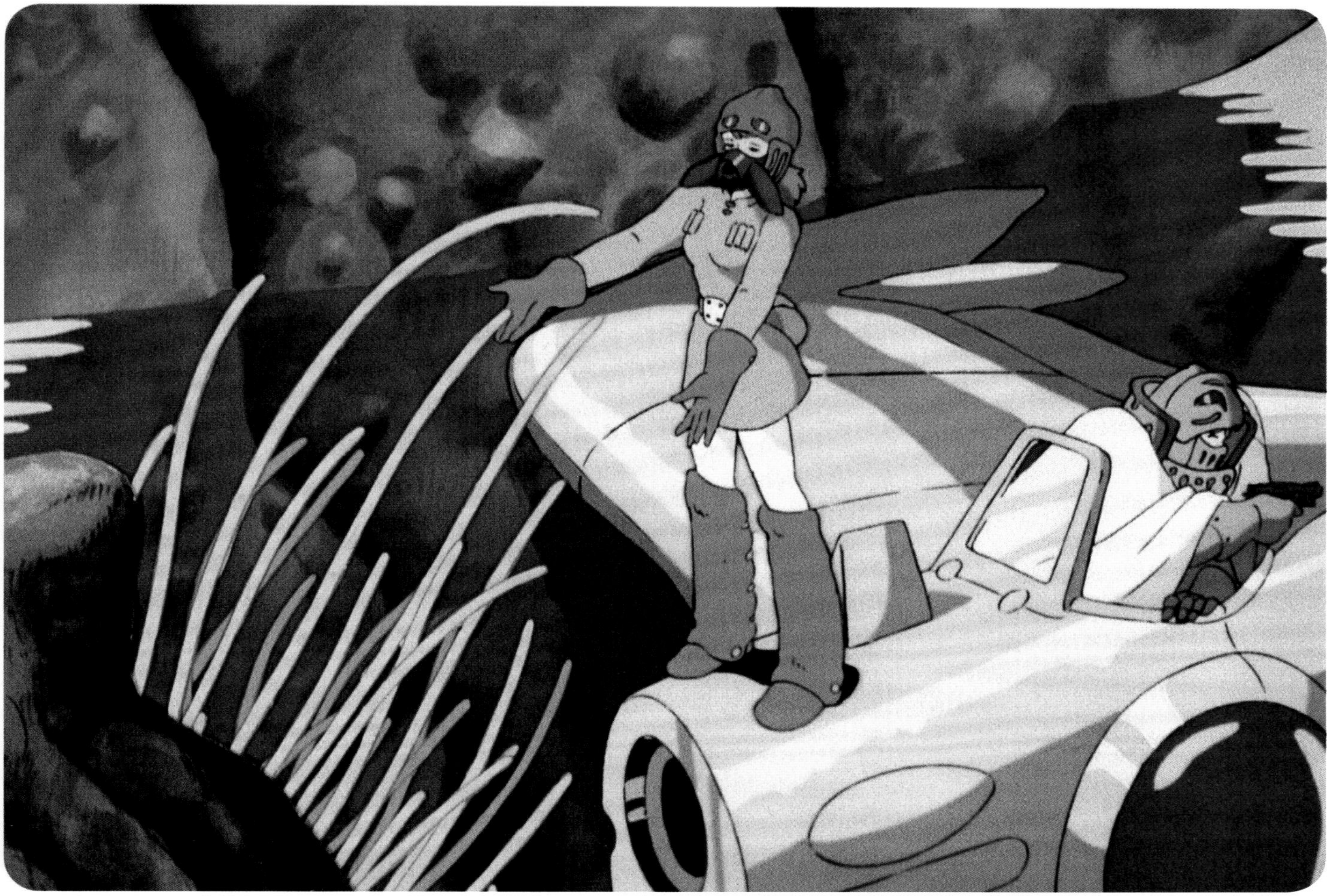

One of the giant insects drew closer and opened its beak. A swarm of golden feelers reached out and gently enfolded Nausicaä.

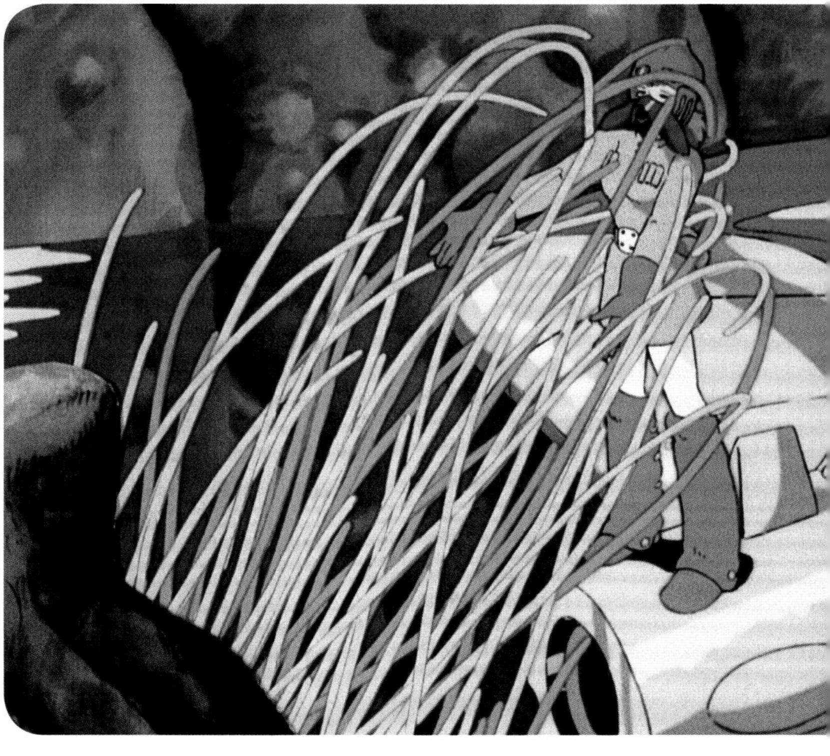

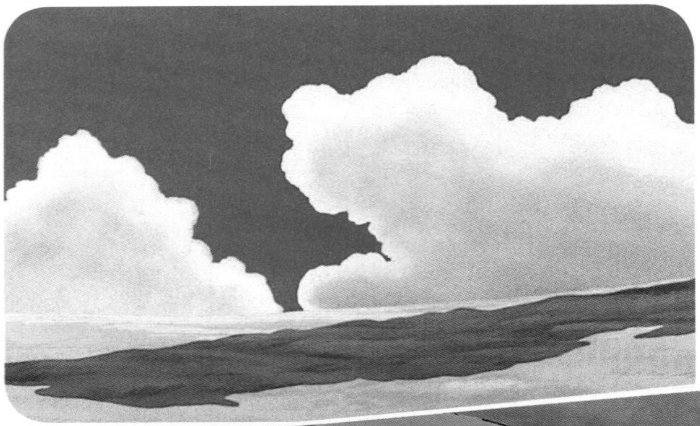

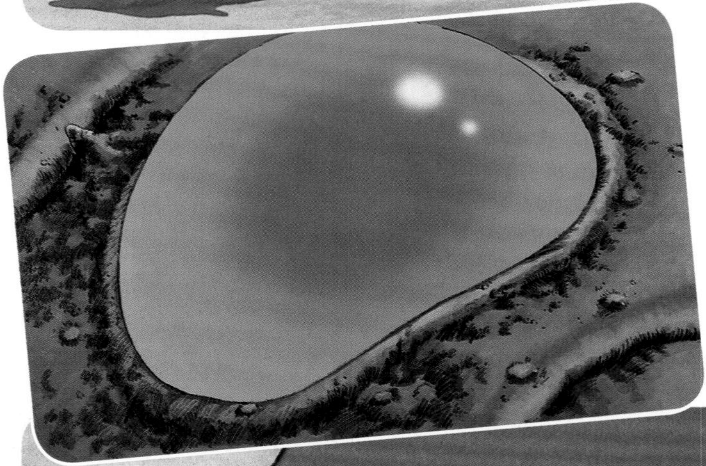

Suddenly she had a vision of a vast plain of golden grass. Above the plain was a deep-blue sky the color of an Ohm's eye, filled with scudding clouds. Was the insect trying to show her something?

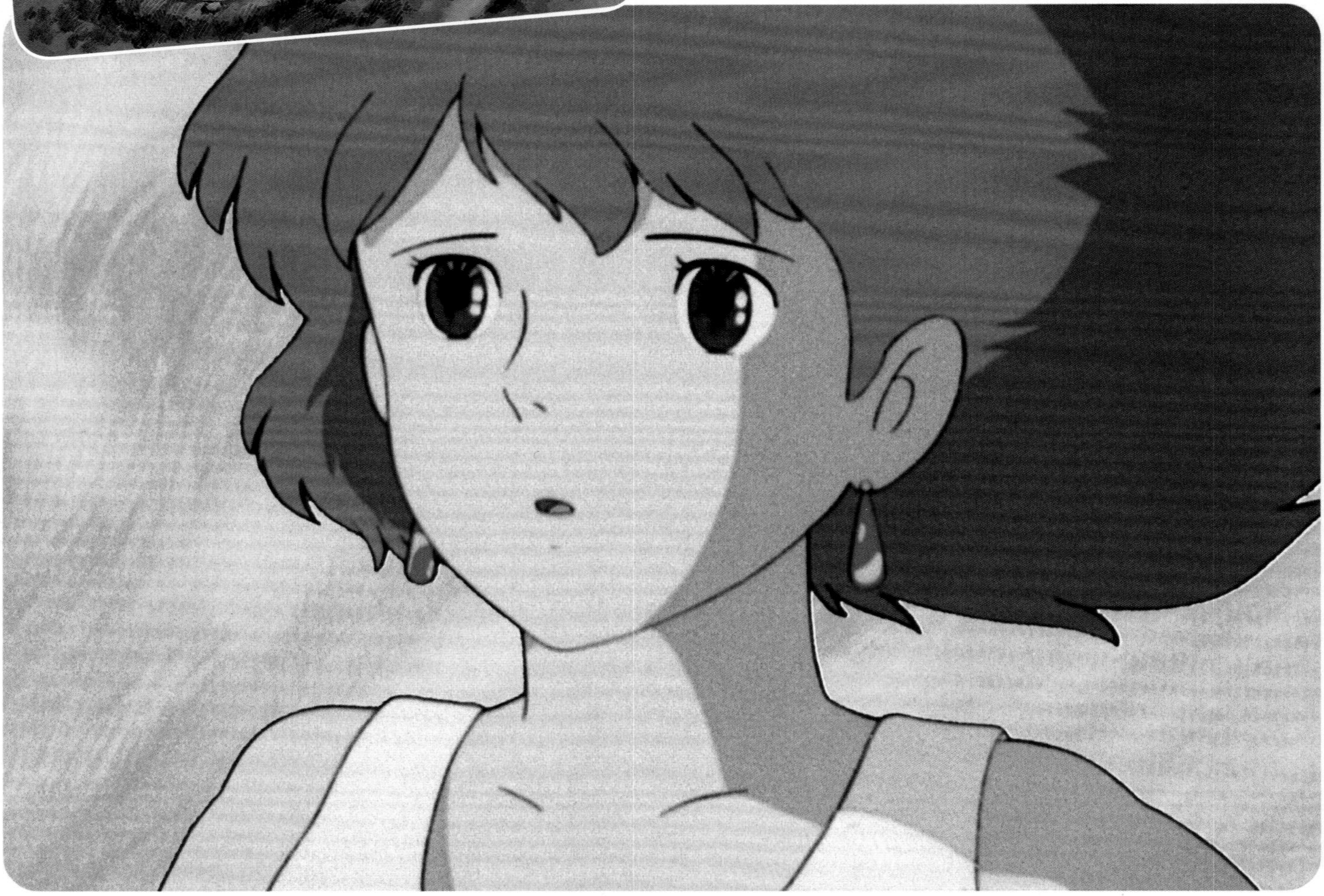

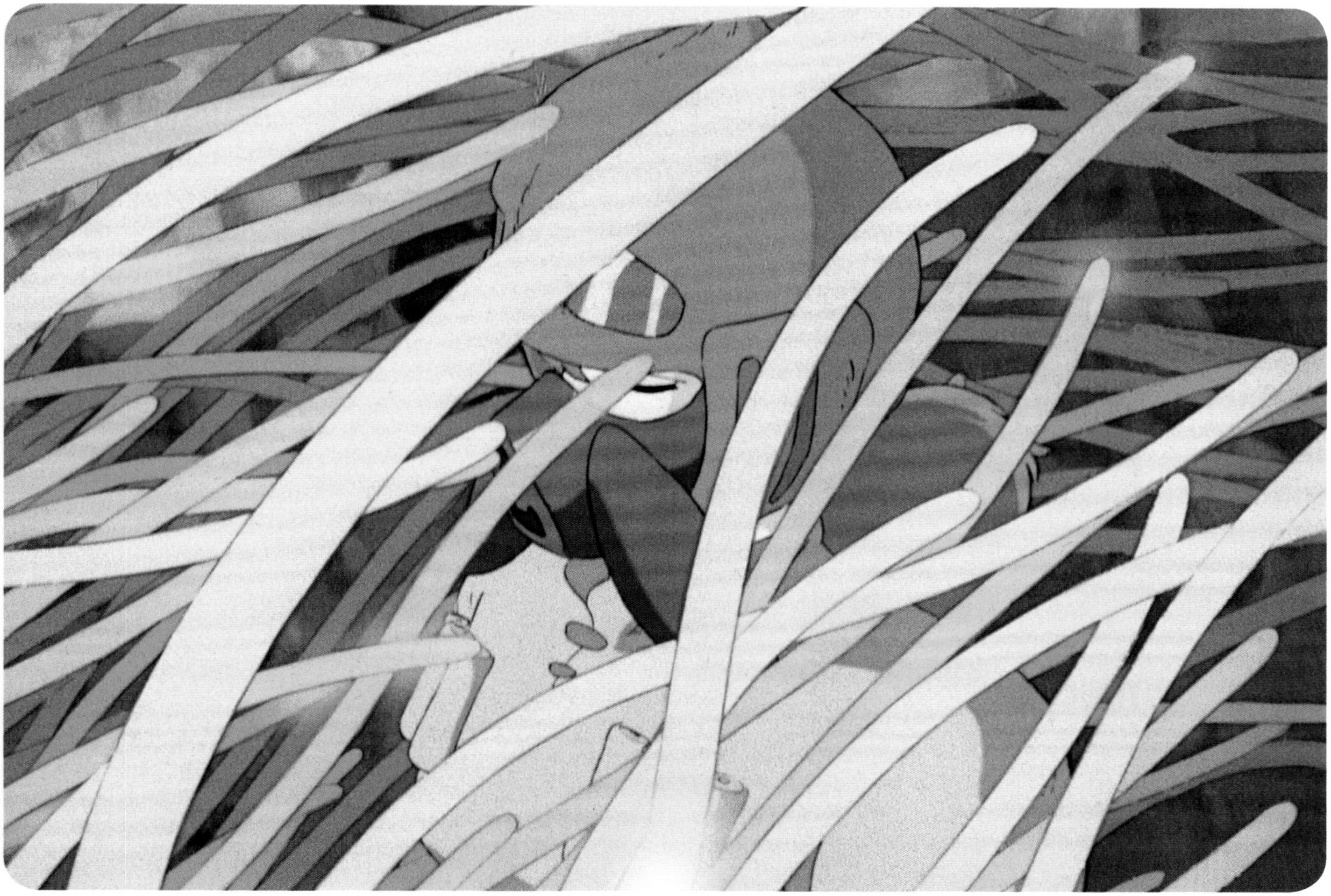

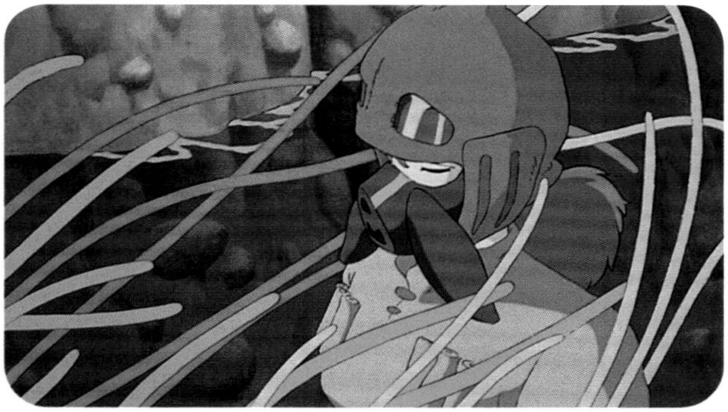

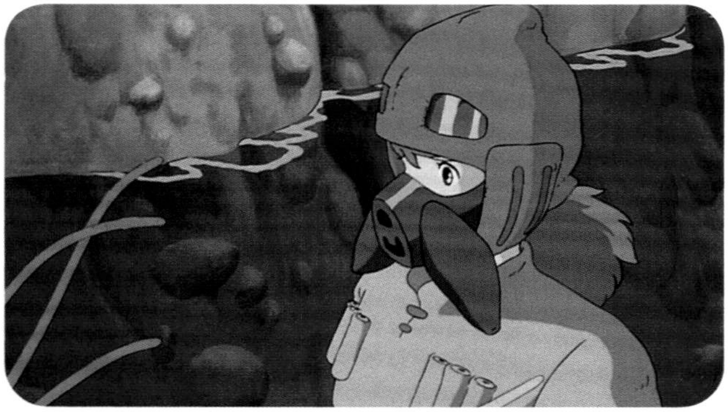

At last the Ohm withdrew its golden feelers. A startled Nausicaä found herself back in the real world.

“The pilot from Pejite—he’s still alive? Ohm, wait!”

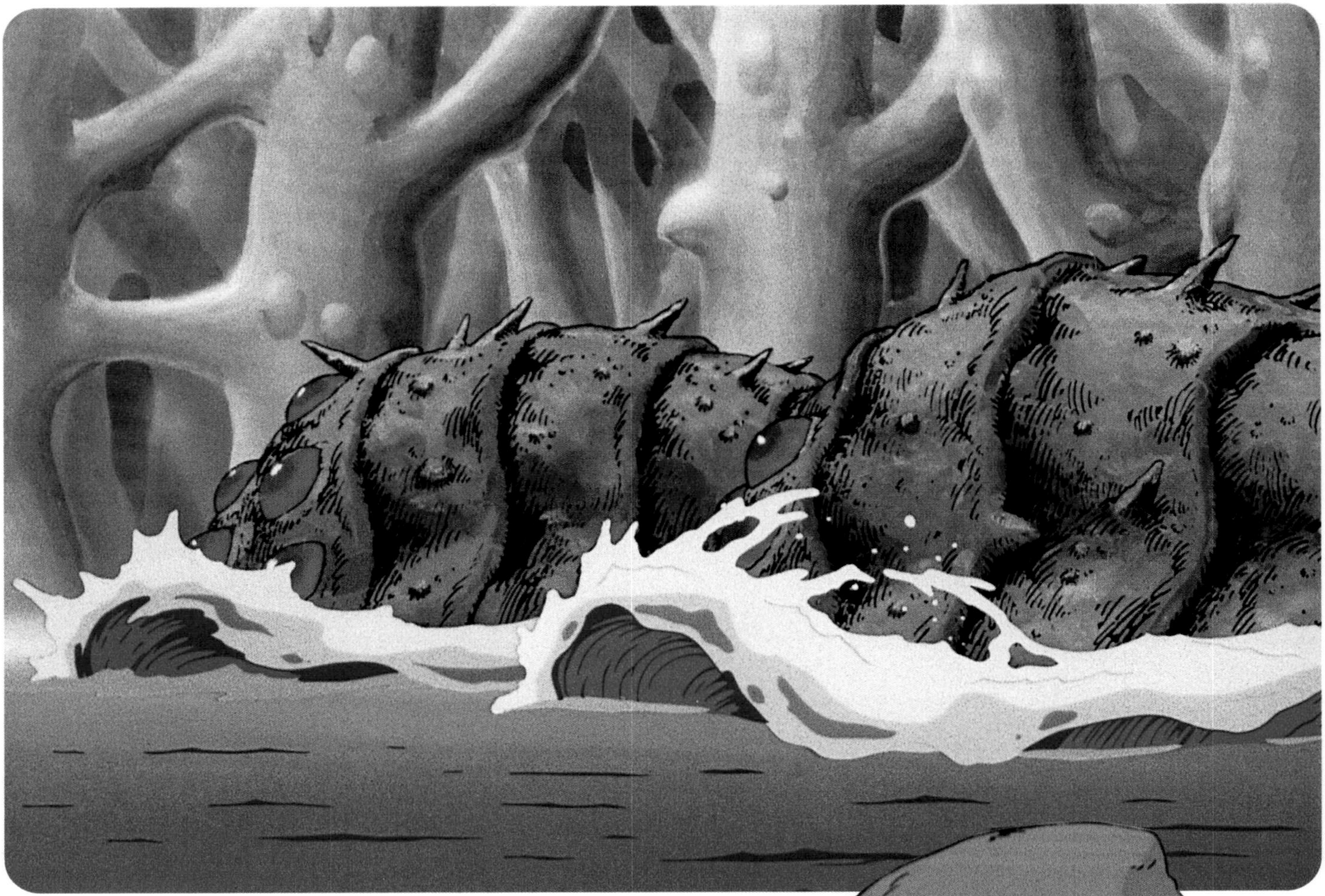

But the huge insects couldn't hear her. Their eyes glowed red as they swam quickly away. Soon more insects came swarming overhead. Their eyes were crimson with rage!

Something was happening deeper in the jungle. Nausicaä hurried to unload her wind rider from the barge.

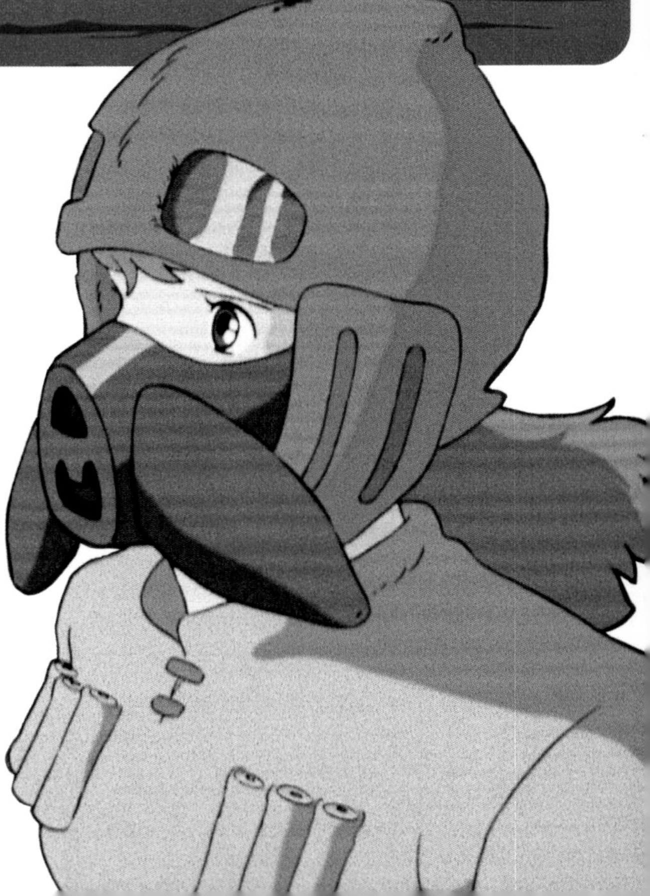

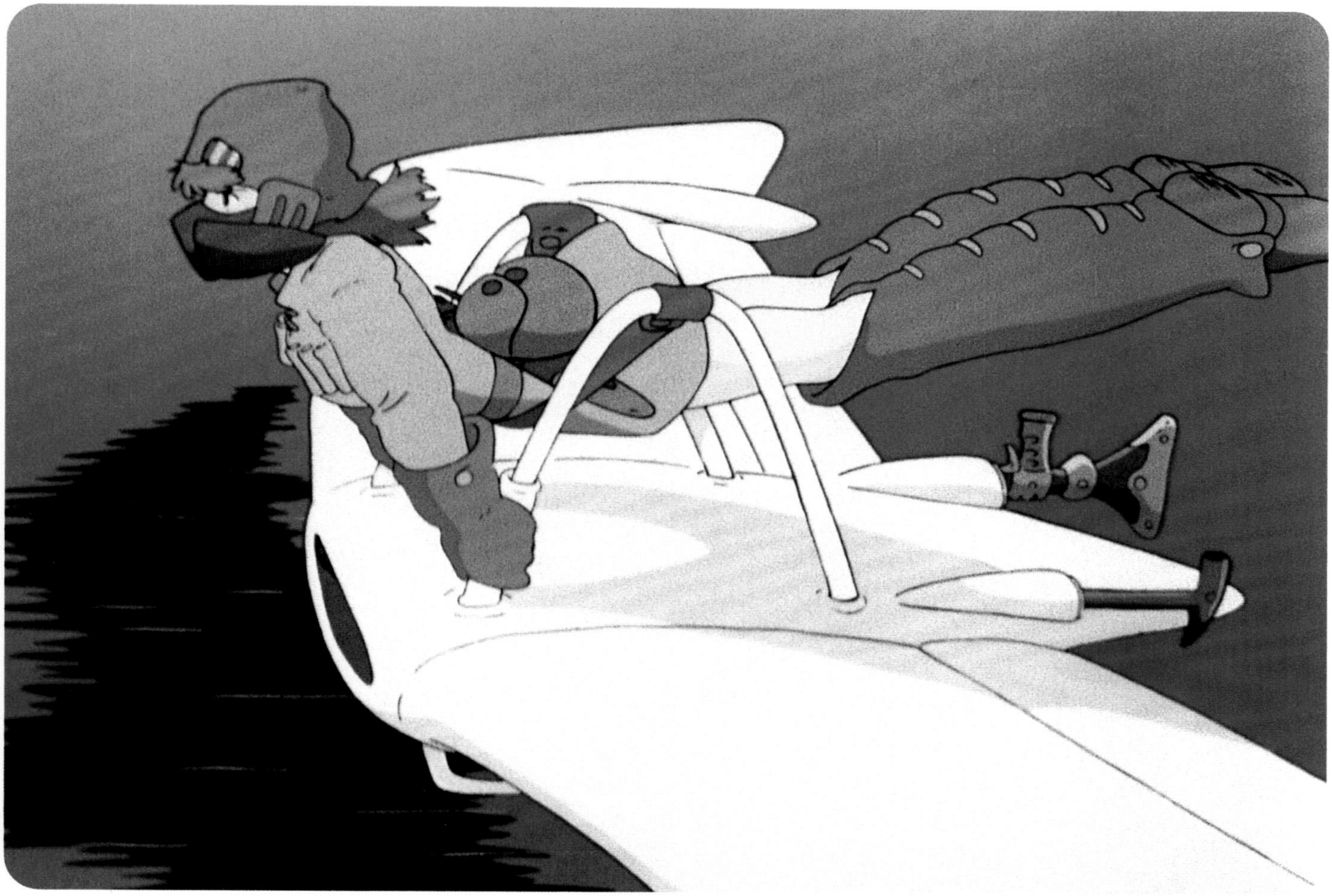

"Take off as soon as the waters are calm and return to the valley," she said to the men as she took off on her wind rider.

"The princess is gone. Let's do as she ordered," Mito said. Then he added quietly to himself, "She'd better be okay."

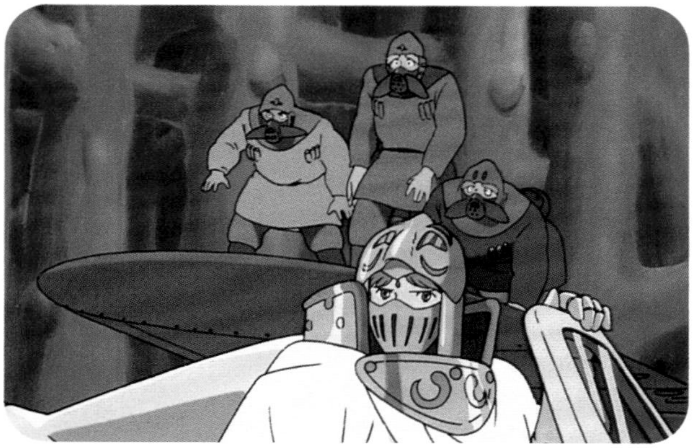

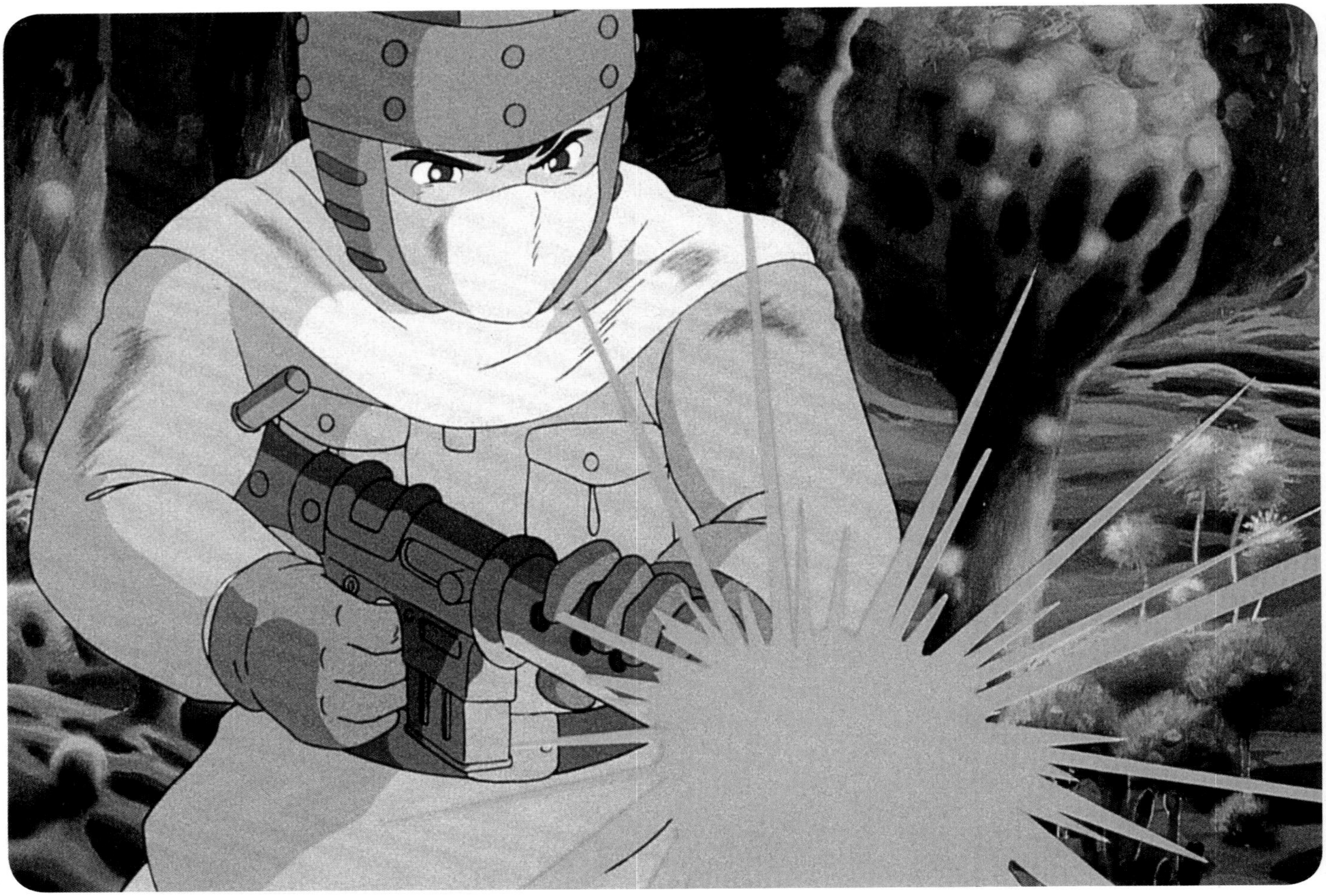

Deep in the jungle, the young pilot was battling the insects. He had survived the crash of his gunship.

He fired his gun again and again, but the enraged insects just kept coming.

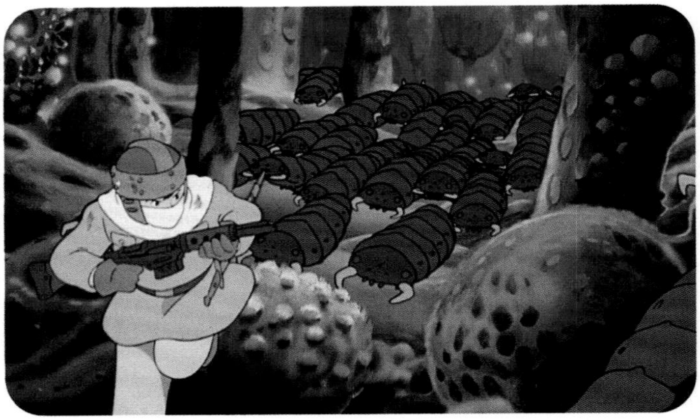

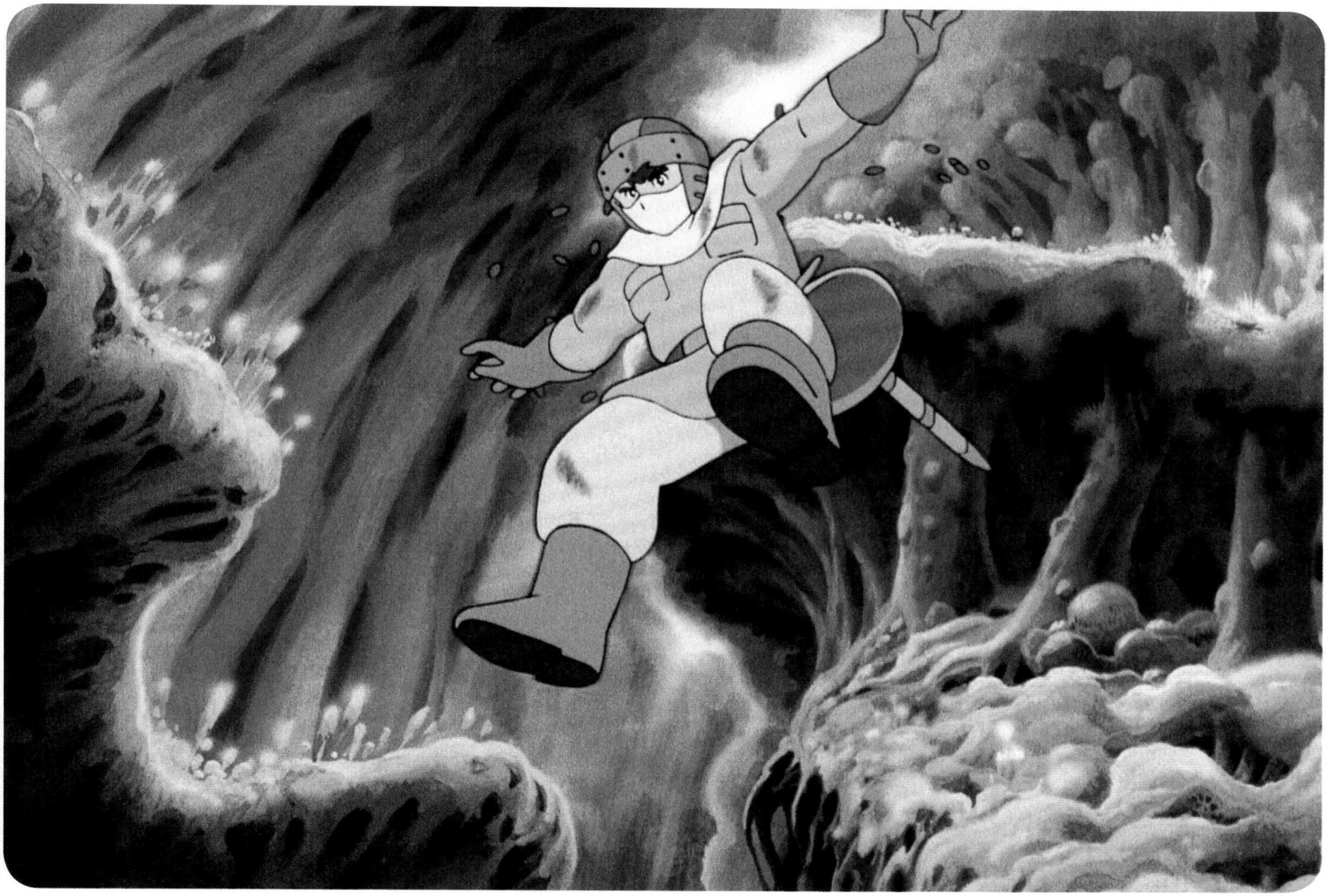

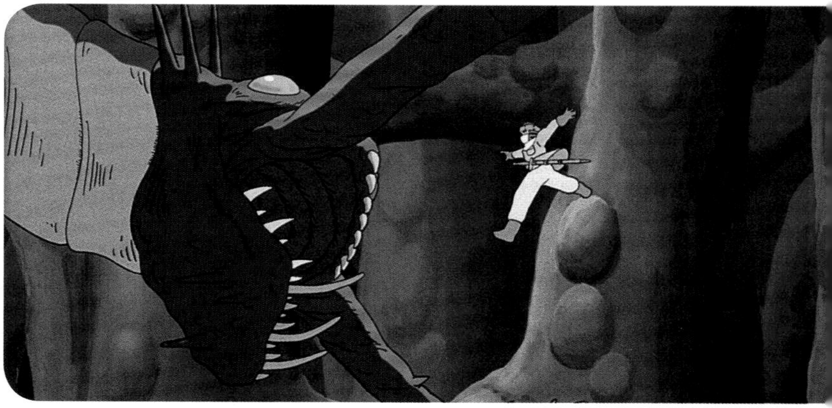

Finally his trigger clicked on an empty chamber. His gun was jammed.

He ran to the edge of a cliff and leaped into the deep valley below. But as he plummeted through the air, a giant hebikera was opening its jaws wide to devour him.

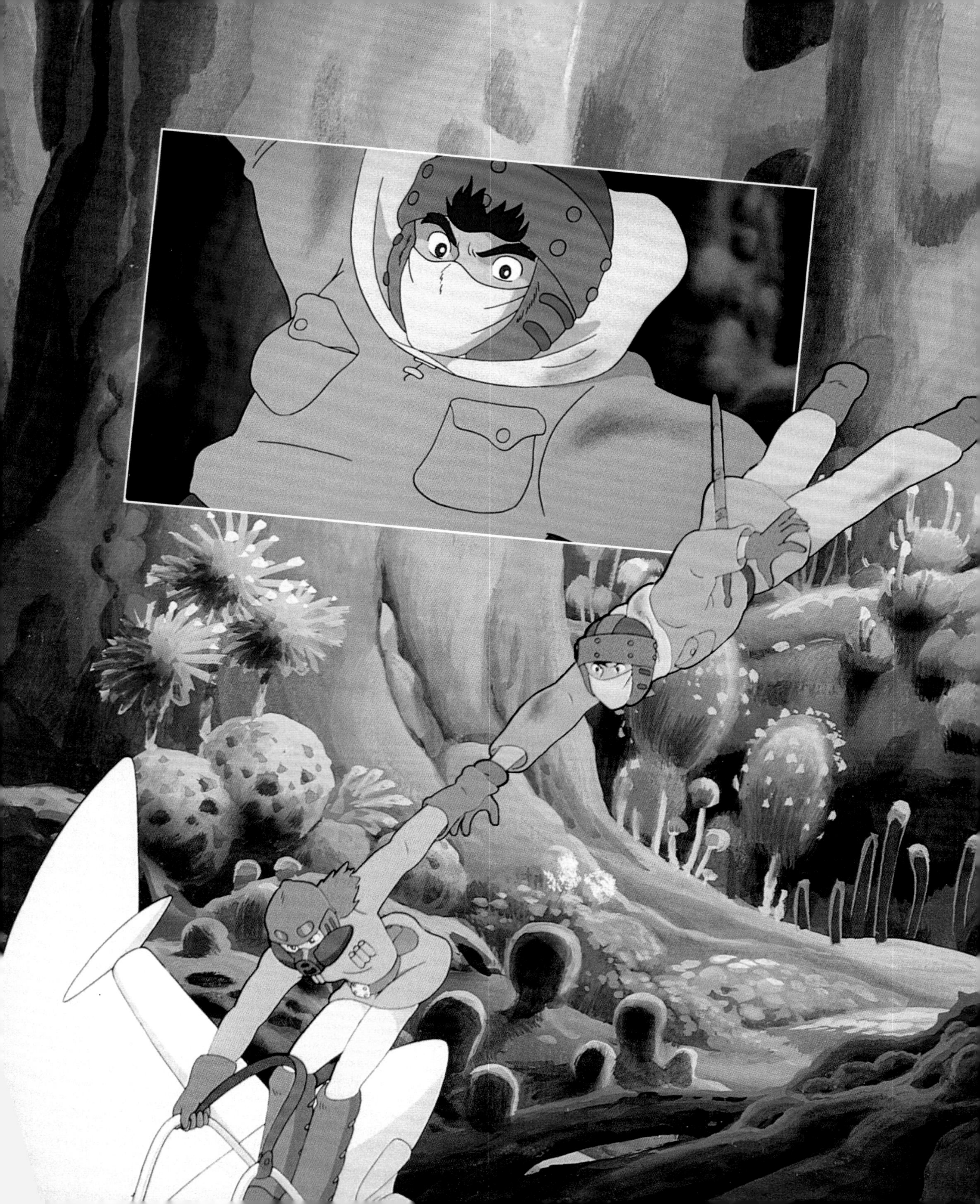

Just then Nausicaä swooped down on her wind rider and caught the young man in midair. The jaws of the hebikera closed with a snap.

"Who are you?" he shouted.

"You've done far too much killing," Nausicaä replied.

By firing his gun at them, the young pilot had enraged the insects. Now there was nothing to do but try to escape. The wind rider banked and turned, fleeing the hebikera.

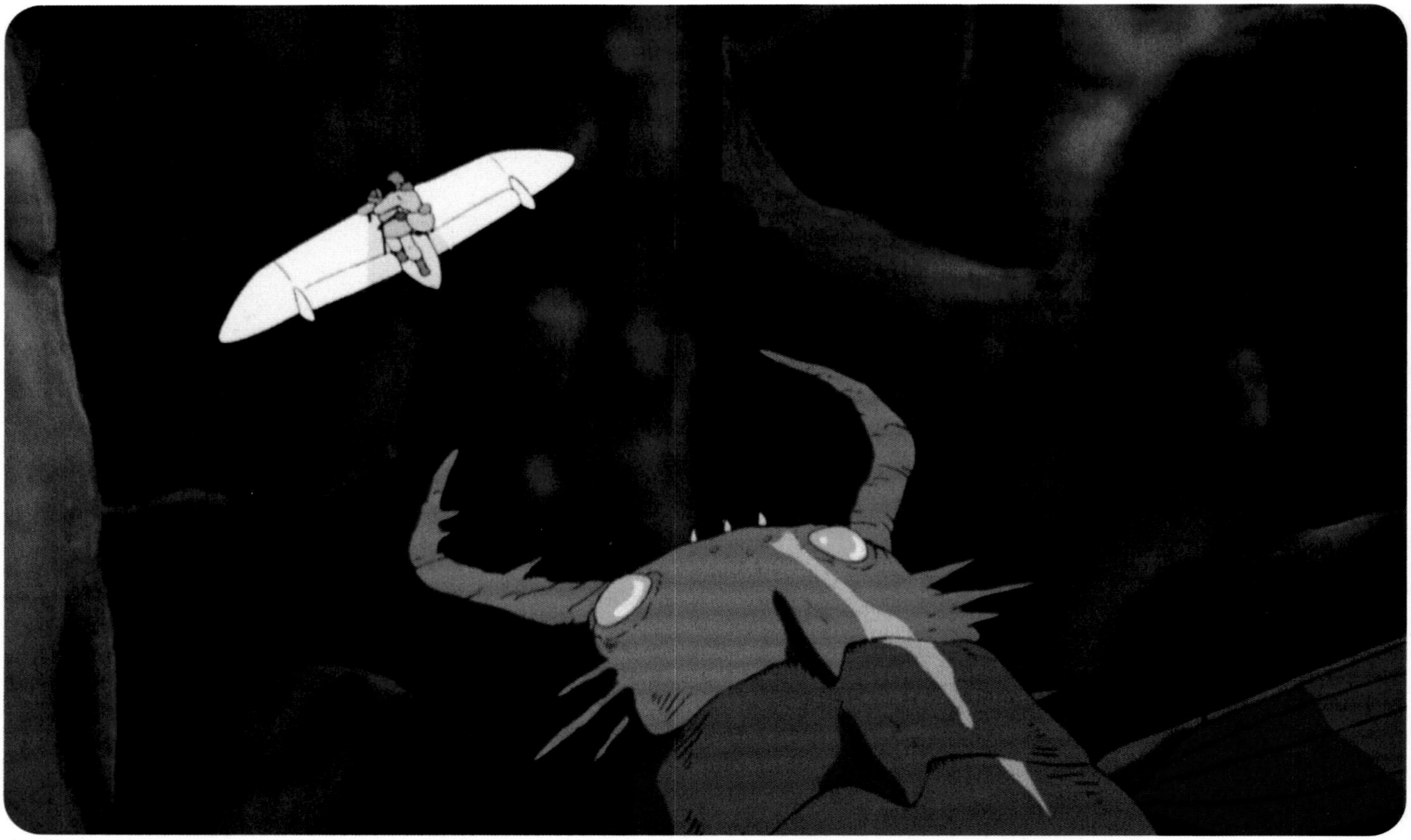

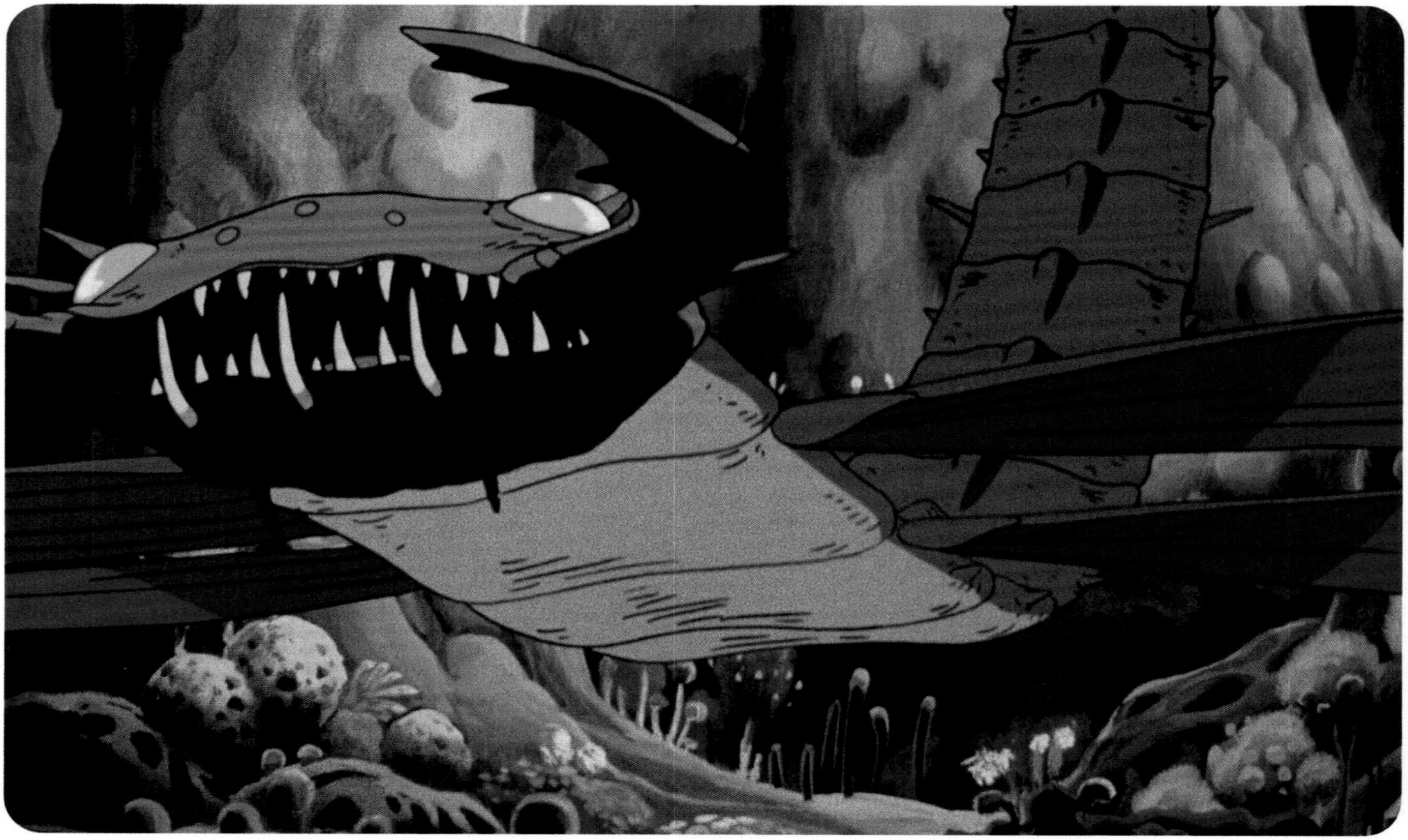

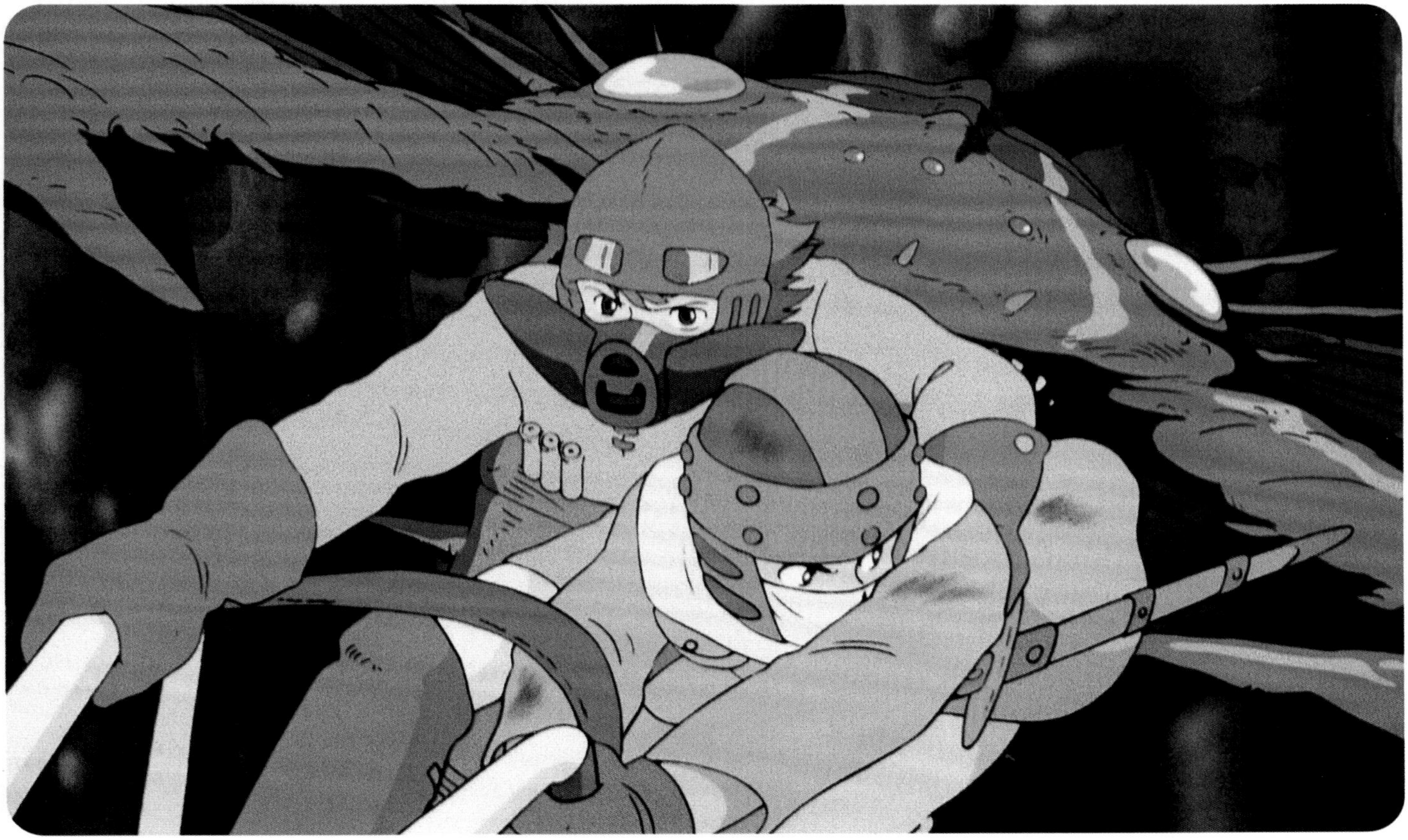

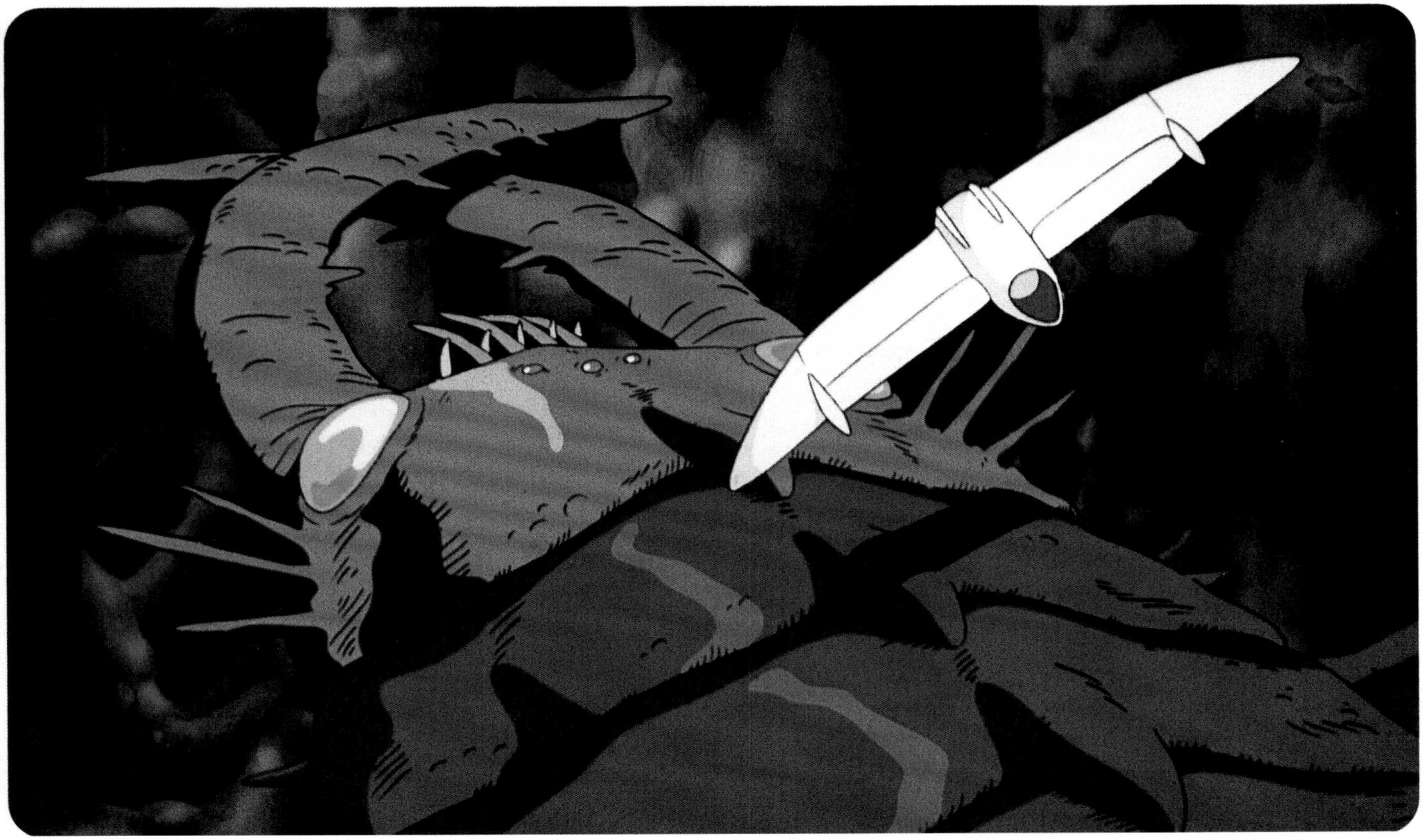

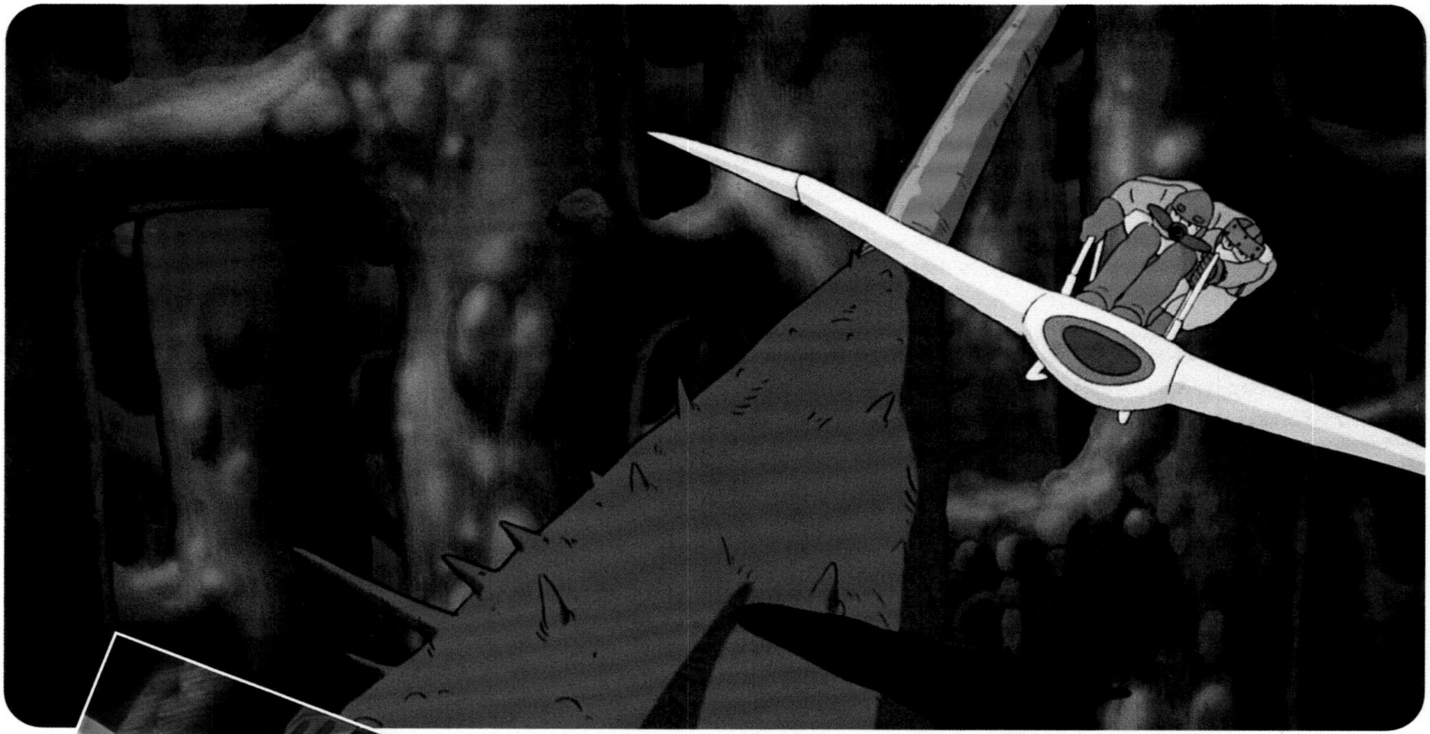

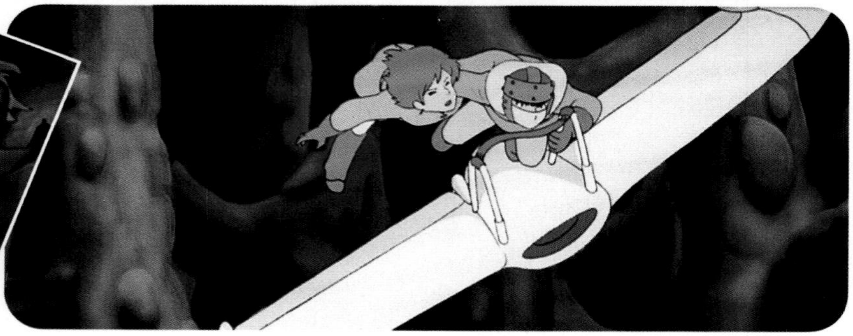

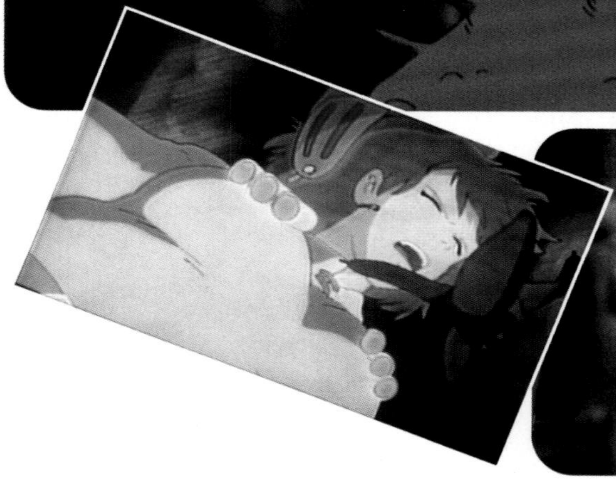

But the hebikera was too quick. With its huge tail, it sent the wind rider spinning toward the valley floor far below. Nausicaä's mask was torn off. She and the pilot were knocked senseless.

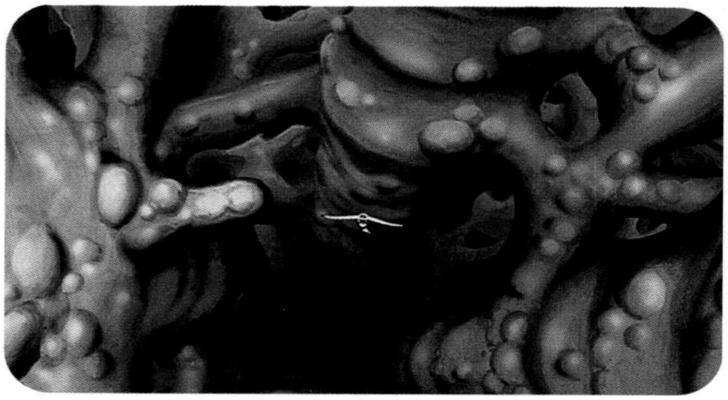

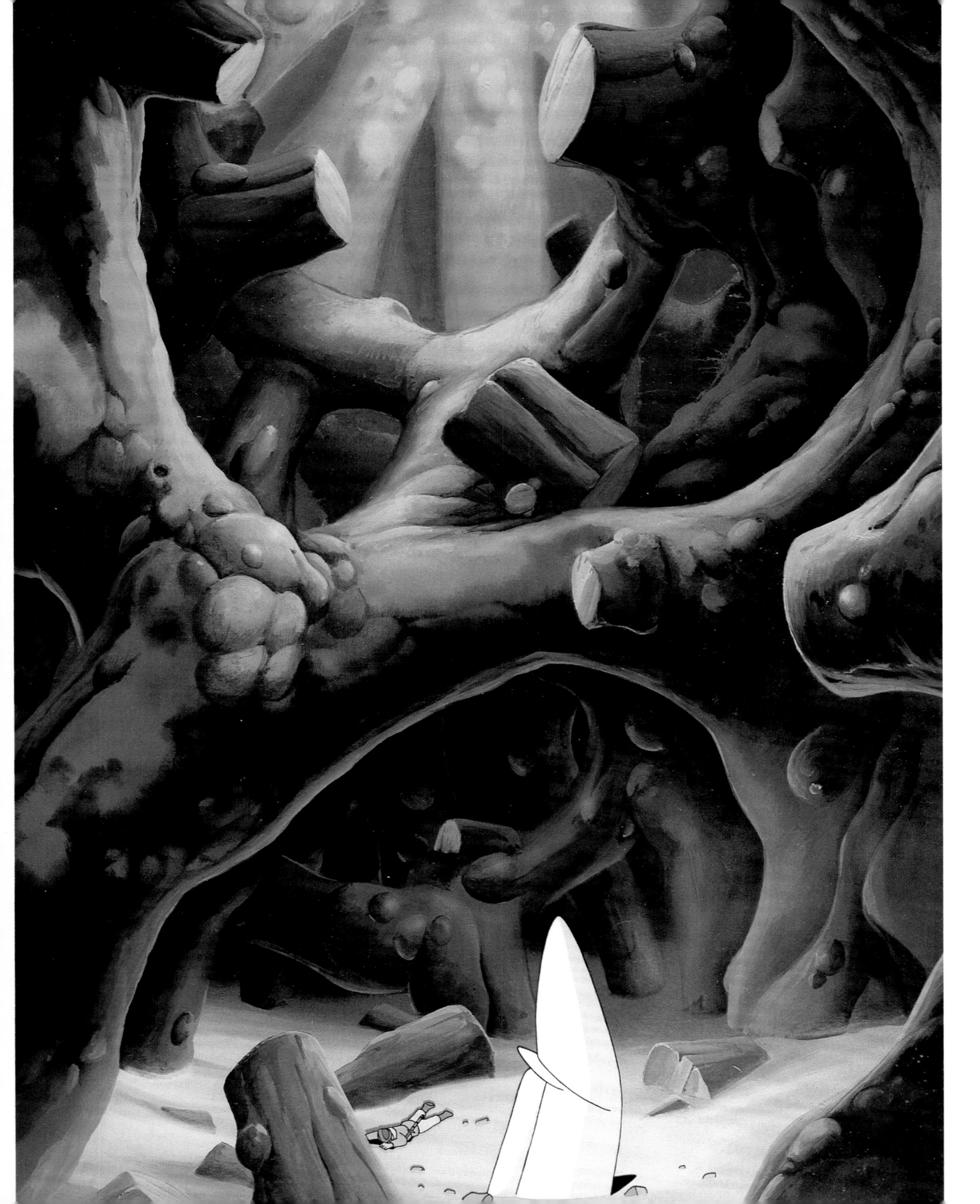

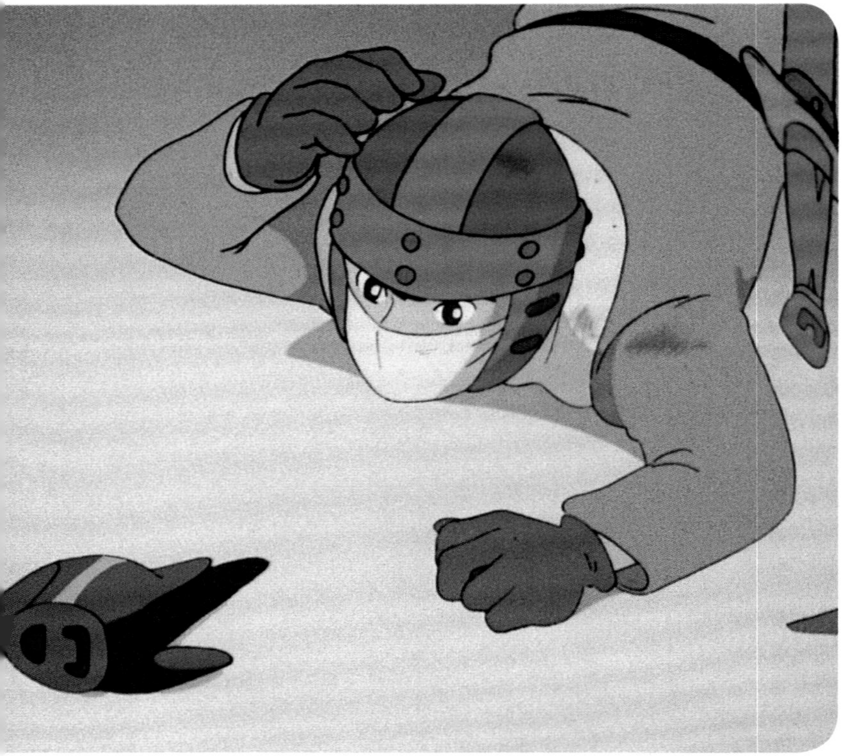

When the young man woke up, he found himself lying on a deep bed of soft sand. Nausicaä's mask was just within reach.

When he saw her lying unconscious not far away, he rushed to help her.

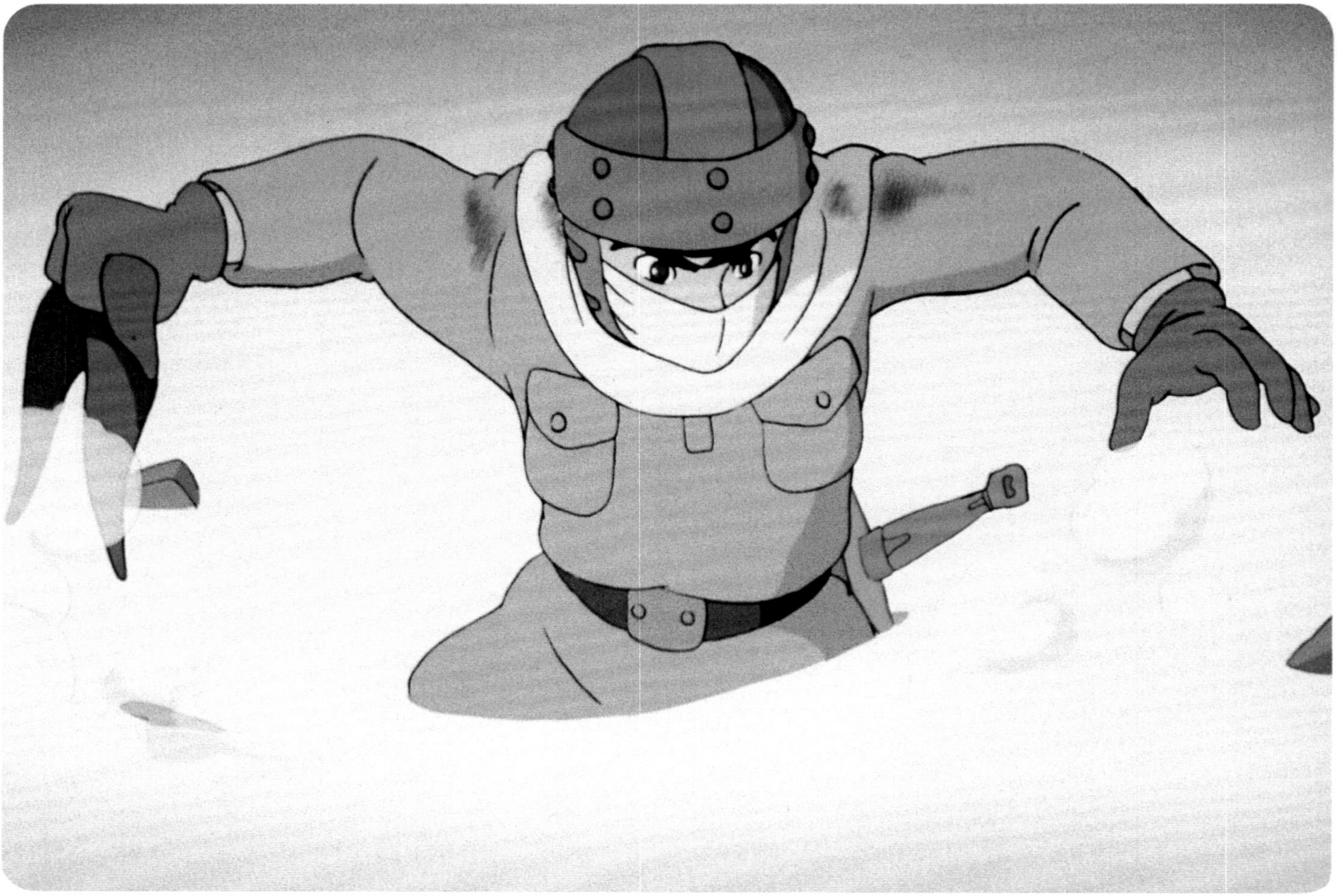

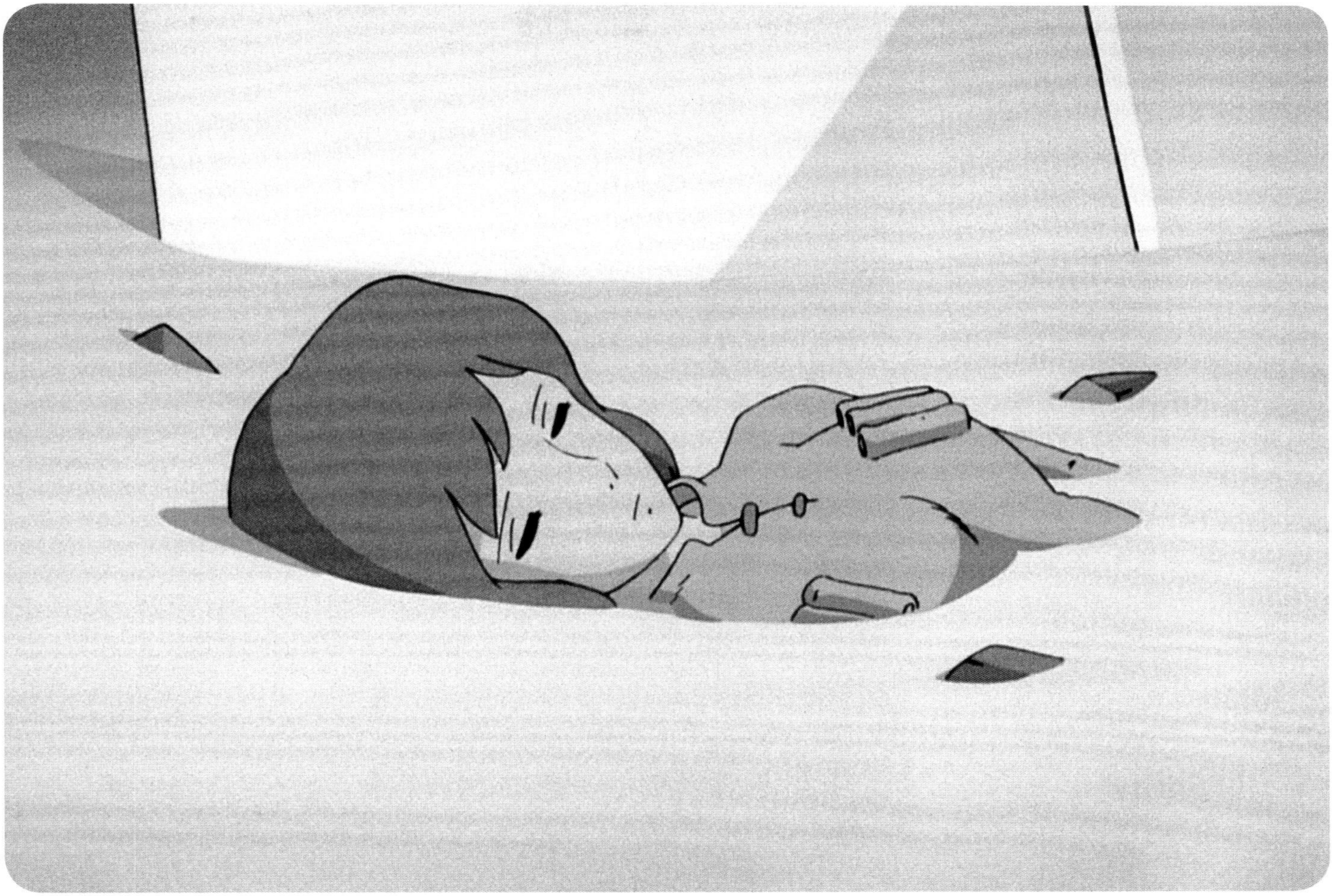

But his legs sank deeply into the sand.

"Quicksand!" He saw that Nausicaä was sinking too.

He struggled through the sand, trying to reach her.
But both of them sank out of sight.

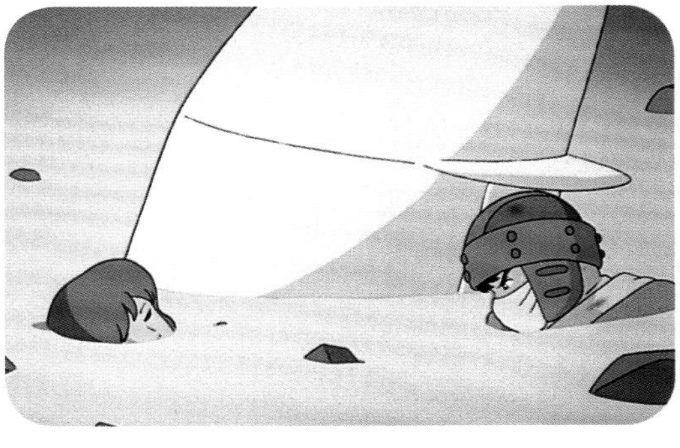

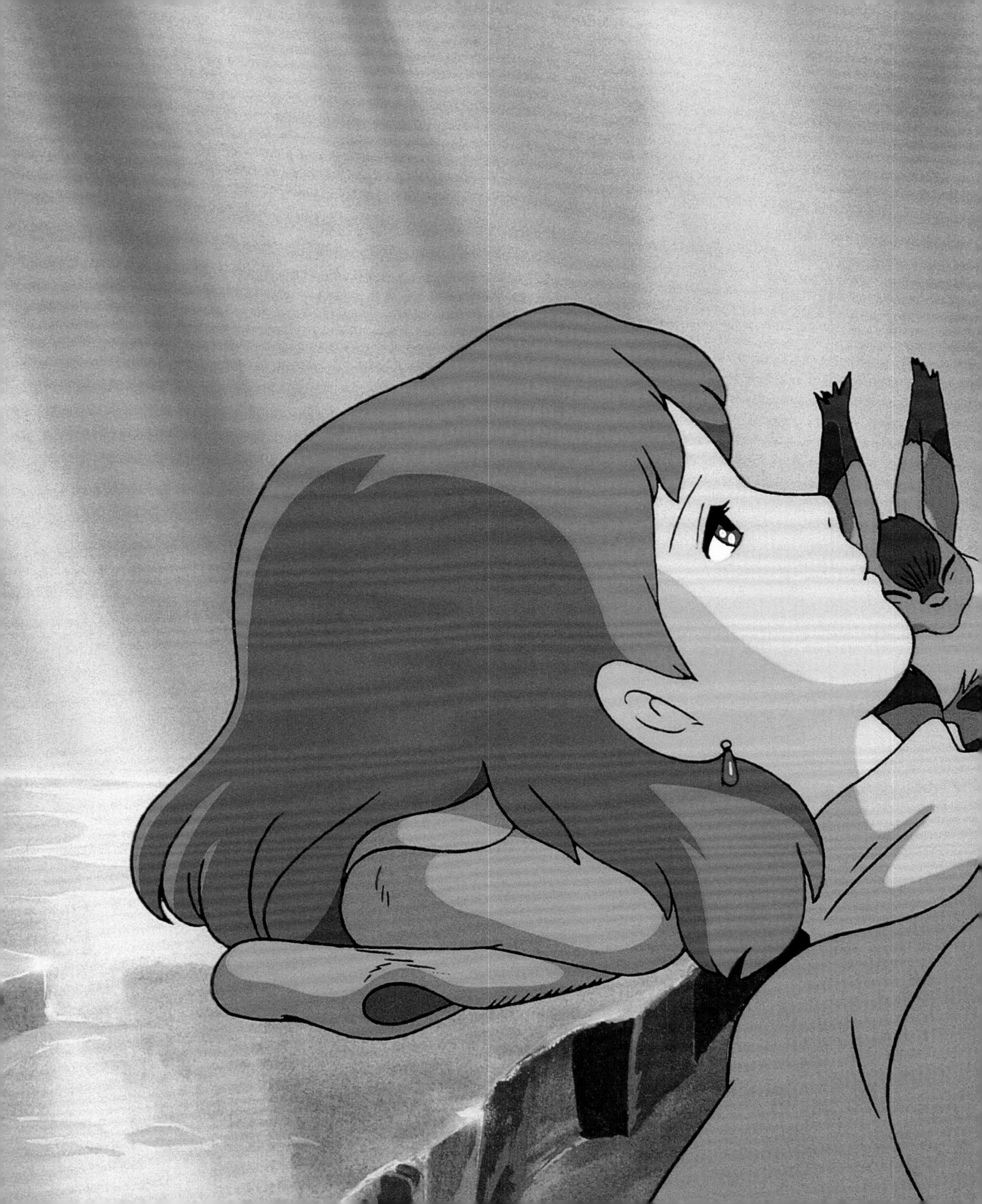

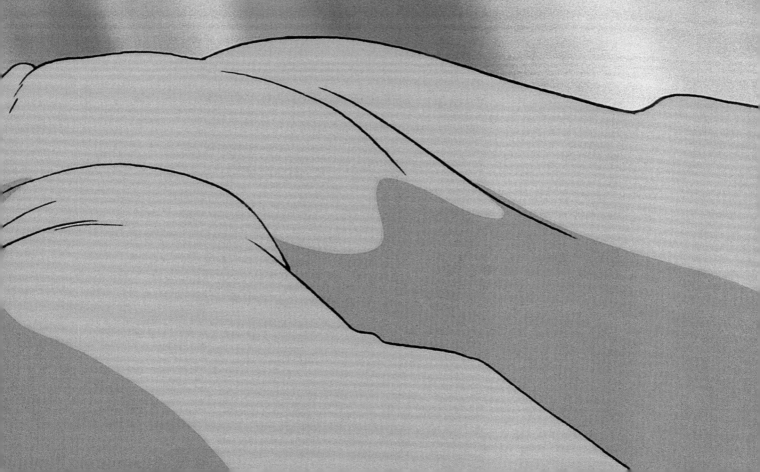

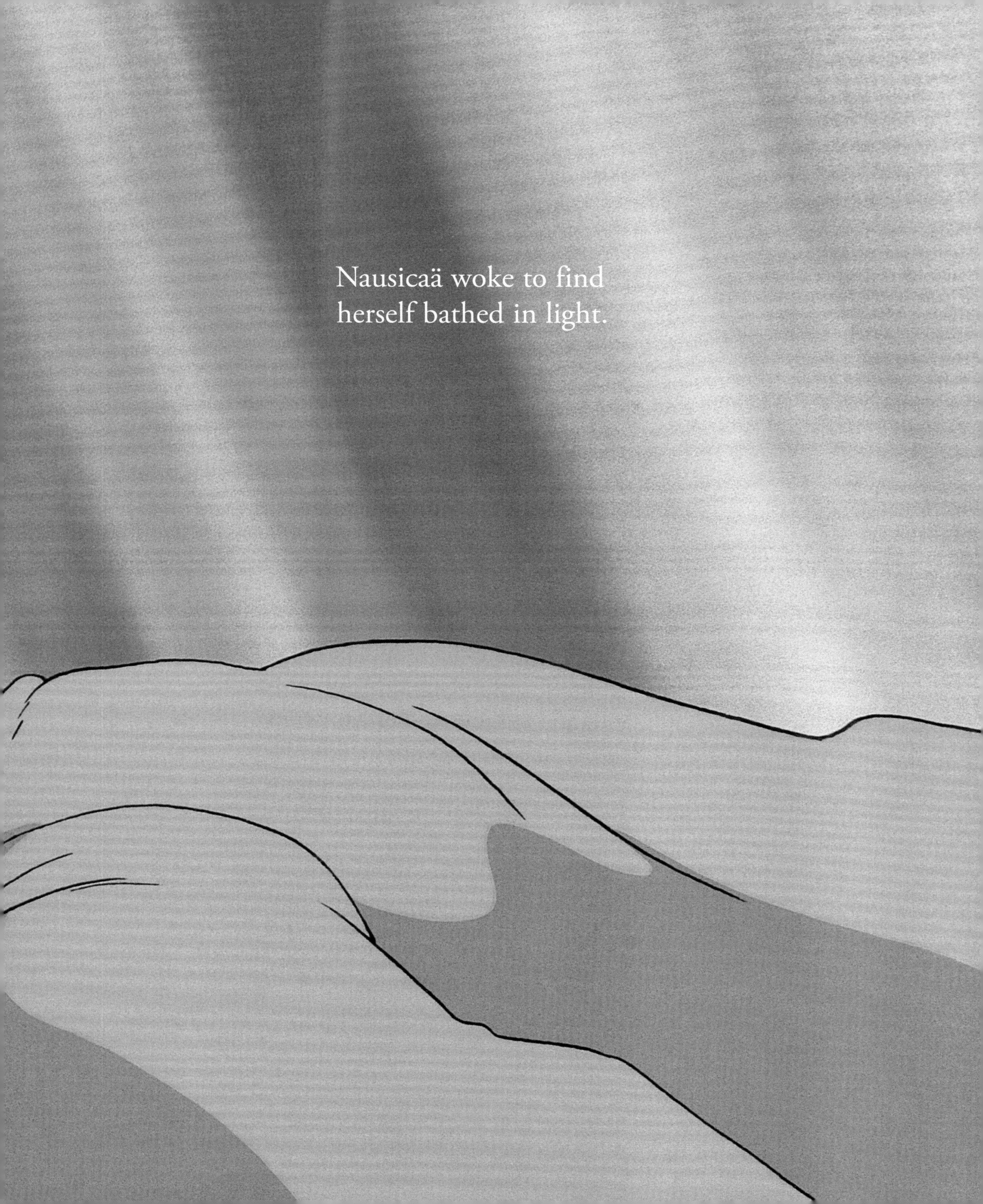

Nausicaä woke to find
herself bathed in light.

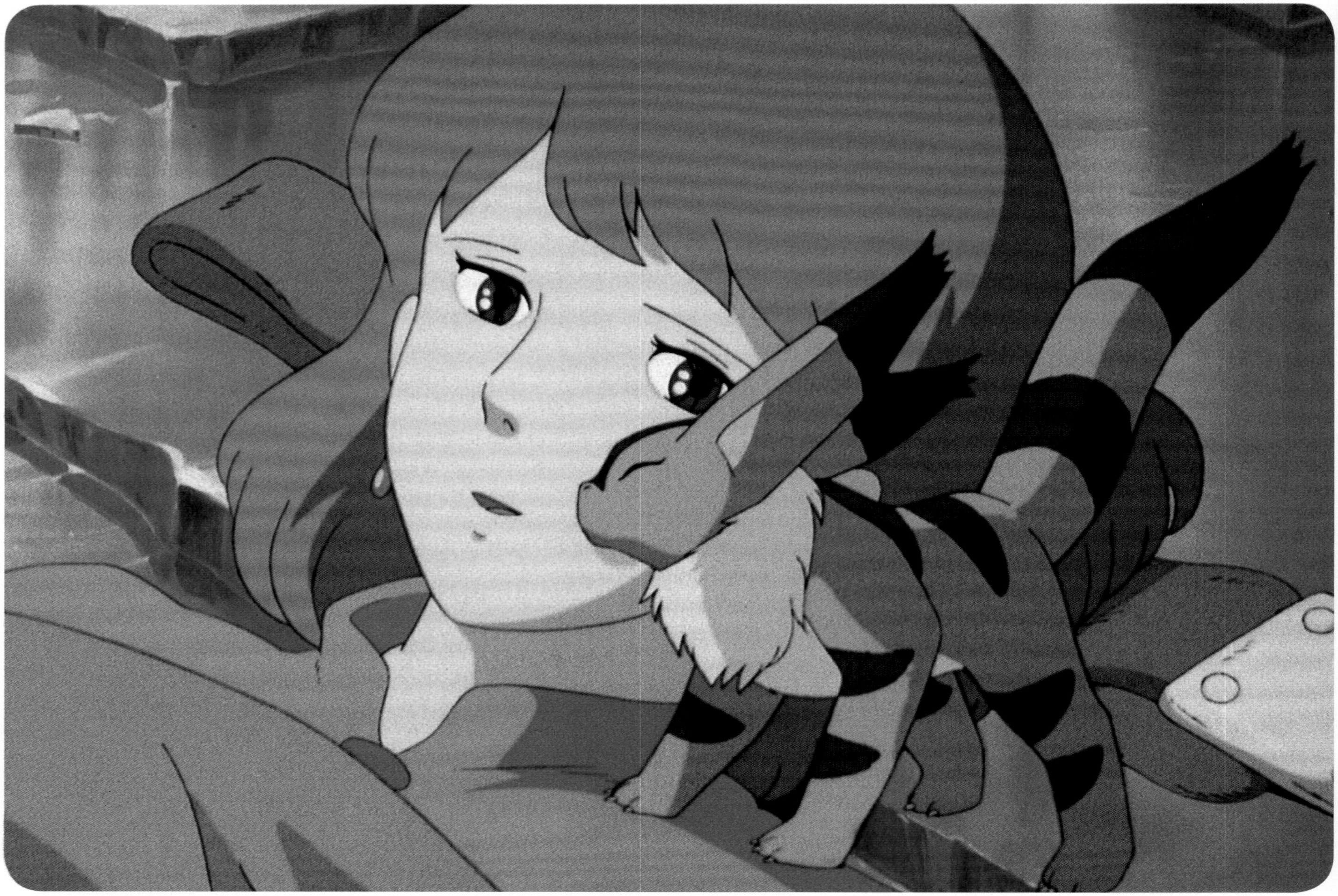

THE SECRET OF THE SEA OF DECAY

She heard the soft gurgle of flowing water.

As she opened her eyes, Teto happily rubbed her cheek.

"Teto…"

She sat up and looked around. She was in a forest of blue trees. Here and there, shafts of light pierced the dimness.

"What a strange place…."

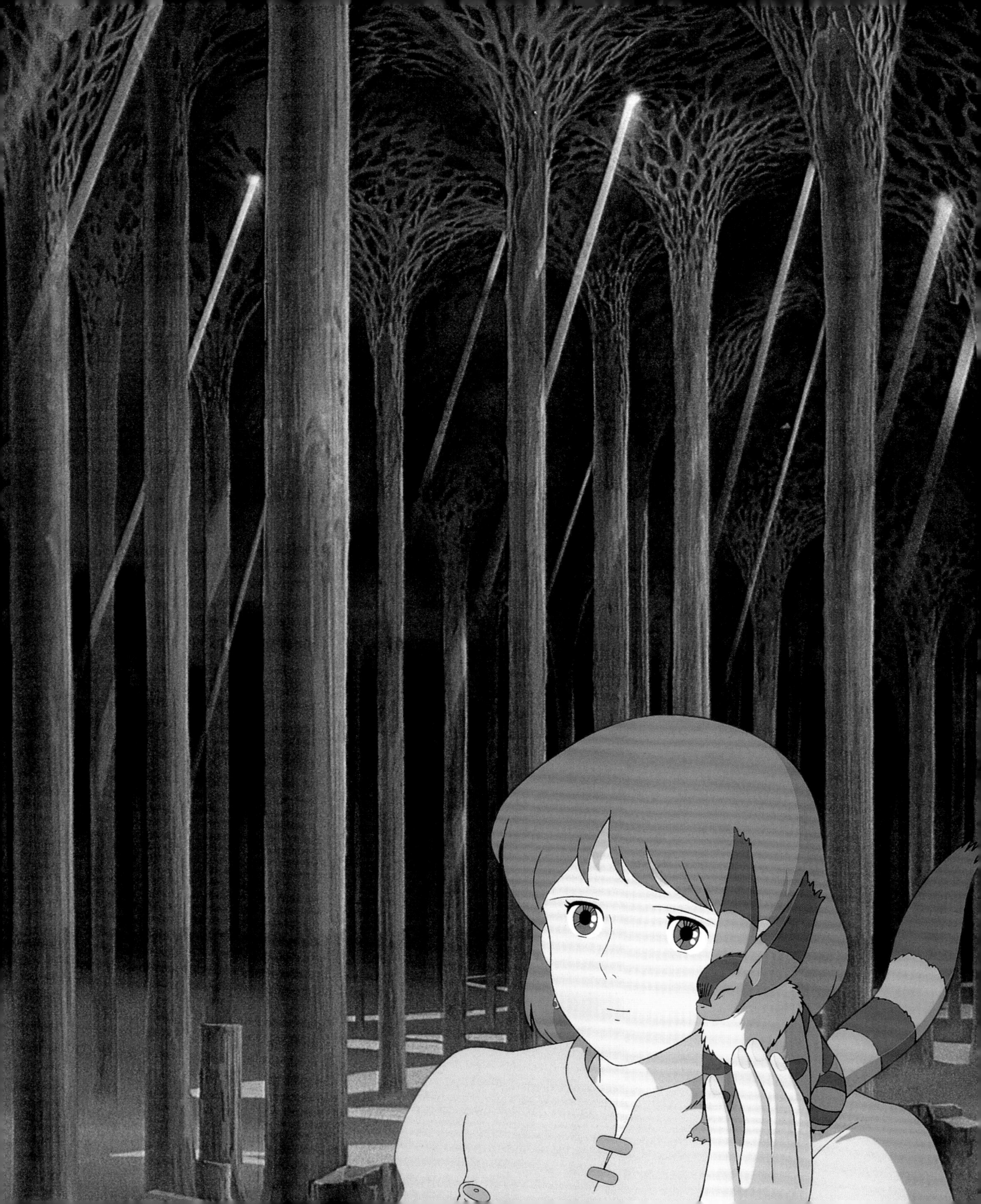

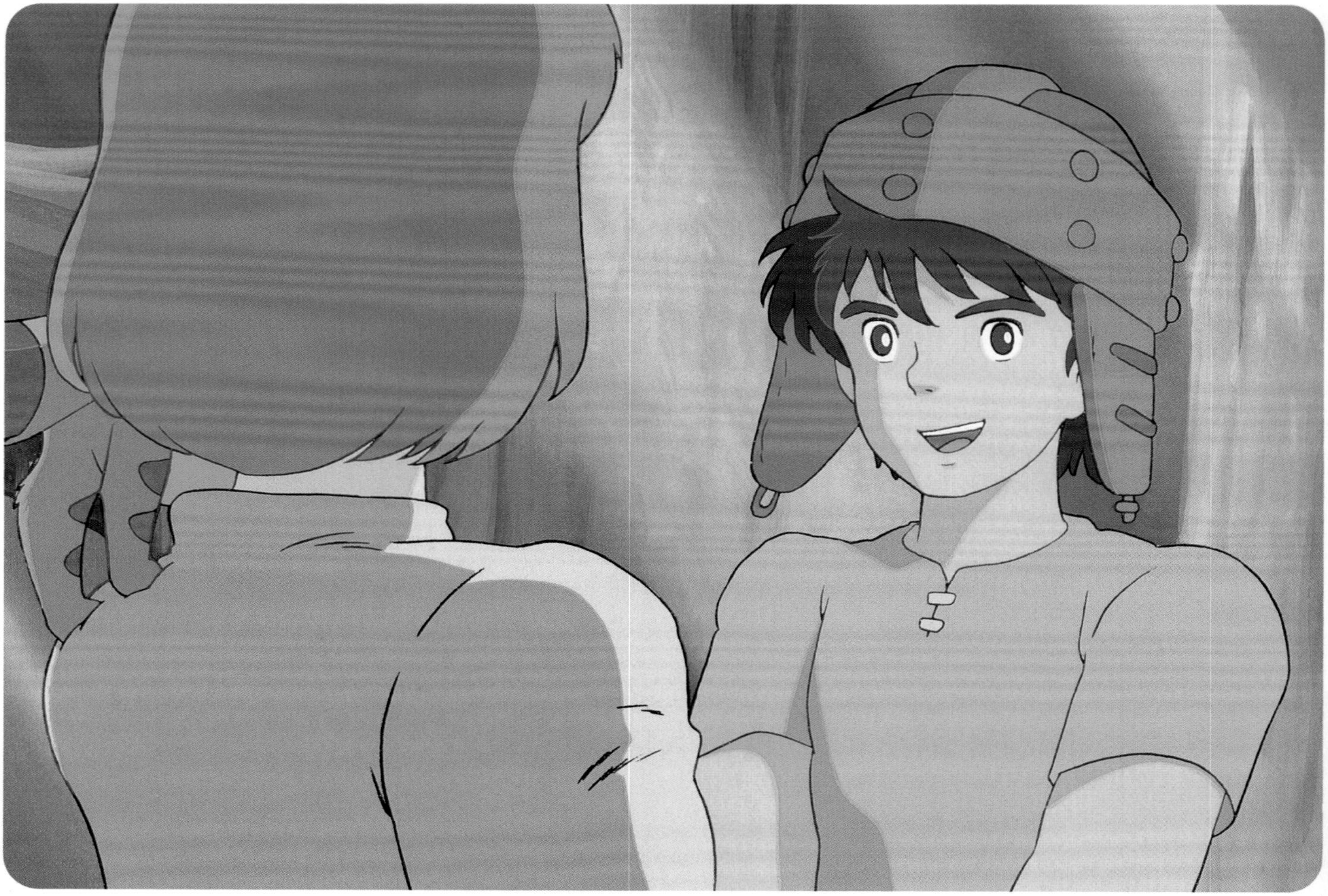

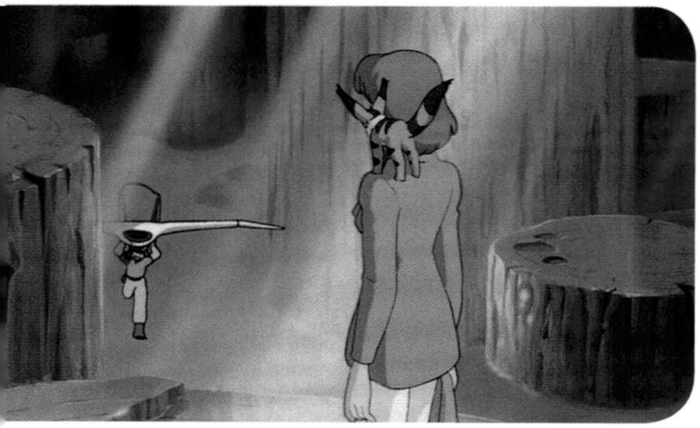

Out of the distance the young pilot came running toward her, holding her wind rider above his head.

"Hey! I found this." He took her hand. "I'm Asbel, from the land of Pejite. I'd like to thank you for saving me."

"I'm Nausicaä, from the Valley of the Wind. What is this place?"

"You're not going to believe this."

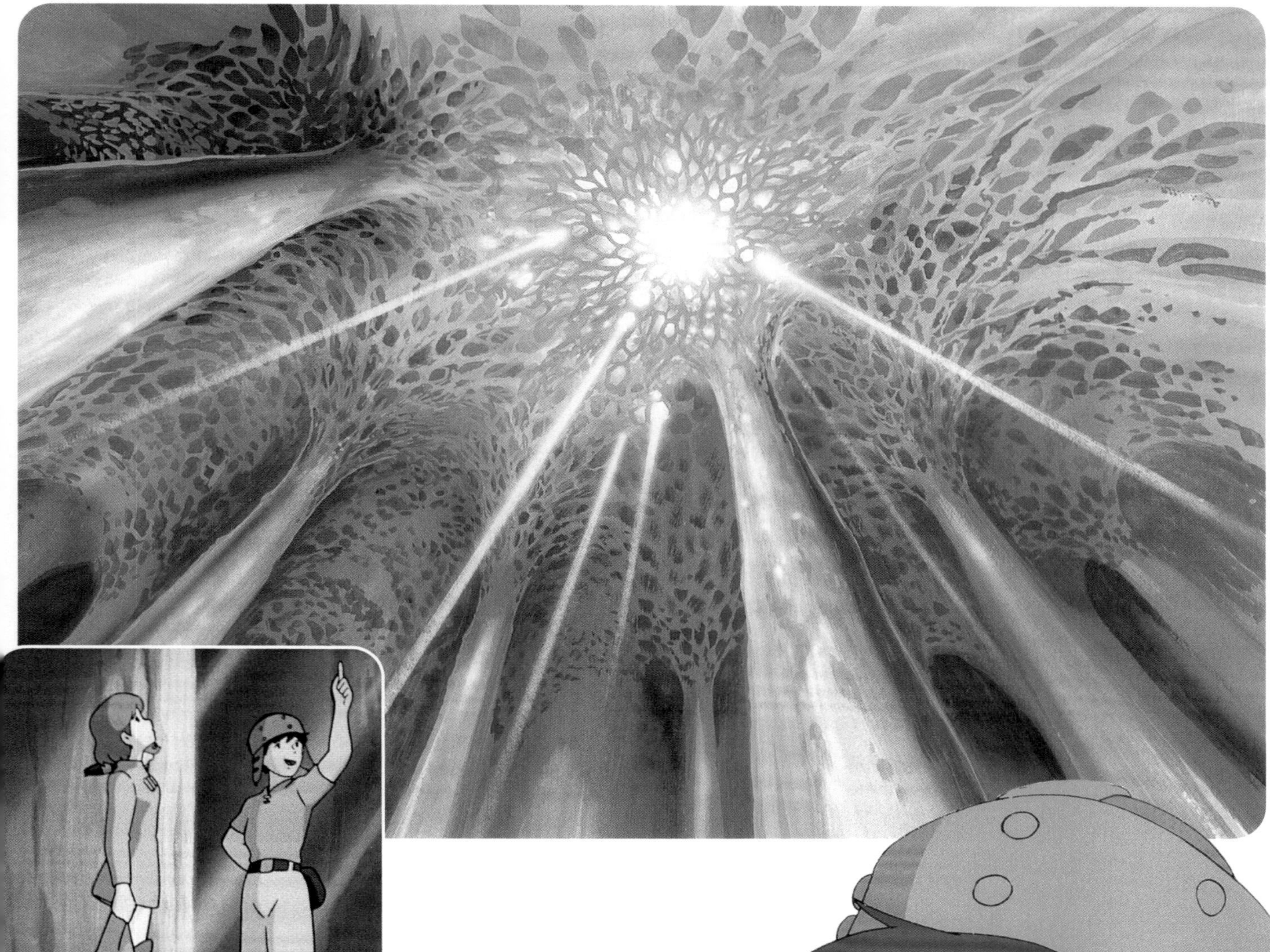

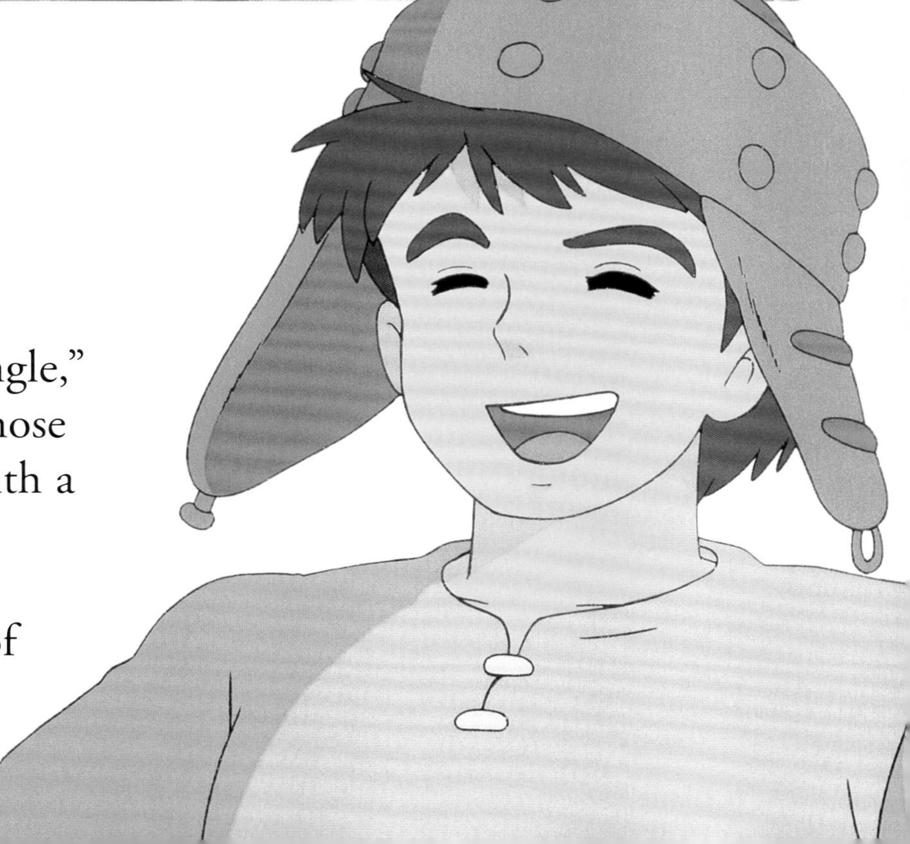

"We're beneath the toxic jungle," he said. "We fell through those branches up there, along with a bunch of sand."

He pointed to the canopy of branches above their heads and smiled.

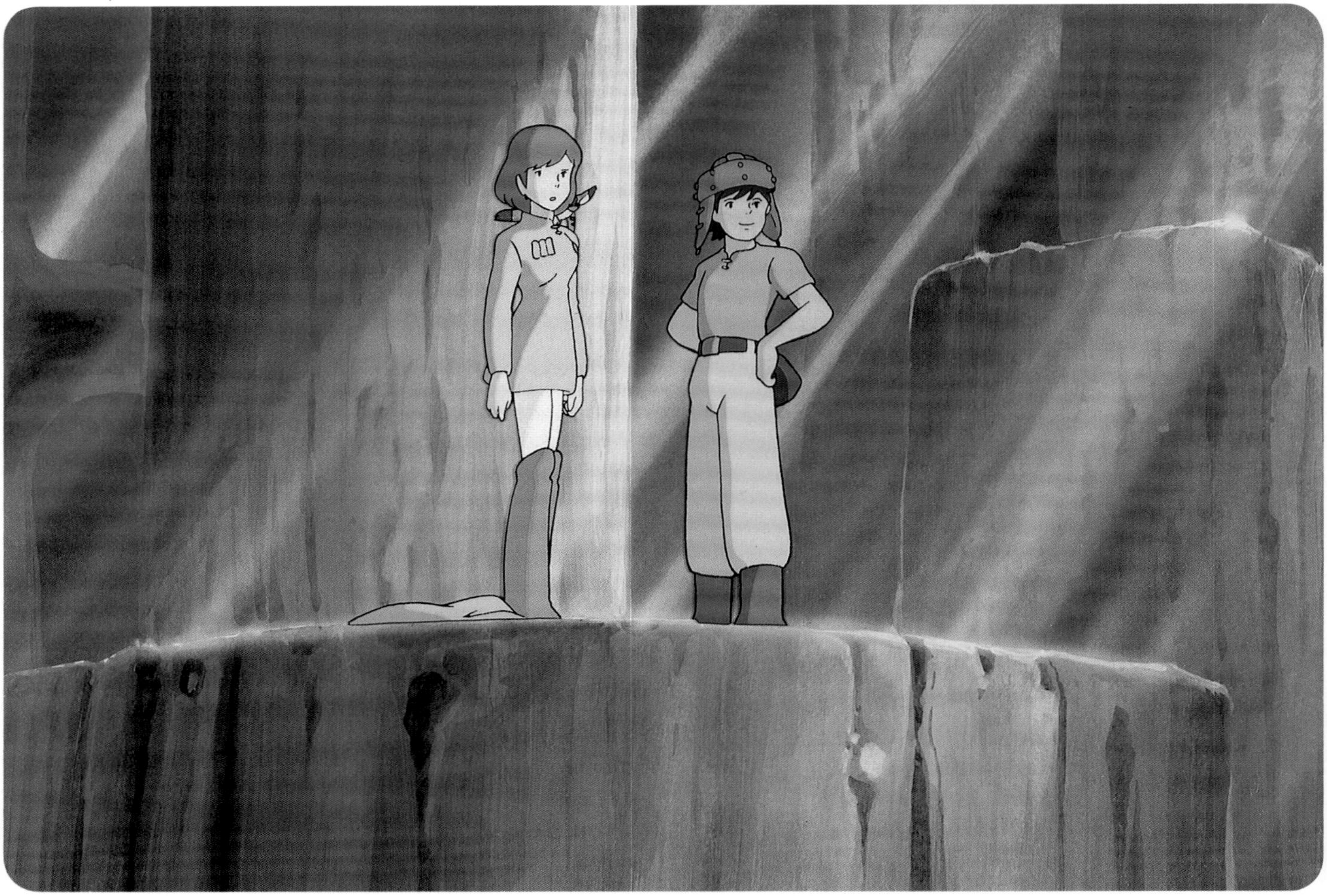

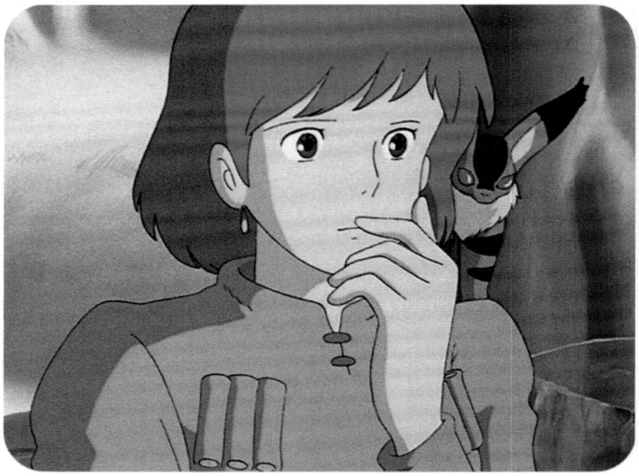

Suddenly Nausicaä put her hand over her mouth.

"Our masks! How can we be breathing without them?"

"I don't know. Somehow the air down here is clean. I couldn't believe it either."

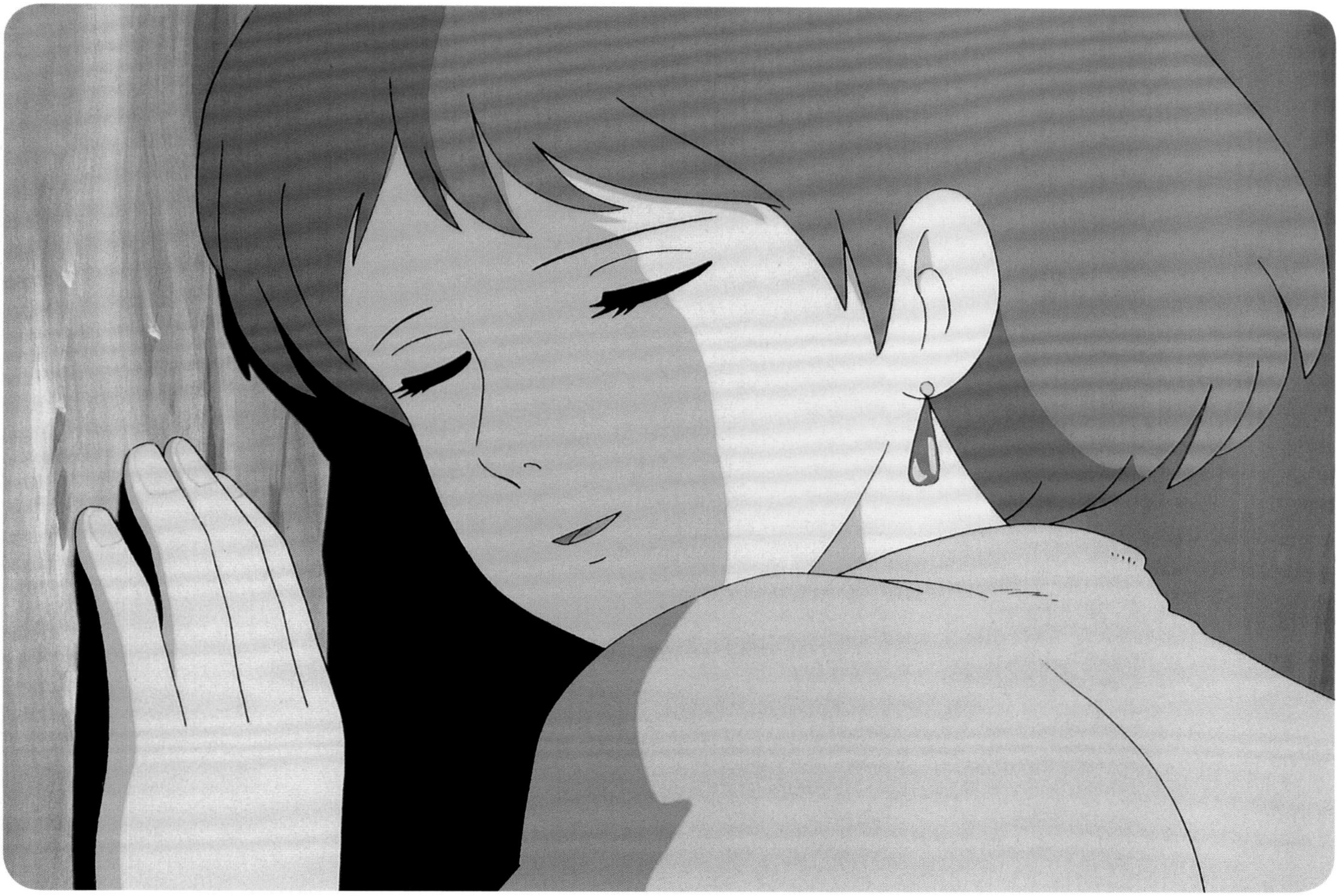

Nausicaä walked slowly among the great trees. They were hard and cold, as if they had turned to stone.

When she put her ear to a tree, she could hear the sound of flowing water.

"It's dead, but the water's still rising through it."

Something came raining down from the canopy. Was it really sand?

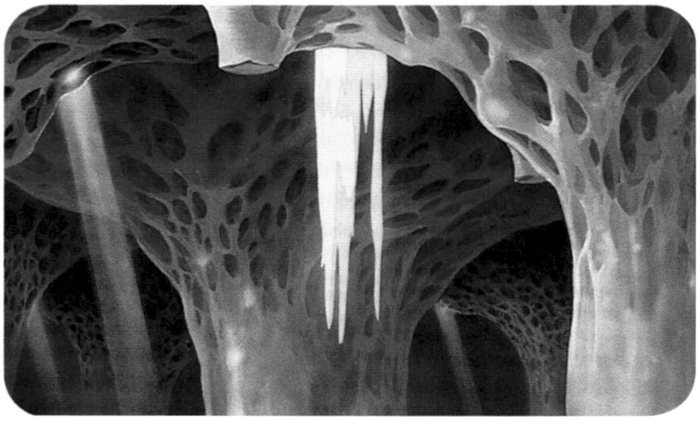

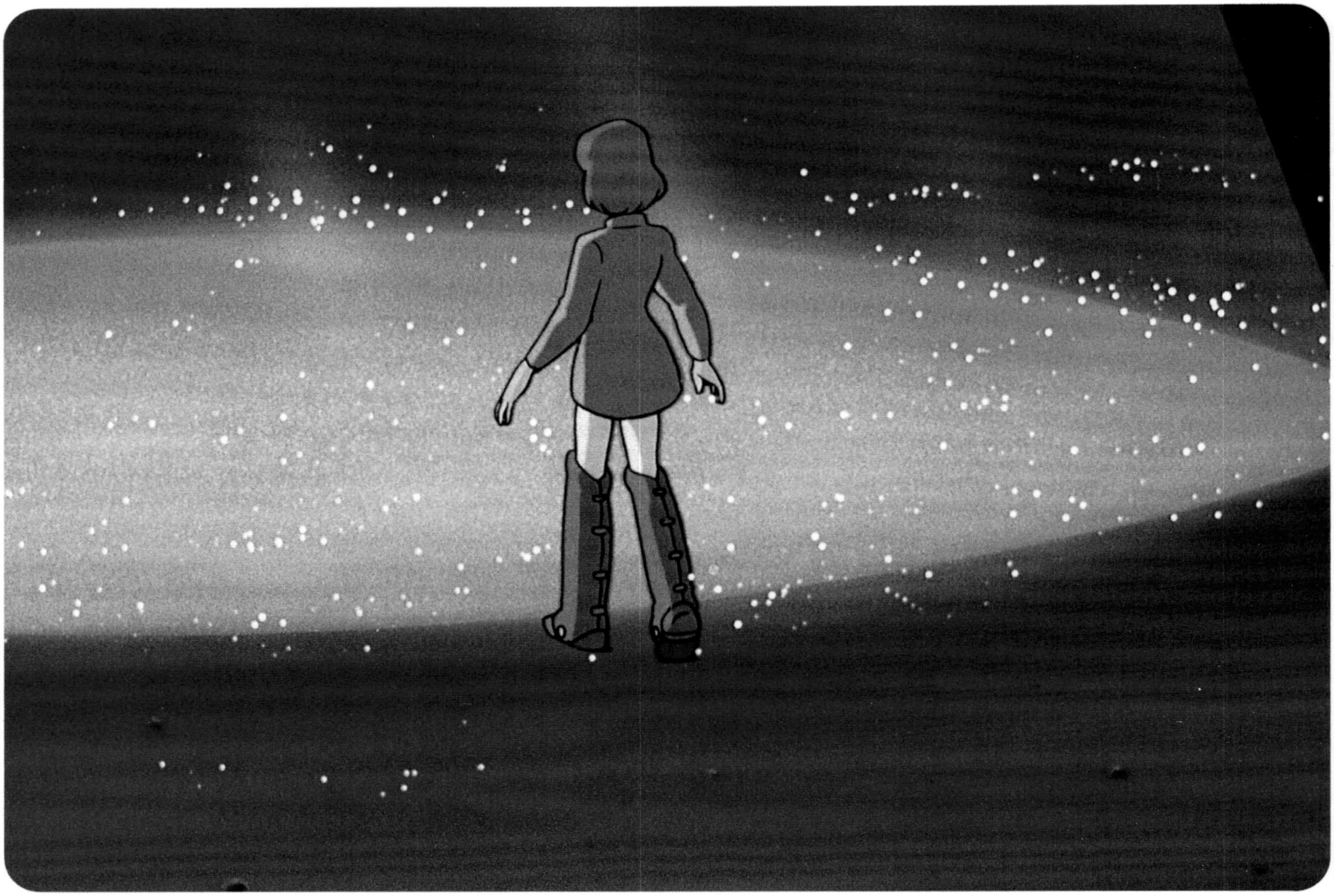

The wood that had turned to stone was crumbling and raining down from above.

Nausicaä picked up one of the golden fragments. It crumbled between her fingers with a clear, ringing sound.

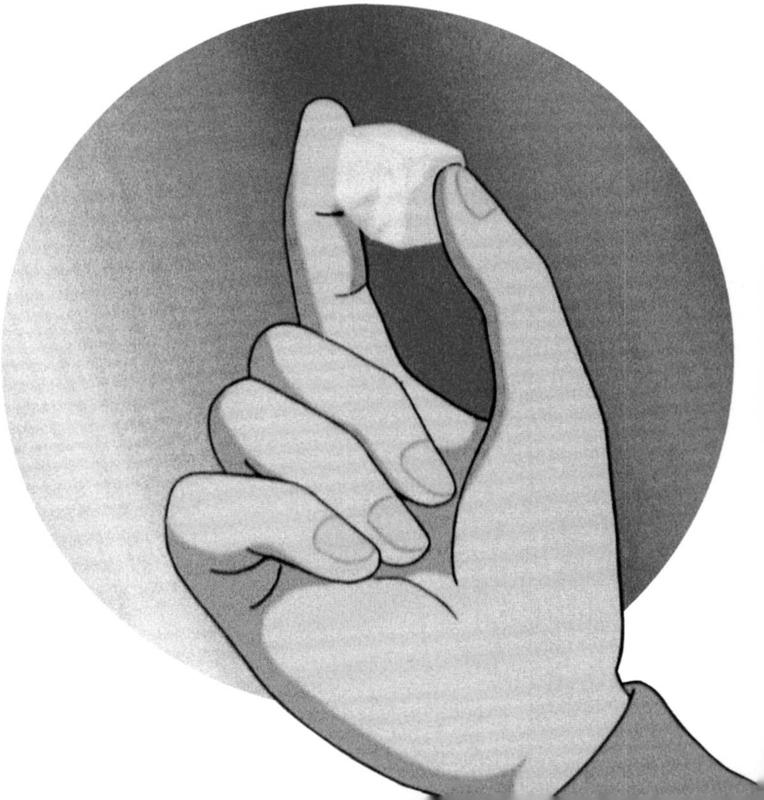

"This is like the sand from the bottom of our well," she murmured with amazement.

It was then that she understood. The Sea of Decay was purifying the soil and water that humanity had polluted.

The trees of the jungle absorbed the poison. After they died, their petrified fragments filtered the water deep underground. The insects were defending the Sea.

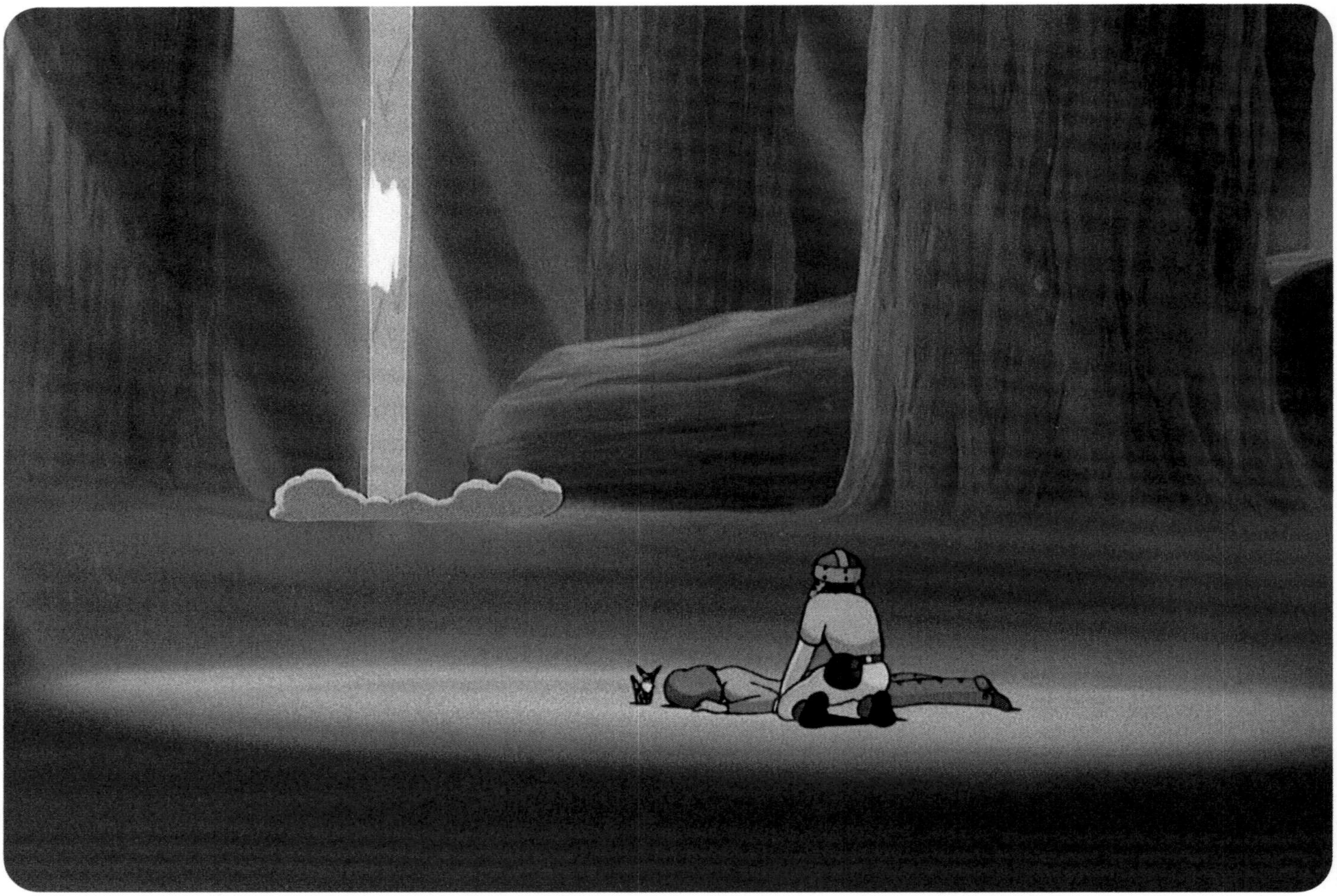

When Asbel found Nausicaä, she was lying facedown in the sand. He peered at her curiously.

"Nausicaä, are you crying?"

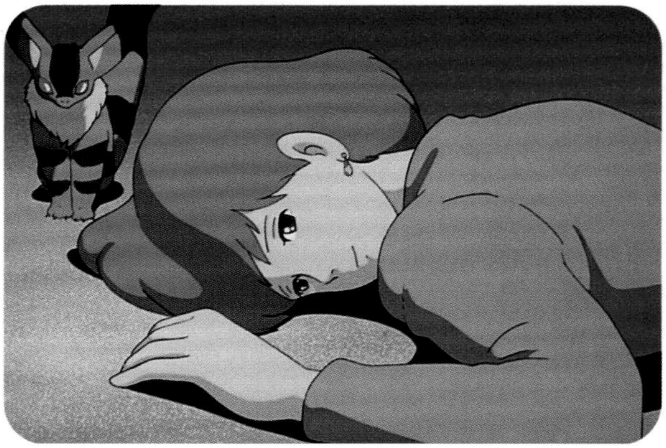

"I'm just happy," she answered softly.

In the dim blue light, tiny fragments of petrified trees kept raining down.

After a little while, Nausicaä told Asbel what had happened.

She told him about the Tolmekian airship that crashed in the valley, and the Giant Warrior it had been carrying. She also told him about Lastel, the Pejite princess who died after the crash.

"I can't believe she's dead," Asbel murmured. "Lastel was my twin sister. I wish I could've been there for her."

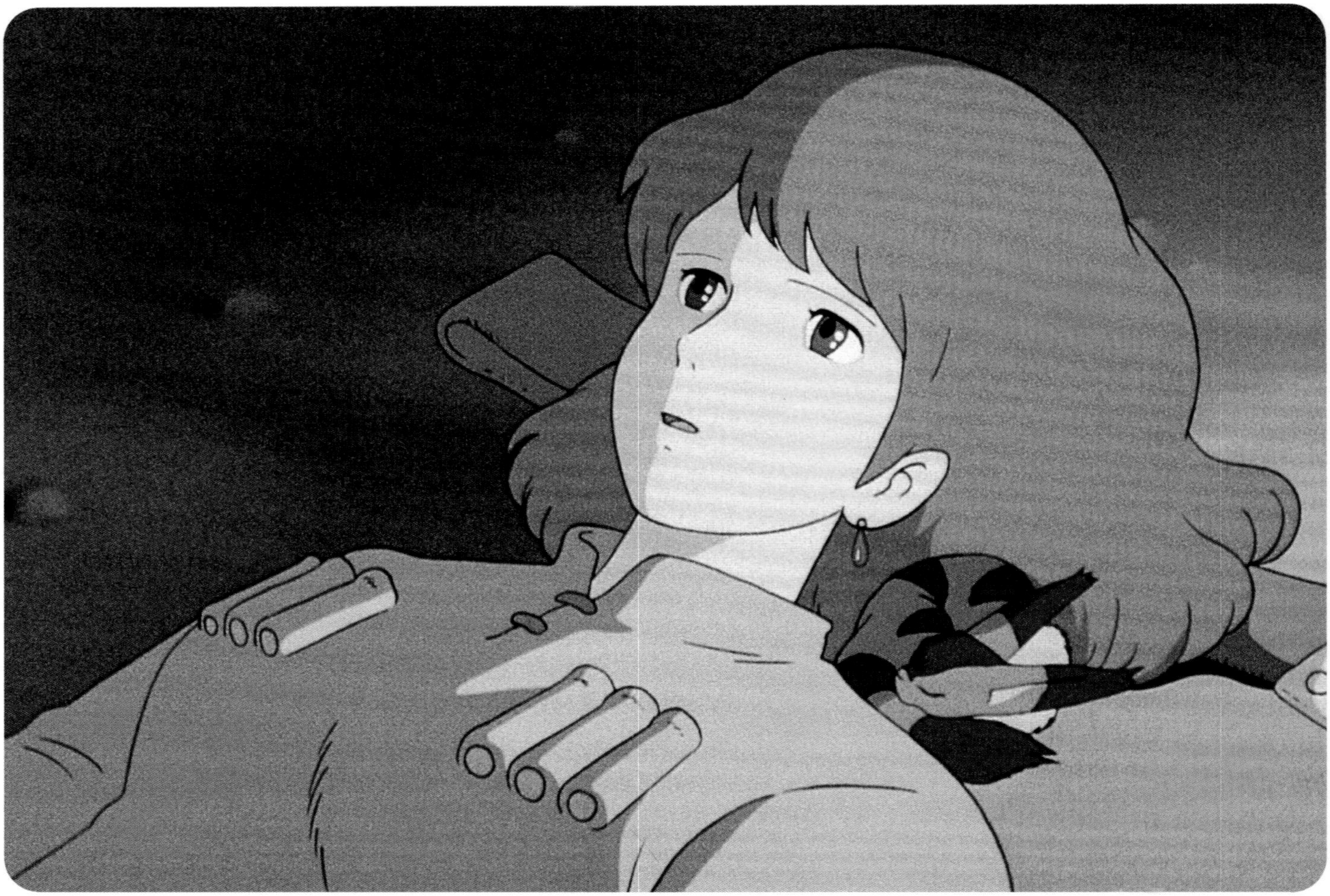

That night, after Nausicaä told him the secret of the jungle, Asbel said, "But it'll take centuries for these trees to cleanse the earth. We're going to have to find a way to stop the Sea of Decay from spreading if we want to survive, too."

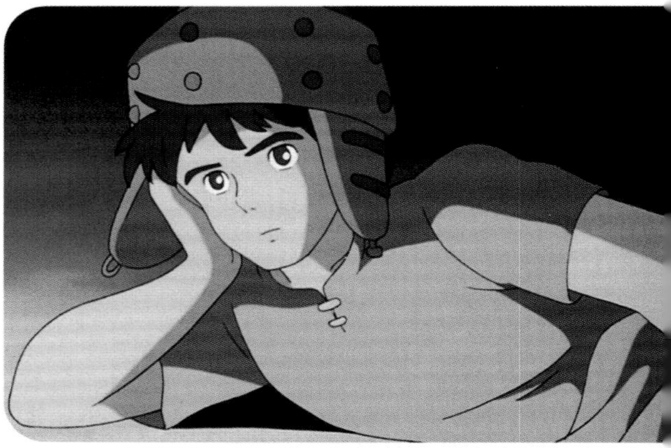

"Stop it? You mean burn it with the Giant Warrior?" Nausicaä
said. "You Pejites sound just like the Tolmekians."

"What?! We'd never use the warrior as a weapon."

He looked sharply at Nausicaä, but she closed her eyes. "Let's get
some sleep, Asbel. We'll need our strength to make it to Pejite
tomorrow."

The two fell asleep in the great forest beneath the Sea of Decay.

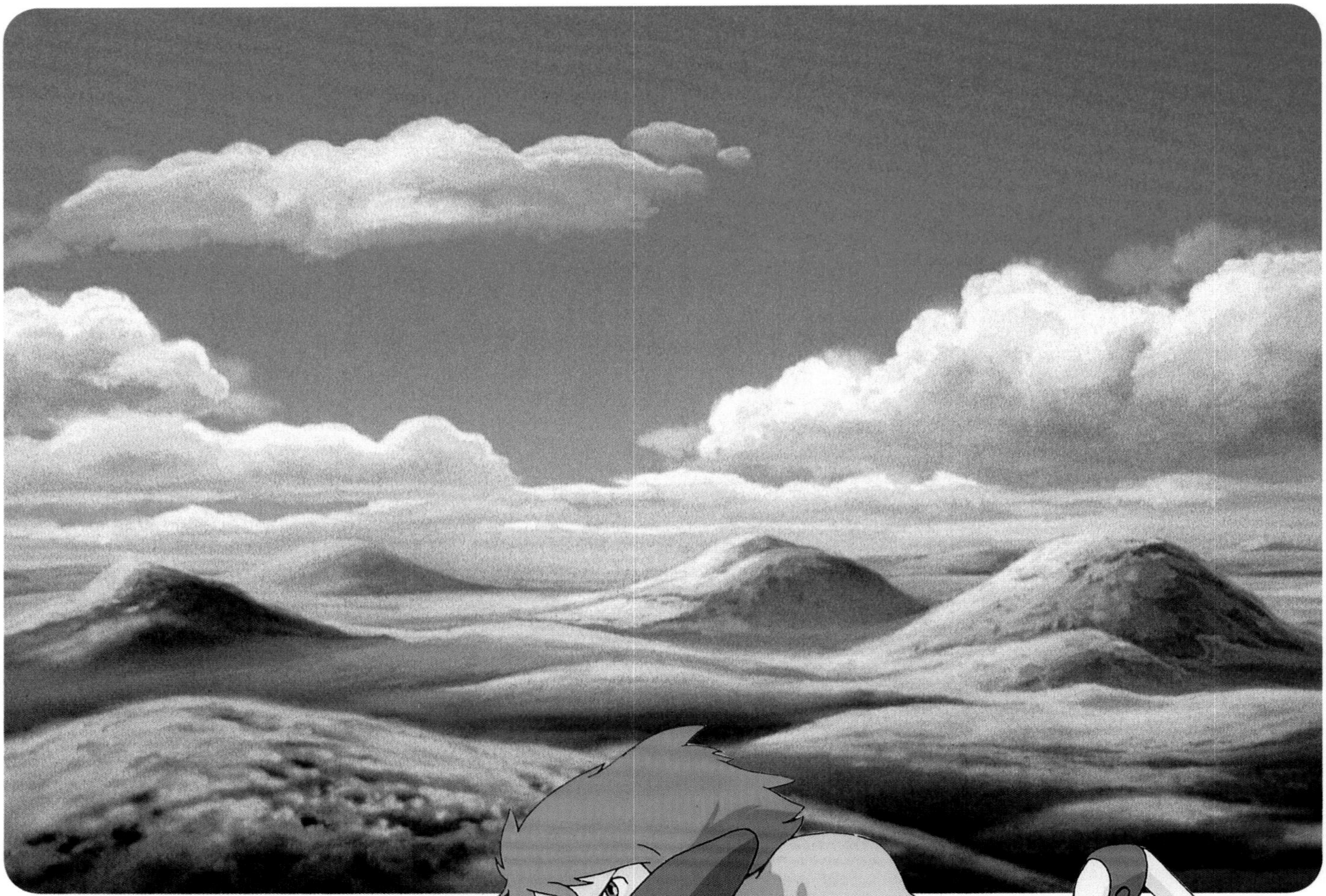

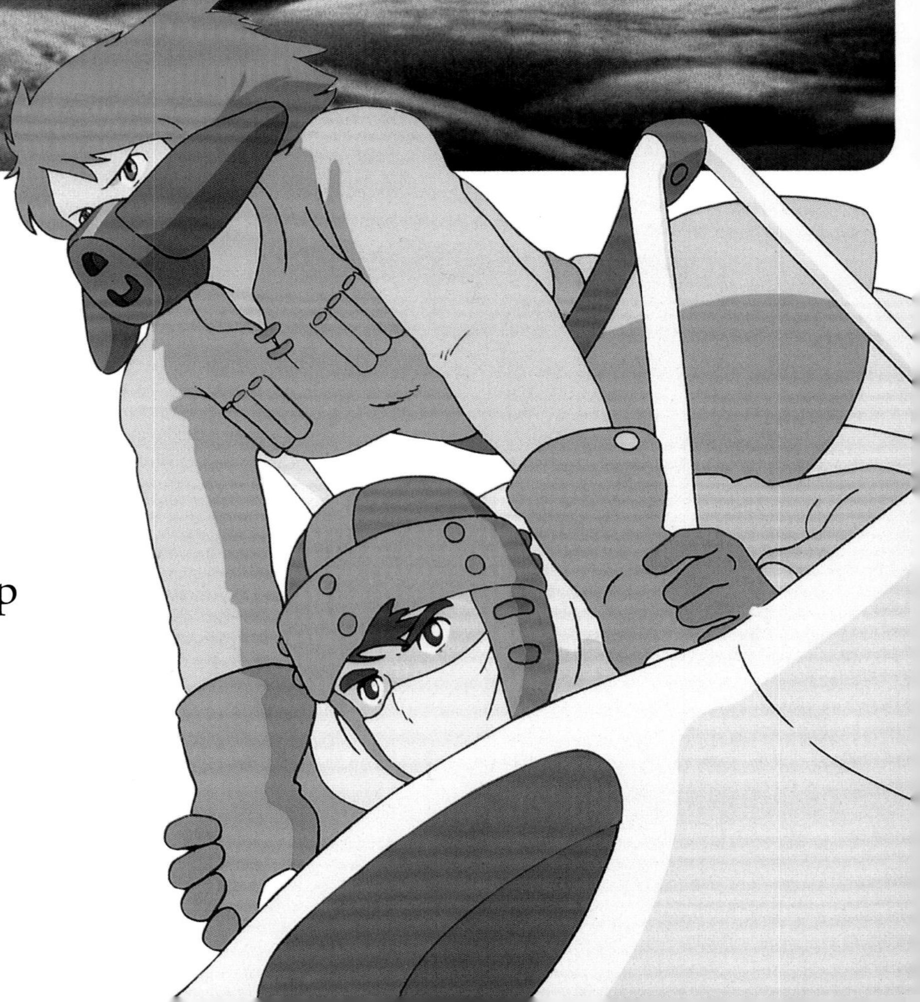

The next day, Nausicaä and Asbel flew to rendezvous with a group of his people gathered near Pejite.

As they neared Pejite, Asbel cried out, "The insects—they're all dead!"

Dead insects littered the ground outside the walls of Pejite. Smoke rose from the city, and the sky was filled with deadly spores.

"We've got to get to Pejite!" Nausicaä shouted.

"Be careful. The Tolmekians might still be there," Asbel said.

They landed in the ruined city and started exploring.

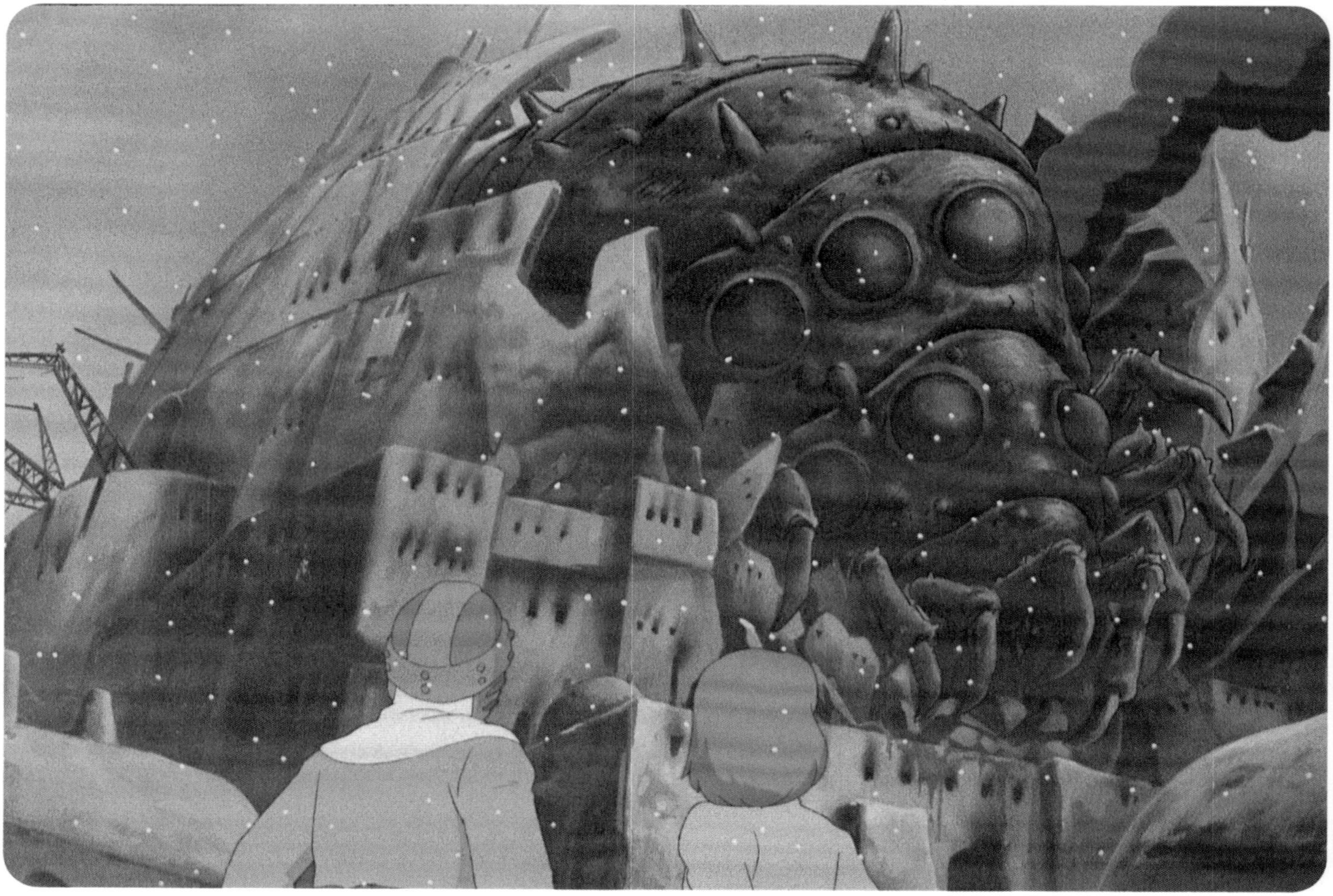

The insects had invaded Pejite. Nausicaä and Asbel saw huge Ohms lying dead amid the rubble of destroyed buildings. It would not be long before Pejite was engulfed by the toxic jungle.

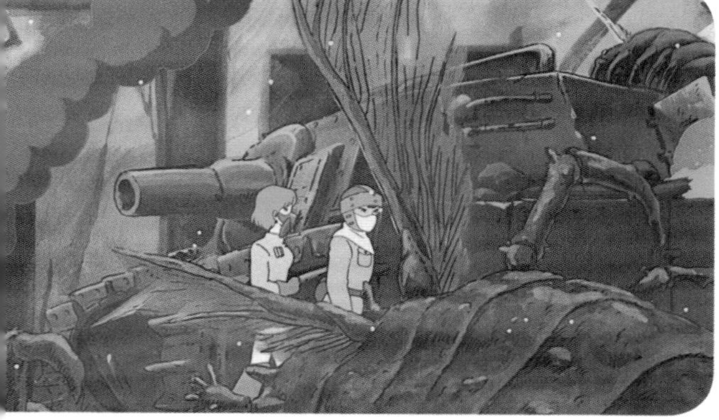

"Pejite is finished," Asbel said sorrowfully. "This was far too much to pay, even if it did get the Tolmekians out of our city."

"Too much to pay?" Nausicaä was astonished. "Asbel, what do you mean?"

As they stood there on the walls of the city, a Pejite cargo airship called a Brig flew low over the city.

"It's one of ours," Asbel exclaimed. "It's landing. Let's go!"

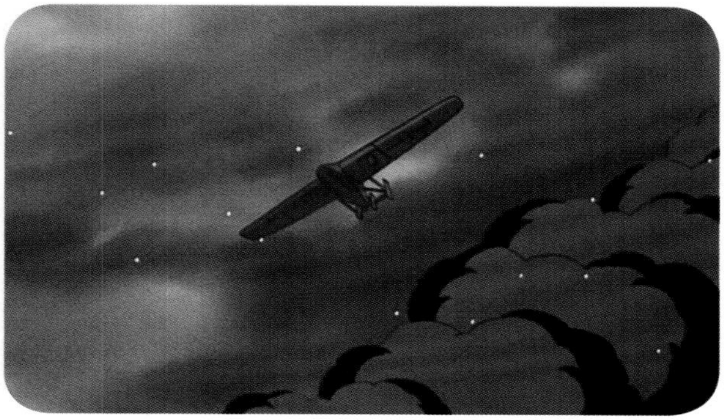

Asbel ran out to meet the Brig as the mayor of Pejite stepped out.

"What have you done to our city?" he said angrily. "It's completely destroyed!"

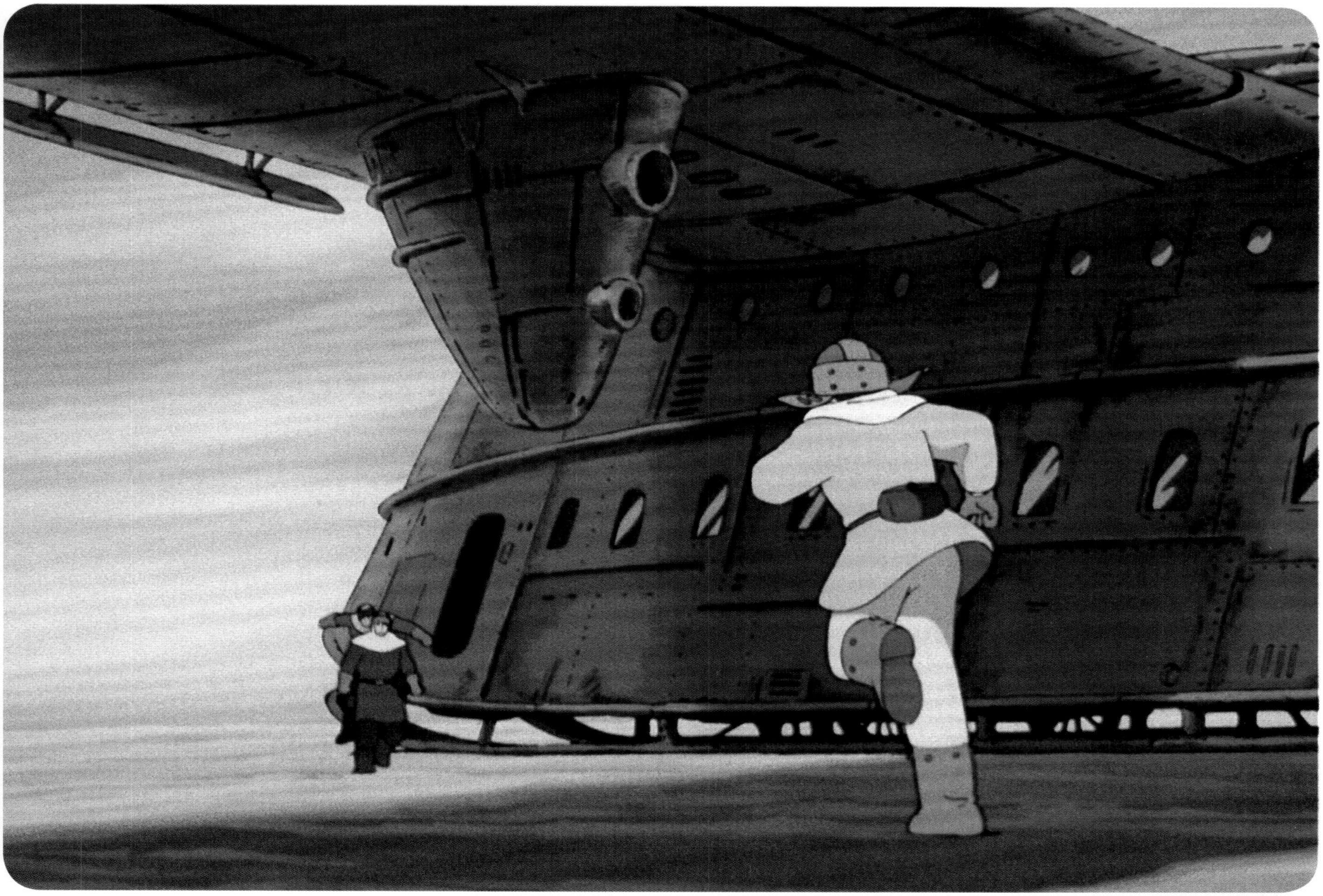

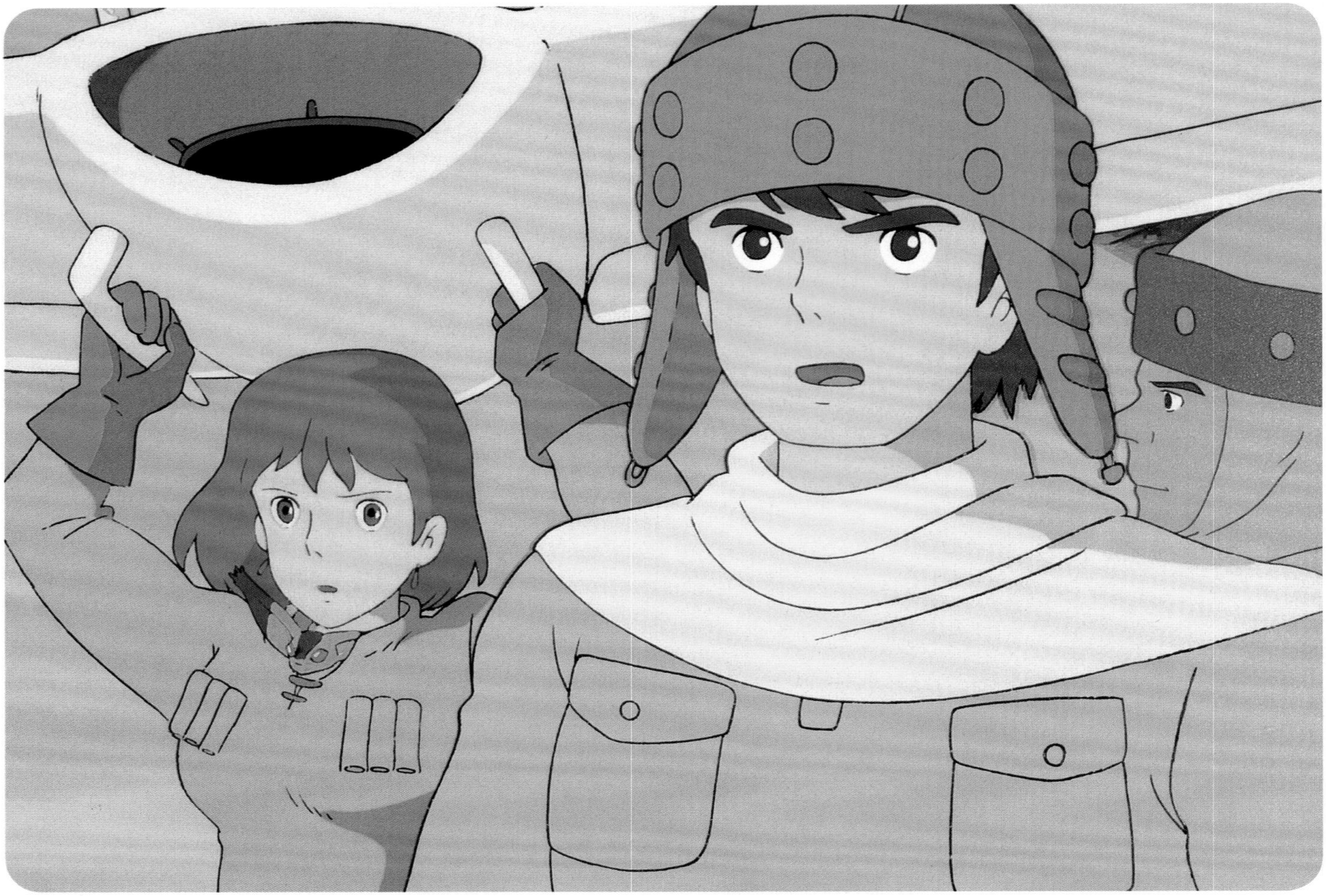

The mayor answered calmly. "Don't worry, we can rebuild it. And if the jungle spreads here, we'll burn it off. We've already made plans to get the Giant Warrior back from the Valley of the Wind. We're sending the insects to destroy the Tolmekians, just as they destroyed them here."

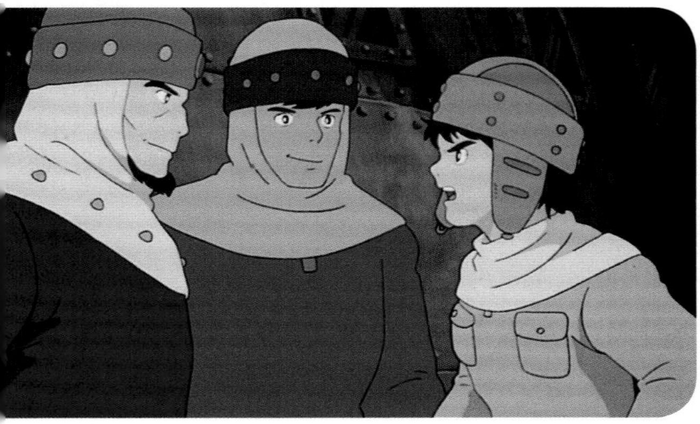

"You sent the insects to destroy your own city?" Asbel was outraged.

Nausicaä stepped forward. "What are you going to do to my valley?"

The mayor stared at her with wonder. "Asbel, who is this?"

Asbel hesitated, then said, "She's the princess of the Valley of the Wind. She saved my life."

The mayor gazed at Nausicaä for a few moments in silence before he spoke. "We have to get the Giant Warrior away from the Tolmekians, no matter what it takes. It's for the good of the planet."

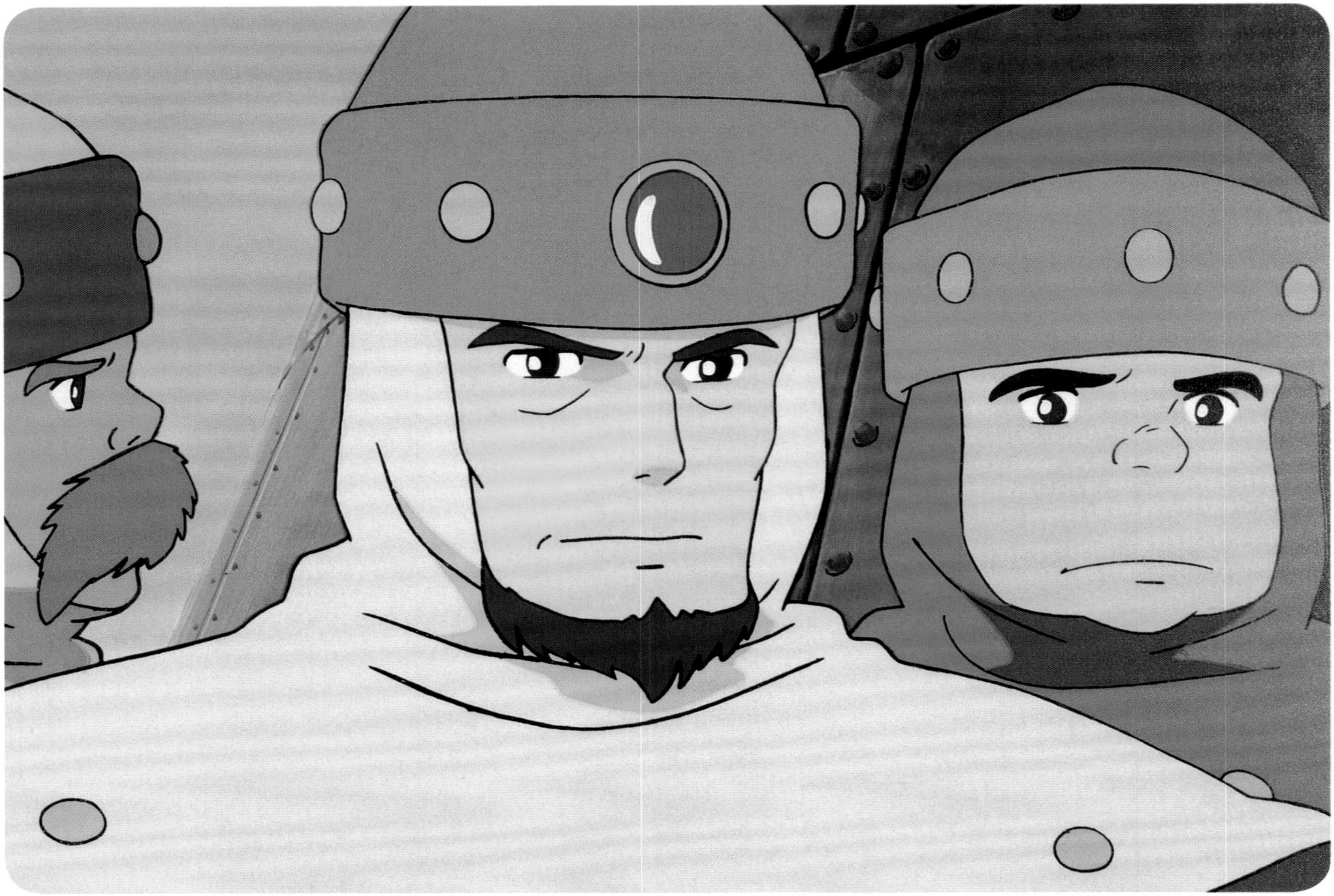

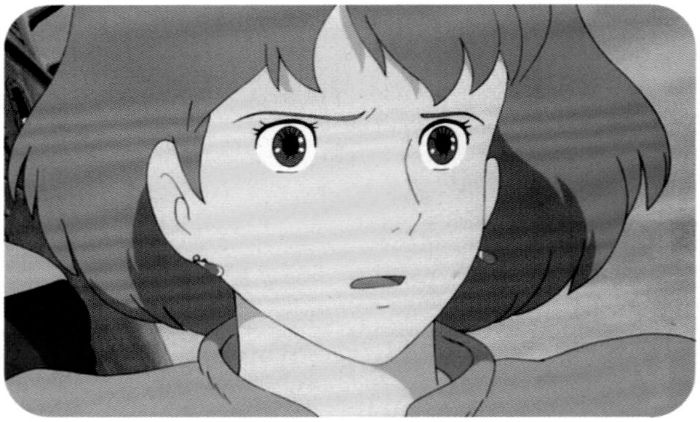

"The good of the planet?" Nausicaä couldn't believe it. "You're killing my people! Stop, I beg you—stop this now!"

"It's too late. The insects can't be stopped."

Nausicaä jumped on her wind rider. She was going to warn the people of the valley, but the Pejites grabbed her and pinned her down before she could take off.

"Once we have the warrior, we'll burn the jungle and take back the earth," the mayor said.

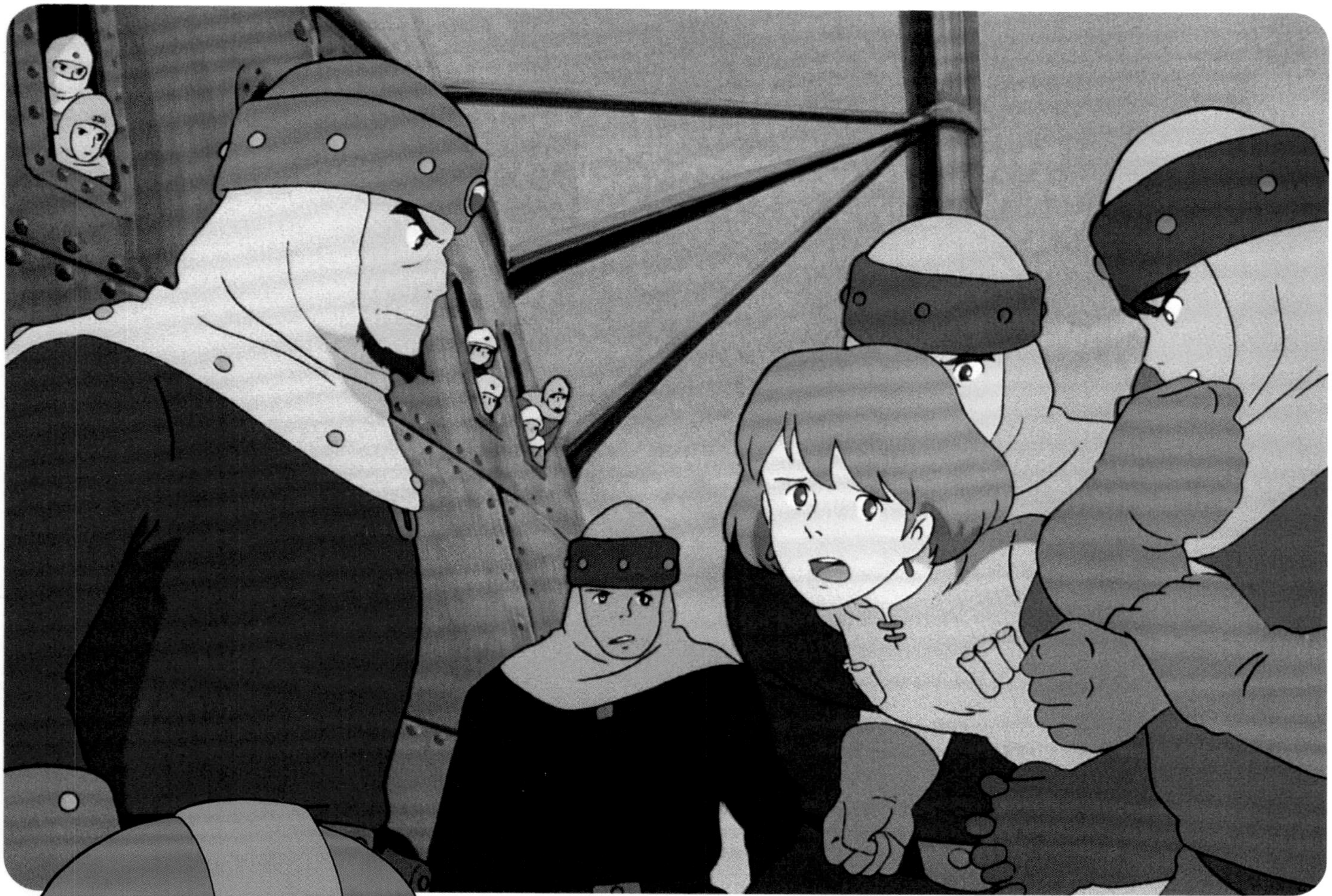

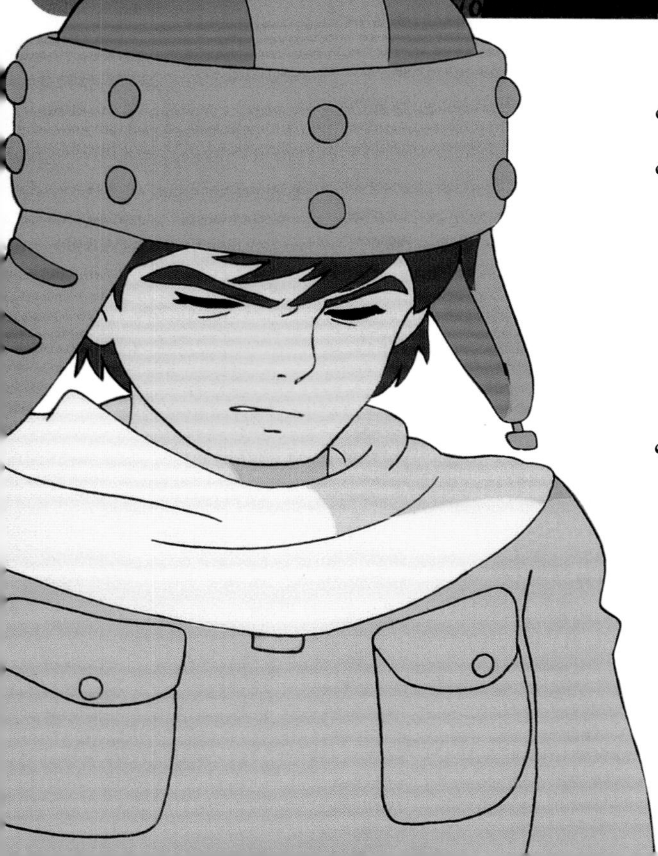

"No!" Nausicaä struggled to get free. "We all rely on water from the wells. But do you know why that water is pure? Because the trees of the wasteland purify it. You can't burn them down!

"Asbel, tell them how the jungle evolved—how the insects are guarding it so we won't pollute the world again. Asbel, please!"

Asbel listened with downcast eyes. When Nausicaä was finished, his expression hardened. Suddenly he rushed the mayor and grabbed his pistol.

"Don't move!" he yelled. "Let go of the princess, now!"

But a Pejite soldier crept up behind him and knocked him senseless with a blow to the head.

Asbel collapsed in a heap.

"No! Let me go!" Nausicaä struggled desperately to break free, but the soldiers dragged her aboard the Brig.

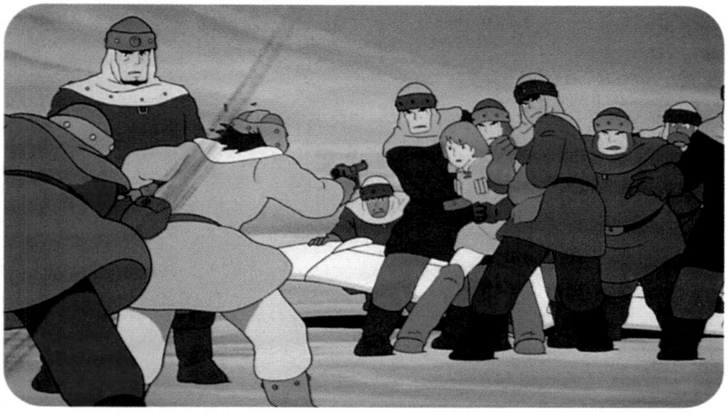

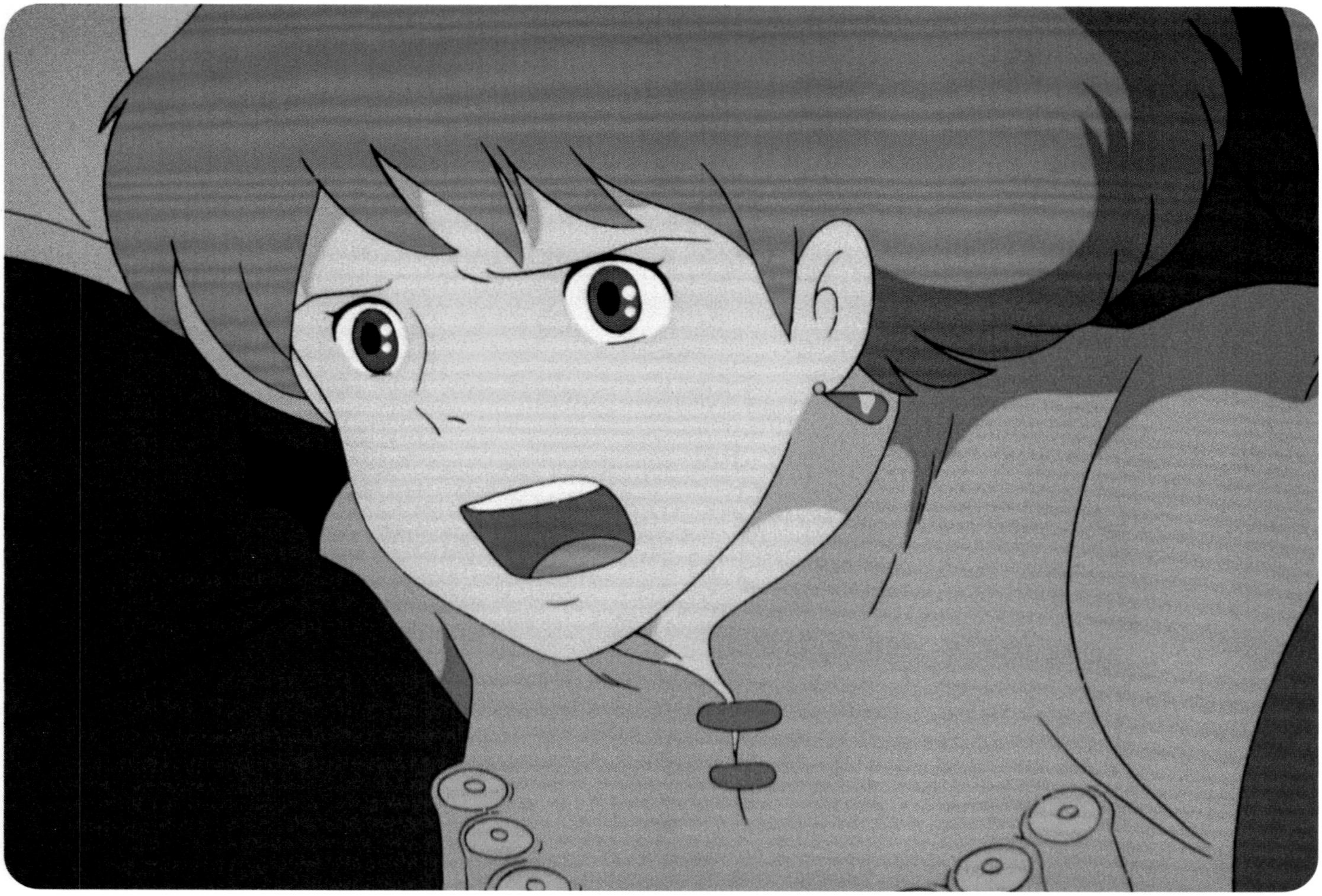

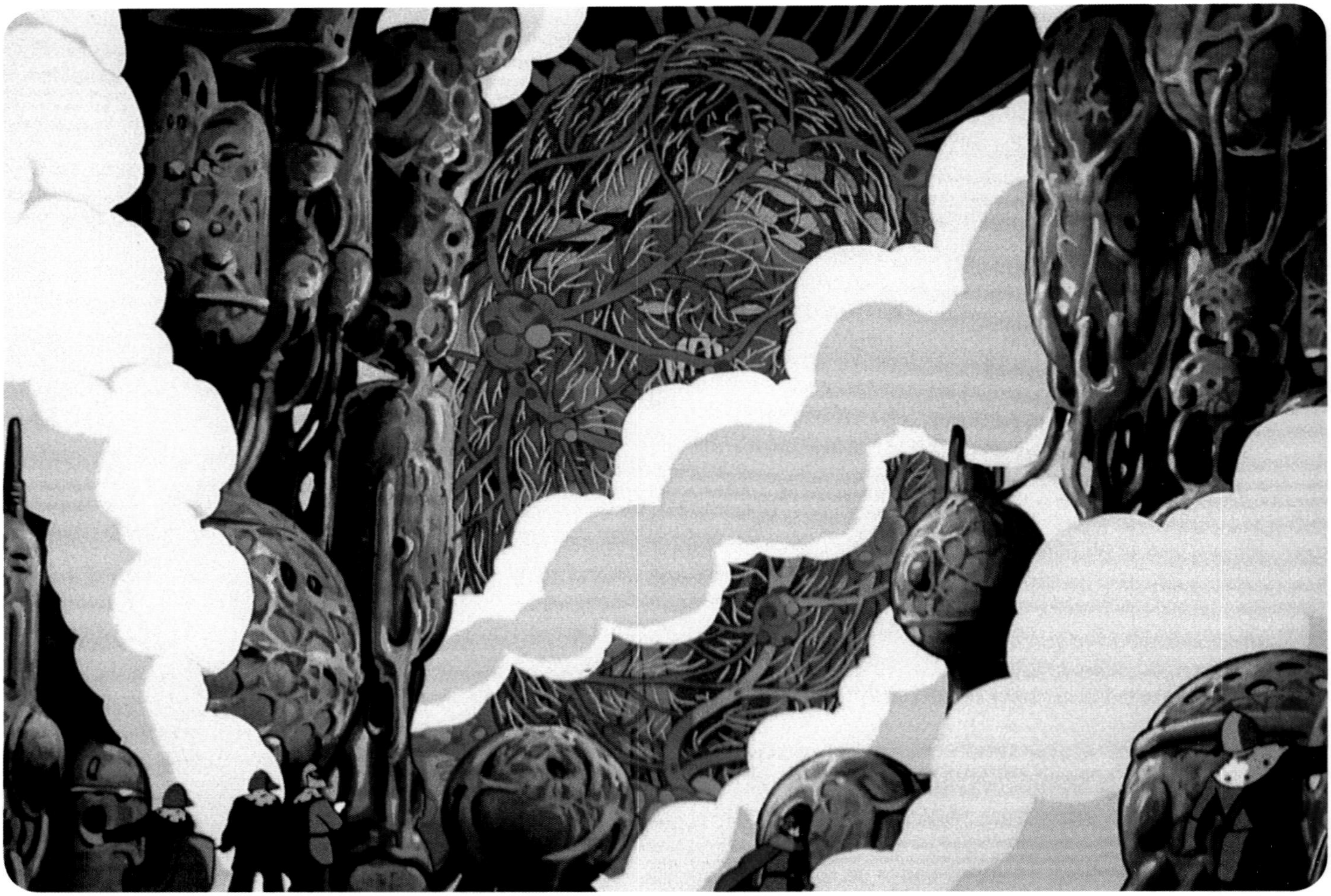

THE GIANT WARRIOR AWAKENS

The Tolmekians in the valley were working hard to awaken the Giant Warrior.

The beating of its enormous heart reverberated throughout the castle. Behind a web of pulsing veins and arteries, a terrifying creature was taking shape.

"I swear—the more I gaze at you, the more attractive you get," Kurotowa said with a smile.

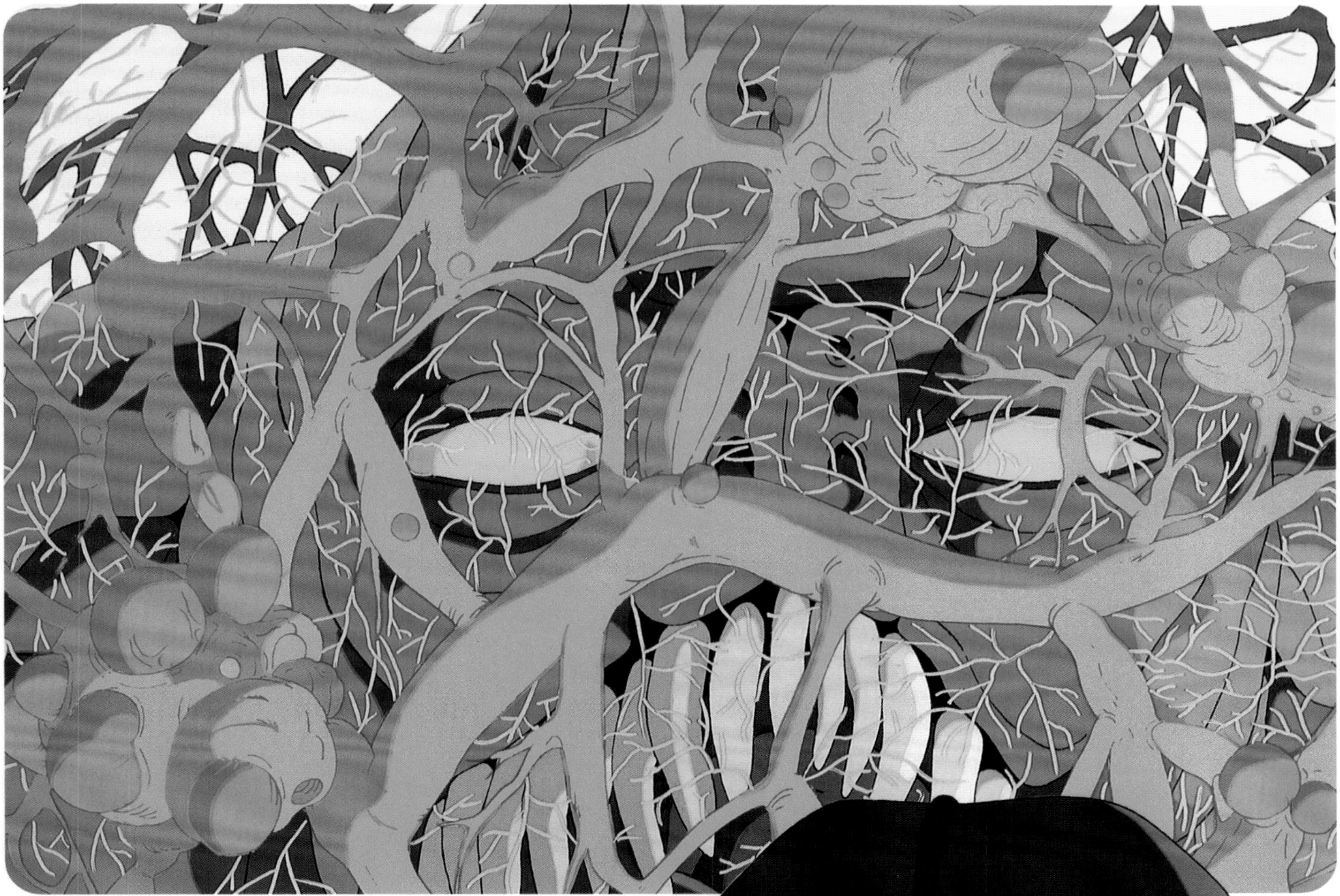

The Giant Warrior smiled back, as if it had understood.

“Ugh! Maybe you should remain buried deep beneath the earth after all.”

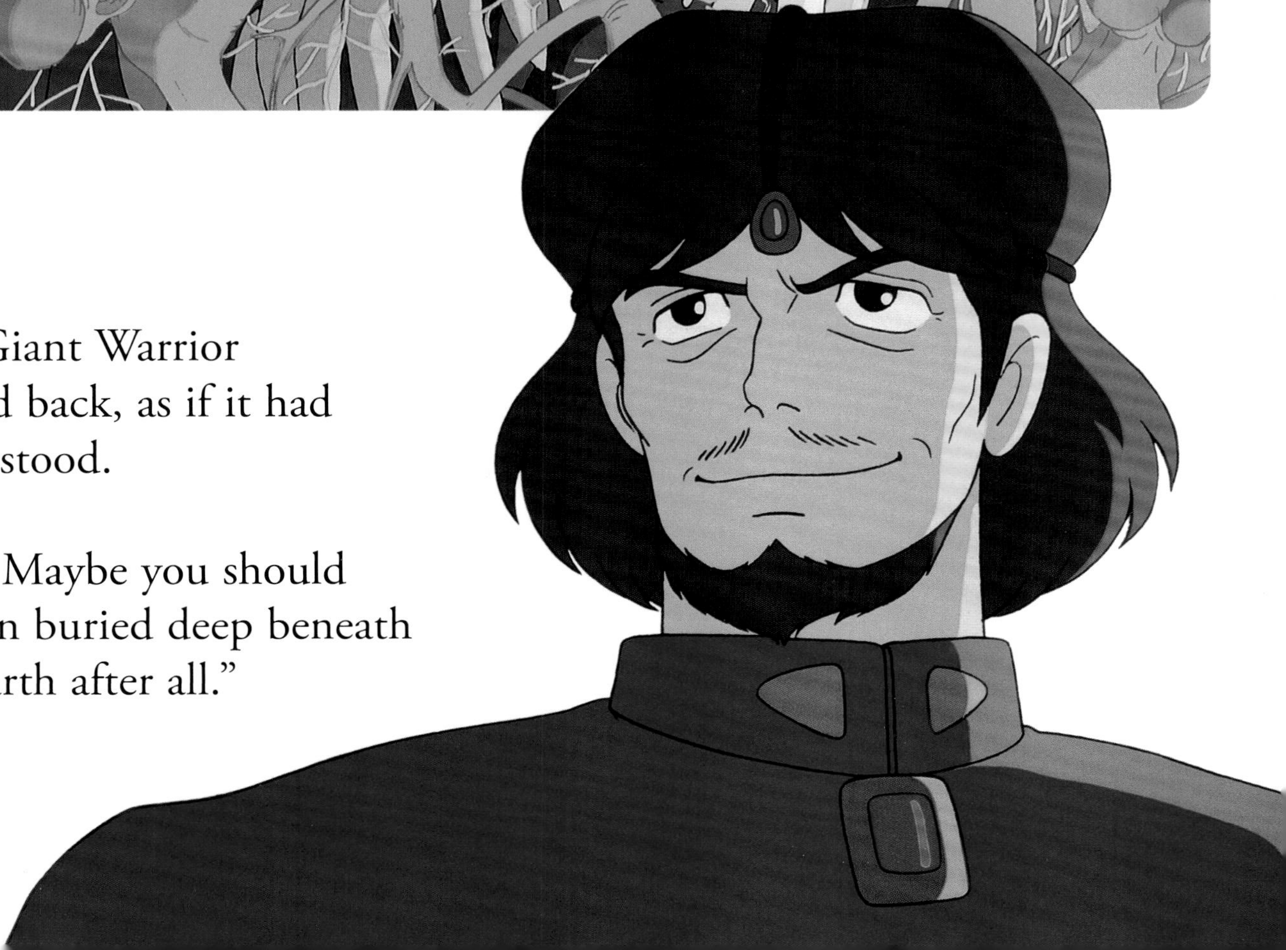

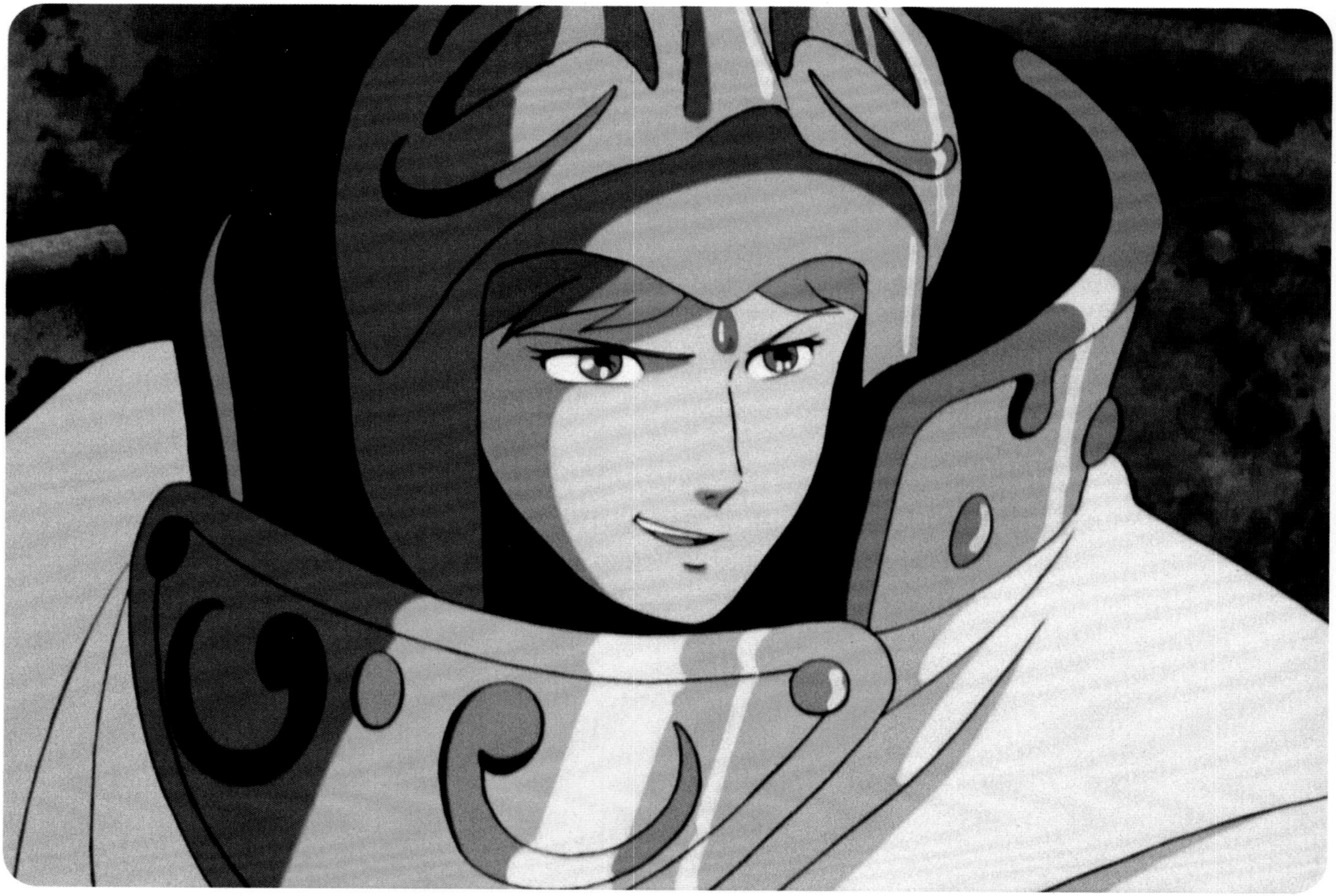

High above the valley was a lake of acid. The old men of the castle had escaped from the toxic jungle and were holding Kushana prisoner on the shore of the lake in an old, rusting airship.

The men brought Yupa to question Kushana about the Tolmekians' plans.

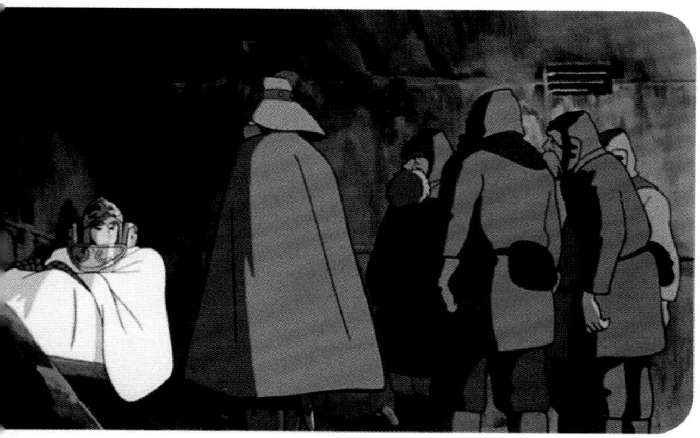

"We'll release you if you drown the Giant Warrior in Acid Lake and then return to your kingdom," Yupa said.

"It can't be destroyed," Kushana growled. "It's too late, there's no turning back. You must use the monster to destroy the jungle and reclaim this world for us humans!"

"The warrior must never awaken," Yupa said curtly.

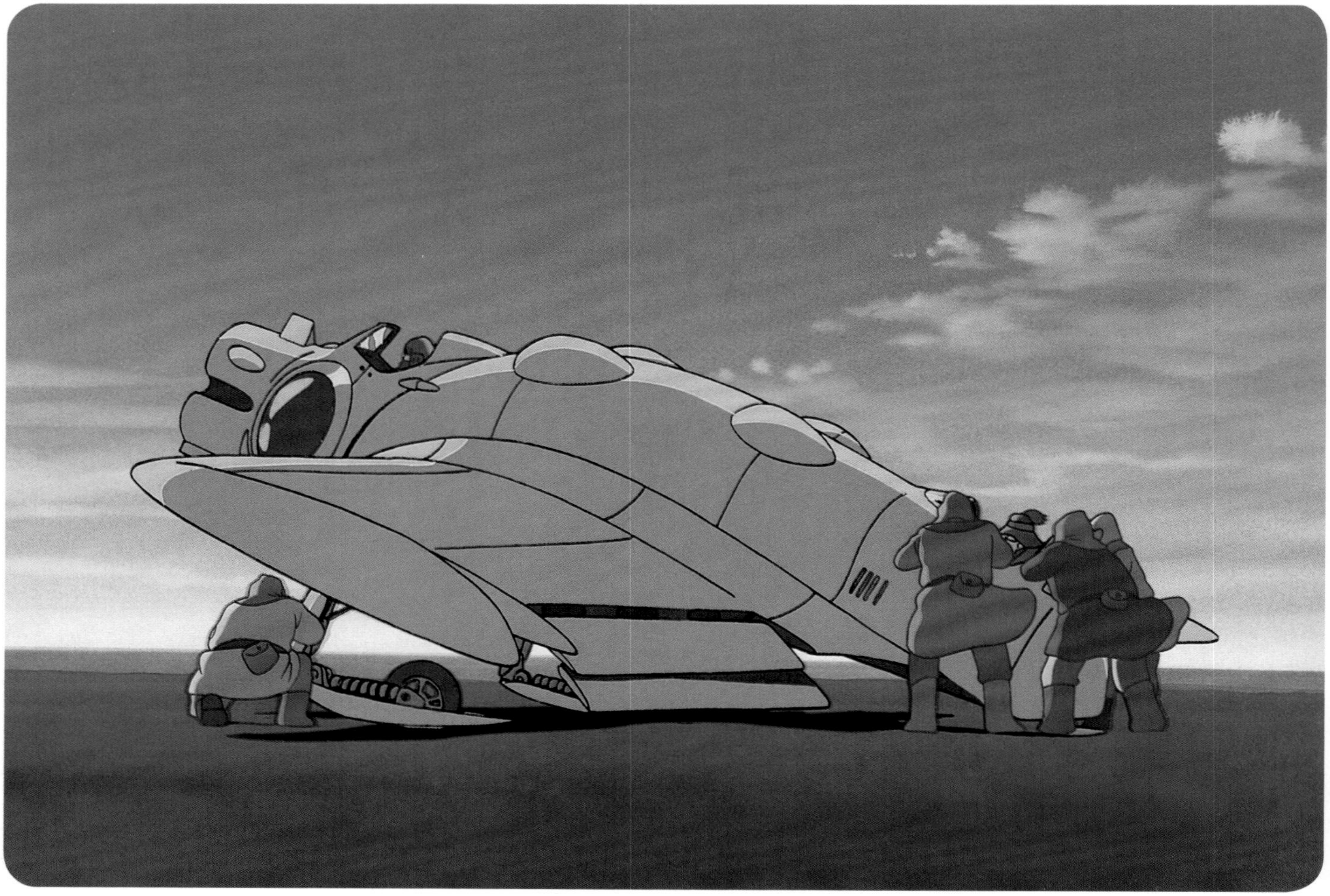

The next morning, Yupa and Mito readied the gunship to search for Nausicaä.

Just before they took off, Yupa told the other men of the castle, "Take care of the valley, and don't do anything rash while we're gone!'

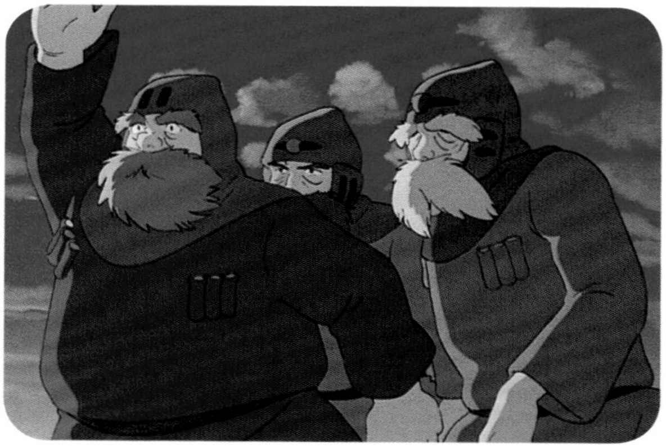

But when the men returned to the valley, they found the people gripped by panic.

Some of the deadly spores had been overlooked. Now the forest was completely infested with them.

The people of the valley hurried to burn off the spores, but it was too late. The toxin had spread to every tree. The spores made a hissing sound as they released their poison.

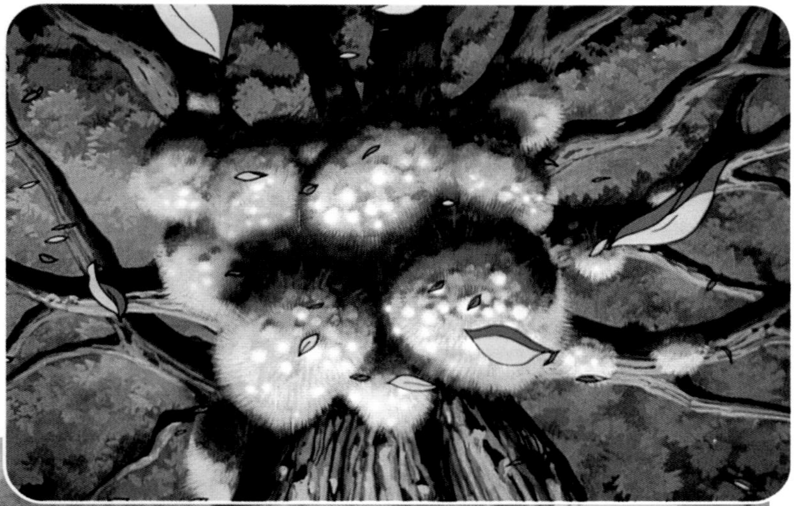

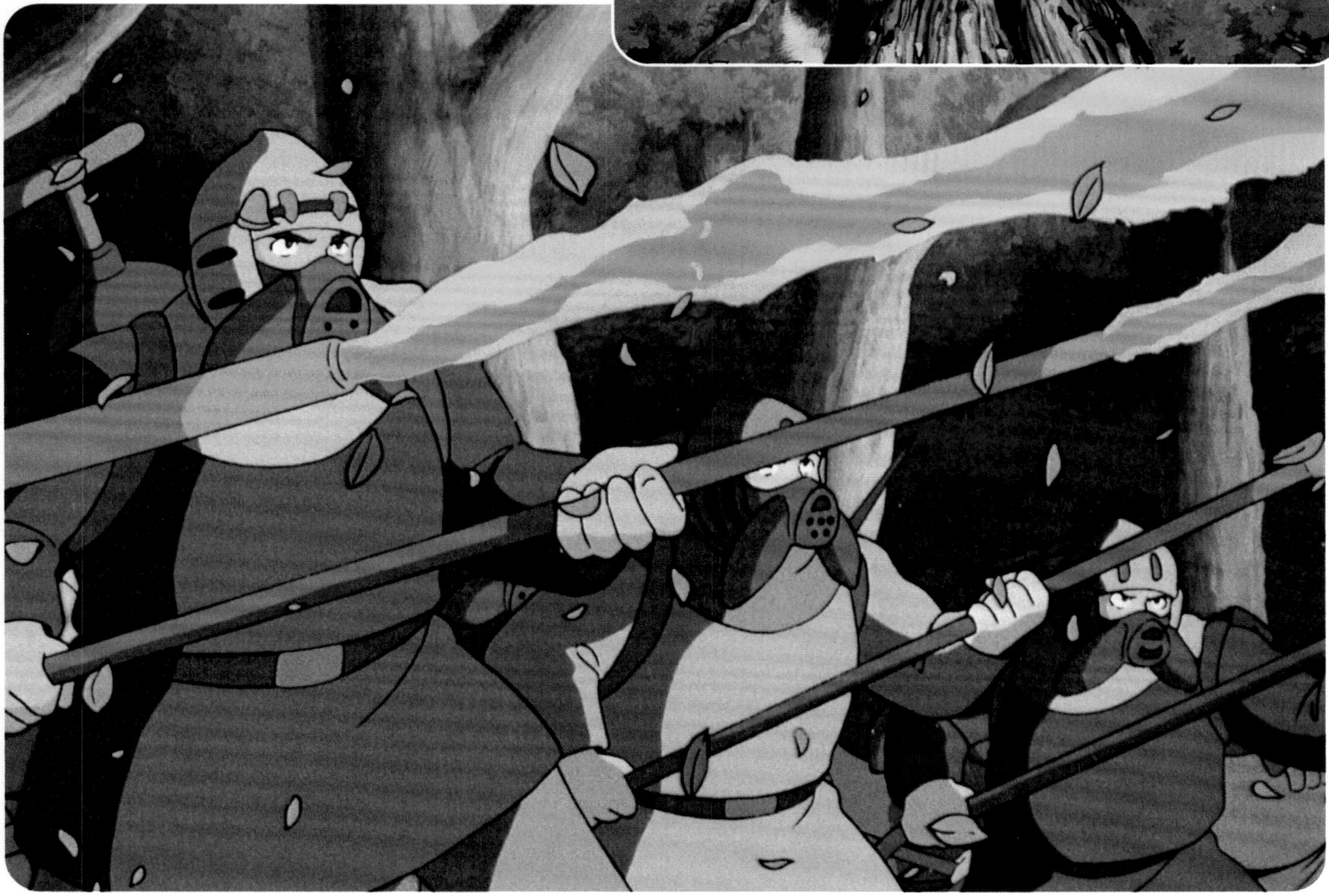

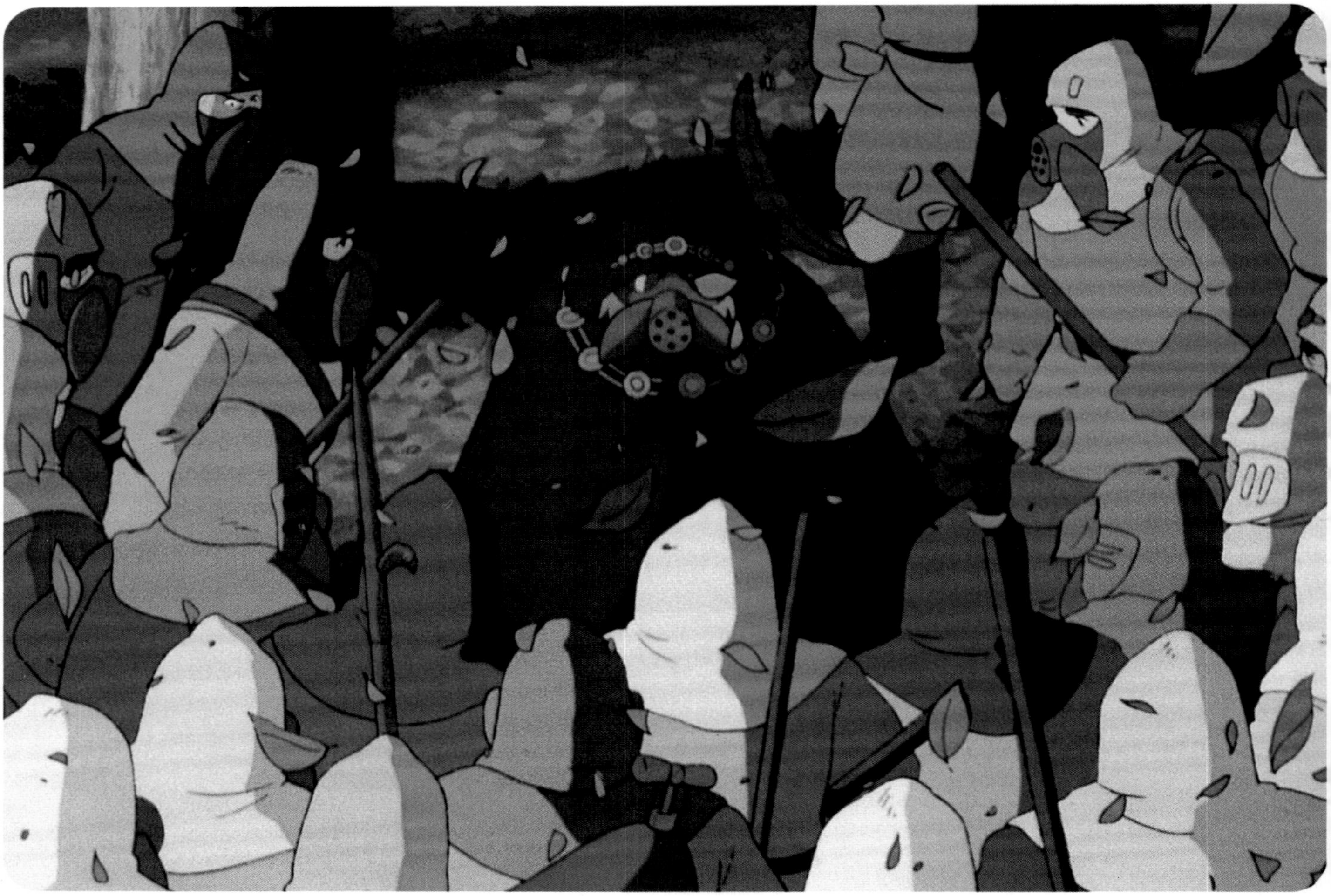

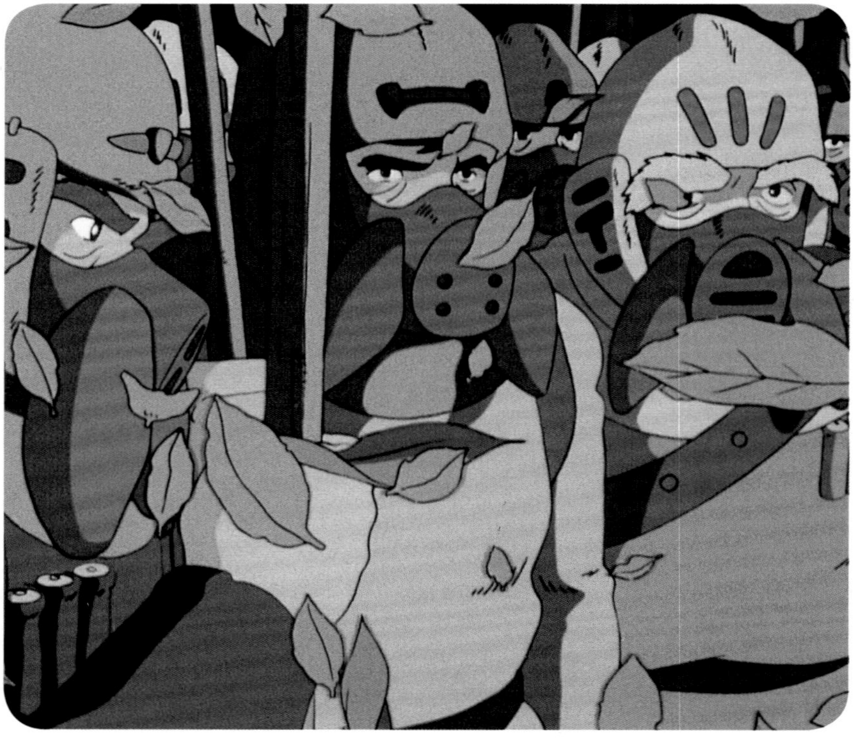

"This forest is doomed," Obaba said. "We must burn it down."

The villagers exchanged stricken looks.

"Isn't there some other way?"

But there was nothing they could do. If they left the forest alone, the Sea of Decay would take over. The people of the valley put every tree to the torch.

Having to burn their precious forest filled them with hate for the Tolmekians.

"Get them! It's all their fault!" they shouted as they attacked the Tolmekian soldiers with everything from farm tools to flamethrowers.

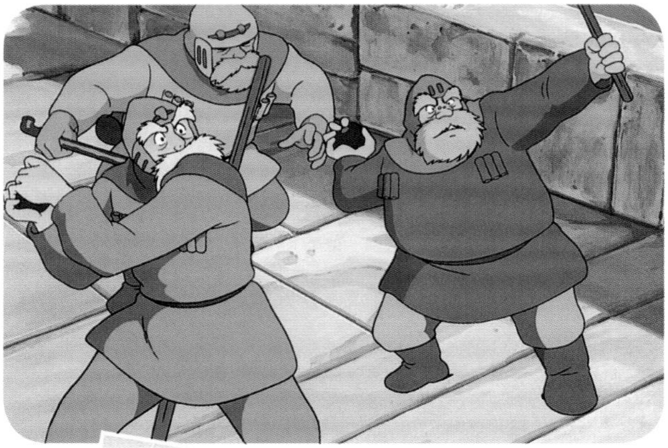

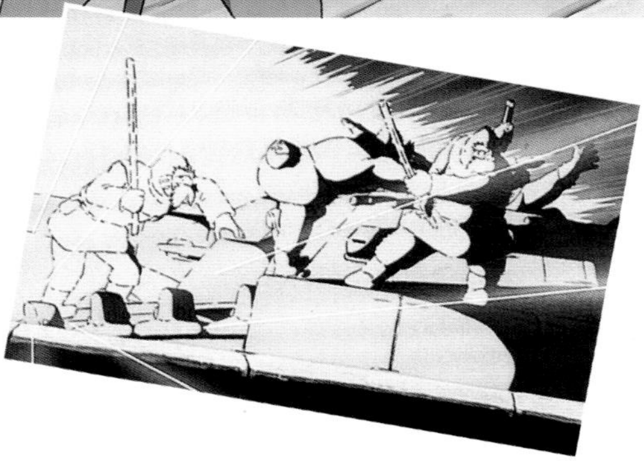

The Tolmekians fought back with their guns and tanks.

"We'd better do something!" said one of the old men. "This is getting out of hand."

The old men of the castle pressed the attack. They threw flash bombs to blind the enemy and stole one of their tanks.

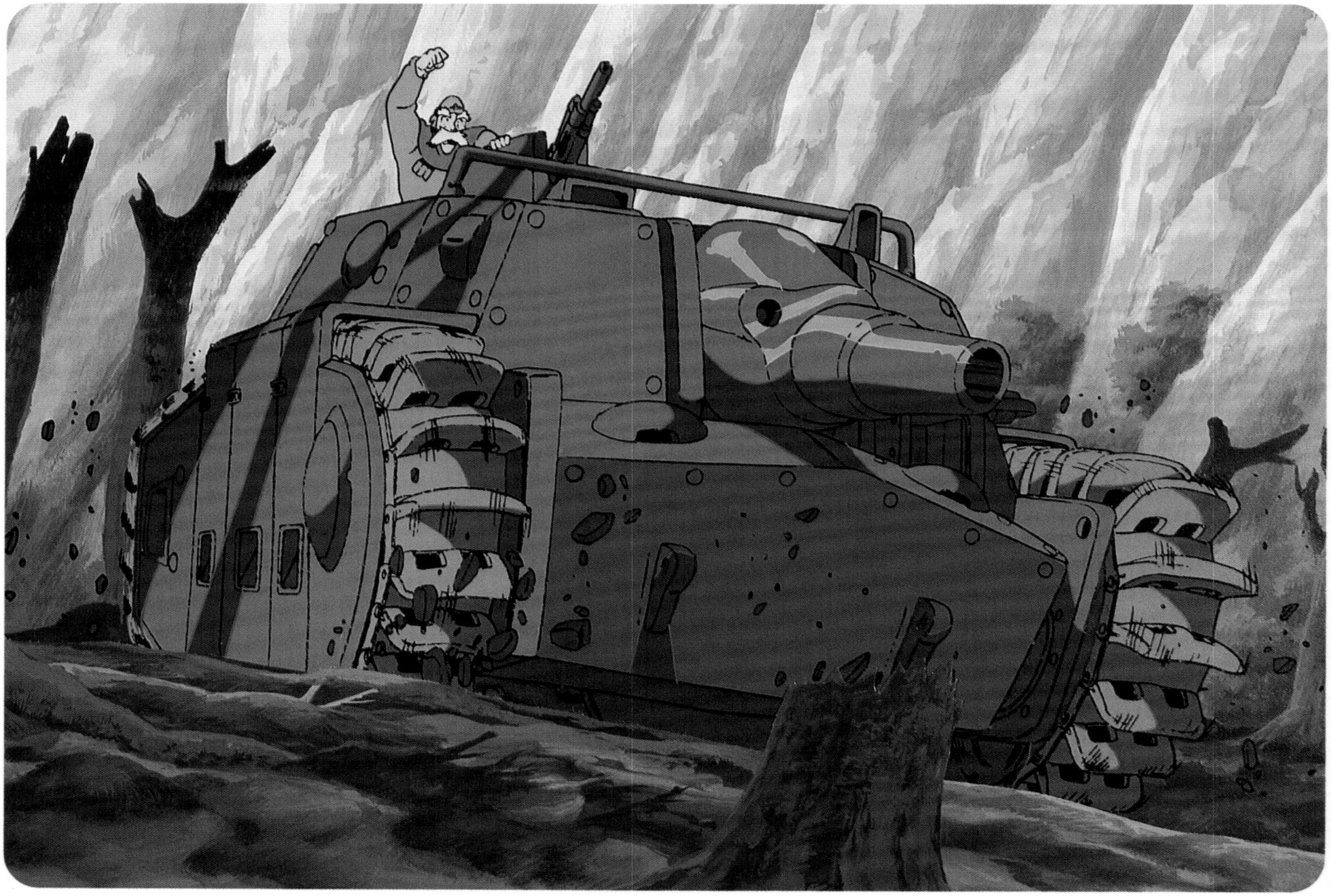

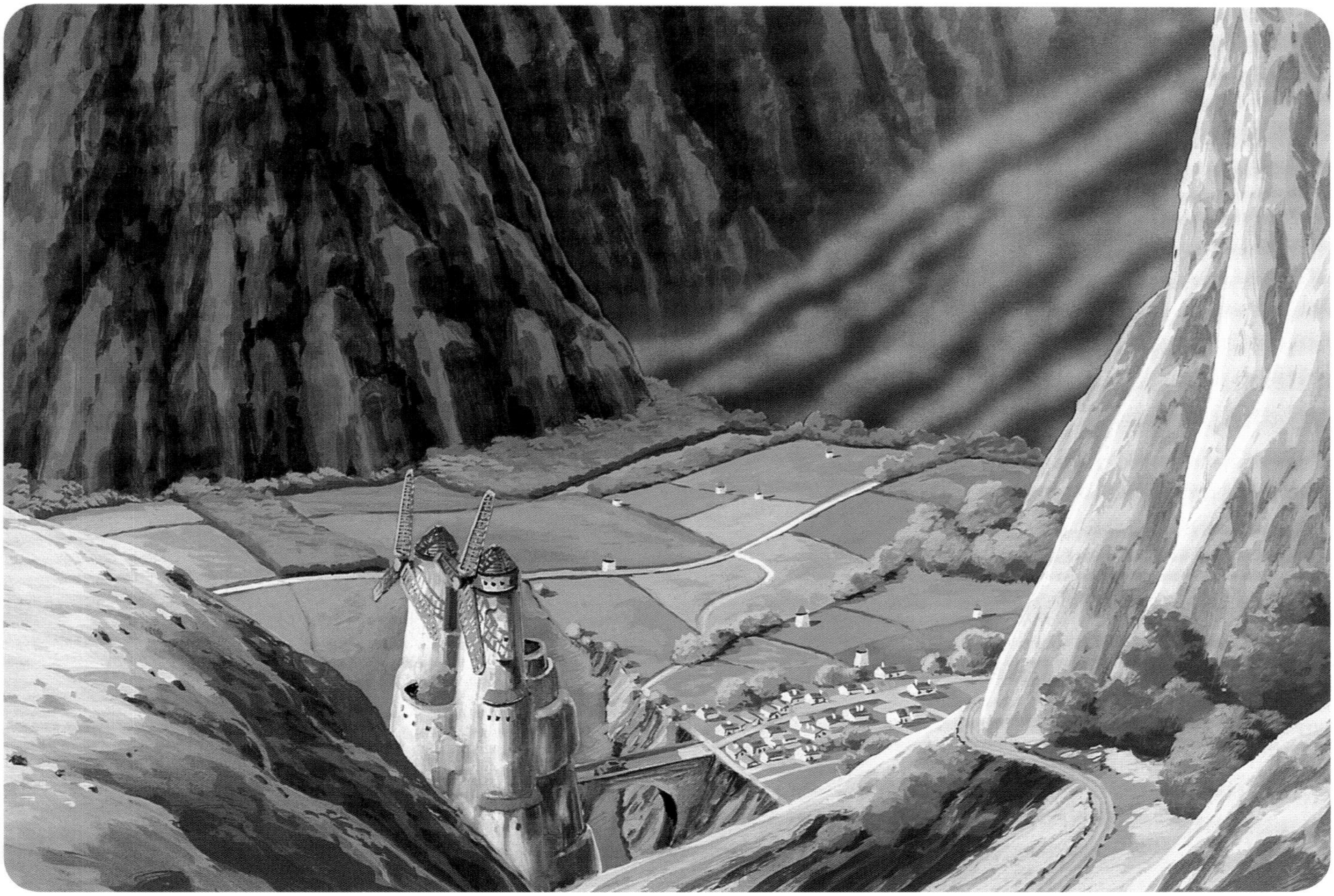

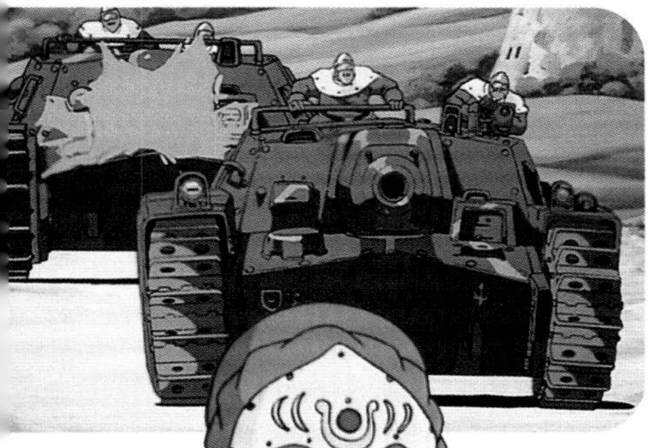

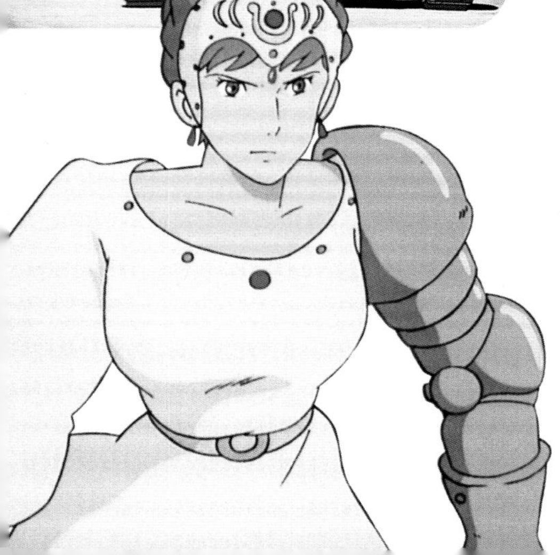

"We'll hold them off. Take everyone else and retreat to Acid Lake!"

Alone in the old airship, Kushana cut her bonds and made her way back to the valley. There she rallied her forces. The fighting between the people of the valley and the Tolmekians had turned into a war.

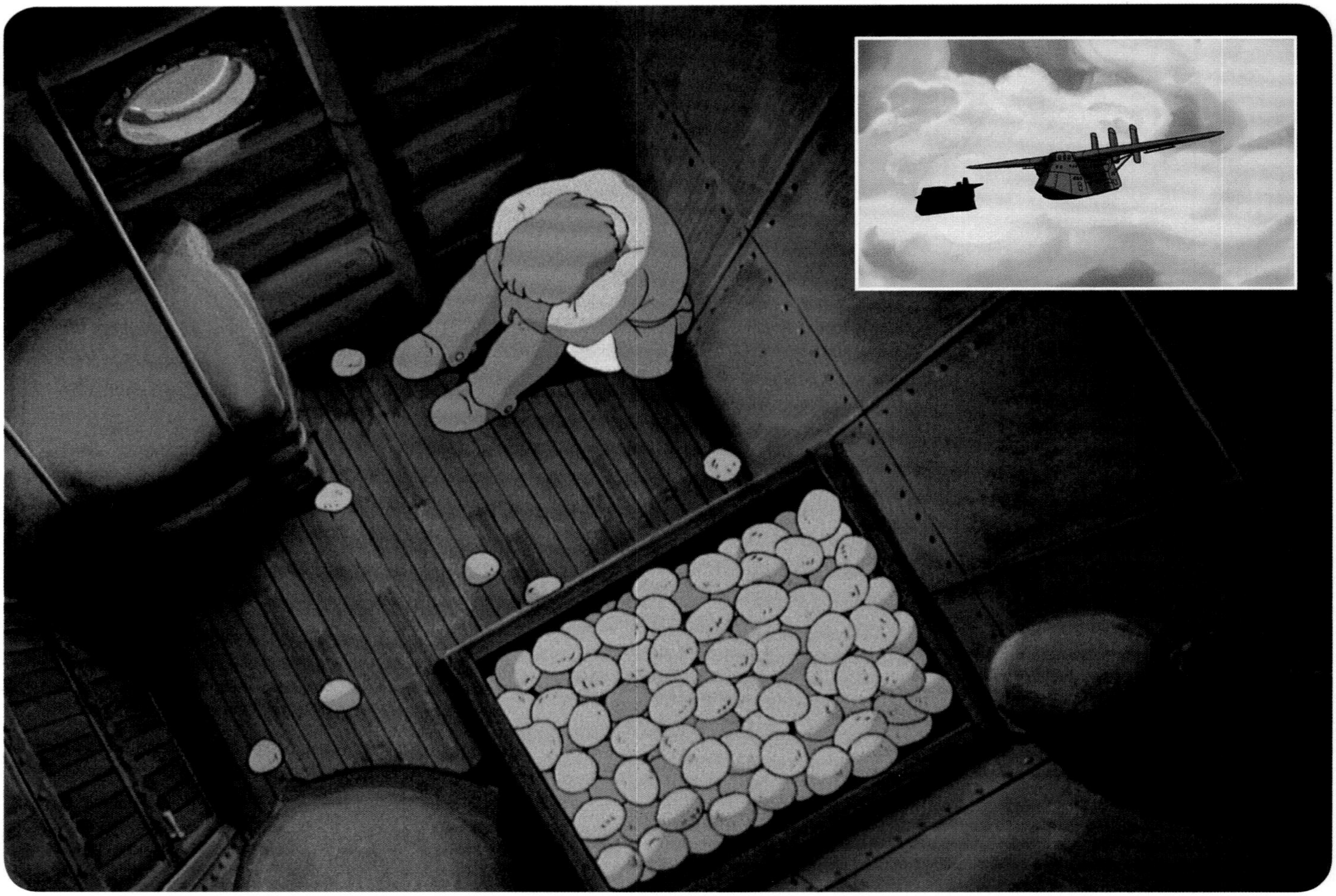

THE RAGE OF THE OHMS

The Pejite brig was flying toward its destination in the valley.

The soldiers had locked Nausicaä in a storage compartment. She sat slumped in a corner, worn out from crying.

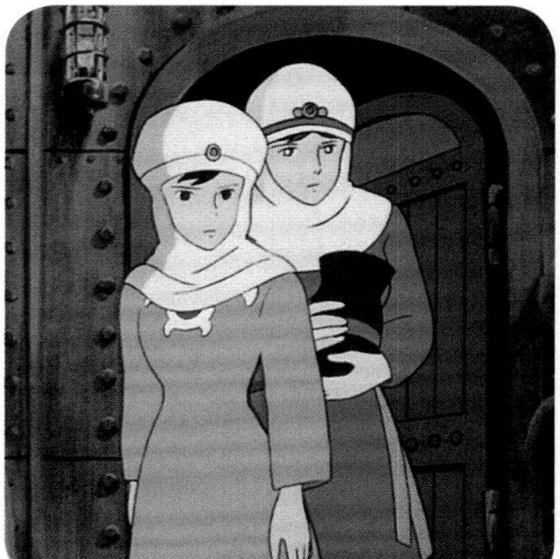

The door of the compartment opened and two women came in. One was Nausicaä's age.

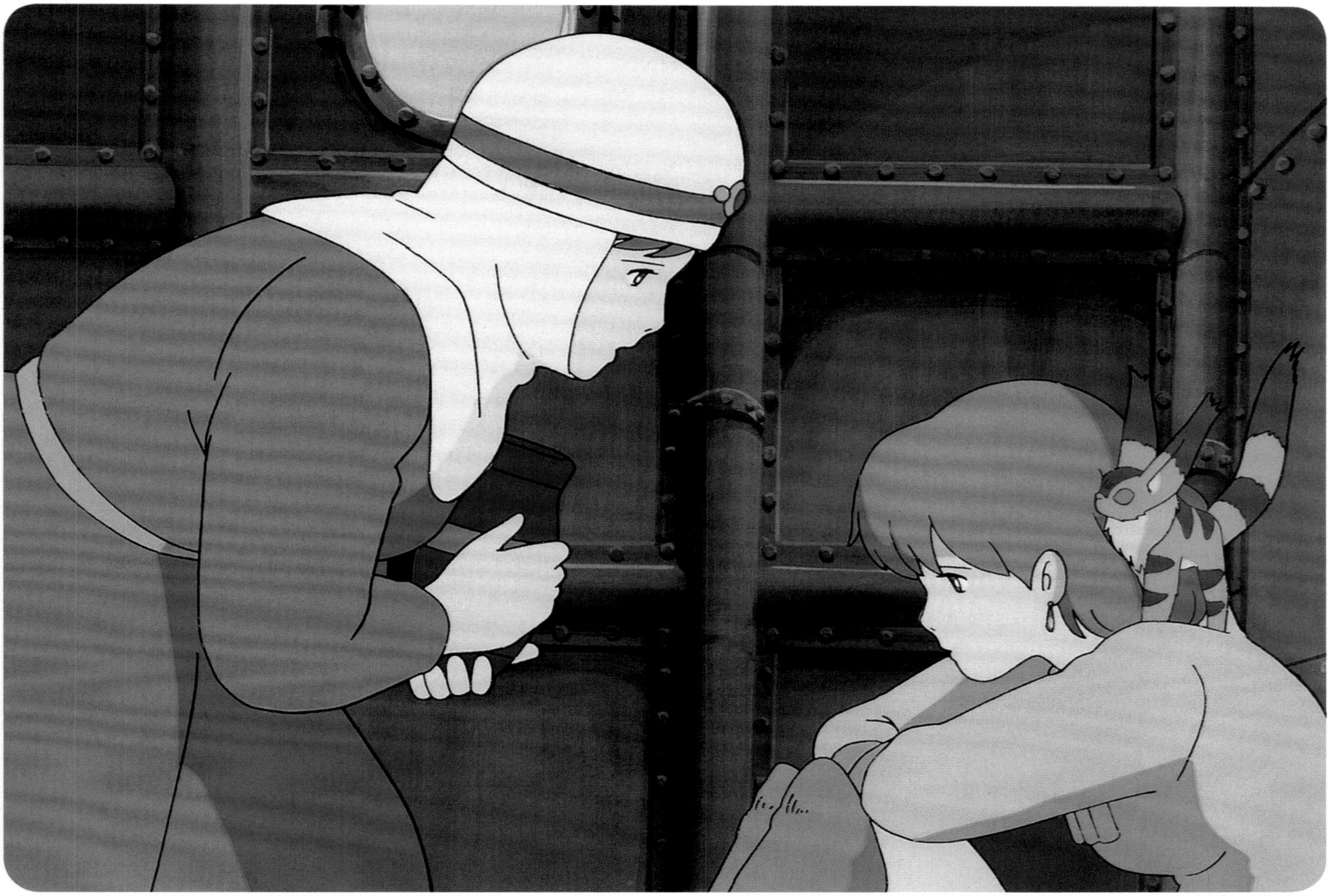

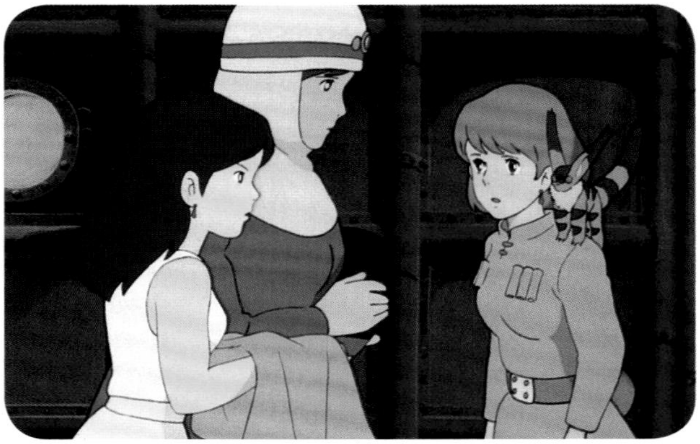

"We're going to get you out of here so you can warn the people of the valley." As the older woman whispered to Nausicaä, the girl took off her tunic. "I'll take your place, princess. Put this on."

"Asbel told us everything that happened," the woman said and gazed kindly at Nausicaä.

"But who are you?" Nausicaä asked in wonder.

"I'm Asbel and Lastel's mother."

Nausicaä's wonder changed to surprise. She had lost her own mother when she was a little girl. Now this woman seemed to be just as gentle and kind. It was almost as if Nausicaä's mother had returned.

"You're their mother?" Nausicaä threw herself into the woman's arms.

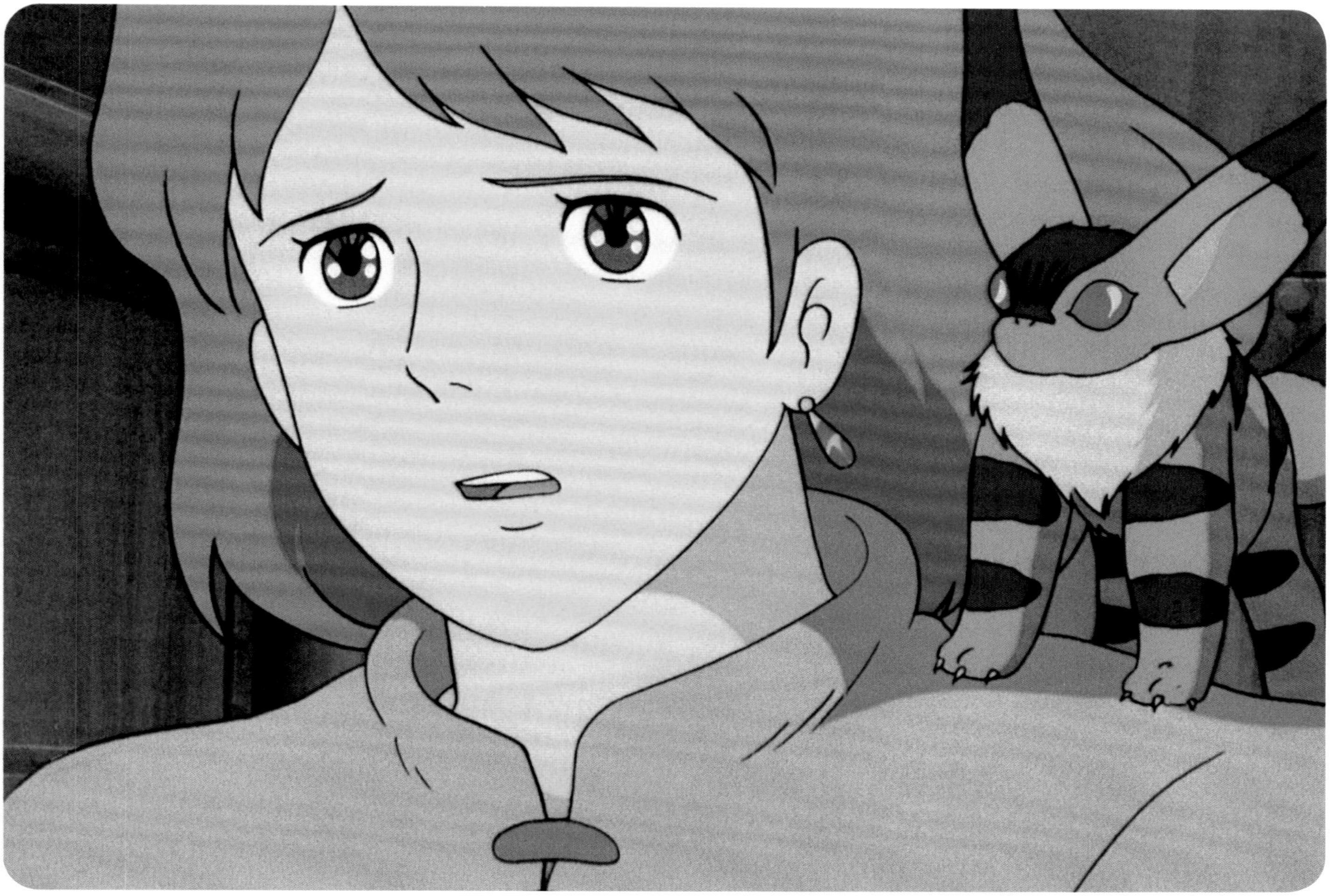

“Please forgive us,” the woman said as she held Nausicaä in her arms. “What our people did was horribly wrong.”

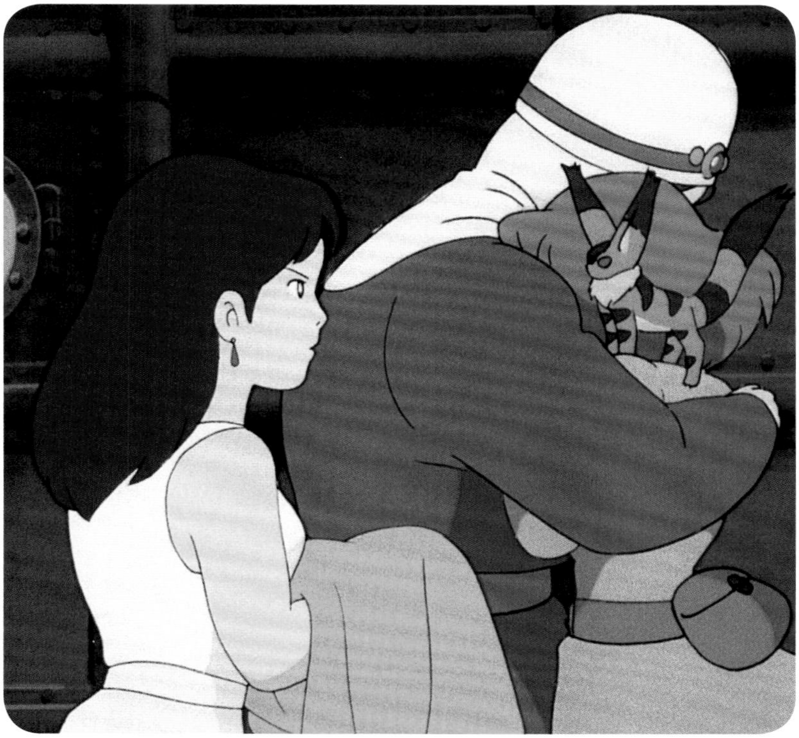

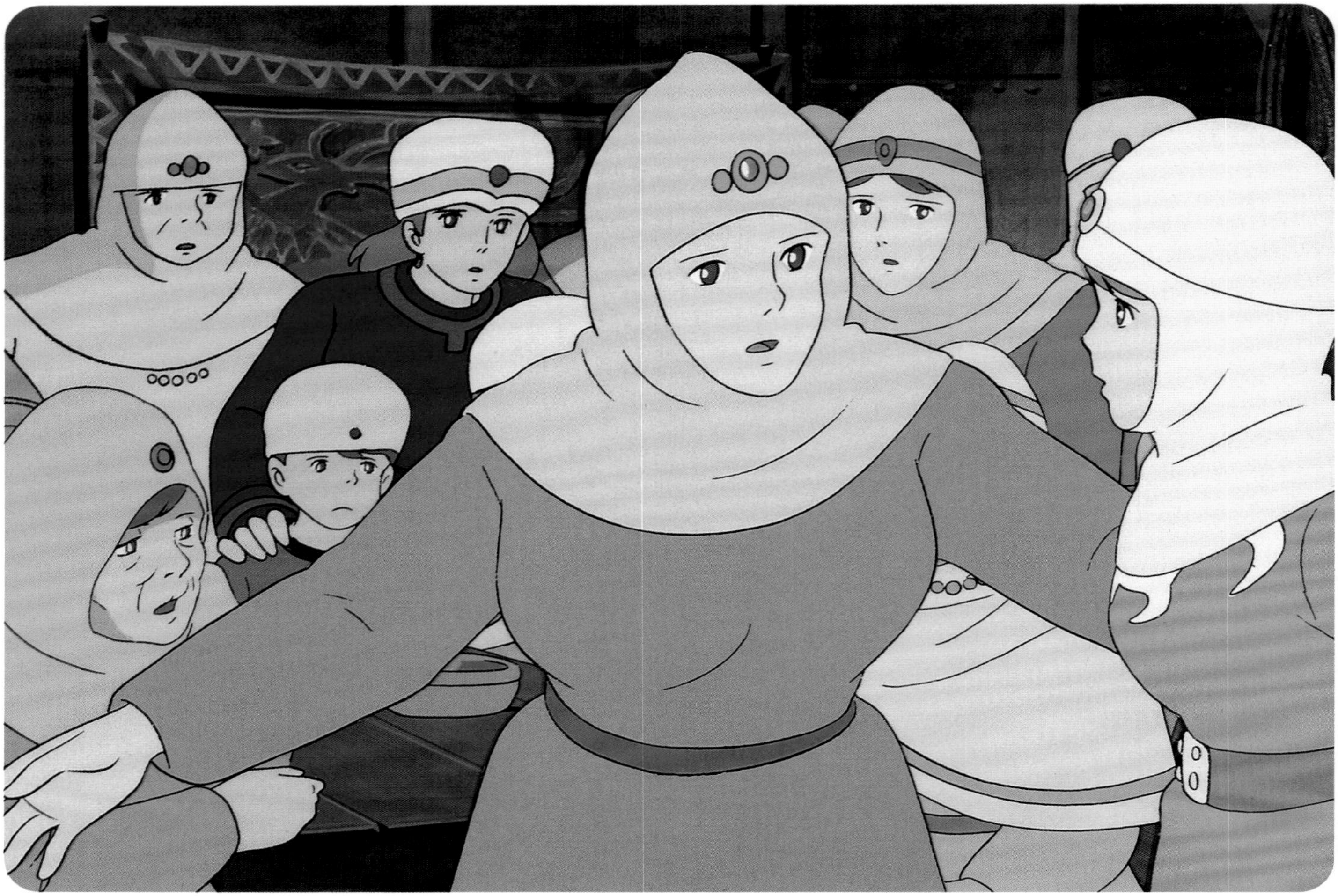

Nausicaä exchanged clothing with the girl, who stayed in the compartment while she and Lastelle's mother joined the other women and children.

"Please be careful. And forgive us for the way you've been treated."

Asbel was there too. He took Nausicaä to the cargo bay where her wind rider was waiting.

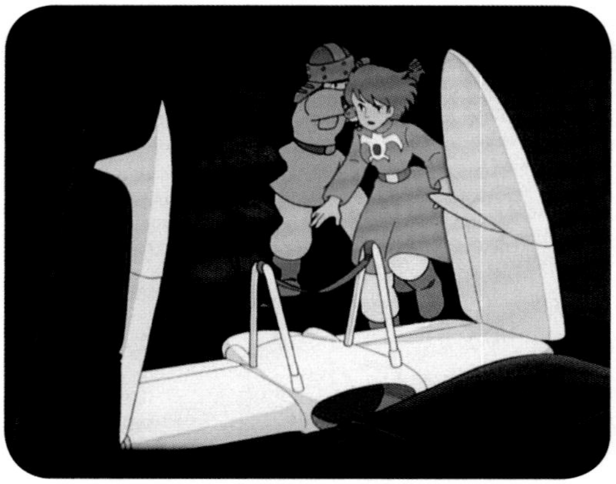

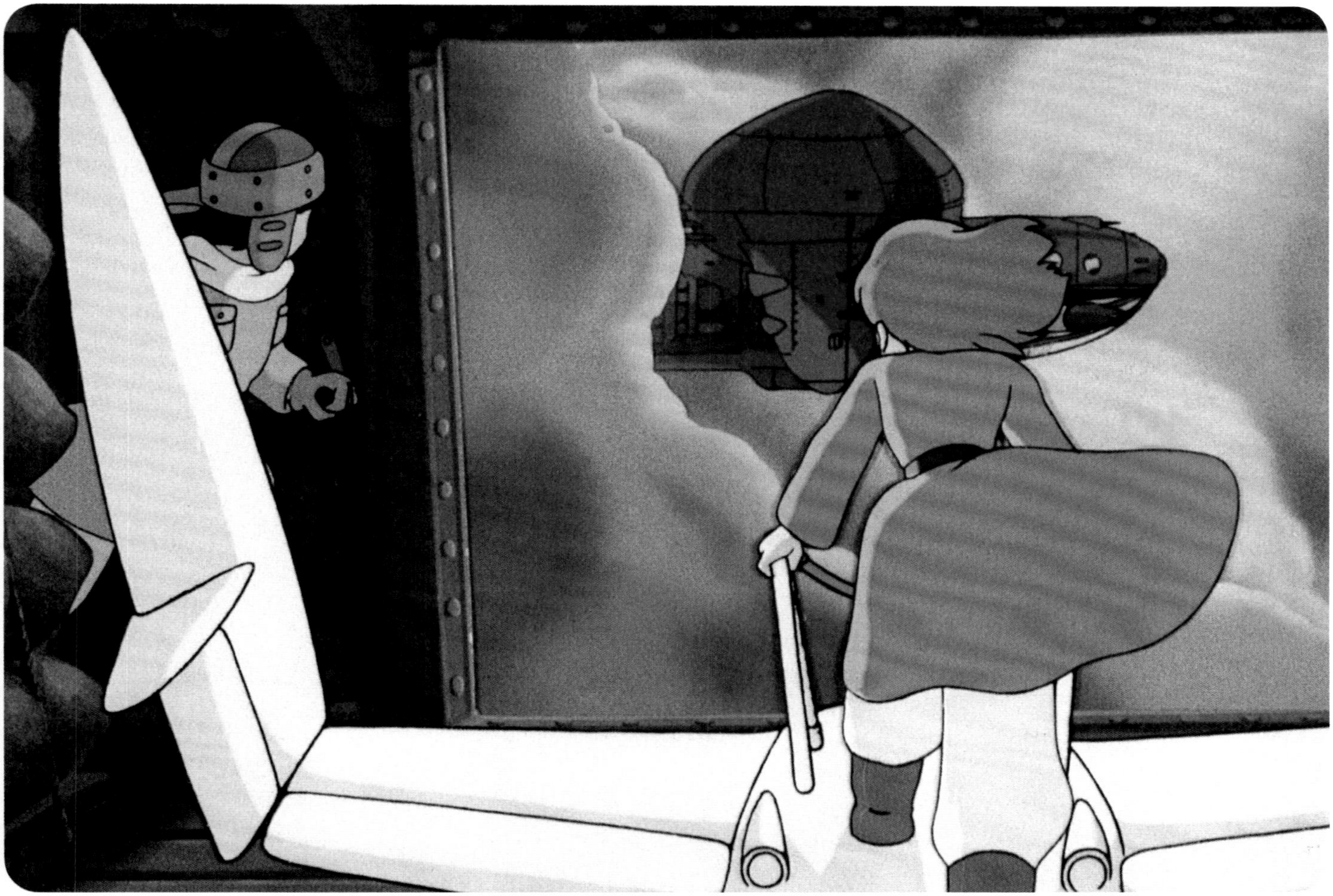

Asbel opened the cargo bay doors. "Can you launch from here?"

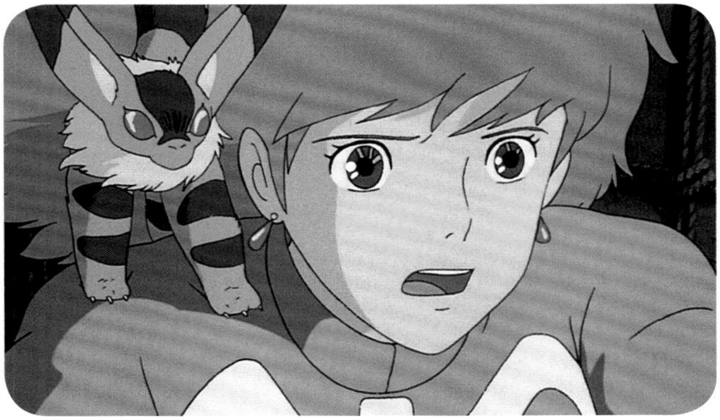

"I'll try!" Nausicaä jumped on the wind rider and was about to take off.

But a gunship emerged from behind a cloud and started shooting at her!

"The Tolmekians!" she shouted.

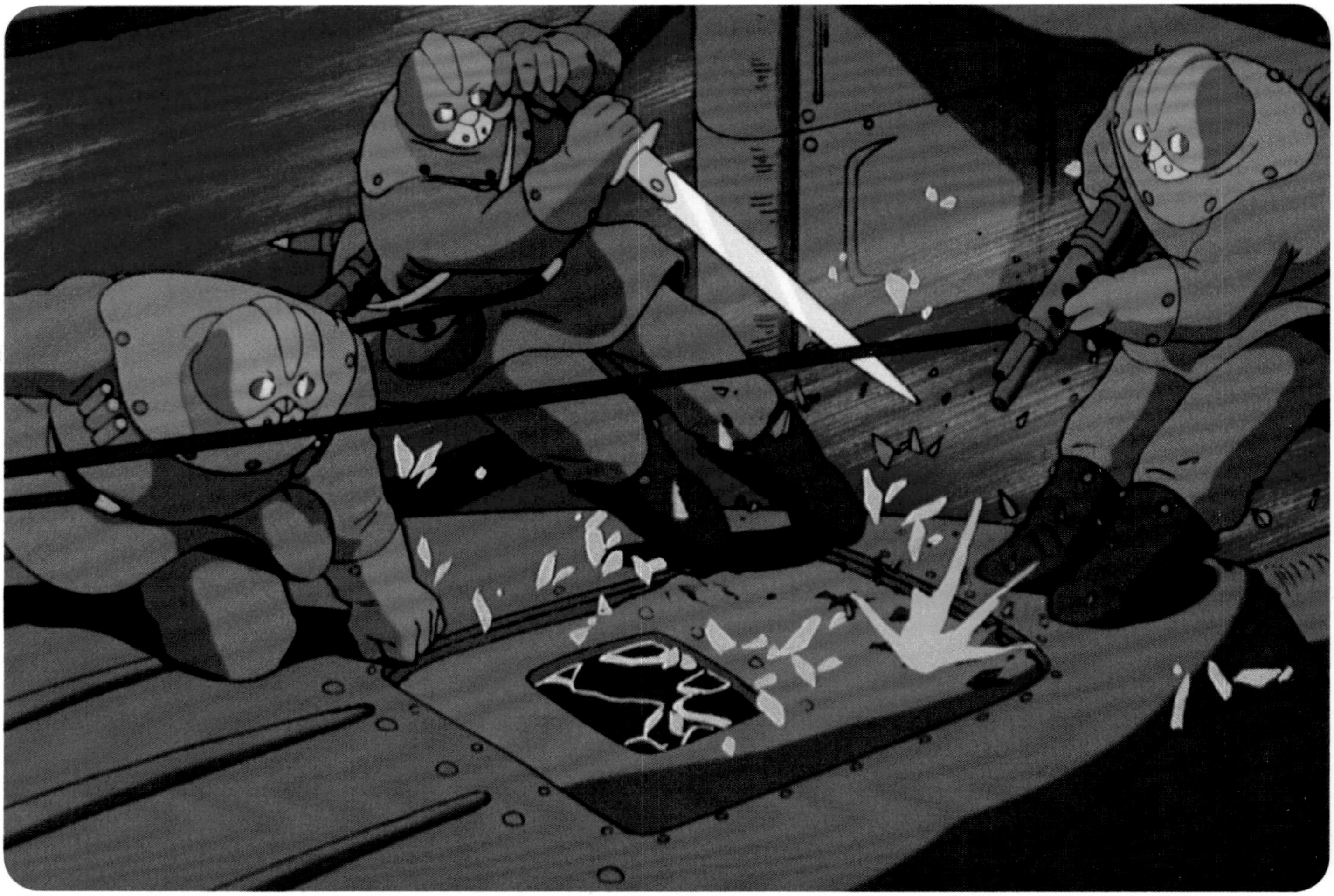

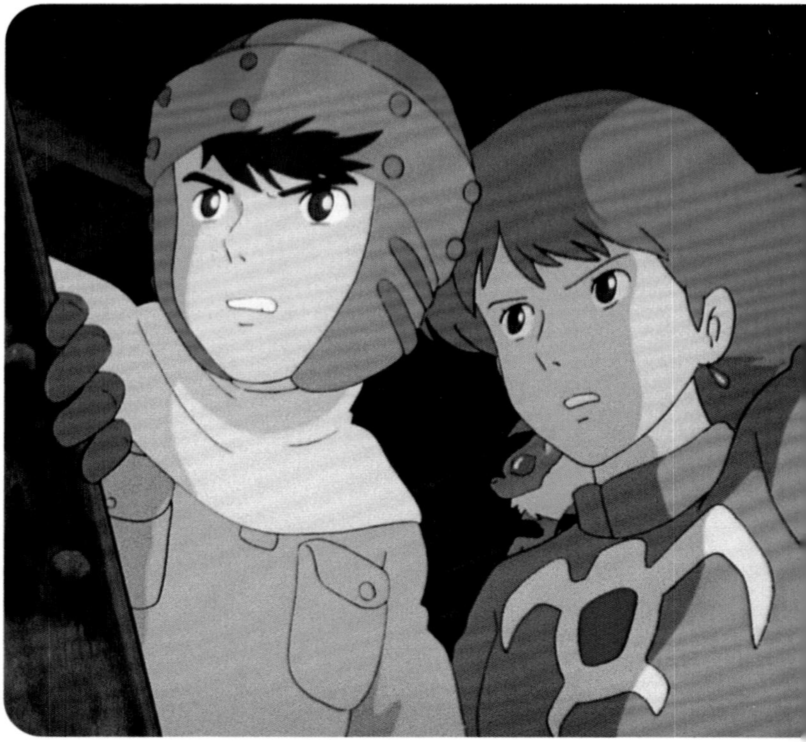

The Tolmekian gunship flew close to the Pejite Brig. Soldiers swarmed from the gunship and used ropes to board the Brig.

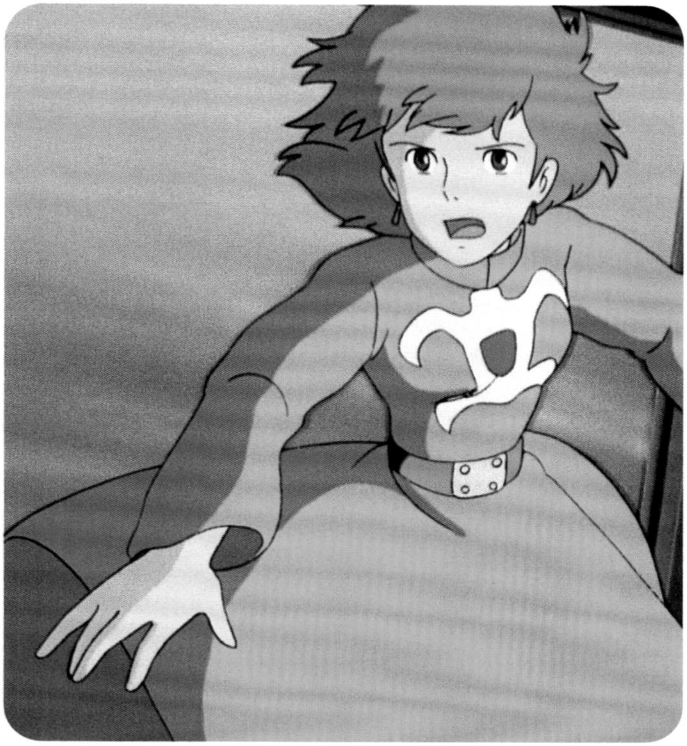

"They're coming," Asbel shouted. "You've got to get out of here now!"

"I can't just leave you and your mother like this," Nausicaä said. "You need all the help you can get."

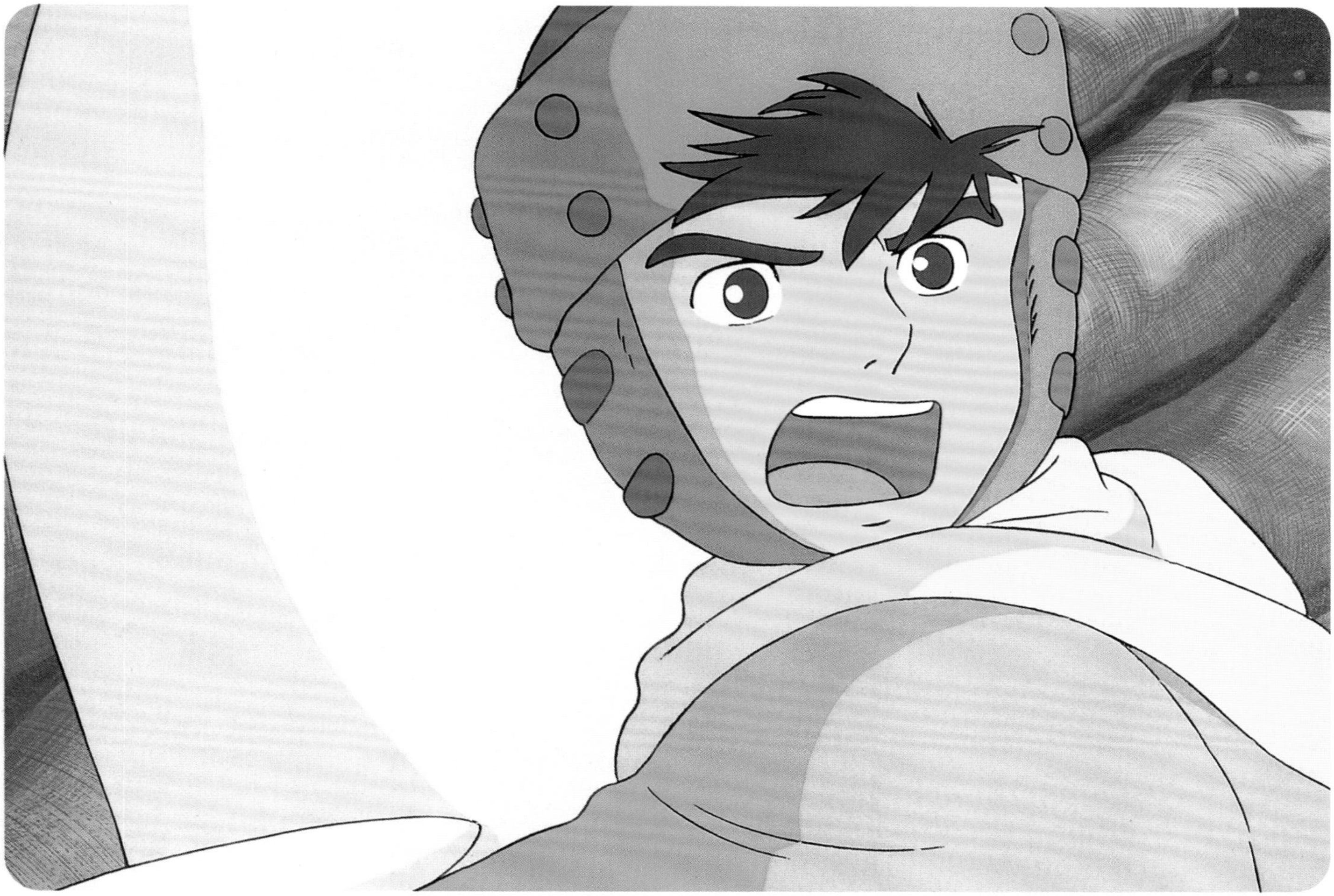

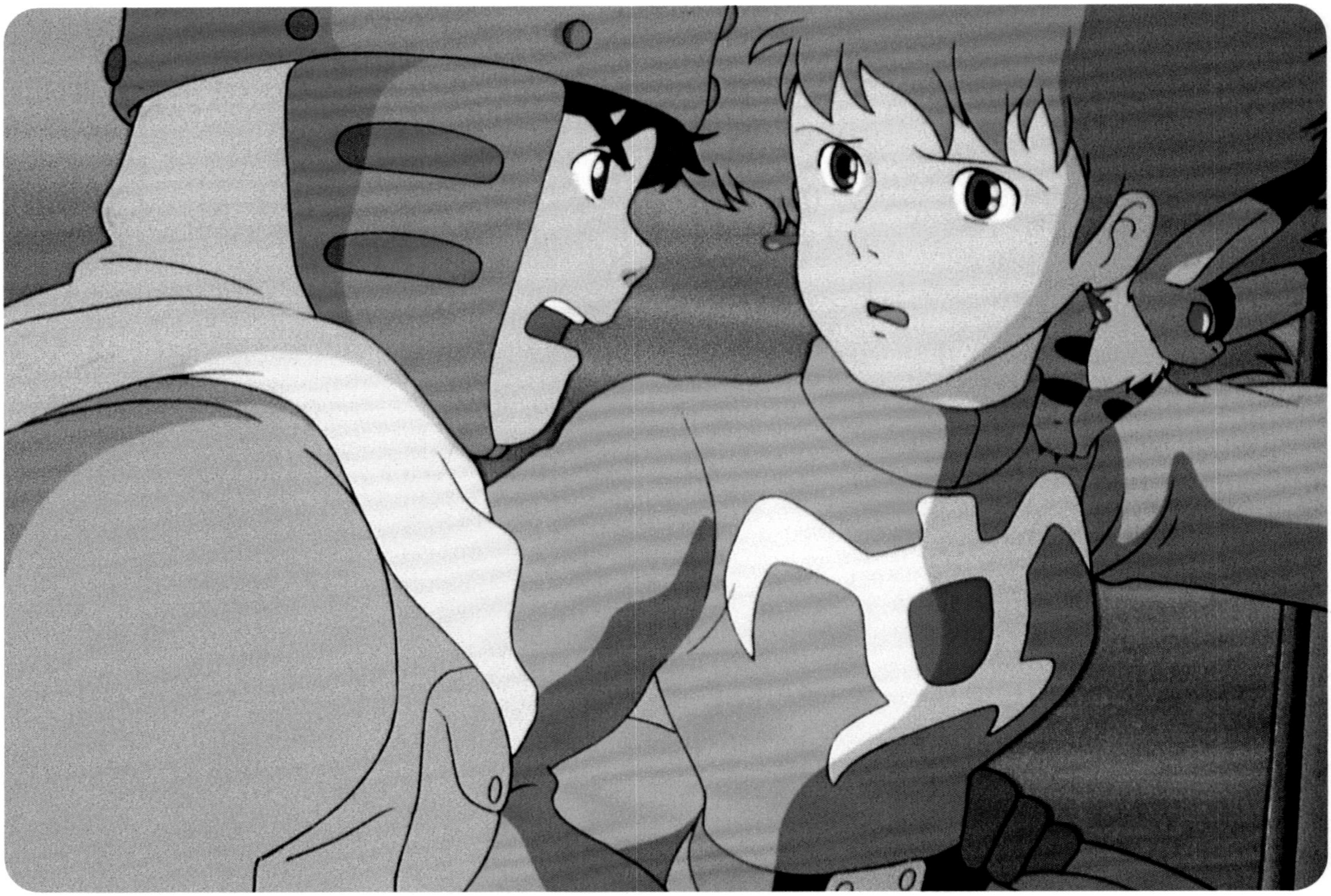

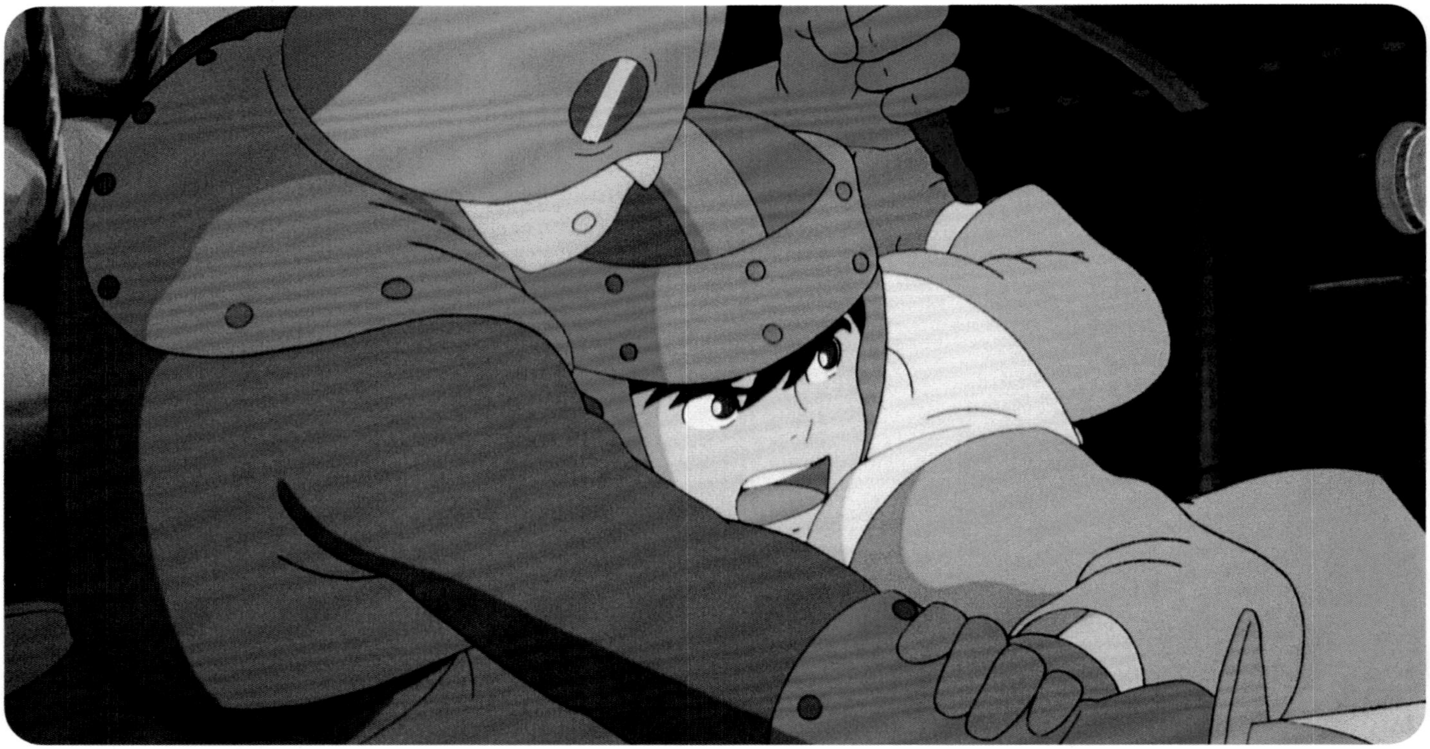

"You have to save the people of the valley," Asbel said."Go, or my people will never forgive themselves."

A Tolmekian soldier burst into the hold and attacked Asbel with a dagger. Asbel held him off as he gave the wind rider a kick.

"Go, Nausicaä—go!"

"Asbel!" she cried out, but she was already flying through the clouds. The Tolmekian gunship spotted her and took off in pursuit, guns blazing.

Nausicaä saw something heading toward her through the clouds ahead. It was the valley gunship!

"Princess!" Mito called from the cockpit.

"Mito!"

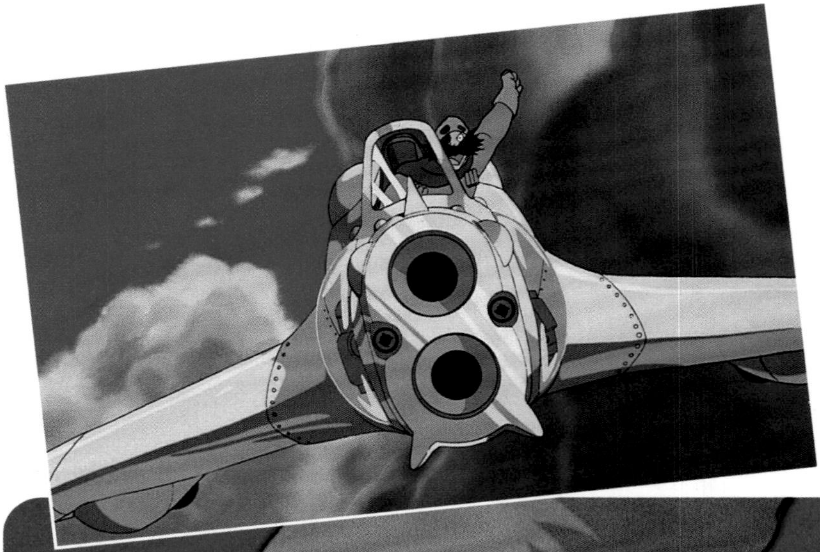

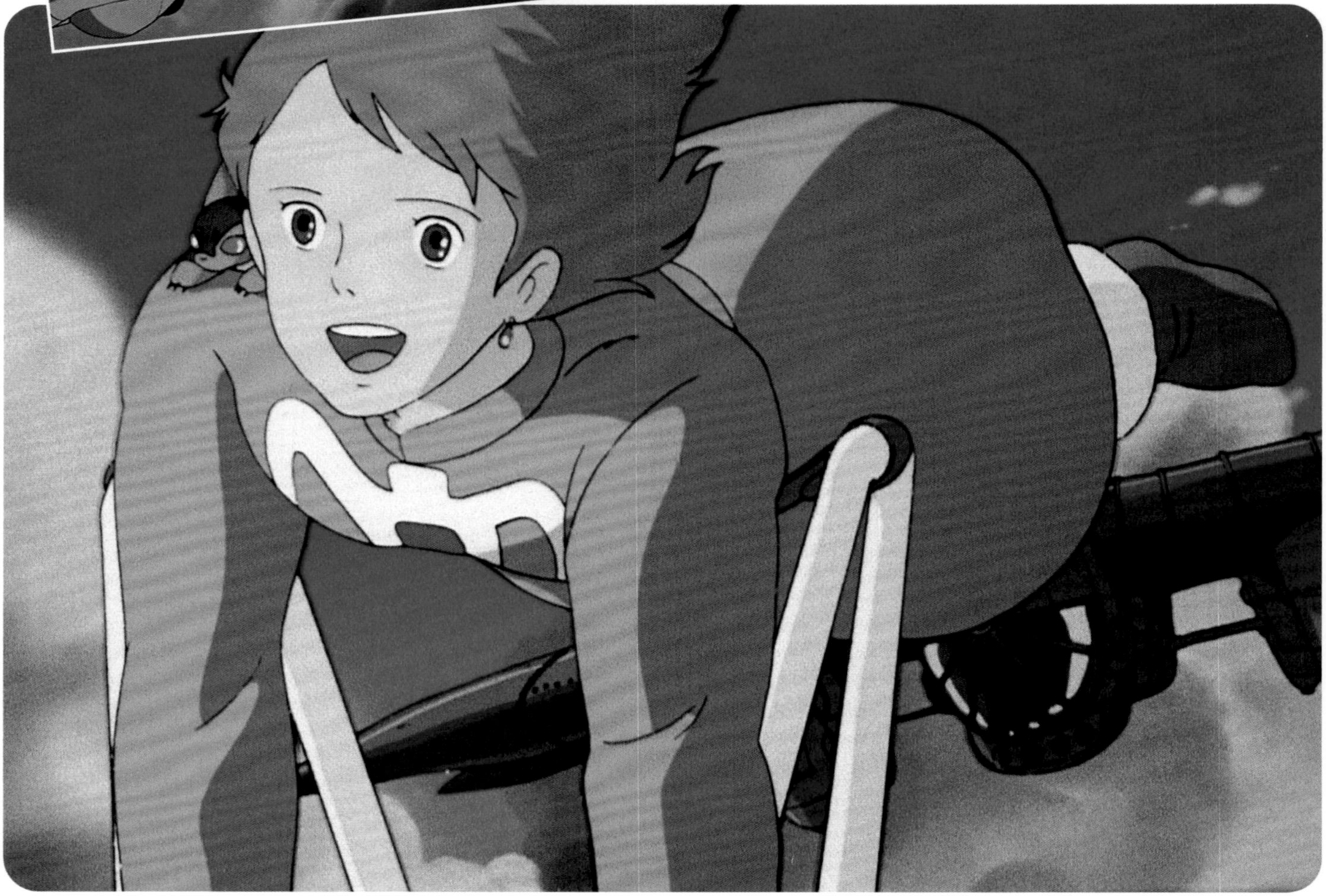

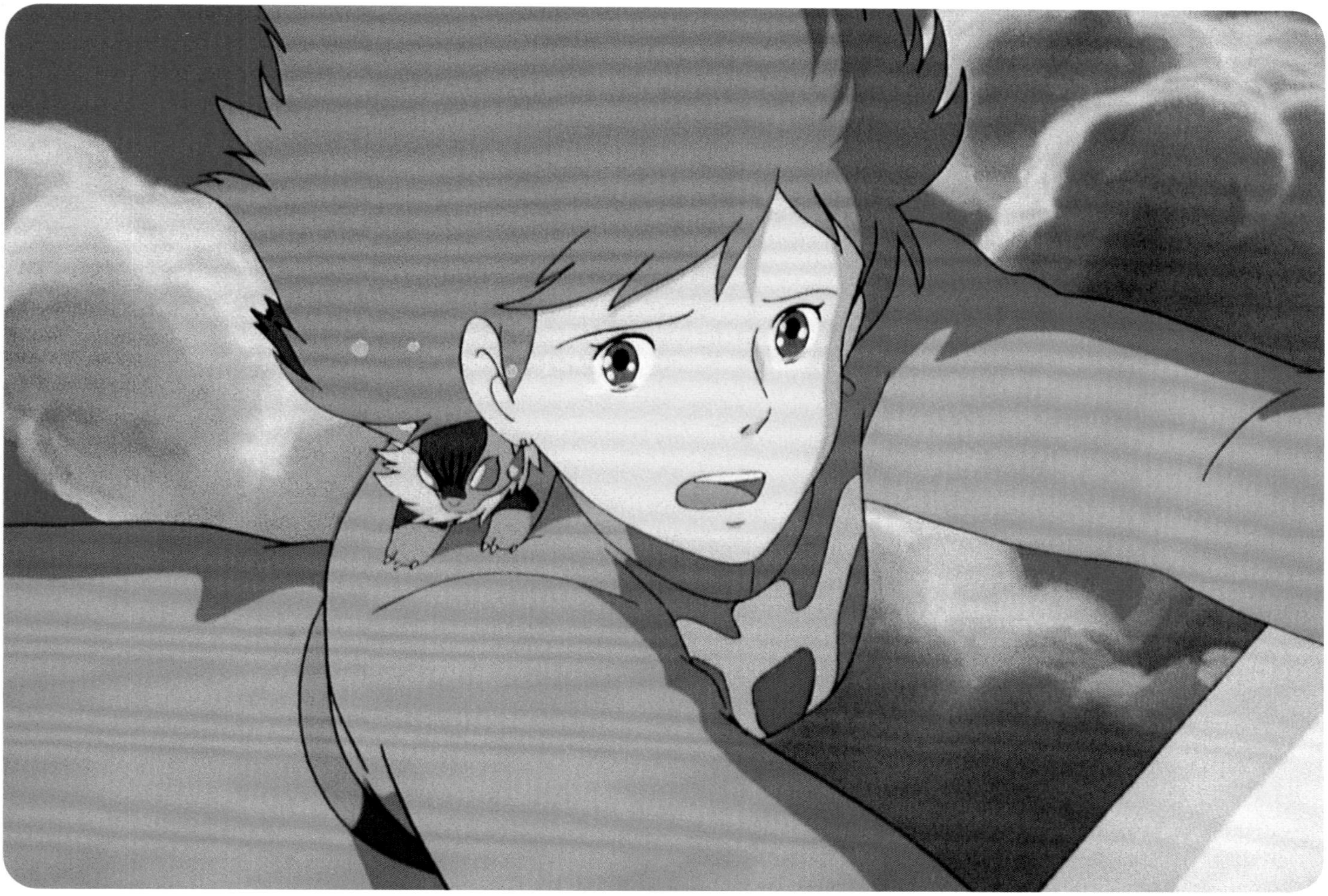

The gunship swooped over Nausicaä and blasted the Tolmekians. The enemy gunship caught fire and plunged toward the earth.

"Mito! Lord Yupa!" she cried. "The people of the valley are in danger. Hurry!" She docked with the gunship and told the two men everything that had happened.

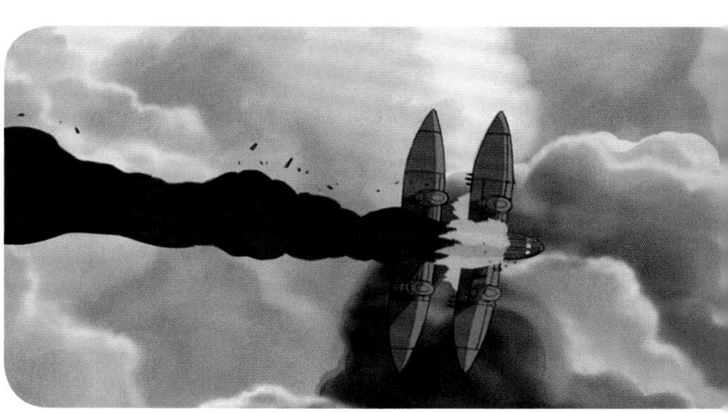

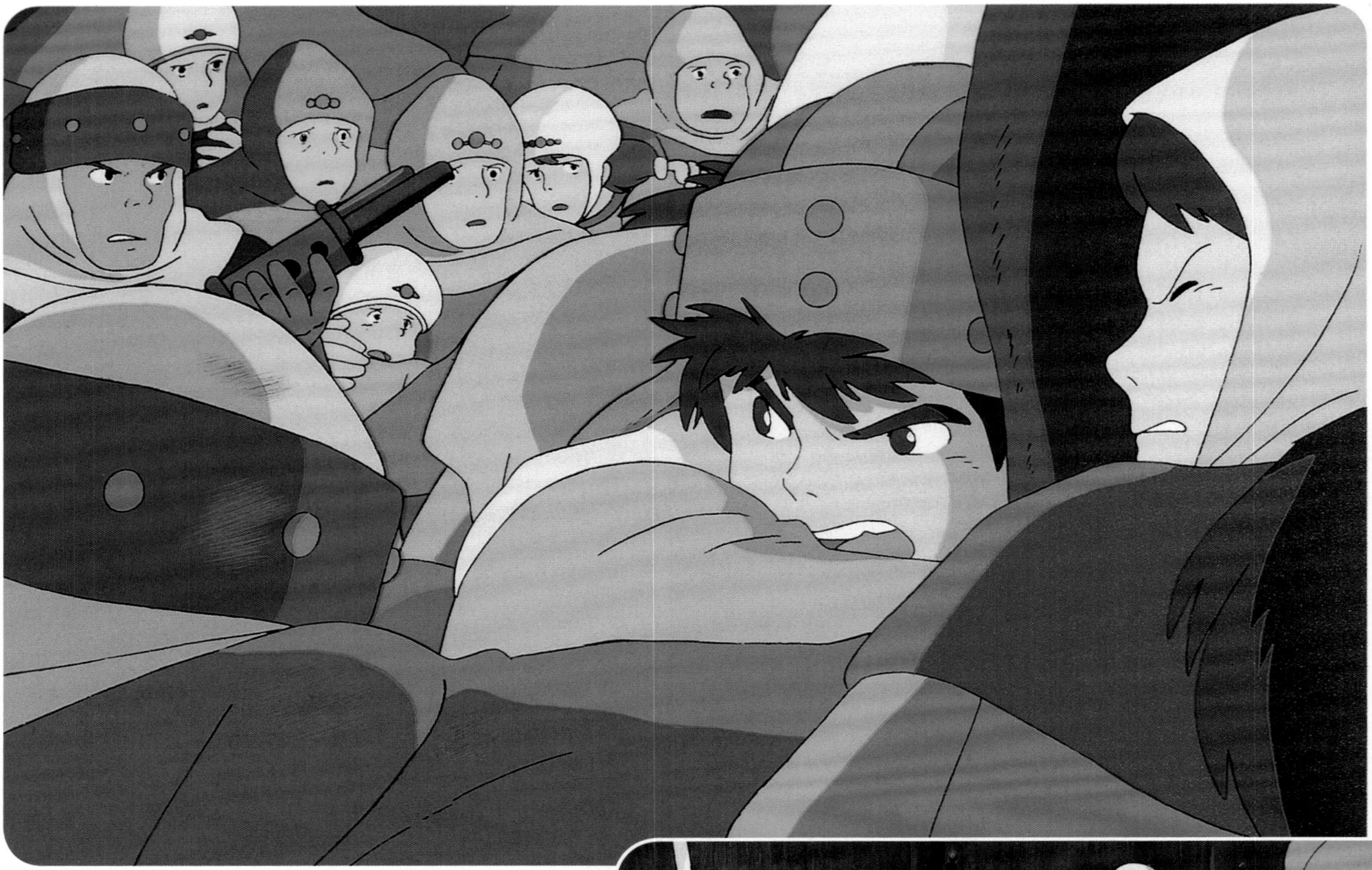

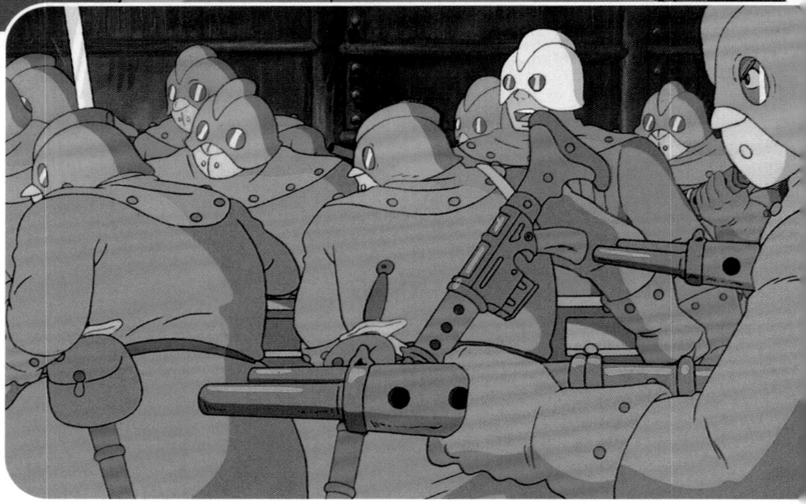

Meanwhile, Asbel and the passengers on the Pejite Brig huddled together while the Tolmekians tried to break down the door. Then one of the soldiers saw a shape like a huge bird bearing down on the brig.

"Look! A gunship from the Valley of the Wind!"

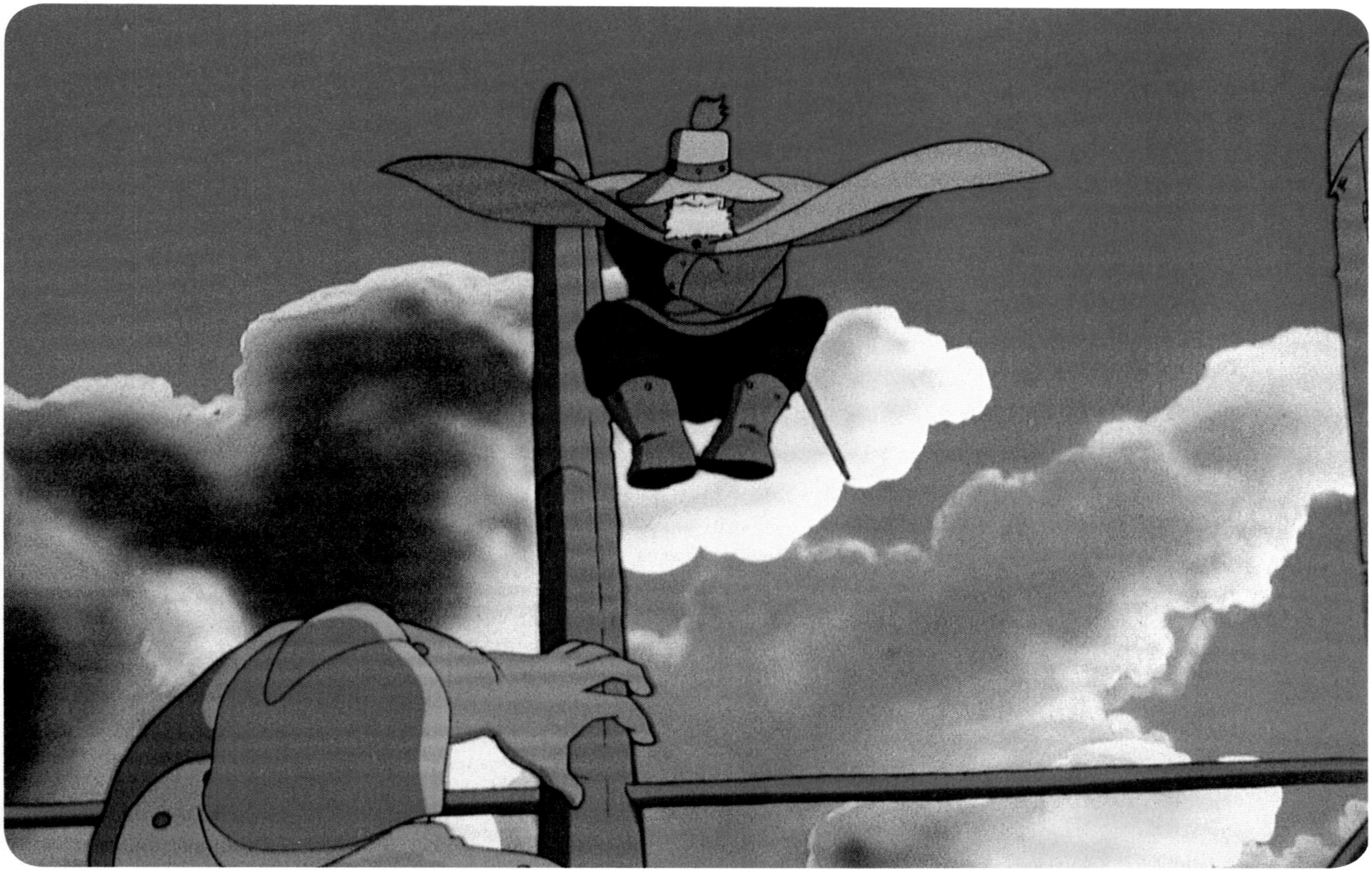

No sooner were the words out of his mouth than Yupa leaped aboard the Brig!

The soldiers rushed Yupa with drawn swords. The sound of clashing steel filled the hold as he parried their thrusts.

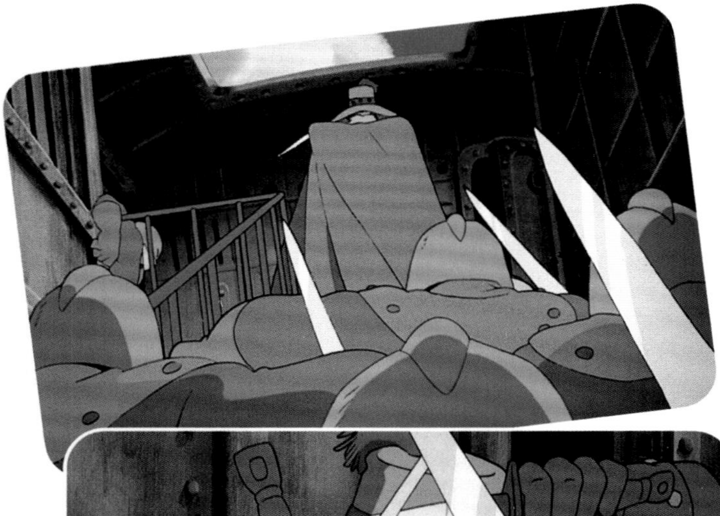

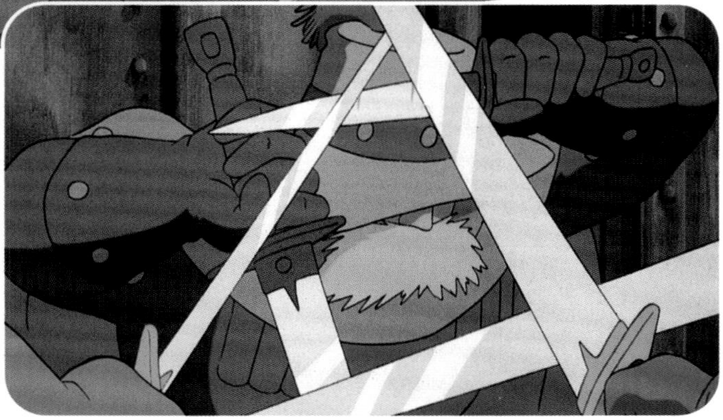

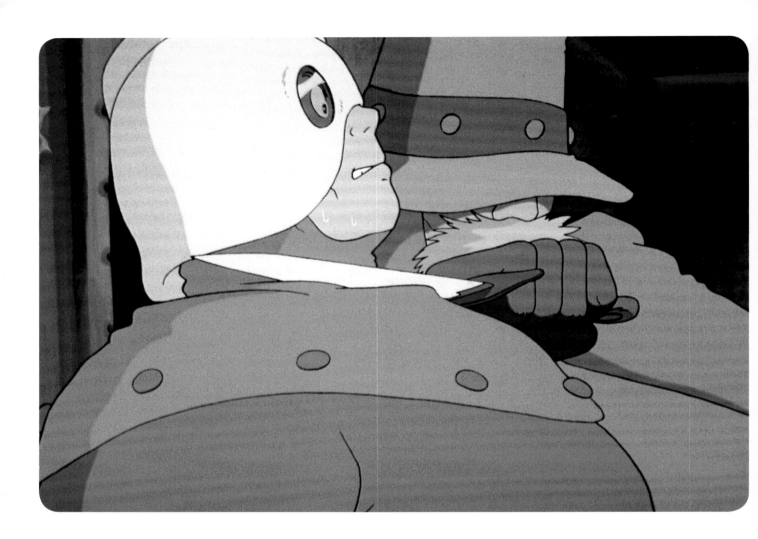

While Yupa was fighting the soldiers, Mito and Nausicaä banked the gunship and headed for the valley at full speed.

Yupa broke through the ring of soldiers and rushed their captain. He put a dagger to the man's throat and said, "I suggest you surrender. There's no ship coming to rescue you."

The Tolmekians knew they were beaten. Yupa took over the Brig and set a course for the valley.

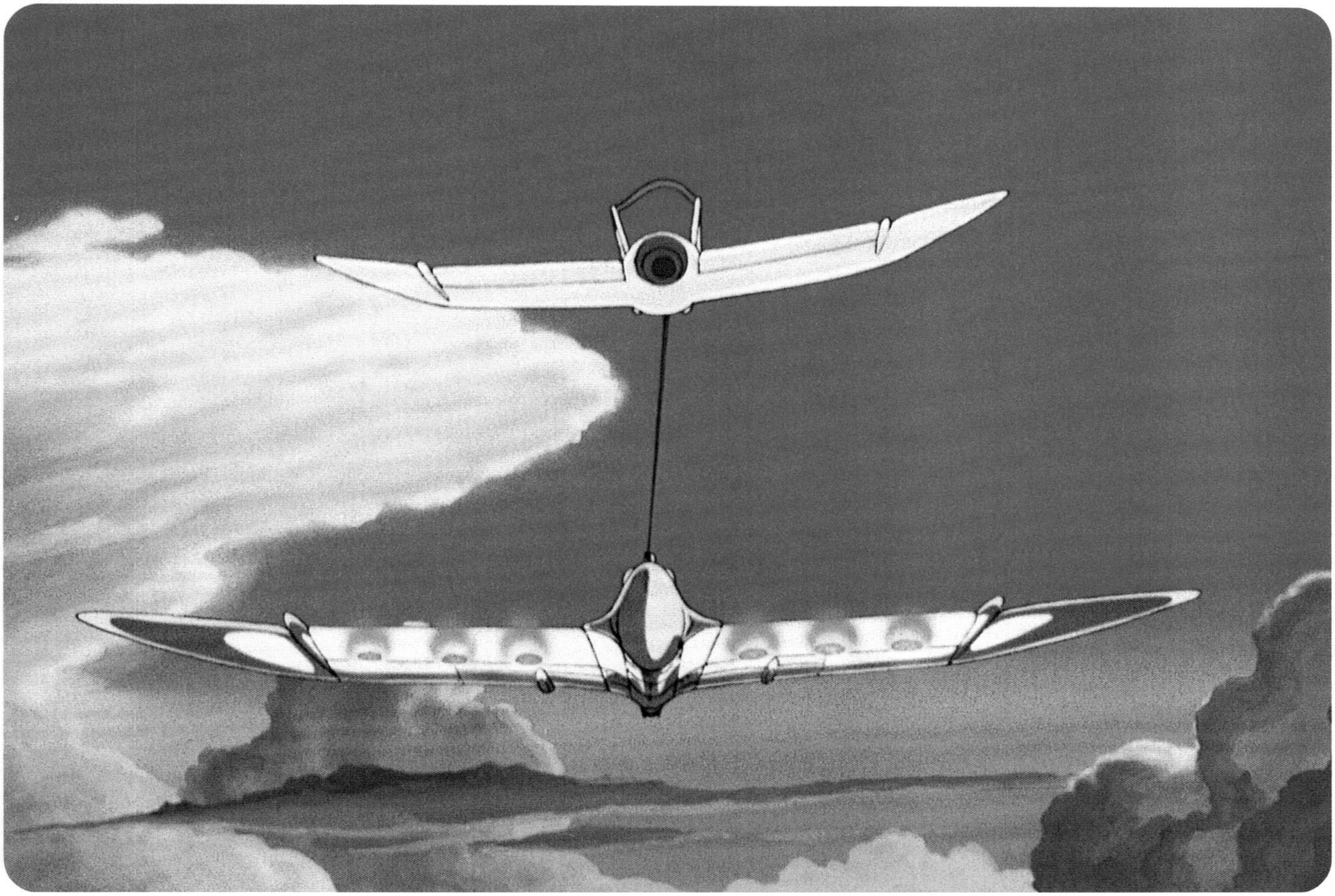

Nausicaä flew the gunship as fast as it would go through the gathering dusk.

"We're going too fast, princess!" Mito shouted. "The engine's gonna burn out!"

But she opened the throttle even more.

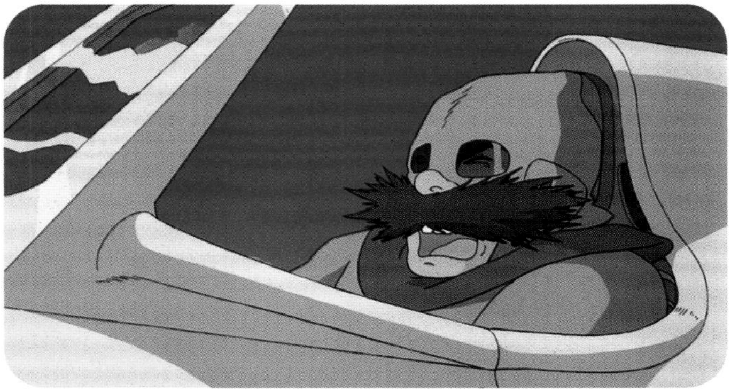

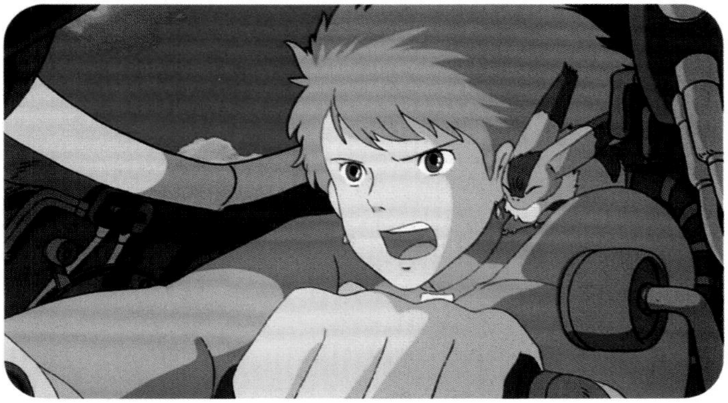

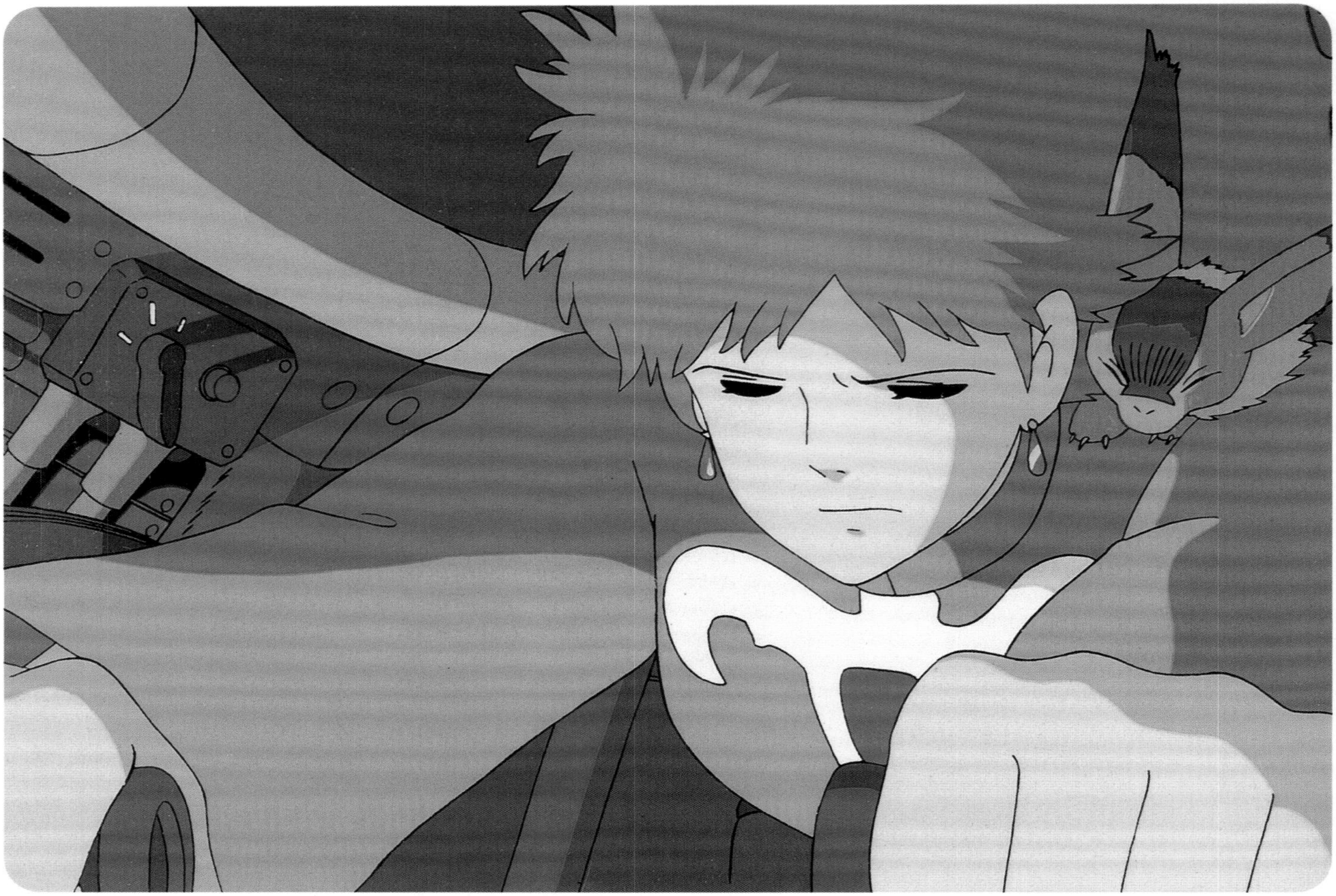

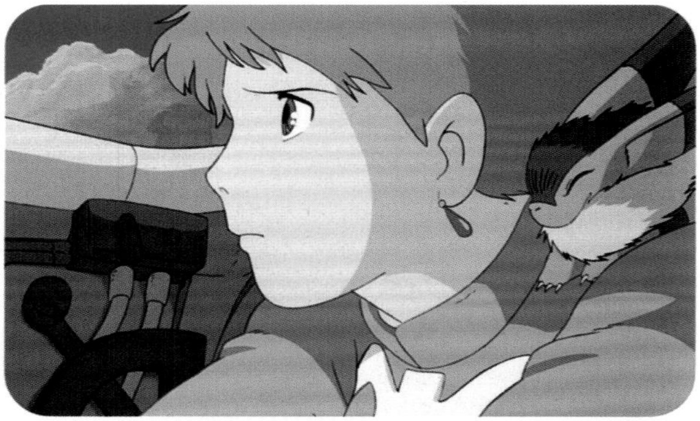

As night fell, Nausicaä said a prayer for the people of the valley.

By now, they had holed up in the old airship by the acid lake and were waiting for the Tolmekians to launch their final attack.

As Mito and Nausicaä approached, they could see a red glow in the darkness.

"The Ohms!"

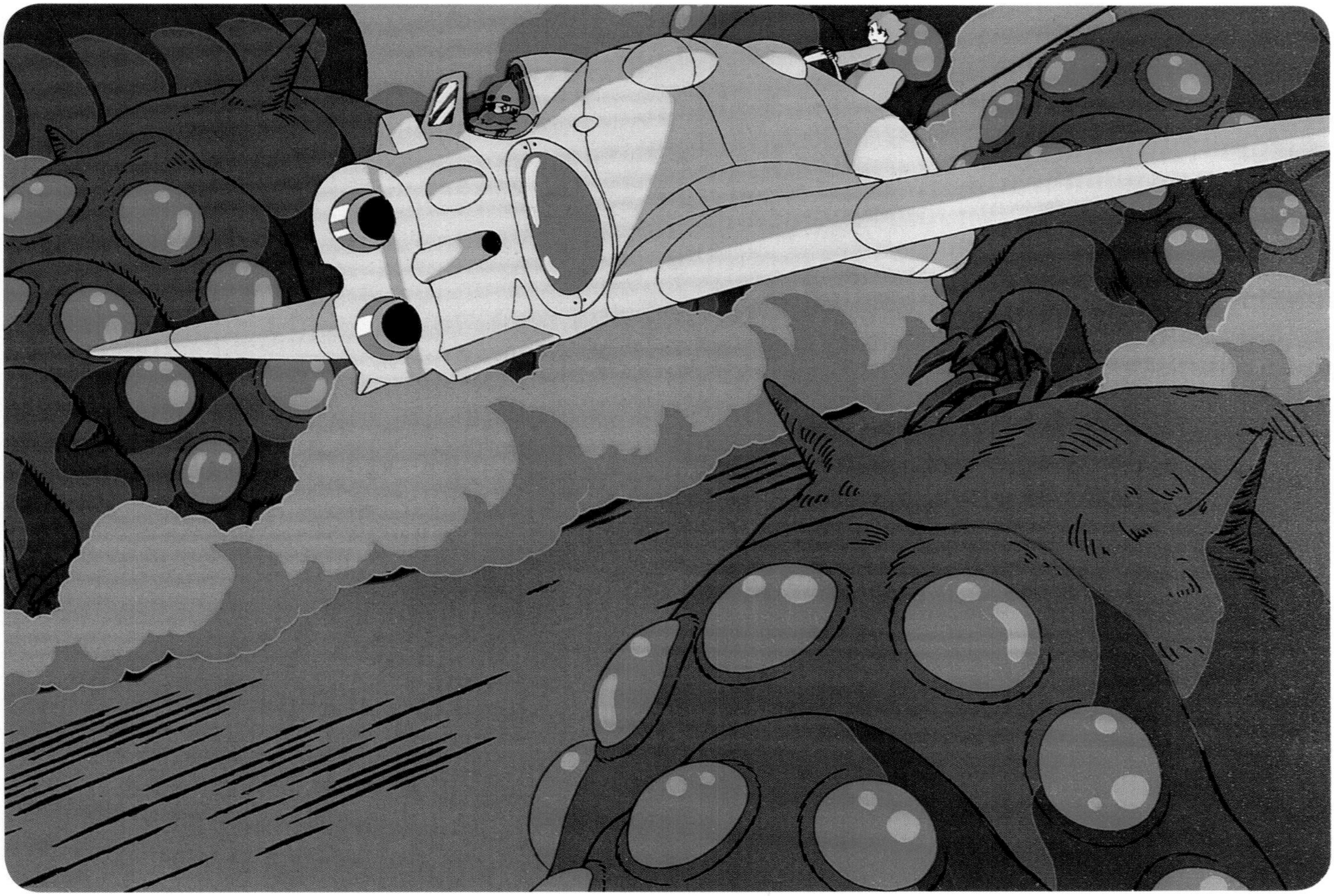

A huge army of Ohms was charging toward the Tolmekians. Their eyes were crimson with rage.

"What's making them stampede like that?" Nausicaä said. She peered into the distance and saw a tiny blue light. "Something out there is calling to the herd. Mito, send out a flare!"

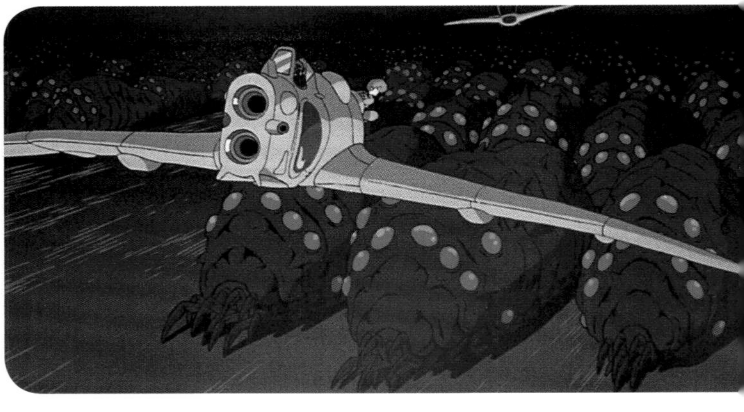

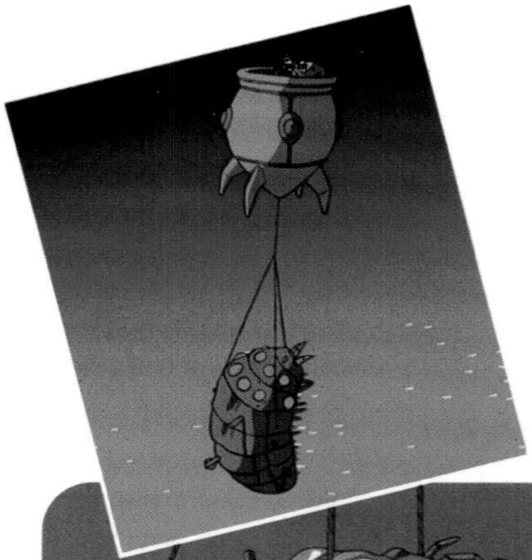

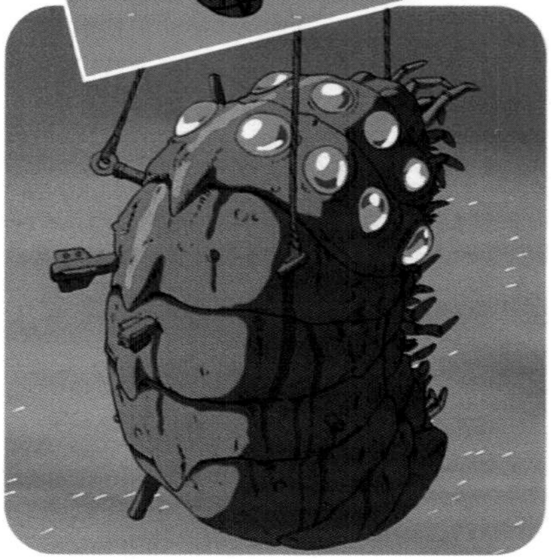

In the light from the flare, Nausicaä saw a baby Ohm suspended beneath a Pejite hover pod.

The baby was hanging from spikes the Pejites had pounded into its body. Blue fluid oozed from its wounds.

"They're using the baby to lure the herd into the valley!" Nausicaä cried.

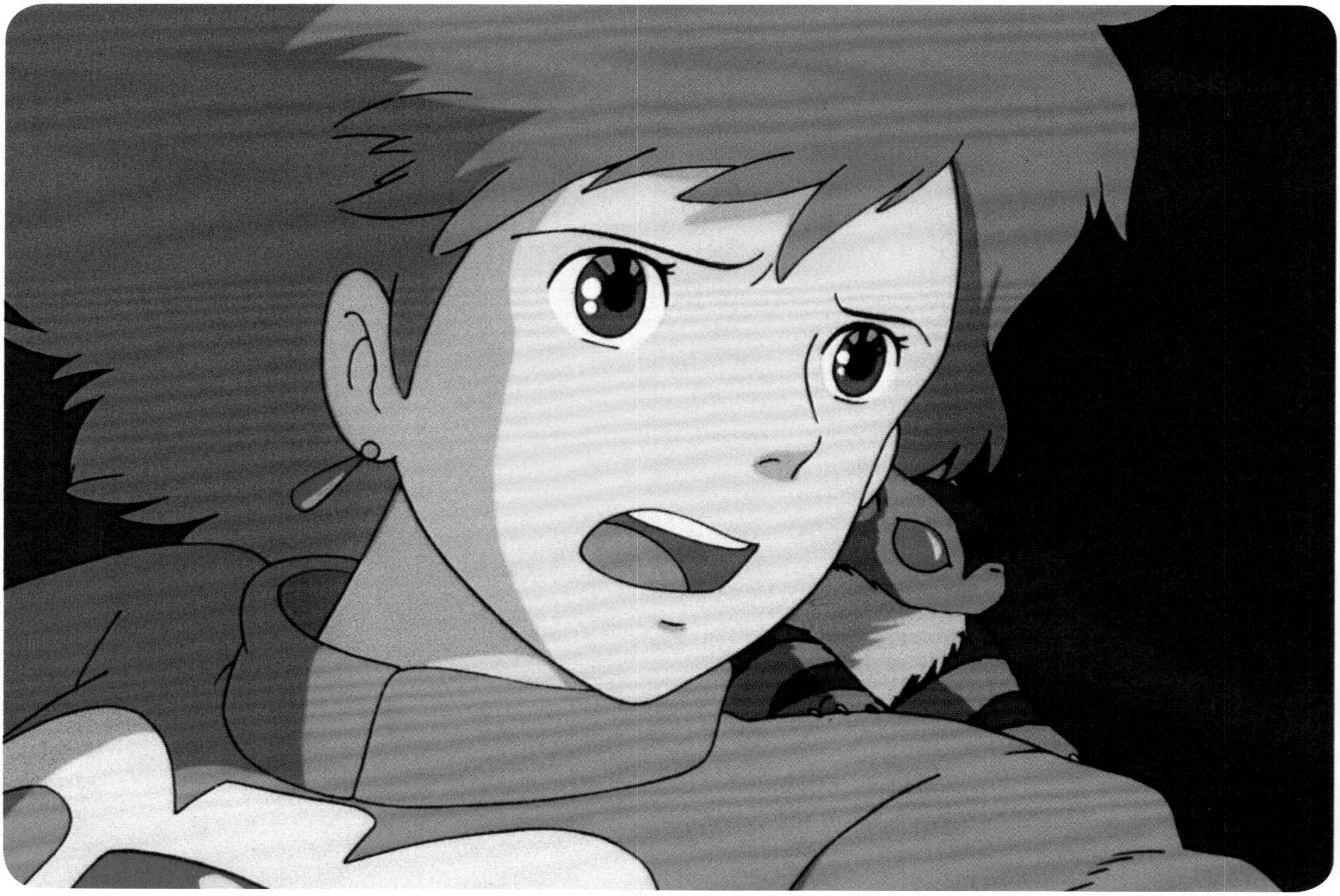

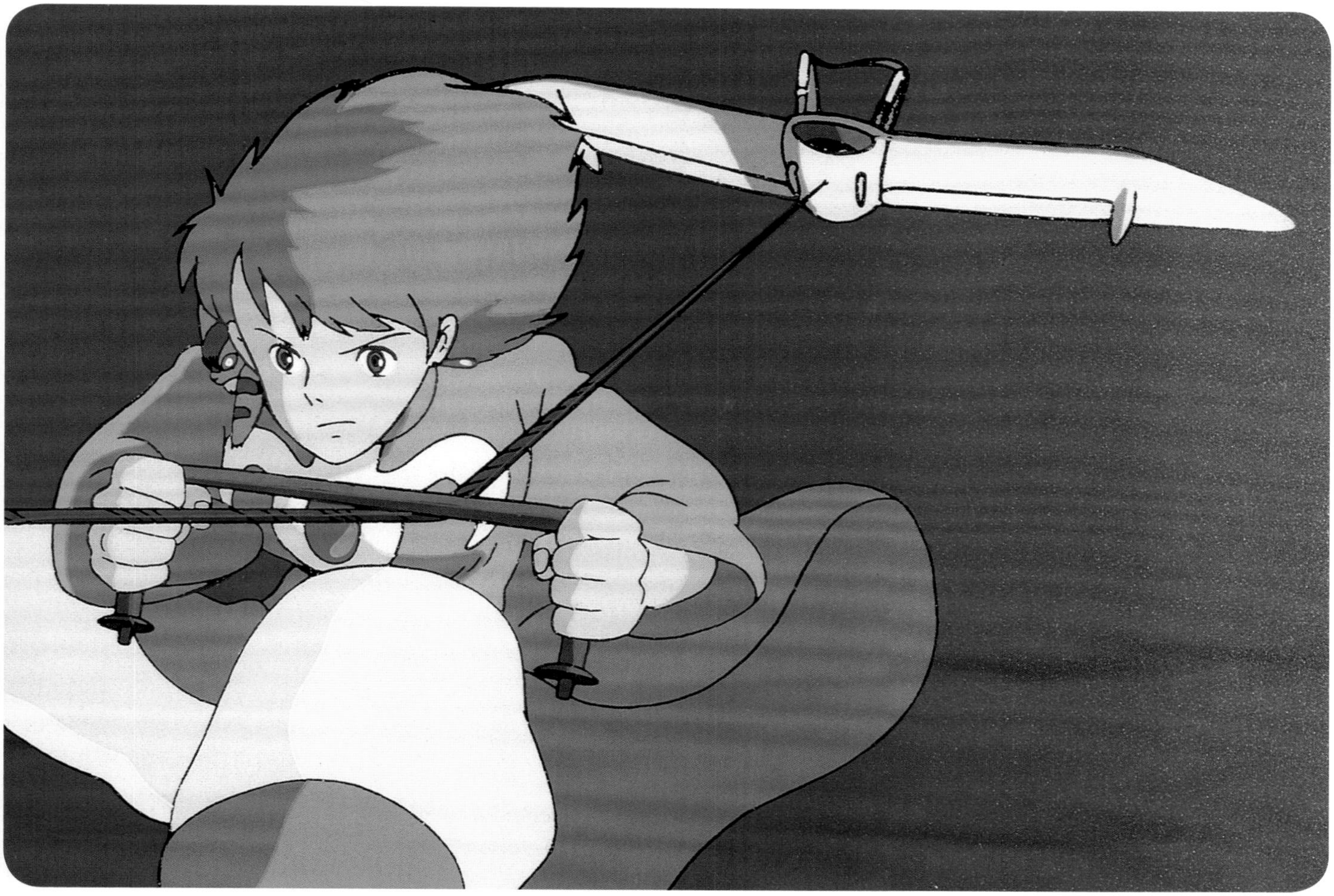

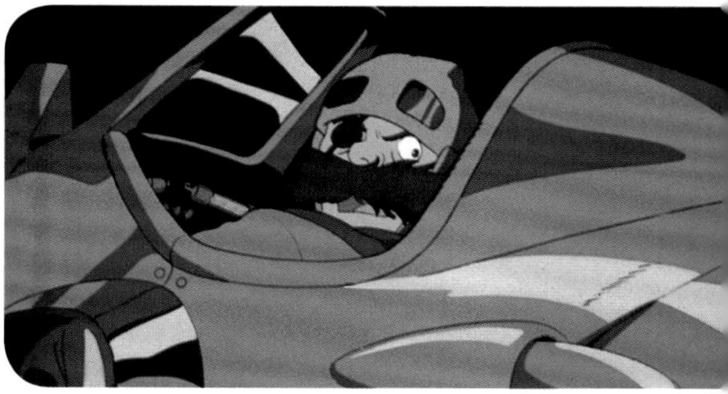

"If the Ohms get to the valley, it's all over. I've got to get that baby back to the herd."

Nausicaä slid down the rope to her wind rider. "But princess, you don't even have a weapon!" Mito called to her.

"Go warn the valley!" She jumped on her wind rider and set off in pursuit of the hover pod.

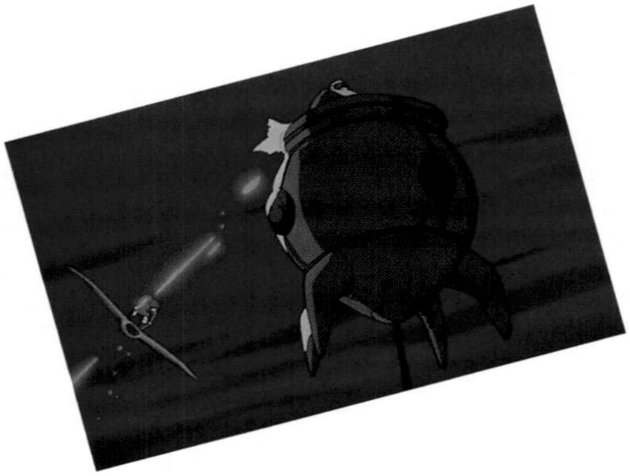

The pod's machine gun opened up with a roar as she flew closer.

Amid the rain of bullets, she stood up and kept coming, arms spread wide.

Suddenly, the young soldier held his fire. "I can't do it!"

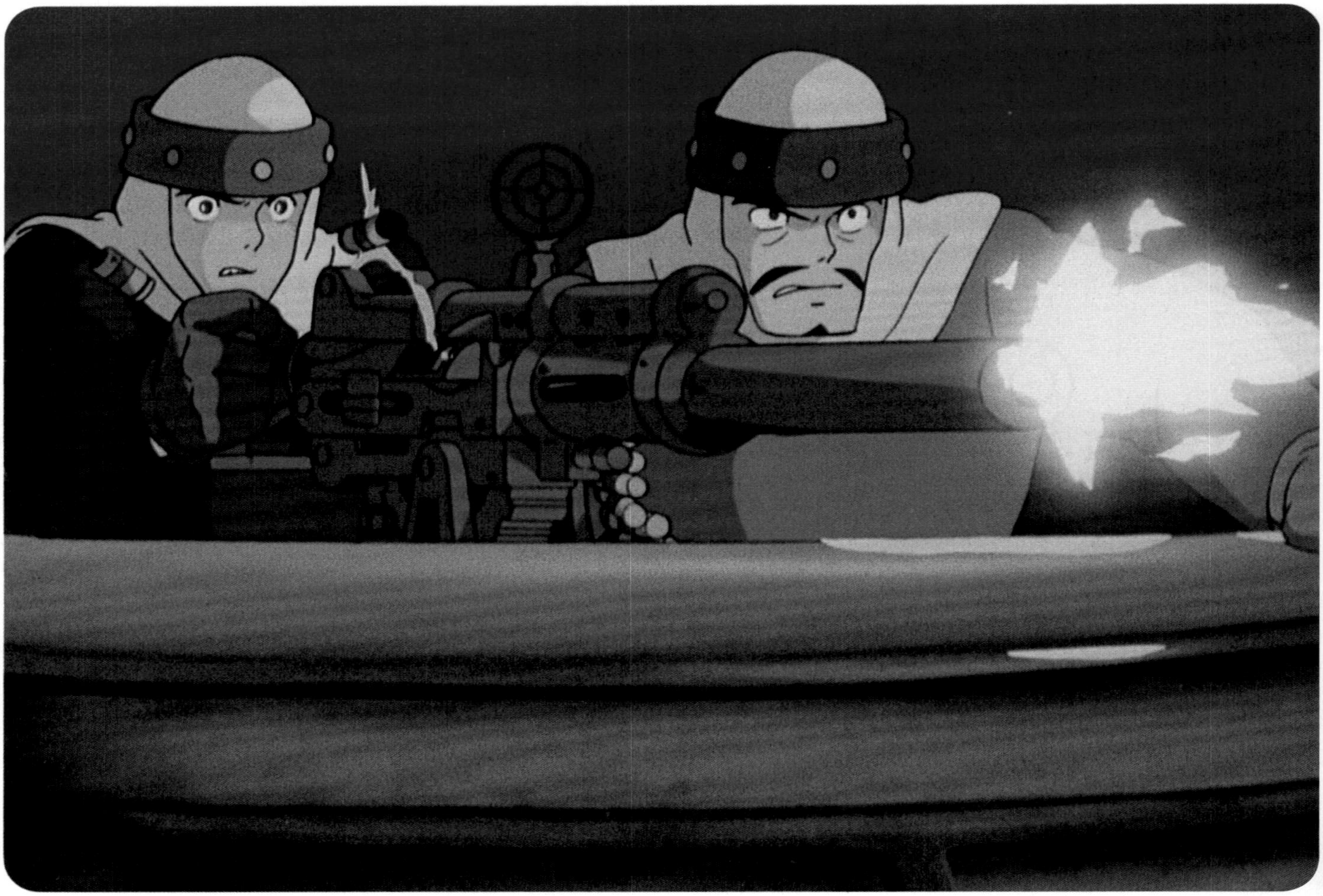

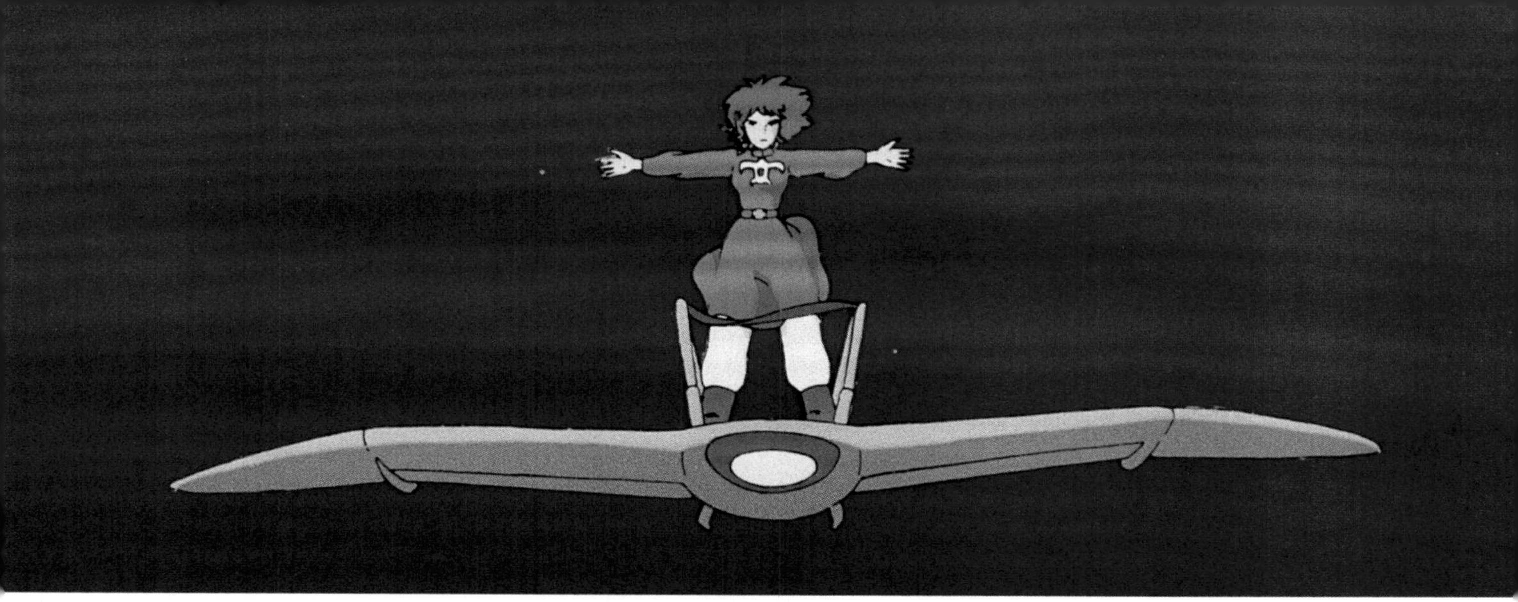
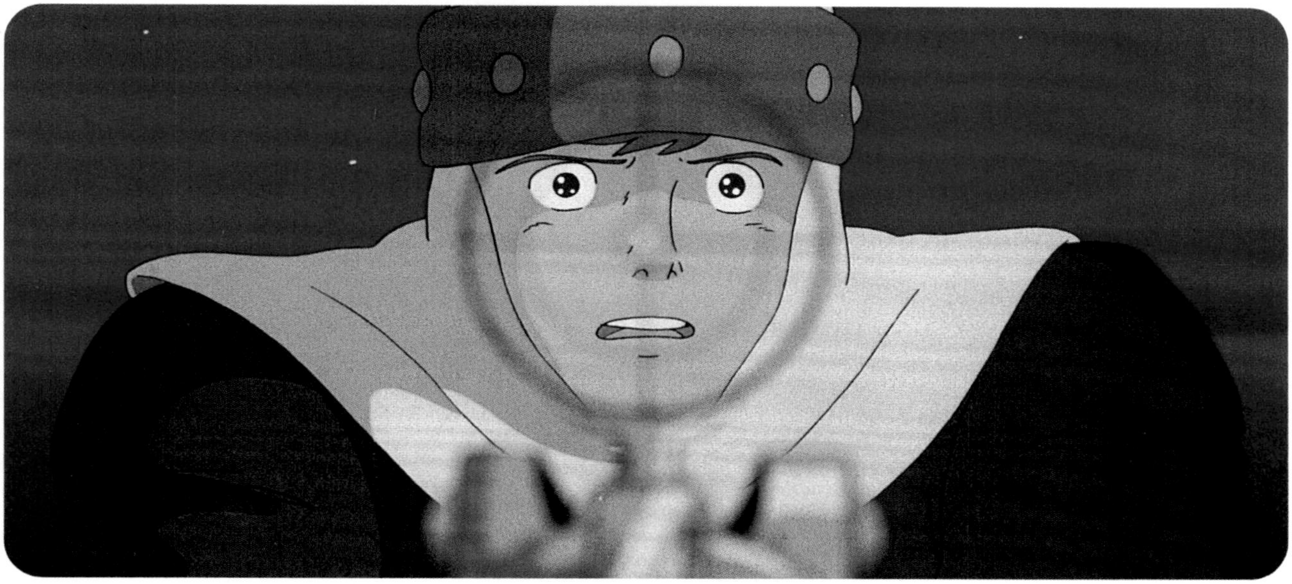
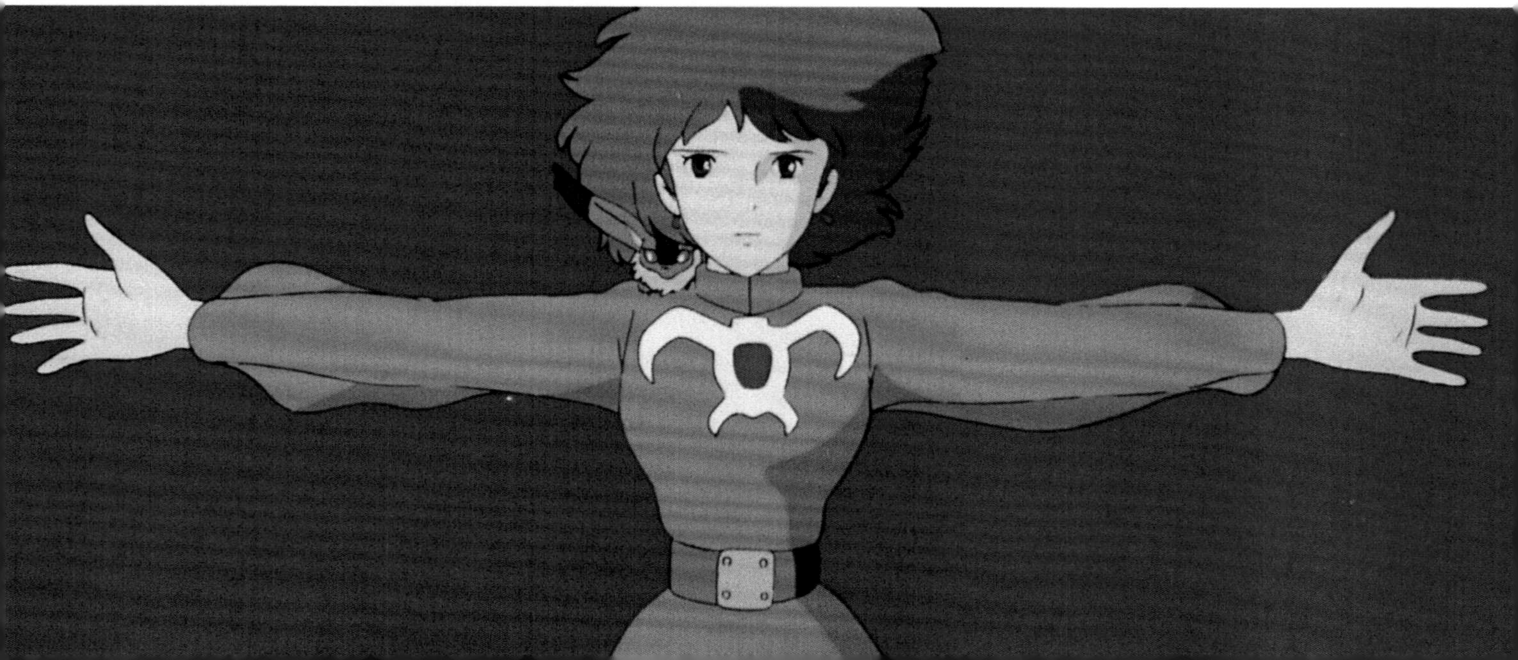

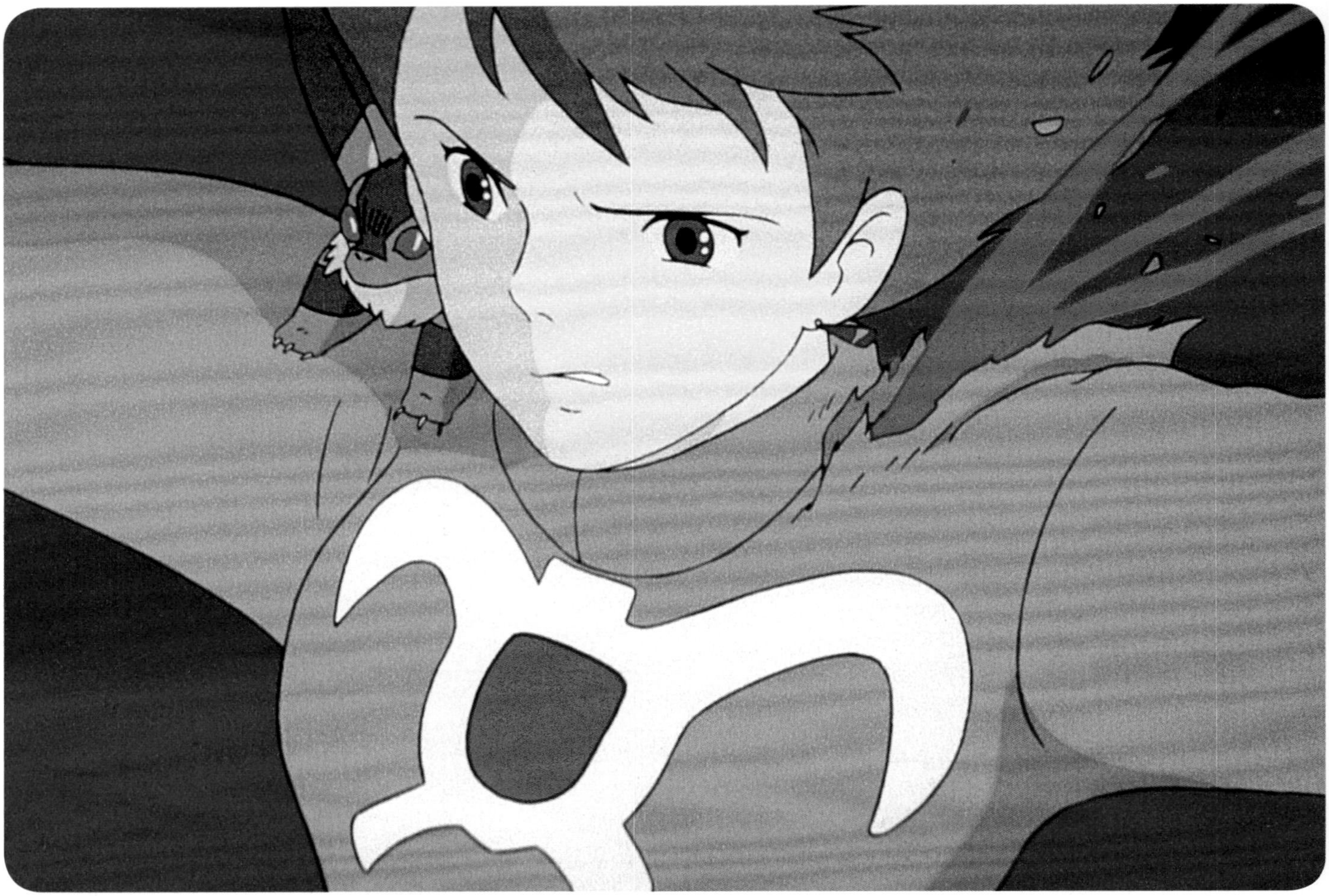

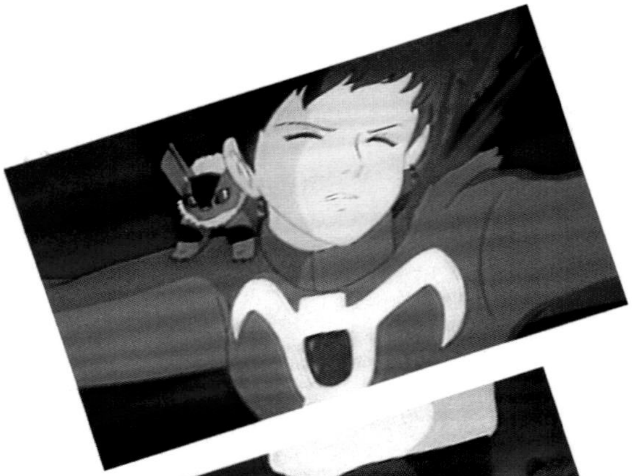

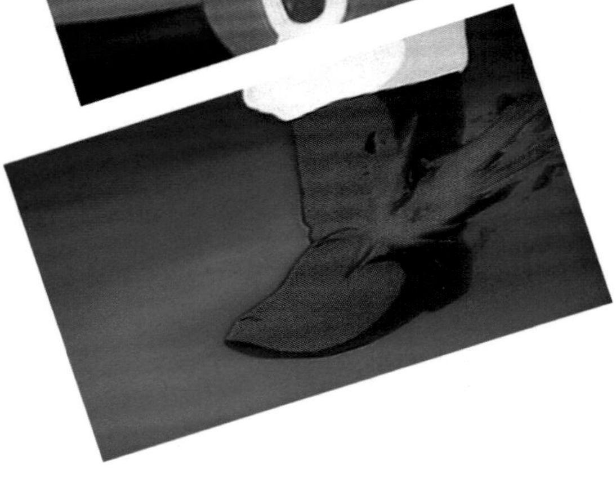

"You fool! Get out of the way!"

His crewmate pushed him aside, aimed the machine gun, and fired!

Bullets struck Nausicaä in the foot and shoulder. Blood poured from her wounds.

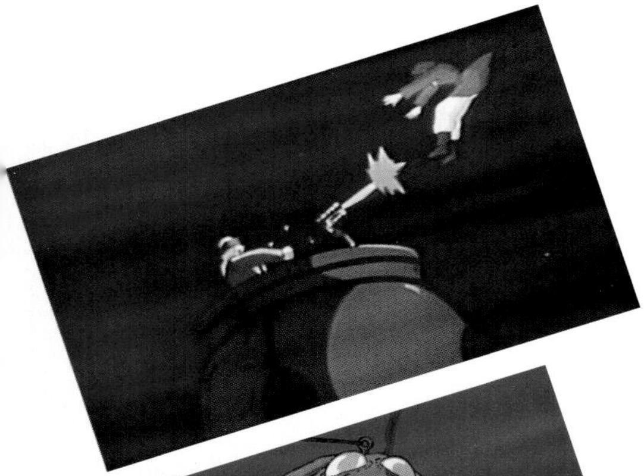

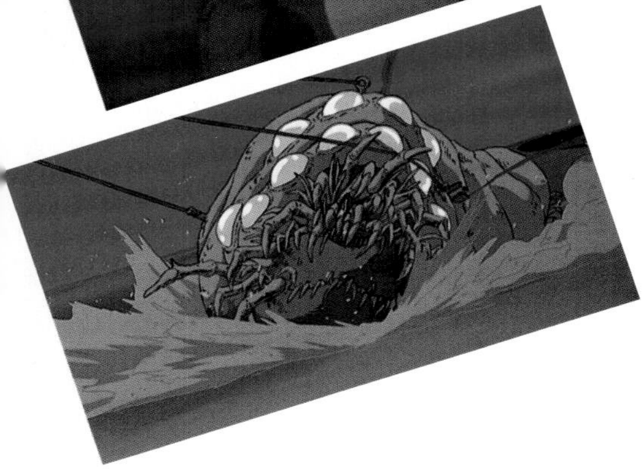

Nausicaä leaped through the air into the hover pod.

The extra weight made the pod lose altitude, and the baby Ohm was dragged along the shore of the acid lake. That brought the pod crashing down.

Nausicaä's wind rider flew off into the distance.

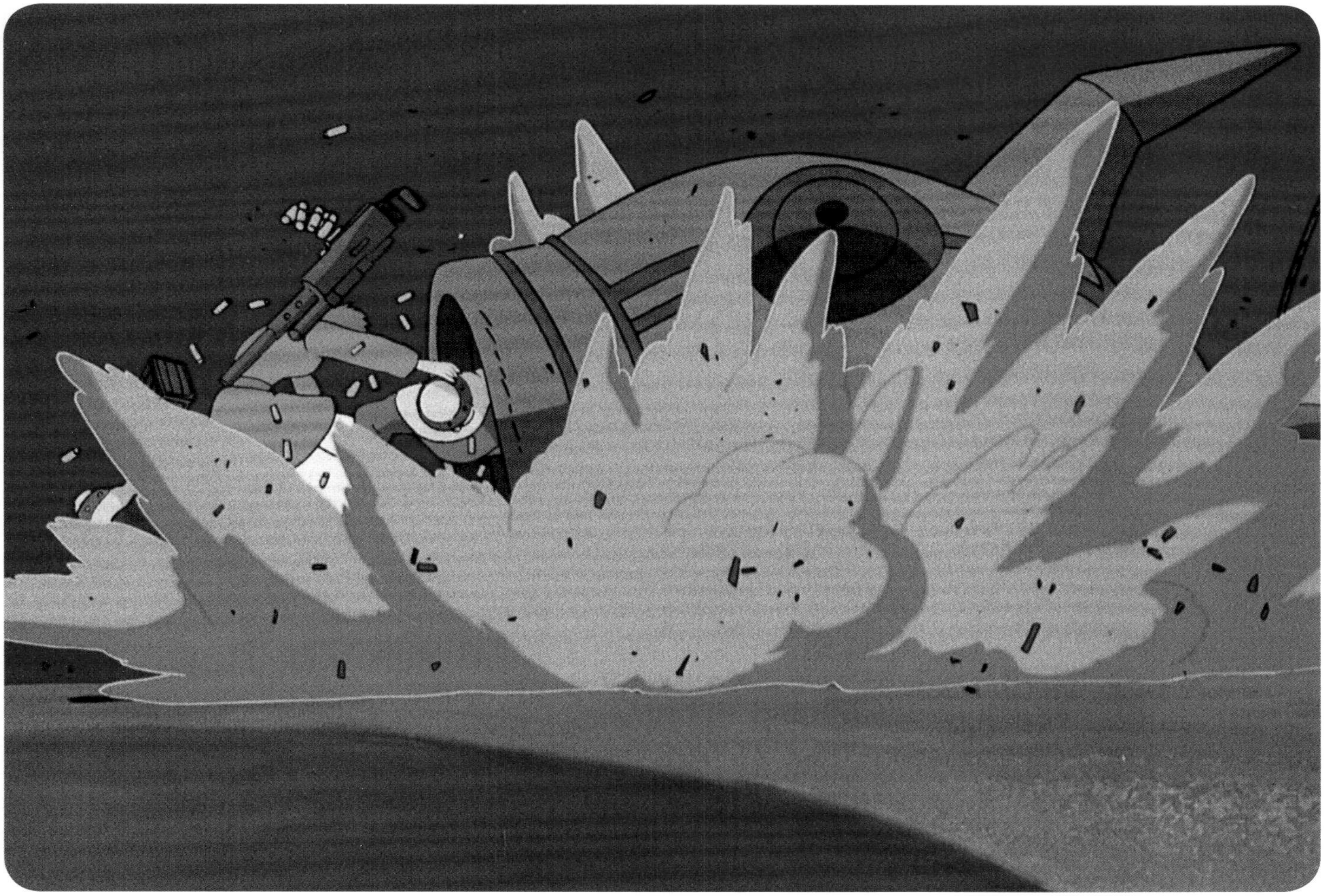

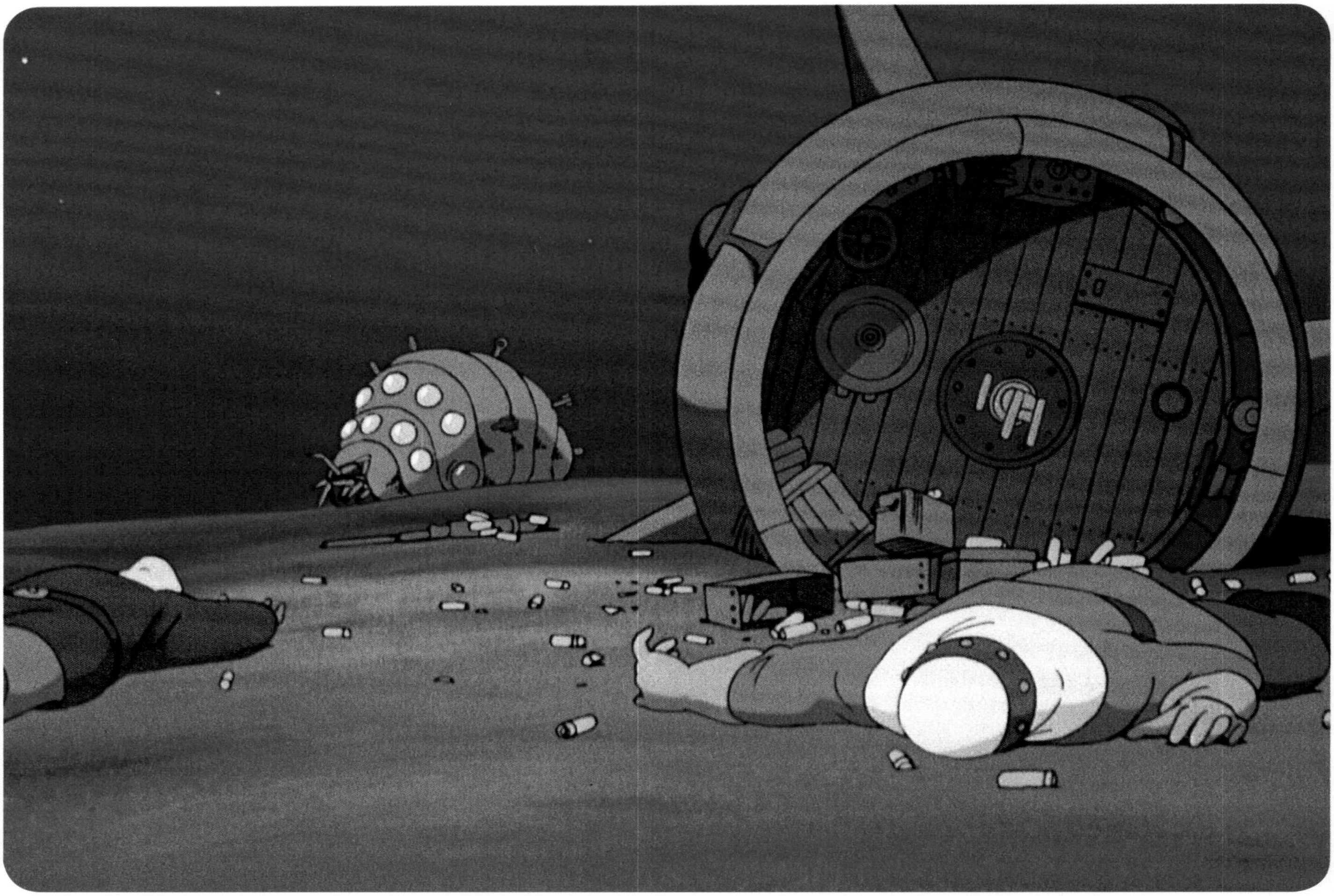

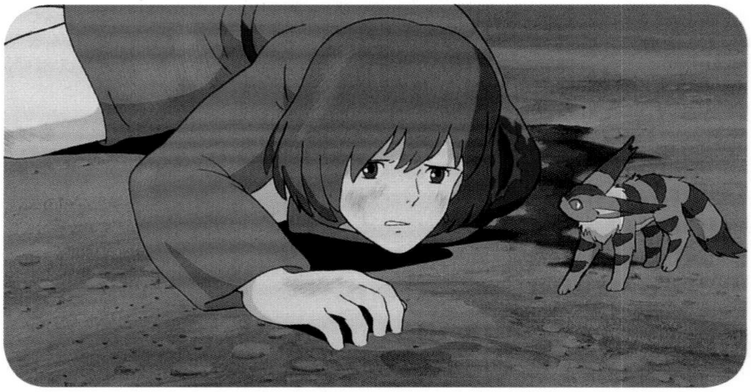

Nausicaä was dazed from the crash. She looked up and saw the baby Ohm nearby. The Pejite soldiers were unconscious.

Groaning with pain, she struggled to her feet and walked closer to the Ohm. Its eyes were glowing red.

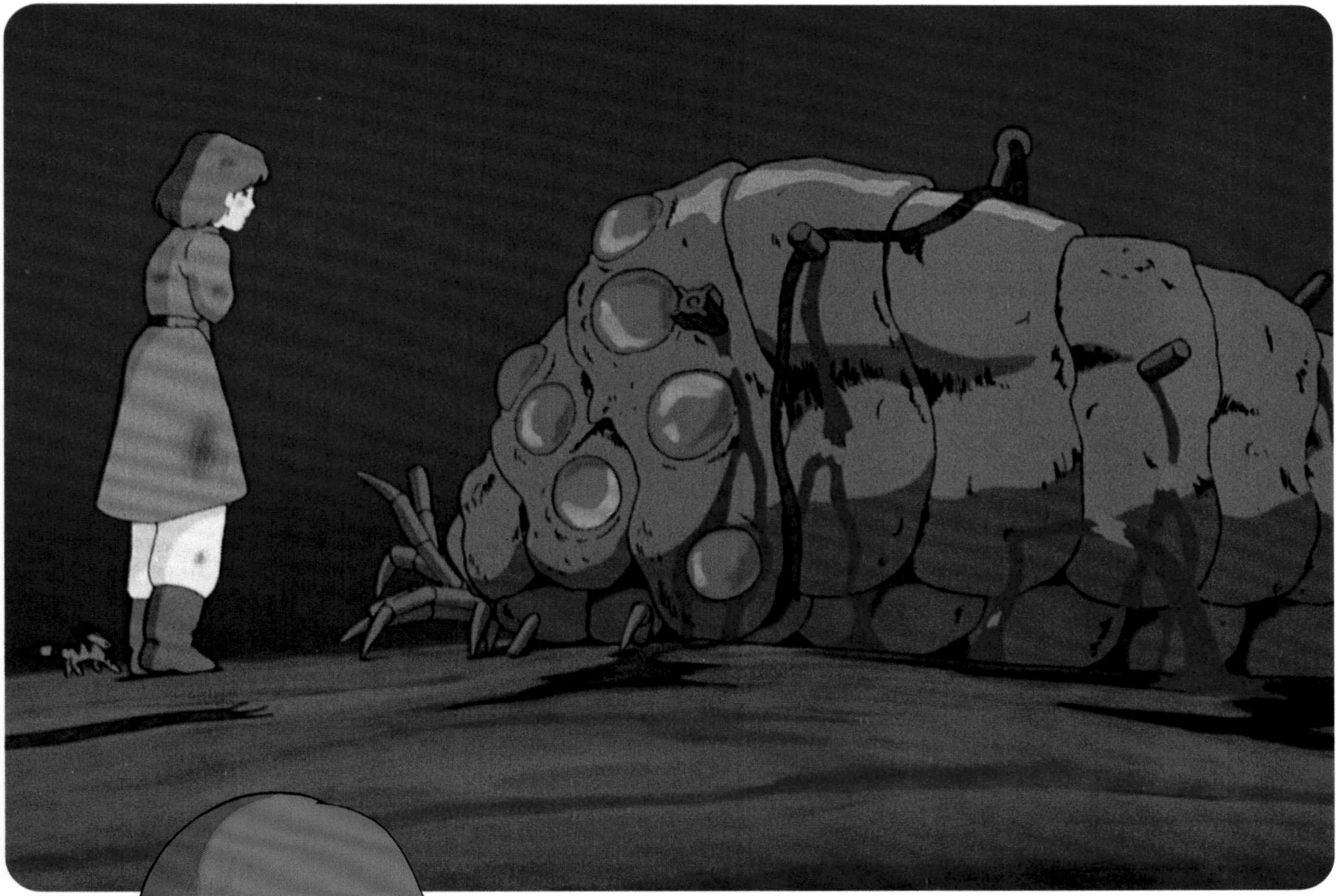

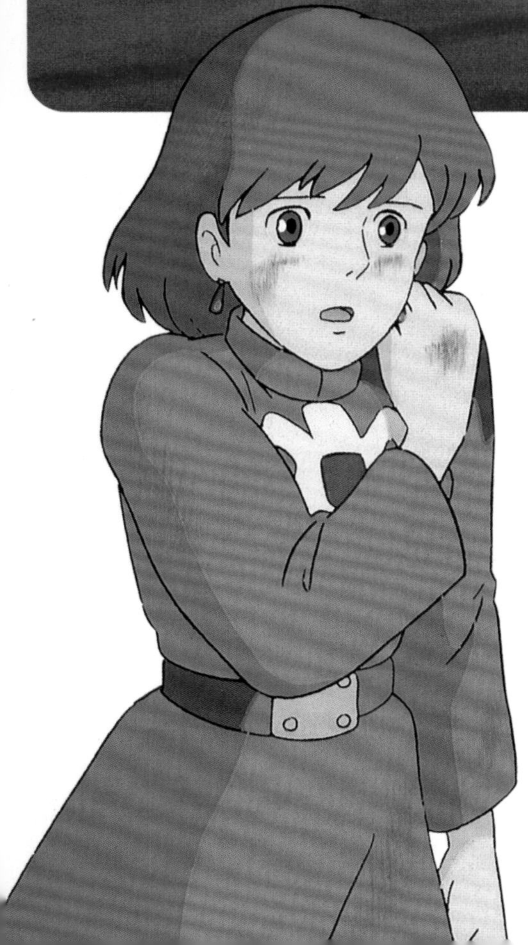

"Don't be frightened. I'm not going to hurt you."

Some of the Ohm's legs had been torn off. Blue blood oozed from its wounds.

"I'm so sorry," she said, and her eyes filled with tears. "Is there any way you can forgive us? We've treated you so badly."

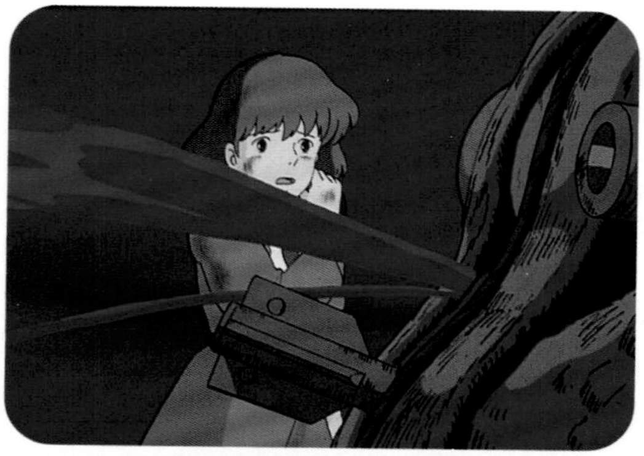

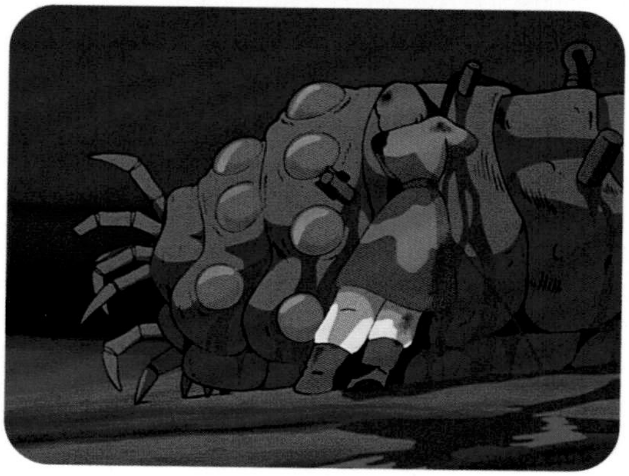

When the baby tried to move, blood gushed from its wounds

"Don't move—you'll bleed to death!" Nausicaä clung to the Ohm and tried to stop the blood. As it poured over her, it stained her tunic blue.

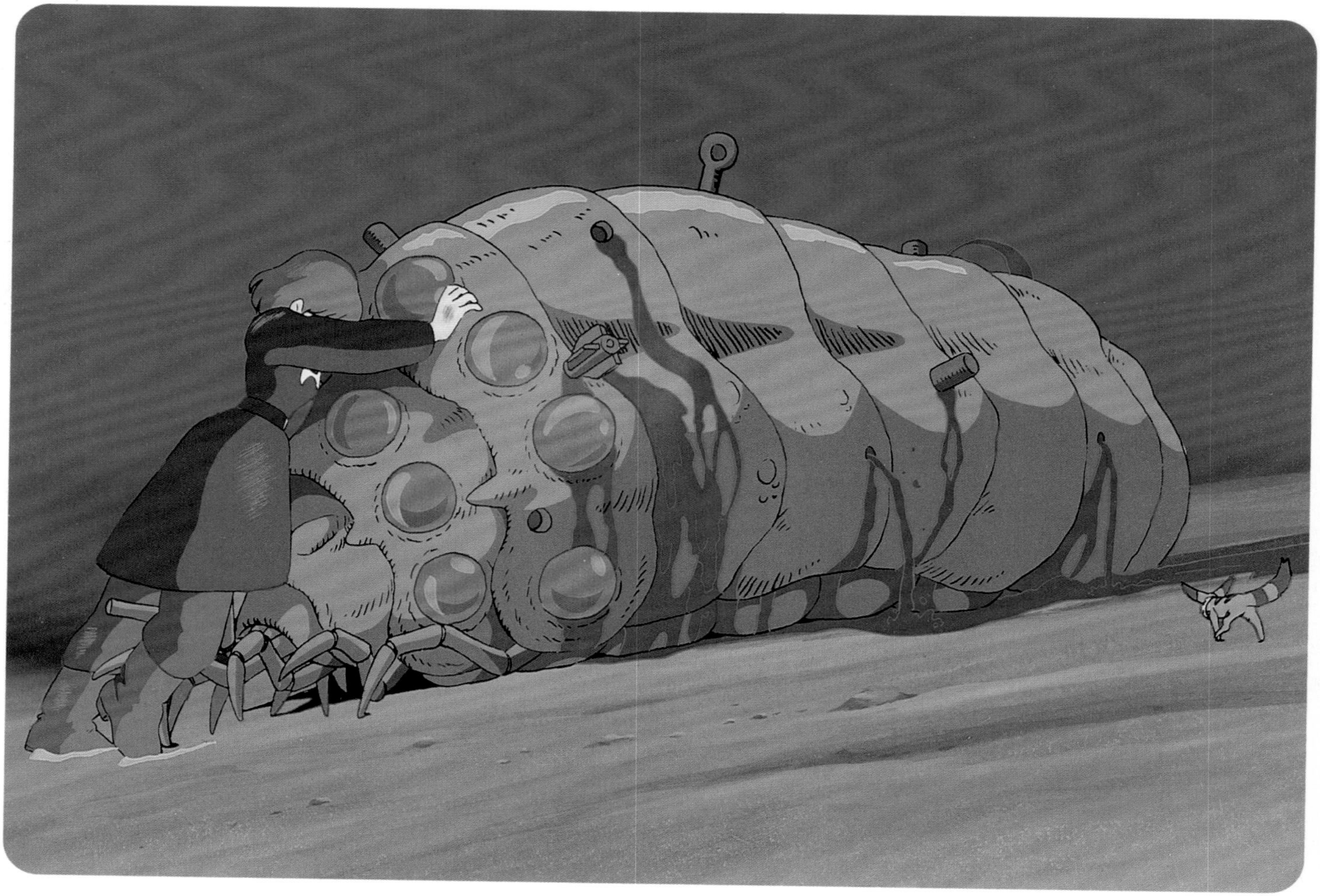

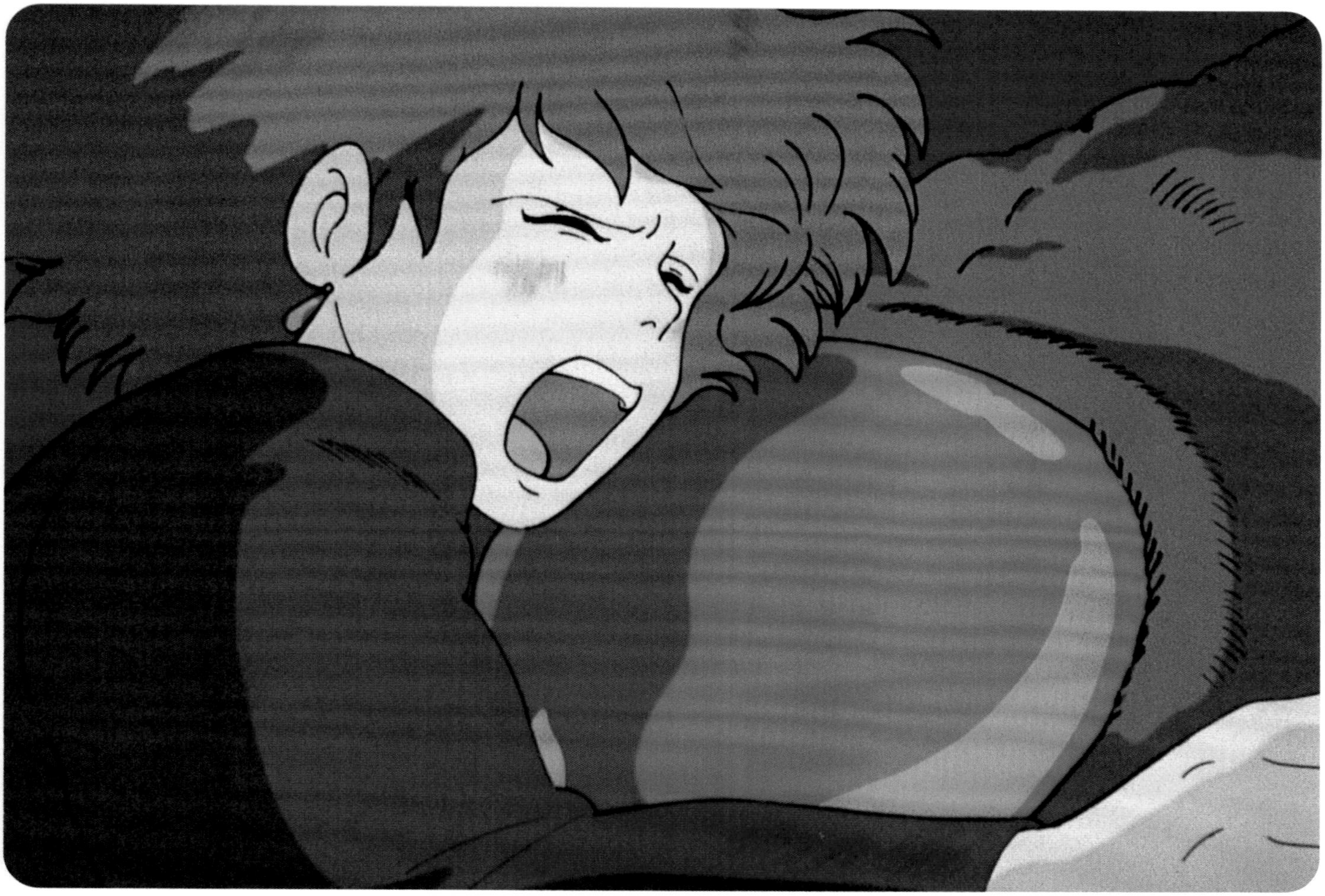

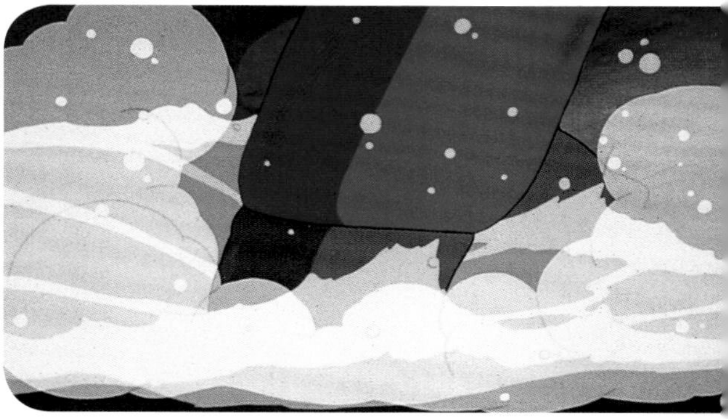

The baby was moving toward Acid Lake.

"No—you can't go into the lake!" The princess pushed back, but the Ohm forced her toward the lake. She stepped backward into the lake with her injured foot. There was a hissing sound as the acid burned her. She screamed in agony.

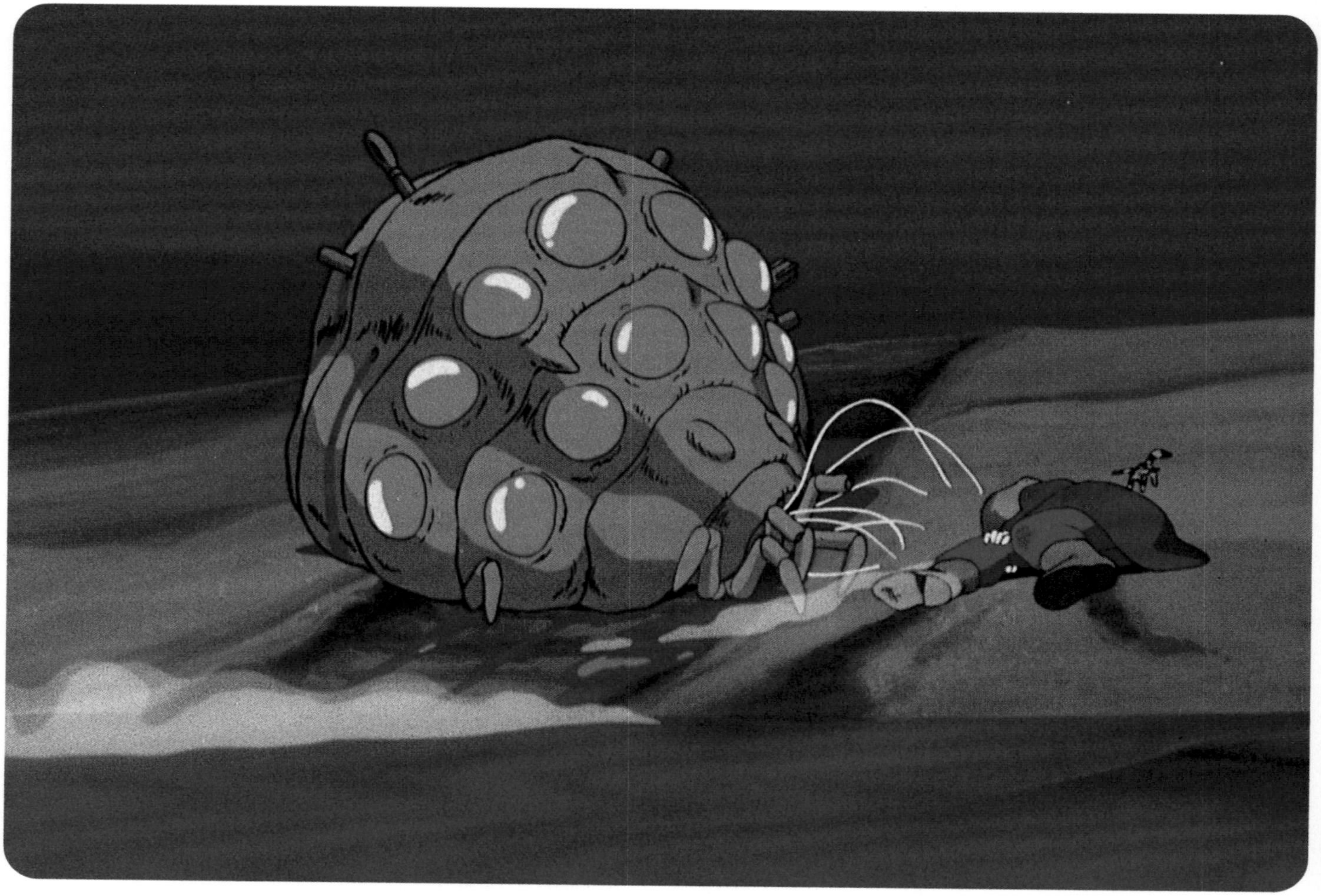

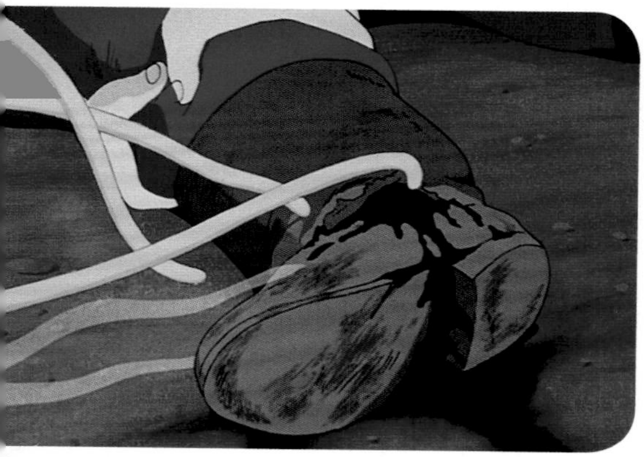

The pain was so terrible that she collapsed on the shore. Her shoe was smoking from the burning acid.

Slowly, the baby Ohm turned and extended its golden feelers toward her. Now its eyes were calm and blue.

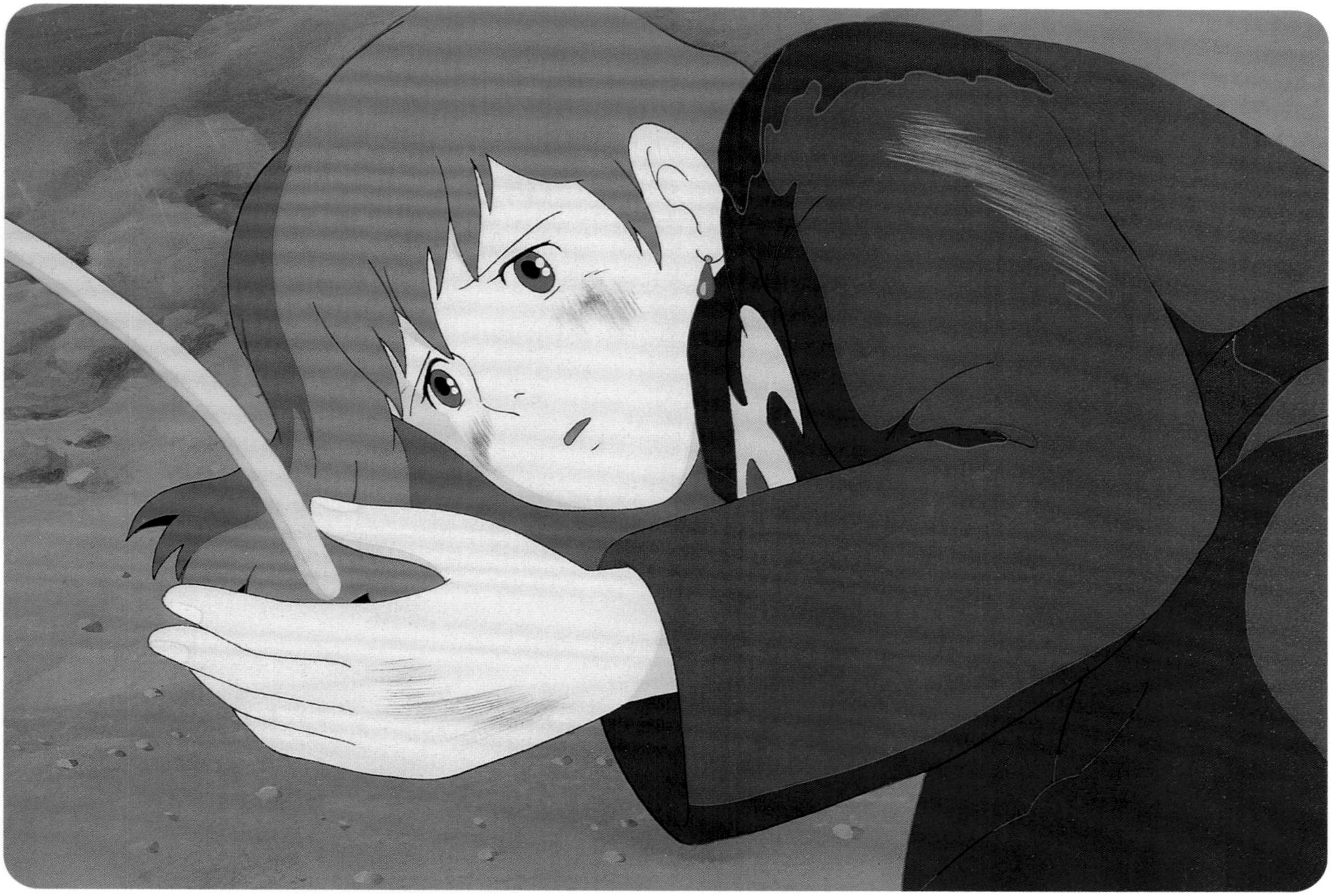

The feelers began to stroke her wounds gently, as though the Ohm was worried about her.

Nausicaä forgot her pain and stood up. Her wounds were healed!

"You're so kind. I'm all right now. Soon they'll be here to take you home."

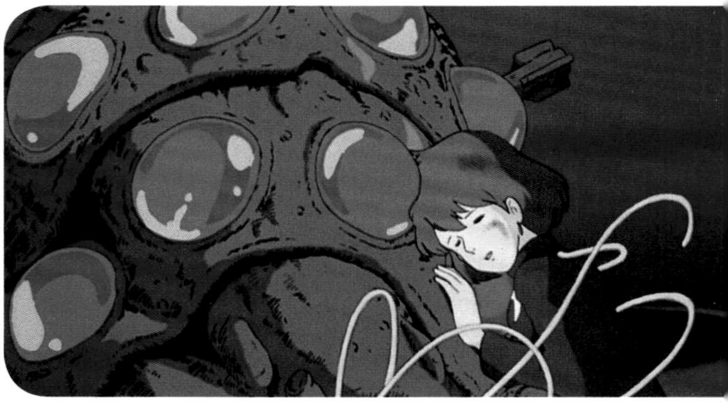

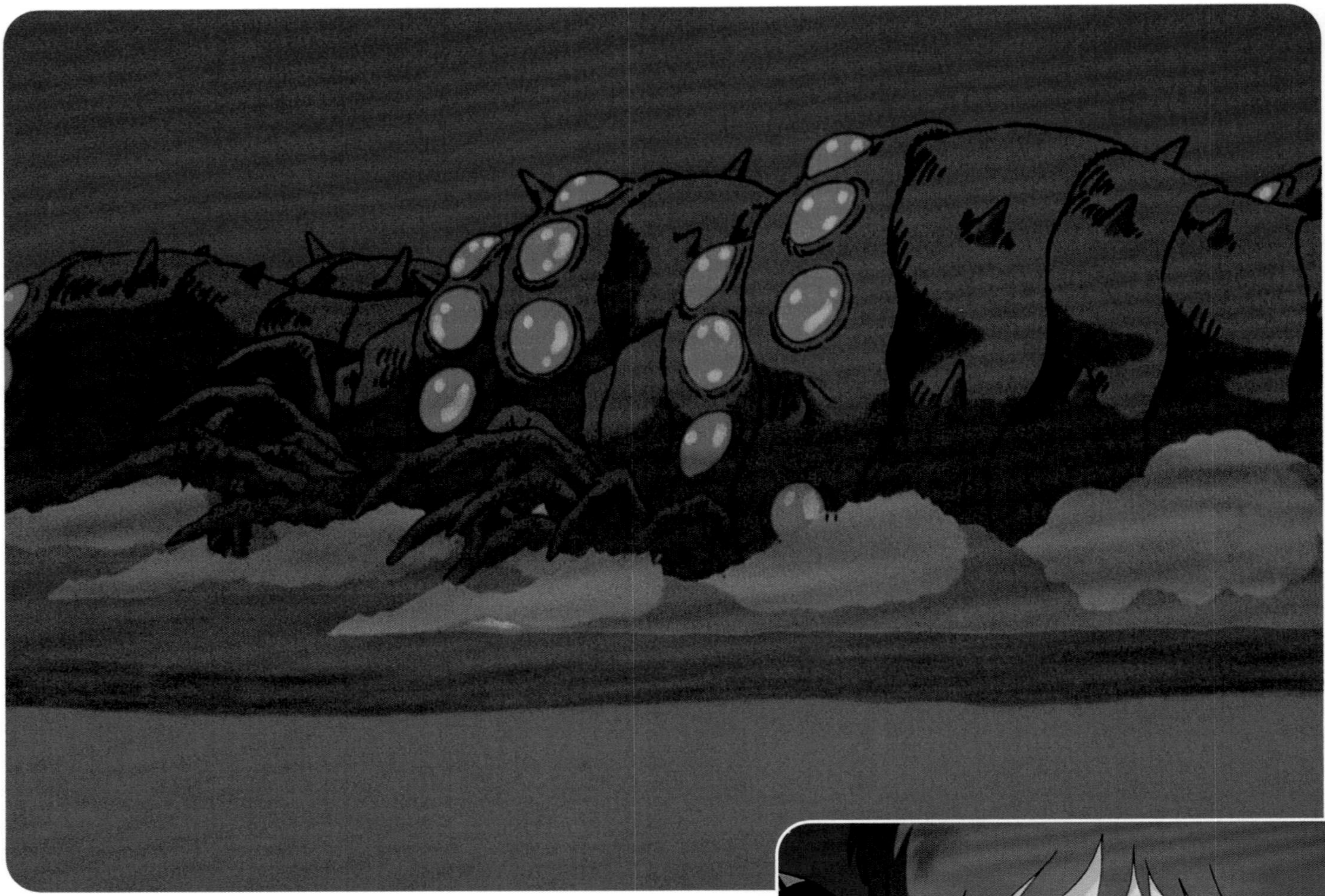

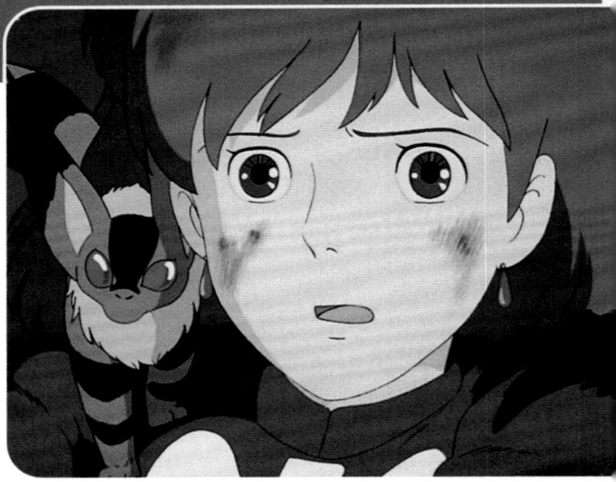

But the Ohms did not come for their baby. The earth trembled as they stampeded toward the valley. Nausicaä begged them to stop, but it was no use.

"They must be blind with rage. If I can't find a way to calm them, the valley is doomed!"

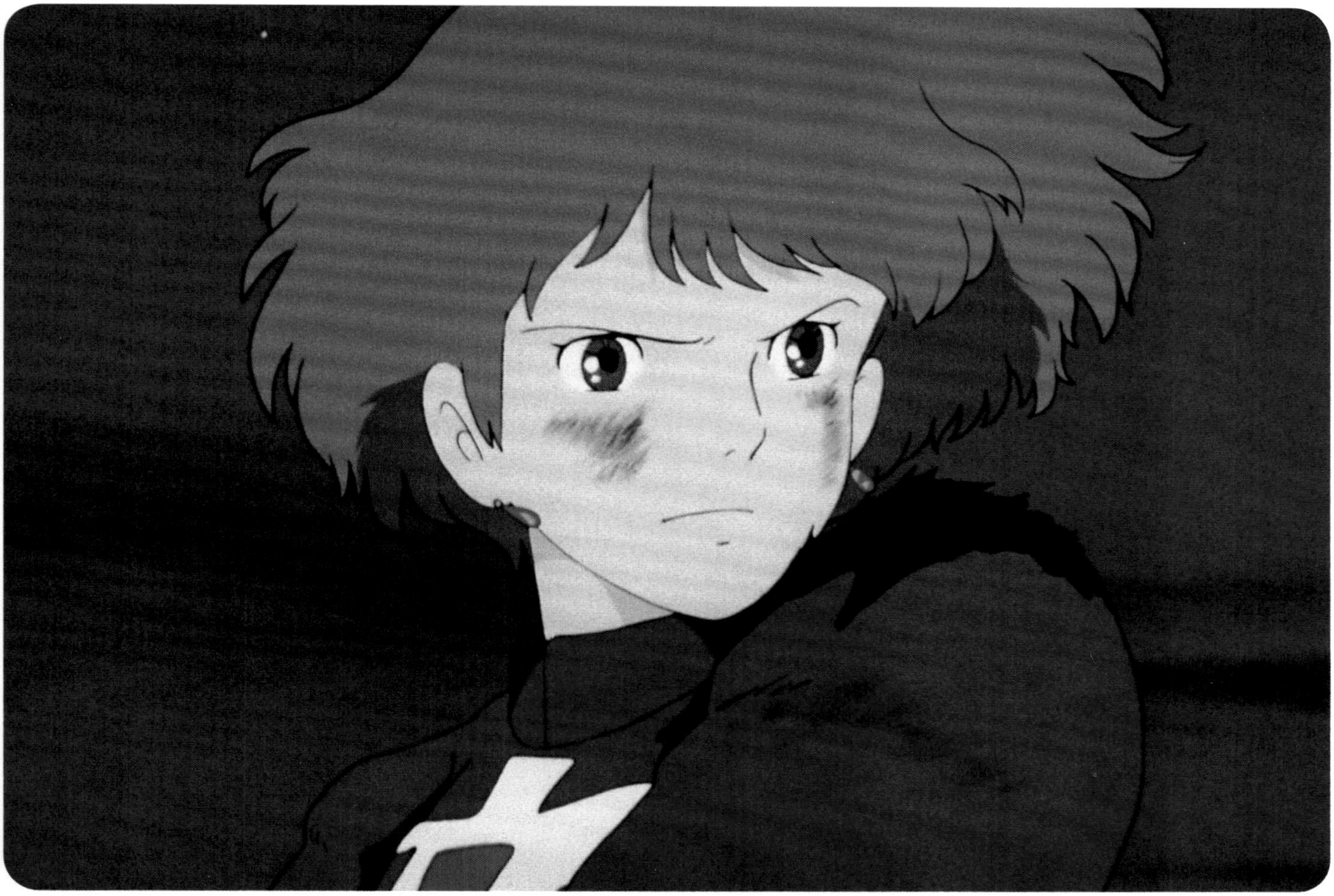

Nausicaä took the machine gun from the hover pod and aimed it at the two soldiers.

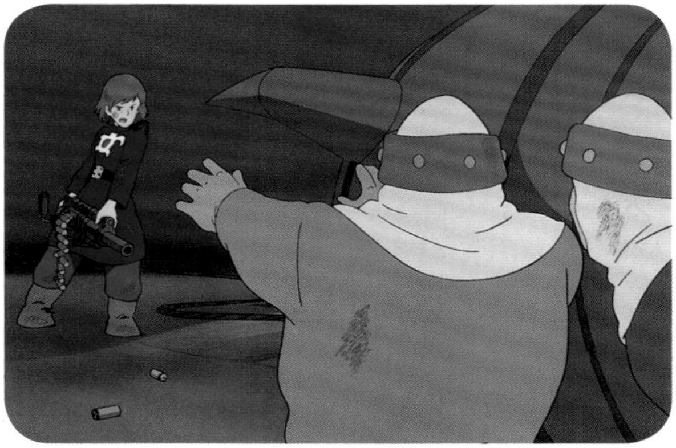

"Fly me back to the herd. We're going to give their baby back to them!"

"It's too late, the herd won't stop…"

She fired warning shots. "Take us there and set us down near the herd. Now let's get going!"

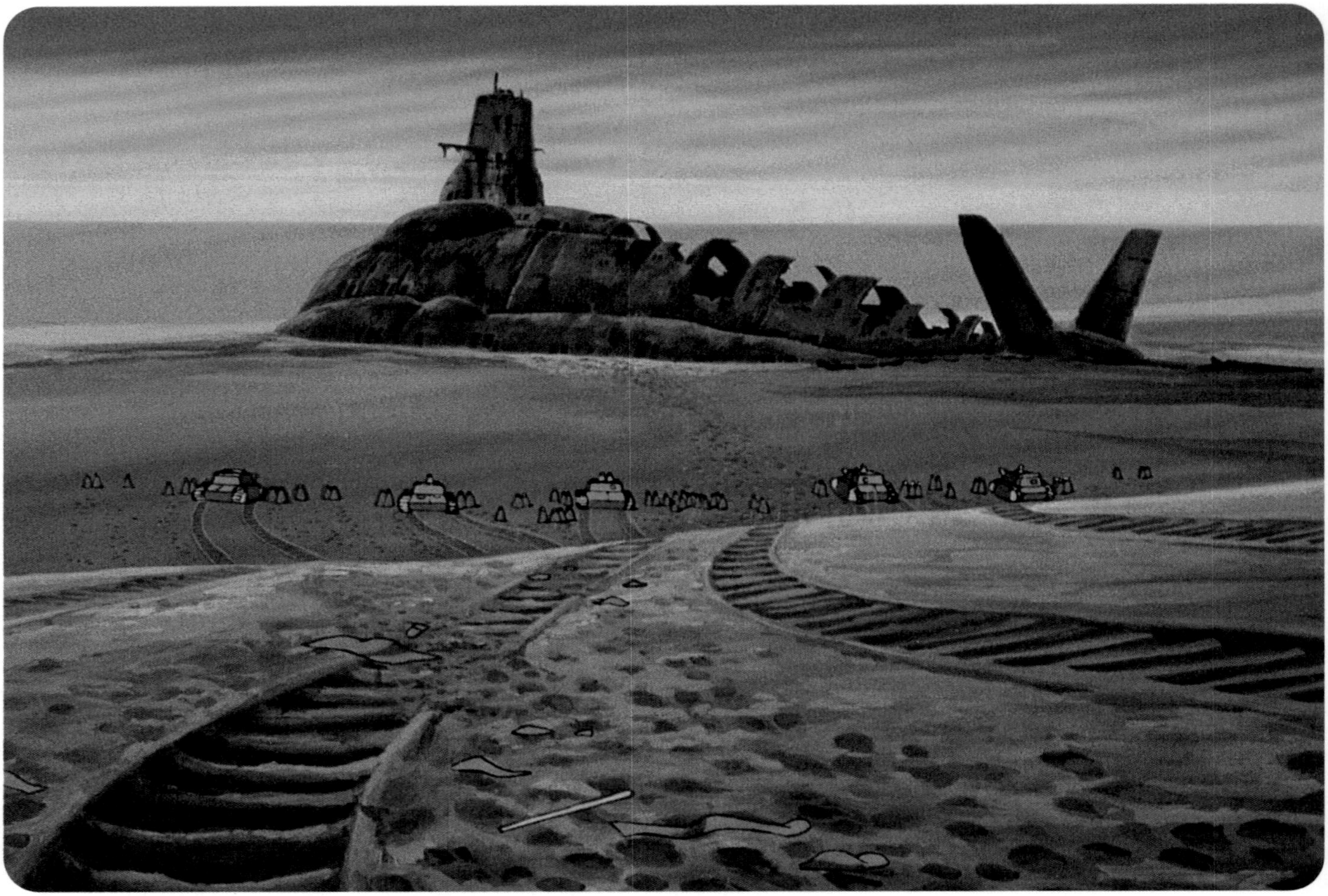

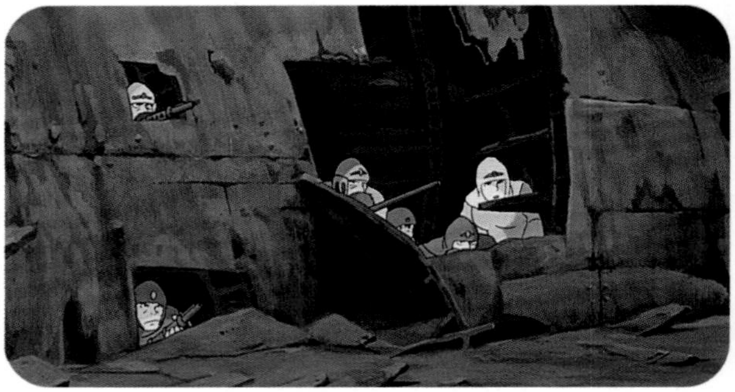

THE PLAIN OF GOLD

On the far shore of Acid Lake, the people of the valley were holed up in the old airship. They had been waiting for hours, hoping Nausicaä would return to help them fight the Tolmekians.

Kushana was holding three old men from the valley hostage.

"Tell the villagers to surrender," she said. "Otherwise, I'll have to kill them all."

One of the old men, who was named Gol, looked up at Kushana.

"It's strange that you're a princess. You're not anything like our princess."

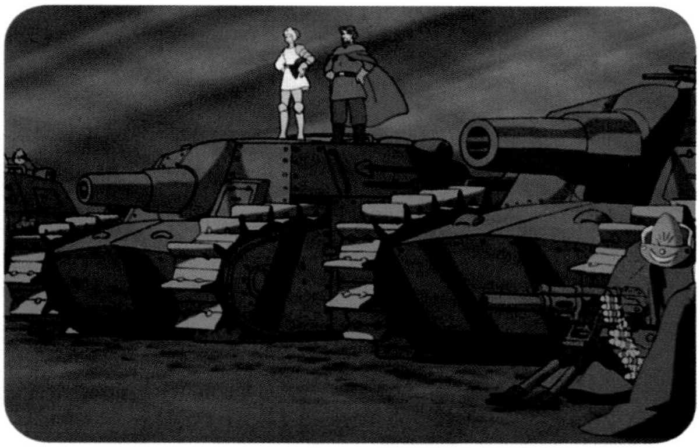

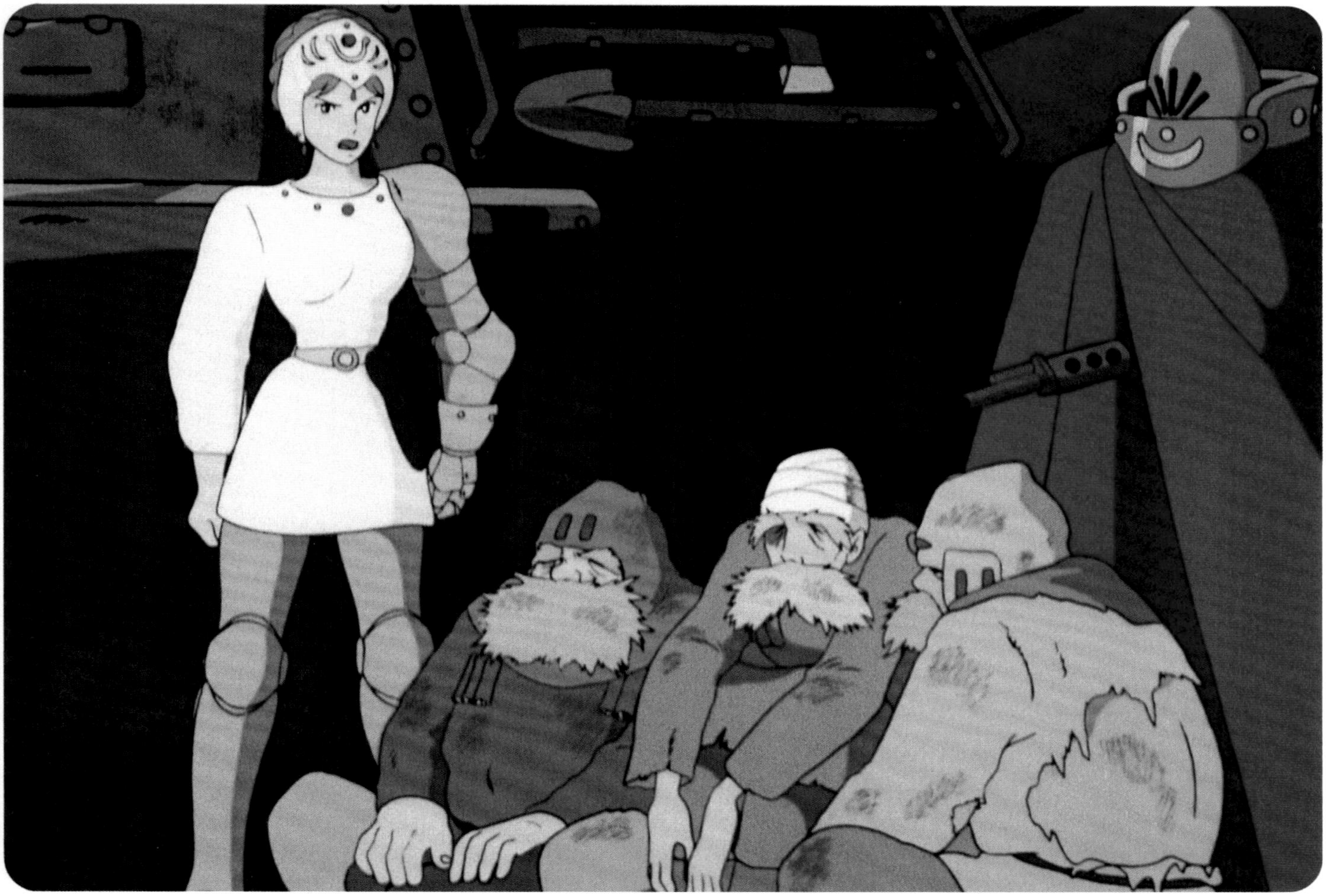

"Take a look at my hands."

Gol rubbed his worn, callused hands. "The poison from the jungle is turning them to stone. But our princess told me that she truly loves these beat-up old hands of mine. She knows these are the hands of a hard worker."

Kushana stared in amazement. "The Sea of Decay is killing you, yet you want to live in harmony with it?

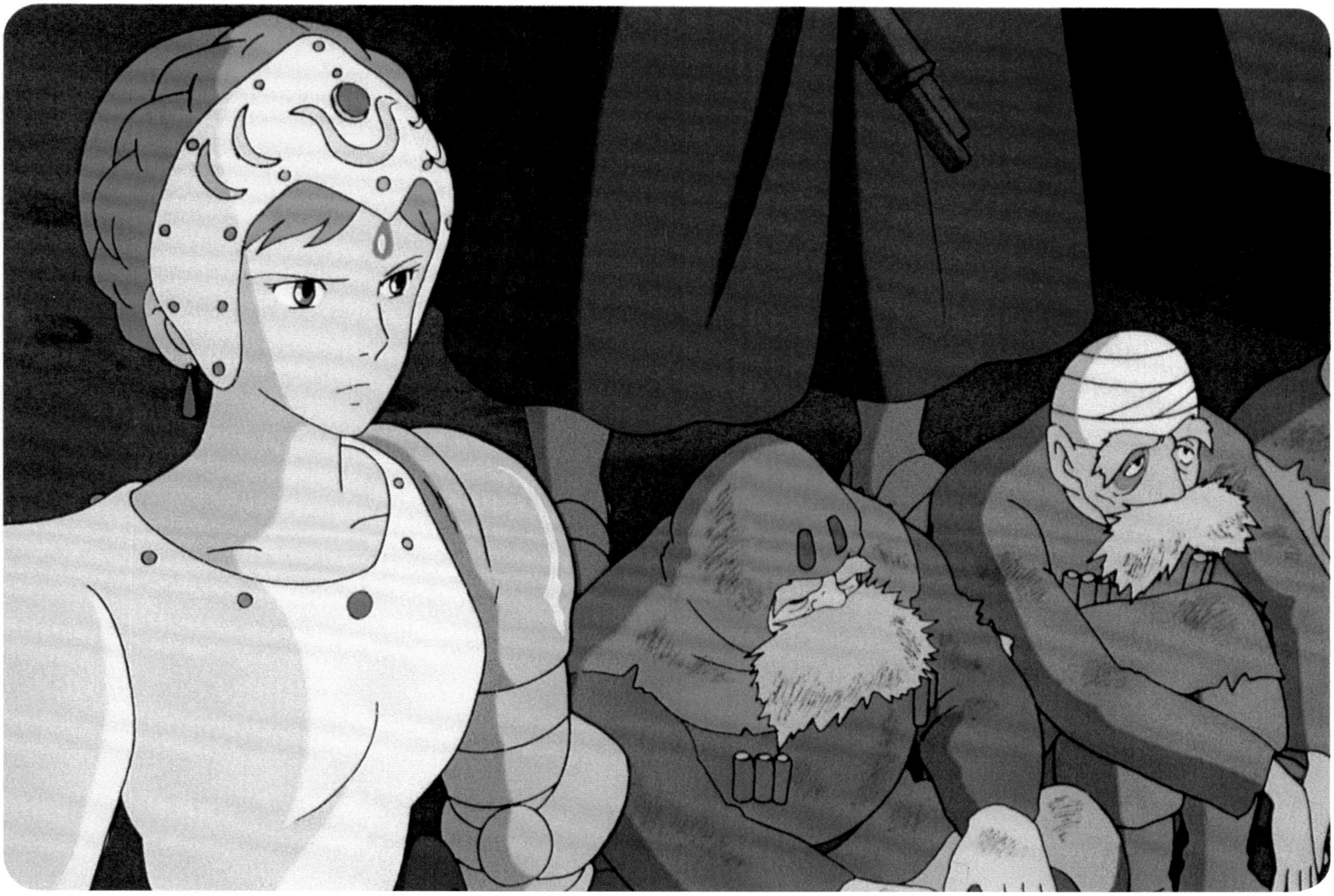

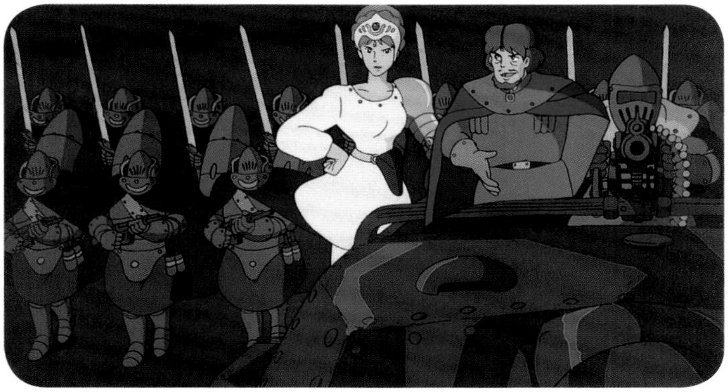

"You want to burn the jungle. Fire can burn a forest to ashes in a day, but it takes the water and wind a hundred years to grow a new one."

Kushana listened quietly, then turned to Kurotowa.

"Prepare the troops to attack!"

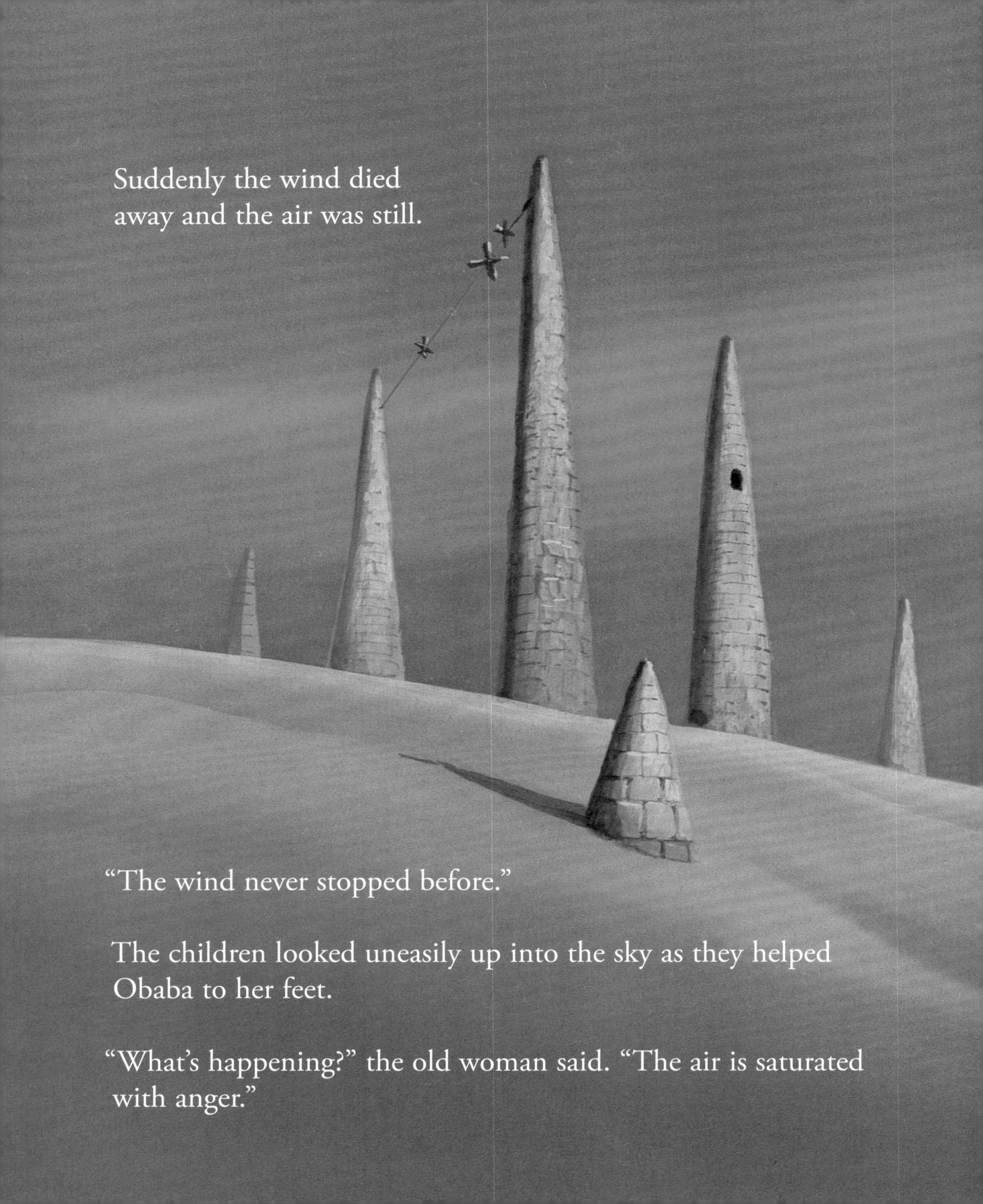

Suddenly the wind died away and the air was still.

"The wind never stopped before."

The children looked uneasily up into the sky as they helped Obaba to her feet.

"What's happening?" the old woman said. "The air is saturated with anger."

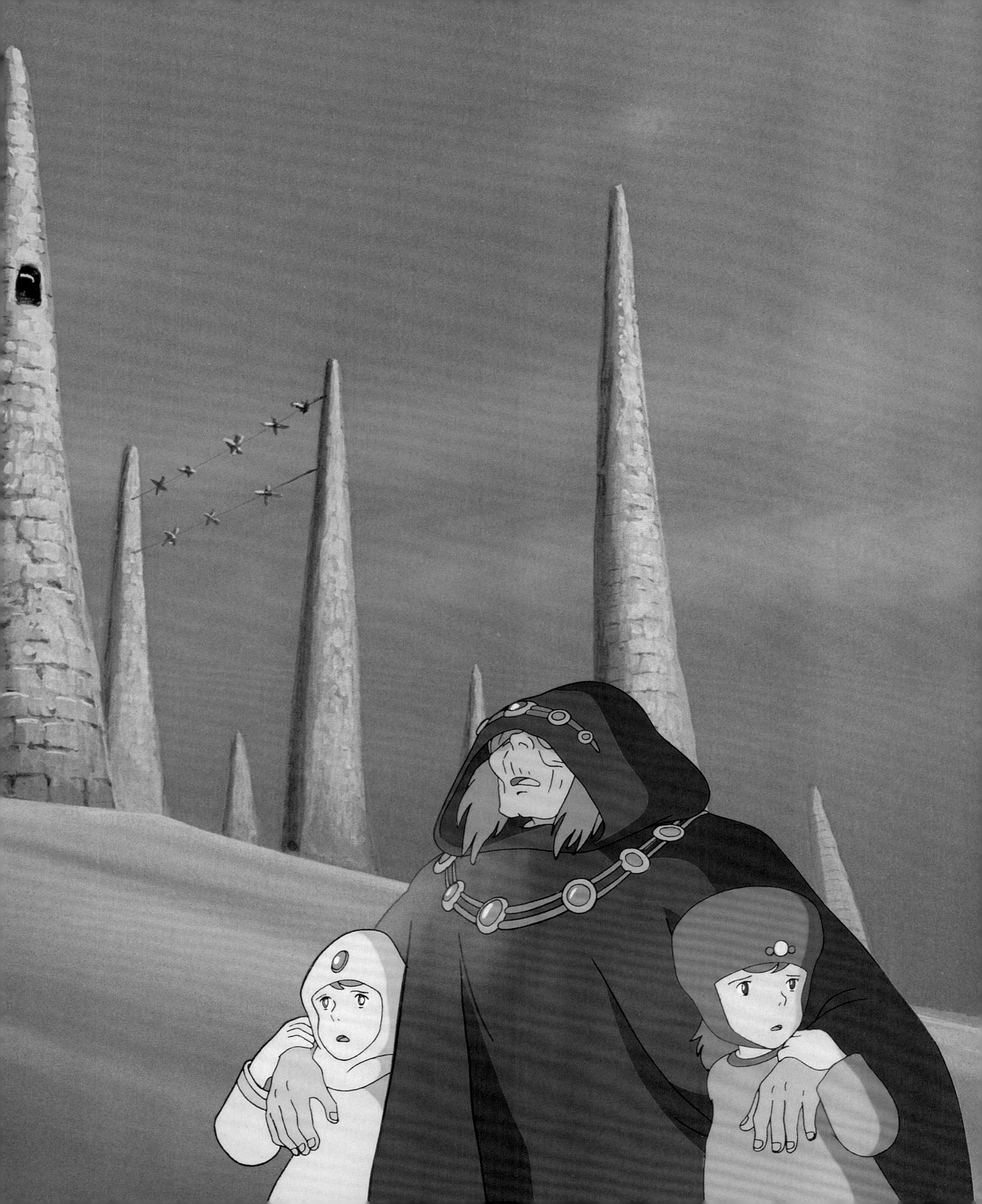

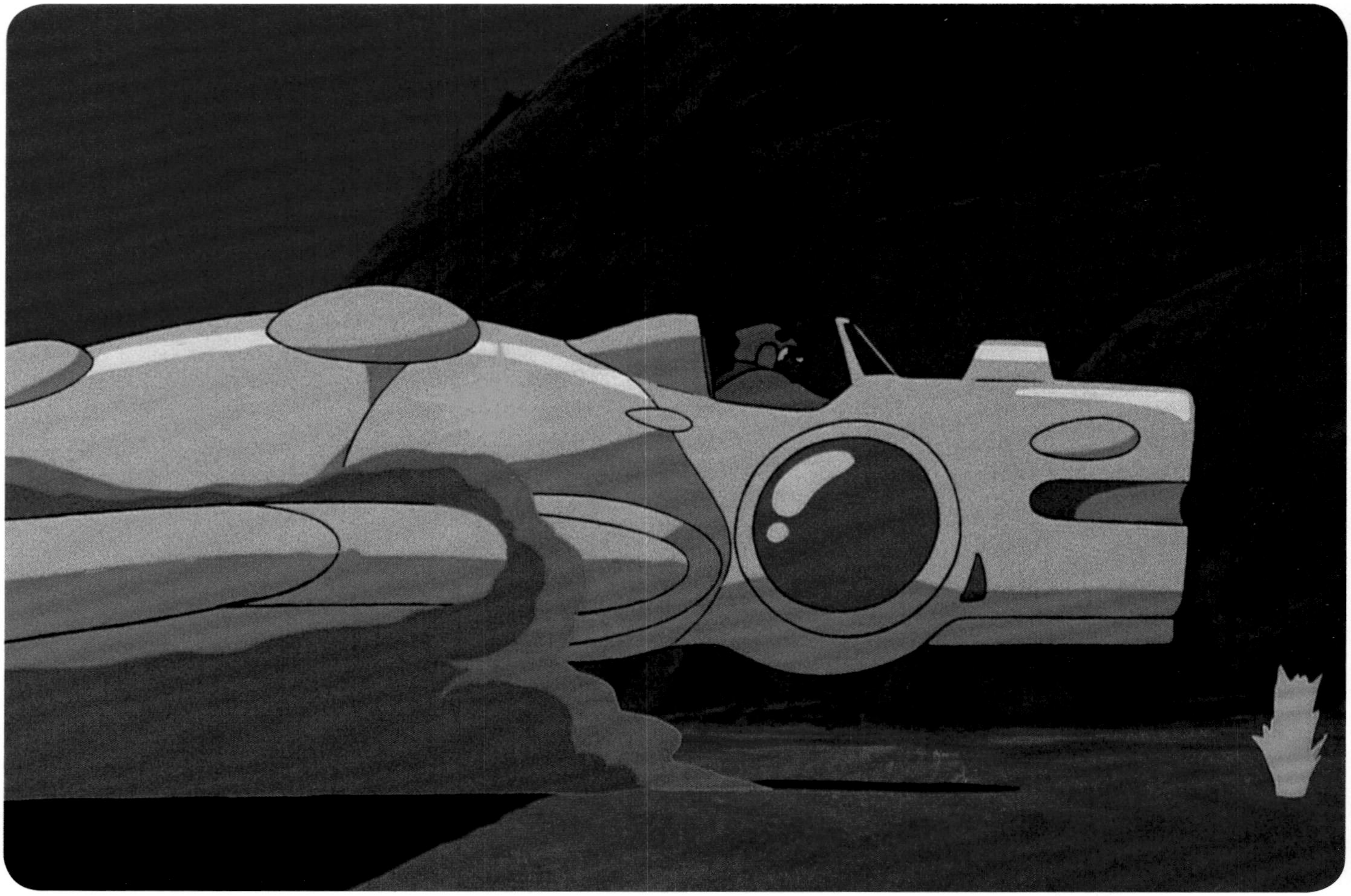

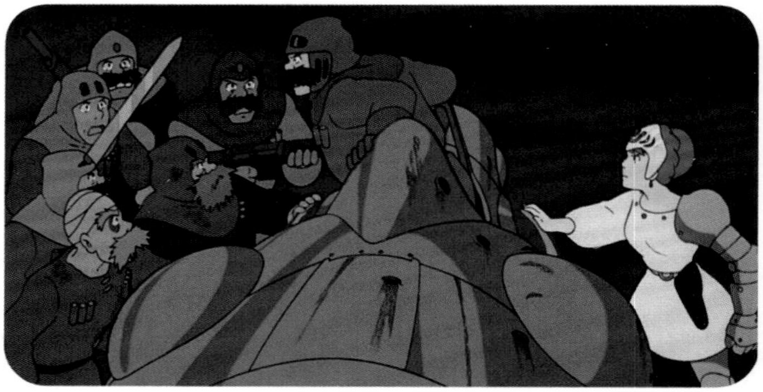

Mito touched down between the old airship and Kushana's forces. The people of the valley quickly surrounded the gunship. Kushana ran out to meet it too.

"What happened to the princess?" she asked impatiently.

But Mito ignored her. "Listen up!" he said to the people. "The Ohms are coming this way. The princess stayed behind to stop the stampede from reaching the valley. This is no time for a battle. Everybody get to high ground—and hurry!"

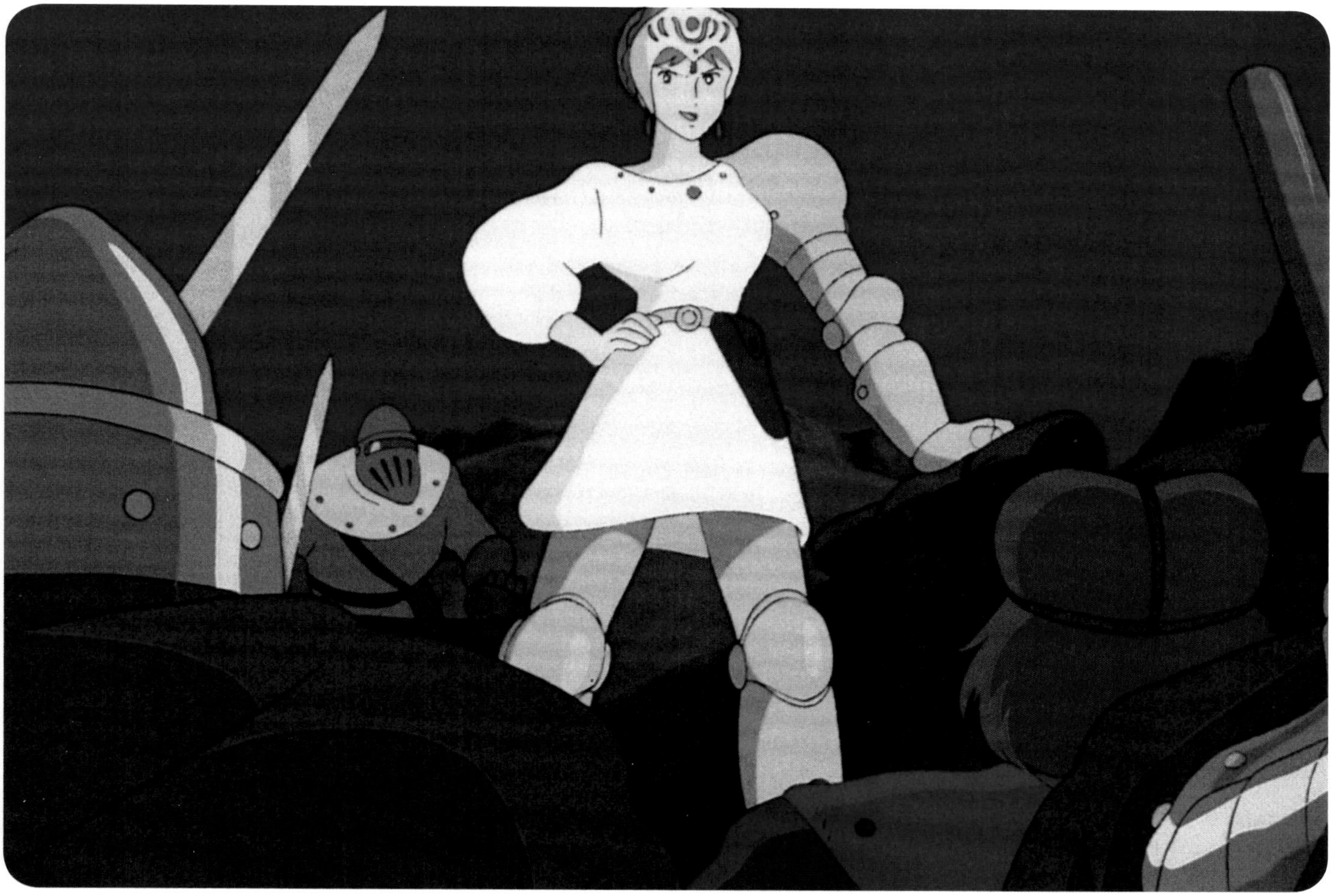

Kushana climbed onto one of the tanks and addressed her troops. "Hold the insects off for as long as you can. I'll be back with help."

Kurotowa stepped forward. "Your Highness, you can't. It's not ready yet!"

"If not now, then when?" She turned to the tank crew. "Move out!"

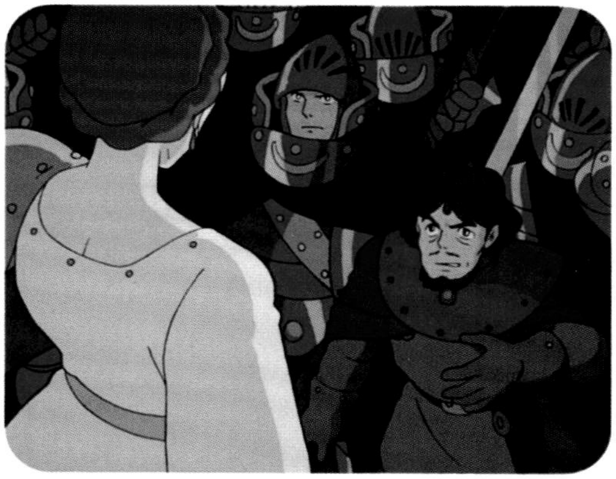

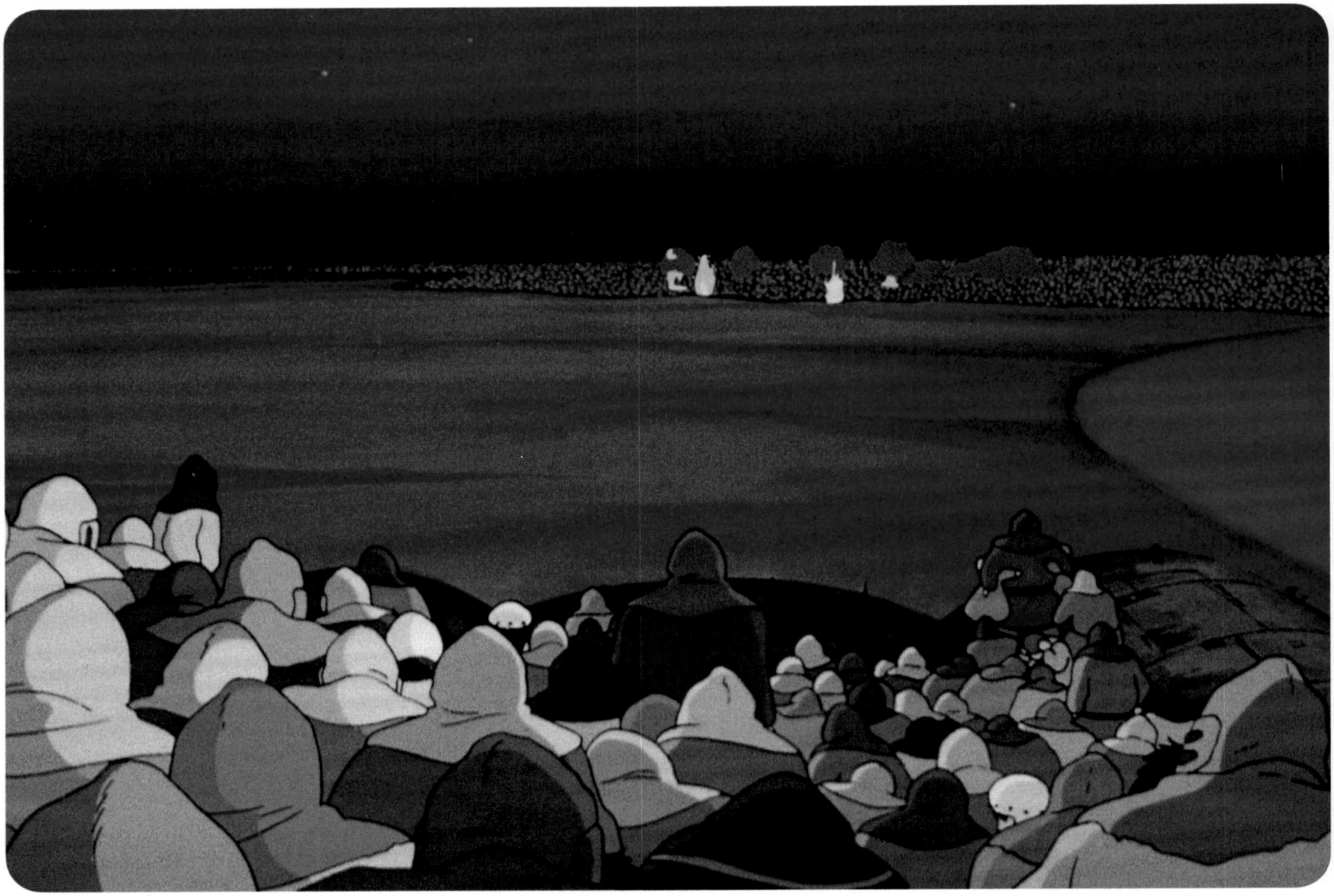

The people of the valley were gathered on the airship, high above the plain. They were hoping for safety from the stampeding insects. The red glow of their eyes was coming closer and closer.

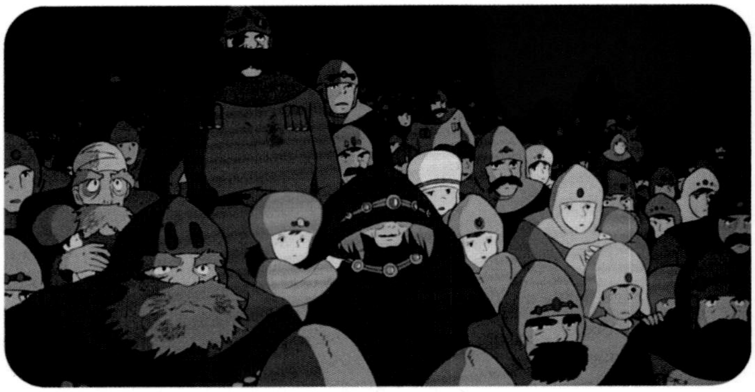

“Are we going to die?” one of the children asked Obaba.

“If that is to be our fate. We can only wait and see.”

The Tolmekians turned all their firepower on the Ohms, but it hardly slowed them down.

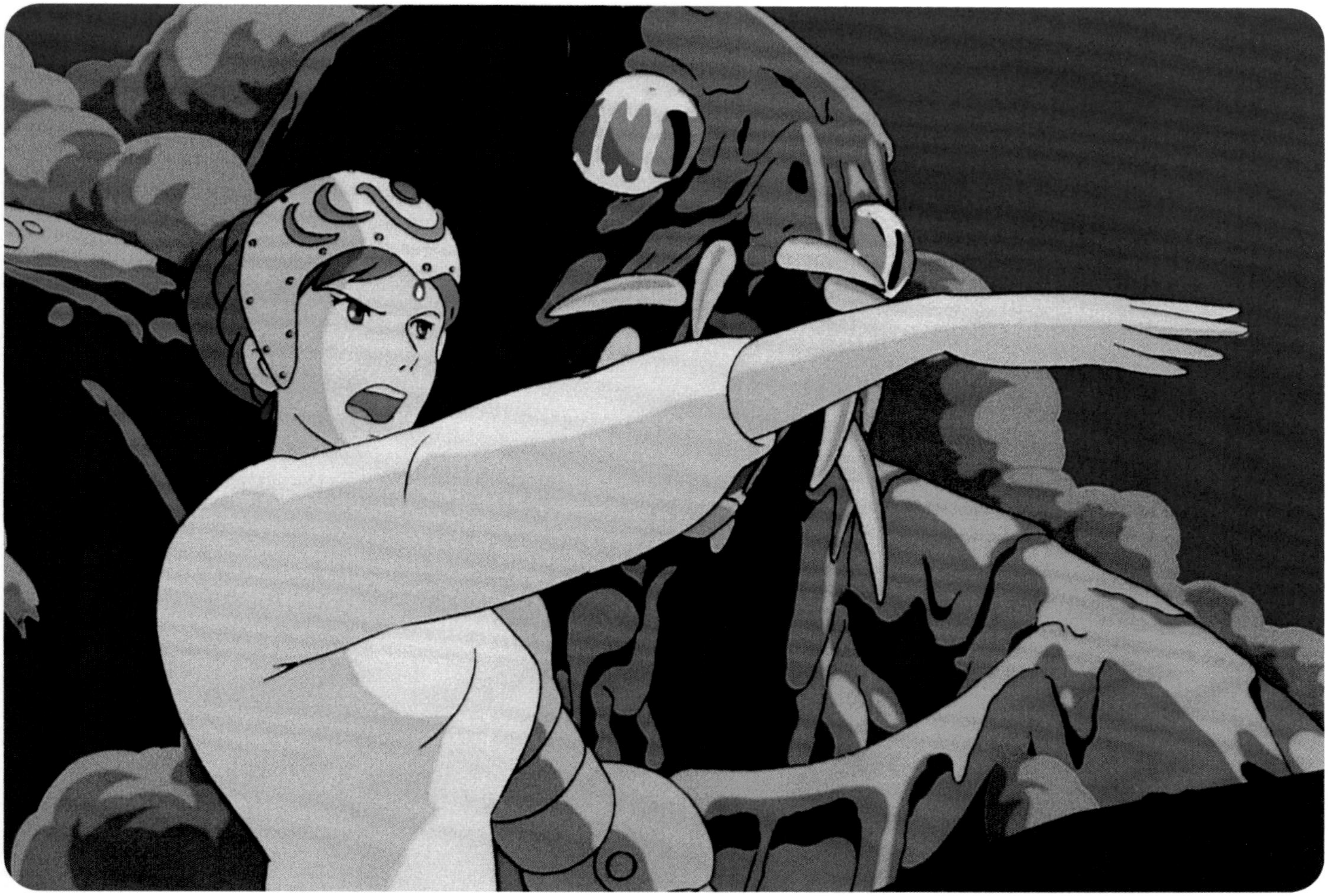

The roar of a tank engine signaled Kushana's return. She had brought the Giant Warrior!

The horrible being crawled to the top of a ridge overlooking the plain. Its body was not completely formed. It seemed to be melting and falling apart.

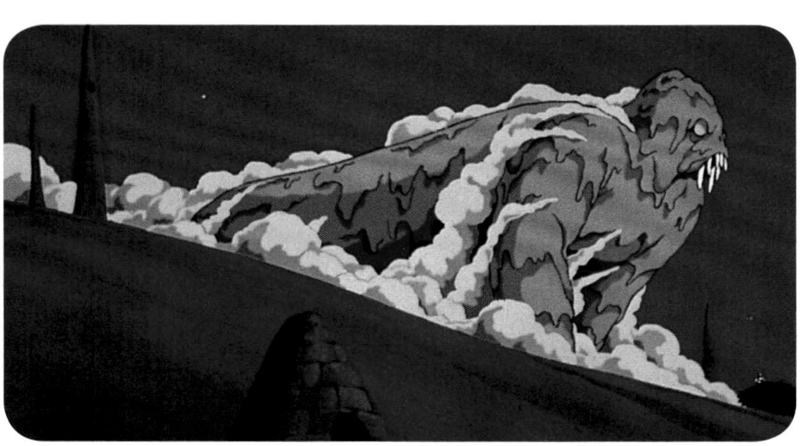

Kushana pointed to the Ohms with a sweeping gesture. "Burn them!"

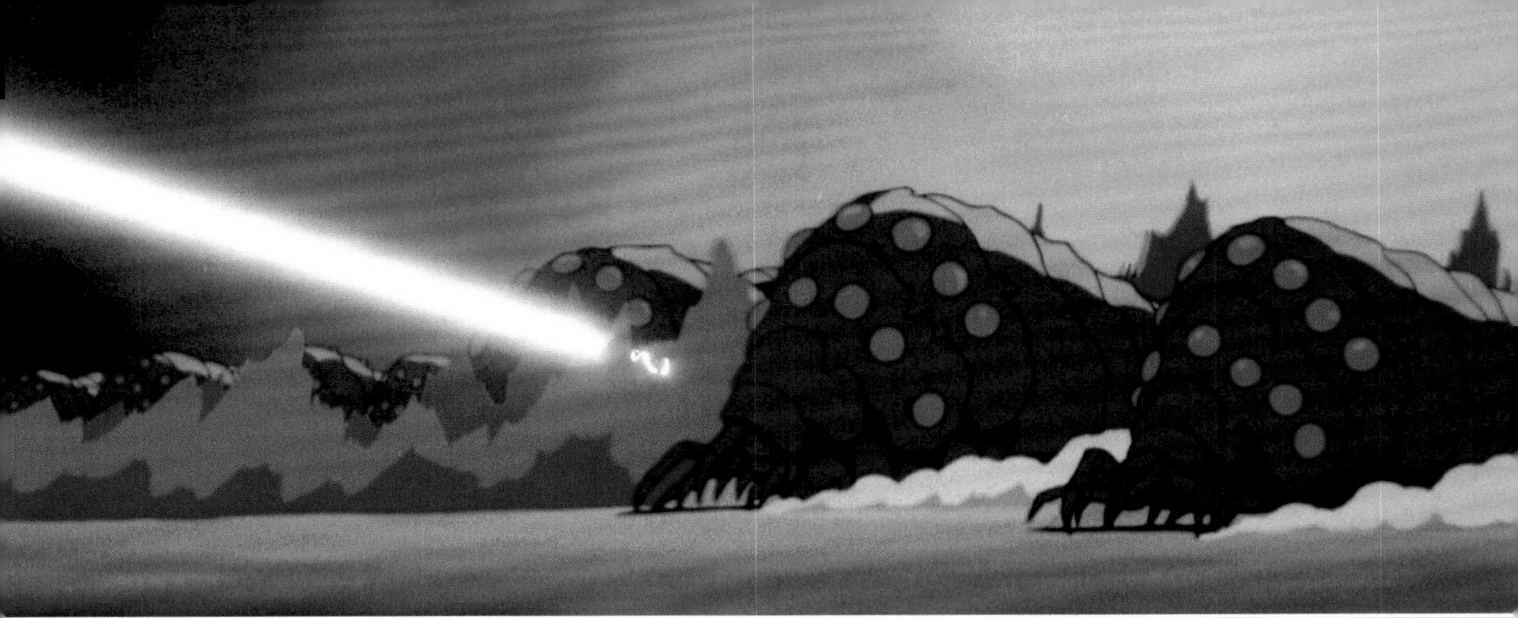
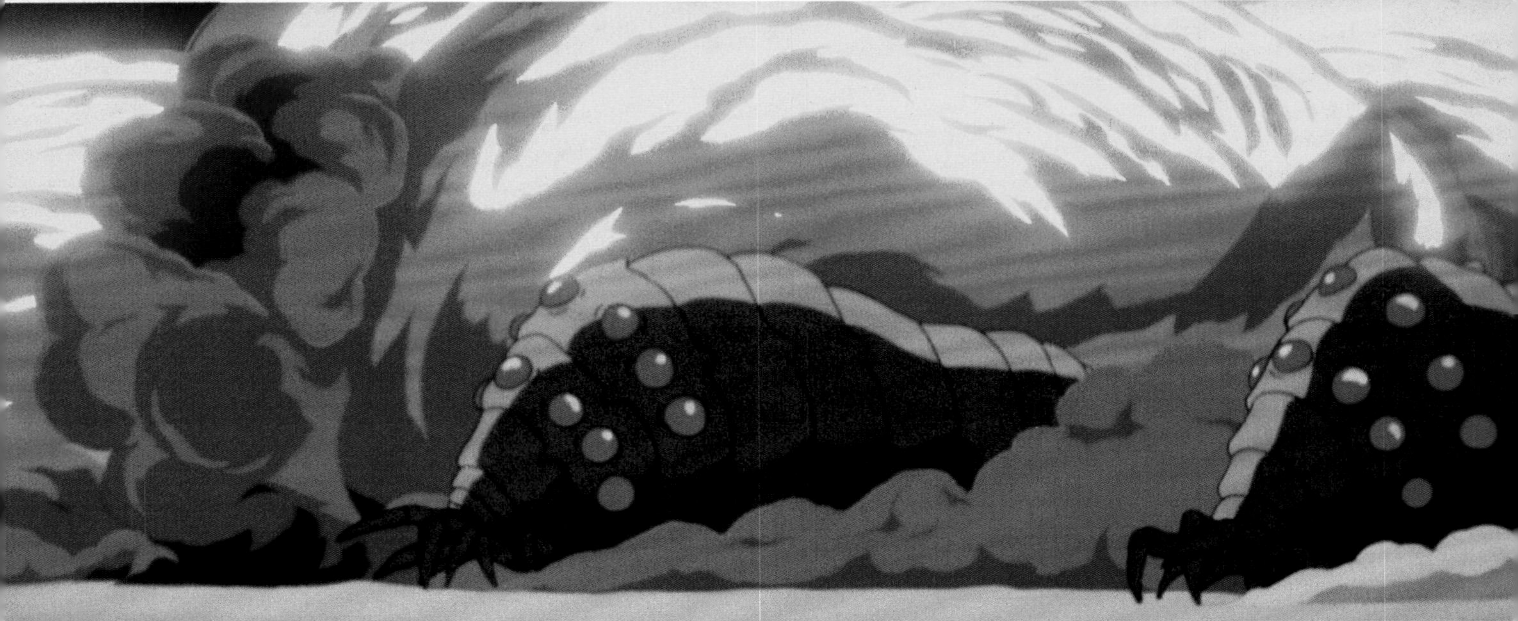
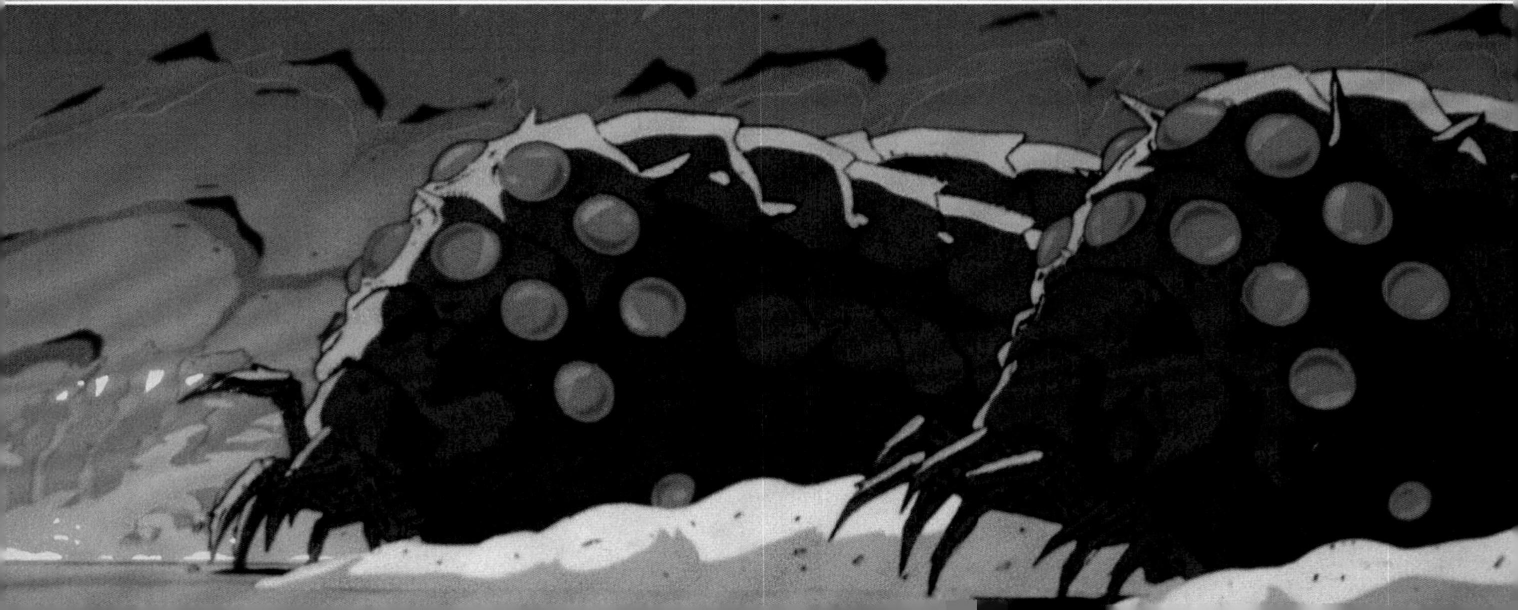

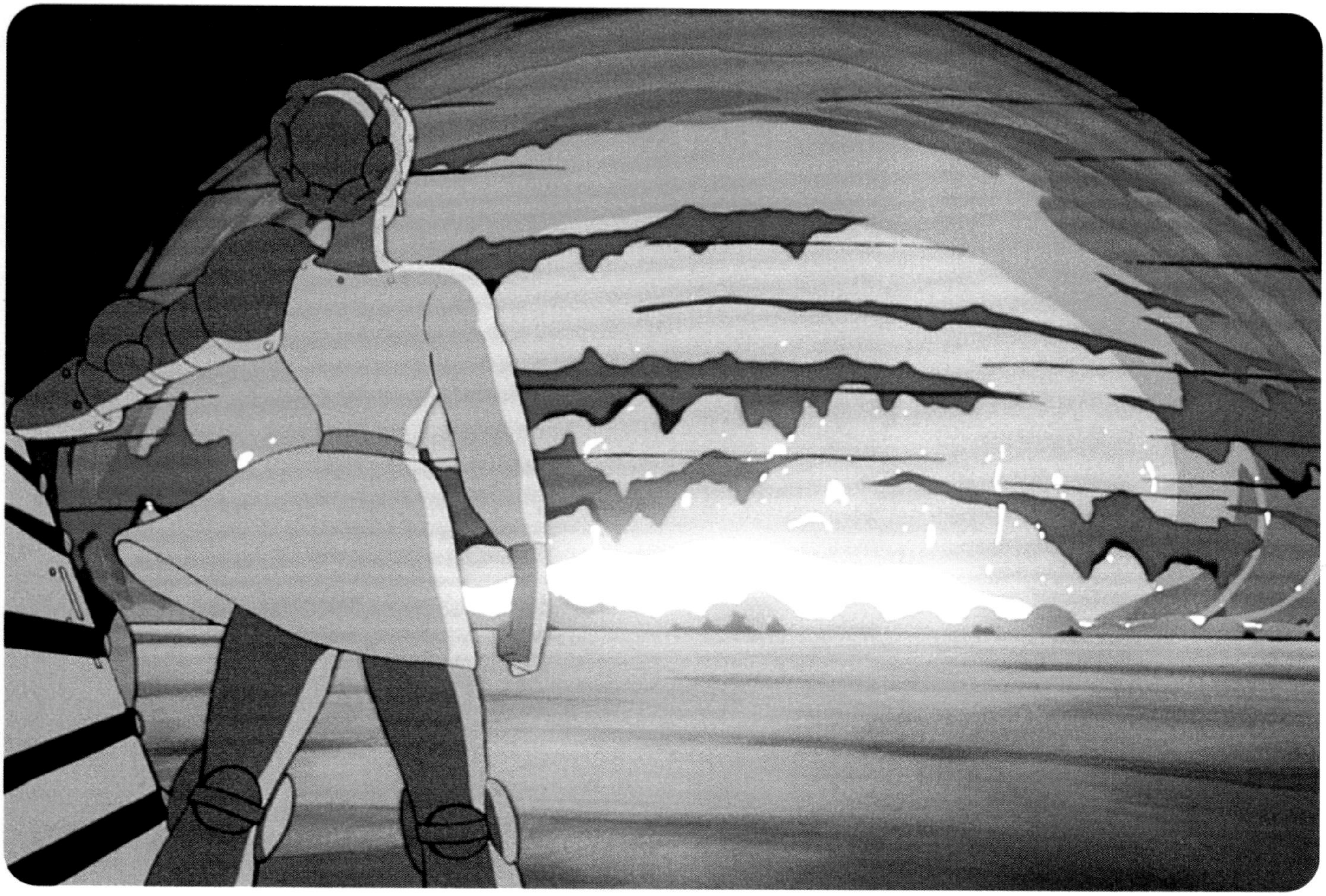

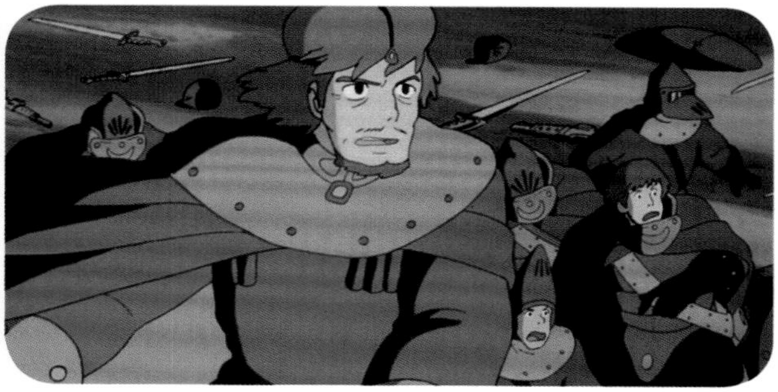

A beam of light shot from the warrior's mouth and raked the charging insects. Hundreds of Ohms were enveloped in fire. It was the same power that had destroyed civilization a thousand years before.

But more Ohms came charging through the flames.

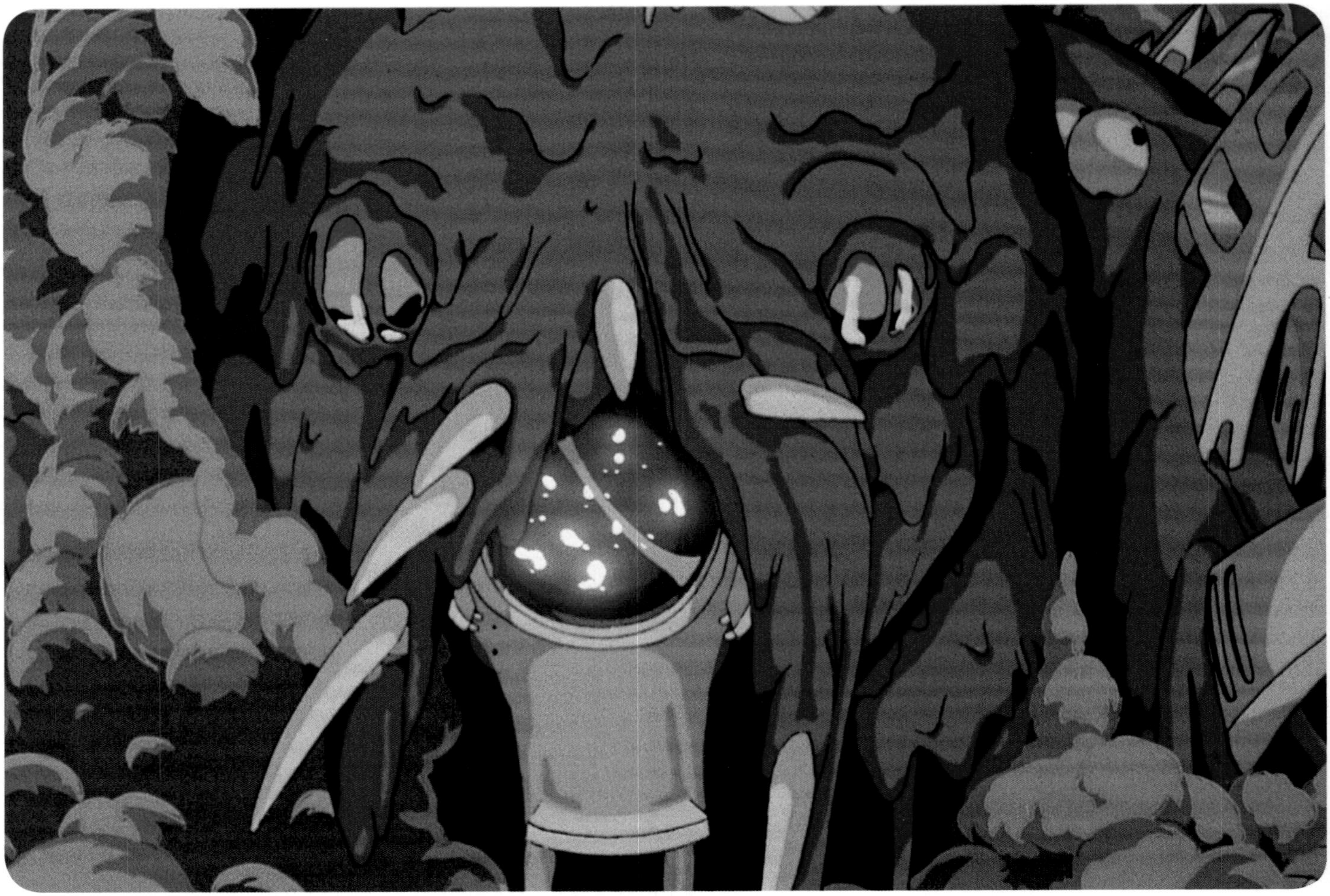

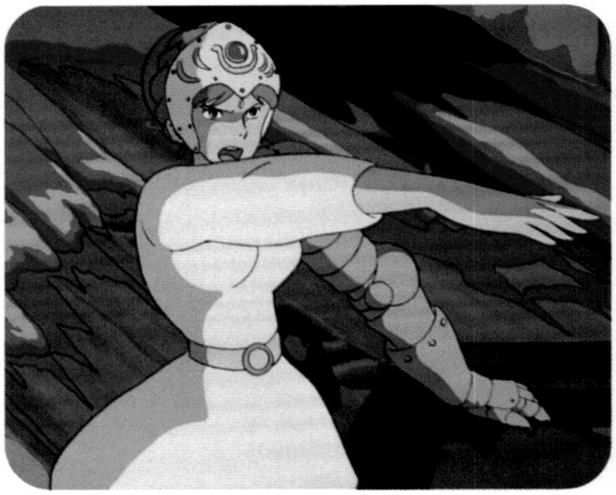

The Giant Warrior swayed and wavered. Great chunks of its body melted and dropped to the ground.

"Hit them again!" Kushana commanded.

The creature groaned and fired another beam of light from its mouth.

A second wave of fire hit the Ohms. But the warrior was dying.

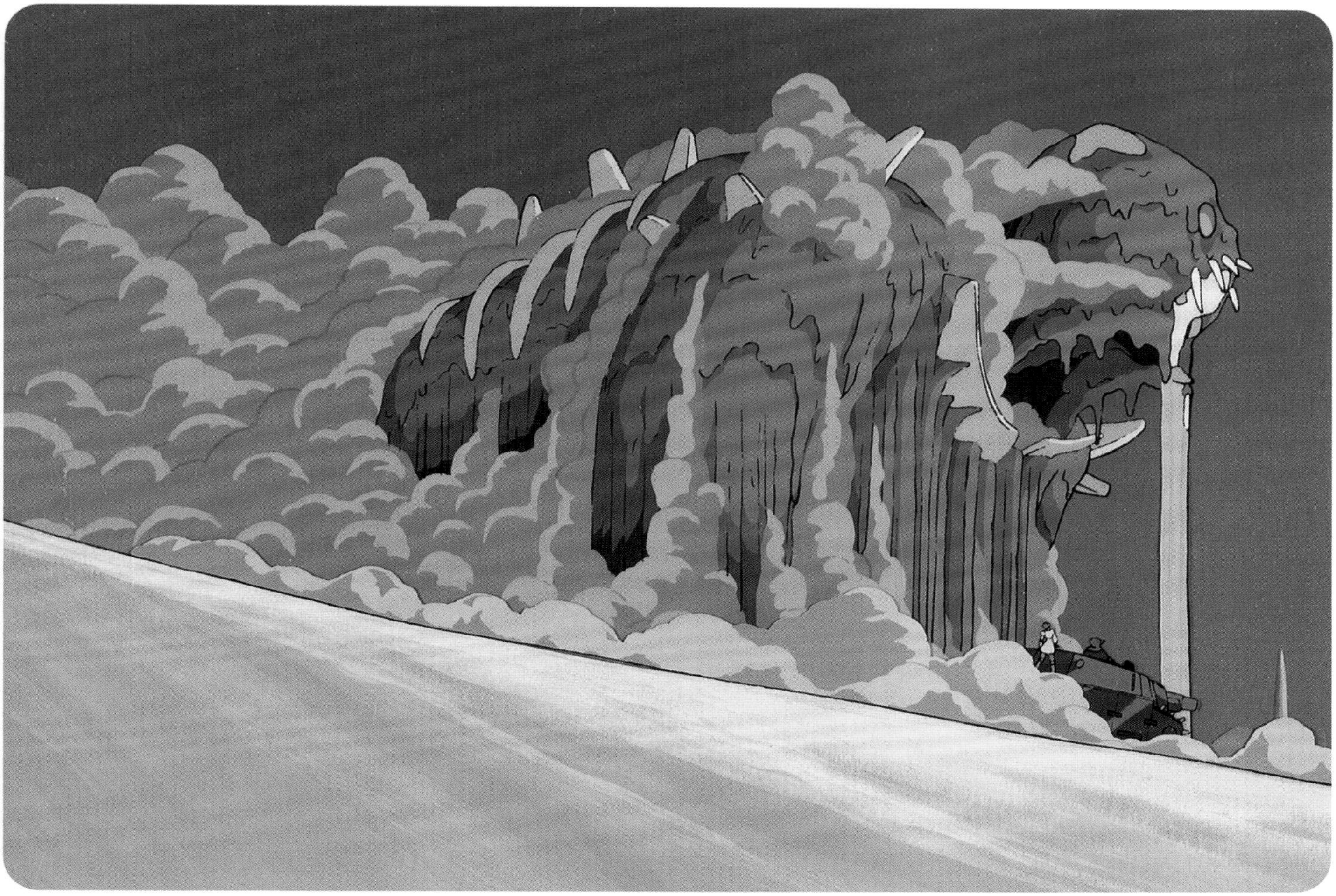

The huge monster collapsed with a roar. Its flesh melted away, leaving only bones. Kushana had woken it too early.

"The Giant Warrior is dead," one of the children said to Obaba.

"That's the way it should be. The anger of the Ohms is the anger of the earth. We don't deserve to survive if we depend on monsters like that."

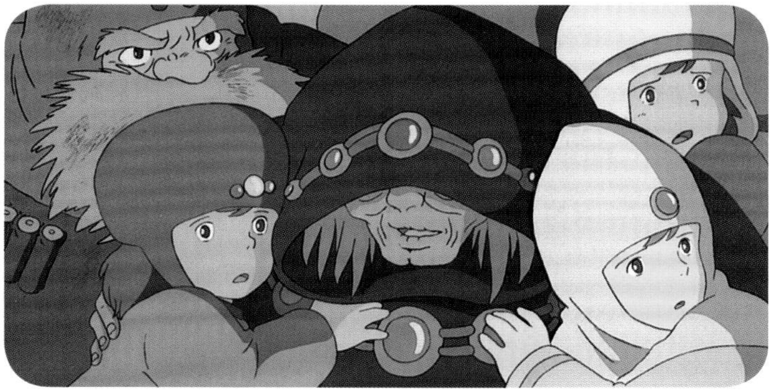

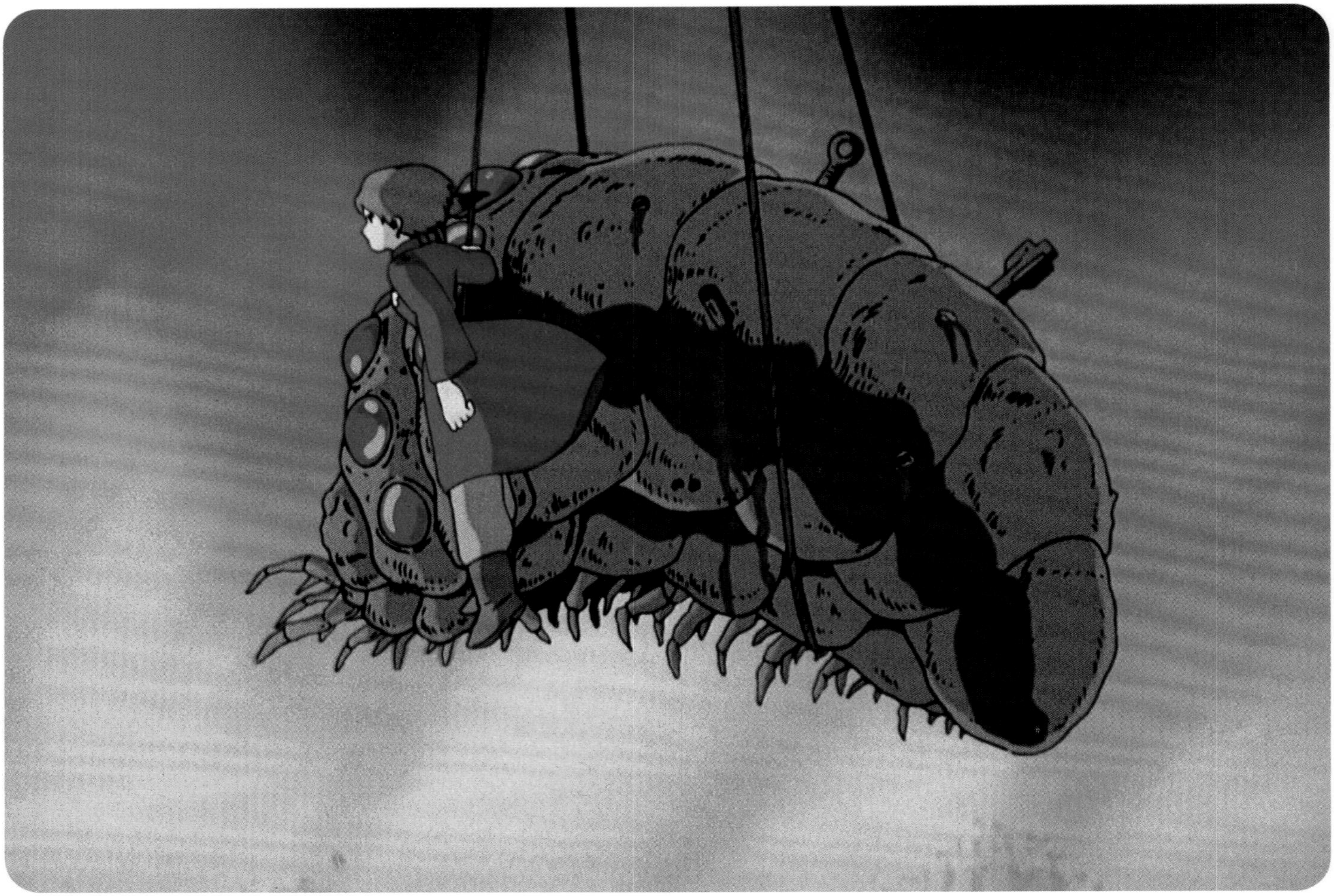

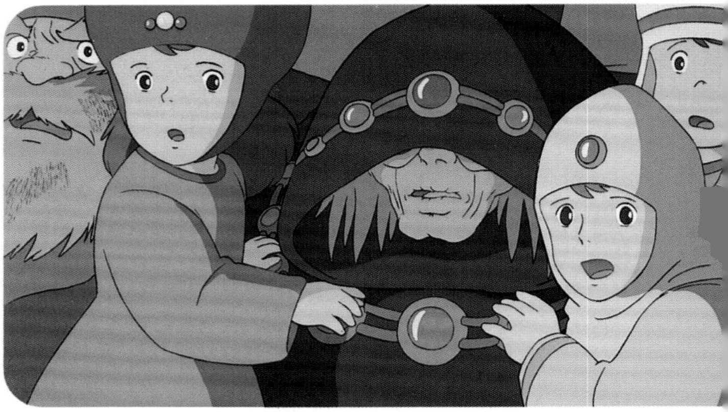

The herd of Ohms was charging straight through the fire toward the old airship. A hover pod was flying just ahead of them. Something was hanging from it on ropes.

As the pod came closer, silhouetted against the flames, the people could see the baby Ohm with Nausicaä watching over it.

"Princess!" the children cried.

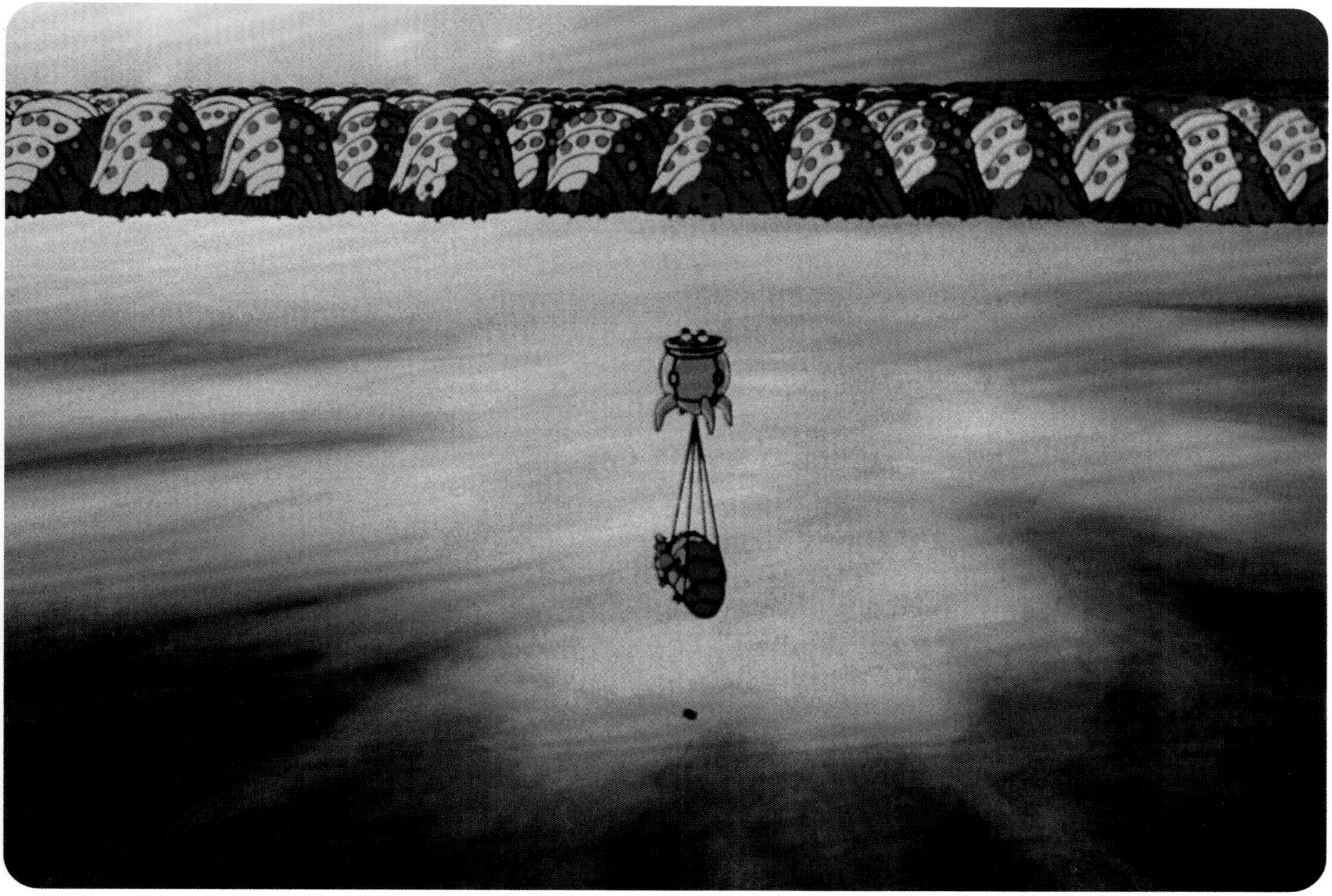

The hover pod stopped in mid-air. Slowly, it set the baby and Nausicaä on the ground before the charging Ohms.

"Princess! What are you doing?" the people called to her. "You'll be killed!"

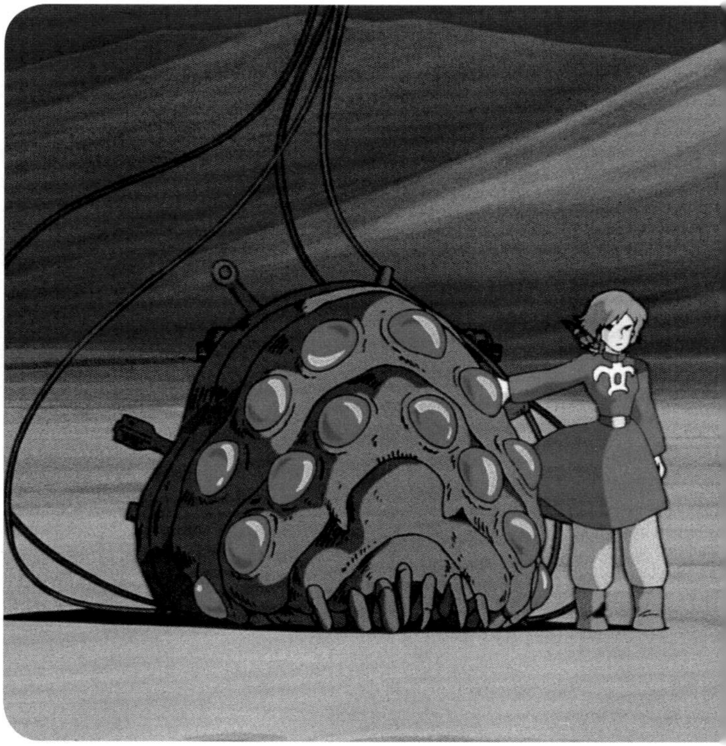

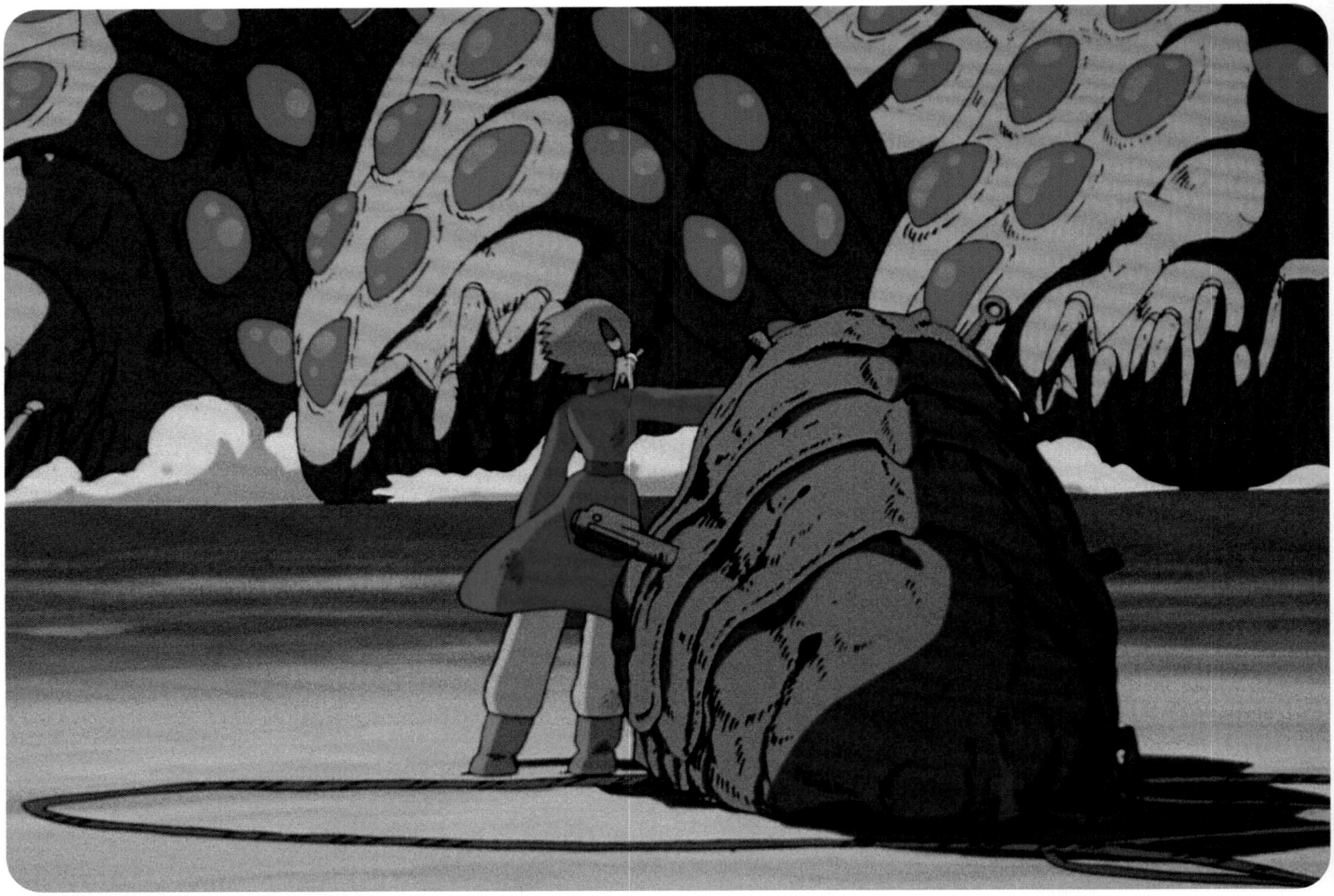

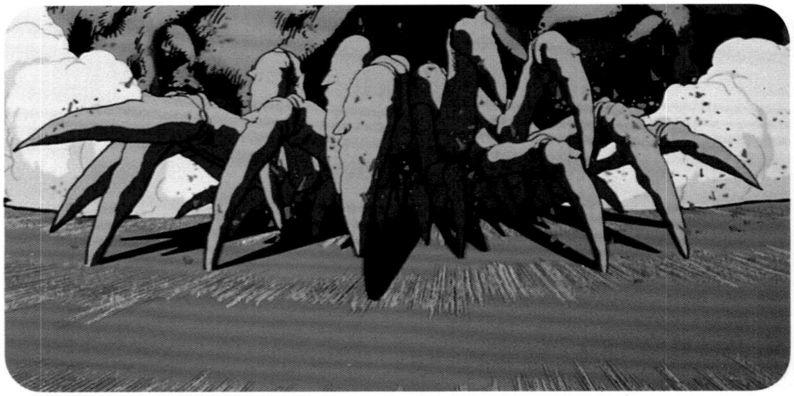

Nausicaä stood calmly next to the baby as the Ohms raced toward her. Her eyes were lit by an unshakable faith in the power of life.

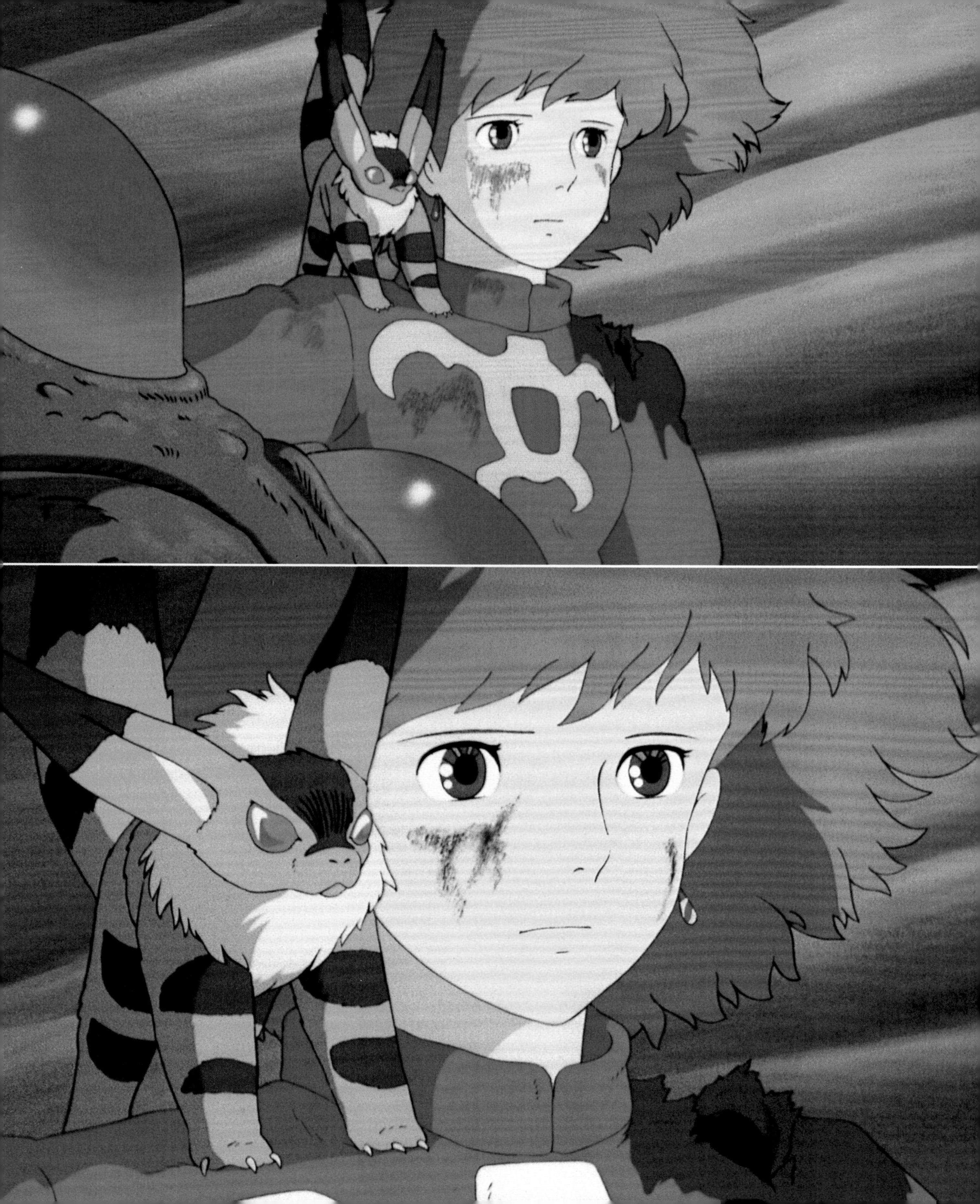

The charging Ohms struck her
and hurled her into the air.

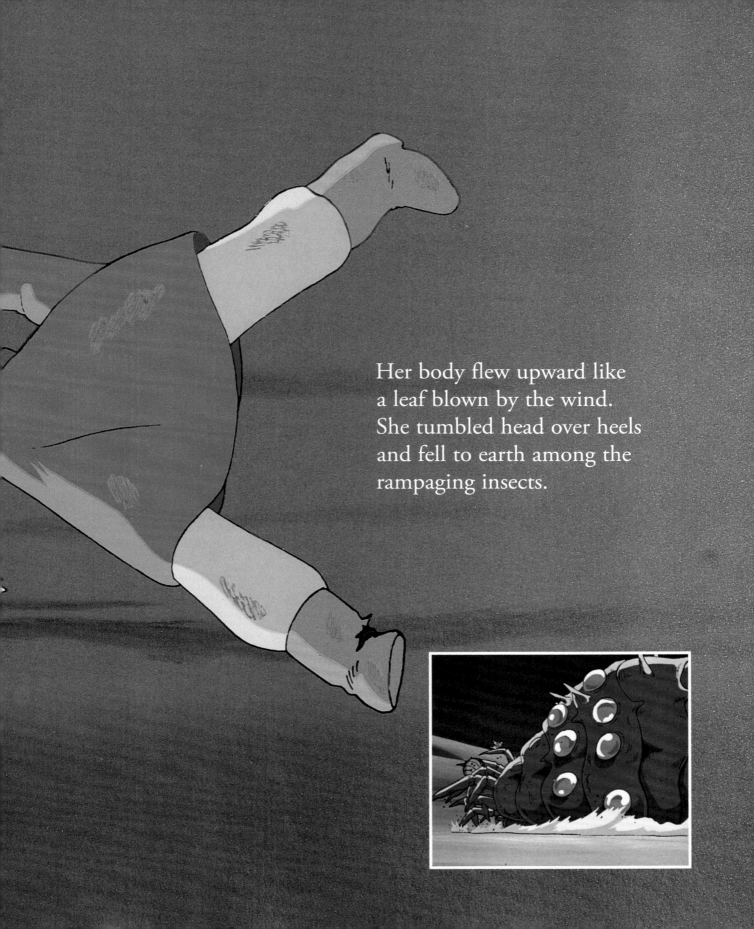

Her body flew upward like
a leaf blown by the wind.
She tumbled head over heels
and fell to earth among the
rampaging insects.

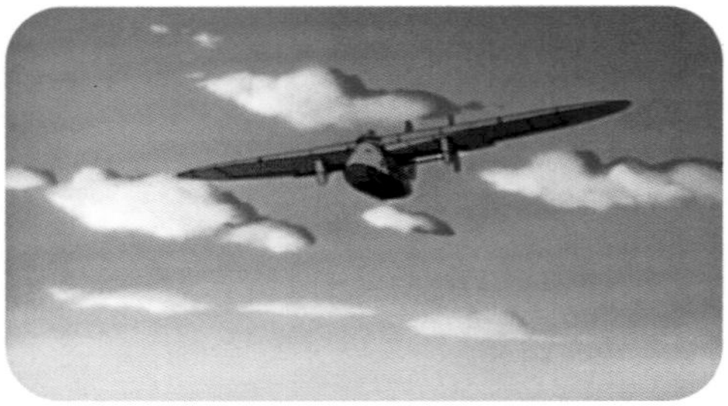

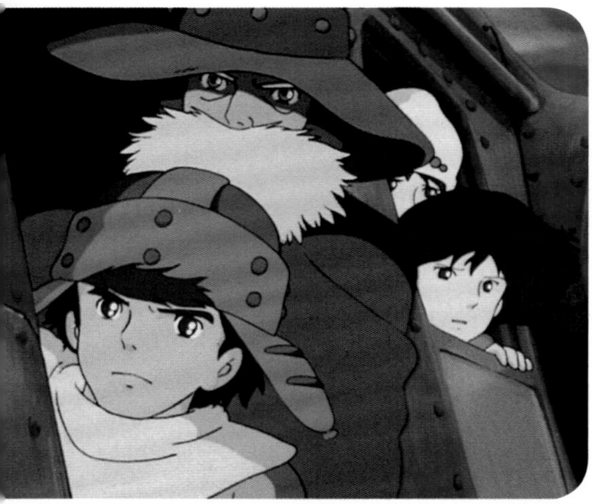

The Pejite Brig with Asbel and Yupa aboard stood out against the dawn sky as it approached the acid lake. Its passengers looked down at the sea of glowing red eyes that stretched across the plain.

But something mysterious was happening. A widening circle of blue light was spreading out across the herd of Ohms.

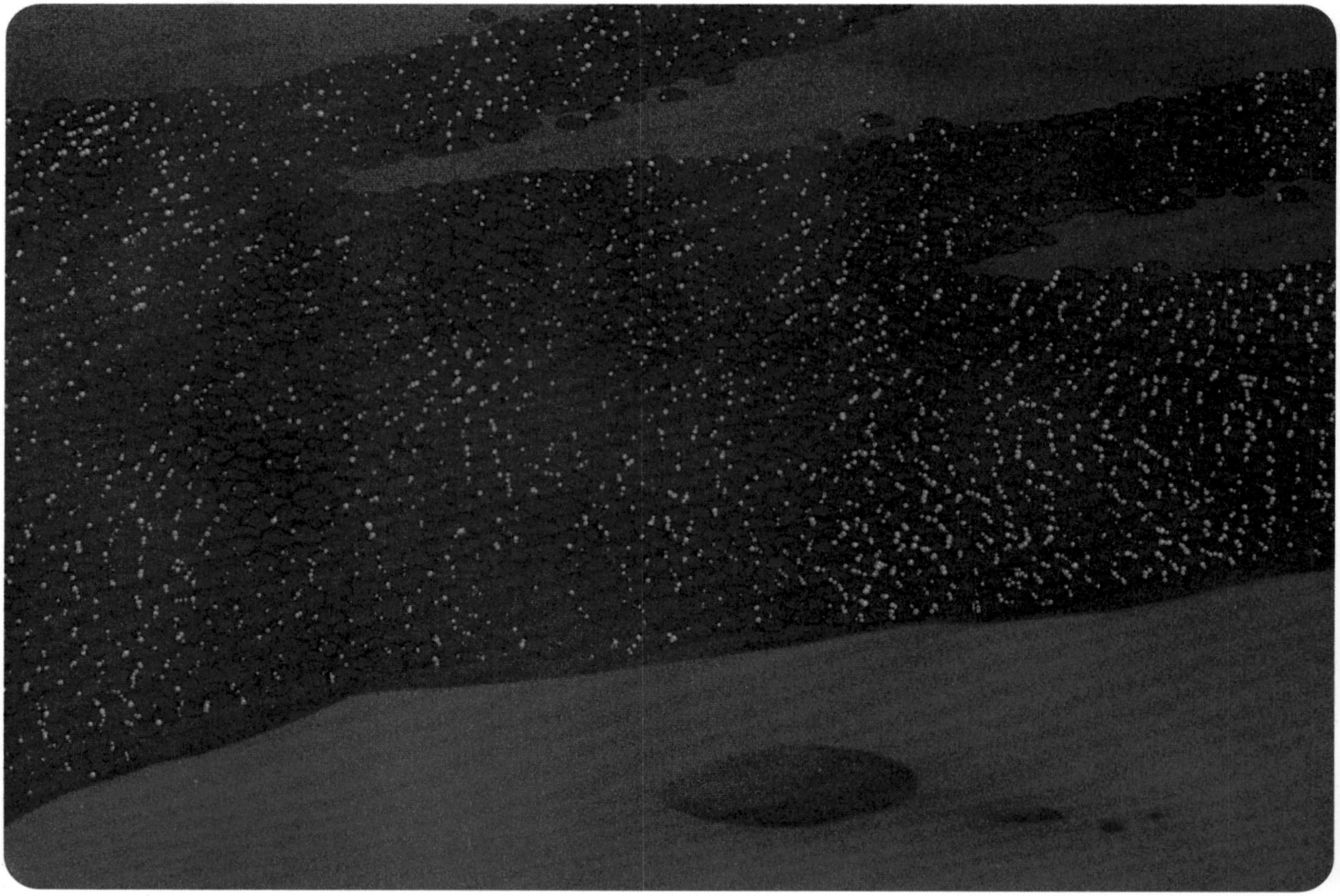

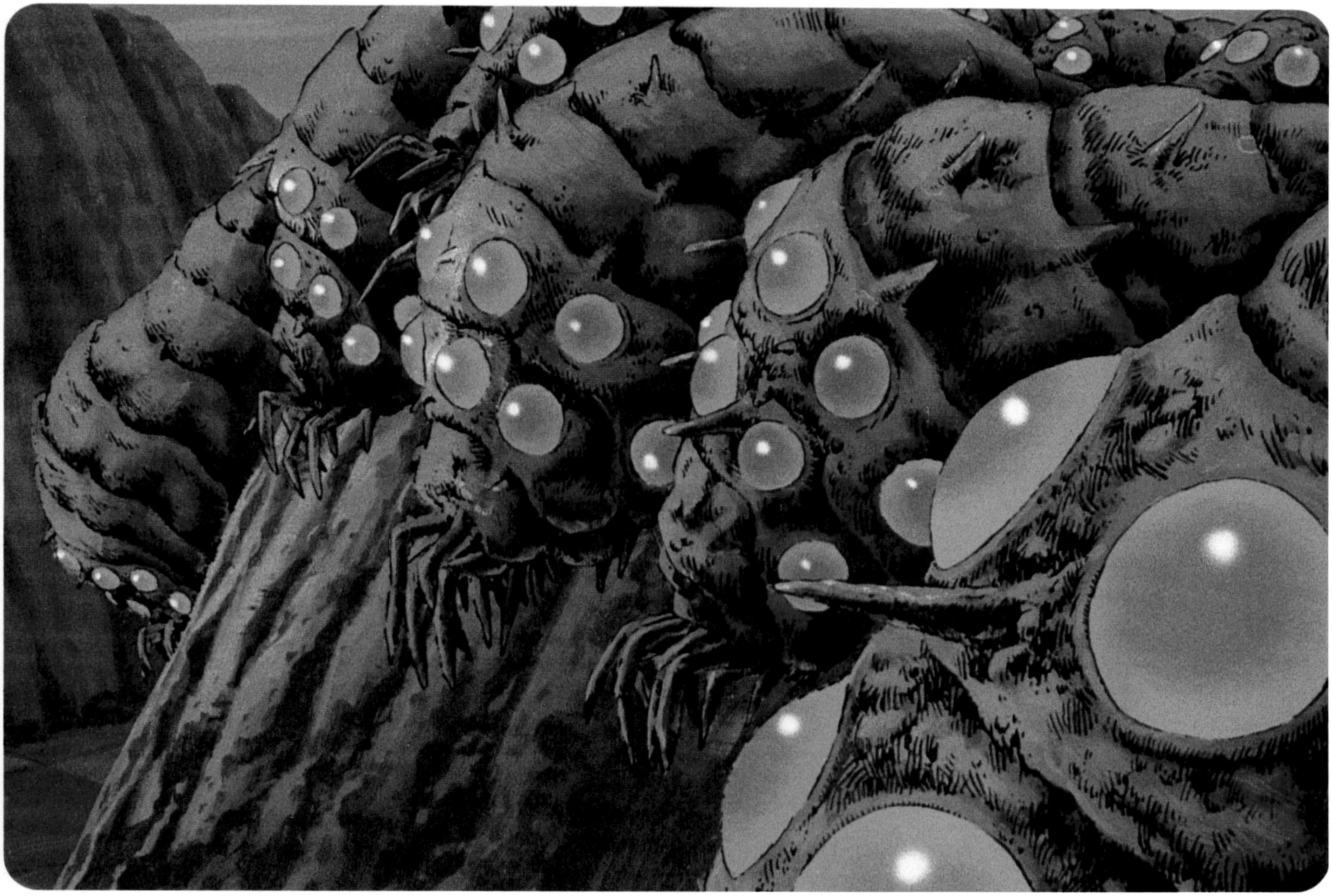

“The rage—it’s left the atmosphere!”

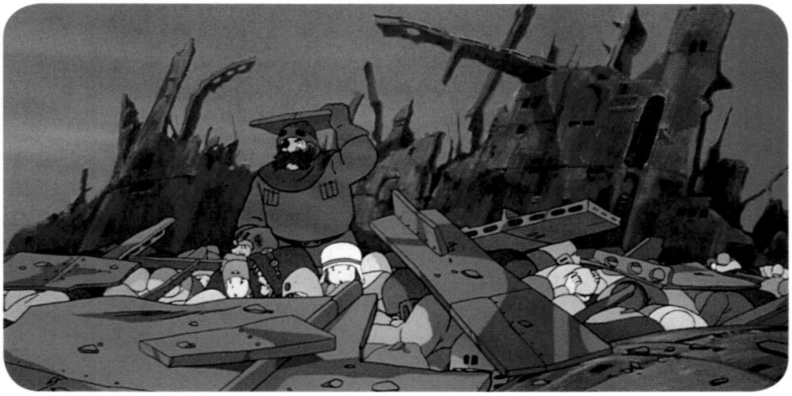

The people heard Obaba, and a look of hope began to appear on their faces.

“We’re going to be all right. The Ohms have stopped raging!” Mito said.

The horde of stampeding Ohms had stopped. Suddenly all was quiet.

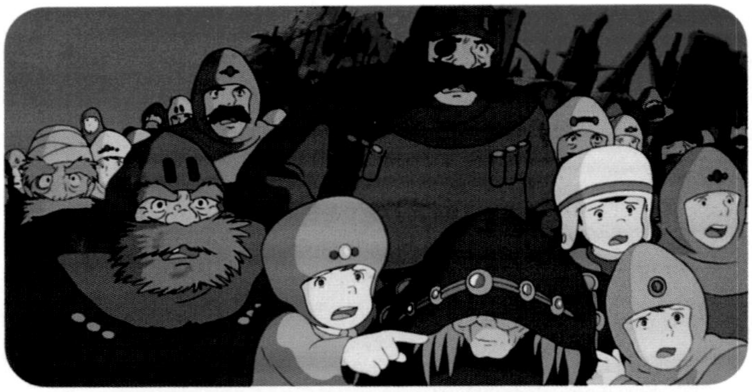

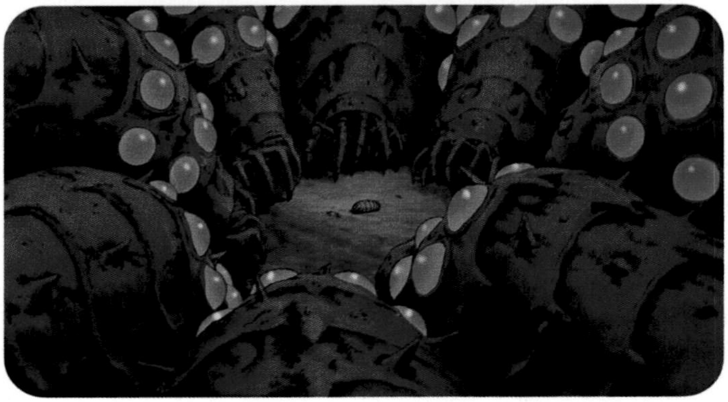

"There's the princess!"

Nausicaä lay on the ground surrounded by the Ohms. She wasn't moving. The baby reached out to touch her.

"The princess is dead!"

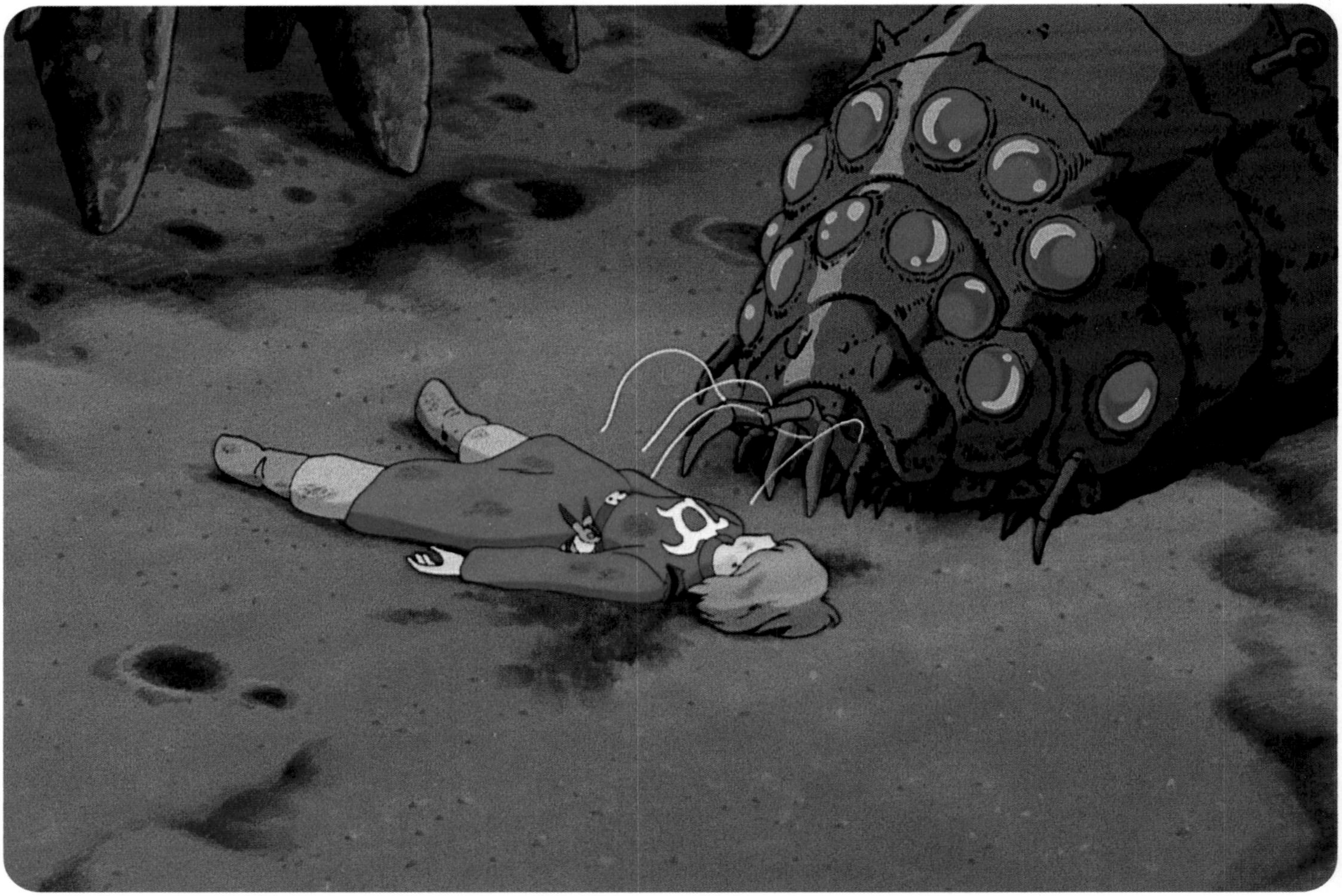

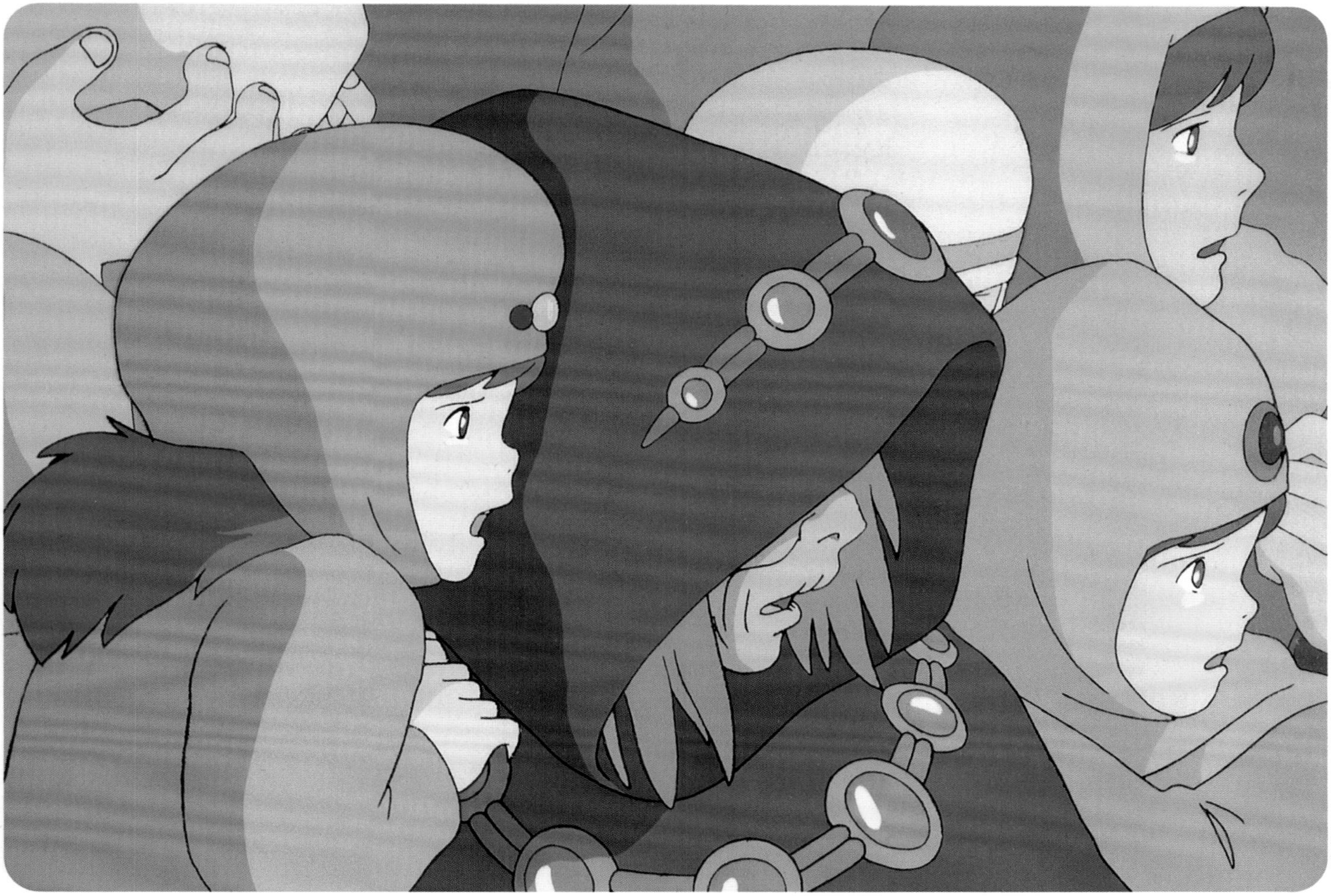

“She quelled the rage of the Ohms,” Obaba said sorrowfully. “She gave her life to save the valley.”

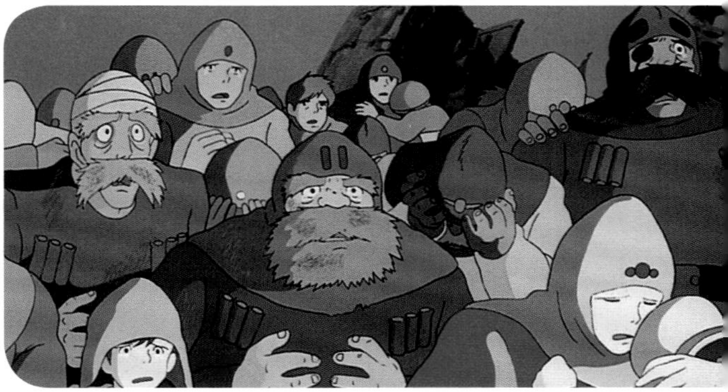

The children burst into tears. The people of the valley began sobbing too.

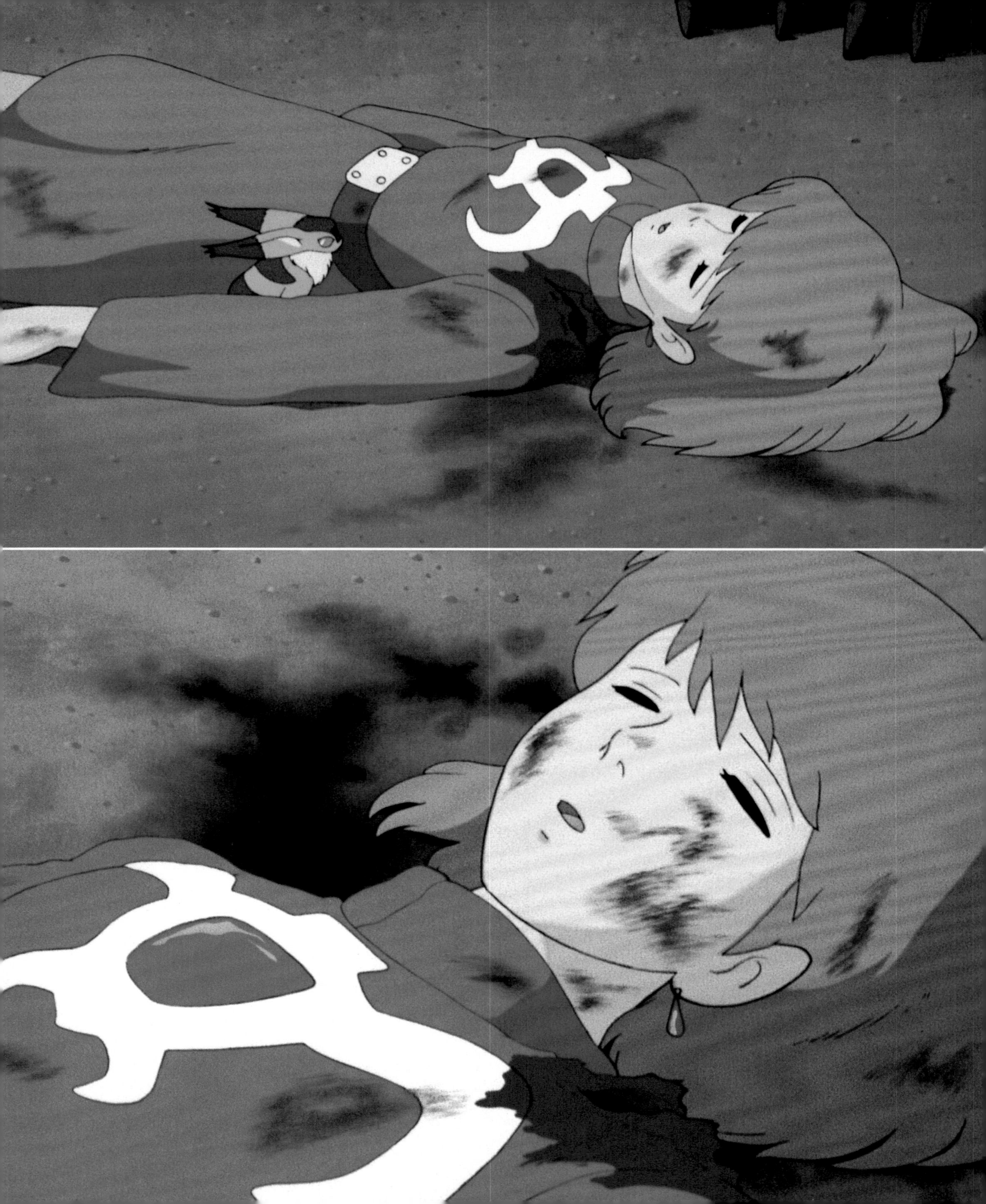

Slowly, the sounds of weeping grew and grew.

One of the Ohms reached out to Nausicaä with its golden tentacles. It grasped her body and gently lifted her into the air.

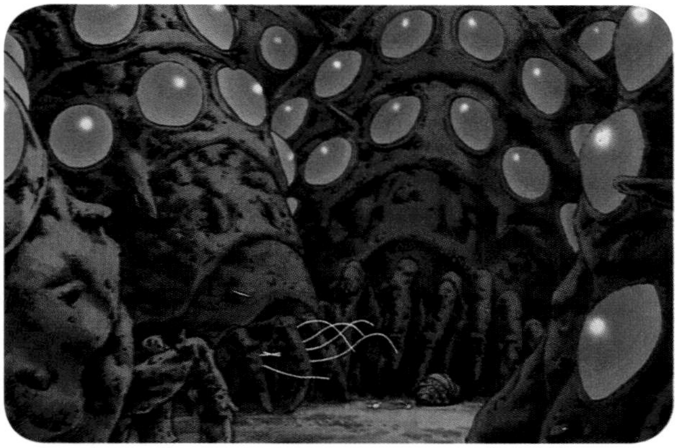

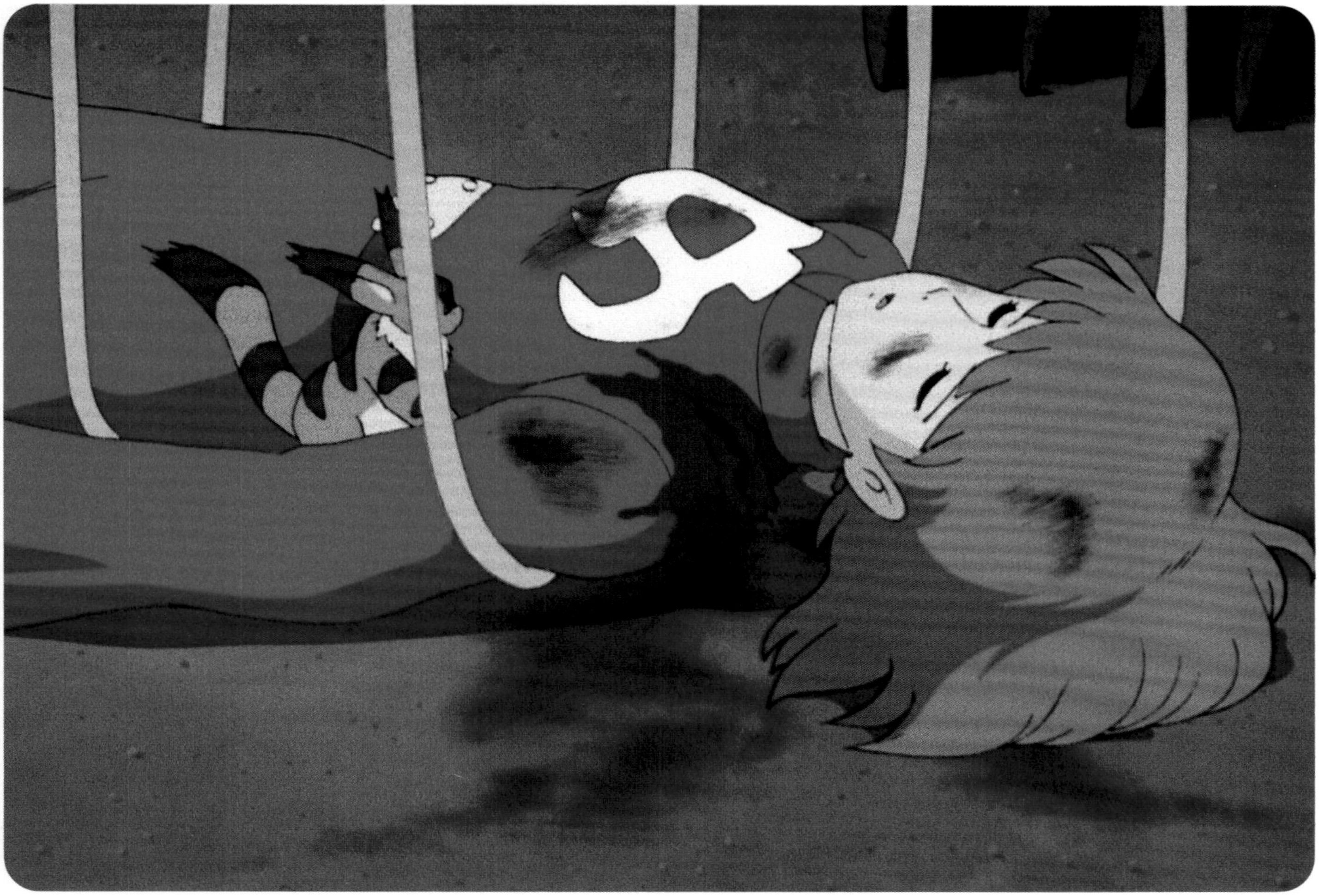

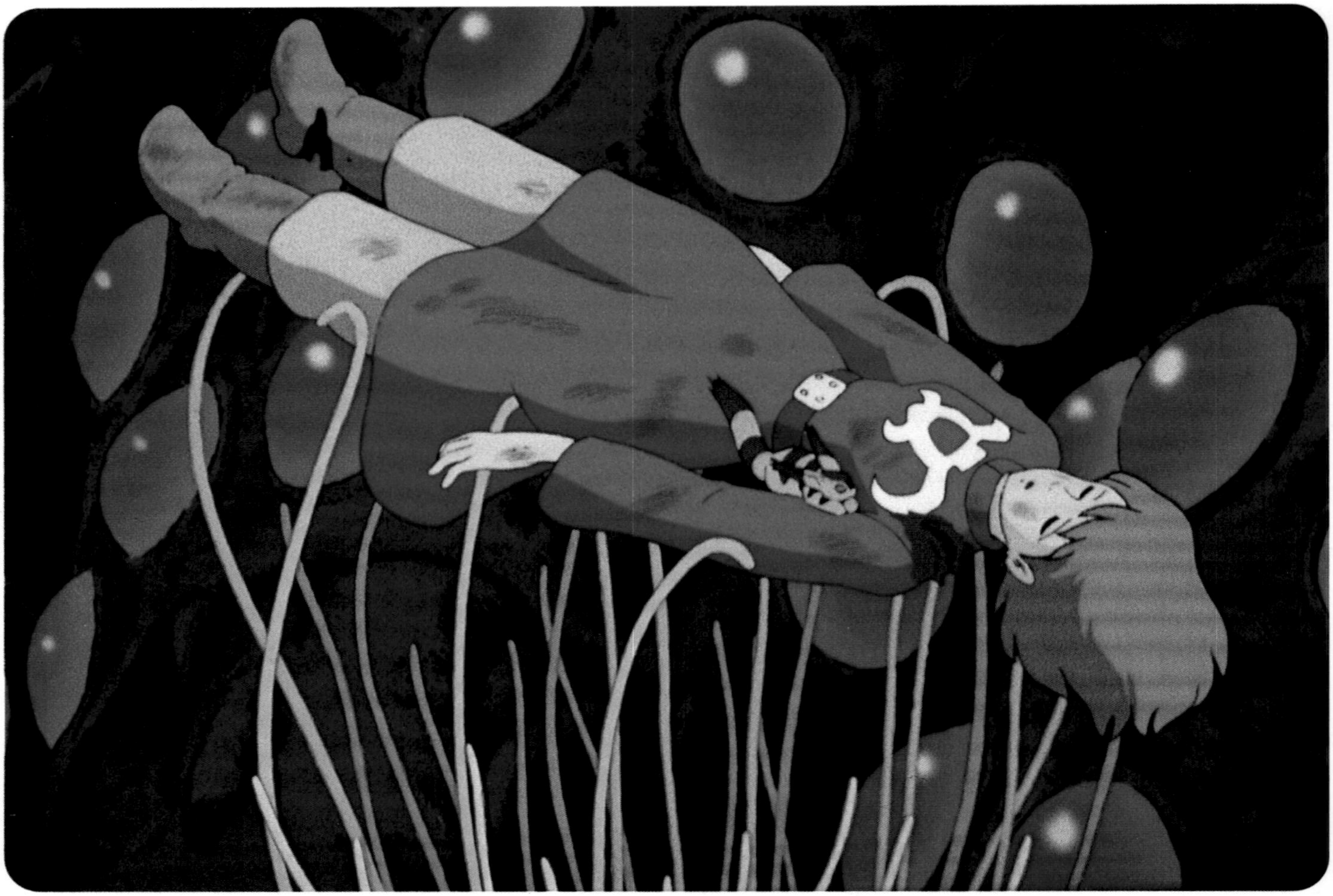

Other Ohms extended their tentacles too, and together they lifted Nausicaä high into the air as the people watched in awe.

More and more Ohms stretched their tentacles toward the princess.

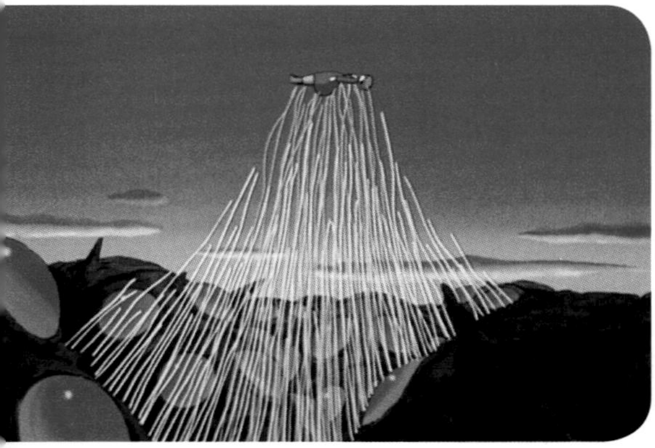

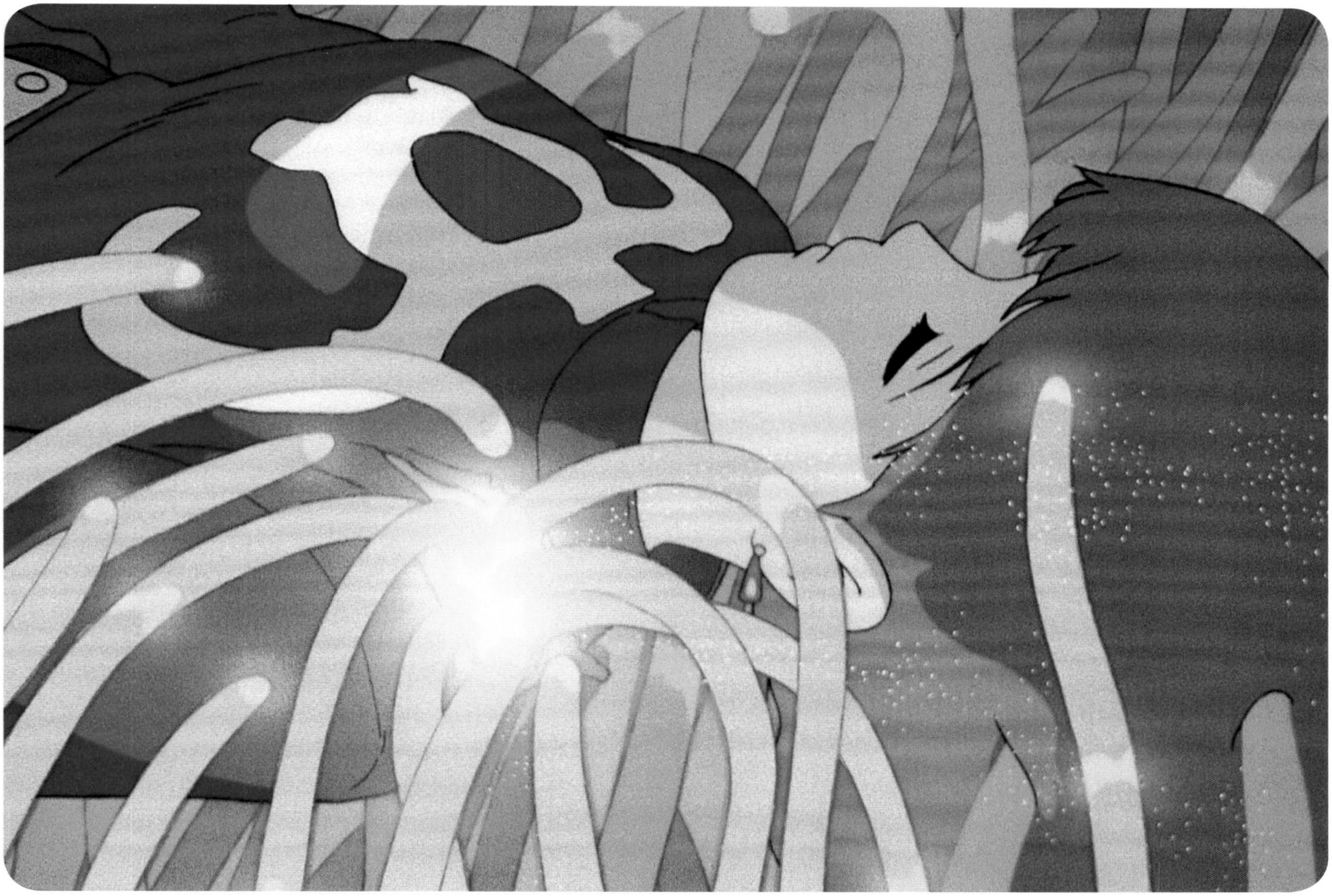

Tiny points of golden light flowed from the tips of the tentacles and enveloped Nausicaä. The tentacles stroked her wounds gently, as though trying to heal her. Little by little, color returned to her cheeks.

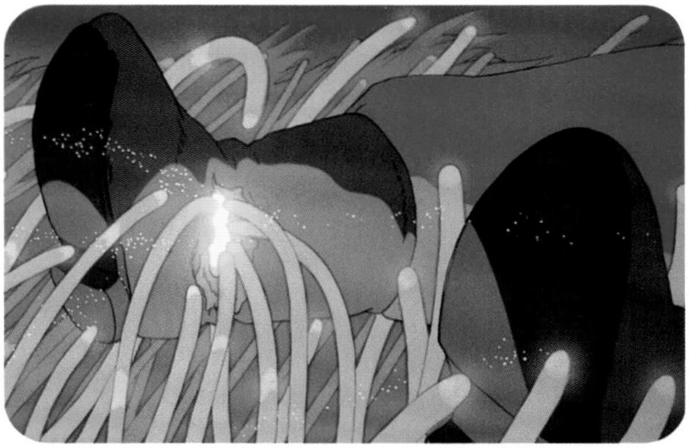

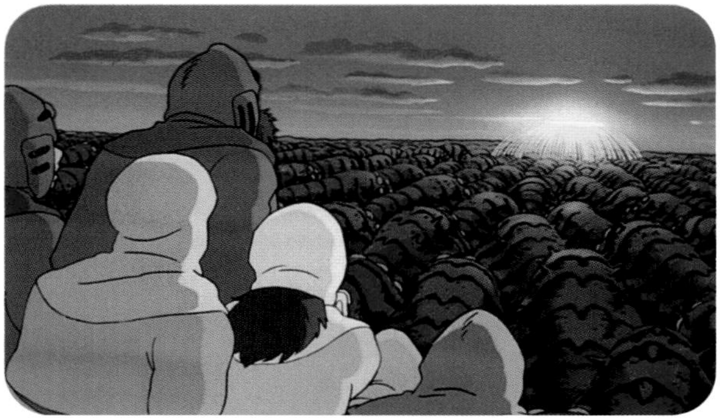

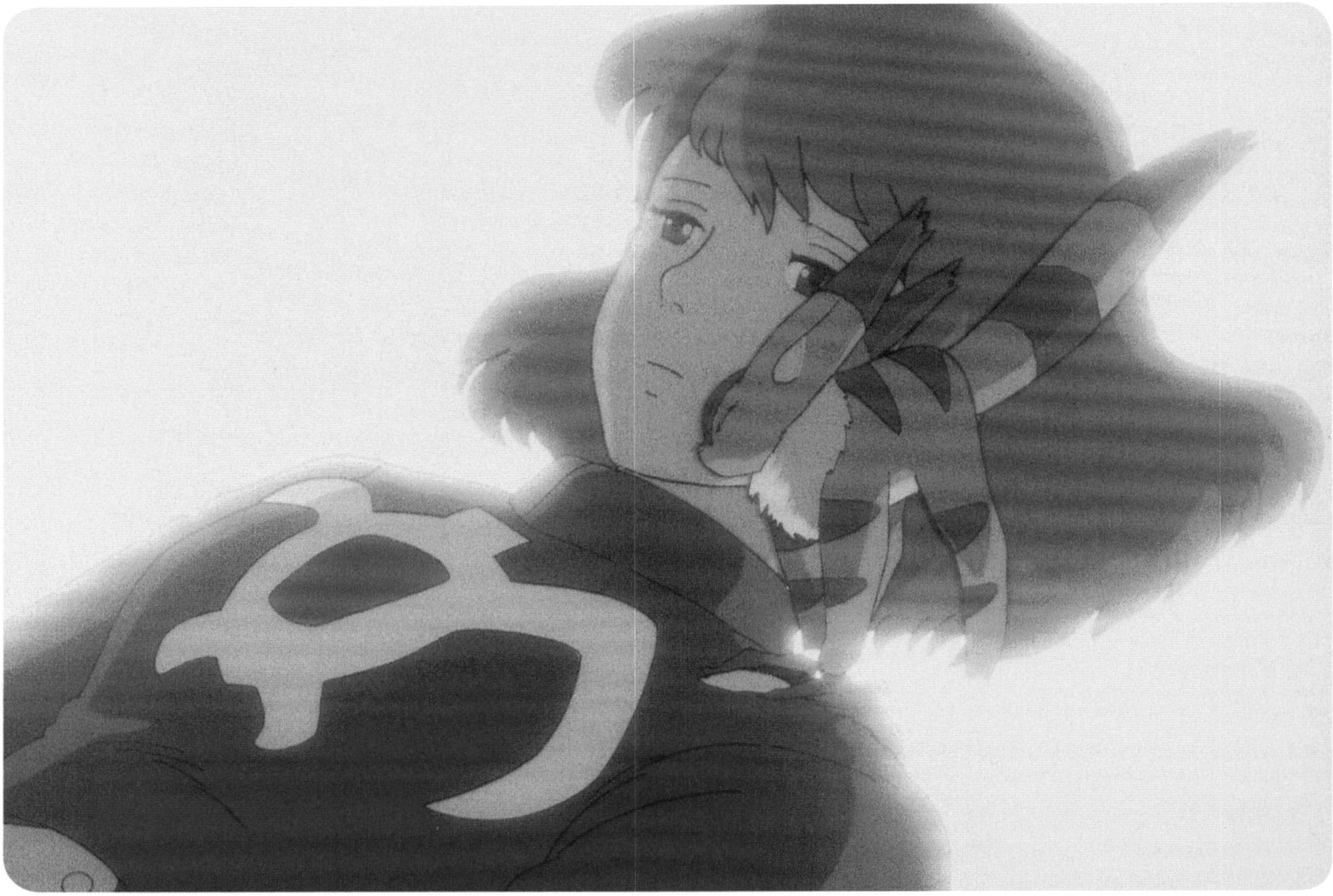

Surrounded by an ocean of light, Nausicaä opened her eyes. Teto was there too, pressing his head against her cheek.

"Teto..."

She sat up slowly and gazed at her surroundings with wonder. She was in a golden landscape.

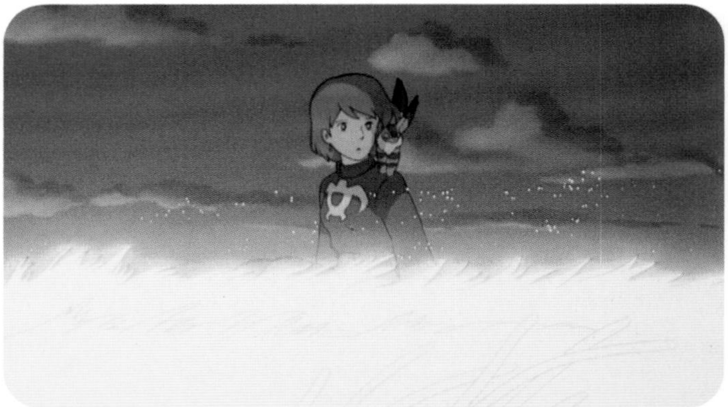

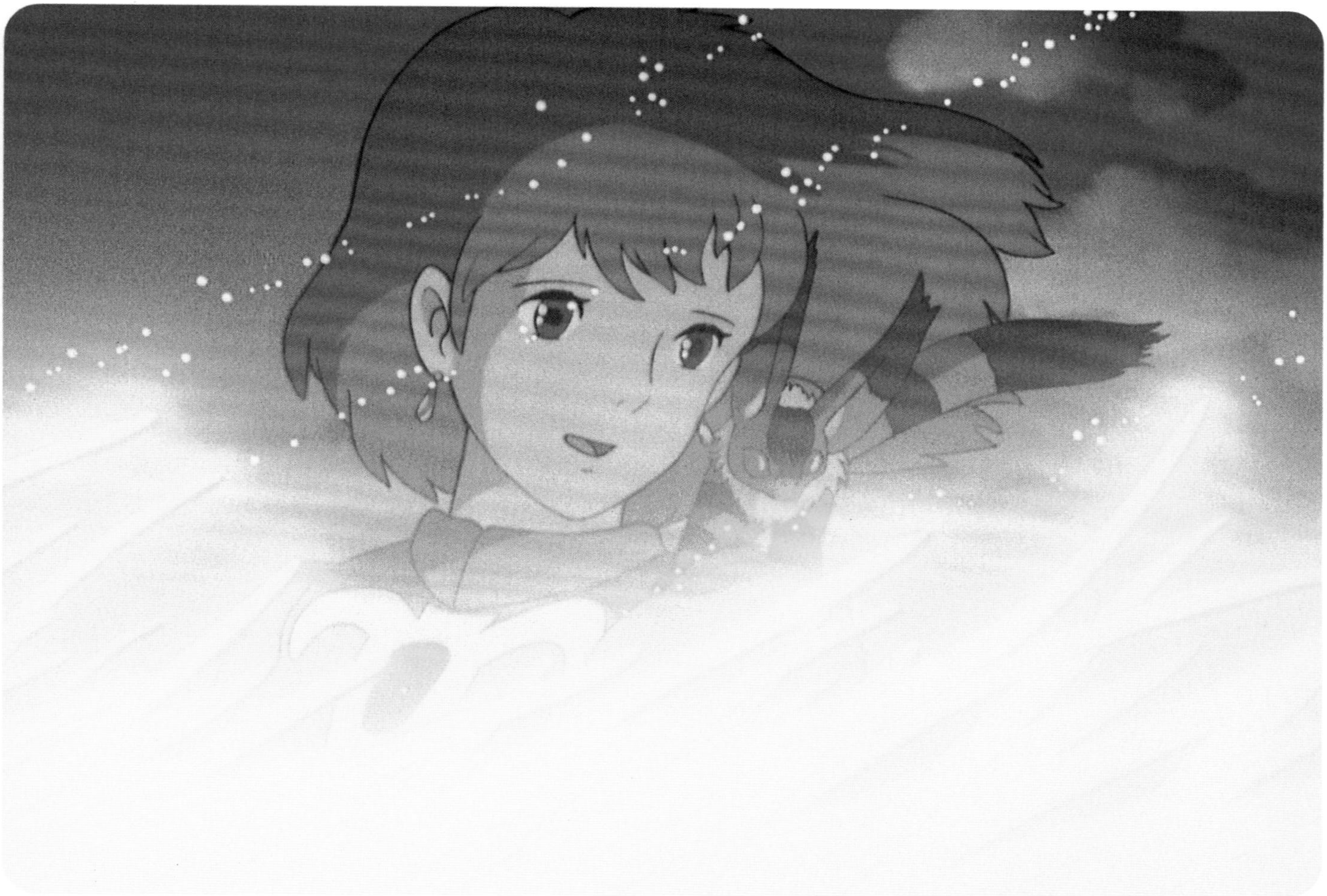

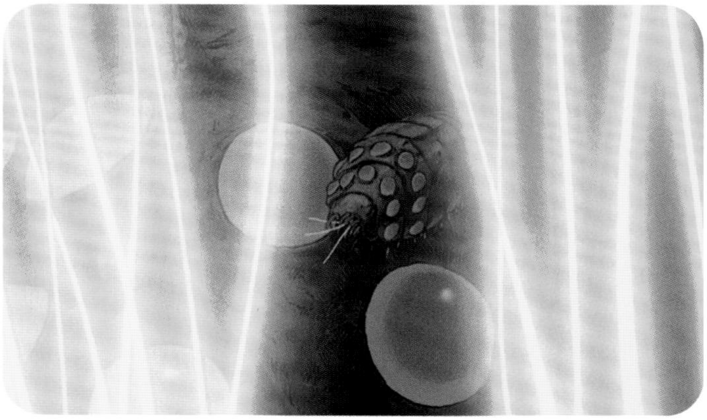

Below her, through the golden light, she could see the baby Ohm. Its wounds were healed, and it waved its tentacles at her.

"I'm so glad you're okay," she said, and smiled.

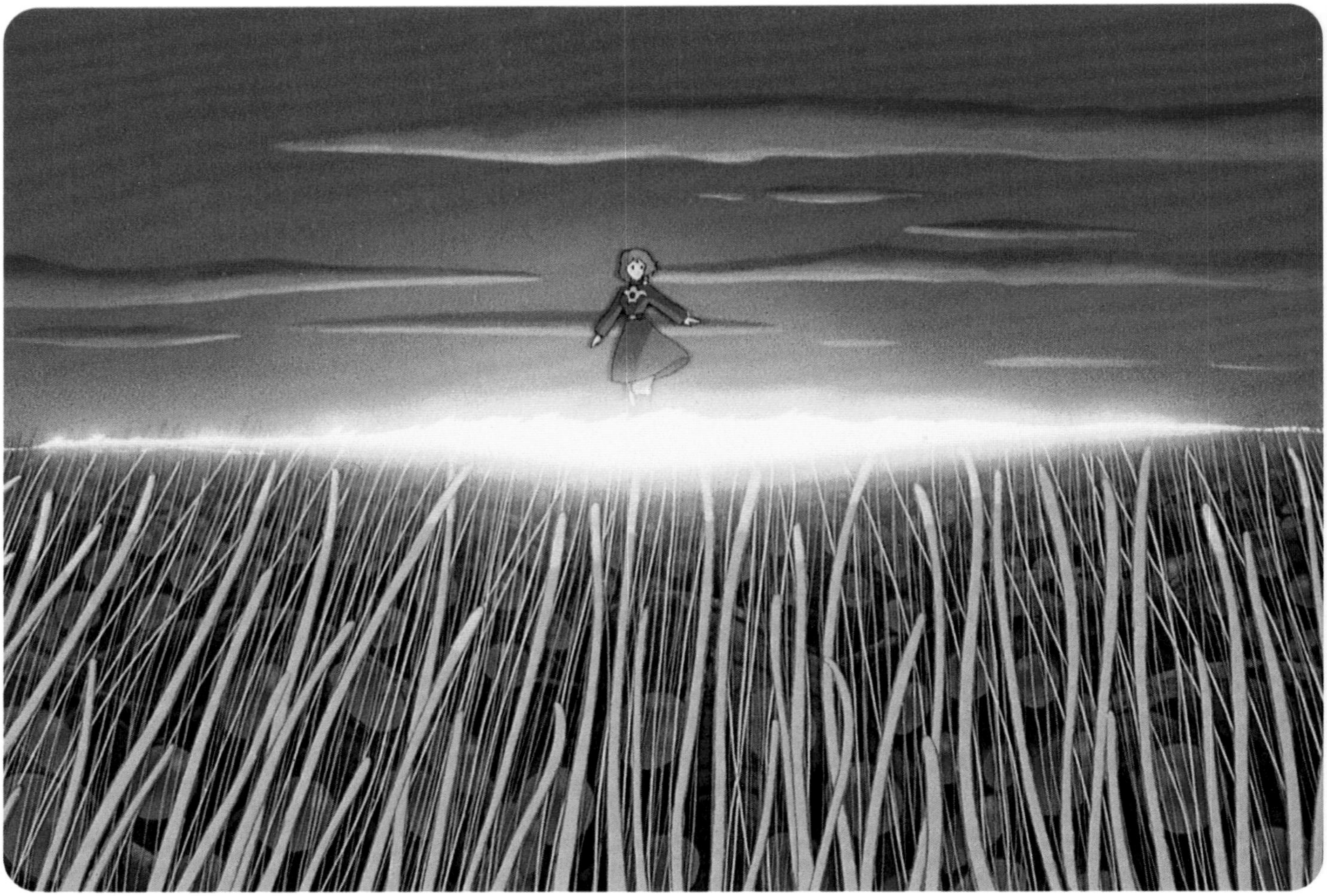

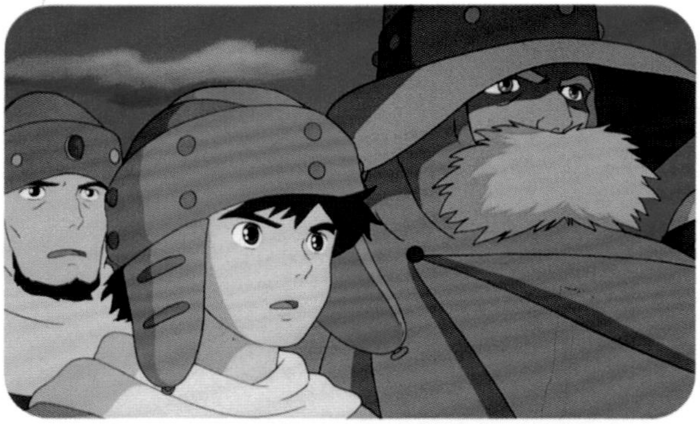

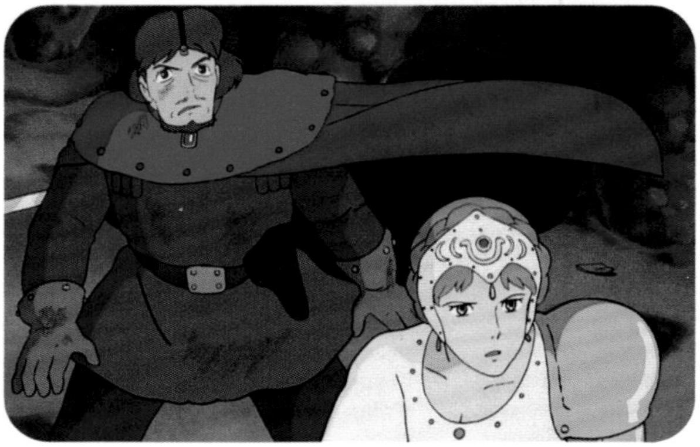

"Ohms…thank you. Thank you!" Nausicaä said. She rose and walked, arms outstretched, across the plain of golden tentacles.

"It's a miracle!" The old men hugged each other with joy. Tears of sorrow changed to tears of happiness.

"Who knew how wonderful the Ohms could be?" Obaba said with deep emotion. "Children, look carefully and tell me what these blind eyes cannot see."

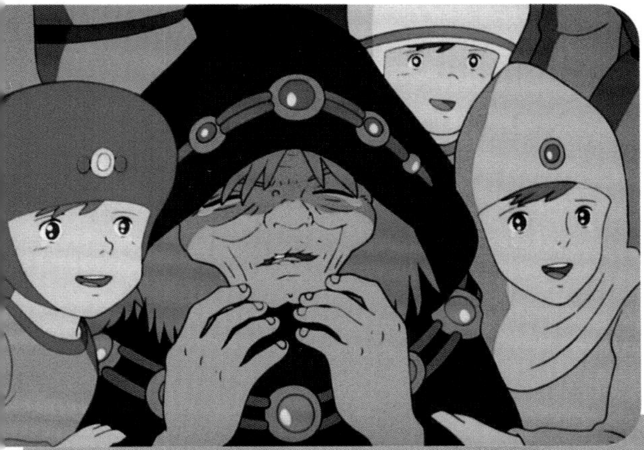

"The princess is wearing a blue tunic I've never seen before. It looks like she's walking through a field of golden grass."

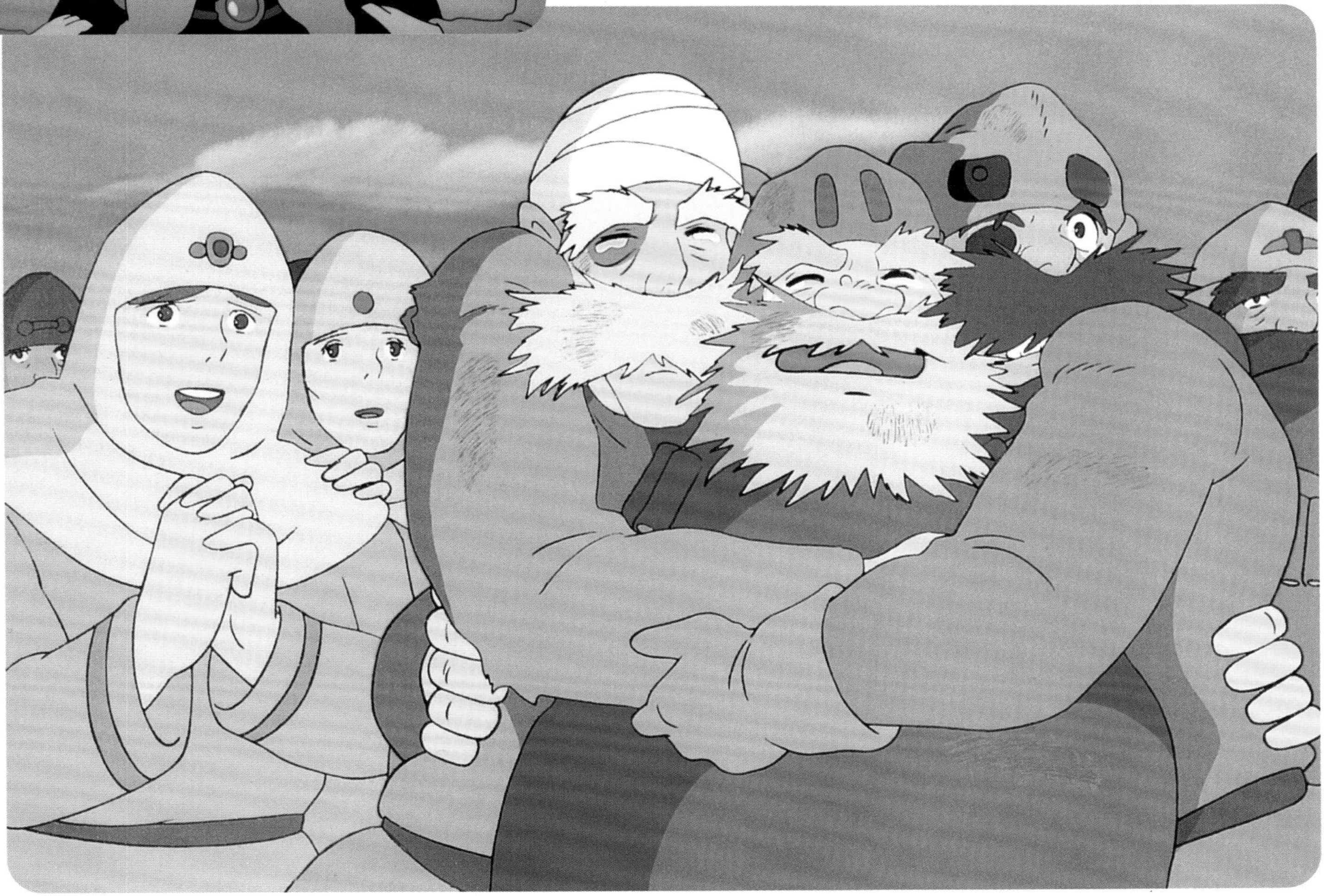

At once, Obaba remembered the prophecy that was woven into the tapestry above Jihl's bed.

"After a thousand years of darkness he will come, clad in blue on a plain of gold, to restore our connection with the earth. The legend has come true!"

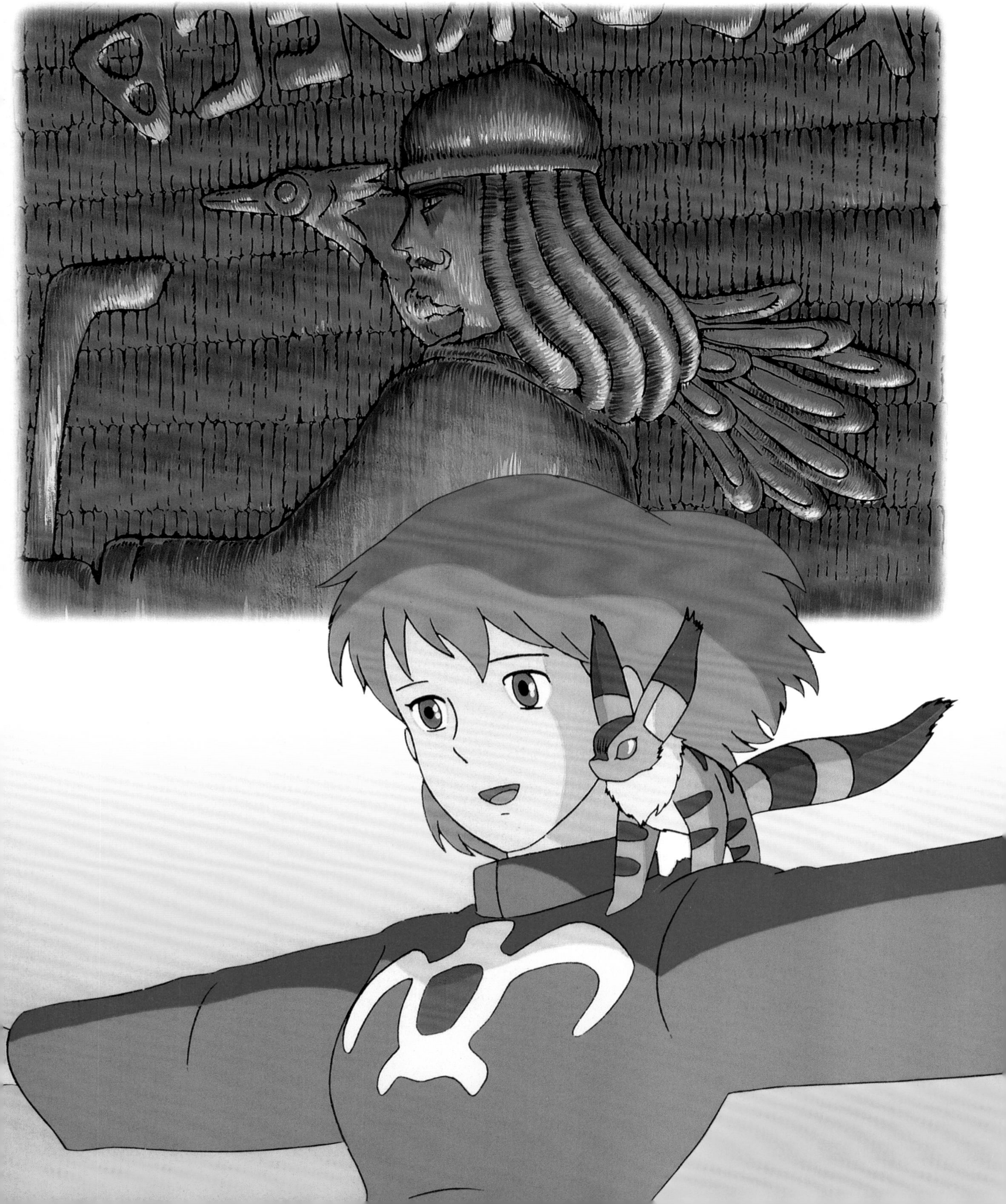

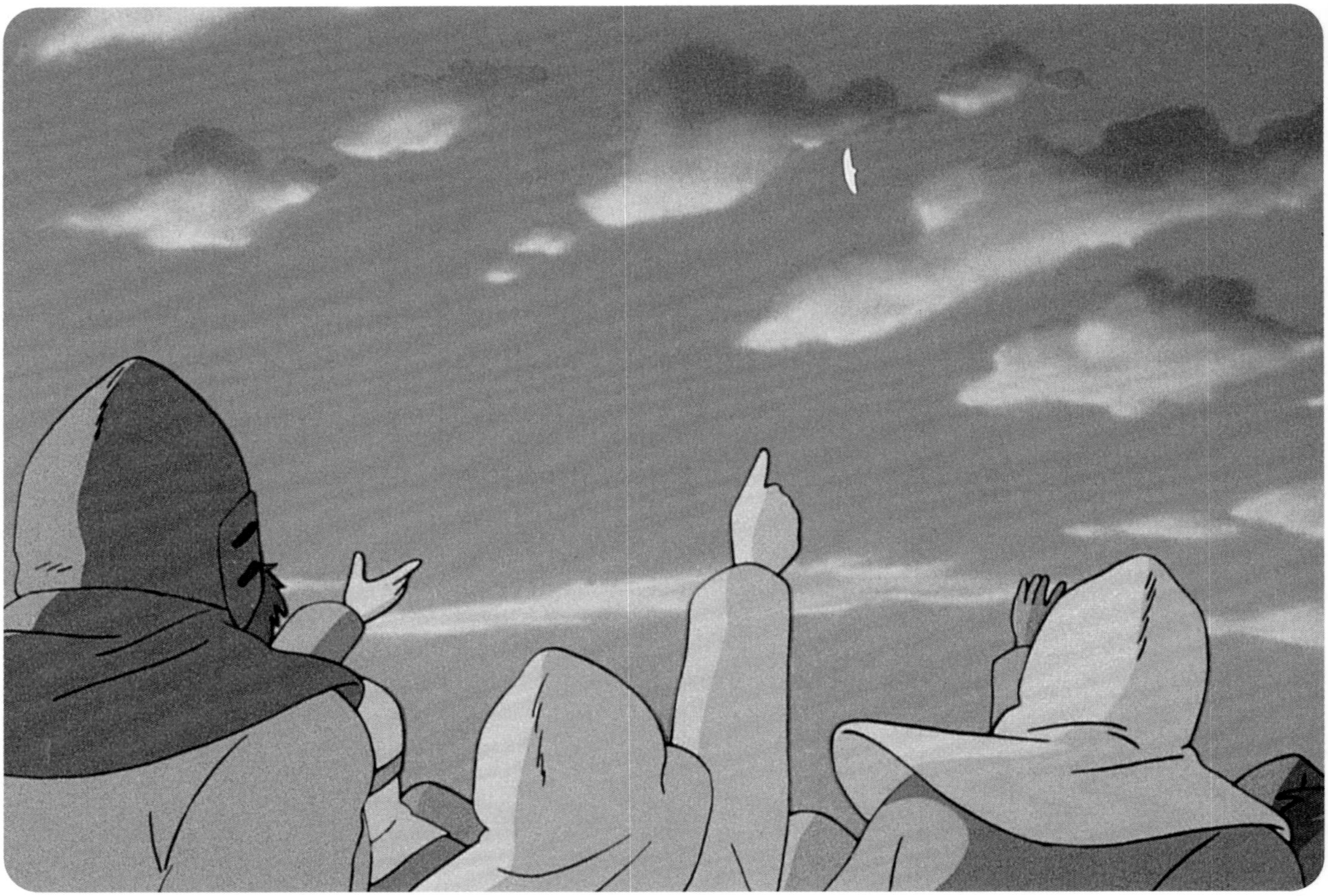

"Look! It's the wind rider!"

The pilotless wind rider flew in lazy circles in the morning sun.

"The wind has returned!"

The Ohms' golden tentacles waved slowly in the breeze. Gently, they set Nausicaä down on the ground. The people rushed forward and embraced her joyfully.

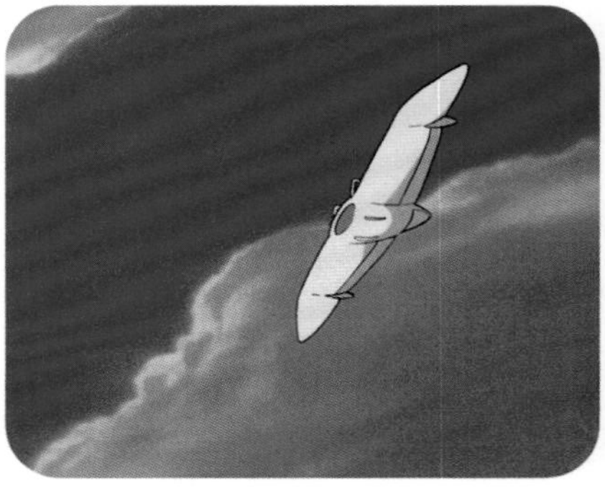

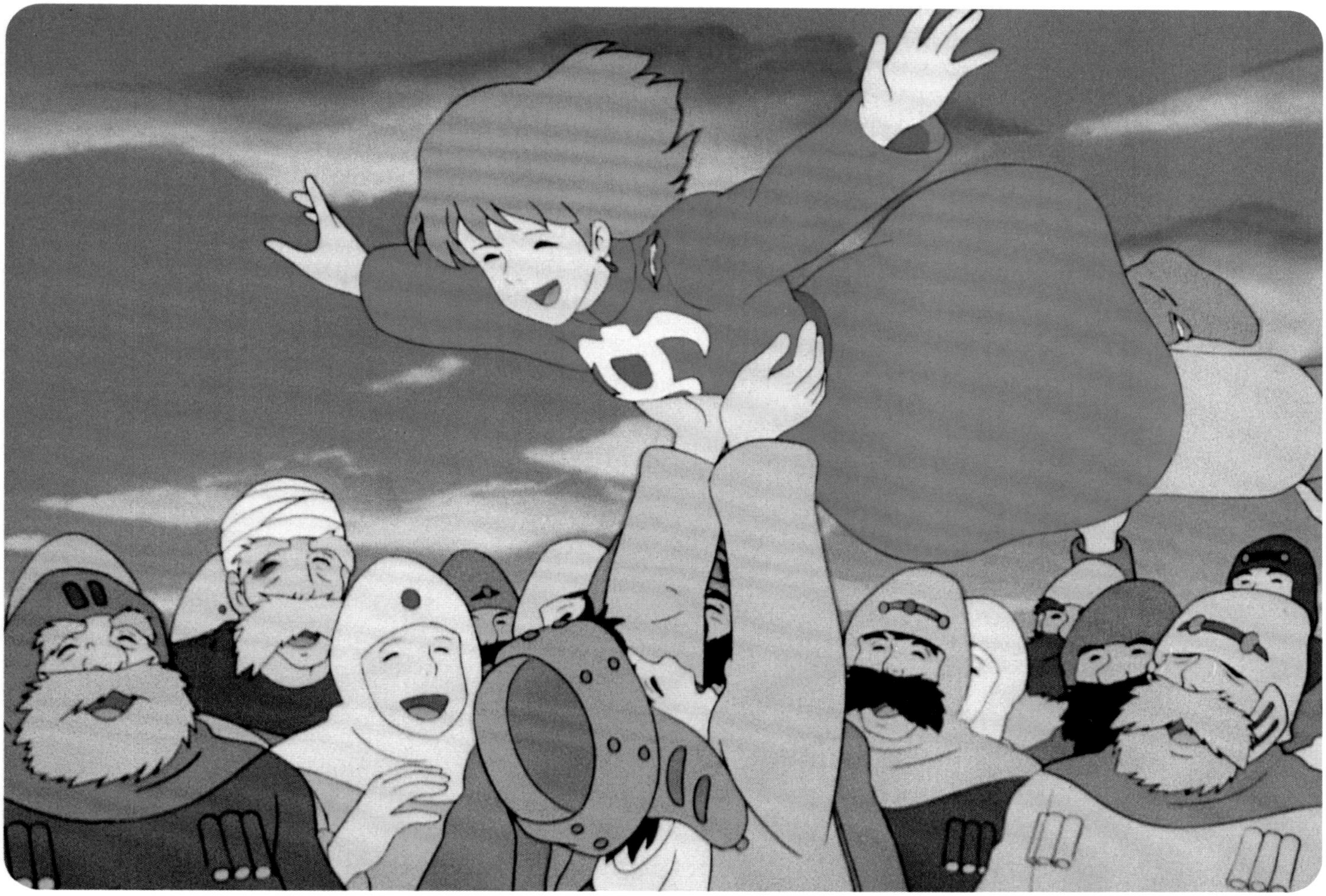

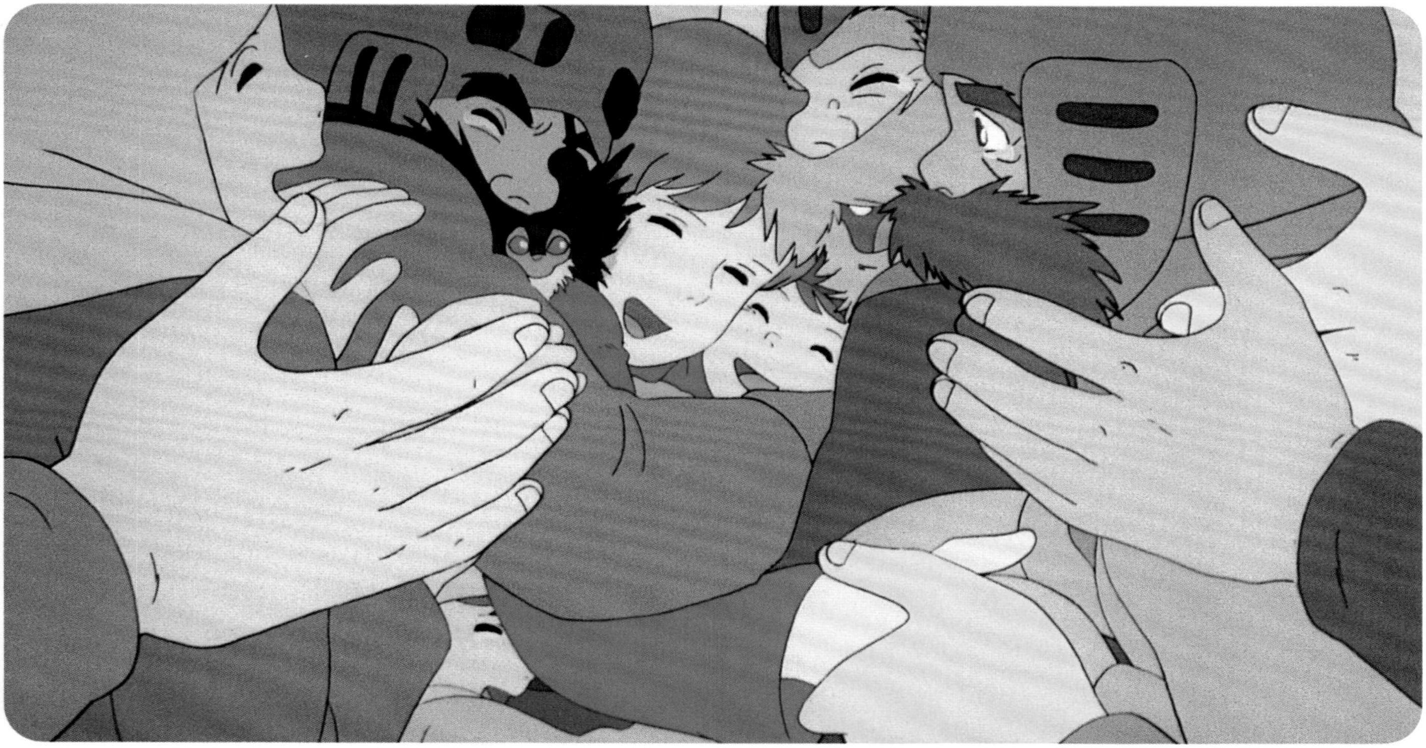

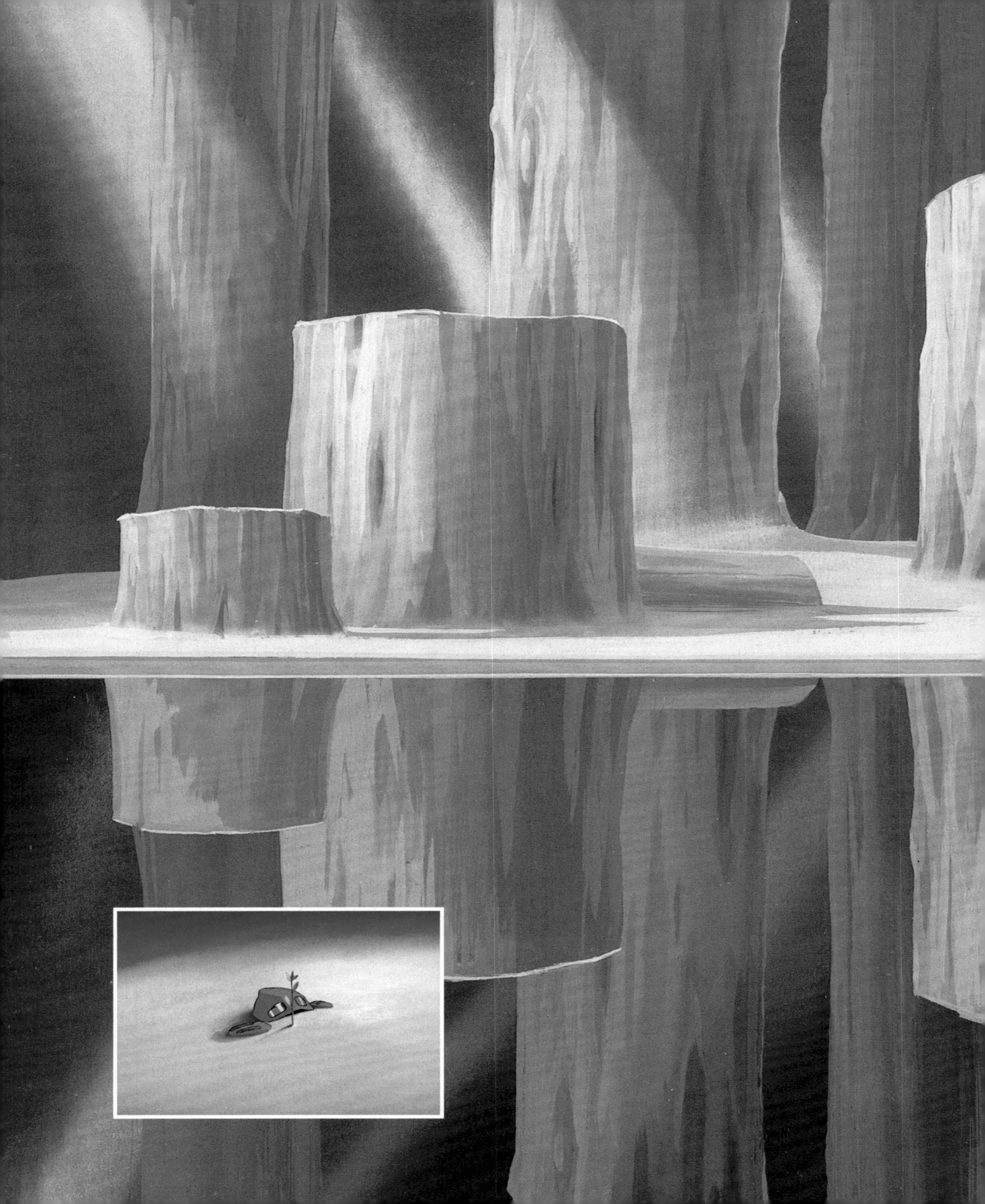

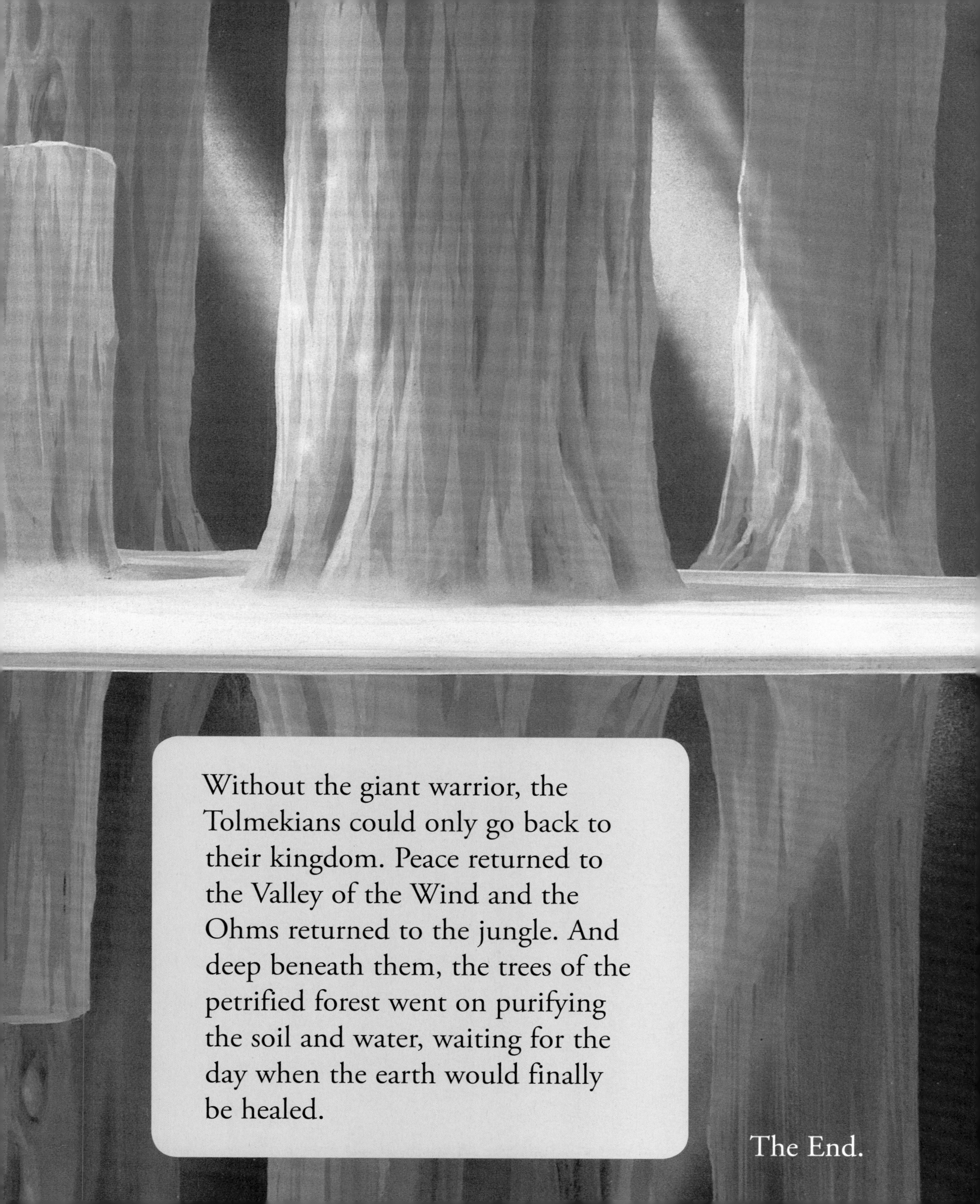

Without the giant warrior, the Tolmekians could only go back to their kingdom. Peace returned to the Valley of the Wind and the Ohms returned to the jungle. And deep beneath them, the trees of the petrified forest went on purifying the soil and water, waiting for the day when the earth would finally be healed.

The End.

NAUSICAÄ
—OF THE VALLEY OF THE WIND—
Picture Book

BASED ON THE STUDIO GHIBLI FILM

ORIGINAL STORY AND SCREENPLAY
WRITTEN AND DIRECTED
BY HAYAO MIYAZAKI

English Adaptation / Jim Hubbert
Design & Layout / Yukiko Whitley
Design Assistant/ Natalie Chen
Editor / Nick Mamatas
Sr. Director, Publishing Production / Masumi Washington

Kaze no Tani no Nausicä (Nausicaä of the Valley of the Wind)
Copyright © 1984 Studio Ghibli - H
All rights reserved.

First published in Japan by Tokuma Shoten Co., Ltd.

Printed in China

Published by VIZ Media, LLC
1355 Market Street, Suite 200
San Francisco, CA 94103

First printing, April 2019